Fall From Grace

Book Four in the Medici Warrior Series

by Emily Bex

Foundations Publishing Company
Brandon, MS 39047
www.foundationsbooks.net

Fall From Grace
Book Four in the Medici Warrior Series
By: Emily Bex
ISBN: 978-1-64583-041-2

Cover by Dawne Dominique
Edited by Laura Ranger
Copyright 2019© Emily Bex

Published in the United States of America
Worldwide Electronic & Digital Rights
Worldwide English Language Print Rights

Dedication

This book is dedicated to all the loyal readers and hopeless romantics who are on this journey with me. Your enthusiasm and love for these characters makes the long hours spent in front of the computer screen writing and re-writing worthwhile.

Acknowledgements

This series could not have been written without the help of my collaborator, Johanna Morisette. Johanna had dabbled in fan fiction, and dragged me reluctantly into a world of vampires, encouraging me to write. She had the initial vision for Shade and was instrumental in the development of that character. Throughout the seven years it took to write this series, she remained a sounding board for the development of the storyline. These characters, and this saga, would not exist if not for her constant support and input which kept me motivated to keep pushing forward.

Table of Reference

Italian to English Translator for Book Four

Italian	English	Italian	English
Addio	Good-bye	*Alzati*	Stand-up
guerrieri	warriors	*Amica*	Friend
Amore	Love	*Bambino(s)*	Baby/babies
Bastardo	Bastard	*Bel*	Beautiful
Beleeza	Beauty	*Bellissimo*	Very beautiful
Bravado	Brave	*Buonasera*	Good evening
Cazzo	Fuck	*Ciao*	Hi/Hello
Dipendenzo	Addiction	*Dolce*	Sweet
Dormire	Sleeping	*guerrieri*	warrior
Familia	Family	*Figlia/Figlio*	Daughter/Son
Fino ad allora	Until then	*Fratello*	Brother
Grazie	Thanks	*Guerrieri*	Warriors
Impavido	Fearless	*Lei e il mio*	She is my
Vero amore	true love	*Madre*	Mother
Meile	Honey	*Mi/Mio/Mia*	My
Mio vampire	My courageous	*Coraggioso*	Courageous
Moltobella	Very beautiful	*Nostra Figlia*	Our Daughter
Padre	Father	*Per Favore*	Please
Per Sempre	Forever	*Rosso*	Red
Scusi	Excuse me	*Si*	Yes
Signorina	Young Lady	*Sorella*	Sister
Stupido	Stupid	*Ti Amo*	I Love You

Re-cap of The Medici Queen, Book 3 in The Medici Warrior Series

Book three begins with the elaborate coronation ceremony for Kate, as she has just been made an immortal and must now assume her role next to Shade as Queen of the Medici Coven.

Shade must help her navigate his world, as they both discover she has not one, but two gifts. She emerges as a day-walker, but also with the gift animalism, a gift long thought extinct among the vampires. It is a gift that gives her the power to communicate and control the animal kingdom. Her conduit to the animal world is a she-wolf named Aegis who appears at Bel Rosso and remains at her side.

Kate quickly discovers she is pregnant again, as the royal couple prepare for the birth of Lorenzo, the long-awaited heir to the Medici dynasty.

Cory has moved back to Virginia and asks that his mother, Rachael, be allowed to visit. When his mother arrives, she recognizes Shade as the vampire she met in the underground clubs in San Francisco and realizes Cory is Shade's half-breed son. As the family overcomes the shock of this revelation, Cory is warmly accepted into family, and Shade insists the Council recognize him as his rightful son.

Not to be undone by Kate, Rissa is planning a wedding ceremony to rival the grandiosity of any royal event. During her grand reception, she and Alec are caught off-guard by an uninvited guest. Max returns with his new mate, Lein, the daughter of a royal master in Asia. While Max is there to goad his former lover, he discovers that Shade has expanded his Bel Rosso estate in Virginia to include a warrior training camp.

Max tries to negotiate with Shade, offering to buy him out at any price, but Shade refuses the offer. Max attempts to blackmail Shade, when he sets him up to be seduced by two feeders. Shade feels he has betrayed his queen, but Kate takes matters into her own hands and delivers the heads of the feeders to Max in a hatbox, and challenges him to war.

When war comes, Max calls on the army of his father-in-law, and his forces outnumber Shade's warriors five to one. The Medici's fight valiantly, but as Kate observes the slaughter of the Medici troops, she draws on her gift of animalism, turning the tide of the battle, and forcing Max to surrender. Bel Rosso is saved, and Max's surrender leaves Shade with the expanded territory of Virginia, but it didn't come at a small price. Many warriors were lost in the battle, included his beloved Fiamma.

Fall From

Grace

1

Kate swung in the hammock, suspended between two trees in the lush garden behind Bel Rosso. Lorenzo squirmed restlessly, playing with his stuffed bear, which he kept tossing out of the hammock to his Golden Retriever, Warrior. The dog shook the stuffed bear before tossing it in the air.

Kate admonished the boy. "Lorenzo, that's not a dog toy."

Lorenzo giggled at the antics of the dog. "Look, Mommy. Look at Warrior!"

Kate smiled at this child, his hair a thick mass of black curls, his eyes the same steel blue as his father's. He was three now, and it took all her energy, as well as all of Theresa's, to keep up with him. He was a day-walker, and even though Kate still slept during the day with Shade, she got up for short periods during the day to spend some daylight hours with Lorenzo as well. The sun was setting on the early spring day, and she waited for Shade to join them.

***

Waking from his death slumber, the soft spring air blew gently through the open windows in the house, now filled with activity. It was his favorite time of night, waking to those he loved, the sun setting, the smell of spring in the air, and the sound of Lorenzo's laughter. Love never felt this good before, and no man should ever have it this good. Closing his eyes, he honed his senses and knew they were outside, enjoying the last of the evening light.

Climbing out of bed, throwing on a pair of sweatpants, he padded down the stairs and out the back door to the gardens. He could hear Lorenzo's laughter, the greatest joy in his life. He was growing so fast. Before long, he'd be training in the camp to become a warrior, and Shade couldn't wait to teach him. Walking out onto the soft grass, it felt incredible under his bare feet, its lushness between his toes. Bel Rosso was their private paradise. Before he got to them, Warrior raced in circles at his feet. Bending down, Shade rubbed his ears. Animals of all species abound here now, and it was finally feeling natural to him. It was just a part of who they were as the animals assimilated into their lives.

His eyes focused in on that beautiful crimson hair, and soft lilywhite skin as she swung in the hammock, her face lit with a smile. He loved seeing her like this, beaming with happiness and contentment. She knew she was well loved.

Walking up to her, he kissed her forehead and climbed in next to her, cuddling her in the large hammock. He saw a pair of eyes, blue as the sky and big as saucers, staring back at him. Lorenzo was such an innocent, and he wished he could hold that inside him forever.

Kate curled into Shade and kissed him, as Lorenzo crawled over the top of him. "You slept well, lover?"

Lorenzo had retrieved his bear and was trying to draw his father's attention. "Daddy, look at Ted. He's got dog slobber on him. Wipe it off, Daddy."

Her kiss ignited his heart, but it was short lived. Spending time alone together had become harder than he ever imagined, now that Lorenzo craved every second of his attention.

"I slept fine, *mi amore*, except... Lorenzo, do you want to explain to me why there is dog slobber on Ted? Warrior does not eat bear."

Laughing, he wiped the bear on his sweatpants and handed the toy back to Lorenzo, who deftly slid his body between his parents. Shade shook his head. No one ever told him this part.

Kate smiled at him. "Are you happy?"

Grunting as Lorenzo beat him on the chest with his bear. "Oh *si, mi amore*. Why do you ask? Are you not happy?"

Kate giggled at the antics of Lorenzo, a constant source of entertainment, but also a constant drain on their time. She couldn't have imagined there was more love to give until this child was born, and now there'd be another.

"I only ask because I'm wondering if you're ready for the

next one?"

His heart skipped a beat and he tried to sit up quickly, almost tumbling all three of them out of the hammock. Letting his hand slide along her cheek, her eyes were glowing with mischief and love.

"I am more than ready for another *bambino*. Are you? Say yes!" Kissing her on the lips, letting his tongue slide inside her mouth, he wanted to crawl inside her and love her forever.

Kate wrapped her arms around his shoulders and surrendered to the kiss, as Lorenzo was tumbled sideways in the hammock. He climbed onto his father's back.

"Eww, kissing."

He tugged at his father's hair, leaning in close and whispering loudly into his ear. "You should kiss Ted. He has a boo-boo."

Kate started laughing and shook her head. "I'm not sure how we found the time, but yes, the answer is yes."

Lorenzo held the bear up over his head and asked, "Time for what, Mommy?"

Kate looked at their son, this beautiful boy who had been the center of their lives, before stroking his cheek. "Time to make your little sister. You'll have a little sister soon."

Lorenzo looked at her quizzically. "Well, how did you make her?"

Kate shook her head and looked at Shade. "Uh, you and your father can have that discussion."

Feeling Lorenzo tugging his hair, the child doing anything with *bel* a struggle. He wanted everyone's undivided attention. Shade's grin went from ear to ear when he heard her say yes. Two, they would have two now.

Pulling Lorenzo off his back and holding him upside down above his head, Shade dropped his leg off the side of the hammock, pushing gently to make the hammock sway from side to side. Lorenzo's laughter was contagious. Shade's own *padre* never had time for what he called nonsense. It was his *madre*'s job to entertain him until he was old enough to begin his warrior training, but this generation of Medici's would be much different.

"My little warrior, it is vampire magic, creating a little sister. Do you think she will look like me or Mommy?"

Lorenzo laughed uncontrollably, as his father held him in the air. "I think she will look like Ted. Can you use your vampire magic to make him a brother instead?"

Shaking him around in the air, Lorenzo dropped the bear and Warrior barked, grabbing up the stuffed toy and leaping over the hammock.

Pulling Lorenzo down onto his chest, the boy calmed down and snuggled his head into his father's neck, his tiny hand tangled in his father's curls.

"There is no magic for deciding brothers or sisters, but I do think you will enjoy having a sister. You need to protect and love her. Can you do that for your sister when she arrives? Perhaps we shall need to get you a sword to make sure no enemies come near her. Big brothers are protectors. I think it is time you took some responsibility and learned some warrior lessons. What do you think?"

Lorenzo lifted his head. "I'm already a warrior, Daddy. You said I protect Mommy when you're in your slumber."

Kissing his massive mop of midnight hair, Shade hugged him tight. "You were born a warrior. Just like me. I love that you protect Mommy for me. You are such a big boy now. Fierce and brave. But you will need to protect all the females around you always. They are very special. You would protect Theresa and Nita, *si*?"

Lorenzo laid his head back down on his father's chest, as Kate ran her fingers through his curls.

"I love Tressa and Nita. I protect them too...just like Uncle Luca. I'm a good protector. But I need a sword."

Kate shook her head no. "Not yet, young warrior."

Shade watched as *bel* responded negatively to weapons, knowing she would do whatever she could to delay the process and keep her beautiful boy within her grasp.

"You are a good protector, but Mommy seems to think it is not time for a sword. Perhaps, we will have to come up with another way for you to protect all the beautiful females in our life."

Lorenzo's mind never stopped. Shade could almost see the wheels turning in his head. Lorenzo sat up quickly, inhaling the air, then squealing at the top of his lungs as he saw his half-brother approach. "Cory, Cory!"

As he scrambled to get down, Shade juggled him, so he didn't fall. As Cory walked up, he kissed Kate on the cheek and messed up Lorenzo's mop of curls with his hand.

Cory laughed, as he asked his father if he was going to work or lounge like a lazy lizard all night.

"I think I deserve some downtime with my family. That includes you too, son. Are you heading into camp?"

Cory nodded yes as Lorenzo climbed him like a tree, screaming to take him along. Cory put his younger brother on his shoulders and started running around. Lorenzo screamed for him to go faster. Leaning into *bel*, Shade took this opportunity to snuggle and steal a kiss.

"Sometimes, two sons are valuable, they can entertain each other."

Kate nuzzled into him, inhaling him, his scent as intoxicating now as the first time she held him. Her desire for him grew with the passage of time, just like her love for him. But the demands on their time were great. He still commanded the camp, now even larger after its third year, and the demands of the Dead House remained. They made frequent trips to Florence, to stay visible to the coven there and for him to coordinate with Marco and check on the running of Castello. They made trips to California, to check on the inn, which stayed full year-round, and the vineyards, which were at full production, as were the vineyards here at Bel Rosso. Kate had planted large fields of lavender and sunflowers, and both had proved to be very profitable crops. Their estates in both California and Virginia had become a mecca on the wine tours, as mortals flocked to see the vineyards, taste the wine, and walk through the fragrant fields of blossoms. Kate had also turned the large mansion they inherited with Max's property into a very expensive inn, and Shade had staffed it with more from his coven in Florence. Everything they touched had turned to gold for them, but it all took time.

Raising Lorenzo had been pure joy, and she'd change nothing. But she knew adding another baby would more than double the demands on their time. Their visits to the Paris house had been infrequent because he had no business interest there, and Luciano managed the French and Greek vineyards, which had been established now for centuries. Kate enjoyed this moment of passion, knowing they must steal time where they could.

She could hear Lorenzo's laughter, as he played with Cory. Lorenzo adored his older brother, and didn't seem to understand, or care, that Cory was a half-breed. When Shade broke the kiss, she stared back at him, the hammock swaying gently beneath them.

"This is the eager one, the child that appeared to me long before Lorenzo. Our Sophia. Are you sure you're ready for this?"

"I will always be ready for the beautiful *bambinos* you give me, *mi amore*. It is the gift I cherish the most."

He glanced as his sons then gave Kate a questioning look, his brows drawn together. "More high energy than Lorenzo? Is that possible? It does not matter, Kate, I am anxious for a *figlia*. I miss holding a small *bambino* in my arms, one that does not wiggle insistently to get away."

Nuzzling into her neck, he licked her vein, his voice husky. "I love you, *bel*, just as I did the first time I saw you. You have me, heart and soul."

Kate stared into those piercing blue eyes. "I sometimes miss those early days, when it was just us, and the house was quiet." She laughed. "I can't remember what quiet sounds like now. Lorenzo is full steam ahead from the time his feet touch the floor every morning. When I look at him, I realize I'd change nothing. He's been such a treasure. When he runs outside in the sunlight, Aegis and Night Stalker run alongside him, and he wears them out. He leaves them both panting. Our Lorenzo is more taxing on Aegis than her own pups ever were. Even

Warrior has to stop and take a nap. But not Lorenzo. I don't think there's an inch of Bel Rosso he hasn't explored. I just wonder how I'll keep up with two of them if they head in opposite directions."

Watching her face light up as she talked, she still took his breath away. "You make me feel guilty. I slumber when you are awake and taking care of things. I am always busy, and now I feel as if I am ignoring you, not giving you time. I never want that to happen to us, to become separated by duties. We have to work on it, *mi amore*, make sure we have time for each other. Do you think we should have another nanny? I am willing to bring one in if it is what you need. I do not want this to become taxing on you." Pulling her to his chest, he rubbed her back. "You will become tired soon. The new *bambino* will wear you down."

Kate snuggled into him, as his arms enveloped her. "I think Theresa would have my head if I brought in another nanny. I think we'll just get another feeder for Sophia, and we'll manage. For now, I'm fine. It's still early in the pregnancy. Perhaps later I'll need you to take some time away from the camp."

Chuckling, he knew Theresa would indeed resist having another nanny. He tried to give her time off to be with Marco at Castello when he could, but with Lorenzo getting older, it was more difficult now than ever.

"Theresa has become quite a necessity in our lives, and I am most grateful for her."

Stealing more kisses, they laughed softly together, as the rest of the world seemed to fade away. He could lay here forever with her, but he knew their life didn't work like that.

"I would advise you to speak with Nita for a recommendation on the wet feeder for Sophia. She will be the greatest resource for you, and she may even know of other wet feeders awaiting duties. Of course, as before, they need to come here to be interviewed."

He felt her snuggle into his neck and he smiled. She was hungry. Her appetite would rise, and he'd need to go to Luca once again during her term. It was the only part of her pregnancy he didn't like, not being able to feed from her.

"Hungry, aren't you? We need to find Theresa, get our son into his bed, and then find our way to our own."

2

Shade shuffled the papers on the desk. The annual meeting with his head accountant, Roberto, had taken most of the night. They had to review the books and examine the profitability of each business unit. All in all, things were progressing well. The Medici had branched out into many ventures, in the last few years. It seemed he had his hands in a bit of everything. But the wineries remained the main stay of their business and kept the money flowing in for the warrior camps and salaries. It would probably spin Kate's head if she knew the true value of their worth.

They had finally gotten through the details of each business, its annual income, and the outgoing expenses. Even Shade was surprised by the number of mortals and immortals he now supported. *Padre* had to be drowning in pride.

Luca was doing well also, bringing in the cash with the sale of his lemons from his property in Italy, and Medici now produced their own brand of limoncello. It was currently the number one selling brand in Italy.

Shade had set up a trust fund for both Cory and Rachael years ago and they too were set for life. Lorenzo, and the children that would follow, would be well established, and the coven secured. By the way things were progressing, they could never spend all the money they had, and for Shade, that was a relief.

As Roberto closed the books on Shade's business ventures, he opened another set of ledgers, and Shade looked at him quizzically. Roberto started reviewing more numbers, as Shade realized the accountant kept a separate record of Kate's businesses.

Roberto cleared his throat before starting to review the next set of figures. "So, Master Shade, that wraps up the details on all the wineries, including the new limoncello production. Everything looks solid there. Now, looking at my lady's business ventures, I'll start with the inns. The California inn is rather small as you know. They can only accommodate a maximum of seven couples at a time. However, the rooms stay booked year-round, and after all expenses and overhead, that inn is showing a profit of four million. The Virginia inn is pricier, and will accommodate more guests, and it has shown a profit of nine million. These two operations are at max capacity now, and they both look sustainable, so I'd say, barring any major change, this income stream can be used as a steady and predictable source for the future, unlike the wineries, where grape production can be impacted by weather."

Shade thought there must be some mistake. Holding up his hand to stop the flow of talk, he interrupted Roberto. "Let me understand this. The incomes for both inns have amounted to thirteen million? Well, that is interesting. I didn't expect them to fail, but I never expected they would produce this much. *Cazzo*, they have done well. Pleases me. Go on."

The accountant nodded. "Very good, master. Now, moving on to the lavender and sunflower productions. My lady planted 800 acres here at Bel Rosso. As you know, year one was a break-even year as the plants were maturing. She expanded the production to California in year two, planting another 800 acres out there. Also, in year two, we started showing profits on the Virginia production, and break-even in California. Now both farms are in full production. The farms yield about $30,000 per acre, once we net out expenses, so we have twenty-four million for Bel Rosso farms, and about nineteen million for California. The California yield will catch up to the Virginia yield as it continues to mature, but for this year, that is forty-three million."

Shade was stunned. Standing up, he paced the floor, running his hand through his thick black curls. Stopping in his tracks, he turned and stared at him.

"There is no way. You made some mistake! Flowers? She made Medici forty-three million planting flowers? *Cazzo.* What in the hell am I doing in the wine business, if this woman can make that kind of money?"

Walking back to his leather chair, he flopped down in disbelief. "To be honest with you, I thought she was just playing around, looking for something to do with her time. She had this idea in her head, and I have not paid much attention to it. We had the land, and it made her happy. The fields look beautiful, and they have helped draw tourists to the winery. I'll be damned!"

Shaking his head, he couldn't fathom the fields of purple and yellow flowers blowing in the breeze produced this type of income. "What in the hell does she do with that stuff?"

The accountant shuffled through his papers, adjusting his glasses. "Uh, well, that figure does include the agri-tourism numbers. As you are aware, visiting wineries is a popular past-time for the mortals. They pay a lot of money to tour vineyards, and both Bel Rosso and California vineyards draw more than their fair share because of the lavender and sunflower fields. Bel Rosso is listed in all the travel journals as a top tourist site with the mountain views, the horses, the vineyards and the bright fields of purple and yellow. People travel from all over the world to see it. You have done well separating your private property from the areas where you allow public access. My lady sells fresh flowers to the tourists who come here to taste and buy wine, but primarily, she sells the oils of both plants to very high-end manufacturers of bath and body care products, and essential oil manufacturers."

Steepling his fingers and resting his elbows on the arms of his chair, he sighed deeply. "I need to pay more attention to these businesses. I knew the tourist venture was doing well. Hell, we might as well go full out and produce these things ourselves. Maybe she needs her own label, her own perfumes and such. Where in the hell was this woman all my life? Is there anything else I need to know about? It sounds to me as if all things are a go and producing income. Are there any properties draining money I need to be aware of? How is Rachael? Does she have adequate funds?"

"Master, Rachael is fine. Her home is paid for, and she has

only to contact our office whenever she has any needed repairs. Her bills come directly to our office; she never sees them. She has the credit card you provided for her personal expenses, and I must say, she has chosen to live modestly. She doesn't travel, but prefers to stay at home, working her garden, knitting, reading, her pleasures are simple. We check with her monthly to see if there is anything she needs. As for my lady...well, she has mentioned that with the flowers, since they attract so many honeybees, she has considered a bee farm. It won't be massively productive from a financial point of view. Probably producing enough honey to be sold locally in shops across the state, but the bees will help with the pollination, and improve the yield on the plants. So, if I might be so bold, I'd never dare to suggest what you should do, but if my lady were to suggest adding a bee farm, I would say, uh, financially, that would be a smart move."

"*Si*, I agree full heartedly. I never refuse her anything, and she does little for herself. She has done a good job managing these ventures, the houses, and the fields. I have also given you a list of raises I want implemented immediately for my staff and my warriors. Marco will send you the list for the Castello leaders. We are moving along rapidly, and I want them to be rewarded highly for their dedication and hard work. I rely on them far more than ever before. I want their income to move with the times. Bees? Honey and bees."

As Shade chuckled out loud, the accountant gave him a puzzled look. "You will have to excuse my laughter, but honey holds a soft spot in my heart."

Roberto blushed as he adjusted his glasses. He didn't live on the property, but he knew everyone in the coven, and they all understood well the song he played for her, "Tupelo Honey."

"Uh, yes master." Their discussion was interrupted by a loud bang as the door was pushed open and Lorenzo entered the room, dragging a toy sword that was two times longer than he was.

"Daddy! Can we play warrior now? I been practicin'. Look!"

Lorenzo swung the long sword, knocking a lamp off the

table and it crashed to the floor. "Uh oh. Mommy said no swords in the house."

Shade looked at his son, who only sporadically remembered the rules about closed doors and manners. He could never be too stern with him. He was so young and there was time to teach him all the things he'd be required to know to be a prince. Watching as the play sword they made together swung through the air and the lamp crashed to the floor, the accountant looked nervous and uneasy around children. Shade bit his lip not to laugh out loud.

"I suggest, little warrior, you lay down your weapon and plead defeat. Your *madre* will not be pleased with either of us. Now come."

Lorenzo scurried to his father, climbing into his lap, his face showing no signs of remorse.

"Let us understand one thing. When you enter my office, you knock, to make sure it is appropriate to enter, *si*? Then you greet our guest and show respect. That is proper etiquette for a young prince and warrior. Now I suggest, before your mommy comes in here, ready to put you in time out, you say hello to our guest. You are a Medici, and you need to learn to be polite and show respect to those of our coven."

Lorenzo tucked his head. "I'm sorry, Daddy." He looked up at the accountant before sliding from his father's lap and approaching him. Lorenzo extended his small hand. "Please to meet you. My name is Lorenzo. I'm a prince but my mommy says I don't need to say that yet."

Roberto shook his hand and bowed his head slightly. "I am quite honored to meet you, Prince Lorenzo."

***

Kate heard the crash from upstairs and didn't have to think twice about who the cause of the commotion might be. She headed down the stairs and in the direction of the study to see what mischief Lorenzo had gotten into now. She stepped into the study to see the smashed lamp, the sword lying on the floor beside the mess, and Lorenzo shaking hands with the accountant.

She sighed and shook her head. "Lorenzo? What have we discussed about playing with the sword in the house?"

Lorenzo turned and ran back to his father, climbing up in his lap.

Rubbing his back, Shade leaned into his ear and in a soft voice, gave him some guidance. "You need to answer your mommy. She is asking you a question. You need to be accountable for your actions, son. Never lie, especially to her. Be my little warrior and do as Mommy asks of you, *si*?"

Lorenzo kept his face buried in his father's chest as he answered her, his response muffled. "You said swords were for outside, but I was just practicin'. I was showin' Daddy."

Kate exchanged a glance with Shade, who was looking away, trying hard not to smile at his son's antics. Kate knelt down by the chair and turned Lorenzo's small face, so he must look at her. "And now Emma will have a mess to clean up. And Mommy must buy a new lamp for Daddy's study. So, what do you think your punishment should be, young warrior?"

Lorenzo looked skyward as he thought about a punishment. "Uhmm..." He looked to his father who continued to look out the window, biting his lip. "Maybeeeeeeeee... uh, no nap?"

Kate raised her eyebrows. "Oh, no nap? But a warrior needs his naps, so I think not. I think time-out for three minutes."

Lorenzo sighed, knowing this was one battle he had lost for sure. Kate lifted him from his father's lap, as they both exchanged a glance and a smile over Lorenzo's head. Kate shook her head. "Just wait until there are two." She carried him out of the room.

Shade watched her as she left. Lorenzo's antics made him want to laugh and he knew he shouldn't encourage him. "*Mi amore*, please wait. Can you bring Lorenzo back here for just a moment?"

Kate looked at him over her shoulder. She wouldn't question him in front of Lorenzo, or the accountant, but she hoped he wouldn't over-rule her discipline of Lorenzo. She turned and carried Lorenzo back to his father. Lorenzo felt freedom in his future and was squirming like crazy to get down and back to the safety of his father's lap. He was small but strong, and Kate released him as he clamored back into his father's lap.

Lorenzo tried to curl up into a ball and snuggle into his father's neck, as he had done since his birth. But Shade had no intentions of letting that happen. Grasping him under his small arms, he lifted Lorenzo, so they were nose-to-nose and the child stared at him. "*Grazie,* for admitting your actions to your mother. But I believe you have forgotten to pick up your sword, return it to your mommy. She will now hold that weapon until she thinks you are ready to have it back. You get three minutes time out, no peeps from you, and then you will take your nap. But there is one other thing you need to know, Lorenzo."

Lorenzo leaned forward, placing his nose against his father's. "What, Daddy?"

"That I love you. I will always love you." Shade kissed his son on the forehead, as Lorenzo's tiny arms went around his neck. Placing him on his feet on the floor, Shade nodded to him. "Now, retrieve your sword, give it to Mommy and walk with her for your time-out and nap. Mommy does not need to hold you constantly. Go." Shade looked up at *bel* and winked.

Lorenzo ran for the sword and Kate told him to be careful of the broken lamp. He picked it up and dragged it behind him, careful not to knock over anything else. Kate took the sword and thanked him but told him she'd decide when he could have it back to play with outside. Lorenzo flashed a look over his shoulder at his father as they left the study. Shade nodded at him, and Lorenzo sighed. Kate took his hand and led him from the room.

"You come get me if I nap too long, Daddy."

Winking at him, Shade nodded. "I will come get you if we need you for battle, little warrior."

Shade heard him ramble on and on, as Kate led him out and down the hallway. Looking up at Roberto, he found him sitting quietly.

"My apologies for holding you up, Roberto. Our house is never quiet. Are we done here? I feel like I have signed my life away tonight. But you have done an impressive job with the accounts. I am pleased."

Roberto nodded. His visits to his master were rare. They usually conducted business by phone. He found it a treat to see for himself what the others had told him, about master, and my lady, and their growing family.

"No, master, we're done for now. I can always call if something comes up."

Standing, shaking hands with Roberto, Shade led him to the door of the office. "It has been a pleasure, as always. Gi will see you out."

Watching as he walked out, closing the door behind him, the figures ran through his head. Fifty-six million dollars...bees, honey and she was still expanding. The Council was eating their words for ever doubting her ability to be queen. His grin was wicked, and pride filled. *She is mine, all mine!*

3

Angelo stood with Shade inside the stables. One of the horses was ready to foal. The stables now housed twenty thoroughbred horses, and they had foaled at least six new colts within the last few years. Angelo informed him the mare would be a while yet before she delivered. He'd let him know, but he expected her to foal during the daylight hours now.

Leaving the stables, Shade headed back to the house, looking for Kate. There were a few things he wanted to talk to her about, mostly her little ventures that had turned into money making machines.

Walking to the patio that ran across the back of the house, he found her planting something in a huge terra cotta pot. He stood back and watched her hands as they worked through the dark, rich soil. She was more beautiful than the first night he saw her.

"You look tempting, even when you are up to your elbows in dirt, *mi amore*. Few more hours and my death slumber will snatch me away from you."

Kate looked up at him as she worked on the many container gardens that would grace the patio and be placed throughout the lush gardens that now made up their backyard. There was open space for Lorenzo to run, and he had a tire swing that Luca had hung for him in the huge oak tree. The patio was bathed in light from the floodlights that gave Shade the opportunity to enjoy this outdoor paradise, she had created for them. Kate reached up to brush the hair from her face, smudging the potting soil across her cheek, as she did so.

"Lover, I can't imagine I look very tempting in these gardening clothes, but you're kind to say so. It sounds like we'll have a new foal by day's end. Is everything okay?"

Walking up behind her, he slid his hands around her waist, rubbing her belly gently. "*Si*, the foal will come during the daylight. I will miss the birthing. But Angelo sees no problems.

The mare is healthy and ready. Tell me I am not dreaming, and we are alone."

Kate leaned back against him, pulling off the gardening gloves and freeing her hands to place over his. "Enjoy the peace and quiet while you can. Lorenzo is sleeping."

Nuzzling into her neck, he kissed her soft skin, and felt her heart beat faster. "Mmm, you smell earthy. I want to talk to you about something. Roberto was here earlier, as you well know. He told me some interesting information. Quite impressive, I might add. It explains to me why the hell you are so tired."

She looked at him with concern. "Is something wrong? Do you think I spent too much? Shade, I've tried to be so careful with our finances."

He shook his head and laughed. "*Bel,* when in the hell are you going to realize, I have more damn money than you can ever spend. But now, it seems you have contributed to that a great deal. Do you have any idea how much money your projects have earned this year?"

She shook her head. "Well, not an exact figure, no. Your people handle the negotiations, selling the plants for their oils. I know the crops have done well. I know the visits to the winery are up and people like walking the grounds and picking the lavender and the sunflowers. They're charged for what they pick. Both inns are doing well. Reynaldo says they have to turn away four out of every five calls because they're booked. When I ask Roberto about the money, he says things are fine. He never shares specifics with me."

"Come, take a walk with me. Let me enlighten you a bit." Letting go of her waist, taking her hand, they strolled casually through the gardens, the fragrant smell of lavender carried on the night air. "The inns are doing very well, their financial gain, a mere thirteen million. But that is not the biggest shock to me."

"Thirteen? I had...wow, that's wonderful! We must reward the staff for that. The places are beautiful, and people love being there. But you know the staff makes the experience, our chefs, and our managers."

Stopping in mid stride, he stared at her. "All you have to say is wow? And yes, I agree, it is about service, they come for a vacation, a break from the mundane, and we give it to them. But *mi amore*, the most astounding thing I learned, is about these flowers, these fields of yellow and lavender. They brought in forty-three million! How did you know this would happen? It blows my mind to think flowers could be so productive financially."

She turned and looked at him as she absorbed the number. She never knew how much money he had. To this day, she didn't know his net worth. He never spoke about money, other than to tell her to buy whatever she wanted, but all she wanted was him, and this life they were building together.

"I knew it was a profitable crop. I found information online, and we had all this land, and then we bought the property next to us. It was just something I saw in my head. Having our home surrounded by these glorious fields of color. And it seemed to fit so well with the vineyards. I never expected... I mean, I thought it would make money, but I never expected this."

Her head was already filling with ideas. "But you know, I wanted to add a bee farm. The flowers draw so many bees, and if we add a bee farm, we can produce our own honey."

She turned and walked backward so she could face him, linking both his hands in hers. "And we're so good at making honey, are we not?"

His heart hammered in his chest. She'd never understand what she did to him. She could ask him for the moon, and he'd find a way to give it to her. He'd give her whatever she wanted.

"Your honey is the sweetest. So, I think bees and honey are perfect." Picking her up, he held her against his chest, her body molding into his. "I love you."

She ran her hands through his thick dark hair and looked into those eyes. She remembered the first time she ever saw him, how he locked her in that gaze and left her dumb-struck and speechless. His beauty still had the power to stop her in her tracks. "And I love you. After all this time, I still struggle to find the words to tell you how much."

"You don't need words. I feel it now. I have felt it since you were turned. We became one for all eternity and now, we feel every beat of each other's hearts. I am so proud of you. How much you take care of me, our *familia*, everyone around us. But I want you to consider something. Think outside the box. Expand the lavender and sunflower operations, make a brand for yourself. Your own line of bath products and perfumes, and other such luxuries women enjoy. Make this your own, Kate. You have this gift. You were in the advertising business. You know what it takes. I am sure Shannon would love to help you. Hell, she could go in with you. I just want you to flourish and be happy in all you do."

"Lover, I'm happy to be behind the scenes. I don't want to run a business full time. Maybe this is something we can think about for the future, for Shannon, if she's interested. I'm happy to create these things for our family and have the people in the coven employed. I'd like to add the honey. That we could brand. And I think in Florence, there is property there that hasn't been developed, and we should expand into olives. The climate is right. You know it would do well. The olives can be harvested for olive oil for consumption, but the oil is also used in bath and beauty products, just like the lavender and sunflowers, and we already have those contacts."

"Woman! Does your mind ever stop? I never met a woman whose mind rolled constantly. Do whatever makes you happy, it obviously works. Anything else you want to do?"

He felt the first effects of his death slumber come over him, as the sun moved closer to the horizon. Brushing back a lock of crimson from her face, her hair still charmed him. She was his siren, and that hair was her calling card.

"Talk to me, *mi amore*. I love Lorenzo, but I see what a demand he is on your time. I do not remember ever being around my own *padre* when I was young. He had little to do with me until I was old enough for the camp. I do not want that for Lorenzo. I want him to come to me always, with anything. I am trying so hard to be a good *padre*. *Cazzo*, he is so smart. He makes me laugh and I cannot seem to love him enough, my heart aches sometimes from the volume of love I have for you both."

"I know that feeling well. He's so hard to discipline because he looks so cute, even when he misbehaves. He reminds me of his father." She chuckled. "But yes, I've been thinking of something. Lorenzo has so much energy, and so much curiosity. Theresa says we should start home schooling soon. It seems early to me, but she says immortals start earlier. Also, I take him with me into town sometimes. He is fascinated with the mortal children, and wants to play, but he still doesn't understand he's different, and there are things he needs to hide from them. I was thinking it's time to put in a swimming pool... well, two actually, one outside for the warm months, and one inside. It could be built underground, next to the bunker and the wine cellar. It will be there for Lorenzo, and for the other children that will follow. What do you think?"

He nodded in agreement. "The pool is a good idea. It will burn off some of that energy. Learning to swim is vital. And yes, Theresa is right. It is time to start the tutors. He will need a sound tutor to teach him the history of Medici, the history of our kind, as well as a mortal education and surviving in their world. He will grow tired of the lessons; I can guarantee you that."

Walking slightly away from her, he lit up a cigarette and shuffled his feet. *Cazzo*, she was exposing Lorenzo to mortals.

Kate continued to talk to him, but noticed he was distracted. "We'll need a professional tutor soon then. Theresa will have her hands full when Sophia is born. Lover, is something wrong?"

Turning his head to look at her before looking up to the lightening sky of the approaching morning, he gauged his time. "*Si*."

Kate was aware of the early dawn light. Their life was dictated by the sun. "Shade, come inside. We'll talk there."

She took his hand as she led him inside the house, brushing the dirt from her knees. "Come upstairs, we have time for a bath together before your slumber." He followed her up the stairs, where she dropped her clothes in a pile before walking to the bathroom and filling the large tub with hot water. She stepped into the tub, as he followed her into the room, shedding his clothes and climbing in behind her.

She lay back against his chest. "Now talk to me. Tell me what's on your mind."

Picking up the large sponge, he dipped it into the hot water before he squeezed it, letting the soapy water run down her breasts. "Mortals, you expose him to mortals in town. Why would you do that?"

"Shade, he travels with us to Florence, to Paris. He sees the mortals when they visit the vineyards. He has to learn to function in their world. He's never left alone, unsupervised. And I talk to him before every outing, reminding him he can't expose his fangs, he can't teleport, or show his strength. He listens, but he doesn't yet understand. He sees children playing, and he wants to join them. It's hard for him to understand he's different, and they'll fear him. But you're not pleased. I can hear it in your voice. Tell me how to teach him. How does he learn about mortals?"

Listening to her, she made sense, but it was such a fine line they walked. One small error could expose them all. Grabbing the rose scented shampoo bottle, he squeezed the thick shampoo into his hand and then rubbed them together, lathering his hands into her hair.

"He needs to learn about mortals and how they are different. He is too young to understand how he will be judged and feared. He will feel the mortal children's fear if he makes a mistake. It could easily scare him as well. He needs to be mature enough to understand why he is different from them. I was never exposed to the mortals until I was much older. I was sheltered inside Castello and taught about the mortals by my tutors. It was drilled into me like my warrior skills. I know he must be exposed, but there is also a danger to him. He is a prince, a Medici, destined to inherit the throne. There are immortal forces out there as well that would do him harm. You expose him without cause when you leave here."

"I'm sorry, Shade. You know I'd never do anything I thought

would bring him harm. I'll keep him here, on Bel Rosso. But he's a lonely child. I mean, he's never at a loss for activity. Theresa and Nita, Luca and Shannon, even Gi plays with him. He follows you into the camp and I know the warriors adore him. And he loves Cory so much. But they're all adults. He has no children to interact with. I guess I never realized just how isolated he'd be. It must have been lonely for you too, when you were growing up."

"I did not mean for you to take this the wrong way *mi amore*, but I need you to understand the consequences. He is so curious, and that curiosity will get him killed, if we are not careful. I just want you to be aware of what could happen. I know you think we are remote out here, but if my enemies want what we have, they will come after it. There are no rules, and they will take what they want. They are not taking our son."

Sighing heavily, sinking further down into the water, he rested his chin on top of her head. "It was lonely for me as a child, but the children of the warriors at Castello were allowed to come and play. We were all protected there. That is why I am so close to Marco, why I was close to Luca's *padre* as well. We were close, tight knit, protected by our own. The times were very different, but we still faced dangers. We can't hide him indefinitely, but we can protect him inside these walls much easier. I am old fashioned. I can't help it, but I know what lies out there."

Kate laid her head back against his chest. The very thought of something happening to their child chilled her to the bone and she shivered in his embrace. No one would take him. She'd call forth the very demons of hell to protect him.

"He won't leave Bel Rosso again, not without both of us. He'll have a sister soon. I'll build the pools, and a tree house. Every boy needs a tree house. He'll have everything he needs right here."

The door creaked open as Lorenzo peeked his head around the door. Kate looked up to see him and could hear Theresa running after him, but it was too late. Lorenzo was fully clothed and running full speed for the bathtub and launched himself at the two of them, landing in a splash. Kate was laughing, when she should be scolding.

Theresa was standing outside the door. "I'm sorry, my lady. He got away from me."

"Don't worry, Theresa. We'll handle it." Kate looked over her shoulder at Shade, water dripping off his long locks. "Like I said, I'll start building a pool."

4

Angelo and the stable hands had had a few long nights. They had just delivered the third and final foal of the spring. He worked to muck out the stalls and move the mother and her new foal into a fresh stall. He'd give them a few days before taking the young foals into the pasture to test their legs. He was shouting orders to the stable hands when he heard Impavido kicking at his stall and getting restless, and almost simultaneously, he picked up the acrid smell of smoke.

Angelo dropped the pitchfork and ran to the other end of the stables where he had left Lorenzo playing. The section of the stables used to store the bales of hay and feed was smoldering, and ready to burst into flames. Angelo called for help, the other stable hands rushed in to move the animals away from the danger, just as the hay bursts into flames, the fire spreading quickly. Angelo screamed for Lorenzo who had been playing on the hay bales, but the child was nowhere to be seen.

***

Kate was inside with Lorenzo who had returned from playing in the stables. His little boots were muddy, as were his hands and face. "Lorenzo, did you leave any mud outside?"

The normally talkative child nodded his head yes. Kate laughed, picking him up, so he wouldn't track mud through the house, and carried him to the tub. She and Theresa were stripping him down and placing him in the tub when Kate felt the fear from the horses.

"Theresa, something's going on in the stables. Can you finish this?"

"Of course, my lady."

Kate kissed Lorenzo on the forehead and rushed out, running to the stables. She could see the smoke starting to rise.

Angelo called out telepathically to Shade. They needed help getting the animals away from the fire, and he couldn't find

Lorenzo!

***

Marcello and Shade had finished the drills held inside the gym with the new recruits. They had picked up a lot of new warriors this spring, and they had been rebuilding their ranks since the battle with Max. Heading outside onto the field, they had split the warriors into three groups, each one concentrating on a specific weapon. Walking toward Marcello's group first, he picked up the smell of smoke. He turned in the direction of the house and saw the smoke rolling from the stables. His heart pounded as he heard the horses, panicked in their stalls. Angelo screamed inside his head that Lorenzo was in there!

Shade called out to Marcello and the other warriors and they teleported instantly to the stables, the hay bales along the back wall completely engulfed. Where is Lorenzo? Angelo was barking orders, as Shade shouldered past stable hands and warriors leading the panicked horses out of the stables, as they screamed in fright.

Shade called out to his son. "Lorenzo! Come to Daddy!"

Shade couldn't see him anywhere and was about to run into the flames, when he heard *bel*.

Kate ran into the stables amid the chaos of screaming horses, as the warriors worked furiously to open the stalls and let them run free. She saw Shade as he ripped at the bales of hay, calling for Lorenzo. He thinks Lorenzo is trapped here!

"Shade, no!" Kate ran to him, grabbed at his shoulders and pulled him back from the flames. "He's safe! He's in the house." She could feel the heat of the flames on her face as she pulled at him.

He felt her trying to pull him free, the flames scorching his arms and the smoke filling his lungs. Suddenly, her words hit him full force. Lorenzo was in the house! Turning, he saw her fear for him, and he picked her up and ran with her outside the stables.

"Stay here. Don't move!"

He headed back inside the stables, and Impavido was

coming at him full speed. "Whoa boy, whoa!"

The horse bolted past him and Shade grabbed his mane and swung onto the horse, mounting him as he fled from the fire. The horse was panicked and wasn't responding to his efforts to calm him. The frantic actions of the other horses didn't help. Impavido was heading straight for the fence line. Gripping his mane, Shade leaned over the horse's massive head as they took the fence together. He leaned into his ear, while using his thighs to grip the horse and tried to slow him down.

"Come on boy, it's okay. We got this. Calm down."

He gradually got the panicked horse under control, but he could see the other horses ready to jump the fence, following behind the stallion. Telepathically, he let Angelo know the animals were out, but they needed to control the horses in the field before they bolted. Shade could hear the warriors. Some were grabbing fire extinguishers, putting out the flames and others rushed to the field to help corral the panicked horses. Telepathically, he called to Kate, *"I need help bel, talk to them! The horses are going to jump, help me control them."*

Kate responded and called for help in controlling the horses, as Aegis, Night Stalker and Warrior surrounded the herd and started to corral them into the pasture. As Bravado ran past Kate, she grabbed the horse's mane, and jumped on, using it to guide him. She rode among the horses, calming them, as she led them away from the fence and out into the center of the field, away from the stables. She glanced over her shoulder to see Shade on Impavido. He jumped the fence and led the massive horse in her direction.

"Shade, what happened? How did the fire get started?"

Shade looked on in amazement as the horses all responded to her, calming immediately, and following her out into the field, grazing, as if nothing had just happened. Riding up to her, Impavido and Bravado rubbed noses, leaning into each other, providing comfort to each other.

"I don't know yet, *mi amore*. Are you all right? *Cazzo*, this happened so fast. Let's go see how bad the mess is, make sure everyone is okay, and see what damage was done to the stables."

Leaning over, he lifted her from her horse, taking her in his arms and sitting her in front of him.

"Tell me you are both fine because I never want to feel that damn fear again. I thought Lorenzo was inside the stables. Angelo said he could not find Lorenzo. Was he inside the stables earlier?"

"Yes, he goes to the stables almost every day. He loves the horses, and he loves being around Angelo. He'd just come back inside, covered in mud as usual. I was getting ready to give him a bath when I felt the horses' fear. Thank God he wasn't in there when the fire started."

Shade shook his head. "I can't imagine how this started."

As they rode to the stables, Angelo came out and they inspected the damage. Although the fire seemed fierce at the time, little damage was done to the stables. The hay had allowed the flames to grow to such intensity so quickly. The rapid response from the stable hands helped to prevent the fire from spreading.

Shade shouted out orders, as the stable hands rounded up the horses and inspected each one, making sure they were all accounted for, and there were no injuries. Angelo assured him they were all fine, and the stable hands started to lead the animals back into their respective stalls once they calmed down. Angelo and the other stable hands would clean up the mess from the fire and attend to the horses.

Angelo told him he had no idea how or why the fire started, and they couldn't see any evidence of sabotage in the mess left behind, leaving them all a bit baffled. Angelo said he'd seen Lorenzo playing near the hay bales and hadn't seen him leave the stables, so he assumed he was still inside.

Looking at Kate, Shade requested her assistance. "Maybe he saw something. Can you ask Aegis if she escorted him back to the house? I want to know if he saw anything unusual."

Kate dismounted Bravado and knelt down, calling Aegis to her. The she-wolf walked forward as Kate leaned in and placed her head against the wolf. "Aegis, were you with Lorenzo? Did you bring him home?"

Kate looked up at Shade. "She says she was lying outside the stables. She didn't go in because the horses don't like it. She said Lorenzo came out of the stables quickly and ran back to the house, and she followed him there. Once he was inside, she returned to the woods. Do you think Lorenzo knows something about the fire?"

"I don't know, *mi amore*. Angelo does not smoke in the stables, and none of the stable hands do either. It is one of my rules. It is dangerous to smoke here for this reason. But we are going to find out."

With the warriors helping to clean up, and things under control, Shade and Kate walked back to the house, his mind rolling. Shade was wondering if Lorenzo could have seen someone in the area that might offer a clue.

"I don't want to scare him, but we need to find out what he knows. It is possible he may have seen someone around the stables, and that is what sent him back to the house. I can't come up with a reasonable answer as to how this happened."

As they entered the house, Theresa greeted them with a freshly bathed Lorenzo in tow. "Is everything all right, my lady? We could see the smoke from here."

Kate grabbed up Lorenzo and hugged him tight. He smelled like soap and sunshine, and she buried her face in his hair. "Everything is fine, Theresa. No real damage. Angelo responded quickly, and the horses are safe."

Turning to Lorenzo, she inquired, "Lorenzo, there was a fire in the stables where the horses live. Did you see anything?"

Lorenzo tucked his chin and shook his head no. Kate looked up at Shade. Lorenzo was a non-stop talker, and his sudden quietness was uncharacteristic. "Lorenzo, it's all right to tell me if you know something."

Lorenzo flashed a look at his father, and then asked, "Can I play with Warrior?"

Shade shook his head. "No, not at the moment. I want to know a few things. Can you help me? Daddy needs to figure out what happened. Come here."

Holding out his arms to his son, Lorenzo hesitated briefly and Shade's heart broke. Looking at *bel*, he knew she could feel his pain.

Lorenzo looked at Kate before going to his father's arm. He laid his chin on his shoulder. "I didn't do anything, Daddy."

Shade gently rubbed his back. He knew something had scared the child, he seemed off his game. "No one said you did, Lorenzo. But I want to know if you saw anything when you were at the stables. Did you see a stranger there? Mommy said you were playing in the stables, so I know you were inside with the horses. You are not in trouble, Lorenzo, but if you saw anything that can help Daddy figure this out, it would be a big help."

Lorenzo shook his head. "No strangers. I would go to Angelo if I saw a stranger. No strangers, Daddy. I was just playin'. I didn't do bad things."

Smiling, Shade kissed his cheek. "Of course, you would go to Angelo. That is the smart thing to do. You are a smart and brave warrior."

Feeling the boy cling to his neck and snuggle into him, Shade closed his eyes. He still had no idea what happened in the stables. "Are you tired, Lorenzo? Do you need a nap? Or hungry? Because if you are, Nita will feed you. You want Mommy to tuck you in, or Daddy?"

Lorenzo clung to his father. "Both. I want both."

Looking at Kate, Shade grinned. "You heard him, both."

Kate smiled at him, but this wasn't her normal Lorenzo. Something had spooked him in the stables, and he wasn't talking about it. She rubbed his back. "Of course, my beautiful boy, we'll both tuck you in, and Theresa will send Nita in to feed you, and sing to you."

Lorenzo held out his chubby hand to her. "You feed me, Mommy."

Kate looked at Shade, and they exchanged a glance. "Of course, Lorenzo. Let's go upstairs to your room, the three of us, okay? You know you're safe here, right?"

Lorenzo nodded but didn't release the death grip he had

around his father's neck.

Shade saw her glance and knew Kate was feeling the same thing he was. Something was very wrong here. But he could think of no reason for Lorenzo to lie. "Come along then, little warrior, time for you to feed and get some sleep. Daddy has work to do before the night is over."

Walking upstairs into his room, Kate sat in the huge rocker. As Lorenzo released his grip, Shade slid him into Kate's arms and Lorenzo immediately curled up on her shoulder, nuzzling into her neck and began to feed. He was way too damn quiet, and that bothered Shade. He took a seat on the sleep sofa and watched as the woman he loved gave nourishment to his son. It was something to behold.

Lorenzo's blue eyes looked at him once in a while as he fed. His small hand fisted around the crimson of his mother's hair, his other hand lying gently on her breast. *Cazzo,* he loved them more than his own life.

It didn't take Lorenzo long to feed, he was still small, and it took little for him to fulfill his need for her blood. His eyelids fluttered open and closed as he struggled to stay awake. Her blood having the complete opposite effect on the child as it did on him. He watched as she rocked him slowly, holding him in her arms, her eyes never leaving him.

Kate could feel how her blood calmed him, soothed him. She could feel her child relax in her arms, as whatever troubled him, left his mind. She gently rocked in the chair, rubbing her hand up and down his back. She could feel him unlatch, as his body relaxed, and she stood and placed him in his 'big boy' bed. He reached up to her with both arms and she leaned over and kissed him. He hugged her and gave her a wet kiss on the cheek.

"I love my beautiful boy. Nothing will ever change that. You understand, don't you, Lorenzo?"

He nodded. His eyes were heavy with sleep. Kate handed him his ragged teddy bear and he clasped the toy tight, holding the tattered bear under his chin. With his free hand, he reached up for his father.

Leaning down, Shade kissed him softly on his chubby

cheeks. Lorenzo gripped his father's long curls and kissed him back.

"Sleep little warrior, tomorrow is another day to conquer. *Ti amo, per sempre.*"

As Shade took Kate's hand, they walked to the door. She turned out the light, closing the door, as they left the room. Shade turned to her. "We need to talk."

Kate nodded and led him to their bedroom where she closed the door. "Lover, he was frightened by something. But I'm sure he's telling the truth when he says no strangers. Besides, you know Aegis and the others would never allow a stranger to wander onto the part of our property we have marked as private. But something is bothering him."

"I feel the same way. Maybe he is just frightened because he felt our fear. He had to hear the horses, the screaming, and the chaos. He is not immune to it, and his senses are more intense than a mortal child. There is something else we need to talk about as well."

"What's that?"

"Feeding. The *bambino* is going to zap your energy soon. You will have to deny Lorenzo as you do me. Nita will have to be his source completely. I can't allow you to get weak. He drains you enough as it is, keeping up with him all day. I see how you look at him, I know it will hurt to deny him, but you have to. We will get through it, I promise you. And if he needs comfort, I can feed him. I do not want you to be upset with me. I'm just making sure you are not overdoing it, si?"

Raising this child had presented so many challenges for her, and sharing the feeding with Nita and Theresa, so she could provide for her mate was only one of them. If he were a mortal child, he would have been weaned from breast feeding or bottle feeding by now. Lorenzo advanced much quicker than mortal children in his physical and mental development, in every area except the feeding. That was something he'd need from her, and his wet feeder, until he was almost an adult. It was her one means to cling to his childhood, but she knew Shade was right. The life inside her now would demand everything, and she'd once again have to give up Shade feeding from her, as well as the rare times her son sought her out for comfort.

"I know you're right, Shade. He usually goes to Nita. He loves her, and she's so good with him. But he was afraid tonight. It was the comfort more than the feeding he sought. But I'll talk to him."

Taking her in his arms, he could feel the pain in her heart. "I understand. I am not dismissing what you did, *bel*. He needs his *madre* for many things. I just need to remind you of what is to come, so you can prepare your heart before it happens. He will not like it. He will push you to your limits to give in to him. You need to stay strong for the *bambino* to survive, si?"

Taking her hand, he led her to their bed where she climbed atop the mattress. He stroked her cheek, staring into those incredible amber eyes. "I should run back to the stables really quick to make sure everything is okay before sunrise, but I want you to feed first."

Kate lay on her back, looking up into those blue eyes. She brushed his hair back from his face as she smiled at him. "Lover, it's early in this pregnancy yet. You would have me in this bed until the baby comes. I'm fine, really. I'll wait for daybreak, when you can join me here."

Leaning on his elbows, he shook his head. "Are you throwing me out of your bed, woman?" Slapping her thigh lightly, he chuckled and climbed from the bed. "You know I love you, and I worry when you are carrying our *bambino*. That is never going to stop."

She laughed softly. "I'll never throw you out of our bed. And please feel free to bring me here anytime. Just be sure you plan to stay when you do."

He chuckled. "I do have warriors and horses to attend to. What are you going to do besides pine away for your savage lover?"

Pulling his t-shirt over his head, he snapped it over her ass as she rolled over and growled. "Do not start growling now, I have been unceremoniously thrown from your bed and told to come back later, so now, you must suffer, my queen."

Laughing, he walked to the armoire and pulled a clean white t-shirt over his head. Standing tall with his arms across his chest, he stared at her.

Kate lifted her face from the pillow, looking back at him through her tousled red hair. "Warriors? You have warriors to take care of? I remember a time, when warriors would not have been a distraction. I must be losing my touch. But get back to your warriors, and I'll be here when you get home."

"Nothing distracts me from you. You have not lost your touch. You inflame my heart more now than ever before. Tell me you still love me."

Kate watched him move about the bedroom, tossing the one shirt aside as he pulled on another. His body as beautiful and toned as the first day she saw him. "I love you even more, if that's possible. You fill my heart. And I'll always be here. Go back to the stables. I'll call the contractors about the pools. I'll see you at sunrise, right here, next to me."

Walking to her, he kissed her passionately. He loved her so damn much. "Deal."

Walking out the door and down the hall, he opened the door to Lorenzo's room and peeped in. His soft regulated breathing told him he was asleep. Walking to the bed, he saw him clutching his bear. Pulling a soft blanket over him, Shade kissed his cheek and headed to the stables. Nothing was ever simple in his life and it sure as hell never would be, but there was one thing he knew without doubt. He was loved.

5

Raven teleported back to the California inn, now his permanent home. For the first time in his young life, he felt he belonged. He was the SIC (second in command) over the five warriors assigned to protect the inn and the inhabitants. He loved it here. He'd grown up a lot in the few years since the Battle of Bel Rosso, and he'd found Mica. They now shared Mica's apartment over the large garage that housed master's collection of expensive sports cars, and Mica fed solely from him.

They weren't mated in the eyes of the Council, since the vampire community didn't acknowledge same sex mating. It wasn't discouraged, just not acknowledged, since the pairing couldn't produce children. Master had approved their living together, and that was all the permission Raven needed. Raven allowed Mica to feed from him, but they had yet to seal their blood covenant, and Raven still needed a source to feed. He'd restricted his feeding to visits to a feeder coven in San Francisco. It was safe, but less than satisfying, and left both he and Mica wanting more.

Raven felt the call to hunt, but he loved Mica, and he didn't want to jeopardize what they had together. It was almost daybreak and he knew Mica would be up, preparing for his day working at the inn. He had a quick smoke and looking like he just rolled in from an all-nighter, still dressed in his slick leathers, he strolled into the apartment.

Mica stepped out of the shower and started getting dressed for the day. The inn was packed as usual, and he was sure Reynaldo was already in the kitchen starting to prep for the breakfast orders. Mica heard Raven come in and he glanced at the clock and sighed. They had been together now for three years, and while he fed exclusively from Raven, he knew Raven still went to the feeders. Mica had no reason to doubt his fidelity, but the beast in them all demanded what he demands.

He didn't want a fight, but things were going to have to change. Mica stepped into the bedroom to find a bedraggled Raven.

In a stern voice, he addressed Raven, "Well, young warrior, looks like you had a good night."

Raven looked up at Mica who was wearing only a towel, barely hanging from his hips, his hair blown dry and styled. Raven whipped his waist-length black hair out of his eyes, as he stared at Mica. Again, with the reprimand, like a father berating a child. Slipping off his leather jacket, he hung it in the closet and held up his hand to Mica.

"We've been through this before. Do you want me to starve? You know what happens when I starve. I tend to go a little, wait, what was the word you used?" Sliding off his leather pants, he shook his head. "Oh yes, animalistic. Come on, cut me some slack, it's just where I go to feed. Nothing more." Flopping down on the bed, he sighed.

Mica put on a starched white shirt and pulled on a pair of dress pants, a stark contrast to the leathers worn by Raven. They were an unlikely pair, but Mica had never been happier, with the exception of this issue of feeding. He stood with his back to Raven. "I don't want you to starve, babe. I'm just saying...I'm tired of sharing."

Raven gave him a soft smile. He loved when Mica called him babe. "I only go to feeders. I do what I have to do. Doesn't mean I like it. You know that." Standing, he walked to Mica, laying his head on his shoulder. "Tell me what you want, I'll do it. I'll do anything for you."

Mica placed both hands on the dresser and bowed his head, taking a deep breath. Their community made no judgments about feeding and sex between same sex vampires. But mating was different. The ritual of mating was reserved for those seeking a life-long commitment, and planned to procreate, so same sex mating was rare. He felt Raven's head against his shoulder and wondered if this young warrior would stay with him for the long run.

"Will you do anything? No, you don't need to answer that. I know the answer. My real question is, for how long? Where do you see us going, Raven?"

Lifting his head, Raven stepped back from him. "Are you asking me if I'll remain with you? You don't trust me. You think I'm too wild. I'm a warrior, that's the problem, isn't it? I'm young, and you think because I live a lifestyle different than yours, I'll find someone else who will interest me."

Turning his back, he walked across the room and finished undressing. He didn't look at Mica but could feel in him the unease about their relationship. "How long, you ask me? What kind of question is that? I've told you I love you. I've never told anyone that."

Raven closed his eyes, as the memories came flooding back to him. He came from the lowest class of vampire and abandoned on the streets. He thought no one would love him because he was different and didn't look or act like the others. "I thought you were different. But you're just like them." He walked to the closet and began to gather his clothes, shoving them unceremoniously into a huge duffel bag.

Mica sighed. He'd grown used to the drama from this young vampire, and knew he responded out of insecurity. He moved quickly, and grabbed Raven's hands, stopping him from packing.

"That's not what I mean at all, babe. Now stop. I have no right to ask this of you. You're still young, but would you consider...would you think about...just feeding from me? It would make this permanent, but I don't know if you're ready to make things permanent."

Raven's head snapped up and he stared back at Mica, the emotions rolling over him as he shook his head, making sure he'd heard correctly. He could feel his chest heaving, his breath coming very hard.

"You have every right to ask. I might be young, but I've lived more than most in my years. Do you have any idea how hard it's been to restrain from feeding from the one person in the world I want the most? If I weren't warrior to Medici, I'd have done so already. It's all I think about. I want to be yours, Mica, yours and no one else. No one else makes me feel this cared for. I'm past ready. I belong to you, and I want to make it permanent. Look at you, you're so beautiful to me, your spirit and love for me... I thought...well, I thought I was too much for you, so I didn't ask."

Mica closed his eyes and said a silent prayer of thanks. "But will your master approve? You should check with him first, don't you think? I mean, you were raised in his coven, and I now work for him. I know he's aware of our relationship. But mating, that doesn't always go over so well in our world. Your master is progressive in many things, but he's still old school too, adhering to traditions. Before we move forward, I think we need his approval."

Raven nodded. "Boss-man might bust a fang on this one. My lady won't be a problem. Yeah, we'll have to ask permission, but I want you with me. We should do this together. Boss-man loves me, he'll see I'm serious, and I'll have to convince him if he has reservations. It won't change my role as his warrior."

He slipped off one of the many gold filigree rings he'd had made in Florence. They were each unique in their design, no two the same. Taking Mica's left hand in his, he slid it over his ring finger.

"In the meantime, until we get approval, you belong to me, and I belong to you for eternity. I know what it means. I've been waiting for what seems an eternity to find someone who understands me, loves me and wants to be with me."

Mica looked at the unique ring on his finger and smiled. It's nothing he would ever have chosen to wear for himself, but he'd wear it proudly as it screamed of Raven. He lifted his hand to his mouth and kissed the ring.

"I'll never take it off. And I'll gladly accompany you to talk with Master Shade. If you think my lady can pave the way, maybe you should tell her first. She seems to be able to talk him into most anything."

Laying his head on Mica's chest, his hand slid up Mica's arm and into his hair, letting his fingers play. "I'll talk to her, I promise. I'll visit there today when master is sleeping, talk to her first. Then we can make an appointment to see boss-man together."

Mica had to tap down his excitement. There was nothing he wanted more than for Raven to feed from him, for the two of them to be able to make their relationship exclusive. But they were owned by their masters, and subject to their approval. Mica wouldn't approach Alec. He hadn't seen or heard from him in years. He doubted Alec even knew who he was. His master was more interested in his mortal pursuits than to concern himself with his coven. Many had left Canton's coven on their own, seeking other covens. Mica felt more like a Medici now than he ever felt bonded to Canton's coven. Everything would hinge on Shade's approval, and until then, Mica could only keep his fingers crossed.

"Then don't delay, babe. The sooner we have an answer, the better. The waiting will surely kill me."

Raven took his face in his hands and kissed him. Moaning, he could barely move fast enough to get back to Bel Rosso. "I'm taking a shower and teleporting straight out. Let me handle my family. I know them best. I won't be too long, I promise. I'll talk with my lady, and make sure we have an appointment with master. I love you, Mica. Don't ever let me go, even if he doesn't approve, please don't let me go."

Mica held him close. "Others won't dictate my choice, young warrior, with or without their approval. I'm not going anywhere."

6

Raven teleported into Bel Rosso, landing at the main house. The place was looking great, and there were times he missed it. He missed all the activity and joking around with his fellow warriors. He was greeted quickly by Aegis, and he ruffled her ears as she curled around his legs. "Missed you too, Wolfie."

Raven was nervous about talking to Kate, but not nearly as nervous as he'd be telling boss-man. He wasn't sure how his master would respond. He'd changed so much since they had come to the States. Everything about his master was changing, and he knew most of that had to do with the queen.

Raven noted Gi's surprise when he opened the door and he asked for Lady Kate. Kate had always welcomed them, and he'd never forget the way she took care of them when they first came here. Gi escorted him to the living room before leaving to find Kate. Raven laughed when he saw Lorenzo's play sword lying on the couch. He picked it up and twirled it around in his hand.

Gi found Kate on the floor inside the teepee that had been erected in Lorenzo's bedroom. She was reading books to Lorenzo, who was quickly picking up the words and reading along with her.

"My lady, Raven is here to see you."

Kate looked up, surprised. She wasn't expecting a visit. She crawled out of the tent and told Lorenzo to play with his toys and she'd be back soon. Kate went downstairs to the living room to find Raven balancing Lorenzo's sword in the palm of his hand. She laughed. "If you get bored with that, there's a train set upstairs."

Raven turned quickly as he heard Kate enter and he spun the sword in the air with a flourish, caught it and bowed. "I believe I'm much better with swords, even small ones. How is the Prince? I hope you don't mind the unplanned visit, but I needed to speak with you on a personal matter, Lady Kate. If

I've come at a bad time...if you were catching a train or something, I can come back." His smile was broad and wide.

Kate motioned for him to sit. "Have a seat, Raven. I needed to get out of Lorenzo's teepee anyway. I was losing circulation in my legs. What brings you to Bel Rosso?"

Shaking his shaggy mane, he got serious. "Well, I've come to ask you something, get your advice on how the boss-man will react. It involves Mica."

He sat down on the couch after she took her seat and fiddled with one of the rings on his fingers, not really looking at her. Suddenly, he wasn't sure of what to say. But then he thought about Mica, and knew this was what he wanted, and he'd stand up and fight for them both.

Kate curled up on the sofa next to him, drawing her legs under her. "Of course! You aren't having any problems, I hope."

His head snapped up. "Oh no, it's nothing like that. I'm in love, for the first time in my life. I love Mica and he returns that love, more than I could ever have thought possible. The coven doesn't disregard us in any way, but it's rare when two of the same sex mates, forming a permanent bond. Our kind doesn't recognize a same sex mating. There's no stigma on the sex, but mating is reserved for well, mating to produce offspring. I want to ask boss-man for his approval of Mica and I mating. I want to be with Mica, stay with him for eternity. I don't know how Master Shade will take it. Five years ago, I'd never have thought about bringing this up to him. His thinking on the matter would have been old school, traditional. But I know he's different now. Mica and I have discussed it and we both agreed we should ask him, get his approval before we move forward."

Kate leaned her head back on the sofa and tried to anticipate Shade's response. "Raven, first of all, coming to him before you made the decision was very wise, and will go a long way. Shade is very old school in some things, and very progressive in others. But he holds tight with the tradition of the coven coming to him first before they make life altering changes. So, I know he'll respect you greatly for that. And when I search my heart, I can't imagine he'd deny you this. He has accepted, even encouraged, Marco and Theresa, as well as Luca and Shannon, and she's a mortal. I have to admit, I never thought of your circumstances before, and I should have. I never considered the idea of you and Mica sealing your bond with one another. But I think you should, if that's what you want. I can't promise you what his answer will be, but I promise if he asks for my opinion, you'll have my full support."

Raven leaned over and hugged her tight. "Mica was right. He knew you'd understand and guide me."

He quickly ended the hug and stood up, walking around the room, fiddling with his hair. "This was more a home to me than any place I lived, even more so than Castello. It will always be home to me. But California suits me. I fit in there. I feel comfortable there. *Grazie* for supporting me, I knew you'd understand that without Mica, I'm lost. He hates that I must go to the feeders, and it doesn't satisfy me either. I want to be his totally. I know you understand that more than anyone I know."

Kate bit her lip. "With all my heart, Raven, I totally understand. And Shade knows of your feelings for Mica. He sent you there because he knew that is where your heart called you to be."

Raven looked at his heavy boots against the warm tones of the plush rug beneath his feet. "He always did seem to know me better than I knew myself. I'll set up a meeting with him. Mica and I want to be together when we see him, so if you have anything you need from the inn, I can make sure Mica brings it along. I'll let you get back to Prince Lorenzo. I know he's probably a handful."

Kate laughed. "Lorenzo is more than a handful, and he keeps us all on our toes. Tell Mica I'm fine, he and Reynaldo do a great job of keeping me up to date on the inn, so I don't need anything. But before you leave, there's one thing. Whenever you visit, Poe comes around, and he seems very happy, very high energy, and after you leave, he disappears for a few days. Aegis says Poe has attached himself to you after the Battle of Bel Rosso. But since my gift of animalism bonds him to me, he'll never leave me, unless I release him to do so. That crazy bird came to me in the Council in Florence, and then showed up here. But I think his place is in California with you. What do you think?"

Looking down at his feet, he chuckled. "Poe is like my spirit animal. He attacked Max, he saved me. Poe kicks ass in battle. And I miss him too. I can almost feel him sometimes."

Walking to her, he went down on one knee and took her hand. "I know it won't be easy to let go of your warrior, but I'd be honored to have him with me. He's fast, like me. He's dark, like me. And you know you love me."

Kate kissed the top of his head. "How could I not? And I want Poe to be happy. There are other ravens here, he was just the first. And it's not like he won't still be part of the family." Kate laughed. "I hope Mica knows what he's getting into."

"Hey, he's taking me on for eternity. He knows I bring the whole family with me. He gets the whole package." Standing up, he hugged her again. "I know I'm not supposed to say this, but..." his voice cracked a bit, and he was almost whispering when he spoke, "I love you, thank you for everything you've done for me." He released her and walked for the door. "I'll talk to boss-man, and set up a meeting, I hope I see you then, Lady Kate."

Kate followed him to the door. As they stood in the doorway, Kate summoned Poe who swooped down and landed on Raven's shoulder, pecking at his long black hair.

"Poe, I release you from your service to me, and assign you to Raven. You belong to him now. I expect you to take care of him, protect him, as you have protected me." She leaned in close and whispered in Raven's ear, "Because I love you too. Now go home and be happy."

Raven smiled down at her. "I promise. Come on Poe, time for your crazy ass to meet Mica and see your new home. No shitting on the guest's fancy cars, and no pecking at the windows. Mica will have you de-feathered, and Reynaldo will serve you up for dinner covered in some fancy sauce."

Poe took off, making a racket of loud and raucous caws, as the bird followed behind Raven. Raven knew she was the greatest queen to reign over Medici, and once again, she had just proved why.

7

Shade waited in his office for the arrival of Mica and Raven. Raven had asked him for a private meeting at Bel Rosso with the three of them, claiming it to be a personal matter. He knew the two of them were happy together, it was one of the reasons he'd sent Raven to California, but he wasn't quite sure what this meeting was about. He hoped nothing had happened that either of them wanted a change of assignment, but with Raven, you never knew what the hell was going on.

He kept in regular contact with him, but their conversations revolved around business. Raven was growing into a great warrior and was a lot more mature now he was around Mica.

As Gi announced their arrival, Shade stood as they both entered. He responded to Raven's fist bump and shook hands with Mica. Gi poured them all a round of Midnight and disappeared quietly as they settled down in their respective seats. Shade looked at them both, complete damn opposites in every aspect, and he couldn't fathom how in the world the two of them got along so well. But then, who'd have ever guessed he'd have fallen head over heels for a mortal. He smiled to himself, acknowledging that love defied all logic.

"Good to see you both. Although, I must admit, I am concerned about what this meeting is about. Raven tells me this is a personal matter. So, you have my full and undivided attention." Taking a sip of his Midnight, he looked over the rim of his glass at the two of them, waiting to see who would speak first.

Raven left the Midnight on the side table, as he and Mica sat facing boss-man at his desk. His dreams had all come true once before sitting in this office, and he could only hope history would repeat itself.

"It's good to see you too, boss-man. Place is looking in top shape. Saw the new warriors out on the grounds when we teleported in. Hell of a lot of them, this time! Word is spreading."

Raven took a deep breath. He'd thought this over in his head, how he'd approach it, what he'd say, and had decided the best approach was just to spit it out. Master didn't play ring-around-the-rosy. He liked knowing the facts up front.

Shade watched Raven, and could tell he was stalling, making small talk. His body language gave him away, telling him Raven was more than a little nervous. What in the hell was going on? He'd play along, but not for long.

"Marcello is kicking their asses into shape, and I am happy with the caliber of warrior applying to the camp now. We have rebuilt our numbers, and we turn away a lot more than we take in. So, stop stalling and spit it out, Raven, I have work to do and so do the both of you."

Raven nodded and knew he needed to say what he'd come here to say. "I've been in California for a while now. I want to stay there. I have… we both need to make a move in our personal lives, together. I wanted to ask your permission, your approval of mating with Mica."

He watched as the boss-man set down his glass and steepled his fingers. Raven recognized the move. It meant he was thinking through the options. Before Shade could respond, Raven continued.

"I'd never do this without your approval. It changes nothing about what I am and how I do my job. This is who I've always been, and I know Mica is where my eternity lies."

Shade looked at Raven, his eyes never leaving him. He listened to his words, felt him deep, and knew he loved Mica. "Before we go any further, I want Kate in on this meeting, Raven. She's your queen. I make no decisions about our coven without her." Raven nodded at him as Shade telepathically let Kate know Raven and Mica were in his office, and would she please join them immediately.

Kate heard him call to her. She hadn't spoken to Shade about what Raven wanted to talk about. She felt it was something Raven needed to approach with him on his own terms, without any interference from her. She turned Lorenzo over to Nita as she headed downstairs, joining the three of them in the study. Kate smiled, nodding at Mica, and winked at Raven. "You needed me?"

Raven and Mica stood as their queen entered the room. They knew their place and showed her their respect.

"*Si*, come join us please." Shade moved from the desk chair to the sofa, making room for her to curl up next to him. "Raven and Mica have come to me with a request. I wish for you to be involved because no one knows about affairs of the heart better than you and I. Raven wishes to mate with Mica. I have a few things I would like to ask them both before I make my decision, but do you understand how two immortals of the same sex are perceived in our world?"

Kate looked at Raven and then to Shade. "I know when you feed it makes no difference if it is male or female, so I have assumed they are welcomed with open arms."

Shade shook his head. "Not exactly. They do not frown upon the sex. But immortal mating is to secure our future as a species. Since they are the same sex, the mating is seen as unnecessary. It is not so much looked down upon, but many in our culture will not acknowledge its validity. Times have changed somewhat, just as with the mortals, and there are those who will accept it." Kissing her softly, he smiled. "Understand?"

Kate thought over what he'd said. "So, reluctantly accepted but not encouraged."

"*Si*. Older masters may resist it. The newer masters will accept it, but quietly. It is not something celebrated or broadcast. Old school."

Clearing his throat, he smiled at Raven. "But Medici is a leader in all things, *si*! We accept and love our coven. This is *familia*. We make the decisions that support our *familia* and move us into the future."

Mica looked at Raven as they exchanged a glance before he addressed his current master. "So, are you saying you approve, Master Shade? You'll allow us to enter into the blood covenant that will bond us together?"

Shade looked at Mica and spoke to him directly. "Let me explain my point of view to you both. I have nothing against same sex mating, not at all. But I have some issues, so hear me out, then Kate and I will make a decision. There is a great deal of age difference between the two of you. Mica, you are older than Raven, but I have known Raven much longer. I know his history. So, I have a few concerns about his seriousness in this relationship. I want to make damn sure he understands what he is doing. That is for your benefit as well, I might add. Have you both discussed this at length? You are willing to take on my warrior for all eternity and understand what being a Medici warrior means? Because if I need him, he is coming, you can bet on that."

Mica nodded, "I understand your concerns. Yes, there is quite an age difference, and, well, look at us. I'd never have imagined I'd fall in love with this wild warrior who seemed intent on breaking every rule. But inexplicably, we did. I have fed only from him in the past three years, but he is forced to seek others. You must have seen with your own eyes how much he's changed. I love Raven, but he lacked structure and discipline in his life. And all that wildness was just a means to cover his loneliness. We are content together, and were he allowed to mate, to complete the covenant of our blood bond, I know he'd continue to be faithful. We have discussed this at length, and he's ready to make that commitment. I understand his role as warrior, and his first commitment to Medici. I'd never stand in the way of his obligation to his coven."

Shade was pleased with Mica's response. He understood Raven, and for now, he was satisfied with Mica's viewpoint. Nodding to Mica, he looked at Raven.

"Somewhere along the line, you grew up, lost your smart mouth, along with some of the antics. I think Mica has a lot to do with that. Raven, this is a huge step for you, one that takes everything you have to keep true to your covenant. This is a lifelong commitment to a mate. Not a game. Not something you can do for a while and then change your mind. I have no doubt

Mica cares for and loves you. His words tell me so. But I need you to speak to me, tell me what lies inside you. Why I should give you what you desire. I am your master. I know where you came from, what you have accomplished. So, talk to me."

Raven stood and walked behind Mica's chair, putting his hands on his shoulders. He looked at boss-man, and for once, he spoke only what was in his heart.

"I grew up on the streets. I was small and skinny and abused. You know all that. You rescued me, gave me a chance to learn and become something far more than I ever dreamed for myself. But I don't think anyone here ever knew all the things I kept inside. I never felt like I was anybody, I felt like the odd vamp out. When I became a warrior, things changed in how I thought about myself, what I could do and where I could go. When you're on the bottom, you can either stay down, or climb your way up. I kept climbing. I wanted to show you I could be something more than a joke. I wanted to show you that pulling me off the streets wasn't a mistake on your part. The pain stayed inside me, because I wasn't sure how to show anyone who I really was inside. I was never attracted to females. I adjusted to the feeders and took what I needed to survive, but I kept other things to myself.

"When I saw Mica for the first time, it was right here in this office, and I knew then, he was what I wanted. There was no doubt in my mind. When I found out he wanted me as well, all the pieces fell into place. I have in Mica all the things I lacked in myself. With him, all the pieces of the puzzle fit together. He makes us complete. This is Raven now. I've grown up, because I have someone of my own, someone who I'm comfortable with, and who's comfortable with me. I don't have to hide the hell from my past inside me. Mica took all that pain from me. He's my home, my peace, and someone I never want to be without. I know what it means, I know better than anyone in this room the difference between love, lust, and sex. This is love, heart and soul, the true deal for me. I want to be done with the feeders. I don't want to hunt. I want to come home to Mica, forever."

Shade was impressed. This was beyond anything he'd heard come out of Raven's mouth. He knew this kid would grow up one day, and he'd tolerated more from Raven than he ever tolerated from any other warrior. Raven stood before him as a man now. One who was in love and he knew Raven was dead serious. Shade had always understood there was so much grief and pain inside Raven, but he needed Raven to work through it in his own way. Shade had helped him cope with it, but it was up to him to face his own demons in his own time. Shade was fairly sure the demons were still there, but Mica would guide him, and that was important.

"First of all, I highly approve of you both coming to me, seeking my approval before moving ahead with your mating. That tells me a lot about your commitment to Medici. Second of all, I don't know when you grew up, Raven, but you did, and I like what I see before me. Your words are coming from a place I know well. Kate is my home. I am never myself unless she is with me, so when you use those words, they hit home to me." Hugging *bel*, he kissed her cheek. "Give me your thoughts, *mi amore*. Tell us what you think, although I think I already know."

Kate looked up at him. "I think love is love, and the heart wants what the heart wants. It rarely makes sense, I mean, look at us. All logic told me to run from you, but my heart said run to you. Everyone advised you against mating with a mortal, warning you I'd never fit into your world. When it comes to love, there are only two opinions that matter, and that is the opinions of the two people in love. I think we need to get out of their way, so they can begin their life together."

Smiling down at her beautiful face, he couldn't help but love her. "Spoken like a true romantic." He stood up facing Raven and Mica. "You have our approval. Congratulations. We wish you all that eternity can give you. I can't add anything more than what *bel* has already said."

Mica stood, and Shade hugged him, slapping his back. "Take care of my boy. He needs you."

Mica returned the hug. "Thank you, Master Shade, for your

blessing and approval. I promise you; I'll take great care."

Shade made eye contact with Raven. Time seemed to stand still, and Shade knew this was the point of letting him go. Raven knew it as well. He could feel the emotion rolling through Raven. They hugged, and it lasted for a while, neither of them letting go.

"It's okay, Raven, it can be scary, but great to move forward. Don't let the past get in the way of your future. Let it go, you choose well in Mica, trust him, and let him show you love and all it can be. I remain your master and will always be here for you. That will never change no matter what happens."

Kate stood to offer her congratulations when Lorenzo came blasting into the room at full speed and wrapped both hands around her knees, his hands covered in a rainbow of paints. Kate grabbed at his hands, but it was already too late as her skirt was covered in a myriad of paint colors.

"Lorenzo! Where... what are you doing?"

"I was painting a mural Mommy, like at Castello."

Kate creased her brow, "A mural? Oh god, a mural? On the wall? You were painting on the wall?"

Lorenzo nodded his head yes as he held up his chubby, paint covered hands. "It looks bootiful. It's a pirate."

Kate picked him up, trying to keep his paint-filled hands from touching anything else as she called for Theresa to get the bath ready. Kate shook her head as she looked at Shade, "Your son... the artist."

Shade threw back his head and laughed. Leave it to Lorenzo to break the ice and change the whole mood. Raven was holding his sides trying not to laugh out loud and Mica was amused as well.

Shade pointed at Lorenzo, "Do you see how when he is in trouble, he is my son and not hers? So, tell me, my little Picasso, where is this mural you have painted of a pirate and I do hope there is a ship, because no pirate is without his ship for all his treasures!"

Lorenzo shook his hands, trying to get free of his mother's

grip. "We got to build a ship, Daddy! A real one!"

Kate looked at Shade and laughed, "Yes, Daddy, build a real one."

Shade took Lorenzo into his arms, his whole body squirming. "A real ship, *si*! Maybe a pirate ship playhouse in the back. We have a sword; we may need a pirate hat to go with it. Now, I think you need to be polite and say hello to someone. You know Raven, but this is Mica, he is part of our coven, and I do not think you two have officially met. You need to welcome him to Bel Rosso."

Lorenzo extended his paint-filled hand to Mica, offering a handshake. "Nice to meet you. My name is Lorenzo. I'm a prince."

Mica looked at his hand as Kate was shaking her head no, but Mica took the child's small hand in his. "It's very nice to meet you, Prince Lorenzo. My name is Mica. And let me know when you get that ship built. I'm sure I can find you some sails for it."

Lorenzo was all grins as Theresa rushed in with a wet cloth for Mica, and scooped Lorenzo up, carrying him upstairs for another bath.

Shade nodded to Mica and watched as Theresa hauled Lorenzo out. He took Kate into his arms. "If you two need replacements so you can take a break with each other, we can arrange that without a problem. Sometimes it is good to be away from everything, and be together, especially on this occasion. Be on your way, take care of each other."

He watched as Raven grinned and then kissed Mica on the lips. Shade felt Raven's happiness as they both walked out of the office heading back to California. Looking down at Kate and her paint covered skirt, he asked, "Where the hell did Lorenzo get paints? We can't leave him alone for five minutes!"

Kate took his hand as they headed up the stairs together. "Your son is quite resourceful. Let's go see whose room now has a mural."

8

It was a beautiful Sunday afternoon and Rissa had decided to go to Bel Rosso and ride. She needed a break from her intense work schedule. Since the wedding several years ago, her business had boomed. It had become more than she could handle alone, and she'd hired several assistants to help her deal with the overwhelming workload.

Alec's focus remained on the Presidency, and they attended every event that would keep them in the public eye, but the time they spent alone together was increasingly rare. If they were together outside the house, they were soft campaigning in regal style. It was all in the plan. There were still obstacles to be removed, so Alec hadn't announced his intentions as a candidate as of yet.

It was rare for her to have some time that she could be alone and ride, so when the opportunity presented itself, she took it. Hyde, as always, was by her side when she left the house. They'd become even closer over the years. She considered him her best friend, as well as her protector and she wondered what she'd ever done without him. She never went anywhere without him unless Alec was accompanying her. Even then, Hyde would make himself disappear in the crowd, keeping a watchful eye. Over the years, she'd come to recognize most of the Medici warriors, and realized just how many of them were actually nearby at all times. Even when she couldn't see them, she could feel them. They surrounded her in a protective cage and there were times she was grateful.

The press was hounding their every move. If Alec made a television appearance, which he was doing more frequently, their lives got even more intense. The press would sit outside, day and night, waiting for one of them to exit. It had become routine for her to always be followed by the press.

She'd been riding for hours, working with Biondo, riding through the fields as well as the mountain trails. The polo season was getting ready to go into full swing and she'd been asked to ride with a group of women, all of them from the socially elite pony set. It was a charity group and they coordinated polo matches to raise funds. It kept her on the society pages of the newspaper and put them both in a great light as she got a lot of press coverage.

Rissa rode back to the stables after she and Biondo had a great workout. The land had changed over the years. There were now fields of flowers and she had to change her riding paths accordingly. Apparently, Kate was obsessed with this landscaping endeavor. What else did a bored queen with a runny nosed brat do?

She'd seen the child more than she cared to. He seemed to always be dirty, playing in mud, or hanging out with that beast they called a dog. Their life here was definitely country. She'd never be able to tolerate all the animals, noise, and dirt.

The main house was beautiful, but she never understood why they'd want to live here. They had huge homes everywhere and still they stayed in this isolated country estate. It was no place for a queen, but then, Kate was a middle class nothing, so what the hell did she know about style. She had all the money in the world and still dressed like a Bohemian.

Dismounting, she brushed off the dust from her expensive designer riding gear. Her custom-made boots alone cost over a thousand dollars, and even though no mortals saw her here, she always dressed the part. The estate was clearly designed so the vineyards and the fields of flowers that drew the tourists were separated from the main house, the camp and the stables. There was a separate drive to the vineyards, and clear signage marked the entrance. The security along the fork in the drive leading to the main house looked subtle, with a small chain across the road and a sign that said 'Private', but Rissa knew there were cameras and motion detectors that would alert them to any trespassers. A warrior would be immediately dispatched to the driveway to politely request any tourist to please turn around. So far, she'd been lucky in that none of the paparazzi had figured out this was her secret retreat.

She led Biondo into the stables and one of the stable hands was immediately there to assist her. Usually, Hyde was around to help, but she didn't mind the stable hands. They were all broad-shouldered men with long hair and dark eyes and made the view quite interesting now that it was beginning to get warm. They were usually shirtless, tan and clad in boots and tight jeans.

She was patting Biondo as the stable hand took the horse away to water when she heard the giggling of the brat. He was playing in the stables again and it was time to get the hell out of there. She had no patience for him.

***

Lorenzo had free reign of the property at Bel Rosso. Once he stepped out the door of the house, Warrior, the golden retriever, would always follow, and Aegis immediately picked up his scent and stayed close. He loved the tree house, and the tree swing that hung from the giant oak. He loved playing in the creek and running through the fields of lavender and sunflowers. He visited the beekeepers, and watched them tend to the bees, extracting the honey. He loved the warrior camp, but he could only enter the camp with his father. Daddy said it was too dangerous, and even Lorenzo could see it was no place to play, although he longed for a day when he could have a real sword and learn to shoot a crossbow like Mommy and Skelk. But his favorite place to play was in the stables, near the horses and Angelo and the stable hands. They always welcomed his visits, and nobody cared how dirty he got. Today, he was climbing the hay bales all the way to the top and calling out for Angelo to find him when he hid behind the bales.

Angelo was chasing him when Lorenzo heard her. Lorenzo crouched down behind the bales and watched as Rissa dismounted from her horse, and a stable hand took Biondo's reins and led him away to be groomed and watered. Angelo stopped his search for Lorenzo and stood to talk to Rissa.

"Ma'am, I hope everything was satisfactory with your ride

today?"

Lorenzo watched as Rissa flipped her blond hair and looked down her nose at Angelo, telling him it was fine, and then she stopped and looked at Angelo from head to toe. She gave him one of those looks Mommy gave Daddy before they went to the bedroom and closed the door. What if Angelo decided he liked her? Would that mean she'd come live here? There was something about this female Lorenzo didn't trust. He remembered, even as an infant, the few times he'd been placed in Rissa's arms he'd scream until his mother or father took him away from her. He climbed over the bales of hay and dropped down to the floor.

"Hi, Miss Rissa."

Rissa looked up as the brat dropped down from the hay. "Oh, hello Lorenzo. Go play." Rissa waved her hand at him dismissively.

Lorenzo brushed the hair from his face, leaving a dirty smudge across his forehead. "I made you something. It's a present."

Angelo looked at him quizzically. He was well aware of Lorenzo's dislike for Rissa and couldn't imagine what kind of present he'd make for her.

Rissa turned and laid her hand across her chest. "You made me a present? Oh well, I love surprises." Rissa looked to Angelo and shrugged her shoulders. "Have you seen Hyde today, Angelo? I was wondering if he'd come out to the stalls."

Lorenzo scurried to get his gift for her, as Angelo answered, "No ma'am, I think he may have gone back to the camp. I can call him if you're ready to return home."

Lorenzo ran up to her. He was holding a small hand-made clay-like figure that roughly resembled a dog. "Here, Miss Rissa. I made this for you. It's Warrior."

"Yes Angelo, please do call him, I'm ready to return home." Turning, she scowled at the curly mop-headed muddy heathen holding out something that resembled an art project gone heinously wrong. *What in the hell am I supposed to do with that thing? Pitch it in the closest dumpster!* Bending down, she took the gift and smiled sweetly. "It's very... lovely. Thank you. Now go play and be a good little boy."

Lorenzo held both hands behind his back. "Do you like it, Miss Rissa?"

She held the figurine with the tips of her fingers as she smiled and nodded. "Oh, well, yes. It's... one of a kind. Original art. Does your Mother know where you are? You should run along back inside." *Fucking brat needs to get the hell away from me. I need to find Hyde and leave!*

Lorenzo, aware he was being dismissed, wasn't ready to end the torture as he tugged at her riding pants, leaving a dirty handprint. "Do you want to know what it's made of?"

Rissa felt the tug and looked down to see his dirty handprint. "Lorenzo! Look what you've done to my riding jodhpurs!"

Backing away, she glared at him. Brushing frantically at the breeches, she was furious. "I could care less what it's made of. You made it for me, now just go back to making mud pies or whatever you do to get so disgustingly filthy!"

Lorenzo placed both hands over his mouth to suppress his laughter. His Mommy had told him about touching things with his dirty hands, but his touch was intentional, knowing it would anger Miss Rissa. "It's not mud-pies, Miss Rissa. It's horse poop. It sticks together better. I made you a dog out of horse poop."

Angelo had to turn his back to hide the huge grin on his face and it took all his willpower to control his laughter, the other stable hands were scurrying for the stalls as they doubled over, clutching their sides, laughing uncontrollably.

Hyde teleported in just in time to see Rissa, holding this glob of horse shit only inches from her face, looking like a volcano ready to explode. *What the fuck is she doing with horse shit in her hands?*

Rissa glared at him as she had to hold back the urge to vomit. Her eyes turned red as she threw down the object and reached for the filthy brat, both hands around his throat. She felt hands grab her waist and she kicked at Hyde as he whispered in her ear to settle down, he was just a small child playing games.

Rissa screamed, "Games? Giving me horse shit is a game? Do you have any idea what these breeches cost? How dare he! I'm not some peasant who stables her horse here, I'm Larissa Canton!"

Hyde spun her around and threw her over his shoulder as she kicked and screamed. "Put me down! Now! Someone needs to discipline that unruly brat!"

Lorenzo picked up the broken figure of the dog and ran behind Hyde as he carried a screaming Rissa away. "Miss Rissa! You forgot your present!"

Hyde sat her down hard on her feet and she screamed at the little creature chasing after her. "Get away from me!"

She made a grab for Lorenzo and the child took off laughing. Hyde tried to grab her as she slipped, but she fell in the muddy yard outside the stables. She screamed in anger, shaking her blonde hair and Hyde held his sides as he busts out laughing.

"All part of riding, Rissa, getting dirty." He reached down to help her up and she slapped at his hand.

"Never in my life have I been treated like this. Someone needs to take that brat and beat his ass! Seriously, he acts like those damn beastly warriors, out of control! I'm going home! Now!"

***

Kate was feeling a sensation of glee and anxiety from Lorenzo as he played. She knew he was safe with the protection of the animals, but she was concerned about what was making him feel so anxious. She teleported herself into the stables to find Lorenzo covered in mud as usual, and Rissa, dirty from head to toe and screaming her head off. She didn't have to think twice to know Lorenzo had something to do with it.

"Lorenzo! What's going on here?"

Lorenzo stopped laughing and looked up at the stern face of his mother. Uh oh! He was seeing another time-out in his near future.

"Nothing, Mommy. I gave Miss Rissa a present... and then...

she fell down."

Kate looked at Hyde and Angelo, both of whom were trying hard not to laugh. Kate approached Rissa, "Rissa, I'm so sorry. We will, of course, pay to have your riding clothes cleaned."

Rissa huffed as she brushed at her clothes. "Oh really! How kind of you. Cleaning them won't suffice. I'll be buying new ones and sending Shade the bill, you can count on it!" Standing up, she went nose to nose with Kate. "You need to discipline that child. I'm a paying customer, this is not acceptable! My god, Kate, stables are a dangerous place for him! I wouldn't want anything to happen to the precious thing. Just look at me, covered in horse shit, he gave me horse shit! What kind of child plays in horse shit?"

Kate reassured her. "Of course, buy new ones, just send the bill." Kate turned her stare to Lorenzo, "Horse poop? You gave Miss Rissa horse poop?"

Lorenzo gave her his most innocent stare with those crystal blue eyes as he told her he made her a present, a dog that looked like Warrior.

Kate bit hard on the tender skin inside her lip, trying hard not to smile. Lorenzo didn't need any encouragement. She gave him a hard stare, well aware of the power he'd have over the ladies with those eyes as he got older.

"I'll deal with you later, young man. And don't think your father won't hear about this."

Lorenzo dove headfirst into the hay bales, hiding from his mother, and exiting the situation as best he could. But he could feel her unexpressed laughter and knew his punishment wouldn't be too severe.

"Rissa, I'm so sorry. If you want to clean up before you go home, please feel free to come up to the house. I can get you something clean to wear before you go home."

Rissa was appalled. *Me, wear anything she owns, what a joke!* Holding up her hand, she faked a quick smile. "No thank you, I just want to go home. I have one request when I come to ride. Please keep your son at a distance. He needs discipline, and a lot of it! Hyde! I'm ready to go now, please get me the hell out of here!"

Hyde winked over her head at the queen and hoped Lorenzo didn't get a bad punishment for his antics. He had entertained the entire stables today.

"Come along, Rissa, you smell!" He laughed as they teleported out and Rissa couldn't wait until she got that bratty kid alone. She'd teach him a lesson he wouldn't soon forget!

Kate was now steaming mad at Rissa as she held a fake smile on her face as Rissa and Hyde departed. Who does this bitch think she is? She doesn't own these fucking stables! Lorenzo will play when and where he wants.

After Hyde had taken her away, Kate turned to the stack of hay bales. "Lorenzo!"

She saw his small face peer around the hay bales, and she raised one eyebrow as she put her hands on her hips. The child climbed over the hay and stood before her, looking up into her face.

"Are you going to make me stay inside when Miss Rissa comes?"

Kate shook her head, "No, Lorenzo. This is your home. And you play wherever you want. But what you did today..." Kate sighed. "Lorenzo, what were you thinking?"

He shrugged his small shoulders, "I was thinking I wanted to give her horse poop because she doesn't like me."

Kate could hear the laughter of the stable hands behind her and she flashed them a look that said, 'don't encourage him!' and they fell silent. She closed her eyes and shook her head, before picking up her muddy poop-covered child and teleporting him back to the house, and another bath.

"You know we have to tell your father about this, don't you?"

Lorenzo tucked his head as he answered, "Yes, Mommy."

As they landed inside Bel Rosso, Theresa was already running the bath water for the second time this day. As Kate walked in and started stripping his clothes from him, Theresa was gathering his clothes for the laundry.

"I swear, my lady, I've never taken care of a child that went through more clothes or had more baths in a single day than Lorenzo!"

Kate laughed as she helped Lorenzo climb into the tub, already splashing water and playing with a toy boat, as if the poop incident never happened. **"Lover? When you have a minute, you may want to come see your son."**

Shade knew something was up as soon as his death slumber ended. He looked out the window to see Rissa and Hyde teleporting out and then saw Kate returning with a very dirty Lorenzo, nothing unusual there. Jumping in the shower, he was almost done when Kate asked him to come see their son. What the hell did he do now?

Drying off quickly, he threw on some jeans and found Kate and Lorenzo in his room. He stood at the door, his feet crossed at the ankles, leaning against the doorjamb, arms crossed over his chest. Lorenzo was refusing, in a very polite way, to get dressed. Shade didn't blame him; he loved being naked as well.

Kate struggled with her willful child as he wanted to run free before she could finish getting him dressed. "Lorenzo, stand still!"

She sensed Shade behind her and looked over her shoulder to see him leaning against the doorjamb, his hair still damp from his own shower.

"You might want to ask your son about the incident with Miss Rissa today."

Shade furrowed his brow. "Oh, we had an incident, did we? That cannot be good. Daddy does not like incidents. Lorenzo, stop your fidgeting and let your mother dress you, it sounds to me like you are in enough trouble as it is. I would not be so eager to add to it."

He watched as Lorenzo rolled his big blue eyes to him and settled down. Lorenzo knew his father meant business. Shade wasn't smiling, and his voice was stern. Finally, after Kate had him dressed, Shade took his hand and led him to the sleep sofa in his room. Shade sat down and pulled Lorenzo in front of him, so he was standing between his knees. He tilted Lorenzo's chin up and stared into his eyes.

"What happened with Miss Rissa today? Start at the beginning and tell me everything."

Lorenzo looked up at his father. He adored his father and always wanted his praise. "I made Miss Rissa a present. It was a dog like warrior."

"Well that was very nice of you to make her a present. And did she accept this present?"

Lorenzo nodded his head eagerly, "Yes, Daddy. She said she liked it, but she really didn't."

Shade scowled. "How do you know she did not like it if she told you she did, Lorenzo? That makes no sense. I think you are leaving out some details or not telling me the truth. I do not accept lying from warriors, even little ones. Never lie, *si*?"

Lorenzo looked at the floor, and then looked over his shoulder. "Where's Warrior? I think we left him outside! I need to go get him."

Shade squeezed his knees together tight, holding him in place and Lorenzo squealed. Shade wanted him to feel a little discomfort and understand this was serious and he wasn't getting out of it.

Picking him up, he let the child stand on his thighs and looked directly into his son's eyes. "I do not think, little warrior, you wish for your Daddy to be angry. Talk. Now."

Lorenzo swallowed hard but looked his father in the eyes. That was what his father had taught him, to look in a man's eyes when you speak. "I made her a poop dog. She doesn't like me and doesn't want me to play in the stables when she comes, so I made her a dog out of horse poop. Then she got mad, and threw it down, but she slipped and fell and got her clothes all dirty, and she yelled at Mommy, and I hid in the hay bales."

Shade choked trying not to laugh. *He gave Rissa horse shit! Now that's my son right there!* Pulling Lorenzo into his shoulder, he felt him curl into his body. He looked at *bel* across the room and grinned. **"How in the hell am I supposed to punish him for that? I want to reward him, for hell's sake!"**

Kate smiled back at him and shrugged. **"I was ready to**

choke her myself. But we can't let him think it's okay!"

Shade rubbed Lorenzo's back. "Lorenzo, Miss Rissa has no children, so she is not used to them. I know you meant for this to be funny, not as a real present to give her. So that was very wrong to begin with. She could have gotten hurt when she fell. But one thing bothers me more than all of this and do you know what that is?"

Lorenzo tightened his arms around his father's neck, holding him tight. He'd work hard to do whatever it was his father wanted. "What, Daddy?"

"When Miss Rissa yelled at Mommy, you ran for the hay bales. Warriors do not run, they defend their beautiful Mommy. Do you understand this? I know you are young, little warrior, but you need to begin to learn the lessons I am teaching you. If you can be creative enough to make a dog out of horse poop, you can learn lessons."

Lorenzo sat up straight. "I can fight, Daddy! You want me to whack Miss Rissa with my sword? I can do it!"

Shade stood him on his feet, trying hard not to laugh. "Lorenzo! You never whack a female."

Shade stood and paced as he ran his hand through his hair. He tried to get his laughter under control. He dared not look at *bel* because she'd surely make him lose it. "My point is to make you understand you always defend the Medici females with your life. That is the rule here. But never pick up a sword in anger. We only use our weapons against a threat. Miss Rissa does not understand you. She can be mean, and if she is mean to you, then you need to stay the hell away from her, not encourage her anger. Does any of this make sense inside that little head of yours, warrior?"

Lorenzo nodded, "Yes. Protect Mommy and stay away from Miss Rissa. Got it."

"Good. Now Theresa will put you in bed. I suggest you stay there. Mommy and I are going to decide your punishment, and there will be one. It will begin when you wake in the morning, *si*?"

Lorenzo looked up at his father and blinked several times,

"Okay, but not too bad, Daddy, okay? Cause it was a present and it's not my fault Miss Rissa fell down."

Shade's heart melted where he stood. Picking him up, he kissed his cheek and hugged him tight. "I love you, Lorenzo. But presents are not made from poop."

Lorenzo squirmed to get down, running down the hall to Theresa. He knew to quit when he was ahead, and before his mother could change his father's mind!

Kate looked at Shade and shook her head. "You are such a soft touch, but I will admit, Lorenzo is a charmer. Heaven help us."

"I love him with all my heart *bel*, but he tests me. I mean, he literally gave Rissa a poop dog? I wish I could have seen that! How in the hell did she fall and what did she say to you? Do I need to make a visit to the Canton residence?"

Kate went to him and slid her arms around his waist, laying her head against his chest. His strength and power still a comfort to her. "He had to have planned it ahead of time." Kate started to giggle. "The poop had dried out and it was shaped like a dog. I'm not sure how she fell. She just turned on her heels in those fancy riding boots and down she went. The stable hands were all laughing, which, of course, only encourages Lorenzo. But lover, she said to make sure we keep him out of the stables when she visits. I already told Lorenzo he could play there whenever he wants. I wouldn't want to dictate his schedule around Rissa. I think he needs to be punished. Maybe he can be restricted from going to the stables for a week. And I think he should be made to apologize to her. He's right about one thing, Rissa doesn't like having him around, and he picks up on that."

He held her close. "He amazes me, *mi amore*. He is so smart already. He does need to steer clear of her when she is here. It is the best thing. I agree with the punishment, and I will speak to Angelo. Everyone needs to be aware of his ways, he can charm already. Cazzo, he will have hordes of females around him when he gets older. As for the apology, that can wait until Rissa is here again, and you or I must be with him."

Kate shook her head. "Oh, don't even talk about him

charming the females. I'm not ready to deal with that yet! But yes, one of us should take him by the hand and go with him to apologize to her. And we'll tell him when he wakes, he'll be on stable restriction for a week. I'll let you talk with the stable hands."

Pushing her hair from her face, he kissed her softly, and slid his hand between them, rubbing her belly. "Mmm, our Sophia grows inside you. So, there are two things we need to get arranged. That Lorenzo feeds only from Nita, and you get another wet feeder arranged soon. Has to be done. One other thing I want to speak to you about."

Laying her weight against him, letting him support her in his arms, she looked up at him. "And what is that?"

"I want you to move ahead with a tutor as we discussed. It will structure his day. He has a lot to learn before he becomes ten and goes to the camp. Then he will be totally occupied for ten hours a night. So, think about it. It might not be a bad idea to get him started before our princess arrives."

She laid her head against his chest. She couldn't believe how fast the past three years had gone by, and their daughter would be here before they knew it. She knew he was right. Theresa was already teaching him to read and do simple math, and he was picking up some basic Italian. He absorbed everything like a sponge.

"You're right, lover. We'll find a tutor to start his home schooling. I already have the room set aside. It won't take any time to get it furnished. And the pools will be done soon. He loves the water, and who knows, it might mean one less bath a day if I can keep him in the pool and out of the mud."

"Good luck with that!" Taking her hand, he led her to their bedroom, where she slid in bed beside him. Without thought, she laid her head on his chest.

"I am happy, *mi amore*. I love you and Lorenzo. Life is as it should be, but if you say Sophia will be a bigger handful than Lorenzo, I think we should enjoy this quiet time while we can!"

9

Alec took his laptop out into the courtyard behind their Georgetown home, and settled into a deck chair. The old brick wall completely enclosed the courtyard, giving him total privacy. He spent his days in Congress, or his office, or this house, and it felt good to breathe some fresh air. If he was going to make a bid for the presidency, now was the time for him to announce he'd be running for office. He'd served two terms as a Senator, and he got high-profile play a few years ago when he and Rissa had their very large, and very public wedding. He'd been careful to avoid involving himself in controversial legislation, remaining a visible, yet likable politician. It had been a fine line to walk.

Rissa had been a great asset in his plan to gain the most powerful office in the mortal realm, and he had a few more things he was going to need her to pull off if he was going to be successful. Santos brought him a Midnight, which he sipped as he smoked a cigarette. He checked his watch. She should be arriving home soon, with Hyde on her arm as usual.

He was aware of how close she'd grown to Hyde, and he'd monitored them both closely, and knew even though Rissa had come on to him a few times, Hyde upheld that 'warrior code' Shade was always ranting on about, and nothing physical had happened between them. He'd kept that knowledge to himself just in case he needed it. With Rissa, he was never completely sure what to expect. He directed Santos to bring her outside to the courtyard as soon as she arrived home.

***

Hyde delivered her home and behaved as the gentleman he was, much to Rissa's dismay. She gave him a soft hug, before telling him goodbye.

He nodded slightly toward her. "See you in the morning, Rissa, get some rest and behave."

She slid her hand along his cheek and smiled in reply. "Only for you, Hyde. Everyone else gets the bad girl."

She saw him shake his head in amusement as he left and waited until he was clear of the house before he teleported out. Santos informed her Alec was in the courtyard and wished to see her. *Does he now? I feel so honored to be summoned!*

She handed Santos her briefcase and tote, as he helped her off with her jacket. She poured herself a Midnight then casually made her way to the pool. Alec looked relaxed, and that was a good sign. Kicking off her red soled Louboutin heels, she strolled outside and sat in the deck chair beside him.

"You look very relaxed and comfortable. How was your day and what happened that you're home so early?"

Alec closed the laptop and turned to her. She was dressed in pale blue for spring, the short pencil skirt showing off her long tan legs and her bare feet. He drank her in with his eyes and thought the mission he'd planned for her wouldn't be a hard one to pull off.

"I was tired of being locked up inside an office, thought I'd do some work from home and enjoy some fresh air. I only seem to come out here when we're entertaining. How was your day, my darling?"

She didn't miss his eyes as they took her in from head to toe, and that excited her. Maybe tonight he'd be interested in more than business. She couldn't remember the last time he'd come to her. She was careful to not display any signs of anticipation, but she didn't have too, he already knew he could wind her up like a toy.

"Well, if you wanted fresh air, you should come out to Bel Rosso and ride with me once in a while. It's great exercise and it's beautiful, all except for that sniveling brat."

Taking a sip of the thick elixir, she laid her head back on the chair and pulled the diamond studded pins from her long blonde hair as it cascaded down past her shoulders. "My day was busy. If I hadn't hired my assistants, I'd be drowning. Business has been booming."

Alec took a sip from his Midnight, letting her ramble on about her day. He knew he'd have to approach this gingerly.

"So, I'll have to throw my hat in the ring soon, to be a candidate. My biggest obstacle is the sitting President, John Ashton. There's no reason to think he won't run for a second term, and if he does, he'll automatically secure the party's endorsement. Then I'd have to wait another four years. I'll wait if I have to, but I'd like to move this process along. The timing is right for me politically. How about you? Are you ready to be First Lady?"

Rissa lifted her head from the chair as her wicked smile spread across her face. "I'm not willing to wait another four years. Let's move on this! Oh Alec, I'm so ready. I think I've proven to you I can handle anything, including being First Lady. We're a good team. I know you have this planned out, so give me the details."

Alec emptied his glass. "What I need, my darling, is a scandal. Something irrefutable that Ashton can't wiggle out of. Are you up for that?"

"A scandal?" Crossing her legs, her skirt hitched further up her thighs. "So, you'll need me to assist on this scandal, I assume. I can arrange anything you need Alec, it's my specialty."

He placed his hand on her knee and slowly slid it up her thigh. "Oh, it will take more than some arranging, my darling. You'll need to be the bait. Ashton ran his election campaign on the whole 'family values' thing. He drags his wife and adult children out for every photo opportunity, and he makes sure they're sitting on the front row in church every Sunday, with the Secret Service and the press in tow, for the entire world to see. I need for you to seduce him. It won't be difficult. He's had his eye on you for some time. We can plant some cameras, get some good video. Once I show him the footage, I can threaten to expose him to the press. There's no way he'd want the public, or his dear wife of thirty years, to see that footage. He'll cave and announce he won't run for a second term for personal reasons or some shit like that. What do you think, darling?"

She felt the heat from his hand as it glided like silk up her thigh and her breathing stopped. He only had to touch her, and she went up in flames. She concentrated hard to hear his words, as his hand lay between her thighs. Bait? Sleep with Ashton?

She cringed at the thought of touching that tiny dick and having it rammed inside her, hell she wouldn't even feel it! She eyed Alec and stared into those pools of blue. Was he serious?

"You'd take the chance of dishonoring my name? Hell, Alec, he probably never even fucks his own wife. I'd bet he's already getting something on the side. Have you checked that out yet?"

"That's rumor and speculation, my darling, nothing concrete and no physical proof. And besides, it would make me look like a typical mud-thrower with nothing to back it up. This needs to be personal, just me and Ashton. Nobody else will ever see these tapes."

Sliding her well-manicured finger across her lips, she was still considering her answer. Let him sweat a bit. He'd force her to do it one way or another, but she refused to give in right away.

"Well, I need to know what I'm walking into. I don't know how easy it will be to lure him in. But how hard can it be. Compared to that mouse he's married to, I'm a fantasy come true." She drained her glass of Midnight and smiled at him.

"I don't think you'll encounter any resistance, but to be on the safe side, I'm sure I can get Shade to use his dream-walking skills to plant a few erotic fantasies in his head, staring none other than the long-legged shapely blonde goddess of one ambitious Senator. By the time you show up in the flesh, his head will be filled with all the things he wants to do to you. All you'll need to do is pour on the charm."

She cocked her head to the side and answered him in a stern tone. "And do I get a sweet reward for doing this nasty little deed?"

He stared her down. If nothing else in her time with him, she'd learned to negotiate. No one got anything for free, not even him. "Of course, my darling, name your price."

Rissa was careful in how she approached this one. "There's something I want. Something I've been thinking about for a long time. I want a playroom just like Shade has at Castello. But I want it inside this house."

He laid his head back against the deck chair and closed his eyes, remembering all the pleasures of that room. He was pretty certain the room remained dormant. He couldn't imagine Shade dragging his precious queen down to that den of sin and depravity and strapping her in the stockades while his beast fucked her in the ass. He smiled at the thought of it. Maybe Shade would like for him to take all those toys off his hand. He'd be doing him a favor! He turned his head and looked at her, "I think that can be arranged, my darling."

Swinging her legs over the side of the chair, she stood and walked along the edge of the pool, her back to him. She dipped her toe into the water and could feel his eyes burning into her back. She turned to face him and reached behind her, unzipping the perfectly tailored skirt. She shimmied the skirt down her hips and slowly stepped out of it, before unbuttoning the white silk blouse. She shook her shoulders and watched the garment float to her feet. She stood before him in a matching baby blue lace thong and bra set.

"Two weeks, Alec. There's a huge polo match for Ashton's favorite charity. He'll be there, his wife won't. I'm sure I can get access to him, get his juices flowing. If you wish to accompany me, to lead the way, that's your choice. Two weeks. You have a deal."

Turning, she dove into the pool, her body sleekly gliding through the water. She unlatched her bra and watched it float to the surface. She swam to the edge of the pool nearest him and emerged from the water. She pushed her hair back from her face, her tits floating on the waters' surface.

"Make it happen."

He smiled wickedly. "I'll call the dream-walker. We'll discuss a plan to get the President's juices flowing again, as well as me helping him empty out all those bad memories from the dungeon beneath Castello. Consider it done, my darling."

Floating backward in the pool, her body rested just below the surface of the blue water. Closing her eyes, she remembered that room, how it made her feel, and she smiled.

Oh, it will be done, my wicked vampire, without a doubt. You get rid of the President and I get you fucking me to the edge of death whenever I want.

10

The Dead House was rocking as usual. The warriors were all in their assigned grids, and Shade knew Alec was contemplating entering the next Presidential election. If that happened, then things would change drastically. For one, he'd need more warriors. Losing so many warriors in the Battle of Bel Rosso, he initially supplemented with warriors from Florence, but he couldn't drain his foreign territories of protection long-term. The new camp had produced some good warriors in the last few years, and this year's group was looking good as well. It troubled him that he had to turn so many of them away. The Medici camp had developed the same strong reputation in the States as it held in Europe, and as a consequence, he was drawing more and better candidates.

Many of the recruits were young, with little experience, but great potential. He'd had to turn away qualified candidates because of space, and also because of age. The Virginia camp couldn't handle the younger breed of warrior. The camp in Florence was designed to take children as young as ten, but he hadn't developed the capacity to handle that here yet. There was so much to teach them, and they required many years of training before becoming proficient. He'd been mulling over a few ideas when Theo walked in with Olivia.

Olivia had returned to him shortly after they lost Fiamma, asking for a second chance, and she'd more than earned the right to stay. She was a dedicated warrior, despite her appearance. She looked almost too delicate. She stood tall, like most immortals, with long brown hair that fell in soft waves around her shoulders. Her eyes were a pale blue, and their almond shape gave her an exotic look. She had high, defined cheekbones, and a peaches and cream complexion. Despite her skill with weapons, and her aggressive tactics as a warrior, her voice and general demeanor remained soft.

It didn't take long after her return for Olivia to adapt and establish a bond with her brothers. Unlike her first visit, she'd been able to win over the respect of her fellow warriors. Olivia worked well in the Dead House and had proven to be a vital part of his team. Theo remained his SIC, and he ran it with precision. He easily adapted to change, never complaining and Shade found he was usually in good spirits. Shade nodded in their direction when they entered.

"You two heading out for the night?"

Theo threw his booted foot up on the chair, tossing his shaggy locks over his shoulder, and slid a shuriken inside his boot. "Usually do a few rounds in G-town, check out the Canton house and then check in on the others. We have a few hot spots now that it's warming up weather wise. But no worries, master, we can handle it."

Shade liked Theo's down-to-earth approach to things. "Well, I may make a few rounds myself tonight. Let me know if any activity flares up, I haven't had a good rogue kill in a while. I will be hanging out here, checking the grids and kill rosters, reading over some of your reports, see if anything gets my attention. Get to work you two."

With a wave of his hand, he dismissed them as both Theo and Olivia teleported out. Flopping down at the large conference table, he spread out the rosters and grids and began checking out what Theo had been up to. Several of Max's Virginia warriors had joined his coven after the battle, and he'd made a point of monitoring their performance closely. They'd taken the blood oath to Medici, and he liked how they'd done so far, but he was still not ready to put them in any leadership positions. Theo had done a good job of rotating their assignments, and giving them a broad range of experiences, working with them on weapons skills, and they were proving to be worthy of carrying the title of Medici warriors.

Hearing boots on the metal stairs, he looked up to find Robert, one of the warrior's he inherited from Max's coven. Robert seemed startled to find the master sitting in the Command Center. Shade smiled at him. "Evening, Robert. Problem? Didn't mean to startle you, I assume you're looking for Theo."

Robert liked his new master. He was fair and always available to his coven. Max had rarely been attentive to his coven. "No problem, master, I was just checking in for my grid assignment before I join the other warriors."

Shade motioned for him to take a seat. "Sit down. Relax. Theo and the others can wait. I rarely get in here anymore. Theo has things well in hand and keeps me informed of anything important. Therefore, I don't get to talk to many of you from the Virginia coven. I know you have a home and family here. How are things going for you? Is there anything I can assist you with?"

Robert didn't know what to think, the Medici was asking him if he needed assistance. "No, master, I'm just dealing with a small argument on the home front. Sibling rivalry, nothing this old warrior can't handle."

Shade threw back his head and laughed. "I am a father myself, two sons, another baby on the way. But I have yet to have those headaches. How many *bambinos* do you have?"

Robert sat up straight, his chest puffing out with pride. "Just the two. A son and daughter. My son is the oldest by only a year. Both of them were born warriors."

Winking at Robert, Shade liked what he heard. "Good stock, bringing up warriors, and never easy. I know my Lorenzo can't wait to become a warrior."

Robert chuckled. "Well, Master Shade, it's not always easy having two warriors, especially when one is chosen to be in your camp and the other turned away. It brings out the true rivalry and a lot of yelling and screaming."

Shade looked puzzled. Robert was a damn good warrior and he'd been around a while. Shade couldn't imagine either of his children being turned away.

"So, your son was accepted into the fold and the daughter turned away? I do not like the sound of that. What is your son's name, I am familiar with the new warriors, but I do not recall knowing one was your son, forgive me."

Robert bit his lip, holding back his laugh. "You have that

backwards, master. My daughter, Rebecca, was accepted into your camp."

Shade raised his eyebrows. "Well, don't I look like the unorganized master? I apologize to you, Robert. Rebecca is a good warrior. She came to us with good skill sets, easily adaptable to Medici code. I have seen her work. She is going to be deadly with a blade. Did your son tell you why he was not accepted? Marcello, Aislynn and I meet with each warrior personally, one on one. We give them things to work on, encourage them to come back again the next spring."

Robert was taken aback by how concerned Shade was. He liked him more and more, as he'd gotten to work under him and saw how he operated. His warriors were all fierce, and there was no bickering amongst them, they worked as a team and all for the cause of Medici and the coven. He wasn't used to such dedication and camaraderie. Max had some cutthroat warriors in his coven, and it was every warrior for himself. Max neither cared nor worried about those he took care of. He was too busy traveling and pursuing other vices to worry about what he already had and those that had pledged their life to him.

"Robbie never said much about it, to be honest. I had no idea you actually talked to him and told him his faults. So, I can't say."

Shade stood and paced as he thought the situation through. He wanted to help this family and keep them together. Hell, they'd been through enough with the takeover. This was a family man, and Shade wanted this family to thrive and stay together in his coven.

"Let me talk to Marcello and Aislynn and see what I can do. I cannot make a decision without the facts in front of me. Once I find out, no matter the outcome, I will get back to you, you can count on it."

Walking to Robert, he slapped him on the back, and they shook hands.

"I'd be forever in your debt, Master Shade, it would calm down my household, but I expect no favors. Being a Medici warrior is a great honor, and if Robbie isn't up to your standards, at least I'll know what he'll need to become better. I can coach and help him."

Shade liked this man. What father didn't want his son to succeed and become the best at his craft? "Let me do the research, and we will see what we can accomplish. No one in my coven struggles alone. Now, you have some work to do. If Theo questions you on being late, you just tell him master wished to speak with you. He will ask you nothing further."

As Shade lowered his frame into the chair, Robert stared back at him. He'd heard this master was extraordinary, as all the legends had told. This master was a family man and a leader, something Max's coven was sorely missing. "My best wishes to your lady, and my family hopes the coming child is healthy. Good night, Master Shade."

Shade smiled and nodded as Robert made his way to the streets of D.C. Pulling out his phone to call Marcello, it suddenly vibrated in his hand. Looking down, he saw Alec on the caller ID. "Hell, what does Alec want?" Answering, he was ready for anything. "Medici."

11

Alec was ready to end his day, but he knew Shade's was just getting started. With Rissa asleep upstairs, he picked up his cell and stepped outside, into the courtyard, to make his call. He paced as he waited for Shade to answer. He heard the deep rumble of Shade's voice on the phone.

"Hey brother, you got a minute?"

"I got all the minutes you need. Problem?"

Alec sat down in the deck chair, draping one leg over the arm as he lit up. "Not a problem, exactly. But I do have another job for you. Need your gift again."

"Is that so? Who is the victim this time?" Shade shook his head. He couldn't imagine who Alec would want to target next.

"Our President has announced he plans to run for office again, just as I feared he would. I could wait another four years, but I'm an impatient man. I think the time is right for me. We're still getting good press from the wedding. Rissa's damn photo is in the paper more than mine these days. The public eats up this whole fairytale romance. But that won't hold for the long-term. I need Ashton to back out of the race. I've already spoken to Rissa, and she's ready to play her part. I just need you to get things started for me with a little dream-walking inside the head of the President. He needs some triple X-rated dreams of fucking Rissa's brains out. Then Rissa will do her part, and I'll take care of the rest. Just need you to prime the pump, so to speak."

Shade sat silently for a while, no idea in hell how to respond to this. "The President? Have you lost your fucking mind, Alec? Even for me, this won't be easy. Dream-walk through his head, give him visions of fucking Rissa? I have to think this one over. I cannot give you an answer this moment."

Alec dropped his leg to the patio, as he leaned forward in the deck chair. "What do you mean? This is no different. Hell, you teleport inside the White House, shadow yourself. No one will know you're there! And come on, brother. This is me you're talking to. You spent enough years wallowing in the depravity of that sexual paradise you had buried beneath Castello. You won't even have to use your imagination to come up with enough kinky shit to fuel his imagination. Work from memory. You forget I've seen you in action, so don't go all mortal on me. I know you calmed the fuck down since then, but you're not convincing me you've gone all missionary position with Kate."

Slamming his fist down on the table, Shade refused to bring his life with Kate into this conversation. He wouldn't take the bait or even respond to that statement.

"That stuff we were into is in the past. Besides, my memories are not helpful. I am going to have to go into his fucking brain box and look for *his* memories, what gets *him* off. He comes off like white bread, but I'm sure there is a lot below the surface. Balls of hell, Alec, how many nights do you expect me to do this, if I do it?"

Alec drew on the cigarette and exhaled slowly. He'd hooked him, now he just had to reel him in. Shade would like to think the darkness inside him was gone, but if there was one thing Alec had learned in his many years as a vampire, the darkness never left. You could push it down, cover it up, but with just a little encouragement, it always returned. He already had Shade thinking about how to get the job done.

"I'm not sure how long it will take. But you know that whole 'family values' front he puts on is part of his public image. There may not be much going down in his bedroom at night, but I guarantee it won't take much to get his mind going. I've seen him look at Rissa when we're at official events. He has the seeds of lust growing, brother, now I just need you to water them. Don't make it too kinky, just make it hot. You know what the mortals like, submissive female, in heat and begging for it. Come on, brother. If you can't come up with a couple of weeks of sexual fantasy, then your ass has definitely been mated too long."

Sighing heavily, Shade wasn't giving into this. He needed time to mull this over in his head. "And you agree to let Rissa do this? Brother, that's cold. You would do anything to get ahead. You sure as fuck haven't changed in the eons we have known each other. Look, I still need to think this through. I'm busy as hell with camp right now. I cannot imagine what you had to promise Rissa for this favor."

"As a matter of fact, my mate did have a little request for me. Once she completes this assignment, she wants her own little reward. So maybe I can help you out. Seems she loves that den of depravity underneath Castello. And I take it from your puritanical response it's no longer in use. Rissa wants a room like that in our house. I'll have to finish out the basement here in the townhouse, keep it below ground and soundproof it. But I'll take all those toys off your hand. Install them here. I'll pay to have it all moved, of course. Just think how happy Kate will be to know you got rid of it all."

Shade paced as the conversation got more bizarre. Getting rid of the sex cult dungeon and all its nasty toys was one thing he wouldn't mind. He sure as hell didn't want Lorenzo to stumble across it any time growing up.

"Give me a few days, brother, I will have an answer. The President isn't going anywhere. I'll get back with you."

Alec tossed the cigarette into the pool, listening to the soft hiss as the hot butt hit the water. "Take your time, brother. Call me when you're ready to get started."

12

Outside in the camp yard, the night was extraordinarily warm for spring. Shade was working with the new group of recruits that had traveled far and wide to be accepted into his fold. It was now up to him and his leaders to train them into Medici warriors. His body covered was sweat, his hair hanging down in wet ringlets, his blood pumping, but his mind was someplace else.

Alec's request, the President, and the task that lay before him had his mind preoccupied. *Cazzo*, he needed to just do this and get it over with. He had mulled it over in his head for days. He hadn't shared the information with *bel*, he couldn't bring himself to tell her. He already knew she wouldn't approve.

Stopping his sword play with the young Rebecca, he stepped aside and told her to rejoin the females with their bow exercises.

He'd spoken to Marcello and Aislynn about Robert's son, Robbie, and reviewed their notes about his performance. He'd not been accepted into camp for the simple fact they'd already reached their quota for the year. Each year, now, they received more qualified applicants than they could accommodate, and he knew he was turning away young vampires with great potential. After reviewing their notes, he'd made the decision to let Robbie into his camp.

He'd called both Robbie and his father to Bel Rosso for a meeting, telling them after a personal review of his performance notes that he'd decided to accept Robbie into the camp. He never let Robbie know his father had spoken to him.

Shade turned his attention to Robbie now as he practiced alongside all the other recruits. He watched him work with his shuriken's. He'd make a fine warrior, and Shade would make sure he kept their family together.

Marcello approached him and Shade smiled. Now there was a warrior who'd someday find a mate that was worthy of him. Marcello was always comfortable around the females, and vice versa. But Shade knew Marcello was in no rush to mate, his focus remained on the battle, and the females were just a pleasant diversion.

Shade nodded in Robbie's direction. "Robbie looks like he is fitting in and taking this seriously."

Marcello turned his head and glanced at Robbie. "He has good concentration, keeps his head in the game, unlike someone else wandering around here tonight. Something bothering you?"

Shade lowered his head, pushing the damp black curls from his cheeks. "Just something Canton wants me to handle. Not a problem, just don't want to give up my time to do it."

Marcello eyed him closely. Whatever Canton wanted, he usually got, but whatever it was, Shade didn't approve, and it was written all over his face, had been for a few days.

"We have this covered. Let us do our job, that's what you pay us for. Go do his work, get it over with and get back here. You know you'll feel better once you get it done. Then you can focus clearly on the recruits again."

Shade locked eyes with Marcello and shook his head, a smirk on his lips. "Since when did you decide to become in charge? You sound more like Marco every day. I know I have to do this, does not mean I like it, but you have a point. Maintain the training routine. I need to call Canton and let him know I am doing this. I will be out of the camp for a few nights."

Marcello fist bumped his master, watching him leave the training field, sword in hand, mind still churning.

As Shade got to the house, he stopped in the back gardens, lit up and pulled out his cell. He reluctantly dialed Alec, getting his voicemail. He left a message, telling Alec to return his call. Hanging up, he snorted, sliding the phone back in his jeans pocket.

He looked up at the lighted window, and knew she waited for him to return from camp. He couldn't tell her about his plans. She was pregnant again, and her hands were full with their son, and this was something he chose not to worry her with. He also knew she'd never agree to any of this.

It tore him apart to keep things from her, but if he told her, it would only result in a battle between them, and he was in no mood to have her upset in her condition. Snuffing out his cigarette, he made his way into the house, straight into their bedroom and the shower. He knew she'd be happy he came home earlier than expected and he wanted to spend time with her before doing what he had now committed to do.

13

Alec had been in meetings with his new campaign manager, Braden Childs. Alec used him during his election bid for Senator, and the vampire was exceptionally devious. They were working now on his campaign for the Presidency. In fact, it had been Braden's idea to use Shade to do the dream-walking. There were other ways to eliminate the President from running, but they were a more 'permanent' solution, and both Alec and Braden would like to avoid that alternative if possible.

Braden opened his laptop, and was looking through a very tight campaign schedule when he asked Alec, "So have you heard back from Shade yet?"

Alec put out his cigarette as his pulled out his cell. "Let me check. I've been so busy. I haven't had time to return calls."

He saw the missed call from Shade, but the voicemail just said to call him. "I'm about to find out." Alec hit redial and waited for Shade to answer.

Shade was back in the camp and agitated he hadn't heard back from Alec. He just wanted this over and done with so he could get back to his warriors and his woman. He'd told *bel* he'd be working in D.C. for a few nights, splitting his time between the camp and the Dead House, so he could check on how things were going there. He was unable to fully concentrate on the new recruits when his cell rang. *About damn time!* He barked into the phone, "So, are you campaigning or fucking someone other than your mate? Took you long enough to return my damn call!"

Alec smirked as he leaned back in his chair. "What has you so riled up, brother? You think you're the only one that has a lot to juggle? I'm here now. What's the verdict, you in?"

Shade paced the training field. "Look, time is money and if you think I have time to wait on your ass, think again! I'm in, but there's a price, brother. I am not going to direct porno films in the mind of the leader of the fucking free world without something in return. So, hands down, no bargaining, this is what I want. I want California, straight out, mine. All of it! I got plans for that bit of territory, you do not have time now to take care of it and will have even less once you get your ass on the throne. So, either you give me what I want, or find yourself another dream-walker."

Alec jumped to his feet, dislodging the laptop balanced on Braden's knee and sending it toppling to the floor. "What the fuck, Shade? That's the majority of my territory! Connecticut is small, and D.C. my power base, but most of my coven is in California. You can't be serious!"

A wicked grin formed across his face. *Yeah brother, I got your ass fired up now, just where I want you.* "Never been more serious. Pick your wars, Alec, you want the U.S., or you want California. What in the hell do you want any more? If you have any fucking confidence about taking the Presidency, you shouldn't care about California. I mean business, brother."

Alec paced, flashing a glance at Braden, who could overhear Shade's end of the conversation. Braden shrugged. "He's got a point, brother. California or the country?"

Alec glared at him. "But I won't be the fucking President forever, Braden. Four years, eight at most. Then I need something to come back to."

Braden picked his laptop up off the floor and waited for it to reboot. "Well, I can always just take him out. But that creates its own controversy and doesn't really solve your problem. The VP takes the Presidency, then he'd probably have the party's nomination, and you're back where you started. Sounds to me like he has you over a barrel, brother."

Alec paced to the window, glaring at his own reflection in the glass. "One condition, Shade. You better fucking make this work. If I'm going to give up my territory, you have to guarantee Ashton caves. If he tries to hang in through the scandal after Rissa fucks him, you may need to perform a few more visits, just to let him know how nasty it will get."

Shade chuckled deep in his throat. "You threatening me?

Not a good idea. I'll start the job tonight."

Hanging up, he looked across the field of recruits, and smiled. He'd just closed one of the easiest deals of his entire life. God help these fucking mortals if they elected Canton.

Alec threw the phone against the wall, turning his anger on Braden. "I better win this thing. Now get busy and do your fucking job!"

14

Shade teleported through the dark of night and across the White House lawn before landing quietly on the roof, still shadowed from view. He saw the Secret Service agents stationed there, with night vision goggles and long-range rifles, chatting quietly to each other, and completely oblivious to him. He figured Ashton would be asleep by this time. His biggest challenge was not having information about the President's habits, knowing when he retired, what time he usually fell asleep, or whether he took any medications that enhanced his sleep but may interfere with his dream activity. Not to mention his target could be roused at any time to respond to a national emergency. Shade would just have to play this one by ear.

He had blocked all images and thoughts from Kate. He sure as hell didn't want her to know what he was about to do. He was taking note of all the security around him before he entered the building, but he remained invisible to them. He had to stifle a laugh. If only the leader of the free world could hire immortals. Telepathy and teleporting would come in handy.

He already had the complete set of blueprints for the White House. He'd secured those some time ago in the event Alec won his bid for the presidency. His warriors were already learning the vast layout of each floor and all the rooms, so they'd be prepared beforehand.

Shade teleported to the third floor which was designated as the family quarters. He made his way to the President's bedroom. He already knew the First Lady slept in a separate room on most nights. That was about the only fucking advantage he had in this gig.

The security was rampant in this place, not that it would do the President any good tonight. Poor fucker had no damn privacy. Why the hell Alec wanted this position was beyond Shade. He stood back and watched the man before him in his bed, sound asleep. He'd have to be careful as to how much stimulation this dream gave him. Shade didn't want him making too much noise and arousing the suspicion of the security stationed right outside his door.

Shade laid his hand on the President's forehead, and then closed his eyes and stepped inside the man's subconscious, curious to see what was rattling around in there. All he could see were flashes of suited men around conference tables, and images of armed military. He almost laughed out loud. What the fuck was he doing here? He got his concentration back and decided to see if Rissa was already lodged somewhere in his subconscious. Shade inserted a vision of Rissa standing sleek and tall, her long legs on display. The image triggered a flash of memories, putting themselves together in rapid succession, like a movie of Rissa as he'd seen her, or imagined her, over the years. Shade walked deeper, pushing the images forward to the front of his brain, and what he saw was rather entertaining. The President had dreamed of her more than a few times. He liked her tits, and he fantasized of fucking her ass. *Well, well, well, why don't we just intensify this little fantasy a bit more and give you all the ammo you need, Mr. President.*

Shade let Rissa walk into his dream naked. She dropped to her knees and sucked his cock like an expert, swallowing him whole. Ashton's body began to respond as his cock rose in his pajamas. Shade filled his dream with the sounds of her sucking and licking, the sensation of her hands, lightly raking his balls. Ashton moaned in his sleep and thrashed around lightly, kicking the sheets free. In the dream, he had Rissa take him to the edge of orgasm, then pull back, letting his rigid cock slip from her mouth. She looked up at him with big blue eyes and gave him a wicked smile. Ashton groaned in his sleep, as Rissa slid his slick, wet cock between her full breasts. Rissa pushed her breasts together as he thrust hard, reaching orgasm and spilling his cum down her tits.

Ashton writhed in his sleep, but Shade kept the movie rolling in his head. He let Rissa push him back on the bed, as she lifted her breasts to her mouth, and licked his thick cum from her nipples and smeared the rest over her body. She undulated before him, hips grinding and tits jiggling, taunting him.

Shade let the President take control of the dream, allowing him to take it where he wanted to go. Ashton pulled her onto the bed, rolling her face down, with her ass in the air as he mounted her and slammed into her ass in one swift motion. She responded with screams of pleasure and begging him for more. Ashton fucked her hard and long, his erection lasting endlessly.

Ashton slapped her ass and her moans of intense pleasure jacked him up even more. Ashton could feel the sting of the slap against his own hand, as it traveled straight to his cock and he came inside her again.

Shade pushed the dream, until Ashton had abused every orifice, and Rissa responded with wanton pleasure, always begging him for more. Shade put the sequence of events into replay, and let it run over and over in his mind, with slight variations.

The President was going to wake up a very happy man and have one hell of a good day. He stayed around for a while, making sure the sequence would keep him stirred. Dreams could be powerful influencers. They could plant seeds of desire, and could be addictive, and this one had more juice than most. He heard something stirring in the hall, voices speaking softly, and he glanced quickly to the window to see dawn was fast approaching.

He took a last look at the man lying in the bed. The President's body still gyrating and the wet spot on his pajamas a good sign. He teleported directly out and headed straight for Bel Rosso. He needed a shower. He felt dirtier than after a night of battle and was disgusted by the images he'd created. He stood under the hot water, letting the images wash down the drain, as he replaced them with visions of adding California to his territory.

15

Shade moved quietly, shadowing his presence, and blocking *bel* for the second night of dream walking with the President. He wandered through the vast famous house tonight before heading to the President's bedroom, taking a private tour. He looked at the portraits displayed throughout the house of each of the mortal men who'd lived here and stood before the portrait of Thomas Jefferson. He'd met Jefferson on several occasions, back in 1785, before Jefferson became President. He'd been the Ambassador to France, and the young emissary from America was looking to expand trade relations with Europe, in a deal that would exchange tobacco for wine. Shade remembered giving him several clippings from his Tuscan vineyards to be taken back to Jefferson's native Virginia and planted at Monticello. Shade never saw the young statesman again, but he didn't miss the irony of the fact his own estate now lay only a few miles from Monticello.

He sighed heavily as he returned to the task at hand. He felt sick about doing this. He'd used his dream-walking skills many times, usually to plant dreams of doubt and failure in combat in the minds of his enemies, undermining their efforts on the battlefield. He'd used dream-walking with Kate when he first met her, when he knew she was attracted to him, but was fearful of moving forward. He'd created dreams much worse than what he was producing for Ashton. But this assignment bothered him. Maybe it was because this wasn't his objective but Alec's. Or maybe because he knew Kate would object. He knew this little detour of the impromptu house tour was just a means to procrastinate.

When he entered the bedroom, he was a little surprised to see Ashton still awake. His pillows were propped against the headboard, as he read by the soft light on the nightstand. Shade hadn't had to push his skills like this in quite some time. He concentrated and shut out all distraction, closing his eyes and going to a dark and quiet place inside his head. He let the powers of his gift send the President a sense of extreme fatigue.

Shade opened his eyes to see the man's head lull back on the pillows, his hands relaxing as the book dropped to the bed. Putting Ashton into a deep dream state, Shade let Rissa waltz in. She started to immediately flirt with the President. Her fingers slid along his arm, her lashes batting flirtatiously, those big blues signaling she could make all his fantasies come true. In the dream, Shade had Rissa speak the words he knew would entice and seduce.

He walked to the bedside, laying his hand on the President's head and intensified the dream, starring Larissa Benneteau Canton.

He let Rissa perform a slow, seductive striptease for him. She played and teased until the President moaned and issued her a command. Shade read his desire and had Rissa pinch and pull her nipples, moaning and licking her lips, just as Ashton had requested. She masturbated herself in a slow methodical dance, her fingers wet with her own juices, bringing herself to orgasm before she licked her fingers clean.

He had Rissa climb onto the bed and slide his pajama bottoms down as she straddled him and performed a delicious lap dance. Although he was orchestrating this dream, he felt a bit of revenge against the bitch that was forever causing him grief in his life. He owed her a few.

Just as the old boy was coming, Shade had her bite hard into his shoulder, drawing blood. Ashton's own desires took over in the dream as he tossed her to the floor. He angrily climbed from the bed and grabbed her hair, dragging her across the room and bending her over a chair. He lashed her ass with his belt as she moaned and begged for more. The President obliged her well and fucked her until he was breathless and covered in sweat.

Shade stepped back from the bed, letting this and the other dream sequences from the prior night continue to stream constantly. He couldn't imagine after a few more nights of this, Ashton could resist any flirtations from Rissa in real life. He'd set the stage, now the rest would be up to her.

The night was almost gone when he teleported out to the Dead House, at least making an appearance there, as if he'd been out on rounds. Theo thought nothing of the unexpected visit, and Shade could at least say to Kate he was at the Dead House. As daybreak neared, he teleported back to Bel Rosso with the rest of the warriors and had a quick smoke before going inside. He'd forgotten to unblock *bel*, so he quickly let his guard down. He walked inside, heading straight to his office and poured himself a huge Midnight. He had no doubt Rissa could make these scenes play out in reality. He'd done his part, and he had earned California.

He heard the electronic shutters go down, darkening the entire house, the lights automatically coming on. He could hear *bel* stirring upstairs. He was usually home, showered and in bed with her long before the shutters dropped for the impending daylight. He made his way to the shower. One more damn night and he was done with this bullshit.

16

Kate heard him in the shower. The blinds were already down, and the sun was beginning to rise. Lorenzo was waking up, just as Shade was coming in. She juggled her sleep to make sure she was always available to meet him when he came home in the morning, so they had time together before his death slumber. She always fell asleep with him, even though she would get up later to spend some day hours with Lorenzo. It was a complex routine, but one she'd adapted to that allowed her to have as much time with him as possible. She understood the demands of spring, and the influx of new warriors who descended on the camp every year made this a very busy time for him, but this was the second day in a row he'd come in at the last minute, showering alone, and quickly slipping into his death slumber.

He joined her in the bedroom as he walked in from his shower and she undressed and slid into bed beside him, as he pulled her close, kissing the top of her head before he slipped into that deep sleep. She lay quietly on his chest. She'd sleep next to him, and wait for the hours to pass, so they could talk. His absence in her life wasn't a pattern she wanted to allow to establish itself.

As the blinds opened wide, Shade began to stir, and he could feel her curled soft and warm next to him. He'd intentionally pushed his timeline at sunrise, arriving just in time for his death slumber, to avoid any conversation. He ran his hand through her hair, her head on his chest, where it should be. Her leg was draped over his and his cock ached for her.

It would soon be time for him to feed from Luca. He hated this time while she was pregnant, but the *bambinos* were worth every second. He looked down at her, hair tousled, so red against her pale skin. Her eyelids fluttered as she moaned softly. Nuzzling into him, she lifted her head and stared at him with amber eyes.

"Sleep well, my walking sin?"

She smiled at him, as she brushed the hair from his face, and tossed her red mane over her shoulder. "Lover, I always sleep well beside you. But I've missed you. You come in so late. We don't have time together."

"I apologize, *mi amore*. Things are a bit hectic this time of year. I have a lot to do at camp with the new recruits. I may have help, but some things I have to do myself. My warriors need to see me. You can't be a leader if you never show yourself to those you expect to follow you, *si*?"

He kissed her. "Mmm, you are the sweetest treat this vampire could ever want. How is Lorenzo? I feel like it's been weeks since I have seen him."

She smiled when he asked about Lorenzo. "Unlike us, Lorenzo never runs out of energy. I'd never have thought one child could keep me, Theresa and Nita busy. But he misses you too, Shade. I know this is a busy time, I do understand. But Lorenzo grows so fast. We won't get this time back with him. Don't get so tied up in your work you forget about us. We need you too."

He knew she was right. It worried him that she thought these things, or even had cause too. *Fucking Alec!* Before the thought left his mind, he heard small feet running in the hall and come to a screeching stop at their bedroom door. He and Kate both stared at the door, waiting for it to burst open, or to see if he'd follow the rules, and ask permission to enter.

They shared a glance as Shade told her, "He wants in, you know. If he comes in without permission, we must be stern, and I am in no mood to be stern, just telling you in advance."

Kate giggled. "He'll knock. He knows he's not to enter our room if the door is closed." They lay quietly, their eyes on the door, when they heard the quiet knock from his tiny hand.

Kate called out, "Who is it?" She had to suppress a laugh as she did so.

They heard the sweetest voice reply, "It's Lorenzo,

Mommy. May I come in please?"

Shade kissed her on the forehead. "He minds his manners, *si*? Come in, Lorenzo!"

The door opened slightly as his little head peeped inside, and all Shade could see was a mass of black curls and two large blue eyes, lit up with glee just as Lorenzo threw open the door and ran for their bed, scrambling to climb it.

"Hold on, little warrior. Do you not think you should ask your *madre* if she will allow you to get in our bed?"

"No, Daddy. I jump on this bed all the time. Wanna see?" Lorenzo scrambled across the bed and started jumping. Kate dissolved in giggles as their son jumped, his curls bouncing, and his own laughter bubbling up. He did a belly flop and crawled over on top of them both.

"Daddy, can you play with me tonight? Can I go with you to camp?"

Shade chuckled at his son's antics. His own *padre* would have blistered his ass if he'd ever thought about doing such a thing.

Shade pulled him into his arms and tickled him softly as Lorenzo's laughter rang out and he struggled against Shade's grip before curling into his neck.

"Daddy is busy. I am juggling the camp and the Dead House tonight, so you can't come along. Once things quiet down, I will make a night for just us warriors, *si*?"

Kate looked at Shade quizzically. "Lorenzo, go find Theresa now, and get dressed. Mommy will take you outside in just a bit and you can see what the workers have done on the pool, okay?"

Lorenzo bounced off the bed, running barefoot out the room. "Okay, Mommy."

Kate turned to Shade. "You're back in D.C.? I don't understand. You have all the new recruits. I thought that was why you were so busy?"

Trying quickly to answer without looking guilty, he swung his legs over the side of the bed, sitting up. "No, *mi amore*, I said I would be spending some time in D.C." Standing quickly, he started getting dressed. "I need to go back into the Dead House. We are preparing for the campaign. Alec will be traveling to different cities. I will need warriors who can follow him, blend in with the crowds, and still provide protection. I know Lorenzo needs my attention, but right now, it is much too hectic. Tonight, will be the last night I will be going into D.C. for a while. I promise I will spend a whole night with him soon."

Pulling on his leathers and a clean black tee, he sat down to lace his boots. "Sometimes, I have a lot of responsibilities to attend to. He has you, and Luca and everyone else. I can't be with him constantly."

Kate was taken aback by his defensiveness. He loved spending time with Lorenzo. Maybe it wasn't Lorenzo he was avoiding. Maybe it was her. "Shade, have I done something wrong? Are you upset with me?"

He swung his head around and stared at her. "Kate, I have no reason to be upset with you. I am just overwhelmed with duties right now."

Sighing, he walked to her and scooped her off the bed and into his arms. Cradling her softly, he kissed her forehead. "I love you and I know you worry, but with Alec getting this close to the campaign, I need to get the new recruits prepared. We have ramped up their training schedule, as I have much to accomplish in a short time. We will need the extra coverage once Alec officially announces he is running. My warriors in D.C. need to be prepared as well. I have to split my time between the camp and Dead House. I do not want to neglect you, so here is my bargain. Let me get a head start with the recruits, we will need them in the metro area, then you choose a place. We will take a little fun night, just the three of us, anyplace you choose. Does that work? Do I not always make it up to you when I am negligent?"

Kate laid her head against his chest. "Of course, lover. I understand."

Kate felt something off in his explanation. It had been a long time since he'd withheld information from her. In their first year together, he'd withheld so much to protect her. But since

Lorenzo's birth, he'd been more open about educating her on the ways of the vampire culture, not shielding her from some of the harsh realities. He knew there were things she needed to know now in order to protect Lorenzo. She had no doubt he was busy, but she felt there was something he was leaving unsaid. Keeping her thoughts to herself, she responded, "I'll hold you to that promise."

"Good, now I need to get moving." Kissing her passionately, he set her down on her feet. "Don't overdo it please, get some rest. Do not wait up, I know I will be late."

He grabbed the gun from the locked drawer, stuffing it inside his leathers as he walked out and down the stairs, teleporting into D.C. Leaving them strained his heart as it was, but he felt *bel's* doubt and his soul screamed. This would be the last night he dream-walked for Alec. Not even the prize of winning California made up for that look in her eyes when she questioned him.

17

The moon was full, and the skies clear. It was a perfect night to be strolling through the White House, and Shade was happy this would be his last trip here, at least until Alec moved in. Tonight, he'd come earlier than usual, wanting to walk the residence, investigate and get a full scope of the inside of this place. Looking at the floor plans was helpful, but nothing beat having firsthand knowledge of the layout. He was able to see where the security was stationed and how heavily armed they were, as well as where cameras were located. He was able to shadow himself and move freely, invisible to the mortal eye, and blocking anything and everyone around him. When he finished his surveillance, he made his way to the third floor.

Shade avoided the Secret Service who guarded the family quarters and teleported into the President's bedroom. He was caught off-guard at what he saw in the bed. The First Lady was lying asleep beside the President. *Cazzo, I was not expecting this!* It wouldn't stop him from his mission, just a small obstacle. Besides, he wanted this damn thing over and done with.

He carefully observed both of them, as they lay in a deep sleep. He laid his hand on the President's forehead, closed his eyes and saw Ashton had already found Rissa in his dreams and was riding her hard. This was a great sign. The dreams were sinking deep into his psyche and working him into a lather.

Shade monitored the progression of the dream, and then slipped the old boy a pair of handcuffs. Ashton cuffed Rissa to the bed posts before burying his face between her legs. He sucked and licked at her, making her writhe with passion, until she came for him. He flipped her over and fucked her in the ass. Shade dropped enough toys into the dream that would allow Ashton to fill every orifice, and play out every fantasy, and Rissa responded with enthusiasm, her moans feeding Ashton's desire.

Shade felt Ashton squirm under his hand and opened his

eyes to see the President groping his wife, as he moaned Rissa's name aloud. He tugged at his wife's nightgown. She rolled over and shook him hard to wake him.

Ashton reluctantly left the dream. He awoke befuddled but craving a certain blonde with big blue eyes and great tits. He looked with some confusion at his wife, her gown wrapped up around her waist as she struggled to pull it back down. She smacked at his hand and asked him what he thought he was doing. An argument was soon underway, as Ashton kept reminding her to lower her voice.

Shade shook his head. Ashton tried his best to explain to his wife he'd had an erotic dream, but she wasn't buying it. Finally, she got up and stomped out of the room, claiming loudly he needed to get whatever that was out of his system, and in the meantime, she'd return to her own bed.

Shade waited patiently while the President stroked himself to orgasm, got up and washed off and returned to his bed alone. When he finally fell asleep, Shade laid one finger on his forehead and the dreams began all over again. There would be no relief in sight for the President. He was going to eat, sleep and dream about Rissa, until that itch got scratched.

Once satisfied the job was done, the sun was on the horizon, and he quickly teleported out, back to the Dead House. There were only a few warriors there, most of them had already left to return back home. He joined the few remaining warriors as they all teleported back to Bel Rosso. He smiled to himself. He was soon to be Master of California.

***

Kate wasn't happy with this pattern of Shade leaving early and coming home late. He fell immediately into his death slumber, and then left on waking. They had no time together. Her worries were quickly dismissed as she was preoccupied with Lorenzo and his boundless energy. She took him to see the construction on the underground pool, as well as the outdoor pool, and like every boy, he started climbing the mounds of dirt that had been excavated for the pools.

When he tired of that, he was climbing up to his tree house, and begging her to follow. She laughed and said, "I don't think so, Lorenzo."

Lorenzo called to Luca, who quickly joined him in the tree house, as Kate sat in the tree swing attached to the large oak. When he climbed down, the three of them walked to the stables as Lorenzo visited every horse, feeding them apples or carrots and visiting with the stable hands.

"Mommy, can we go see Daddy in the camp?"

Kate paused, looking at Luca. "I'm not sure that's a good idea, Lorenzo. The new recruits are there. It may be dangerous."

Luca scooped him up, lifting him to his shoulders. "I think we'll be okay. Come on, little warrior. Let's get you to camp."

Lorenzo lifted both hands in the sky as he rode high on Luca's shoulders, and Kate followed them to the camp. Once they entered, Marcello saw his cousin and slowly walked over. He gave Luca a hug. "Bringing us a new recruit, cousin?"

Luca lowered Lorenzo to the ground. "Yep. He's a little small, but I think you can work with him."

Lorenzo yelled out, "I forgot my sword!"

Kate flashed Marcello a look. "Don't you dare give him a real sword!"

Marcello laughed. "No, my lady."

Kate inquired if Shade was busy, and Marcello informed her he wasn't in the camp tonight, that he'd been in D.C. the last few nights. "Oh...right."

Kate watched as Skelk worked nearby, impatiently showing a new recruit how to use the crossbow. "I thought Skelk was assigned to the Dead House?"

Marcello cast a glance in Skelk's direction. "Oh, he is, but it's been so quiet there he's been coming home early and helping us with the training."

Kate gave him a smile as she felt a tight grip on her heart. Shade had told her they were really busy in D.C., and the inconsistencies were starting to pile up. **"Lover? Where are you?"**

Marcello took Lorenzo by the hand and led him off to watch some of the new warriors' train. Skelk lost patience with the new recruit, and cuffed him on the back of the head, sending him on his way, when he noticed Luca and joined them. The two warriors fist bumped, as Skelk turned and nodded to Kate. Kate smiled at him. They had a special bond after she broke through his barriers and worked with him to hone her own crossbow skills after the Battle of Bel Rosso.

"Skelk. You're looking well."

He bowed and said, "As are you, my lady. Will the daughter of Medici also be a warrior?"

Kate laughed. "Not if I have anything to say about it. Or Shade, either, for that matter."

Luca shook his head. "No way would that happen."

Kate changed the subject, asking Skelk about his workload in D.C. He told her things had been very light. "So, are you working with Shade then?"

Skelk shook his head. "No, my lady. I see him when he comes in, but then he leaves on his own. He's not in the Command Center with Theo."

Kate nodded and said nothing. **"Lover? Can you hear me?"**

He always answered her. Since Lorenzo had been born, he'd never blocked her from his thoughts, always remaining open. But tonight, she heard only silence. Kate flagged down Marcello, waving him over, indicating she was ready to take Lorenzo back to the house.

Returning back home, Lorenzo rode on Luca's back, as the child chattered endlessly about the warriors. Luca noticed Kate was silent. When they reached the house, Lorenzo scrambled down, and Kate told him to go find Theresa. He ran up the stairs in search of his nanny, already in need of a bath.

Kate turned to Luca. "May I ask a personal question?"

Luca looked at her quizzically, not sure what was coming. "Of course."

She looked at the floor, embarrassed she had to ask, "Is Shade feeding from you yet?"

He creased his brow as he answered, confused as to why she was asking. "No, not yet."

She gave him a half smile and nodded as she followed her

son up the stairs. Theresa was already filling the tub with water. She didn't need to see Lorenzo to know he'd need a bath. Kate found Lorenzo in his room, pulling down toys when she herded him into the bathroom, and helped him strip from his clothes. Kate heard the whir of the electronic blinds and wondered again where he was.

"Excuse me, Theresa."

Theresa had a firm grip on Lorenzo as he played in the tub, "I've got him, my lady. Go to master."

Kate left the bathroom and walked down the hall to their bedroom. She didn't feel him yet and her heart raced. He wasn't in danger. She'd feel that immediately. Her heart was breaking as she could only think of one reason why he'd block her. She entered their bedroom and heard him teleport into the bathroom, followed by the sound of the shower. She wondered whose scent he was washing away. She stripped from her clothes and slid beneath the sheets in the room made pitch black by the blinds. She turned on the lamp by the bed and waited for him.

He entered their bedroom with a towel draped low on his hips, his hair still damp, as he slid into bed beside her. She wondered for the hundredth time where he'd spent the last few nights.

"Shade, I tried to reach you tonight."

He pulled her to his chest. "What? Oh, I must have been busy, Kate. Was it... important?" The slumber slammed into him, his body drained by the sleepwalking and the lack of feeding.

Lifting his arm, he laid it across her shoulders, the blackness taking him down and he gave in to it. "Slumber."

Kate felt her heart break as his slumber dragged him down, stealing away even the few seconds they had together.

18

Kate slept fitfully, getting up several times to check on Lorenzo before climbing back in bed, lying next to him. The images of those long-destroyed photos of him with the Asian feeders flashed through her head. Where did he feed, and from whom? She felt him stir beside her as the blinds rolled up, letting in the light of early dusk.

Hearing the whir of the blinds, the slumber was slow to leave him. Moaning, he threw his hand over his eyes. Slow to break free of the grogginess from the deep slumber, he felt a hard knot rise in his chest. He could feel *bel* was bothered by something. He couldn't read her thoughts as she was blocking him. *She never blocks me! Cazzo, she is pissed off.* Wracking his brain, he was trying to remember last night, and all he could remember was her being in bed when he came out of the shower.

"Sleep well, *mi amore*?"

Kate lifted her head and looked at him. He stared back at her with those piercing blue eyes. She remembered his anguish when he succumbed to the feeders, his anger with himself that he felt he'd betrayed her. She saw none of that now and was so confused. "No, I didn't."

As he stared at her amber eyes, he also saw flecks of red, ready to flame into a full-blown beast. *What the fuck did I do? She is still blocking me!* "No? Is Lorenzo okay?"

Kate sighed in frustration and sat up, tossing the blankets aside as she slid from the bed, grabbing her robe from the foot of the bed. "Lorenzo is fine. It's not Lorenzo that has me worried. I tried to reach you last night. You didn't answer me. Where were you?"

"First of all, woman, stop blocking me from your thoughts. I don't like it. Get back in this bed, you are about ready to explode, and I don't like that either. When did you try to reach me? I didn't hear you. I was in D.C., I told you that, Kate." *Cazzo, she is pushing me on this one.*

She snapped her head around, her red hair flying, "You don't like when I block you? Really? Exactly where in D.C., and please don't say the Dead House. I know better!"

Sitting up, slowly getting out of bed, he felt like hell, and this was the last thing he wanted to deal with. Putting his hands on his hips, his voice was low and quiet, because what he saw before him was one pissed off mate and that beast of hers was going to be aimed at him, and not in a good way.

"Oh, so you know better. That tells me you have been investigating, asking questions...whatever you want to call it. Means you do not trust me. You're pissed off, so come out with it, and tell me what is really eating away at you. I have no time for these games, Kate."

He'd volunteer nothing. He was forcing her to make the accusation. She looked at him with tears in her eyes. "Where do you go? Where do you go to feed? Are you hunting?"

Feed? Hunting? What in the hell? "*Mi amore*, you have this all wrong! I am not feeding anywhere. I do not hunt, ever. What in the hell has your mind been chewing on?" Rushing to the other side of the bed, he took her in his arms, but she struggled against him and that really threw him off. She'd never done this to him!

He took a step back. "Don't do this, *mi amore*. Don't. You can't push me away when everything in your head is mixed up and confused. I know I haven't been here. I know that upsets you. I promised you I would take you and Lorenzo anywhere you want to go, and we will be together, I still mean that. Please, *bel*. I only want to feed from you. You must know that."

She pulled away, but his words felt sincere and a part of her was relieved he wasn't leaving her to feed, but there was still something he was hiding. "So, I'll ask you then. What is it you're hiding? Why have you blocked me?"

Sighing heavily, he walked to the window, the sun had set but the light in the sky was beautiful, the colors streaming across the horizon. He laid his forehead on the windowpane. He had no idea how to approach this. He couldn't even look at her.

"I trust you with my heart and soul. Never doubt that. But I blocked you because of what I had to do, something I wished for you not to know. A job for Alec. I mulled it over a bit before I did it because it was something I wrestled with myself. I did not wish to do it, but in the end, I did it for our *bambinos*, for us, for our *familia*. I don't expect you to understand some of the things I do and why I do them. Sometimes, they are heinous, but I assure you, I harmed no one physically. I blocked you from my thoughts because I never want you to see me in that way. It is so you never look at me in disgust or disappointment. It was wrong for me to do that to you. I have tried to involve you since you have become immortal, to include you in everything."

Kate looked at his back as he stood at the window. What deeds could be so horrible he wouldn't share them? "Lover, my imagination is running wild. I've seen you on the battlefield. I've seen you kill. What could you do that you think you must hide from me? I assure you, the things running through my head could be no worse!"

Kate looked at him with hurt. "Shade..." She reached for him. "Please. No secrets. I don't want to fight. You said you didn't feed, and I believe you. But something is bothering you. There's something you hide from me."

Turning around, he saw how much she hurt. "Take a good look, you are looking at the soon to be Master of California. That is one secret."

Kate raised her eyebrows in surprise. "What? Doesn't California belong to Alec? Did something happen to Alec?"

"No. But he asked me to do this one job. I bargained and that was my price to do it. He agreed but there is one condition. Rissa has to do her part. Once done, he gives me California. So, kiss me and tell me you still want your savage lover."

She went to him and slid into his embrace, but her mind was reeling. *What job would be worth Alec's entire territory?* She kissed him and saw the strain in his face. He was tired, and clearly, he hadn't fed, and it was taking its toll. "Shade, what exactly did Alec ask you to do?"

Looking down at her, she still maintained the sweet innocence she'd held as a mortal, the face he fell in love with. How could he withhold this from her? "Can we please lie down? I will tell you. *Bel,* I am tired, I just want to hold you, *si*?"

She read the concern on his face and felt a sense of foreboding. Taking his hand, she led him back to their bed, climbing in ahead of him, and opening her arms to him. "Lay next to me, lover. I don't want secrets between us."

Climbing in without another thought, he snuggled into her neck. Her scent was intoxicating, and his mouth watered. He swallowed hard to keep from taking what he wanted.

"Alec wants to escalate his timetable. He wants to run in this election, but there is a major obstacle in his way, the President. He needs Ashton to withdraw, to not seek a second term. Alec has planned a scandal, a means to blackmail him. He has convinced Rissa to sleep with the President, get it on film. He will threaten to make it public if Ashton does not withdraw. He asked me to make sure the President is more than ready for whatever Rissa has planned. To use my gift of dream-walking to fill his head with visions of sexual depravity of him and Rissa together. That's what I have been doing and where I have been." He leaned close to her ear and whispered softly saying, "Don't hate me for this."

Kate pulled away, sitting up in their bed, absorbing what he'd said. "You dream-walked on the President? You were in the White House? Why would he ask you...no, never mind, I know why he asked."

She covered her face with her hands. Dream-walking was his gift, and he rarely used it, except to bring her dreams of pleasure. She knew it was designed as a weapon, just as her gift of animalism could be used as a weapon. She hated that he was pulled into Alec's world, that Alec had exploited him to achieve his own goals. She lay back down beside him. She couldn't deny his nature, for she was vampire now too. She'd done things she never thought possible, but this was a bitter pill to swallow.

"Well, at least you extracted a high price. I wish you weren't so aligned with him."

Rolling over on his stomach, he lifted his head and looked at her. "Alec was my way to make it here in the States. You use what you have, contacts. He was well established here, I was not. We go back a very long way. When I came here, it was to explore new territory. I bargained for everything I have here. The dream-walking was not a hard task, but it went against my grain to do it. But what I got in return builds upon our strength here. We have gained a lot of territory in the last year. But it also means more of my time away. I can't change that. I can't change how much I want to do well, see our *bambinos* have something. It is important to me to secure the future of our coven. This is my gift to my *familia*, my coven, to you, because I love you. I cherish you. I want you to be proud of me, proud of my accomplishments."

Kate stroked his face. "I'm always proud of you, but none of these things mean anything if you're not here. I understand your obligations, I know we both have a responsibility to the coven, but please don't become so absorbed in your responsibilities you no longer have time for me, or your children. I miss you, and Lorenzo misses you, and there will be another soon."

He sighed heavily. "I get lost in my work, *mi amore*, it is all I have ever known. There was nothing else for me. I try to come home to be with you and Lorenzo, but with camp, it is never easy. Guide me, Kate. This is the only place I feel at peace and when I upset you, there is no peace of mind for me. I wish I could spend every moment with you. Perhaps someday that will happen. Did you think about where and what you wanted to do on our date?"

She ran her fingers through his hair, as her eyes explored his face. She never tired of looking at him. "All I want is your time. Just spend the whole night with us. Lorenzo loves when you're home. We can all ride, maybe swim in the grotto. We live in paradise. You don't need to take me anywhere else."

Closing his eyes, he moaned. He loved when she touched him, her hands so soft and gentle. "That sounds like heaven to me. But I think there is something we both need first."

Placing both hands on either side of her face, he kissed her. His need was intense. His tongue explored inside her mouth, gliding over her teeth, and then nipping her lip, he pulled her lip into his mouth. "You taste like heaven and sex and exotic fruit grown just for me."

"Feed, lover. Feed from me."

19

Shade had let Marcello and Theo know he was taking the night off. He'd promised Kate a date night, and she was content to spend it here at Bel Rosso. They were taking Lorenzo along as well. Both of them needed his attention. Hell, he needed some attention too.

While Kate was in the bath, he walked down to his office to give Alec a call, he wanted this done. He was ready to put the dream-walking assignment behind him. The rest was up to Alec and Rissa, but even if they failed, he was taking California. No excuses, he'd kept his part of the bargain. He felt better having this done with and finally letting Kate know where he'd been. They still had so many lessons to learn together.

Grabbing his cell off the desk, he rang up Alec, and hoped this wouldn't take long. His mate and his son were waiting for a long night together. After a few rings, Alec picked up. Shade spoke into the phone, "It's done, brother."

Alec smiled when he answered the call and heard Shade's message. "I couldn't be happier. Anything I need to know?"

"Not really but something you might find amusing." Chuckling, he couldn't wait to lay it on the line with Canton.

Alec smirked. "I think the only thing that will amuse me is having him withdraw from the campaign, but what have you got?"

"Rissa shouldn't meet any resistance. Seems the old boy was already having a few dreams about your mate, didn't take much to get him there. Tell Rissa to bend over and let him fuck her in the ass, he likes that. He also likes to talk dirty to her. Throw in some handcuffs, and a few other toys and both of them will have a good time. Guarantee it. Get the papers drawn up, this is over."

Alec shook the images from his head. "The last picture I want in my head is Ashton with a boner. Rissa can handle this one, and I'll have my lawyers draw up the papers, send copies to the Council. When I'm President, I'll invite you and Kate to the White House."

Shade rolled his eyes, he couldn't fucking care less about the White House. "*Grazie*. Good luck. Checked out the place while I was there, we will need to figure out how we get a few warriors placed on your Secret Service detail. You just get there and let me worry about the rest. My regards to Rissa."

Laughing out loud, knowing Alec could hear him, he hung up. Poor Rissa, that Ashton cock was one small little worm compared to the cobra she was used too.

***

Kate was rushing to get things done for the night since Shade had decided to stay home with them. Lorenzo was feeding with Nita, Theresa was cleaning his room, and Kate was trying to get some laundry done. She was bent over the laundry basket, sorting through the dirty laundry, most of which belonged to Lorenzo. She shook her head, as she was tossing his clothes into the washer. He easily went through three wardrobe changes a day. If there was dirt, Lorenzo would find it. Having the pool construction didn't help, because Lorenzo was always in the middle of everything. She poured in the detergent and bleach and turned on the washer.

Taking the steps two at a time, Shade followed her scent to the laundry room. Peeping around the corner, he found *bel* still in her nightgown. The silk fabric clung to her curves as she bent over the laundry basket. The washer began to shake and rattle and seemed off kilter with the load inside it. Kate bent over the machine, trying to shift the wet laundry, as the washer shook her whole body, moving it to a rhythm he'd seen before. Stepping inside the room, he closed the door and slid up behind her, his hands gliding from her thighs up to her ass, as he flipped the red silk gown up over her hips, laying it over her back. Cupping her ass, he moaned softly, nuzzling into her neck. "I want you, right here, right now. I need you."

Kate felt his hands slide under her gown and gasped in surprise. The noise of the washer had masked his entry. She cast a glance over her shoulder to notice he'd closed the door. She hoped Theresa could pick up on their vibe and keep Lorenzo out because she recognized that husky tone in Shade's voice and knew the beast had been aroused and there was no turning back. She pushed her backside against him, feeling the hard steel of his cock through his jeans, as his hands gripped her hips.

"You rile my beast woman, like no other." He unzipped his jeans and his cock, thick and long, sprung forward. His jeans hit the floor and he stepped out of them, kicking them behind him and taking a spread leg stance. His hands roamed back over her ass, then up her spine as he wrapped one hand in that luscious silken hair and pulled her head back. The washer began to really shake, pushing her hard against his hips. Grasping his cock, he slid the head inside her, wet and warm. She was ready for him. She needed him as much as he needed her.

Turning her head to the side, his tongue slid up the pulsing vein in her neck. He slammed his cock deep inside her, matching his motions to the timing of the washing machine that bucked and vibrated with the uneven load. Growling, he nipped at her shoulder as his cock glided in and out. He cupped one plump lily-white breast in his hand and pinched her nipple. Her moans ran through his body like a siren calling him home. Sinking his fangs deep into her soft flesh, he fed like a starving vampire, as he rode her from behind.

Kate gripped the side of the washer as he grabbed a handful of hair and lifting her head, sank his fangs deep. She felt the surge of heat between her legs that accompanied his feeding, and she moaned in response. His lips were hot and wet as they drew her blood, his breath ragged, as he drank with abandon.

Unlatching his fangs, her blood dribbled down the side of his mouth, but his beast had yet to be satisfied. He wanted his due and was enjoying this stolen moment of fun. Pulling from her, he spun her around, not prepared for what she did next. Her tongue snaked out and licked the blood from his chin. He lifted her onto the washer, and pulling her to the edge, he slid his aching cock back in that sweet honey. Kate wrapped her legs around his hips and gripped his shoulders.

"Ride me, my crimson beauty. Take all of me. Make me come inside you."

The washer bucked and jarred, rhythmically slamming her hips into him, the racket from the unbalanced washer drowning out the sounds of their lovemaking. She clung to his broad shoulders as she nuzzled into his neck, feeling the pulsing of his vein against her tongue. She bit hard, feeling the burst of his blood against her tongue, as his cock pounded into her. The wave of heat rolled through her, as the orgasm hit and she unlatched, throwing her head back, screaming to the heavens.

He felt her body respond as her orgasm shook her. He loved watching her cum hard for him. She was beautiful in her passion, never holding anything back from him. He felt the tightness in his balls as he came hard, throwing back his head, his mouth open as his beast roared his approval. He pulled her to his chest, both of them panting and catching their breath.

"*Cazzo*, you make me crazy with wanting. I could not resist. You should do laundry more often, *si*?"

The washer shuddered as the load was balanced and it moved into spin cycle. Kate could only giggle when he said she should do laundry more often. She heard tiny feet running to the laundry room door, and Lorenzo's voice calling out.

"Mommy, are you okay?"

Kate bit her lip as she tried to re-arrange her gown. "Mommy is fine, Lorenzo. Just doing laundry. Go find Theresa." She laid her head against Shade's shoulder, trying not to laugh and praying Lorenzo didn't open that door.

Burying his face into her hair, he was trying not to laugh, he whispered, "You know he is standing right outside this door. Tell him to get dressed. Daddy has a surprise for him. Distract him." He felt her body shaking against him as she giggled into his shoulder. "Stop laughing, damn it."

They were laughing like teenagers caught red-handed. Kate slid off the washer and pulled her gown back into place. She backed Shade into the corner behind the door, as he struggled to get his jeans back on. She opened the door and scooped

Lorenzo up in her arms, closing the door behind her and carrying Lorenzo back to his bedroom.

"Where's Daddy? He said he was staying home tonight."

Kate curled him up, and blew on his belly, sending him into a fit of giggles. "Your Daddy will be along soon. Now let's get you dressed so we can all play, shall we?"

Theresa ran out of the nursery, taking Lorenzo from her arms. "So sorry, my lady, he got away from me."

Kate smiled, "It's fine, Theresa. Keeping up with Lorenzo takes a team effort."

Kate entered their bedroom to find Shade had teleported there. She wrapped her arms around him as they both collapsed on the bed, laughing.

20

Shade and Kate were going over plans for hiring a tutor for Lorenzo. They were snuggled up on the couch, talking and sipping Midnight. Shade had a surprise for Lorenzo, and he was waiting for their son to join them. It never took him long to find them.

Shade laughed. "I think you are going to have your hands full getting him to sit still for long. He may have to start slowly with his tutor." Hugging her close, he felt relaxed just to be home. He smiled as he remembered their earlier encounter in the laundry room.

Kate nodded. "He'll need a patient tutor for sure. Lorenzo can't sit still for five minutes. We have some appointments scheduled next week to start looking at tutors. I believe Theresa has scheduled a gentleman named Enzo. She said he was one of your tutors when you were young. She said if he could keep up with you when you were a boy, then Lorenzo would be a piece of cake."

He looked at her with surprise. "Damn, Enzo is still tutoring? I remember him well, stern but patient. I had to sit my ass down for my studies. *Padre* would not tolerate any foolishness. Now Lorenzo, he is worse, much worse than me!" Laughing, Shade watched her smile. She looked so radiant when she is pregnant.

Kate shook her head. "Not according to Theresa. She said the apple didn't fall far from the tree. I'm sure Lorenzo has more freedom, and perhaps he has a few more things to get into than you had access to, but I'm pretty sure that mischievous spirit he comes by naturally. And speak of the devil... "

Lorenzo was jumping down the stairs, holding onto the rail, and landing hard on each step.

"Lorenzo, what are you doing?"

He yelled back to her, "It's not Lorenzo! It's a giant!"

Shade watched his son as he pounced hard on each step.

"Giant, what have you done with our Lorenzo?"

Lorenzo hit the bottom step with a thud and roared loud before running full speed and launching himself at his father.

Shade stood and caught him in mid-flight, swinging him around in a circle. Lorenzo's giggles were contagious, and Shade couldn't help but laugh with him. Shade stopped spinning him and held him close to his chest, as the boy's head kept bobbing around as if he were still spinning.

"Serves you right to be dizzy in the head after eating my Lorenzo. Well, now I am so sad, because I had a surprise for Lorenzo. If he is gone, I should tuck this giant into his bed and take Mommy out for a surprise."

Lorenzo screamed, "No!" He placed his hands on either side of his father's face. "I'm Lorenzo. This is just my giant disguise!" He leaned his head against his father's. "See me, Daddy?"

Squinting his eyes, Shade grunted. "I think I see Lorenzo in there, but I will not be sure until I have a kiss. That will tell me for sure."

Lorenzo planted a big, wet kiss on his father's cheek and started kicking his legs. "What's my surprise, Daddy?"

"Ah! I see Lorenzo. Well, first, let us discuss something before we have the surprise. Miss Theresa is not your maid. She is not here to clean up your messes. She is your nanny. Therefore, you need to pick up your toys, your dirty clothes and keep all of your books on the shelves. If you can do that, I think we might be able to go for a horse ride tonight with Mommy."

Lorenzo looked at him with surprise and raised both hands palms out. "I always clean up, Daddy. Tressa says I pick up things just like my Daddy."

Kate was laughing out loud. "Yes, he has you on that one."

"I think Mommy is making fun of me." Sitting him down, Shade crouched in front of him. "You need a jacket before we can leave. It is a bit chilly outside. Mommy will ride Bravado, and you can ride on Impavido with me."

Kate put his jacket on as he squirmed. Shade picked him up and put him on his back. Lorenzo wrapped his chubby little arms around Shade's neck and whispered in his ear, "I love you, Daddy."

"I love you too, little warrior." He grabbed Kate's hand as they strolled out to the stables, where the horses were already saddled and waiting for them.

"First thing to remember when riding with a lady is, she always mounts first. So, you need to climb down so I can help Mommy mount and then we will get mounted, *si*?"

Lorenzo scrambled down from his father's shoulders, running in Angelo's direction. "I'll get a carrot!"

Shade laughed. "Now I know why Impavido is gaining weight, he feeds him constantly."

Kate was laughing as Shade helped her mount Bravado. "He loves to feed them. Angelo says he has to keep a close eye on him when he's here. He'd feed them the whole bushel of apples."

Lorenzo came running back with a carrot in each hand. Shade stopped him. "Here is the deal, little warrior. I will let you give them each a treat. But they do not get treats until after the ride, you will spoil them and then they will not listen to commands because they already had their treats. Understood?"

Lorenzo nodded his head the whole time his father was talking to him, his dark curls bobbing. "I thought they might need energy, Daddy."

He turned to Bravado as Kate steadied the horse, holding his reins. Lorenzo held his hand palm up, tucking his thumb under his palm as the horse took the carrot from his small hand. "See Daddy, Angelo teached me how to feed them."

Kate smiled at him, correcting his English. "You mean he taught you."

Lorenzo nodded. "Yep, that's what I said."

Shade looked at his family. Life was good for the Medici, and she was right, he needed to be home more, with them. "I am impressed, a good warrior is always a great horseman, now come on before the night ends and we never leave the stables."

Picking up Lorenzo, Shade sat him on the saddle. "Hold onto the pommel, so I can mount." Shade stepped in the stirrup and swung his leg over the massive horse, one arm going around his son. "We ready to ride, little warrior?"

"Go fast, Daddy!"

"If we go fast, you will fall off. And Mommy will never be able to keep up with us. Impavido is much bigger and faster than Bravado. I always beat her when we race!" Shade looked over at *bel*, wiggling his eyebrows and grinning.

Kate winked at him as she led Bravado out of the stables, the large black stallion following. Once outside, they cleared the pasture, and the horses walked side by side down a well-worn trail that winds through the woods, around the vineyards, and across to the huge fields of lavender and sunflowers, all sprouting the early spring growth. Kate reached out and took his hand, as he lifted it to his lips and kissed her palm. Lorenzo started twisting in the saddle, trying to keep an eye on his parents, as Kate let go of his hand so Shade could steady him.

Shade admonished him. "You will twist your neck off. Now, we are farther out from the house, so let's play a game. I think you will like it. Let's see how many animals you can see from atop Impavido. You have the ability to sense them, even when you can't see them. And for each one you find, Daddy will give you a reward. Ready?"

Shade picked up the pace as they moved closer to the mountain range. He wanted Lorenzo to practice the use of his skills and start to hone his night vision and hearing. He was born with these skills but must learn to master them.

Lorenzo loved the attention and set himself to the task. He was quick to point out that Aegis and Night-Stalker were following them along the tree line. "That counts, right, Daddy?"

"*Si*, that is very good, Lorenzo, you are observant of your surroundings. Being a warrior, you must always know what is lurking in the shadows. Oh, I see something quite interesting. See if you can see what I see."

Lorenzo swung his head, looking to see if he could spot what his father spotted, and focused his senses. He looked up and saw the falcon in the tree. He pointed skyward and all three of them looked up as he shouted, "Danica!"

"Good job. You make Daddy very proud!"

As they headed up the mountain trail, the trees became thicker, the blackness even deeper. Vampire sight adjusts to the dark, like daylight for mortals, and he waited for Lorenzo to adjust to the darkness.

Lorenzo continued to look skyward and pointed in another direction. "Look, Mommy, do you know that bird?"

Kate laughed as she looked in the direction he was pointing. "Lorenzo, all the animals respond to me, but that doesn't mean I know them all by name. But I do know this one."

Kate held her gloved hand up over her head and the large white owl swooped down from his perch high in the pines and landed on her hand. Kate looked at him as he tilted his head. "Lorenzo, I'd like you to meet Wizard."

Lorenzo was bouncing in the saddle as he tried to pet the huge owl, and Shade had to grab him around the waist to keep him from falling off the horse.

"Can I keep him, Mommy?"

Kate shook her head. "They are wild, Lorenzo. They want to live in the wild. But I'm sure he'll visit you."

Kate lifted her hand skyward again as the bird took flight, his huge wingspan creating a breeze they could all feel. "What else is out there, Lorenzo?"

Lorenzo turned his attention back to the forest and concentrated hard.

Shade could barely keep a hold on his son, his head swiveling from side to side, his body squirming. Shade's heart filled with love for this child and he wondered why he needed Kate to remind him he should be home more. "Lorenzo, close your eyes, feel and listen without looking, see if you can sense something without using your eyes. Try it for Daddy."

Lorenzo closed his eyes and threw both hands over his face. He focused his energy and concentrated only on his sense of smell and sound. "I can hear it, Daddy."

He concentrated harder, picking up the scent of an animal he wasn't familiar with. This wasn't one of Mommy's warriors either. But it was on all fours and stayed close to the edge of the tree line. His senses told him the animal was smaller than Aegis and Riparo. He opened his eyes and pointed. "Over there, Daddy."

Kate had picked up the animal as well and knew what was there, but she'd let Lorenzo discover it. As they turned the horses in that direction, the small red fox darted out of the trees and ran across the open field.

Lorenzo clapped his hands together. "A fox! I found a fox!"

"*Si*, look at him run. Now, how many does that make, little warrior? You found so many, were you keeping count as you found them?"

"Five, Daddy. Do I get five surprises?"

"You will once we get back to the stables, but for now, I think we need to let Impavido stretch his legs and run. You can ride with me if you can sit still and hold on tight. I will not let you fall, but you need to pay attention. You have to feel the horse beneath you, anticipate his moves." He turned to Kate. "I want to let him ride faster, but I do not want you to feel you have to keep up, can you handle it?"

Kate smiled at him. "After laundry? I think I can keep up." She gave Bravado a kick with her heels and snapped the reins as the horse took off, and Kate's laughter drifted back to him.

Lorenzo leaned back against his father's chest and looked up at him. "Is Mommy taking Bravado to do laundry?"

Shade threw his head back and laughed like hell. "No, little warrior, but I think Mommy is racing us back to the stables. We should try to beat her, *si*? Now lean over Impavido's mane and hang on tight. We are about to go fast."

Lorenzo giggled with excitement as Shade slid his arm around his son to hold him tight in the saddle, his little hands gripping Impavido's mane. Shade kicked the horse with his heels as the stallion took off at full speed. The wind blew through their hair as Shade leaned over Lorenzo, so he could hear him. "Let's catch Mommy and win this race. Medici *per sempre!*"

Lorenzo squealed with excitement. "Go fast, Impavido!" He clung to the horse's mane, secure in the knowledge his father held him in place as he shouted to the horse to go faster. The large stallion quickly gained on the smaller horse, as they both raced to the stables. Bravado picked up his speed without coaching, as he worked hard to maintain the pace of the black stallion.

Turning the reins, Shade veered off the path and along the fence line close to the vineyards. Lorenzo was laughing and yelling the whole way, no fear of speed. Pulling up slowly on the reins, Shade brought Impavido to a stop.

"Okay, little warrior, it is your turn to lead Impavido to the stables. Now, take the reins in your hands, let's show Mommy you can take control of this big horse."

Shade took his little hands within his and gripped the reins, teaching him how to manipulate the reins to turn the horse. They galloped slowly back to the stables where Kate waited for them, and Shade let Lorenzo have full control of the reins. He knew Impavido would respond appropriately. He could feel Lorenzo's excitement and happiness in having the reins.

Angelo helped Kate dismount and led Bravado away to the water trough, as Kate beamed at Lorenzo leading the huge stallion into the stables. "Good job, my beautiful boy!"

Lorenzo had a smile from ear to ear, as Shade dismounted and lifted Lorenzo down. "Are you tired yet, little warrior?"

Lorenzo was bouncing up and down. "Nope! I need my surprises."

"Ah yes, how many was it again? I think it was fifteen. I owe a lot of surprises."

Lorenzo looked up surprised and then looked to Kate. He knew it wasn't fifteen, but he'd love to have fifteen surprises. Kate held his gaze and could see the wheels turning before he turned to his father. "It's only five surprises, Daddy."

"I like your honesty, little warrior. Medici warriors are always honest."

Crouching down, Shade pulled out five small cards from his jeans pocket. "Now these cards are promises for surprises. You need to collect them, save them up. The more good deeds you do, the more cards you earn. I will make you a deal. I will give you five more to go with these five since you were so good tonight. You learned a lot of things, you listened well, and I was very proud of you. If you can save up fifty cards, I will let you get your own pony. Deal, *si*?"

Lorenzo looked like a bouncing ball as he took the cards. "I can do good deeds! What's a good deed, Daddy? Tell me and I will do it."

"A good deed is helping to keep your room clean. Helping Mommy when she needs it and also behaving, listening when you are told to do something. Rules, we have them for your safety and you must abide by them. But remember one thing, little warrior, if you do not abide and do good deeds, cards will be taken away. So, you need to earn a lot of cards to get that pony. Now come along, let's get back to the house."

Grabbing *bel's* hand, they began to walk back to the main house. He could hear the warriors at the camp, the sound of swords and grunting and he didn't miss it at all. Being with his son and Kate was time he cherished.

"Is there something else you would like to do with Daddy tonight? This is your night, so you pick what you wish to do next."

Lorenzo picked up his feet, letting his parents carry his weight as he dangled between them. He kicked his feet out and swung forward, before landing on his feet again. "Can we play ball then? You and me and Mommy?"

"That is a good choice, little warrior. Let us see your coordination. I have a feeling it is pretty good."

Lorenzo broke free of their hands and took off running for the house. Shade pulled *bel* into his arms, kissing her passionately.

"I love you. And I love this night with you and Lorenzo. *Grazie* for reminding me of all the things I miss."

21

Lorenzo found his ball in the front yard and returned to the back yard to join his parents. He tossed the ball to Shade who tossed it back to him as Kate curled up in a comfy lounge chair on the patio.

Shade called out to her, "Are you bailing on the ball game already?"

Luca and Shannon emerged from the house and Lorenzo came running, grabbing Luca around the knees.

"Uncle Luca! Come play with us."

Luca picked him up, as Lorenzo squealed. "And what are we playing tonight, little warrior?"

Lorenzo held up his hand with the ball. "Mommy and Daddy are playing ball with me. We can all play!"

Kate felt a momentary sadness as she realized her child had never known the joy of playing with other children. His world was populated, and highly protected, by adults. She ran her hand over the small swell of her tummy, glad that soon he'd have a playmate.

Luca turned Lorenzo upside down, holding him by his ankles as Lorenzo squealed with laughter. Shannon looked at Luca with surprise. "That's not how you hold kids."

Luca laughed as he swung Lorenzo, making him laugh even harder. Kate just shook her head, knowing Lorenzo loved the rough-housing play with the warriors. Luca finally set him down, and Lorenzo retrieved the dropped ball, grabbed his father's hand and headed for the open back yard.

"Come on, Mommy. Come on, Uncle Luca and Aunt Shannon. Come play!"

The adults followed him into the yard, lit by spotlights mounted in the trees. They formed a small circle in the grass, standing close enough to allow for Lorenzo to throw to them.

Shade directed him. "Lorenzo, throw the ball to each person in this circle, have them throw it back. Let's see your skills."

Lorenzo immediately threw the ball to Shade, and he returned it. The child proceeded to throw the ball to each person several times, going around the circle. Shannon missed it the second time and Shade laughed at her.

"Do we need to send you to warrior camp, Shannon?"

She threw the ball hard at Shade. He caught it in one hand and rolled it back to Lorenzo. Finally, after they had done this exercise a while, Shade wanted to test Lorenzo's strength.

"Little warrior, let's see how far you can throw this ball. I am going to back up and you throw it as hard as you can at me. Show me what you got!"

Running backwards out in the yard, Shade watched as Lorenzo prepared to throw. Lorenzo scrunched up his face, concentrating hard, as he threw the ball to his father hard, easily reaching the distance. Kate clapped for him. "Good job!"

Shade tossed the ball back under-hand, sending the ball in an arc that was easy for Lorenzo to catch. "Again, little warrior! Daddy wants to see that again."

Lorenzo beamed at him, confident now he could throw the ball hard enough to reach his father. He used a side arm throw his Uncle Luca had taught him, the ball picking up speed. Shade caught the ball and felt the mild sting in his hands from the speed.

Damn, kid has an arm on him. Shade wondered how he learned that technique and rolled his eyes to Luca who just stood there, arms crossed over his chest, grinning. Tossing the ball back to Lorenzo, he caught it easily. Shade held up his hand for him to stop.

"That throw made my hand sting, little warrior, so let's see if you can throw it even further." Backing up another five yards or so, he squatted down with his hands on his knees. "Put some heat on that ball, warrior!"

Kate watched her child. He was only three, but his mental development was closer to six or seven, and his physical skills were still being discovered. He was stronger than a mortal child, but it wasn't something they had encouraged him to explore.

His face was a study in concentration as he judged his father's distance from him, watching as Shade backed farther away. Kate was wondering if he could throw that far, and from the furrowed eyebrows on Lorenzo, it looked like he might be wondering the same thing.

Luca cheered him on, "Come on, warrior. You've got this!"

Lorenzo focused all his attention on the ball, and stepped into the pitch, throwing hard. As the ball left his hand it seemed to glow slightly, and Kate looked puzzled as the ball burst into flames, hurling at a rapid rate of speed in Shade's direction.

Lorenzo shouted, "No!"

Shade saw the ball leave his son's hand as it came straight at him, when it burst into flames. He was wondering what the hell was going on and before he knew it, the ball of heat was coming at his head and he dropped and rolled away from it. The ball landed on the ground, igniting the grass around it. Luca ran to the small fire and started stomping it out, as Shade ran for Lorenzo.

Shade picked him up, holding the boy to his chest, frantically checking his hands to see if he was hurt. Shade could feel the boy's fear as Lorenzo started to cry.

Shannon and Kate had both run to him, surrounding him, and grasping at Lorenzo.

Shade waved them away. "Stop, he is fine. Just let him calm down please. Daddy has you, little warrior. It is okay. We are both okay."

Lorenzo burrowed into his father's chest, his hands clinging to him, trying to crawl into his father's skin. He was confused and fearful of what he'd done. "I didn't mean to, Daddy. It just happens sometimes. Like the stables. I'm sorry, Daddy."

Lorenzo sobbed quietly on his father's shoulder as Kate stroked his back, trying to calm him, but her heart was pounding in her chest.

Shannon shouted, "What the fuck was that?"

Kate shook her head, and looked at Shade with a question, and mouthed, "What was that?"

Shade stroked Lorenzo's hair as Kate rubbed his back, the

child's fear building. Shade soothed him, understanding his son's confusion and fear. His son would be a fire-thrower. They hadn't looked for a second gift once he displayed his gift for day-walking. But like his mother, he'd have two gifts. Fire-throwers were a rare breed, and made powerful warriors, but it would take a lot of training to help him master this skill.

"You do not need to be sorry, little warrior. Daddy is not mad, so calm down. I will explain it to you, but I think we need to settle down first."

Looking at *bel*, he could see her confusion, and he spoke to her telepathically, "**It is another gift. He is a fire-thrower. He can make fire appear with the sheer thought of it from his own hands. It is somewhat rare, but this scares the fuck out of me that it has manifested so soon.**"

Shade saw the fear in her face, as Lorenzo clawed at his shoulders, trying to get closer. He sank his fangs into his father's neck and started feeding, seeking comfort and reassurance. He was troubled, and Shade completely understood.

"*Mi amore*, we need to go inside. We need to talk to him alone."

Kate nodded. *Talk to him alone? Who's going to talk to me? Now he has two gifts, like me? A fire-thrower? I've never even heard of that.* Her head was spinning with questions. Luca was with Shannon, he nodded to Shade and steered Shannon back indoors and to their suite. Kate could hear Shannon peppering Luca with questions. The same questions were swimming in her head. She fought to maintain her calm, so as not to further upset Lorenzo.

"It's okay, Lorenzo. Don't cry, my beautiful boy. You did nothing wrong."

Lorenzo fed heavily from his father's neck as they walked back into the house, his body relaxing, his mind settling. Getting inside, they took him straight up to his room and Shade sat in the rocker with Lorenzo in his arms, still feeding.

"Little warrior, do not gorge your belly. Unlatch, easily."

Lorenzo did as he was asked and looked at his father. Shade kissed him softly on the cheek, as Kate sat on the floor next to them.

"It is okay. Tell Daddy how you feel. Tell me everything about the fire. The fire is your gift, Lorenzo. It is normal. We just have to learn to control it."

Lorenzo slid his thumb in his mouth as he curled against his father's chest, pondering the question. "I don't know, Daddy. I just think real hard and it happens. I wasn't trying to make the fire happen. I didn't do it on purpose, I promise."

"I know you did not do it on purpose. It is your gift, Lorenzo. All vampires have a gift, something special they can do. Your mommy has two gifts, and it appears you do as well. Your mommy is a day-walker, like you. And she can communicate with the animals. Daddy only has one gift. I am a dream-walker. I can walk into your dreams. Make them good or bad. You have two gifts, Lorenzo, day-walker and fire-thrower. That is what you just experienced. If you concentrate very hard, you can start a fire with your own two hands. But it is very dangerous. It is designed to be used as a weapon. So, we need to practice and build your skills, so you do not get hurt, and you don't hurt innocent people. Do you know what happens when people get near fire?"

Lorenzo nodded. "I know it's bad, Daddy. I know it scared the horses."

"*Si*, little warrior, fire is a very scary thing, it can damage many things. For all vampires, the fire will burn us, destroy us, and turn us to ash. Only the fire-thrower is immune to the flames. So, you must understand what you have is very dangerous. I do not want you to be scared but we have to be careful of this gift until we can control it, and I will help you."

Lorenzo started to sob, clinging to his father's chest. "I don't want to hurt you, Daddy. Can you take it away? I don't want to be a fire-thrower."

His heart broke for his son. The gifts were both a blessing and a curse. Pulling Lorenzo to his shoulder, hugging him tight, Shade wished he could take his son's pain and anguish from him.

"You did not hurt me, Lorenzo. But I need you to

understand how dangerous it is, and why both of us need to help each other to learn to control your gift. I can't make it go away, but I can teach you to master it. We are Medici men, so we will always control our gifts for the good of our coven, *si*."

Lorenzo sniffed hard as he tried to get his tears under control. He nodded his head. "I'll work hard, Daddy. Can I still be a warrior?"

Smiling down at his sweet face, Shade nodded. "You will be a great warrior. This Warrior King needs his Prince by his side. Nothing will ever hold you back from being a warrior, Lorenzo, you were born to be one, just like me."

Still holding him, Shade stood from the rocker. "Now, I think we need to get Theresa in here to get you a bath, and Mommy and I are going to talk a while. When you are ready to be tucked in, we will come kiss you good night, *si*."

Lorenzo wiped his nose on the sleeve of his shirt. "*Si*. I got snot on your shirt, Daddy."

"I can see that, but it is a good thing. This means Mommy will have to do laundry again." Looking at Kate, he grinned and gave her a wink. Setting Lorenzo down on his feet, Shade crouched down in front of him, taking his face in his hands. "Will you be a good warrior and do something for Daddy?"

Lorenzo nodded his head.

"Mommy is upset too, so you need to give her big hugs and kisses, tell her you are okay."

Standing, he spoke to Kate telepathically, **"I will be outside having a smoke. Once Theresa gets his bath underway, come back outside, we need to talk."**

Kate picked up her child as his small arms encircled her neck, and he clung tight. "Come on, my beautiful boy. Let's go find Theresa."

She carried him to the bathroom where Theresa was running a bath. The news had already traveled through the household that their son was a fire-thrower.

Theresa smiled at her and said, "Don't worry, my lady. He's not the first."

Theresa helped her undress Lorenzo and lifted him into the

tub. Lorenzo was grabbing at his toy boats, and already seemed oblivious to the startling news that was about to change their lives. Kate smiled at him and kissed the top of his head. "Be good for Theresa, and I'll be back soon."

He was splashing water and playing as he answered, "Okay, Mommy."

Kate left and headed outside to find Shade on the patio, smoking. She approached him and slid her arms around his waist. "Please tell me all your words of re-assurance weren't just to calm him down. Is he going to be okay?"

"I will not lie to him, Kate. What I said is true, but I left out a few details. Some of them startling even to me. This is a rare gift, and it does not usually manifest until the child is around the age of seven or eight years. Lorenzo is so damn young for this to be happening. I don't know if that means his gift will be extraordinary, or if it is the combination of our blood together. He inherits traits of us both, and I had hoped he would dream-walk, but that is not the case. Fire-thrower is a tricky thing to teach them to control, and I am worried, I won't lie. He is our son, and if your visions of our future children are correct, he is the only son we will have. So, his existence for our coven is vital. When he threw that ball, I could not believe my eyes."

"Lover, I couldn't even understand what I was seeing. And clearly, neither did he. At least that explains the mystery about the fire in the stables. Do you know how to teach him to control it?"

"I know some. I have seen other immortals with it, but it is not common. All vampires have met at least one fire-thrower in their lifetime. Now I am not claiming to be an expert, I will have to call in some help and do some research on this one. But managing the gift is much like managing dream-walking. He must visualize what he wants to happen, focus his energy and concentration, and his gift will appear. It is a lethal gift, *mi amore*, very lethal. He will be an extremely dangerous vampire. He can wreak havoc with fire. His enemies will fear him for the damage he can do to them and their covens. We have to approach this carefully."

Kate looked at him and had a vision of her son as a man. She knew already he'd look much like his father, and he'd have Shade's skills as a warrior, but add fire-thrower to his list of powers, and she knew he'd be formidable. She felt concern, but also pride. She knew this was a gift that Lorenzo would master. "We'll find the right people to help him, and he'll be legendary."

Taking her in his arms, he hugged her tight, laying his head atop her fiery crimson. "Legendary. I just want him to love his life, love his coven. I want him to feel the happiness I now feel, because there is so much love in my life now. Let's go upstairs, he is probably driving Theresa mad with his shenanigans. And then I think Daddy should tuck Mommy in."

22

The discovery of Lorenzo's fire-throwing gift had spread through the camp like wildfire, and everyone at Bel Rosso knew about it. The night following the discovery, Shade called all the warriors together in the gym. A hush lay over the room as the warriors stood about, looking a bit nervous. Marcello gave a loud whistle and all eyes turned to Shade as he made his way to the front of the room to address them. Marcello, Aislynn, Theo and Skelk all joined him.

"First, welcome to the new warriors. We will have periodic meetings whenever I feel there are circumstances of which you all need to be aware. Just listen, then you will be given a chance to ask questions."

Pacing back and forth, arms crossed over his chest, his eyes scanned both the new recruits as well as his tenured warriors, all representing the future of Medici. His son would lead some of these warriors someday.

"Your Prince had quite an evening last night. He discovered a second gift which has been bestowed upon him. I know you all know what I refer to. This rumor has spread like a disease at Bel Rosso, and if you haven't heard it, you have been living under a rock. Lorenzo is a day-walker and also a fire-thrower. He possesses two gifts, just like your Queen. Fire-thrower is a rare gift, and I suspect, with the average age of the warriors in this room, most of you have never seen one. Your Prince can produce fire with his hands, and with time, will be able to throw fire at any target. This gift can be deadly, it can kill immortals instantly. I have little experience with it myself. I have witnessed it several times in my travels, but none of my warriors ever held the gift.

"Lorenzo spends much time here in the camp. Therefore, I suggest we keep a careful eye on his progress. He has no control of his gift as yet, and this scares him. We all understand now the source of the stable fire. So, I ask that you help him as best you can as he learns to control his deadliest weapon. I will seek out the help of Council, but we will not speak of his gift to others. The Battle of Bel Rosso was won with the element of surprise of your Queen's rare gift, and surprise is a valuable asset to have."

Shade stopped pacing as he looked out over the crowd and saw heads bobbing up and down in recognition of his words.

"Any questions?"

No one responded and Shade chuckled, as the new recruits still looked a bit intimidated by him. Turning to his leaders, he spoke directly to Marcello. "Any other business we need to discuss?"

Marcello shook his head to the negative.

"Well, that is a damn first. If we have nothing else, you are dismissed. Go to your assigned stations and get your asses to work."

Walking back to the small office Marcello used to hold the files on the warriors, Shade rummaged through the papers.

Skelk pushed through the crowd of warriors moving back to the training field, working his way toward Shade. He stood in the doorway and cleared his throat.

Shade looked up at him. "Need something?"

Skelk shook his head, shuffled his feet, and slung the crossbow over his shoulder. "Master, it has been some time, but I worked with a warrior who was a fire-thrower. He was young, had to learn to manage this gift on his own. I would practice with him and helped him hone his skill. I'm no expert, but I would be happy to help the prince master this skill. I worked with my lady on crossbow and she said I was a patient instructor."

Shade suppressed a smile. Skelk was one damn good warrior, but a loner, and patience wasn't a virtue he was known for. But Kate had gotten along with him immensely, spoke highly of him, and he had honed her crossbow skills to perfection. Shade sat down on the edge of the desk. "Skelk, I have to be honest, I can use all the help I can get. I have seen it in action, but I need to tell you, when he threw that ball and it came at me like a fucking firebomb, you could have knocked me over with a feather. I have tried to explain to him what it is, but he is frightened of it now. The accident in the stables happened without provocation. Lorenzo is an even-tempered boy, but once he gets older and gets pissed off, he could burn the damn house down. Are you sure you want to tackle this? Lorenzo will drive you mad with his endless curiosity."

Skelk looked at the floor. He'd seen Lorenzo in the camp and playing at Bel Rosso, and the kid was one ball of non-stop energy. Skelk had lived a life of solitude, isolating himself even from the other warriors, and he'd never admit he looked on with envy at the life his master led, with a mate and a child. He had lived his life as a mercenary, never intending to pledge allegiance to any one coven, until he met the Medici. Now he called Bel Rosso home, and even though he didn't socialize with them, he called these warriors his brothers. He'd watched the relationship between Lorenzo and Marcello blossom, as well as the bond Lorenzo had with Luca, and secretly, he'd love to be included in that inner circle, but it was a desire he'd never give voice to. "If you and my lady will trust me, I promise I can work with him."

Shade could see the wheels turning in his head. He slapped Skelk on the back. "There is no question about trust, brother. You have proven yourself with me, with all of us. And my mate has a special place in her heart for you. Do not be surprised if she joins Lorenzo when he comes to you to train. She will help keep him under control. I will speak with her about it, but I have no doubts she will agree. I am grateful, Skelk. I see what you do here, how you work with the warriors, things they will carry with them for the rest of their lives, skills that could easily save their life. Never think I do not see what you do here. You are loved and appreciated, brother."

Skelk kept his eyes on the floor as his master heaped praise on him. He felt pride but wasn't comfortable with the attention. "Okay, well, talk to my lady then. And if you both agree, just let me know. I will be happy to work with him."

"I appreciate it, Skelk. I will get back to you on this one. Go on and bust some heads out there tonight. Oh, by the way, how is Robbie doing?"

Skelk had turned to leave when Shade threw the question at him. He stopped and turned. "Oh, Robbie. He'll do fine. Picks up weapons quickly. Not quite as aggressive as some. Confidence issue, I think. A little experience is all he needs. Some of the young ones come in all cocky, act like they know it all, when underneath they are pissing their pants. Robbie wears his emotions on his sleeve, shows his fear sometimes. He'll learn to mask it with age."

Shade watched the hulking warrior retreat and knew he was one lonely warrior. Although Skelk never lacked for female company, he might as well have been alone. Like most warriors, Skelk's life was solitary but Shade thought this one had a deep dark past, one he wasn't sure he'd ever know.

23

Since the fire-throwing episode, Lorenzo hadn't been left unsupervised, and that was fine with him! He was still confused about this discovery, in spite of his parents' reassurances that everything was fine. Tonight, his father was in the camp, meeting with all the warriors, and his mother was with him as they both made their rounds on the progress of the indoor and outdoor pools.

Kate noticed her child lacked his usual exuberance over climbing on the excavated piles of dirt, and she knew he had misgivings about his gift.

On their way downstairs to the indoor pool, they encountered Cory, who gave Lorenzo a high five. "Hey, little dude! What's happening?"

"Did you hear about me, Cory?"

Cory laughed. "Dude, everyone heard about you!"

Lorenzo looked like he might cry, and Cory responded to the child's conflict. "Hey, Lorenzo." He picked him up and held him close. "Don't be sad about it. It's all cool. What's wrong?"

Lorenzo's voice quivered. "I could hurt people. I didn't mean to do it."

Kate rubbed his back and shushed him. "Lorenzo, you'll learn to control your gift, and when you do, there's no danger. You'll use it as a weapon, but only when you need it."

Lorenzo looked uncertain. "Who will teach me?"

Kate was wondering that herself, but she couldn't show him any doubt. "Your father will teach you, and I'm sure the other warriors will help. You know, Lorenzo, when I discovered my gift with the animals, I didn't know how to use it either. I had to learn how to channel my power, how I could use my gift to help protect us, and you'll do the same. You were born a warrior. Our coven is vast now, and it grows bigger every day. There are so many who depend on us. As you grow, you'll follow in your father's footsteps, and he'll train you to be a great warrior, just like him."

Cory rocked back and forth with him, as Lorenzo calmed down. "Your gift will be awesome, little dude. Can you imagine? Once you're grown, you'll fight battles like our father. Fire is deadly to a vampire, and yet you're somehow immune to it. You'll be able to use it as a weapon. It's a powerful gift, little brother. Don't be afraid of it. Dad will teach you to channel it, don't worry."

Kate took his chubby cheeks in her hand. "But promise me, Lorenzo. Tell me you understand. This isn't a toy. You don't explore this gift without supervision and direction. You don't use it in anger and revenge. You use it to protect yourself and your coven only, understood? Once something, or someone, is destroyed, we can't bring it back."

Lorenzo nodded as he sniffed away his tears. "I understand, Mommy."

"I know we've let you play outside in the yard with just the supervision of Aegis, but until you learn how to control your gift, someone will always be with you. This isn't a punishment. This is to protect you, okay?"

Lorenzo nodded and was relieved he didn't have to carry the burden of this gift alone.

24

Mica had spent his lifetime in servitude to a master, moving from coven to coven, never feeling at home. It was only now, with Raven, that he felt the need to establish some roots. In the past three years he and Raven had lived here together, they had worked to make their apartment into their home. For Raven, who'd spent his life as a warrior, living in a barracks, it had been a paradise.

Mica had always served in a master's home, or overseeing an inn, but this was the first place that had been truly his. The first place he'd been allowed to mold and shape to his own taste. He knew this came as a result of the generosity of my lady. It was clear whenever Mica was around her that she made no class distinctions, which was a sharp departure in their culture. Still, even with all the freedom they'd been given, they'd dared not make the decision to mate without Shade's approval. They had been back in California for a number of days now, and they had both been busy catching up. This was a busy time at the inn. Actually, it was always a busy time at the inn, but Reynaldo had been informed of their decision to mate, and Shade's approval, and he was encouraging them to take a few days to themselves. He said he could take over the managerial duties for a few days, and they had enough warriors to provide security. And, of course, if anything major went down, he and Raven were right here on the property.

Mica had had one of the housekeepers helping him clean the apartment. He wanted to make sure everything was special. Reynaldo had delivered several bottles of Midnight. Mica had draped their bed in a canopy of sheer tulle, in a pale ivory color, and filled the room with candle light. He was running the oversized claw-foot tub full of steaming water and had filled the tub with night blooming jasmine. He knew this was over the top, but underneath the leather and the tough exterior Raven projected, he knew, beat the heart of a romantic. He took one last look around their apartment, making sure everything was in place for the two of them.

***

Giving out the final orders for the evening to the warriors, Raven was feeling anxious. He felt his beast kicking him hard. They'd been back in California for a few days, and nothing had happened between him and Mica. They could never leave the inn for long as this place was nonstop work, including protection around the clock. He didn't mind the work, he was used to it, and so was Mica. But it gnawed at him that he and Mica had still not mated. It seemed as though once the boss-man had given the go ahead to mate, Mica was satisfied, and acted like there was no rush.

It had been a warm day, and Raven had pulled his long hair up in a twisted bun on his head. Maybe he could talk Mica into joining him for a late-night dip in the pool. Wrapping up, he headed back to their apartment, ready for a shower and to be out of his jeans. He loved Mica, now he just needed to find time to mate with him and seal their blood covenant. Climbing the stairs to their apartment, he smiled. He'd never been happier in his life. He had freedom, he had a mate, and he had free reign over the warriors. It was worth all the blood, sweat, and tears he'd spent to get here, and he was grateful for all of it.

Swinging open the door to their apartment, he was struck with the most exotic fragrance. *What is that? Jasmine?* His eyes adjusted to the dim light as he saw candles everywhere, giving the whole place a soft golden glow. Feeling his heart race, he stopped inside the door. It was like a little paradise inside their home.

"Mica?" He walked into the living room but got no response. "Mica?"

Mica poured the Midnight into the crystal wine glasses he'd ordered for the occasion. He'd had their names etched into the glass. He heard Raven enter and call his name. Mica left the small galley kitchen and entered their living room. "Welcome home, warrior." He handed the glass of dark elixir to Raven and held his glass up for a toast. "To us."

Raven took him in as he offered him the glass of Midnight, wearing a pair of loose, relaxed, white linen pants. His bare chest was bronzed from the rays of the sun, and his hair smelled like the ocean air. Taking the wine glass, Raven spun it around, admiring the etched details of their names. Holding up the glass, he tipped it slightly against Mica's. "To us."

Taking a sip, Raven never lost eye contact. They peered at each other. His longing reflected back to him in Mica's eyes. He felt suddenly nervous. His stomach rolled. He'd waited for so long for this mating and now it was in front of him, he felt undeserving of this gorgeous man, offering him an eternity of love and companionship. Looking down at his booted feet, he shuffled them slightly. "Are we celebrating something I should know about?"

Mica smiled. "Oh, I definitely think it's something you should know about. I think it's time we sealed our covenant. We've both been so busy. Are you ready, my young warrior? There's no turning back."

Raven raised his eyes to him, and knew he was in safe hands. They'd made love so many times, but this time, it would be different. He'd never feed from another after tonight. He'd belong to him, for all eternity. Raven had spent a lifetime before he'd been taken in by the Medici when his body had been abused, used and tortured. He still bore those scars. But if it led him to Mica, then it was all worth it.

Leaning in, kissing him softly, his lips felt soft and sweet. "I don't want to turn back. I feel nervous. I don't know why. I want this, and I know you want this, Mica. Why do I feel like it's the first time I've ever made love?" Raven refilled his glass and knocked it back in one gulp.

Mica smiled to himself at his young lover's nervousness. "You're nervous because it means something, babe. Casual sex means nothing. No commitment. It's like hunting, devoid of emotion. Take what you need and move on to the next one. But we've both had enough of that, yes? We've both lived long enough to know when we've found the right person. I know we're unconventional, in more ways than one. But you're my choice, Raven. I choose you above all others."

Raven struggled to control the overwhelming love that spilled from his heart. His body shook slightly. "I want to be your choice, don't ever think this isn't what I want. I never...." Stumbling over his words, he couldn't believe how inept he felt. "I always knew I'd be with boss-man for eternity. He saved me, gave me a life with structure, discipline and direction, something to strive for. I was happy to be Medici, but I was lonely too. Meeting you gave me so much more. I never thought this would happen to me. Look at me, I don't fit in anywhere. Even as a warrior, most think I'm too small, too young, too everything."

Taking Mica's hand, he slid his fingers over his knuckles. Mica's hands were soft, not callused like his. They were so different in so many ways and yet, they were drawn to each other. "You'll be stuck with me forever, leather, hair, bling, and everything else. But I promise you, it will be an adventure. This is forever for me. I don't want to be with anyone else, ever. So, kiss me already, and make this happen before someone calls you away from me."

Mica gave him a light kiss and led him by the hand to their bathroom, bathed in candlelight, the steam rising from the tub. Mica set the wine glass down and took the glass from Raven, before he began to help the young warrior out of his clothes. "No quick shower tonight, my young warrior."

Raven removed the jeans as Mica released the drawstring on his linen pants and let them fall around his ankles. He stepped into the tub, and slid down into the water, the petals of the white jasmine floating on the surface. Mica held his hand out to Raven. "Come join me."

Stepping into the tub, Raven released his hair from the bun and let it cascade around him. Feeling Mica's hands on his hips, he was gliding down into the scented water, and nestled between Mica's legs. He couldn't help the moan that escaped as he lay back on his chest, the warmth of the water easing his body to relax. "The jasmine is nice, exotic. I could lay here forever with you. Did you do all this yourself?"

Mica stroked his fingers through Raven's long black hair as he laid his head back against his chest. "Oh, I had a little help from the staff to get things ready. And no need to rush, Reynaldo will oversee everything, so we won't be interrupted, so just relax, my young warrior. We may not be able to afford an exotic getaway like our master, but there's no reason why we can't create our own paradise right here."

Mica slid his hand down Raven's chest, as they both lay back in the large tub, enjoying the relaxing heat of the water, and the intoxicating scent of the jasmine.

Raven closed his eyes. He'd built such high walls around his heart. It had taken a long time to completely let his guard down and let Mica in. Mica understood him like no other, understood he wanted to be loved, but also had needed to protect his heart. Mica had been a patient lover, giving Raven the time he needed to heal, and learn to trust. He picked up the pearl white flower floating on the water and brought it to his nose, inhaling the exotic scent. "So, the staff knows what's going on in here tonight. I don't care. All I care about is being with you, I love you, Mica."

Mica let the warrior relax into him. He was still young, much younger than the men Mica was usually attracted to. In fact, there was nothing about Raven that was remotely close to the men Mica had been attracted to. But, somehow, for the two of them, they seemed to be able to put all the broken pieces back together. With Raven, Mica felt whole again. And he knew, for Raven, it was the same.

"I'm afraid we have no secrets tonight, babe. But they all wish us well." Mica kissed the top of his head, before sliding his lips to his ear, and running his tongue around the soft shell.

Raven whispered, "No secrets." Turning his head, he pulled Mica's lips to his and kissed him long and slow. "Hungry? Careful, I bite back, and this time, I intend to."

Grinning, he let go of Mica and slid his hands over his thighs under the water. They weren't muscular like his, but there was strength in him. "And remember, I'm a lot younger than you, so

I promise to take it slow. Hope you can handle me!"

Mica picked up a sea sponge as Raven slid beneath the water. He poured a liquid soap on the sponge and started washing Raven's back when he resurfaced. "Oh, I think I can handle you. I think I can handle you just fine." He proceeded to run the sponge down Raven's arms and chest.

The sponge and the water felt energizing and yet relaxing all at the same time. "Have you done this before? Bathed another male? Please just tell me I'm the first warrior, because I think I might get pissed if I'm not. I like knowing my sword is the one that is the mightiest in your army."

Mica laughed out loud. "You're my first warrior, babe. Not many warriors out there who are attracted to men. And quite honestly, I had very few opportunities to cross paths with many warriors. I never worked for a master with a coven as extensive as the Medici. My life has been spent with other vampires born into servitude."

Raven took the sponge from his hand, and continued to bathe himself, scrubbing away at his legs, as Mica teased him. "So, I guess you can say you're the only sword in my army."

Raven ran the sponge down Mica's leg. "We've been together a while, but I don't think you've told me what you were really attracted to in the past." He playfully splashed the water back on Mica and laughed as he felt Mica tug at his hair. "I know it's the past, but what were they like. I'm curious. Other than the fact they were older, and born into servitude, am I the most gorgeous hunk of vampire you've ever seen? Admit it, my blood energizes you, makes you feel young. And naturally, none of them were stylish like me, so tell me. Just humor me." Holding up the sponge, Raven handed it back to him without looking back. "More soap please."

Mica sensed his nervousness as he listened to Raven chatter. He knew him well, and knew he covered his nerves with humor. "Fact, you are the most gorgeous hunk of vampire I've ever seen." Mica kissed his neck lightly. "Fact. Your blood does energize me, young warrior."

Mica nipped his shoulder, drawing blood which he licked

away. He slid his hand between Raven's legs, grasping his hardened steel cock. "Fact. Tonight, and every night thereafter, it will be my blood that energizes you."

Mica sank his fangs deep into the strong but lean muscle on Raven's shoulder and sucked slow and deep, letting the warriors blood seep into his mouth. He began a long, slow stroke of his hand along Raven's cock.

Raven's head lulled back and to the side as he felt Mica's sharpened fangs sink deep, and his beast was within inches of escaping his control. His hand stroked his cock, as Raven gripped Mica's thigh. Growling deep, the need to taste him was overwhelming. His voice sounded foreign as Mica's name escaped his lips, breathy and raspy. "Don't stop. Take all of me."

Mica unlatched and stepped from the tub, lifting Raven up with him. He dried him off, and then wiped himself dry with the thick white towels used by the inn. "Come with me, warrior."

He took Raven's hand and led him to their bedroom, and the bed that was draped in the soft tulle. Mica pulled back the curtain of tulle and allowed Raven to enter. Raven crawled across the sheets into the middle of the king-sized bed, his dark skin and black hair in sharp contrast to the snow-white sheets.

Mica climbed in behind him and pulled the soft veil of tulle closed around them. Mica lay down beside him in the room lit only by the flickering light of the many candles, and the moon that was visible in the skylight above their bed.

"It's just us now, my sweet warrior. You need no pretense with me." He held Raven close to his chest, sliding his hand up his back, cupping his head in his hand, and pulling him close to his neck. "Now take from me, what no other has taken. Seal our bond, and mate yourself to me."

Raven inhaled deeply. His eyes glowed a bright red as his fangs punched through. Licking Mica from his shoulder to his neck, his tongue followed the vein. "From now to eternity, I belong to you."

Sinking his fangs into the tender flesh, Raven felt that first explosion of his lover's blood in his mouth. He drew and swallowed, letting Mica fill him deep and the power of their connection slammed into him like a bolt of lightning. They both moaned as Raven drank deep and felt like he wanted to crawl inside him, be him. He felt like he was alive for the first time. He never wanted to stop this feeling, a high more powerful than battle. His cock throbbed as Mica's blood mixed with his. Raven could barely breathe from the intense pleasure screaming through him, taking him to a level never felt before.

Mica slid his hand down Raven's chest and took his cock in hand. He stroked him as he fed. Mica's own head thrown back, as he experienced the sensations of having Raven feed from him for the first time. His own cock throbbed for relief as he wrapped himself around Raven. He folded himself over top of the lean and lanky warrior, and once again bit deep into his shoulder, completing the circle. They fed from each other, and Mica stroked him, following the pace set by the rocking motion of the young warrior's hips.

Their bond was sealed, and Raven was claimed, belonging now to Mica. He surrendered to the stroking as he unlatched, his head thrown back as Mica fed and Raven was lost in the passion. His orgasm shook him to the core as his roar was deep and guttural, calling out Mica's name.

Wrapping his arms around him tightly, Raven gasped for air, his breath ragged. As Mica unlatched his fangs, Raven could feel his need rising hard and fast. Pushing him down on his back, sliding on top of him, slinking down his body, kissing his flat, taut stomach, his hips responded. Raven raked his hand down Mica's chest as he slid his tongue around his cock. Mica gripped his hands in Raven's hair as Raven took him deep into his throat, needing and wanting to give him so much pleasure.

Mica gave himself up to the talented ministrations of his lover's warm, hot mouth, as he brought him to orgasm. Mica clutched a handful of Raven's dark hair in his fist as he cried out, his head thrown back on the pillow. Raven crawled up over his chest, and kissed him on the mouth, before dropping down beside him, their breathing ragged, their hearts pounding. Mica turned to him, pushing the coal black hair back from Raven's face. "You are mine now, warrior."

They were distracted by a frantic pecking at the skylight above their bed, as they both looked skyward, to see Poe peering through the glass at them. Mica laughed. "Well, no secrets now. That damn bird will tell all."

Raven laughed. "That damn bird is my gift from the Queen. And you can bet she already knows we're mated. It's like a fucking wild beast telecommunication system straight to the big house."

He cuddled into Mica's neck, letting his hands glide slowly all over his body. "Poe is like me, we both soar now. Nothing can stop us." Softly turning Mica's face to his, he kissed him and smiled. "That could not possibly feel as amazing to you as it did to me. I never felt anything like that in my entire life. Tell me that's going to happen every time I feed, because your blood tastes like explosions going off in my head, my heart, and my cock, simultaneously. How did it feel for you?"

Mica chuckled. "Like explosions going off in my head, my heart, and my cock, young warrior."

Grinning, Raven licked his hard nipple and rolled over, lying flat on his back. The moon was beautiful as it beamed down on them through the skylight.

"I love you, Mica. I never said that to anyone before. Without you, I won't survive. Don't let me down, don't let me go. There's much to accomplish yet, for me. I want to keep rising. I want to keep being the best warrior I can be. And I want to be the best lover and mate for you. I was scared to commit, scared you'd never understand me, but I know different now."

Raven stopped speaking as he heard his master in is head. **"Congratulations to you and Mica. Sounds like a wild kingdom out here, brother. We are behind you. *Per sempre.*"**

Raven smiled to himself as he answered, ***"Grazie,* boss-man."** Turning to Mica he informed him. "Boss-man says congrats."

Mica laughed. "You know this is the weirdest fucked up coven of all time, right? I mean, my breathing is barely back to normal and the east coast already knows we consummated our union."

Raven grinned. "Welcome to Medici. And we might be fucked up, but we fucking rock! I know you're not used to it, but boss-man and my lady take care of us. We take care of each other. It's what we do best. When we say *familia*, we mean it. I'm proud everyone knows. Are you ashamed of us?"

Mica rolled over on top of him and cradled his face in his hands. "I'm never ashamed of you, warrior. You make me proud, and I'm proud to call you mine."

"The feeling is mutual. So, shut up, kiss me and since we have the night off, I'm ready for round two. See if you can keep up, old man!"

25

It was the night of the annual White House Correspondents dinner, the night where the D.C. power players rubbed shoulders with the Hollywood glitterati and members of the Press. It was a purely social event, raising funds to award scholarships to young, upcoming journalist, but really more about being seen.

Alec was in a tux and Rissa was wearing a floor length gown that glistened under the light. She could hold her own with any of the A-list starlets who floated through the room. Alec kept his eye on President Ashton. If Rissa was going to approach him, she'd need to make her way through the crowd during the cocktail hour. Once the dinner started, the President would be swept away to the dais at the front of the room. They each had a drink in their hand, one neither of them could drink, as they pretended to sip and mingle with the crowd. As Alec inched closer to the President, he bent his head to Rissa. "It's now or never, darling. Why don't you work your magic?"

She smiled as she turned to Alec. "Time to turn on the charm."

Kissing him softly on the cheek, she casually made her way closer to Ashton, nodding at a few familiar faces as she went. The First Lady was occupied with other guests when Rissa saw she'd caught the President's eye. Locking eyes with him, she watched the smile that slowly crept up the corners of his mouth and she nodded and cocked her head to the side, letting her hair fall over her shoulder. Taking a deep breath, she approached him and watched as he turned in her direction.

The President had a smile plastered on his face and shook the hand of every person that approached. He felt tired already, and the evening was just getting started. The First Lady had moved to the other side of the room, as she also worked the crowd, giving them both maximum exposure. He had to give her credit, while they rarely slept together any longer, she enjoyed the perks his power brought, and she remained a valuable asset. She knew how to handle herself with the press, and the public adored her motherly, if somewhat matronly, image. Ashton looked up to see the object of his erotic fantasies approaching and immediately got a boner. He chuckled to himself. He hadn't felt that kind of attraction since he was a frat boy at Yale. He was careful not to look overly interested as the lovely Mrs. Canton slinked up beside him and slipped her arm into his. She was a clever politician's wife too. She knew to make the gesture look friendly, and not overtly sexy.

"And how is the lovely Mrs. Canton this evening? I must say, you outshine any of the movie stars here tonight."

"Well, I do thank you for the compliment, Mr. President. You look rather dapper yourself. But you always cut a handsome figure. I like powerful, distinguished looking men. Power and control can be a wonderful aphrodisiac. I'm rather bored, but we must do our duty, as is the way of the world in Washington."

Sliding her fingers casually along the lapel of his tailored tuxedo, Rissa was mindful of the press. "I'm sure this evening is much the same for you, but then again, it must be an exciting time if you're going to run for reelection." Licking her lips softly, her smile was brilliant yet sexy. *That's it Rissa, reel him in slow and easy.*

He placed his hand over hers as it rested on his arm. "Yes, I'm afraid campaigning is inevitable. It takes so much time, not to mention the fund-raising. But I still have a lot to accomplish before I give up my seat in the Oval Office, so it's unavoidable, I'm afraid. But I hear the talk on the Hill too. I know your husband is thinking he'll throw his own hat in the ring someday, and wouldn't you make a delightful First Lady. My dear, I think you'd outshine the legacy of Jackie Kennedy."

Rissa dramatically threw her hand across her heart and blushed. Leaning in closer to him, she whispered in a breathy voice. "Oh John, you do know how to make a lady blush."

Leaning back, Rissa cocked her head to the side and watched his eyes slide over her low-cut designer gown. "Alec may throw his hat in the ring when he's ready, and of course, I'll be right by his side. But then, we all know that schedule will pull him even further from me. But your wife is quite adept in doing her job as First Lady. You're a lucky man, Mr. President."

Ashton basked under her attention. "Yes, well, we all make sacrifices to get what we want, don't we? You know, if you'd like a private tour of the White House some evening, I'd be more than happy to oblige. The First Lady will be on a press junket, promoting her preschool educational programs for the next few weeks. I'd love some company, and you can see firsthand how it might feel to be First Lady."

Well, haven't we made a great impression this evening? Our ticket inside! "Oh, that would be such an honor. I'd love that very much, John. To walk in the footsteps of Jacqueline Kennedy would be so exciting." Biting her lip, she beamed a smile at him. "I'll accept that invitation."

Reaching into her small beaded handbag, she withdrew a business card and laid it inside his palm. "My personal number is on the card. I very much look forward to seeing you."

The President discreetly palmed the card and slid it into his pants pocket. Alec had been surreptitiously watching the interplay between Rissa and the President as he maintained a conversation with his colleagues. It looked like Rissa had closed the deal, so he moved in their direction, and slid his hand onto the small of her back, bending to lightly kiss her cheek.

"There you are, my darling. We mustn't monopolize the President's time. He has a lot of guests to greet tonight."

Alec extended his hand to the President. "And the best of luck to you, Mr. President, on the upcoming campaign. We need to make sure our party stays in power, so you will have my full support."

The President took his hand and felt the strong grip of the young Senator from Connecticut. He didn't need an enemy in Canton, so he'd have to be discreet. "Thank you, Alec. You've always been a strong advocate for my policies, and I appreciate your support. Now, if the two of you will excuse me, I do need to shake a few more hands tonight."

The President nodded in Rissa's direction, and caught her

sly wink as he moved away. Alec pretended to sip at his drink before turning to Rissa.

"That was successful, I hope?"

She spun on her heels toward him, sliding her hand down his chiseled cheek. "You expected anything less?"

Chuckling, Rissa knew she had this in the bag. "Like a small boy in a candy store, eyeing up the candy. This will be easy." Kissing him on the cheek, she took his hand, as they strolled casually amongst the powerful and beautiful. Rissa could already envision herself in the White House, and not as a visitor.

26

Marcello had been keeping an eye on Cory. He seemed happy enough, but he never left the damn estate. He kept to his room in the house, more than likely eating pizza and playing those video games. Marcello felt guilty leaving him behind. He occasionally took advantage of his freedom to hunt and sought out the young coeds on Fraternity Row in C'ville, and he thought maybe it was time for Cory to tag along. After all, he had Medici blood in him. He needed to experience the world outside of Bel Rosso.

Charlottesville wasn't exactly the world, but it was a world Medici now ruled and protected, and Cory needed to see more of it, vampire style.

Cory reluctantly joined him as they teleported onto Rugby Road. They walked the street of stately old homes that had been converted to fraternities, looking for one where the party had spilled out onto the street. Marcello zeroed in on his target and pushed ahead. Cory didn't look thrilled. Marcello shook his head. The kid was always so quiet in public. He knew Cory relied on the feeders for food and sex, but it was time he learned how to really get laid.

They entered the frat house with its wall to wall people. Marcello nudged Cory's shoulder. "Grab a drink. Settle in, brother, plenty of eye candy here and a good feeding ground. Music isn't half bad either. You look like you are scared out of your mind. Relax, they're just women."

Cory felt uncomfortable, not scared as Marcello claimed. He wasn't a big party person. He'd been in this scene a million times in California, in the underground clubs where, for him, it was a matter of survival. He had a hard time associating this crowd with fun. The place was jammed with college kids his own age, and he wished he could be more like Marcello and just come here, enjoy the bounty, and leave.

"Not scared, just not my thing, Marcello. I prefer a more

intimate group. This reminds me of a sex den in the underground clubs, been there done that. But don't hold back 'cause I'm here."

Cory grabbed a cold beer and popped it open. He watched Marcello go to work, and he was amused. It was so easy for him. His good looks and confidence drew the females to him, and Marcello knew how to use his looks like a weapon. Cory knew he didn't exactly have that look, or the charm. He found himself a quiet spot along the wall and leaned against it, keeping his eyes peeled. Why in the hell did he come here?

***

Madison pushed her way through the throng of drunken students. She was annoyed with herself that she'd let some of her friends talk her into coming. She'd made the rounds of the frat parties her freshman year, and quickly determined this wasn't for her. The object of these parties seemed to be to get as drunk as possible, as fast as possible. The beer bong was flowing freely as the crowd lined up to guzzle beer from the funnel. The floor felt sticky under her feet as another drunken frat boy stumbled into her, almost knocking her over. Madison pushed him away as she made her way for the door. The music was so loud everyone must shout over it to be heard and she'd had enough. She had almost reached the door when another couple, dancing frantically, smashed into her, knocking her off balance. She threw out both hands, looking for anything to break her fall when she felt strong hands reach out and grab her, pulling her to safety. She looked up to see a boy with long, dark brown hair and soulful brown eyes. She'd seen him earlier, standing near the door, his back to the wall, clearly feeling as out of his element as she did. He asked if she was okay and she nodded yes, the music making any conversation impossible.

Madison motioned for them to go outside, and the sweet faced boy followed. They stepped out onto the wide porch, and even from here, the smell of beer and weed followed them. Madison turned to the boy. "Thanks for breaking my fall. I'm afraid I'm just not frat party material. I'm heading out. You want to join me?"

***

Cory watched the girl as she tried to get to the door. He was captivated by her, despite the fact he could see how annoyed she was with the crowd. He could see she was as uncomfortable here as he was. As fate would have it, she almost landed on top of him, but he was quick to respond and caught her before she could fall. Being a half-breed vampire did have some advantages.

When she stumbled forward, her face was covered by her long, dark blonde hair. Once she regained her balance, she brushed her hair back from her face and looked up at him with her large blue eyes. Cory was reluctant to let her go, but slowly let his hands glide from her shoulders to her hands, under the pretext of steadying her.

She looked nothing like the other students here. Her hair was almost to her waist, with a single braid secured with beads and a feather. Each finger bore a ring, lots of silver and turquoise. She was wearing a white lace tank and a tie-dyed skirt with soft calf-skin moccasins on her feet. She looked like a throwback hippie from the 60's, not a college preppy. He even wondered if she was a student here. As they screamed at each other over the music, she nodded toward the door and he followed.

"No problem, it's not easy maneuvering in that crowd. Came with a friend myself, not of my own choice, believe me. What exactly did you have in mind?" Cory pushed his long hair from his face and shuffled his feet as he looked back at her. "My name is Cory Medici, by the way."

Madison smiled up at him. He was tall and slender, dressed in jeans and a t-shirt with a faded logo of The Clash, and an unusual brown leather vest. "Cory. Nice name. It suits you. My name is Madison. Madison Barnes. There's a nice coffee house down on the mall. It's quiet there. Want to join me?"

"Thanks, nice to meet you, Madison. Coffee sounds good, but I didn't drive, so I have uh, no ride. You have wheels, or do you mind walking?"

He was already telling Marcello telepathically he was out for the night and would find his own way home. But he left out the detail he was leaving with a female. He didn't know yet if there would be any more details to share, but he liked Madison Barnes already.

Madison pushed the mop of hair back from her face, her long earrings dangling, catching the light. She slung the fabric purse with the Moroccan design over her shoulder as she headed away from the frat house. "It's a bit of a hike, but I don't mind the walk. Java Java. Do you know where that is?"

Cory didn't take long to follow her, watching her petite figure move ahead of him, not bothering to wait to see if he was joining her or not. Picking up the pace, he was quickly at her side and liked her style, she owned it. He liked how she decided in a moment what she was going to do, and would do it with or without him.

"I'm rather new to the area, I live in White Hall. But I know there are a lot of shops there. Do you live close to here? Go to school here?" They continued to walk, reaching an intersection and Cory placed his hand on the small of her back and led her safely across. She didn't shrug him off, and Cory took that as a good sign.

Madison turned to look at him. "I'm an art major. Third year. I have a place over off of JPA. Do you go here?"

Cory suddenly felt out of his element. *JPA? What the hell is that? A bar, a frat house, a sorority?* He knew he had to respond, and he tried to keep the panicked look off his face. She'd think he was some moron.

"Don't judge, but what's JPA?" He laughed, trying to lighten the mood and how uncomfortable he felt around her.

Madison laughed, "Well, you just answered one question. You're not a student here. JPA. It's short for Jefferson Park Avenue. There are a lot of apartment buildings there, but I have a small apartment inside a house. I prefer the privacy. So, White Hall. I've seen signs. Out in the county? Where all those vineyards are, right?"

Cory began to breathe again. "That's right. Horse country and all the vineyards. I'm not a student. But I love art, fashion, leather mostly. It must be nice to have your own place. I noticed your rings before, they're very unique. I like them. You own that style." Casually grabbing her hand, he looked down at her rings.

Madison hadn't spent any time visiting the vineyards, but she knew they were a big tourist attraction in the area, and the estates were quite large. She led them down Main Street in the direction of the mall. This boy didn't look like he came from money. Maybe he worked on one of the estates.

"Thanks. I'm afraid I don't fit in with the preppy culture of this campus, but they have a great art school. So, what is it you do?"

Cory wasn't sure how the hell to answer this. He couldn't just say, oh yeah well, my father is a vampire, so is my stepmom. I make leather outfits for a bunch of vampire warriors. We live in this huge house, we have more money than God and yeah, I can bite you if you like. "Just a leather artisan. I make custom leather goods. I'm originally from California but came here to live with my father and stepmother." He kept up with her, enjoying the conversation, but hoped she didn't probe for too much detail.

Cory had kept her hand in his after examining her rings, and they walked together toward the coffee shop. Madison led him inside and they both walked toward the back of the coffee house, past the private alcoves that held other couples. They found a quiet place in the back on a sofa, and Madison dropped down, tossing her bag to the side.

"You make stuff from leather? That's cool. Like, belts and stuff?"

Cory was intrigued by this Madison Barnes. She was nice, pretty, and different from the other girls he'd seen on campus. He tried to answer her questions truthfully, but not in much detail.

"Leather is my thing. My birth mother wasn't a rich person, so I had to learn how to make my own money. I bought a lot of leather clothes in second hand shops, and then I'd take them apart and make my own stuff. I do mostly custom work for people, like pants and jackets, but I can do anything with leather."

Cory loved looking into her eyes. She seemed totally interested in everything he said. He wasn't used to talking about himself, and he knew he'd need to be careful, but he felt so comfortable with her. "What can I get you? My treat, so here's your chance!"

The waitress approached and Madison ordered a green tea and asked for the humus plate before turning to Cory. "You can share the humus plate with me. It has cucumbers, carrots, peppers, pita chips. All organic. What do you want to drink?"

He chuckled. "I think you were born in the wrong place. You sound like the girls from California." Grinning at her, he turned to the waitress, "I'll have a cafe latte." Turning back to Madison, he decided it was time to fire out his own questions. "So, you're an art student. Do you have an artist or period of art you like the most?"

Madison shook her head. "I don't really paint much. I'm more interested in pottery. I have my own potter's wheel. That's one of the reason's I got my own place. I can work when the mood strikes me, and I don't have to worry about roommates. But I like a lot of art. I love the Impressionist, but also a lot of the realism from the Renaissance. I sell some of my stuff down here, a few shops down. I don't make a lot of money from it yet, but I'd like to be able to make a living at it someday. How about you? Do you sell your work?"

Cory took a deep breath. There was no way to find out about her without having the conversation turn back to him. Trying to relax, he tried to turn what he actually did into something more on the scale of a little white lie. "Yes, my dad has some contacts in Italy, and I make custom leathers for them. Sort of like sportswear. It's hard to describe."

He pulled at the leather vest he wore over top of his t-shirt. "I made this. I came up with the design, cut the pattern, and stitched it. But I don't sell anything in a private store or specialty shop."

Madison ran her hand over the vest. It was finely crafted and felt soft as cloth. "Get out! You made this? You could totally sell these down here! If you need the money, I can introduce you to the shop owners."

The waitress delivered their order, and Madison used a pita chip to scoop up the humus. A large dollop dropped from the chip and she laughed and caught it in her other hand. She held her fingers to his mouth, allowing him to lick the humus from her fingers. He locked eyes with her as he took her fingers in his mouth, and she felt a shiver run through her. Her offer to feed him from her hand was spontaneous, but she didn't anticipate her own response to the erotic feel of her fingers in his mouth. She smiled back at him, sensing his shyness.

"So, what do you think? You want to meet the store owners?"

Cory couldn't take his eyes off of her. He loved how she dug right in, not worried about trying to appear dainty in her eating. He was shocked when she lifted her fingers to his lips, but he snaked his tongue around her fingers and sucked softly as his eyes locked with hers. He looked down quickly when she withdrew her fingers. Sipping his latte, he shrugged about her comment.

"Never really thought about selling to the shops, to be honest. I do okay right now. It's not about the money for me, but more about pride in seeing my creations used. People feel different when they wear different things. But I wouldn't mind meeting some of the owners. All I have to show of my work is what I'm wearing right now, but I'd like to go and see your work."

Madison shrugged. "Yeah, sure. I'll show you my work. But the shops are all closed now. We'll have to come down in the daytime." She swallowed down the green tea and pondered her next question. She'd only just met him, but she had good instincts about people. "You can come back to my place, if you want. I have a lot of my stuff there. I mean, if you want to."

Cory almost choked on his latte, her place? She seemed

sincere in her offer. Why not, he was just going to sit at home and play video games and she was much more interesting and pretty. Popping a few cucumbers in his mouth, he looked over and nodded.

"Not a problem, I don't think I've even seen a potter's wheel before. And I'd really like to come back down here and go through the shops when they're open, this is a cool place to hang out, and I have my own personal tour guide."

Nudging her shoulder, his laugh was a bit loud and she giggled as well. They both looked at each other when the couple sitting across from them snuggling and kissing shot them a dirty look and they both really began to laugh.

"I think maybe we should leave before we get thrown out." Standing, he grabbed the bill and took her hand to help her up. Walking to the check-out, Cory paid the bill and they headed outside. "Lead the way. I have no idea where JPA is."

Madison led him to a bus stop. "It's a bit of a hike, and we already walked here from Rugby. Wanna take the bus? It's pretty cheap."

Cory could remember a time when he could only afford a bus. She was frugal with her money, he could tell. Some of her clothing looked like it was secondhand, and he admired that in her. He knew what it was like to not have money to eat, but he now also knew the other side of that coin.

"Cheap is good, but let's get a cab. I saw some cabs on the main drag down by that theatre. You don't mind, do you?" Taking her hand, he blushed and began to walk in that direction.

Madison let him take the lead toward Water Street. "Well, yeah that's great. But I can't afford a cab. My parents help with my expenses, and I make a little money working part-time and selling my stuff. Are you sure?"

"No problem, I got this. Come on!" As they walked hand in hand, Madison didn't let go of his hand and she was smiling. He liked making her smile. Hailing a cab, he minded his manners and opened the door, helping her in before sliding in beside her, and slamming the door.

Madison gave the driver her address and leaned back

against the seat next to the mysterious new boy. "So, you live with your parents then? In White Hall?"

"Yes, my dad's place. He just got ma... oh um, he just got married a few years ago to my stepmom. My dad is Italian, my stepmom is American, and I have a baby brother who's energetic to say the least. You have any brothers or sisters?"

Madison watched as the lights from the passing street lights illuminated his face, before plunging them into darkness again. His features were soft, almost androgynous. He had a sensual quality about him, and yet he was shy around her. He lacked the loud, boisterous cockiness of the boys on campus, and for that, she was glad.

"No siblings. I'm an only child. I have one more year of school and then I may end up living with my parents again too. At least until I can figure out how to make a living with my art."

The driver pulled over to the curb as Madison pointed out the house. "This is it. You coming in?"

Cory looked at the house and smiled. "Well, if you don't mind, I'd like to see you inside, make sure you get home safe. My dad taught me manners and Kate would never allow me to just dump you off. Kate is my stepmom."

Opening the door, he handed the cabbie a ten and told him to keep the change. He reached in and took her hand, helping her out. He had no idea what lay inside for him, but he didn't care, as long as he was with her. He suddenly had an urge to know everything about her and discover all the mysteries of Madison Barnes

.

27

Kate lay awake next to Shade, as he slept in his death slumber. Cory didn't come home last night, and although Kate reminded herself he was a man and not a child, it wasn't behavior that was common for Cory. He worked in the camp, hung out with the warriors, fed at the feeder compound, and occasionally went out with Marcello, but he always came home before sunrise. She knew he wasn't in any danger. Shade would have felt that, and he slept soundly beside her. But still, she worried. She was wondering if maybe she should get up and go to the camp to see if Marcello had any idea where he might be when she heard his footsteps on the stairs. Slipping from Shade's embrace, she left their bed, grabbing a robe and walked barefoot up the stairs to Cory's suite. She tapped lightly at his door.

***

Cory left Madison's apartment to find the streets were already buzzing with people. He knew Bel Rosso ran on a schedule, a strict one, and he was late! He walked away from Madison's house and found a quiet spot between two old houses, protected from view by overgrown landscape, and teleported back home. He landed right inside the front door and stood still. He heard nothing, not even Lorenzo, and he breathed a quick sigh of relief. He quietly made his way up the stairs to his suite, closing the door softly behind him and flopped down on the sofa, pulling out his cell phone and finding her number. He smiled remembering her goodbye kiss, and how she'd felt in his arms before he fell asleep with her last night. He'd never been with a mortal girl. When he dropped out of school, he lived on the fringes of the vampire community. They didn't really accept him, but at least they understood what he was. A vampire female would never consider him for a mate, and he had more or less resigned himself to a life without a mate. But Madison was so different from other girls. There was something special about her. She made something come alive inside him. Cory was so lost in his thoughts that the tap on the door startled him and he jumped to his feet. *Who in the hell is that?*

"Uhhh, yeah?"

"Cory? Are you okay? Can I come in?"

Kate! Dude! You are so busted! Cory looked down at his wrinkled clothes and berated himself for not going straight in and taking a shower. He probably smelled like weed and Madison. "Oh yeah, I'm fine. Um sure, come on in."

Kate entered the suite to find him sitting on the sectional sofa in his living room, looking a little disheveled. She joined him on the sofa. "I'm sorry. I don't mean to intrude, but you didn't come home, and I was worried. I mean, not that you have to check with me or anything. You're not a child. It's just you've never stayed out all night before. I just wanted to make sure you were okay."

Kate could pick up the strong scent of incense and the distinctive smell of pot in his hair and clothes.

Cory's eyes darted about the room, trying not to make eye contact with Kate. "Yeah, I'm okay. You're not intruding. I went into Charlottesville with Marcello and uh, we kind of got separated. And well, I met someone."

Kate knew Marcello was one of the few warriors who had permission from Shade to hunt, and he went to the campus to target the young girls there. She was aware Cory had gone with him a few times, but they'd always returned together.

"So, this someone. This sounds like something more than feeding then. Do you want to talk about it?" To the best of Kate's knowledge, Cory hadn't been in a relationship with anyone in the few years he'd lived here at Bel Rosso.

Cory looked directly at Kate, shaking his head strongly back and forth. "I didn't feed! I promise I didn't. I wouldn't do that to Madison, she's different."

Cory flopped back against the sofa, sighing. If he told Kate, then his dad would know. He wasn't ready for all these questions yet. "I just met her, she was at this frat house Marcello took me to, and I didn't approach her or try anything.

I could see she was bored being there, like me. Someone bumped into her while she was trying to leave and knocked her into me, and I just kept her from falling. She is..." Cory shrugged. "Mortal."

Kate listened as the words tumbled out. Cory had found a girl, a mortal girl. She knew a female vamp would never be drawn to him. He'd never have the power and skills of a full blooded vamp, and a mating would produce a child that was not full vampire. His only chance for a relationship lies with a mortal, but Kate was acutely aware of the pitfalls.

"A mortal. You didn't...say anything, did you?"

Cory lowered his head and fiddled with his leather vest. Quietly, he answered her, knowing he'd probably told Madison too much already. "No."

Kate lay back against the sofa, closing her eyes. "Cory, I want you to have love in your life. I want that for you. But I'd be lying if I said this was going to be easy. Just... take it slow. Let her come to you on her own terms. Only you will be able to judge if she'll be accepting of... who we are."

Kate took his hand and squeezed it. "Talk with your dad, and maybe Luca. If this is someone you want in your life, you're going to have to be prepared for the fact she may reject you. Reject us. And you know we must be so careful."

Cory scrunched his forehead. "Talk to Dad? I don't know. I just met her, and I really like her. She's different, like me. She's easy to talk to and seems to understand me. I don't want to do anything to hurt my family or her. But Dad?" Cory shook his head. "He won't like this. I don't want to bring her here, not yet. I left the party with her and we went for coffee, then she took me back to her place. We were just talking and talking and we fell asleep. I know that sounds made up, but really, I swear, I was honorable. We both woke up this morning and realized we fell asleep.

Cory leaned forward, placing his head in his hands. "She's different than any other girl I've met." Sitting up, he looked at Kate. "I thought about it, feeding from her. I thought about all the things I could do to her, then just erase her memory and she'd never know. But I didn't, because I want to see her again, get to know her. The warriors are like brothers, but I can't be like them, I can't do the things they can do."

Standing up, Cory began to pace. "I want more than hanging out with them. I want... I just want someone of my own."

The depth of his loneliness broke her heart, and she was aware of just how isolated he was, living between two worlds. She watched him pace. "Cory, your dad will be concerned about our exposure. But he'll want you to be happy. Just go slow. Let her get to know you first. See if her feelings for you are mutual. You'll gain a sense of her over time, and you'll know if this is something she can come to terms with. It didn't matter to me what your father was. Well, that's not completely true. It mattered, but Shade mattered more. My desire to be with him was greater than my fear of what might lie ahead. And look at Shannon and Luca. It can work, Cory. Just go slow."

Shuffling his feet, looking down at them, she didn't understand, and he tried to make her see. "You forget I'm not like you and Dad. I'm not like Luca or Shannon. I'm not mortal, or immortal. I'm always rejected and stuck in the middle. I hate it. I hate me. I don't fit. But I feel at ease when I talk to her, just being around her. Going slow is the only option I have. I also know I hope I never see that horror in her eyes when she finds out what I really am. I should probably just leave her alone."

Kate jumped to her feet and wrapped him in her arms. "You are a beautiful man, with a beautiful soul. You have a kindness and a gentleness that shines through you. And you'll find someone, Cory. If not this girl, there will be others. Don't walk away from this. If you like this girl, then see where it goes. Will you do that?"

Cory was startled by her hug. He wasn't used to being held. It felt comforting, maybe she did understand. But his dad...that would be another story! He didn't feel like he could tell Shade yet, and besides, this relationship with Madison might not go anywhere.

Cory embraced Kate hard, laying his head on her shoulder.

She'd been more of a mother to him than his real mother, even though there wasn't that great a difference in their age. "I want to, I want to try. Please don't tell Dad. I know you tell each other everything, but I'm not ready yet to tell him. I just met her. I want some more time with her. Please."

Kate rubbed his back and shushed him, just as when she held and calmed Lorenzo. "I'll keep this to myself for now, Cory. But you must promise if this relationship looks like it's going somewhere, you'll talk to him. Don't fear your father. I know he reacts strongly at times. But he loves you. You must know that."

It felt good to allow someone to hold him. "He can blow the roof off this house, let's be honest here." Laughing, he pulled away from her embrace. "Thank you. I feel better. I promise if I get to that point with Madison, I'll talk to you both. She's an art student at the university and she makes pottery. We have some things in common. She actually thinks I could sell my leather stuff at some of the shops downtown, and I think I might want to try that."

Kate smiled at him. "You *could* sell your stuff. Easily! Now let me get back downstairs. He doesn't wake up, but he knows when I'm not there." Kate turned to leave then looked back at him. "Madison and Cory, it has a nice ring to it." She winked at him as she opened the door to leave.

Cory smiled, knowing she got the situation with Madison and him. "Mom... wait. I know Dad loves me. I don't fear him. I just never want to disappoint him. I love him so much, he gave me a new life, and he taught me respect and caring. I want Madison to feel special. I want to have with her what you have with Dad. I see how much loving someone can make you come alive and give you something to live for. I have a real good example in you and Dad. I love you both."

Kate looked back at him, biting her lip, hoping this girl could see past the obstacles and open herself to the love Cory had waited all his life to share. "And we both love you."

28

Santos brought Alec another Midnight as the Senator looked through several budget appropriation bills. As he set the glass down, Alec looked up, so engrossed in his work he was unaware of how much time had passed.

"What time is it, Santos?"

Santos checked his watch. "Almost 10 p.m., master."

Alec drank down the thick elixir and swiveled in his chair, fishing the cell phone from his pocket. He dialed Shade's number. He'd meant to call earlier in the evening, hoping to catch Shade before he left for the camp. Now he's sure his call would interrupt his schedule. The phone rang several times and Alec was expecting it to go to voicemail when he finally answered. "Brother! Sorry to bother you. But I'm going to need your help in this next phase of the plan."

***

Shade was watching the new recruits. The camp had just started with the new group, but they were already indoctrinated into the routine, and knew where they should be on the field. He noticed Marcello and Cory in deep conversation and wondered what that was about. Cory looked up and momentarily locked eyes with him before he quickly looked away. Before Shade could explore this further, he felt his cell buzz. Dropping his sword to the ground, point down, he fished the phone from his leathers. Seeing Alec's name on the ID he took the call, and heard Alec asking for another favor.

"I already did what you asked, brother, you owe me. If Rissa is not coming through for you, that's not my problem."

"Hang on, brother." Alec motioned for a refill as Santos filled his glass again. "Rissa has an invitation to join the President while the First Lady is out of town, so the plan has been set in motion. But it won't do me any good if I have no way to prove it. This is an easy request. I just need some cameras planted. As long as Rissa knows where the cameras are, she can orchestrate the situation to make sure it's all caught on film. This won't take long."

Closing his eyes, Shade lowered his head and tapped the cell phone on his thigh. *Has he totally lost his fucking mind?* Walking to the high enclosed wall around the camp, he took his time, making Alec wait. Stepping outside the locked gate, the noise was less intrusive, and no one could overhear him.

"Let me make sure I understand. You expect me to go inside the White House again, plant cameras so your mate can fuck the President? I suppose you want me to watch as well, maybe assist? I am afraid that is out of the question. We made a deal, it did not include me installing cameras, nor taking them down."

Alec stood up so quickly he knocked over the glass of Midnight. "Let's be clear, Shade. You are walking away with the largest chunk of my territory. The dream-walking set the stage, but if I don't have something to hold over Ashton's head, something I can threaten to share with his wife, then this is all for nothing. I suggest you find a way to make this happen, brother. You have an entire fucking army over there. Surely someone can plant a few fucking cameras."

Shade paced outside the camp enclosure. "Relax, bro. Damn, you do not make my life easy. Okay, we have one good option. Hyde is her protector. I will assign this to him. Besides, he should be close at hand anyway, just in case things go wrong. Consider it done."

Alec sighed and sat back down as Santos cleaned up the mess and brought him a fresh glass. He ran his hand through his hair, glad to have this settled. He was in no mood for a fight tonight. "Glad to hear it, brother. Knew I could count on you."

Shade looked at his watch. "Speaking of which, is he with her now? I want this over and done with."

Alec propped his feet on the desk before he took another sip from his glass. "She's home for the night. She got back from the gym about an hour ago. So, you can talk to Hyde tonight, or I can have Rissa tell him tomorrow."

Shade shook his head. "Hell no! I will speak with him. Leave her ass out of this. Hyde would not take orders from her to begin with. This needs to come from me. He won't like it, but he'll get the job done. He can easily install the cameras and get them back to you with the needed evidence. Let me deal with him, you deal with Rissa. I am busy tonight, I need to move on."

Alec heard the impatience in his voice and knew to quit while he was ahead. "Just let me know when it's done, brother. I'd say I owe you one, but you're getting all of California, so you're still coming out ahead."

"Damn right I am." Hanging up, Shade stared at the phone, then slipped it back in the pocket of his leather pants. Looking up at the moon, he slid his hands through his hair. "This is some messed up shit. Don't let me down now, Hyde." **"Hyde, where are you, brother? I need to speak with you immediately. Come see me in the camp."**

Shade strolled back in through the camp gate, retrieved his sword and waited, as he wondered how in the hell he got himself into these predicaments.

29

Cory knew he'd have some questions to answer from Marcello. As he made his way to his leather shop, he saw Marcello on the field. Marcello raised his hand to acknowledge him, and then walked in his direction.

"What happened to you last night, brother? You didn't stay very long at the party. Everything okay?"

Cory scuffed his boot in the dirt, avoiding Marcello's stare. "Yeah, I'm good. I met a girl, that's all."

Marcello slapped him on the back. "Well, that was the point, wasn't it?"

Cory smiled and kept his eyes on the ground. "No, not to feed. I mean...I met someone. You know. Someone I really like, a lot. I got her number."

Marcello laughed. "Oh hell, brother. I'm afraid I can't help you there. You should talk to Luca, or master. They're the experts on mortals around here."

Cory flashed him a look. "I can't talk to Dad yet! But yeah, Luca." He looked over his shoulder back in the direction of the main house. It was still daylight, and he knew his dad would be deep in his death slumber. He turned toward the house, and thanked Marcello for the advice, and heard Marcello shout "Good luck."

Cory entered the house and could hear Lorenzo upstairs playing under the watchful eye of Theresa. He took a deep breath and knocked lightly on Luca's door. "Luca? Its Cory, are you busy?"

Luca looked up from his canvas as he heard the tap on the door and heard Cory on the other side. Creasing his brow, he started to wipe the paint splatters from his hand as he dropped his brush into the jar. "Nothing that can't wait. Come on in, Cory."

Cory realized he'd been holding his breath and released it in a big sigh. Walking in quickly, he closed the door behind him and saw Luca had been painting. "Oh man, sorry, I didn't mean to interrupt." Stammering, Cory looked down at the floor, then around the suite. He didn't prepare well for this encounter and now he felt like an idiot.

Luca sensed his nervousness. Cory rarely came to his suite, so Luca knew something was on his mind. Luca dropped down on the sofa and invited Cory to take a seat. "Sit down, brother. What's on your mind?"

Cory took the seat across from him, flopping down hard, throwing his left leg over the padded armrest of the chair. "I just need someone to talk to that isn't Dad or Kate. Marcello was kinda useless, but he suggested I talk to you since you'd know more about mortal females." Cory laid his head back on the overstuffed chair and sighed heavily. "I met someone, and I really like her a lot. Go ahead and drill me."

Luca laughed as he lit up a cigarette and offered the pack to Cory, who shook his head. "You met a mortal girl, and let me guess, it felt like you were struck by lightning? She leaves you tongue-tied, makes your palms sweat? Is that your problem, little brother?"

Cory wasn't expecting the laugh, he was expecting to get drilled with questions, but he grinned as Luca described exactly how he felt. "Exactly. But she's so different, you know. She, like, gets me. She's not like other girls I've ever met. She's sexy, smart, and talented and she doesn't look at me like I'm a freak." Sitting up, he rested his elbows on his knees and stared at Luca. "I went with Marcello to Charlottesville, to the campus. He took me with him to feed. Then I saw this girl. But I didn't want to just feed from her and walk away. We hung out all night and ended up at her place. We slept together, I mean, not sex, we fell asleep. I slept next to her all night, holding her. When we woke up this morning, I didn't want to leave but I knew I needed to get my ass back here or I'd be under interrogation. Kate heard me come in and talked to me a while. I told her some things, but I'm still confused. Luca, I could have done a million things to her in her sleep, and I thought about it, but I couldn't. I felt something for her, and she's so damn beautiful."

Luca laid his head back against the sofa and exhaled, remembering the first time he saw Shannon and smiled. "So how can I help you, brother? You think you love this girl?"

Cory shook his head. "I don't know. I've never loved a girl. But I think I could easily love her. She doesn't know I'm a half-breed, or anything about my family or where I live. I tried not to give her too much information. It's tricky. And what happens when she finds out? I'm afraid, once she knows; she will run screaming in the other direction. How did you let Shannon know, when did you let her know?"

Luca leaned forward and put out the cigarette before locking eyes with Cory. "I had a bit of an advantage because Shannon was friends with Kate, and Kate was still mortal. I knew the minute I saw Shannon I wanted to be with her. I asked her out, and we went on a double-date with Kate and Shade. So just be happy your first encounter with this girl didn't require Shade as a chaperone."

Luca chuckled at the memory of their first date together. "I can only tell you what Kate told me. Go slow, let her get to know you. Make sure she's as interested in you as you are in her. I was able to let Kate explain to her what we were. What we all were. But Kate knew Shannon, and knew if she decided to walk away, she wouldn't do anything that would put her in jeopardy. You won't have that advantage, so you'll need to move slower. You don't have a beast to the same degree as we do. So, you'll have to figure out if you think she's the one you want to be with for the rest of your life, Cory, and if she feels the same about you. Until then, I'm afraid you'll have to keep the truth under wraps. I know it seems deceptive. And in a manner of speaking, it is. But none of us can afford to expose ourselves to a mortal who's going to freak out when they discover what we are. So, tell me about her. How you met her."

Cory listened intently before he responded. "Slow is how I want to go. This is all new to me too, but I want to get to know everything about her. She wants to see me again."

Cory stood and walked slowly around the room, tugging on

his jeans. "I went to a frat party with Marcello. I felt awkward from the beginning. I mean, I just didn't fit in there. I saw her in the crowd, and she didn't fit in either. I could see her moving in my direction, toward the front door when some people bumped into her and almost knocked her over. I just reached out, stopped her from falling. We walked outside together, and she asked me to go with her for coffee. We walked to that outdoor mall place in downtown C'ville and we just talked. She's an art student at the university. She makes pottery, really good, beautiful pieces. She sells her stuff in some of the shops on the mall. We had a drink, food, laughed, it was fun. Anyway, she asked me in when I took her home. She has her own place. It was so different, I love the space. We smoked some weed and fell asleep together on her bed. Nothing happened, I swear. I just felt something come together inside me when I held her in my arms. Like, I don't know, like... I mean, it felt like she was meant to be there. Fuck, Luca, yeah I could stay with her."

Luca smiled as Cory paced, as he remembered all his own doubts when he first fell in love with Shannon. "Does this mystery girl have a name?"

"Oh yeah, Madison. Awesome, huh? She's so pretty, long blonde hair, big eyes. She dresses like a hippy, like she's from another era, lots of rings and jewelry. Oh, and she wants to take me to the shops where she sells her pottery and introduce me, so I can sell some of my leather. I think that would be great."

Cory sat down again across from Luca and punched him on the arm. "You should sell your paintings. Those shops down there are a gold mine. I might get rich, who knows!" Cory laughed. "Seriously, I hope I can pull this off without her finding out too soon. So she can get to know me before she figures out what I am. I'll have to hold her off from coming here. That might not be easy. You had it easy with Kate knowing Shannon. Kate said I should talk to Shade, like he would get this! I would be dead."

Luca laughed and shook his head. "First of all, little brother, you're already rich, if you haven't figured that out yet. I'd lay odds there's a trust fund with your name on it. Shade wouldn't leave anything to chance. And your father fell in love with a mortal himself. Trust me, he'll understand. He'll have concerns for you, and for the family. You already know that. We all have to be careful. But he won't keep you from this girl if she's the one. I can promise you that much."

Cory eyed Luca and thought long and hard about what he was saying. "I won't compromise my family, ever. I know Dad would understand, but I'm not ready for that confrontation yet. Let's face it. He's going to drill me with a million questions. I want to be able to answer whatever he throws at me and right now, I can't do that. If I need someone to talk to, can I come to you?"

Luca nodded. "Of course, brother. You can keep it under wraps for a while. That will give you a chance to see how she feels, and if this goes anywhere. And you know you can come to me anytime. You'll be fine, little brother. Kate says we all need to have the shit kicked out of us by love. And believe me, there will be times you'll feel like you've had the shit kicked out of you."

"Thanks, Luca." He walked toward the door but turned to look at Luca. "Dad says he knew it was Kate. He knew. Nothing was stopping him from having her for eternity. You knew with Shannon. And you had an ace in the hole with Kate helping pave the way. But I don't know if she's the one, and I'm out here alone. I feel like Madison can make me whole, a better person. And I don't want to screw this up. If she's the one, I sure hope to hell you're right about Dad, because I don't want to have to choose between him and someone I love and can call my own. Thanks for everything, brother."

Luca leveled him with a stare. "He'll never make you choose, Cory. I grew up with him. I know him better than most. He'd never make you choose."

Cory stared at Luca for a long time. He knew Luca was close to Shade, they were tight, and Luca wasn't of his blood. Cory was of his blood, but nothing had ever come between him and his dad in the years he'd been living here. He knew deep inside there would come a time when they wouldn't see eye to eye on things, and he hoped that Madison Barnes wasn't it. "I hope you're right, Luca. I want to sell my leather at the shops. Should I ask him first?"

Luca nodded. "Yes, absolutely. It involves you making a business deal with mortals. Anytime our paths cross with the mortal world you want to make sure he is aware."

"That I can handle!" Grinning, he threw up his hand and walked out, closing the door behind him. Instead of going back to his room, he walked down the lane and into the camp, entering his workshop. It was daylight and the activity in the camp was low. It was the perfect time for a phone call to a certain Madison Barnes. He missed her voice already. Pulling the phone from his pocket, he searched for her number and stared at it a long while. Looking around the shop before he hit dial, he decided he'd spend the daylight hours making her a unique gift crafted from his own hands. But first, he needed to hear her voice.

•

30

Madison made her early class on time, just barely, and was now back home with some time to spare until her afternoon classes. She was preparing to spend some time at the potter's wheel as she got the clay ready. Cory had been on her mind all morning. She liked this boy, but he was sending mixed signals. And although she was glad he hadn't pressured her to have sex last night, she was surprised. She was wondering again if he might be gay when her cell phone rang. She dug the phone from the bottom of the fabric handbag and didn't recognize the number. "Hello?"

"Hi Madison, it's Cory. I hope I'm not bothering you. Just wanted to call and say hello."

"Cory!" She balanced the phone on her shoulder as she wiped the wet clay from her hands, then walked to her bed, and stretched across it. "I'm glad you called. I have a break between classes. Did you get home okay?"

Cory grinned at the sound of happiness in her voice. He could tell she was glad he'd called. "Sure, I did, sorry I haven't called before now, but I had to work. Now you have my cell number, so don't be a stranger. Listen, ummm, I'll text you my email, you can email me your schedule for classes, that way I won't interrupt you. Wait, do you have a laptop? Didn't think about that. Sorry."

She smiled at his nervousness. "I have a laptop. It's hard to be a student without a laptop. Text me your email and I'll send my schedule. So, are you seeing anyone special?"

Cory could feel the blush creep up his face. Then his grin was as big as his head. "I sure am." *Wait, did I just say that? Where in the hell did that come from?* He'd been hanging around the brothers too long. He was beginning to sound like Raven.

Madison felt a lump in her throat. Of course, he'd be seeing someone. That would explain why he didn't make a pass at her.

So, was he just looking for friendship? "Oh. Uh, is she a student too?"

Cory panicked. Madison thought he was talking about someone else. Shit, how was he going to get out of this mess? "Yes, she's a student. She's beautiful too, and has a very unique style. I like being around her, and I want to spend more time with her. Oh, and I should tell you, her kiss, sweetest thing ever." Cory hoped she didn't hang up.

Madison twirled her hair around her finger as she listened to him describe the girl he was already taken with. "Well, she's very lucky to have you."

"No, not really, but I'm very lucky to have met her and hoping she wants to see me again. So, what do you say, someone special? Can I ask you out on a date, a real date?"

Cory waited a moment, she didn't respond right away. He could feel his heart rate accelerate. "Say yes Madison Barnes, because no one is more special in my life than you."

Madison sat upright. He was talking about her. "Yes, of course. My answer is yes!"

Cory chuckled. That's what he was waiting to hear. "So, what do you say, maybe Friday night? What would you like to do? Lady's choice. I'll pick you up in my truck, and we can roll into town, dinner, movie, shopping?"

"Uh, there's a great place for Italian food on the mall, and Ry Cooder is performing at The Paramount on Friday. He's an old blues singer. Not everyone's cup of tea, but I really like him. Or did you want to take some of your stuff to the shops?" Madison paced the floor, twisting her hair around her fingers in anticipation of his response.

Cory didn't think he really had anything ready for the shops yet, so he'd avoid that for now. "I love Italian, and Ry Cooder, great! I like blues. How early can you go because we can just check out the shops first, I need to see what kind of stuff they carry, then I can gauge what I should be making to appeal to the market. If you don't mind? Then we can grab some grub and hit the Paramount. This is all at the mall, right?"

"Yeah, right. My last class on Friday ends at two, so any

time after that works for me. I can show you the shops, maybe introduce you to some people, then we can grab an early dinner. The show is at eight, I think. You want me to get the tickets?"

Cory shook his head. "Look, Madison, I know money is tight and I'm asking you out, so I want to pay. I can get online and get the tickets. It's not a big deal. And how about I pick you up at like three on Friday?"

Madison nodded. "Yeah, you can order them online. But Cory, I get some money from my parents and I sell stuff and work part-time, so I have a little money. You don't have to pay for everything. I don't expect it."

"I know you don't expect it, but you deserve to be treated special. You're beautiful, and you're mine. Keep your money for what you need it for. So, I'll see you at three on Friday. Sound good?"

"Yeah, I guess I'll see you Friday at three then."

Cory could hear a change in her voice. Maybe he'd pushed too hard on the money issue, but he knew what it felt like to have nothing. "Madison, don't be angry with me, I want to pay. Spend more time with you, get to know you. I hope you want the same."

"I do, Cory. I want to get to know you as well. But you just, uh, referred to me as yours. I don't mean this to be hurtful, and I don't want to scare you off of anything, but, I don't *belong* to you, or anyone else. I struggle hard to maintain my own independence. I set my own rules. I hope you get that. And I hope I haven't made you change your mind about going out with me."

Cory felt his heart fall to his feet. He'd already opened his big mouth and gone too far. But he understood her, knew that independence was far more important sometimes than anything else. His past life in California taught him that above anything else.

"I'm sorry. I'm really nervous, Madison. I don't date much, but I understand about independence. So, let's make a deal right now. Equals. We belong to the earth, the moon, the universe. You didn't change my mind, I respect you speaking up. Accept my apology? Please?"

She laughed. "Accepted, Cory Medici. See you on Friday."

"See you then." He didn't hang up right away, and neither did she. If he hung up, he had to wait until Friday to hear her voice again. Finally ending the call, he stared at the walls. Yeah, Luca was right; this wasn't going to be easy. He wanted to make something for her, something special. He was never a flowers and chocolate sort of person, and he was pretty sure Madison wasn't that type either. The grin on his face began to spread. This required something as unique and genuine as she was.

31

Alto drove, as Hyde escorted Rissa to the White House where she was expected. The big evening was about to begin. Alto passed though the security check points and pulled the car around the circular drive. Hyde exited the car and led her to the entrance where she was instructed to enter.

"Rissa, there shouldn't be any danger inside. There will be Secret Service everywhere. Once you get to the private chambers, they remain outside those doors. I've placed video cameras strategically throughout the President's living space, but have the majority of them in his bedroom, so try to lure him there. Every angle is covered. Once you go through these doors, I won't follow, but if anything goes wrong, I'll respond as best I can without exposing what we are. You're somewhat on your own here."

Rissa eyed him slyly and smiled. "Never underestimate my power as a woman, Hyde. He's putty in my hands. "

Hyde grunted. "I have no doubt. When you're ready to leave, just send me a message telepathically. The staff will escort you back here to the door. I'll be with Alto over at the Willard Hotel, and we'll drive here to meet you. It's only five minutes from here. I'll shadow myself, so I can retrieve the cameras."

Rissa inhaled deeply, just wanting to get this over with. "Let's do this."

***

The head butler had been informed to expect a visit from Senator Canton's wife. The White House staff was used to keeping secrets, and not asking questions, but the staff had been a buzz all week over this news. What reason could the President possibly have to meet with Senator Canton's wife, in his private quarters after hours, while the First Lady was out? The butler greeted her on arrival.

"Mrs. Canton, follow me please. The President is expecting

you."

The butler led Rissa to the private elevator that took them to the third floor. He escorted her to the door leading into the family quarters flanked by the Secret Service and tapped lightly. The President answered the door and extended his hand to Rissa, giving it a firm shake.

"So happy you could accommodate me on such short notice, Mrs. Canton. Please, come in."

As Rissa entered the room, President Ashton nodded his dismissal to the butler and closed the door. "Now, can I get you a drink, my lovely?"

Rissa glanced around the room and smiled to herself. One day very soon this would all be hers. "What a beautiful room, Mr. President. I'd love a red wine."

Ashton was nervous as he poured a glass of wine for her and a double shot of bourbon for himself. He downed the drink in one gulp and refilled his glass before turning to her and offering her the wine. "Please, sit down, and call me John. Make yourself comfortable. Can I get you anything? Have you had dinner?"

Taking the glass from his hand, Rissa could sense his nervousness. The stupid fool probably never fucked anything this hot in his whole miserable life. She sat elegantly on the upholstered chair, her tight fitting dress hugging every curve. Crossing her legs with a dramatic flair, her skin was shimmering. She tossed her long blonde hair over her shoulder and rolled her huge blue eyes up to him, the smile spreading across her face.

"Oh no please, I've had dinner, but thank you for the offer. Imagine having dinner privately with President John Ashton, the most powerful man in the world. I'm so honored to have this invitation. I couldn't possibly ask for anything more than your wonderful company." Taking a sip of the wine, Rissa was careful not to ingest too much, this wasn't Midnight, but a small amount wouldn't harm her.

The President sat down next to her, taking in her long tanned legs. Unlike his wife, Rissa didn't wear hosiery. He was wondering what else she might have left off under that skirt. He let his hand rest on her knee as he tested the waters. "Well, maybe next time I can arrange for us to have a private dinner." She didn't pull away from his hand, so he moved it slowly up her bare thigh before stopping.

Rissa resisted the impulse to move away from this repulsive man. She knew she had to let him make the first move as that was what Alec needed. "A private dinner would be wonderful, John. I'd look forward to it. And, the Secret Service? Do they stay outside that door?" Rissa gave a nervous laugh, loathing every minute of this charade. She hoped he didn't take all damn evening to get to the bedroom.

"The Secret Service always stands just outside the door. But don't worry about them. They won't enter the family quarters unless I call them or push the panic button. I don't think there will be any need to push the panic button, do you?" He slipped his hand further up her thigh and under the edge of her fitted skirt.

Rissa laid her hand on his thigh and licked her soft red lips. "No panic at all, Mr. President." Lifting her hand from his leg, she slid it along his sagging jawline. In a breathy voice, she spoke to him, "You're so handsome and powerful. I adore powerful men, how they handle every situation with such ease and grace."

Ashton's heart raced as she responded to his advances. He was well aware of the men who used their power to attract women, but he'd never played that game. It had been a very long time since a young woman flirted with him, and he felt clumsy. He downed the last of his bourbon and set the glass on the table before taking her hand. "Maybe you'd like a tour? The family quarters aren't open to the public."

Rissa could sense his nerves and his anxious need to take her. Setting her wine glass down, she stood and reached for his hand. "Well, that's an invitation I'm most eager to accept. It's not often such a powerful man offers me a personal guided tour."

As Ashton stood, she wrapped her arm around his elbow and leaned into his ear whispering in a husky sexy voice. "Lead on, show me all of the dark corners and special places I should see."

He almost stumbled as she whispered in his ear. He led her in the direction of his private bedroom, which would put a little space between him and the Secret Service. He pushed open the door and held his hand out for her to enter ahead of him. "After you, my lovely."

"What a beautiful room." Walking ahead of Ashton, Rissa wandered slowly around the room, stopping to kick off her heels, and quickly spotting the cleverly positioned cameras Hyde had placed earlier. Sauntering to the bed, she could feel his eyes burning a hole in her back. Letting her hand slide along the finest linens on the bed, her eyes swept to his.

"Do you sleep alone, John, or does your wife join you? I can only imagine that a man in your position of power can be under so much stress. It would be a pity not to have someone to comfort you on those nights."

Ashton joined her and sat down on the bed. "I'm afraid my wife has her own bedroom. She says I toss and turn at night and it keeps her awake." He brushed a stray lock of hair from her cheek. "I can't imagine you'd ever sleep alone, my lovely."

Sighing heavily for effect, Rissa had him right where she wanted him. "I sleep alone quite often, more than you could ever imagine. Alec...is so busy. He's absorbed with his career. We barely see each other and I...."

She let out a soft sob as she sat beside him and curled into his shoulder. "Oh John, you don't know the loneliness I feel. Alec's attention is always on his work, not me."

Ashton placed his arm around her shoulder, stroking her arm. "Then I have sorely misjudged him, my lovely. What man in his right mind would ever let you sleep alone? Clearly, he needs to re-assess his priorities."

He nuzzled against her cheek, his breath hot against her skin. She was wearing a delicate perfume that intoxicated him.

Rissa could feel his breath against her cheek and resisted the impulse to recoil. She must give him a sign she accepted and wanted his attentions. Sliding her tongue softly around his ear lobe, her hand glided down his chest. She grabbed his cock through his pants and felt his hardness. "You'd never let me sleep alone, would you?"

With a quick intake of his breath, he almost jumped when she slid her hand between his legs. He knew she'd be an eager one. "My lovely, I can't understand how any man could ever leave your bed. I confess, I'd never get any work done if you were mine."

He kissed her neck, leaving a wet trail on her skin as he worked his way to her lips.

"John...show me how you'd never leave me lonely."

She slid her hand in his hair, and felt his lips close to hers. Snaking out her tongue, Rissa licked around the edges of his lips, and then kissed him softly. Releasing the kiss, she jumped off the bed and stood with her back to him, her hands over her face. "Oh, I can't believe I said that. What must you think of me? I'm so sorry. I just need someone..."

Ashton couldn't believe his luck! She was practically begging him to take her. He stood and removed his tie, letting it drop to the floor. He started to unbutton his shirt. "Please. Don't apologize to me. I can't believe what a fool Canton is. I promise you, my lovely, you won't leave here tonight doubting how desirable you are."

Rissa moved in for the kill. Reaching around to unzip her dress, she moaned as she pretended to struggle with the zipper and watched as he moved to help her. "Your hands, their so strong, so commanding."

He quickly unzipped the dress and let it drop to the floor. He removed his shirt, oblivious to the graying hairs on his chest as he pulled her hard against him. He fumbled with the hook on her bra, finally releasing it and freeing her of the garment. She was helping him to remove his belt, and unzipped his pants playfully as they slid over his rounded hips. He stumbled awkwardly stepping out of his pants as she tugged at him, leading him to his bed. She was everything he'd dreamed of. He climbed in bed over top of her, leaning his weight on her hair and she yelped.

"Oh, sorry! So sorry." He quickly shifted his weight from her hair.

Fucking old goat! Rissa wanted to spew when she saw his wrinkled old cock. How in the hell did she ever let Alec talk her into this? Then she reminded herself to keep her eye on the prize. She'd be the lady of this house soon.

"Wait John, let me help." Putting her palms on his shoulders, she rolled him on his back, letting her hair fall forward onto his face as she straddled him. "Let me show you what it can be like."

She ran her tongue down his neck and onto his chest as she grabbed his cock and stroked him, and felt him ready to cum. This would be one short fucking ride. Sliding him inside her, she took him fully. She could barely feel his small cock inside her when she started to move her hips.

Ashton laid his head back on the pillow as she straddled him. He gripped her hips as she deftly slid onto his cock and started riding him hard. He gritted his teeth and moaned as he came hard inside her. Huffing and puffing, he let his hands slide down her thighs.

"Oh, my lovely. I didn't mean to cum so fast. Was it good for you? Please, lay down beside me. Let me rest a minute and I'm sure the next time will be better."

Rissa had only ridden him for two seconds and he came, at least she thought he did. *For fuck's sake, is that it?* She stared down at him and he looked like he was having a heart attack. *Oh, hell no, you old goat, there's no way in hell you are dying with that piss ant little cock inside me.* "Oh John, it was wonderful."

Rissa wanted to run as fast and as far as she could. She wanted nothing more than a shower! Sliding off him, she couldn't even look at the shriveled little inch worm that lay dead and spent beneath his round belly. "John, I can't stay long. Alec has made arrangements for some company. I made my excuses to meet with a client this evening, but I must get back to him as soon as possible. He relies on me to entertain. Please forgive me."

Sliding off the bed, she gave him a soft kiss on the cheek and moved away from the bed before he could grab her. Hell, what was she worried about, he didn't have enough strength to sit up! She quickly grabbed her bra and dress, and stepped into her shoes. *I need to get the hell out of here now.*

Ashton sat up on his elbow. She was already out of his bed and dressing. To be honest, he knew it would take him a few hours before he could go again, but there were so many things he wanted to do to her. "Are you sure, lovely?" He struggled to sit on the side of the bed. "Another night then? I can call you when I have another night free."

Rissa's head swiveled toward him as she finally got herself together. *Not a chance in hell, you old fart.* "Oh, of course. I hate leaving you like this, but I must go."

Walking to the door, her hand on the doorknob, she stopped and turned. "Please rest, don't bother to see me out, I know the Secret Service will make sure I'm safely seen out." Smiling at him, she gritted her teeth as she did so. **"Alec Canton, you better have that room finished for me very soon, because there is no way in hell I am ever doing this again!"**

Walking out of the room, she straightened her dress, sliding her fingers through her hair and sending Hyde a message to let him know she was finished, as the Secret Service called for the head butler to escort her out.

Alto had just parked the car when Hyde informed him Rissa was ready. Both men chuckled as Alto restarted the engine and returned back to the White House. "Well that was the shortest trip ever."

32

Alto made the short drive back to the White House, as Hyde teleported inside Ashton's bedroom, shadowing himself from view. Watching as the President stumbled to the bathroom, Hyde waited impatiently. He had little time to get this job done. He heard the water from the shower and quickly gathered the cameras and dumped them into the leather satchel.

Hyde wrapped up and teleported back outside to the waiting car, just as the butler arrived at the door with Rissa. He tossed the satchel in the car, and stepped forward to take Rissa's arm, assisting her into the car. As Hyde slid in beside her, Alto started the engine and they headed back to the Canton residence. Hyde could feel her fuming already. "That didn't take long. Alto barely had time to find a parking space. I was prepared to wait a couple of hours at least."

Rissa huffed. "Don't even start, Hyde. What in the hell did you expect? He must be at least seventy years old!"

Hyde started to laugh, a slow chuckle that rolled from deep inside him. Rissa turned and belted him on the arm. "This isn't funny. He almost had a damn heart attack when he was done. It was like fucking a limp dick, seriously, why the hell Alec thought he needed Shade to dream-walk is beyond me."

Hyde consoled her through his laughter. "If this is the worst he ever asks you to do, I'd say you got off easy. Oh sorry, no pun intended." He bit his lip to stifle his laughter again.

Rissa screamed in frustration as she slammed her hands on the seat, her hair whipping around, her embarrassment rising. How dare he make fun of her, she was doing what her master asked her to do and this was a small price to pay for getting the sex chamber in their own house. "Enough! Just shut up, Hyde."

Alto guided the car easily through the traffic and pulled into the Canton residence. Hyde slid out of the car and reached in to help Rissa when she slapped his hand away.

"Get off me, you oaf!"

Hyde laughed as she stormed for the door. He grabbed the satchel from the back seat and followed her to the house.

Rissa whipped open the door and slammed it in his face. Hyde chuckled as he opened the door and walked in behind her as she screamed out for Alec. Santos appeared, and she snarled at him.

"Get me a Midnight. Now! A double and don't take all night." Kicking off her heels, she knew Alec was home but where in the hell was he.

***

Alec heard her as she stormed inside, and he could feel her anger from here. He polished off the last of the Midnight and slid the laptop off his long legs, stretched out along the leather sofa. He walked to the foyer to see an angry Rissa, and Hyde with a smirk on his face. "Did you have a good evening, darling?"

"How nice of you to join us, Alec. No, I certainly didn't, but I won't discuss this in front of Hyde. He's had enough fun at my expense for one evening. Get your cameras and dismiss him. Santos! Where's my Midnight?" Rissa stormed for the living room and almost plowed into Santos as he handed her the Midnight. "I've had about enough of old men this night."

Alec bit his lip to keep from smiling, and noticed Hyde was struggling to keep a straight face as well. He retrieved the satchel from Hyde who indicated all the cameras were removed and the footage was inside. Alec thanked him for his service as Hyde turned and left. Alec carried the satchel back into the living room, and removed the cameras, plugging them into the laptop to download the footage.

Rissa continued her pacing, having kicked off her heels, gulping down the Midnight. Alec chuckled. "Come on, my darling. You weren't gone very long. How bad could it be?"

The laptop pinged to indicate the video had downloaded and Alec started to play back the film. He was laughing so hard tears streamed down his face. "Well, this isn't what I expected, but it will do the job. It may be even more humiliating. Ashton will drop out just to make sure no one sees this pitiful performance. This would make him more a laughing stock than a scandal."

Rissa was fuming, pacing, and gulping down the Midnight. "Go ahead, laugh! It was definitely not funny from my standpoint. Alec, he was pathetic. I thought the old goat was going to have a heart attack and die before I could get out of there. I did as you asked, humiliated myself with that...that...limp dick old bastard, now I want satisfaction!"

Slamming the glass down, Rissa went for the box of cigarettes and lit up. Inhaling, throwing her head back, she sighed. "I feel filthy."

He took the cigarette from her hand and inhaled deeply before handing it back to her. He held her gaze as he exhaled. He slapped her ass hard as he directed her. "Then get upstairs and shower. And I'll join you shortly."

33

Shade carefully scripted his invitation to *bel* on the scrolled paper. He was asking her out on a date, just the two of them. Chuckling to himself, he remembered not so long ago, when he'd teleport into her condo and whisk her away to exotic places. But Lorenzo had brought an end to their spontaneous rendezvous, and Shade wanted to recapture some of that romance.

He'd arranged for Theresa, Luca, and Shannon to be home with Lorenzo. With Kate in the early stages of pregnancy, and the camp taking off, he knew he had a limited window of time for the two of them to enjoy a night out. As much as they both doted on Lorenzo, it came at a price, as they had little time for just the two of them, and he felt guilt for that. She deserved the world and he planned on getting it for her.

Finishing up the invitation, he let the ink dry before rolling up the scroll. "Damn computers have taken away the romance in this world."

Tucking the scrolled paper inside his leather jacket, he honed in on her whereabouts in the house, and felt she was asleep. He knew she tried hard to wait for him to return from the camp every morning, but with Lorenzo, and the pregnancy, she was getting tired more easily now.

Creeping up the stairs, he made a beeline for Lorenzo's room and found Theresa exiting. She gave him a smile, letting him know she'd just put Lorenzo down for a nap. As she left the room, he walked inside to check on his son. It was his habit now, one he enjoyed. Kissing the toddler softly on his cheek, brushing a stray curl from his eyes, Shade took a deep breath. The future of the Medici coven lay on the shoulders of this small boy, his one and only full-blooded son.

Quietly leaving the room, he closed the door behind him and made his way to the master bedroom to find his *bel* asleep. She lay stretched out in their bed, her soft curves covered in a white nightgown, her flaming crimson trailing across the white pillows and her lashes like crescent moons across her cheeks.

He walked silently to her side of the bed and laid the scrolled parchment on her bedside table, along with a perfect red rose. Smiling to himself, he knew she'd love getting out of the house and being alone together for one night. As he undressed, he heard her stirring and quickly slid into bed beside her, his death slumber coming on quickly. Curling into her, pulling her close in a protective embrace, he whispered to her. "Your warrior is home, *mi amore*."

Kate felt him as he slid into bed beside her, felt the heat of his body as he pulled her close and she nestled into him, her head on his shoulder, his arm encircling her. She'd fallen asleep waiting for him. She knew he'd slip into his death slumber soon. She felt him kiss the top of her head and sigh, his body relaxing, as they both drifted into a deep sleep.

The next sound she heard was the soft whir of the shutters, as they opened to the setting sun, and she felt him stir beside her. She was in the habit of getting up at least once during the day to be with Lorenzo, but she'd slept through the entire day. It made her aware of the new life growing inside her. She'd forgotten how much being pregnant had drained her energy, and she wondered, for a moment, how she'd ever keep up with two children. Lorenzo kept both of them running at full speed. She slowly stretched out beside him and felt the glorious pull in her muscles as she raised both arms over her head, and extended her legs, pointing her toes. She felt him nibble at her shoulder as he pulled her closer. She curled back into him, giving in to the feel of him and the warmth of his skin.

"I don't want to get up, lover. I want to stay here all night. I never get you all to myself anymore."

Shade stared at her as she woke and he knew this would be the last time he'd feed from her during her pregnancy, and he wanted the evening he'd planned to be a special one before he once again must feed from Luca. "I feel the same way, but I intend to fix that." His hands tangled in her mass of crimson as he snuggled into her neck and groaned.

She squealed and squirmed as he gripped her tighter and she started to giggle. She rolled on her side, trying to escape as he pulled her close, her back against his chest, as he threw one leg over her. They were both laughing when she saw the scrolled paper on the bedside table next to the long stem rose. She reached for the scroll. "What's this?"

He pulled her away, keeping the scroll just out of reach. "That is a message for my *dolce amore*."

She laughed again as he tickled her, and she lunged for the scroll. "Well, since you left it next to my side of the bed, I guess it is mine now."

She unrolled the scroll and read his hand-penned message, holding the red rose under her nose as she read. "Hmm, I guess *dolce amore* is out of luck, because I'm stealing her invitation for a night out."

Shade loved playing with her, he thrived on these rare moments they were alone. "Everything is taken care of as far as Lorenzo goes. He has a sitter, several as a matter of fact, all capable of handling him. We just need to be alone together, *mi amore*. That time will become even rarer, I am afraid, with Sophia on the way."

Kissing her neck, he wondered if she was up for this venture. Her energy was waning already. "How are you feeling? If this is something that will tire you, then we can easily just do something here at home."

Kate laughed. "Lorenzo is the one who tires me. I'd love an evening away, just the two of us. I love him to pieces, but we never have a minute alone anymore."

As if on cue, there was a tiny rapping at the door. Kate looked at him and shrugged. "Like I was saying..."

Shade tried not to laugh out loud. "Who dares try to enter this warrior's lair?" Shade's voice boomed loudly; as they both awaited the answer. They heard a growling sound from the other side of the door as Lorenzo answered, "It's the dragon!"

Shade looked at Kate and winked. "Quickly, *mi amore*, get

behind me, there is a dragon!"

Lorenzo bursts through the door, both arms extended, his hands claw like as he growled and catapulted himself onto the bed and into his father's arms. "I'm a Medici dragon, Daddy! I will eat all the bad people and fight with the warriors!"

Shade grabbed him up and wrestled with him on the bed. "Well, it seems as though you have become a vicious dragon. Now that you have that in hand, perhaps we should concentrate more on your studies. Mommy has lined up a tutor for you. Learning books is as important as learning dragon skills, *si*!"

Lorenzo was still anxious to play, and Shade held him tight across his chest. "Settle down, I have something to discuss with you, little warrior, while your Mommy is here with us."

Lorenzo stopped his struggle and settled into his father's chest. "What would you like to scuss, Daddy?"

"Discuss." Shade shook his head, chuckling. "Now this is serious, so I need you to listen. Daddy is taking Mommy out on Saturday, for some alone time. Luca, Shannon, and Theresa will be here with you. But, you must be on your best behavior. No dragon fights, no swords. And what is my rule about going outside the house if we are not here?"

Lorenzo threw his hands in the air. "But Daddy! It's warm outside! Uncle Luca can protect me, and Warrior and Aegis. What if something exciting happens and I'm stuck in the house?"

"I know it is warm, but you should be in bed by the time we leave, and no matter what happens, we have rules for your safety. I need my little warrior to be safe. Your baby sister is on her way, she needs you to protect her, so you need to grow into a fine warrior. You will listen to Luca while we are gone, or there will be a great punishment."

Lorenzo struggled from his father's grasp. "Okay, Daddy. I don't want a great punishment. Will I get more cards?"

"If you behave like a good little warrior, of course you will. I will make you a deal."

Throwing his feet over the side of the bed, he realized he was buck naked and quickly grabbed a sheet, tugging it free to wrap around his waist before standing. Lorenzo was already scrambling across the bed to snuggle with Kate, as Shade walked to his dresser, fumbling for something to wear. "I will double the cards if Luca gives me a good report on your behavior."

Looking over his shoulder, he already saw Lorenzo in his mother's arms, snuggling into her neck. "And your mother will not change these rules no matter how much you wish it."

Lorenzo nestled into his mother's embrace as his father left the bed. He whispered to her, "I love you, Mommy," as his mother covered his tousled curls with kisses. He broke free and stood on the bed, jumping up and down. "I think I need a trampoline."

Shade took a deep breath. His son wasn't taking anything seriously lately. "*Bel*, I think it is time you call in Enzo. We need to get our *figlio* on a schedule before the arrival of Sophia."

Kate laughed. "Poor Enzo. Does he know Lorenzo has an attention span of three seconds? I'll talk with Theresa and get it scheduled. I've been working on the school room already."

"*Grazie*! Lorenzo needs to learn how to concentrate. Enzo will teach him those skills. It won't happen overnight. Are the pools completed yet?" He slid a t-shirt over his head, and quickly slipped on a pair of low slung jeans.

"The outdoor pool is scheduled to be finished this weekend, but the indoor pool will take about two more weeks, which is fine. The outdoor pool is the one we'll use first. They'd probably finished sooner without Lorenzo 'helping' the workers so much." Kate slid from bed as Lorenzo continued to bounce up and down. She slipped on a robe and walked to Shade, sliding her arms around his waist. "I don't know where he gets all this energy. And what will we do with two?"

"We will learn as we go, *mi amore*. No one said this would be easy. One day at a time. Theresa is here for you. You do too much, but you must learn to juggle them and cut back. He will never forget he needs you. I have not forgotten, now have I?"

She gave him a squeeze, knowing he'd leave for the camp soon. But she'd be counting down the hours until their private date. "I'd never let you forget."

Spinning around, he kissed her, his arms holding her tight before turning his attention to Lorenzo. "Lorenzo, would you like to go to camp with Daddy tonight?"

Lorenzo responded by jumping higher on the bed, "Yes!"

"Then go get on some shoes, so you can come with me."

Lorenzo didn't need a second invitation. He loved to go to the camp! "Okay, Daddy!"

He leapt off the bed and ran to his bedroom. "Tressa! I need my shoes. Quick!"

Kate laughed at her son's enthusiasm. "I hope your warriors can handle him."

"You let me worry about him tonight. Do something for yourself, that is an order! I will bring him back when he is exhausted, have no fear, I can manage that." Kissing her long and hard with passion boiling, he slapped her ass and headed for the bedroom door.

"Come along son, we have young pups that need to be turned into warriors!"

34

Shade thought Saturday night would never come, but it was finally here, and he was more than ready to take *bel* out for a night alone. The spring evening was beautiful, the air was cool, and everything was in bloom. The scent of newly sprung flowers permeated the night air. He dressed casually in jeans and a white dress shirt, and loafers with no socks. Walking to the garage, he decided to take the red Alfa Romeo Spider. Driving the car to the front door of Bel Rosso, he spotted Aegis and Night Stalker roaming quietly around the grounds, stopping to glance his way. Willing a red rose in his hand, he walked to the front door, holding the rose behind his back and rang the doorbell.

Kate was pulling a light shawl from the closet to carry with her on their date when she heard the doorbell. They weren't expecting company, but she stepped into her sandals and grabbed her handbag before heading down the stairs. She detoured to Lorenzo's bedroom to find Shannon sitting inside the teepee, reading Lorenzo a story. Kate crawled on the floor in her sundress and poked her head inside the tent, "Give Mommy a kiss and be good for Auntie Shannon."

Lorenzo planted a wet kiss on her cheeks and nodded. "Okay, Mommy."

Kate looked at Shannon and said, "I owe you one."

Shannon laughed and said, "You owe me more than one, now get out of here. Go have fun."

Kate backed out of the teepee and heard the doorbell again and wondered why Gi hadn't answered it. She scrambled down the stairs and opened the door to find Shade waiting for her. "Can I help you, sir?" Shade's grin was as big as his head.

She answered the door in a beautiful sundress, and her crimson hair down. She looked relaxed and ready. He bowed his head and pulled the rose from behind his back, presenting it to her. "*Si*, my lady, I am here to escort the beautiful Kate Medici on our date. Is my lady ready?"

Kate took the rose and held it under her nose, smiling up at him. "Lead the way." She took his hand as he escorted her to the bright red sports car.

Opening the door for her, he held her hand and she slid inside, as he fastened her seat belt for her. Once he was satisfied she was safely locked in, he closed her door and walked around, climbing inside the driver's seat. Firing up the Alfa Romeo, he loved the sound of the Italian sports car.

"*Mi amore*, I left the top down, but I can easily put it up if you feel the air is too cool for you. Now, have you decided where you wish to spend the evening?"

"The night air feels perfect, and I think I want to go to the Skybar, so we can be under the stars."

He nodded. "Good choice, it is a beautiful night." Leaning over, he kissed her cheek, and her rose scent overwhelmed him. "You look beautiful, and you smell... edible."

Putting his hand on the gear shift, they took off slowly down the long drive leading away from Bel Rosso. "So, Main Street, Charlottesville, it is. How did Lorenzo take you leaving?"

"Lorenzo was being entertained in the teepee by Shannon. He was fine. He loves Shannon and Luca. He should go to bed soon, so I'm sure he'll be fine."

Kate leaned her head back against the seat as the wind blew through her hair. She was thinking she should have worn it up, as it would be a tangled mess by the time they arrived.

Glancing sideways at her, he saw her running her hand through her hair as it started to blow in the breeze. "You know I love your hair down. So, stop stressing, you look sexy when that crimson blows around your face. I will have to be on my toes tonight. Every damn man in the place will have their eyes on you."

As they reached the main road, he laid his hand on the soft swell of her tummy. "I love you so much, *bel*. When you are with *bambino*, you look radiant. I am like a moth to your flame."

She placed her hand over his. "Yes, well, that moth to flame is what got us in this condition."

He chuckled as he peeled out, heading into town. He took the curves, never slowing down, and Kate gripped the door and the seat and squealed. He drove almost as fast as he teleported. He slowed down as they approached the city limits and drove through town, parking on Water Street. Shade raised the top on the convertible, not wanting to leave the car open in a public parking lot as Kate took a minute to brush her hair and re-apply her lip gloss.

He stepped around the car and opened her door. She took his hand as they walked together toward the open-air mall, already crowded with other people enjoying the return of warm weather and looking for a night out. They walked slowly up the mall, looking in shop windows, before they reached the restaurant. There was a band playing at the far end of the mall, and the music carried on the night air.

As they approached the restaurant, the place was teeming with people. The moon and stars were brilliant in the sky as they entered, and the hostess escorted them to the Skybar that sits atop the popular local restaurant. Shade slipped the hostess a very large tip to secure a small table that looked out over the mall. The hostess flashed him a huge smile as she led them to their roof-top table and told him to enjoy the evening. Pulling out a chair for *bel*, he smiled and kissed her. "My lady."

Sitting across from her, he tried to shut out the thoughts of the men seated around them as their eyes took in Kate who remained oblivious of their stares. Their waitress arrived at the table and was young, and full of energy. He ordered them a bottle of Midnight, informing the waitress they wouldn't be ordering any food tonight. She winked at him, and scurried off, when he felt Kate's hand on his thigh under the table. "I see my date is frisky this night, or are you just claiming what belongs to you?"

She smiled at him, his eyes piercing blue in the festive lights strung over their heads. If they lived a million years, she'd never get tired of looking at him. "Always. I will always claim what belongs to me."

"I belong to you heart and soul. You have shown me true love, in all its forms. Do you have any idea how rare that is? I searched so long, and then this crimson haired minx came along, stumbling over her words, falling over herself when she was around me. It was quite amusing at first, and damn if you didn't make me work for it."

Reaching under the table, he grasped her hand and squeezed it tight. "But once you found your voice, I could not shut you up." Laughing, he watched as the waitress returned with the Midnight, and poured a small portion into his glass. He lifted the glass and sniffed at the thick elixir before taking a sip and nodding his approval. The waitress never took her eyes off of him as she poured the wine into their glasses and set the bottle down, asking him coquettishly if there was anything else he needed. He gave her a quick glance before looking back at Kate and answering, "I have everything I need."

The waitress raised a brow and smiled at him. "Well, just flag me down if you change your mind."

Kate didn't miss the exchange and shook her head as she marveled at the effect he had on women of all ages, as he raised a glass to her.

"I think this special date deserves a toast, *si*?"

Kate lifted her glass to his, never taking her eyes from him, as she whispered, "To us."

They sipped at the wine, oblivious to the sounds of the other couples seated at the nearby tables, as the music from the band drifted on the night air. They sat holding hands across the table, talking about everything and nothing, enjoying the rare opportunity to have an uninterrupted moment.

The night progressed and the moon seemed to have disappeared behind the clouds. He never wanted this night to end. They had so little time alone anymore. Reaching across the table, he let his hand glide along her cheek. "I believe we should take a walk. Perhaps head toward the music, it will probably be ending soon. I have not been this relaxed since..." Chuckling, he winked at her. "Since before Lorenzo's birth!"

She finished the wine in her glass as he left several large bills on the table. Kate pulled the wrap over her shoulders as he placed his hand at the small of her back and guided her through the crowded tables. Their waitress flashed him a mega-watt smile and told him she hoped he'd come back again soon. Kate shook her head and smiled to herself. She didn't miss the fact the waitress's invitation didn't include her! *Dream on, sister. This one is mine.* They made their way down to the brick covered mall, and wandered in the direction of the band.

As he took her hand, they strolled among the young couples out and about at this late hour. A small clap of thunder rang out and he saw a streak of lightening flash across the sky, as they felt the temperature dropping suddenly. The band ended the song and quickly started packing up as the crowd started dispersing.

"I think perhaps there is a storm coming, *mi amore*, you know what this means?"

"An end to this date?"

A sly grin slid slowly across his face as he turned to her and placed his hands around her waist. "Not on your life, woman! It just means this dance I was anticipating, will have to wait until we get back to Bel Rosso."

As she stood on her tip toes, he kissed her with passion as people started to stream past them, in a hurry to get indoors. Leaning in for another kiss, the lightning struck again, lighting up the entire area and he felt her jump in his arms.

"I think perhaps we should head to the car. This storm means business." Grabbing her hand, they began to walk to the car, when suddenly it began to pour, huge sheets of rain falling like a waterfall and there was no escaping it now. He yelled at her over the sound of the pounding rain and earth moving thunder. "Run!"

She grabbed his hand as they ran back down the mall, turning on the side street that led to the parking lot. They were both drenched, their wet clothes clinging to their bodies, as their laughter rang out between the booming thunder. A loud crack of lightning lit up the sky, and they heard a large boom as a transformer was knocked out and the area was thrown into darkness. Kate squealed and squeezed his hand. "Don't lose me!"

"Never happen!"

Their laughter rang out among the many people thrown in absolute chaos in the pitch dark, running and screaming for their cars. But Shade was in his element in the pitch dark, the raging storm arousing something primal inside him, his blood rushing and his beast knocking. He was taken aback by how excited the bastard was. He lifted her into his arms, her legs wrapping around his waist, her arms tight about his neck as he took off running.

As they reached the car, Kate slid down his body as he set her down. He looked at her in the thin cotton dress as it clung to her body, her nipples standing out beneath the material and he had no reservations. The night was dark, and the smell of the rain was like an aphrodisiac. He bent his head to suckle her nipple through the dress and felt the sharp intake of her breath as his warm mouth enclosed her cold, hard nipple.

Kate gasped, and backed up against the hood of the car, her hand in his hair. She looked about, but the parking lot was plunged into darkness, although she could hear the sound of other couples running to their cars. He lifted his face to her, and they kissed, the rain pelting hard, bouncing off the hood, creating its own rhythmic beat.

He laid her back over the hood of the Alpha Romeo, his hand sliding up her thigh, pushing the wet skirt up her hips as he squeezed hard before gripping her panties, ripping them away. His fingers glided inside her as he leaned over her, kissing her fervently, biting her lip and sucking her tongue into his mouth. The storm had unleashed his beast, like a fever that ran in his blood. Shade wanted her, here and now.

She felt the sharp tug as her panties tore away and his hand slipped between her legs. She started to utter a protest when his mouth covered hers and she was swept up in his passion. She wrapped her legs around his hips as he pushed her back on the hood of the car. She clung to his shoulders as she responded to the heat of his tongue as it explored her mouth. She dropped her head back and could feel his lips as they slid down her neck, his tongue tracing the rapid pulse in her veins.

Shade had never taken her in such a public place, but there was something magical in the violence of this storm, and they both felt it. Sliding his hands around her hips, he pulled her closer, as the rain pelted them. Unzipping his jeans, his cock sprung from its cage, hard and ready. Leaning over her, as the rain beat down on his back, he slid his cock home and heard her moan loud and clear as the storm raged around them. He thrust into her as he grabbed her wrists and lifted them above her head, and buried his face in her neck. "Ride the storm with me, *mi amore*."

Kate felt him enter her and she cried out, her voice muffled by the storm. Her body responded to him, matching his timing, their bodies in tune with each other. Her hands pinned over her head, she felt the sharp sting of his teeth as they sank into her neck and he drank from her. She felt the power of him unleashed and knew it was the beast that ruled, as she felt the explosion of heat between her legs that always accompanied his feeding. She struggled to free her hands, and cling to his back, pulling him closer, oblivious to their surroundings. The lightning strike was close, as the thunder accompanied the bright light that turned night to day, flickering on and off, and exposing them to the few stranglers, still making their way to their cars, but she was too caught up in the passion to stop now.

Without thought, the beast took what was his. Sinking his fangs deep, and his cock deeper as her heat encompassed him. The beast encouraged her actions, wanting her beast to come out and play, as he felt her nails dig into his back.

Flashes of lightening revealed quick images of her, lying beneath him, her face contorted in passion as she clung to him and the beast satisfied his lust, her blood filing his mouth and sizzling in his veins. His heart was pounding, and he couldn't get close enough to her. He pulled her into a sitting position as she straddled him, and he pushed deeper inside her. She threw her head back, the water streaming off her face as her hair hung behind her, and he roared into the night.

They surrendered themselves to the violence of the storm, as it matched the power of their passion. She clung to him as he thrusts deep and she cried out as the waves of her orgasm hit her. She dropped her head back, feeling the rain pound her face. The lightning flashed again, and she could see him, his own face contorted in passion as he came deep inside her. She felt his body relax as he laid her back against the hood of the car, his own body draped over her, his breath hot and rapid in her ear.

The explosion of them together gave Mother Nature a taste of her own medicine tonight. Leaning over her, the rain still coming down, he could barely breathe, waiting for his beast to subside. Sliding his hands on either side of her face, he kissed her, knowing this would be the last time he'd feed from her now for months, her pregnancy once again forcing him to seek out Luca. "*Ti amo.*"

Standing, he helped her off the hood of the car and into the passenger seat before walking around the back of the Alpha and sliding into the car. As he slammed the door, another flash lit up the sky as they assessed each other, their hair hanging in wet ringlets, and their clothes disheveled and clinging, as they both broke into laugher, puddles already forming on the floor and seats.

"Good damn thing this interior is leather."

Kate leaned her head against the back of the seat and sighed, reaching for his hand as he started the engine and placed his hand on the gear shift. She shivered slightly as the chill from the wet clothes set in. He leaned over the console and kissed her, pushing the loose strands of hair from her wet cheeks. Breaking the kiss, she stared back at him. "Well, that will give the locals something to talk about."

He couldn't stop laughing as he peeled out of the parking lot and away from the city. "We might as well let them know who rules the night!"

Just as they got out on the highway, the rain seemed to dissipate as the storm moved west. Luca spoke to him telepathically, **"Little warrior was asleep but there was one hell of a storm raging here and he's up now. Shannon is a bit distraught as how to calm him down and he'll have nothing to do with Theresa. Any suggestions?"**

Shade looked over at *bel* and shook his head, water spewing everywhere. "It seems our son is not very happy at the moment."

Kate smiled as she placed her hand on the slight swell of her belly. "Tell Luca to let Warrior get in bed with him and let him know we're almost home. He'll be fine."

Shade kept his eye on the road as he put his foot down, picking up speed as he conveyed the message to Luca, but wanting to get home to Lorenzo.

Kate turned on the heat to take off the chill of sitting in her wet clothes, and sang a lullaby to Lorenzo, telling him to cuddle with Warrior and be her brave boy and she'd be home soon. She felt the child calm himself and knew he was in safe hands. As they approached the long, private drive to Bel Rosso, the lights looked warm and inviting in this home they had created for themselves, filled with all the people they loved.

Shade pulled the car into the garage, exited, and opened the door for her. She slipped into his arms and he held her close, feeling her shiver. Grabbing her hand he led her inside. "Let's get you inside and into something dry."

Theresa greeted them as they entered. "My lady! Are you all right?"

Kate giggled as she knew they were both soaked to the skin. "We're fine, Theresa. How is Lorenzo?"

Theresa smiled. "He's fine. Warrior is in his bed, and he is pretending to sleep so he can get more cards."

They laughed as Shade took the stairs to their bedroom. "Come with me, *mi amore*. A hot shower will warm you up."

They stripped from their wet clothes and stepped into the hot, steaming water of the shower as they washed each other, hands gliding over wet skin.

"Did I tell you how much I love you, Shade Medici?"

He kissed her as the water rinsed away the suds. "I don't

think you have mentioned it, *mi amore*."

He turned off the water as they stepped from the shower, drying each other with the thick towels.

"Then I have been remiss, because I love you more than life." She dried her hair as he kissed her neck and rubbed her rose scented lotion on her back. She followed him back to the bedroom where he slipped on a pair of jeans and she pulled on a soft robe.

"Come. Let's check on Lorenzo. I told him we were on our way home. He'll wait to go to sleep until he sees we're back."

Walking quietly to his room, the door was open just a crack and Shade peeped in. Putting his hand over his mouth to not laugh out loud, he winked at *bel*. Whispering to her, "Someone is definitely playing games. Take a peek."

As Kate moved to the door, Shade stood behind her to watched Lorenzo trying to keep one eye open and the other closed. He followed Kate as she opened the door and went to their son's bed, playing along with Lorenzo's charade of sleep. Warrior jumped off the bed and jumped up on Shade, as his hand went into his furry mane, and he scratched the dog's ears.

Kate sat on the side of the bed and brushed Lorenzo's thick curls back from his forehead, where she kissed him. She whispered, "Lorenzo, are you asleep?"

He answered quietly, "I was sleeping, but Warrior got scared in the storm, so Uncle Luca let him sleep next to me."

Kate smiled at him. "Well, I'm sure that made Warrior feel much better." She tucked the blankets around him as he curled into a warm ball. "Mommy and Daddy are home now, and the storm has passed, so I want you to sleep." She kissed him again on the cheek as he yawned and nuzzled into the soft warmth of the blankets.

"Can Warrior stay?"

Kate patted the bed as the large dog jumped back on the bed, circling several times before lying down next to the small boy.

Shade watched *bel* do what she had always done best; provide comfort to everyone around her. How many times had she comforted him, taken his warriors in hand and made them feel the same? Her compassion and heart were so enormous. As she stepped back, he smiled at her and went silently to the side of his son's bed, letting his hand slide along Lorenzo's back.

"Sleep, little warrior, *Padre* has everything covered."

35

Cory couldn't get Madison off his mind. It was going to be a gorgeous Sunday and he wanted to spend more time with her. He gave her a call and she suggested a picnic. He liked that idea. He'd never been on a picnic with a mortal girl, or any girl for that matter. He checked with Luca to see if he could take out one of the motorcycles and Luca tossed him the keys to his Harley.

Cory retrieved the package wrapped in plain brown paper from his room and stuffed it in the saddlebag. He grabbed a few cords in case Madison packed a basket or something. He wanted to make sure he could accommodate everything. Grabbing an extra helmet, he strapped it on the back and headed into C'ville. The sun was beating down on his back and it felt good. It was going to be a great summer if he had Madison to spend it with.

Parking the Harley on the street, he pulled off his helmet and headed for her door, hoping she wouldn't mind riding on the bike.

Madison couldn't remember the last time she'd been this excited about a boy. She'd made a commitment to herself to stay focused at school, and not get sidetracked. It had been an easy promise to keep since she didn't fit it with the culture of this campus. She put a few bottles of wine, along with some cheese, a couple of pears and some fresh baked French bread into a basket. Grabbing a straw hat, she heard the roar of the engine in her driveway. She peeked out the window to see Cory straddling a Harley, pulling off his helmet, and throwing a long leg over the bike as he kicked the kickstand down with his booted foot. The motorcycle was an unexpected surprise. She ran to the door and opened it before he could even knock, greeting him with a smile.

Cory was surprised when the door flew open and Madison stood there in her usual boho style with a cute hat on her head. Leaning in, he kissed her cheek and then turned to look at the bike. "I hope you don't mind taking the bike? You like to ride? I have a helmet for you."

She flashed him a broad smile. "I love to ride. I haven't been on a bike in a long time. I thought we'd just go up Observatory Mountain. It's not far." She tucked her hat in the basket. "You got room for my basket?"

"Sure do."

Grabbing the basket, he walked to the bike and tied it down. Handing her the helmet, he helped her adjust the strap tight and made sure it was comfortable before putting his helmet back on. "You'll have to tell me how to get there." Straddling the bike, he kicked back the kickstand and looked at her. "Hop on!"

Madison climbed on the bike, sliding her arms around his waist, her chin resting on his shoulder. She gave him some initial instructions as they headed out. It was a beautiful day, and there were a lot of students walking or on bikes. Madison guided him through the campus to the small, winding road that led up the mountain. The mountain laurel was in full bloom. She pointed out a small dirt trail, as Cory left the paved road, slowing down as they entered the trail into the woods. They reached a clearing and Madison indicated this was the spot. He stopped the bike and she slid off, unhooking the basket and pulling out an old quilt that she laid out on the ground.

Cory was a little saddened when they got to the mountain so quickly. He liked the feel of her so close to him, her arms around him. He checked out the area around them and no one was anywhere around. As she spread out a patchwork quilt on the grass, he set the basket down on the quilt and flopped down, patting the spot next to him. "This is a great spot and good view. How did you know about this place?"

Madison shrugged. "It's right on campus, and the observatory at the top belongs to the university. It's really more of a big hill than a mountain, and it's within walking distance, so a lot of the students come here. It's a quiet place, and it doesn't take long to get here. I come up here and read sometimes, or just sketch."

She opened a bottle of wine as she talked and poured them both a glass. "There's cheese, and some pears in the basket. Help yourself."

Cory took some wine and then pulled out a pear. Rubbing it against his jeans, he cleaned it off and pulled out a pocket knife. He carefully cut the pear and held out a slice to Madison, watching as her tongue wrapped around his fingers. He could feel his heart hammering in his chest. This girl had him enchanted. Cutting a wedge for himself, he popped it into his mouth.

"This place is so peaceful. So, what are you going to do when school is over? I mean, do you get the summer off? Are you going home?"

She shrugged. "I'll probably just stay here. I can work on my pottery and build up some inventory for the shops. Next year is my last year, and my class schedule is unpredictable. Besides, I don't like sub-letting my apartment. I don't like people messing with my stuff, you know? And I don't want to have to pack it all up and store it."

She let him feed her the small slices of pear as she sipped on the white wine. Lying back against the tree, she looked up through the branches at the dappled sunlight as it filtered through. "What a beautiful day. I'm so glad you called."

Cory thought about what she'd just told him, she'd be leaving school next year. He wondered if he could possibly hold onto her that long. What if things got serious, would she stay in C'ville after graduation?

"I'm glad you accepted. This was a great idea. Oh, I have something for you!" Quickly getting up, he hurried to the bike and opened the saddle bag, taking out the wrapped package. Walking back, he sat down cross legged next to her, placing the package in her lap. "I made something for you. Go on, open it."

She looked up surprised, wiping the pear juice from her lips. "For me?"

She took the plainly wrapped package, smiling to herself, appreciating that he'd recycled a paper bag instead of buying fancy wrapping paper. Opening the package, she found a leather hand bag with a shoulder strap, adorned with tassels and beads. "You made this? Cory, I love it!"

She stood up and slipped the bag across her shoulder, modeling it for him. "It's the perfect size for me. I carry so much junk!" She dropped back down on the blanket and planted a kiss on his lips.

Cory watched her face and could tell the moment she laid eyes on the bag she loved it. Watching her model it, he smiled but he didn't see the kiss coming. She kissed him and he fell backward, his hands going around her waist as he pulled her on top of him.

He couldn't resist the nearness of her and lifted his head, kissing her lips, slipping his tongue into the sweet warmth of her mouth, tasting the wine she'd just swallowed. She smelled so good, and the sun felt good on his skin. He felt himself falling for her.

Madison returned the kisses, but then broke away and rolled onto her back, lying next to him. She really liked him, but she didn't want things to move too fast.

Cory felt her reticence and tried to fill the void. "I'm taking that as you like the bag? Your laptop should fit in there as well."

"I do love it, thank you. What about you? What will you be doing this summer?" She rolled over on her side, so she could see his face.

Turning his head, he looked at her. "Working mostly and hoping I can spend more days like this with you. My stepmom is having a baby in the fall. That will change things up a bit. I'd like to get some things made for the shops."

He watched as she dumped the contents of her old patchwork fabric purse out onto the quilt and started to transfer the contents to the leather bag. He laughed. "I am beginning to wonder if all your stuff is going to fit in that new bag. What exactly is in there?"

"Stuff for class, my keys, a pair of shades, money when I have it." She laughed, sliding close to him as she pushed the bag aside and pulled his head into her lap, running her fingers through his hair. "Do you mind?"

When he shook his head no, she proceeded to create a single braid close to his face. Pulling odds and ends from the items emptied from her old bag, she wove a few beads and feathers into the braid. When she finished her work, she planted another kiss on his lips.

"There, now you look like we belong together." She immediately blushed as the words left her mouth.

Cory let her do as she pleased with his hair. He loved the feel of her hands on him. She had a very delicate touch and it felt good to have someone paying attention to him. When she kissed him again, he loved how sweet and easy being with her was. There was no pressure to perform. Looking up at her, he liked her blush. She was so naturally beautiful.

"Are you saying we're a couple?" Letting his hand play with her painted toes, he smiled at her.

She smiled and looked away, dropping her head back. "Couple? I've..., I don't know, I've never been a couple. I'm not sure I even know what that means. Are we a couple? I just met you, but I really like you..., a lot."

Sitting up, he took her hand. "Madison, I don't mean to scare you. I don't know if couple is the right word. I know we're friends, but I know I'd like more. Maybe I'm moving too fast. Maybe I want more than what you want to give. All I know is, I never met anyone like you, and I want to spend more time with you." Letting go of her hand, he looked away. "I've never had a tight relationship with a girl before."

Madison loved his directness. She sat up and pulled her knees to her chest. "Well, that's okay. I've never had a tight relationship with a guy before. I had some boyfriends in high school, but nothing serious. And I've tried to stay focused while I was here at school. My mom met my dad in college. She ended up dropping out when they got married, and then she never finished. She says she always regretted that. Not the marrying my dad part, but the dropping out part. She says she wished they'd waited. I know it's going to be hard for me to make a living as an artist, so I'm hoping that getting the degree will help a little. I want to spend time with you too, Cory. But I have to finish school. I have to make that a priority. I hope you can understand."

Scooting up behind her, he stretched out his long legs on each side of her and laid his hands on her thighs. "Work is a priority for me too. My work is just as important to me. School is like a job for you, so I understand. I think if we just go slow, like we have been, things will be fine. I guess I just wonder if some other guy is going to get your attention." Cory grunted. "I sound like an idiot saying that. Sorry."

Madison laughed as she laid her head back against his shoulder and felt him lean his head against hers. "I don't think you have anything to worry about, Cory Medici. Besides, I'm definitely big on monogamy, and I've never bought into the friends with benefits lifestyle that exists on campus."

As she leaned back into him, he couldn't help but smile. He played in her long hair. "I like how we are for right now, and I'm glad we can find time to do things together. Even simple things like this."

Reaching for the wine, he took a chug straight from the bottle before handing it to her. As the afternoon progressed, they ate the cheese and fruit, talked about their art and their dreams for the future. As the sun set, Cory knew he needed to get her home soon. He'd be expected back in the camp. "We should be getting back. The sun is almost set."

"Yeah, I still have some art history homework to finish up tonight."

She started to gather the items and stuff them back in the basket, carefully folding the quilt. "My great-grandmother made this quilt. It's the only thing I have of hers. I love old things, things with a history."

She slung the new handbag over her shoulder as he secured the basket to the bike and threw his long leg over the bike, steadying it for her. She climbed on back and slid her arms tight around his waist. On impulse, she nibbled at his ear and whispered, "I could get used to you."

"That's a good thing because I like being around you. Now

put your helmet on, I want to make sure I get you home safe."

Firing up the Harley, they made their way back to her house and Cory did a few spins around town, delaying the inevitable. Someday, she would be his. He had his mind set on that. As they pulled up to her place, he shut off the bike and climbed off, removing the helmet carefully. Madison handed him her helmet and he untied the basket.

She took his hand and leaned in and kissed him. "I had a great time today. Don't wait too long to call me."

Holding her hand, not wanting to let go, it felt like the day had gone by much too fast. He knew he needed to get home. He had to get into the camp. There was no such thing as a weekend for the warriors.

"Don't worry, I'll call you later. Sweet dreams."

Letting go of her hand, he stood and watched her unlock her door and go inside. Once the door was closed, the grin remained on his face all the way back to Bel Rosso. Returning the bike to the garage, he put away the cords, hung up the helmets and headed for the house, the grin still plastered across his face.

36

Cory left the garage and headed straight for camp. He was a little late getting back. He didn't have regular work hours, but he did try to be in the shop when the warriors were training. That was usually the time they'd choose to stop in for repairs or to talk about new leathers. As he crossed the training field, he saw his dad working with the new recruits from this spring. They'd be making the cuts soon, and then Cory would be really busy. His dad looked up to see him pass, and Cory waved at him, continuing on to his shop.

Shade was barking instructions at a new group that were trying their turn at the bow. It was never his art form, the bow, but he did know how to use one and he tried to instruct with a firm hand. Stepping back to observe, he saw Cory heading for his shop and he stared at his son. *What the fuck is that shit in his hair?* Shade saw Cory's single braid embellished with beads and fucking feathers. Cory threw up his hand to him, as he headed for his shop. Shade nodded but couldn't take his eyes off his son's hair.

Taking a deep breath, he headed in that direction, wanting to know what the hell was going on. Cory had been acting a bit strange for the past few weeks and now this? As he stepped into his shop, one of the warriors was inside talking to Cory. "Out! You can do this later. Your ass needs to be on the field."

As the warrior scrambled from the shop, Cory stared at him and said not one word. He felt his father's tension and knew something wasn't right here.

"We need to talk, son."

"What's wrong? I know I was a little late, but you haven't made cuts yet. I didn't think we'd be very busy."

Shade slid his hand through his hair and leaned against the long cutting table. Crossing his arms over his chest, he stared at Cory's hair. "You tell *me* what's wrong. You seem to be avoiding me lately. And now, you come to work with braids, beads, and fucking feathers in your hair. Cory, there are fucking pink feathers in your hair, son. You need to talk to me."

Cory's hand flew to the braid. He'd completely forgotten the braid. "Oh that, it's nothing. Just...uh, it's really a pink feather?"

Shade looked sideways and squinted. "More than one. So, you think coming to work with pink feathers in your hair is nothing? Is this a new trend, or something else? I know you were close to Raven, and if that's what's going on that's okay. Just spit it out, whatever it is."

"Dad, you think I'm...like Raven? I mean, I love Raven, like a brother but I'm not gay. I let, uh, someone else braid my hair. We were just fooling around, and I forgot it was there."

Shade pushed himself off the table and stood back and stared. "I didn't say you were gay. And if you were, so be it. But now, I'm more concerned. Someone else braided your hair? Elaborate, please."

Cory sighed; he'd hoped to put this conversation off a little longer until he knew where he and Madison stood. "Okay, well, can we talk, you know, man to man, without you going all parental on me?"

Shade walked to a chair and plopped down. He threw his booted feet on the table, crossed at the ankles and lit up a smoke. "First of all, being parental is my job. Get over it. Look, just start from the beginning. Tell me what you think I need to know and I will listen. But, then, I get to talk. Man to man, let it go."

Cory took a deep breath before he started talking. "Okay, well, I went into town with Marcello a few weeks ago. We went to a frat party on campus to, you know, feed. Only, I met this girl. I mean, we were there to meet girls, but not to, you know, meet them."

Cory scuffed his feet. "Anyway, I met this girl I really liked, so we hung out, had coffee and stuff, and I went back to her place. I ended up falling asleep there. I didn't feed from her. I was attracted to her and I wanted her, but I didn't feed or have sex, you know? I didn't want to just feed from her. I didn't want to erase her memory and have her not remember me. So, we just slept. We've seen each other a few times. I was with her all day today. She braided my hair while we were on a picnic. I still haven't made love to her, but I can tell we're headed in that direction. I really like this girl, Dad, a lot. And I don't know what to do because, well, look at me. Look at all of us. How can I let her in? How can I tell her what I am, what we all are? That's why you've seen me talking with Luca. Since Shannon is still mortal, I was hoping he could help me. But I'm so confused and afraid, because she might bolt when she finds out. So there...that's my big secret."

Shade listened to his son and read his body language. He felt him deep inside and knew Cory was far more than gone on this girl. His next words needed to be spoken with love, care, and guidance.

"You could have told me to begin with, Cory. I am not the enemy. I love you, more than you can ever imagine. Going to be honest, it hurts me a bit you went to Luca instead of me, but I can't blame your choice. I know Luca guided you in the right way. I'm proud of you. You showed this girl respect. That shows me how much you care about her and she means something to you."

Shade stood up and hugged his son to his chest. "Relax, we can figure this out together. Luca never saw Shannon coming, and I admit, I feared we would be exposed, but I was wrong. And with Kate, I didn't care if I had to move mountains and pull the stars from the sky for her. Both mortal, and things turned out fine."

Shade released Cory from his arms. "Listen to me. It's still new, and you don't need to expose her to everything at once. You will know when the time is right to tell her what she needs to know and when she needs to know it. Believe it or not, you have it much easier than I did."

Cory looked at him in disbelief. "Easier? Not possible. I see how women look at you, and the warriors all talk. You had experience with women. I've been with men and women, but always for money. Trust me, it's not the same, and never easy.

I've never been with anyone when it was for real, so I feel like a blind man right now. But thanks for listening and understanding. Luca said you'd understand."

Shade chuckled. "I didn't come into this world having experience, I had to learn the ropes like everyone else. I could never have talked to my *padre* like you are talking to me. He arranged for me to be mated once, and if it were not for my *madre*, I would have lived a very different life. You are what you are, a half-breed. You can mingle with mortals much easier than I can, you can eat their food, drink their drink, and appear mortal. Your beast doesn't claw for release when it sees a female you desire. So, you do have some advantages that can give you more time before exposing who and what you are to her. You may feel blind, but you are not. Look around you, there is plenty of guidance here, and we will get you through this when the time comes. In my heart, I know you are struggling, but relax. Take your time, don't expose anything yet. If you have been with her this long and nothing's happened, she wants this to go slow as well. If she starts to push for answers to questions you aren't sure how to answer, come to me. We will go from there, put our heads together and figure out a plan. So, does this female have a name?"

Cory grinned. "Her name is Madison. Madison Barnes. She's an art student at the University, and she's so beautiful. She has long blonde hair and blue eyes, and I can't believe she didn't already have a boyfriend. We have a lot in common. She makes her own pottery, so we both work with our hands. I made her a leather handbag. She really liked it, I think."

Shade smiled. "Did she kiss you when you gave her the bag?"

Cory blushed. "Yeah, she kissed me."

"She liked it, trust me. Just remember, females, whether mortal or immortal, are never easy."

Giving Cory a huge hug, he pounded his back lightly and headed for the door. "Just do me one favor, check your damn hair before you come home and walk in this camp, you will get a lot less ribbing if you do."

Walking out the door, he could almost hear Cory sighing with relief. Shade lit up another smoke. This father shit was going to turn him gray.

37

Shannon walked through the lavender fields with Kate, as Lorenzo was clinging to her hand, talking non-stop. It was another beautiful day with clear skies and a bright sun, making the thick new growth on the plants appear even greener. Kate had just informed her she was pregnant again, and as happy as she was for her friend, her first thought was, she'd have to share Luca...again.

She walked in silence, looking at her feet as they stepped carefully between the rows of lavender. Last year, Kate had opened a farmer's market, a cooperative among local farmers nestled between the many vineyards spotted throughout the Virginia countryside. The Bel Rosso Vineyards had gained a strong reputation for their quality wines and was a big draw for tourists who were drawn to the wine country. In addition to the beauty of the vineyards, the tourists drove past the horse pastures where the thoroughbred horses grazed, and the brilliant fields of bright yellow sunflowers growing next to the mounds of purple, as the soothing scent of lavender filled the air. Kate had sold some of the fresh flowers in the market, along with a section dedicated to the wines that were sold to the mortal market and had extended an invitation to local farmers to sell their fresh produce. It was good business for the farmers, but really good business for Bel Rosso.

Shannon remembered asking Luca about the decision to allow mortals such access to the property, even though the vineyards and fields of flowers were located in a direction away from the main house and the camp. He'd smiled and reassured her that the best strategy had always been to hide in plain sight of the mortals. They had enough security on the property to be alerted immediately if anyone wandered onto the sections of their property marked as private.

Kate was watching her friend, and saw she was lost in thought. "Did you hear me? I'm pregnant again. It will be a girl this time. Sophia."

Shannon looked at her and smiled. "Sorry, yes, I heard you. I was just lost in the beauty of this day." She stopped and gave her friend a hug, as Lorenzo pulled at her shirt-tail. "I'm so happy for you, for both of you. I know this is what you've always wanted."

Kate returned the hug but felt her reticence. "Are you okay, Shannon? With…you know, the whole feeding thing?"

Shannon shrugged her shoulders. "Of course…"

Kate looked closely at her friend's face. She'd known Shannon a long time, and knew she wasn't speaking her mind. "So, what are you not saying, Shan?"

Shannon stopped walking and picked up Lorenzo, balancing him on her hip as she turned to Kate. "Please understand I'm sincerely happy for you. And I understand the feeding situation. I've come to terms with it. But I sometimes wonder…I just wonder, when will it be my time?"

Kate reached for Lorenzo as he squirmed in Shannon's arms and lifted him to her own hip. "What do you mean, your time? You can't possibly doubt how Luca feels about you."

"No, I know he loves me. I've never questioned that. But we've been together over three years now. I'm still mortal, and he never speaks of turning me. He never really refers to our future, other than to say he'll love me for eternity. But I don't know what that means anymore."

Kate stood quietly and listened, feeling her closest friend's doubt. "Shannon, have you ever asked him? Have you asked to be turned?"

She shook her head no. "I just figured if he wanted that, if he really wanted eternity with me, he'd bring it up. I don't think I should have to ask."

Kate bit her lip and placed her hand on Shannon's arm. "Turning a mortal isn't something they take lightly. The process itself is dangerous. The mortal may not survive. It's a big decision, for both the vampire who must turn you, and the mortal being turned. Of the thousands of vampires I've met or seen since coming into Shade's life, only a handful weren't born vampire. Talk to him. I know Luca's heart, he's a man of honor and loyalty above all else. He may be waiting for you. He may need to know this is what you want too. I know he'd never pressure you to take this path. And if he has reservations, he'll tell you. Talk to him, Shannon."

Shannon nodded yes. "I will. I know you're right. But what if...what if he does have reservations? This life with him, it's both charmed and cursed. You told me that once, and I didn't understand. But having been with him now for so long, I get it. But Kate, there's no way I'd go back. I can't imagine a life without Luca."

Kate leaned her head against Shannon's, as the soft wind blew through their hair, mingling the bright red with her light brown locks. She kissed Shannon's cheek. "Then tell him."

The women hugged, with Lorenzo squeezed between them, as his hands tangled in their hair. Kate broke the hug and took her friend's hand. "Come on. Let's walk back to the house. Lorenzo and I can check on the progress of the pools, and you can go find Luca."

38

Shannon entered through the back door of Bel Rosso, stepping over some of the remaining tools and equipment that were used to put in the new outdoor pool. The pool was accessible from the patio, allowing you to step down into the crystal clear water. The deep end of the pool was designed to blend into the landscape, with large flat landscape rocks that overhung the edge of the pool, and thick plants that created a rich garden around the rocks. One side of the pool had a long pergola built over the new patio, and had wisteria planted, which would soon be climbing the pergola, creating a canopy of dark foliage and flowers.

Entering the house, Shannon encountered Gi who nodded in her direction. "Luca is in the bunker, Miss Shannon."

"Thanks, Gi. You read my mind."

The ancient butler smiled as he passed her in the hallway, and she headed in the direction of the stairs leading to the underground bunker, as well as the new indoor pool. Luca was emerging from the doorway, brushing dirt from his jeans as she approached. Looking up, he flashed a mega-watt smile that never failed to make her heart skip a beat.

"*Mia belleza.* Looking for me, I hope."

Taking his hand, she beamed back at him. "I was. Do you have time for me, right now?"

He pulled her close and kissed her. "For you, always. What's on your mind?"

Shannon's smile faded as she shifted gears, realizing the serious nature of their talk. Leading him into his suite, she plopped down on the sofa, as he sat beside her. He brushed the hair back from her face, noticing the hint of sun on her cheeks, and picking up the fresh scent of lavender. He knew she'd been walking in the fields of flowers.

"Talk to me, Shan. I see concern in your eyes."

She sighed as she lay back against the sofa. "You see

everything in my eyes."

He chuckled. "Well, not everything. If I could see everything, I'd already know what's troubling you. Talk to me, *mia belleza*. Whatever it is, we can fix it, yes?"

Shannon stared back into those pale hazel eyes, in sharp contrast to his dark, olive skin. "I talked to Kate today. She told me she's pregnant again."

He nodded at her, never breaking eye contact. He knew how much she struggled with Kate's first pregnancy, and the fact Shade had to come to him for feeding. "Are you not happy for them?"

She closed her eyes tightly. "You know I am. I want only the best for them. Kate is like a sister to me. But Luca...when is it our turn?"

Luca leaned in to her, his lips brushing her cheek, his breath hot against her ear as he whispered, "Tell me what you need, *mia belleza*. If it is mine to give, I will give it."

Shannon melted under his spell, and swallowed hard as she answered, "You talk about eternity for us, but you never mention turning me. I need to know what you see for us. I need to know where I fit in."

He felt her inner turmoil and took her hand, placing it on his chest over his heart. "You fit here, *mia belleza*. Here, in my heart. I have moved slowly with you. I needed you to see my life, understand my life. It's rich in many ways, but restricted, and yet there is nothing I would change. I needed you to find your own way here. Understand my role, my obligations and commitment to this coven, to my master. I needed to make sure you could share this space with me. I'd never ask to turn you. It's too great a sacrifice to ask of any mortal. It's something you had to desire for yourself. Something you had to accept with no pressure from me to do so, because there's no turning back. I think of it often. But it has to be your choice, not mine."

She placed her hands on either side of his face and spoke softly, "How could you ever doubt this isn't what I'd want?"

He kissed her lightly, his lips barely touching hers. "I never doubted your love. Never. But I have watched you struggle with our lifestyle. I know you accept Shade feeding from me, but I also know it pains you. I feed from you, so I feel your pain, *mia belleza*. There are still challenges for us. There is this new baby, and Kate has foreseen a third. Shade will come to me to feed with each pregnancy."

She nodded her head. "I know that. I can deal with that, Luca. Did you think my attitude about that would change?"

He shook his head. "No, but if I were to turn you now, then I couldn't feed both of you. Shade is a master, and a warrior. His body demands much blood from me. I couldn't sustain you both. You, too, would need to feed from someone else while Kate was pregnant."

Shannon stood suddenly from the couch, pacing in front of him. "What? Luca, I wouldn't want to feed from anyone else. I love *you*!"

He reached out and touched her hand. "It's another reason I haven't approached you. It's not impossible for us to do. You could rely on the feeders when I'm committed to Shade. The concept isn't foreign to me, but I know it would feel awkward for you."

She looked at him with surprise. "Awkward! Awkward doesn't begin to describe it. It's not just the feeding, but the whole sex thing."

He tugged at her hand, pulling her back down on the sofa beside him. "I've thought about this a lot, Shannon. We should probably have discussed it sooner. I shouldn't have left you guessing. But my thoughts were to wait until all three babies were born. Shade will no longer need to come to me, and you wouldn't need to seek another. For an immortal, this is but a moment in time, but I realize, for you, I'm asking you to wait several more years. Is that too much to ask, *mia belleza*?"

She turned her head and looked at him. "And in the meantime, Luca?"

"In the meantime, I will talk to Shade. He knows my heart, and yours. He won't stand as an obstacle in our future. I will ask his permission for you to feed from me. That will seal our blood covenant. And once the last baby is born, I will turn you."

Her hand brushed his cheek. "The blood covenant. Will it change me?"

He shook his head. "Yes and no. You'll be bound to me. You'll feel my emotions, but not as strongly as I feel yours. It will start to prepare your body for the turning, making you stronger. Say yes, Shannon, and I'll talk to him. Asking Shade's permission is only a formality now. We've been together so long. Say yes, and you can feed from me, be bound to me. Move here, live with me."

She sat up straight on the sofa. "Wait...move here? I have a job, and you just said it could be years before you could turn me."

Luca shook his head in frustration. "Shannon, these are just details. You don't need to work. I can take care of us."

She stood and started pacing again. "But I like my job. And what would I do?"

His eyes followed her as she walked back and forth in front of him. She was strong-willed. It was one of the characteristics he was drawn to, but he knew she wasn't a woman who'd sit idle at home and be taken care of. "We'll find a solution, Shan. If you need to work, we can figure something out. If you need to maintain the charade, then keep your condo in Alexandria. I or one of the other warriors can teleport you back and forth. These are just details. The bigger question here is whether this is what you want, the blood covenant, the turning."

Shannon stood still and let the memories of the past three years float through her head. Every memory of pleasure and beauty and joy had been a moment with Luca. She couldn't even envision a future that didn't include him. "It's what I want. It's the only thing I want."

He stood and pulled her to his chest, kissing the top of her head. "Then you'll be mine, *mia belleza*."

39

Shade walked slowly around the perimeter of the training field, it was well past midnight and there was a lot to get done with the new recruits. He lit up a smoke, keeping an eye on the young ones now in his charge. His mind wasn't completely on the task at hand. Hell, he couldn't even remember the last time he was on the streets fighting, getting bloody and kicking some rogue ass. A part of him missed the action, but he knew he was where he was supposed to be in his life.

Looking up, he sensed something coming in his direction and saw the arrow aimed straight at him. He ducked his head to the side as the arrow whizzed past him. He glanced immediately to the source of the arrow and found a young male warrior, cringing in terror, his eyes bugging out of his head. "Not a good idea to kill your master!" He shouted with aggravation.

Throwing up his hand, he motioned to the warrior he was fine and watched him slink back to his group. Shade shook his shaggy mane. Only a few years ago, he would've killed the young bastard.

Luca entered the camp, looking for his master. With the new recruits in training, he knew if he wanted to talk to Shade he'd have to track him down here. He saw him duck the errant arrow that was on a misguided course for his head, and watched as the young recruit went pale. Luca had to laugh to himself. He remembered his own days of training in the camp at Castello, and how long it took them all to become proficient. Luca approached his master with a smile. "I see some things never change, master."

Chuckling, Shade threw Luca the pack of smokes and nodded to him to take a squat beside him. "And I was just sitting here thinking about how I missed being on the streets, hell, I think this is worse, they are supposed to be on my side."

Leaning back against the wall, giving Luca a sidelong glance as he lit up, Shade knew something was up. Luca only sought him out in the camp when he needed to talk. "Everything all right at the house?"

Luca nodded as he inhaled deep on the cigarette before letting the smoke escape his lips, tossing the pack back to his master. "Yeah. All good. Lorenzo had to make a last minute inspection of the workers on the indoor pool before Kate put him to bed. You got a minute?"

Shade took a long look at Luca, the most valuable vampire warrior in his life. Luca had something on his mind, but Shade couldn't get a read on it. "For you, I have all the time in the world. Spit it out."

Now that he was here, Luca wasn't sure where to start. "It's about Shannon. She's been with me now for over three years, and I feed only from her. I've done all you asked of me, and we've moved slowly. We needed to know if she could accept our lifestyle, and I think she's proven she's up for the challenge. I'm here to ask your permission to allow her to feed from me, to seal our blood covenant. I've discussed this with her, and I think she's ready for this next step. I wouldn't ask to turn her until the third child Kate has foreseen is born. That way, Shannon won't be placed in the position of having to feed from another. It's time, master, and with your permission, I'd like to seal my bond with her."

Shade listened carefully while keeping his gaze on the warriors training on the field. Luca was right, his relationship with Shannon had been a long one, and Kate's best friend had taken all the obstacles in stride. Shade slid his hands through his curls as he grunted. "You have shown great patience, Luca, I could not have waited that long for *bel*."

Shade pulled his long legs up to his chest and rested his elbows on his knees. "She understands what this entails? The bonding, the turning? This is not a game and she needs to know what will happen to her. There is great pain for her in the turning, and it is not without risks."

"She's aware, master. And I'm sure she will discuss it in detail with Kate when the time comes. But she has assured me this is what she wants. And I think you know it's what I want.

From the moment I saw her, I knew she was the one. It was the same for you, was it not?"

Shade grinned with memories of his *bel rosso*. "*Si*, the moment I saw her and that fiery red hair. She grabbed my heart and never let go. If someone had told me I would fall in love with a mortal female, I would have laughed my ass off."

Standing, Shade reached down and grabbed Luca's hand, pulling him upright. "I won't give you an answer until we talk with Kate. We make all decisions together and I want her to be with us. Let's go up to the house and have a drink, see if she can join us and talk, *si*?"

Luca stood beside his master and his oldest friend, as they turned to walk back to the house. He knew Kate would offer no objection to this union. Entering the house together, Emma informed them Kate was in Shade's office, on a conference call with Reynaldo and Mica over plans for the peak tourist season for the inn in Napa.

Nodding to Emma, he and Luca proceeded to the office. "That would be my queen, making money hand over fist."

As they entered the office, Shade strolled in and saw Kate sitting in his large leather chair behind his desk, and he chuckled. She looked like a small girl in that huge chair. Walking to the bar, he poured two large tumblers of Midnight, handing one to Luca. Standing with his ass against the bar, he sipped and listened to her conversation.

Kate looked up as her mate and her protector entered the room and she smiled at them. She quickly wrapped up the conversation with Mica and turned the chair to the two men. "To what do I owe the pleasure of this visit? It's so rare to have the attention of both of you."

"It's your lucky night, *bel*. Are you comfortable?"

She laughed. "I'm quite comfortable. But please, bring me only good news."

Shade stepped closer to the desk and leaned in to Kate, going nose to nose with her. "I think, *mi amore*, you would be much more comfortable sitting in my lap in that big chair, *si*?"

He kissed her lips gently and gave her a smile and a wink.

She stood as they switched positions, Shade settling in the chair, and Kate curling up in his lap. Luca took a seat in the leather arm chair near the desk.

"What have you come to discuss? What's important enough to bring you both?"

His hand went immediately into her crimson, letting the silken strands curl softly around his fingers. "Luca has come this night to ask permission for something. I wish not to answer him alone but for us to give our decision together. Do you wish to ask her, Luca?"

Luca leaned forward in his chair. "I asked my master for permission to allow Shannon to feed from me, to seal the blood covenant."

Kate sat up straight and looked quickly at Shade and back at Luca. "Why are we even discussing this? Have you asked Shannon? If this is what you both want...why are we having this conversation?"

"Relax, *mi amore*. We are discussing this because it is serious business, this blood covenant. Shannon has agreed, of course. And, eventually, she will be turned, as were you. That is a big obligation for them both. Luca is only following orders. He must ask his master first before bonding with another. But I think, perhaps, you do not realize everything Shannon will have to endure."

Kate looked at him with surprise. "I realize better than most what she'll have to endure. What do you mean?"

Shade's gaze fell on Luca before turning back to Kate. "I feed from Luca when you are pregnant, *bel*. This has been a struggle for Shannon, as it was for you when you were mortal. Luca can't feed Shannon and I at the same time. They have made the choice to bond now, but to wait for Shannon to be turned until our last child is born. Shannon can survive on mortal nourishment through that period. This is a big step for them both, and I have one concern."

Peering back at Luca, Shade locked eyes with him. "If you have a blood covenant, you will feel her more intensely, and she will need to be with you more frequently. I think it is time we look at the living arrangements. You will have little time to go back and forth to Shannon. We need you here, Luca, and once Sophia is born, more so."

Luca nodded. "I want her here. I asked her to move in with me if you agreed to the covenant. She knows we'll not move forward with the turning until the third child is born, and she knows that could be a few years away. The time is of no consequence to me, but Shannon is concerned about her job, and what she'd do if she moved here. I don't have all the answers, but I assured her we could find a solution. I or one of the other warriors could teleport her to her condo if she feels the need to keep a presence in her mortal life."

Kate stood from Shade's lap and walked about the office, deep in thought. "Lover, you once suggested to me I expand my business interest, develop my own brands for the lavender and sunflower oils. I wasn't interested in taking on more projects, especially with the demands of the children. But Shannon could do this. She'll be a part of our coven soon, a part of our family. Why not make her a partner in this business? I can think of no one better to expand on what I've already created."

Shade watched her pace back and forth. He knew that expression of determination. He glanced at Luca and winked, steepling his fingers together. "I have always thought you would enjoy expanding what you so carefully created, *mi amore*. And since Shannon worked with you at the ad agency, I think she would be an excellent partner. If she accepts, she would be a welcome addition to this house, not only for Luca's comfort but yours as well. I know you miss her, and so does Lorenzo."

Shifting his gaze to Luca, he inquired, "Can your suite accommodate Shannon? And what is your take on this idea *bel* has come up with? Do you think Shannon will agree to this? I know it will be a big change for her, but I would prefer she reside here with us. There are benefits to all of us if she did."

Luca sighed with a sense of relief. He knew his master wouldn't throw up any barriers, but it was still a weight off his shoulders to have his approval. "We never discussed any other alternative to her working, but I know how much she loves Kate. I know they'd work well together. We can certainly present this idea to her. As for my suite, it's more than large enough for the two of us, and provides us with privacy, especially if she has free rein over the rest of the house."

Kate beamed at him. "Of course! This would be her home as well, just as it is yours."

Shade smiled at Kate's happiness and knew deep inside, she missed her best friend. He beckoned her onto his lap. She snuggled against his chest and kissed his neck softly.

"So, shall we say yes or no to Luca and Shannon sealing the blood covenant, or do you wish to see, first, how Shannon will respond to our offer?"

"Yes, to the blood covenant, regardless of whether she decides she wants to be a part of our businesses. It's time for her to seal her covenant with Luca."

Shade grinned at her and kissed her. Looking at Luca, he nodded his head and smiled. "Luca, you officially have our permission to seal the blood covenant with Shannon. I thank you for being patient. Our lives have interfered with yours greatly. Don't tarry on getting this done. The time is coming soon when I will need to feed from you. But, I will say one thing. Do this when the time is right, in the right place, wherever that is. This will be a great night for you when it happens. If you need some time off, to be alone, just let me know. We can arrange things here in your absence. I am proud of you and your choice. She is a beautiful and intelligent female."

Luca felt like his life was just beginning, knowing Shannon would now hold a permanent place in it. He couldn't wait to tell her, and to bring her here to Bel Rosso to live.

Shade pulled Kate from his lap and stood, going to Luca, and gave him a hug. "Go, find your female, tell her the good news, and what we have offered. Get back to us when you know something."

Luca seemed lost for words as Shade watched him head out the door of his office.

"It never ceases to amaze me how you seem to make

everything perfect in my warriors' lives." Kissing her with passion, he grabbed her hand. "Come along, *mi amore*, I wish to check on our son."

40

Shade teleported over Washington, D.C. It had been a while since he'd made the rounds over the political city, teeming with people on the move. He hovered over Georgetown, his old territory when he first took over protection for Alec. He was pretty sure he knew the reason Alec has requested this meeting, since the dream-walking sessions had been completed for some time now.

He landed, unseen, outside the home of the Cantons. As he raised his hand to ring the bell, Santos opened the door and nodded. "Master Shade, you will find Master Canton in his study. He is waiting for you."

Shade smiled at the ancient butler. The old bastard had been with Alec for eons, he had to be older than Gi. He strolled to Alec's study and found the door open. Rissa was just leaving as she paused, arms crossed over her chest, a smirk on her lips.

Shade nodded. "Mrs. Canton."

He watched as she unfolded her arms, cocked her hip to one side and blurted out in a sarcastic tone, "Shade, big bad ass warrior. You kept Alec waiting, very rude."

Shade grinned and leaned into her ear. "The King is worth waiting for."

Rissa slapped his arm and tried to move from Shade, but he blocked her path. "By the way, nice work. I am assuming since Alec called me here, you fucked his way into the campaign."

Rissa growled and raised her hand to slap him when Shade shook his head. "I wouldn't if I were you, I can take Hyde away any time I like, and I think you might need him."

Winking, he turned his back to her and headed into the study. He could hear her stomping out of sight.

Alec overheard the ongoing quarrel between Rissa and Shade and shook his head as he poured Shade a drink. There was certainly no love lost between those two. "Come in, brother. Have a seat." Handing Shade the glass, he nodded toward a chair. "We have some business to discuss."

Shade took the drink and swirled the dark sweet elixir around in the glass. Settling himself in a chair, he grinned. "So, what the hell is going on, brother? I am assuming this is about the campaign." Shade took a deep drink and then locked eyes with Alec. "Are you really going to go through with this?"

Alec sat across from him, lighting up a cigarette. "I had my little meeting with Ashton, showed him the feed from the cameras we had planted. That was all it took. I told him I could destroy the footage, or destroy his career. His choice. The old man broke down and cried, begged me not to expose him. It was all pretty easy after that. He has a special press conference scheduled to announce he won't run for a second term due to some health issues. As soon as it's official, I'll announce my intentions, and then we'll start with the campaign. That's where you come in."

Shade sat forward in the chair, leaning his elbows on his knees, his drink still in his hands. "Well, D.C. is covered, brother, no matter what. Rest easy with that one. Fill me in, what do you need? And be specific."

Alec took a deep drag on the cigarette, exhaling the smoke. "Once I announce, I'll need to get on the campaign trail. I won't be the only one vying for this position, so I want to get out there quickly. I'll need to take Rissa with me. Having a wife with you on the campaign is important. People want to see that. So, we're going to need to have Hyde available to travel with us. I'll use Alto as my driver, even when we're in one of those god-awful campaign buses. He's always acted as my bodyguard in key situations, and he's good, but he's not warrior bred. I think I'll need more security than he's trained to handle. Plus, I'll be leaving the safety of my own territory. The mortals won't see anything, but I'll have to operate inside the territories of other masters to campaign. So, I need another warrior to watch my back. He'll have to be clean cut, like Hyde. Someone who's skilled yet polished and who can blend in with the crowd. You got anyone that fits the bill?"

Shade stood and paced back and forth, getting himself

another drink before answering. "Well, I trust you know what the hell you're doing going into other master's turf. Bro, you need to make sure they know you are coming and why. That could get really ugly. Hyde is no problem. He is in." Shade ran through his roster of warriors in his head, weighing each of them as a potential candidate to serve as a protector for Alec.

Alec nodded, sipping at the Midnight. "It goes without saying he'll need to be a day-walker, and he'll need to be male. I can't have the distractions of another female around, especially with Rissa. I can't afford to have the press see her pissed off over my bodyguard. Some of the events will be in the evening, but a lot of the campaigning is done during the day. I already have my campaign manager working on a schedule. He'll run interference with the other masters; let them know where I'm going to be. Braden ran my Senate campaign. He knows what he's doing."

Shade took his seat once again. "I have a warrior in mind. Mateo, he has been with me a long time. He has long hair, but he can keep it pulled back, tall, damn good warrior. Has a good street sense, and he can handle anything that comes at him. He trained at Castello since he was a boy. He helped Marco quite a bit before I brought him to the States. He knows Hyde as well, and they both work well together. Do you need to meet him before I assign him? "

Alec shook his head. "I'm no judge of warriors. You know what I need, and I trust your judgment. We'll be on the road several days at a time. I'll be coming back home for brief periods, and the campaign will last a good eighteen months. Just make sure I have the same person for the duration, so they learn my schedule, how I operate, how I work the crowds. If Mateo is your choice, that's good with me. Although, if his hair is long, then I think he'll have to cut it. This is a conservative party. He can always grow his hair back after I'm elected."

Shade sat back. "Mateo can cut his hair, he cleans up well. He will be informed he takes all direction from you, as does Hyde. Damn, eighteen months? I will be a *padre* again before this is over. You know I will have to take Kate back to Castello for the birth, but that won't interfere with any of your plans. Everything will be in order while I am gone. Theo is over the Dead House, Raven is in California and Marcello is in charge at the camp. Mateo and Hyde can handle this, and if they need back-up, they have plenty of resources. Besides, I doubt Rissa would leave if I said Hyde couldn't go along." Shade chuckled at the rib and emptied his glass of Midnight.

Alec grunted. "You'd have a hard time ever getting Hyde away from Rissa. I'm not blind to her devotion to him. Whatever works, brother. She's happy with him, and they seem to get along, so let's not mess with that. As for Mateo, have him call my campaign manager, Braden. He has my full schedule, and Braden can give him all the information he needs. I'll need to get started within a week, so no time to lose."

Shade stood his full height and set the empty glass on the polished wood table beside the chair. "I will call Braden, get the schedule. I usually have complete instructions in a folder when I give my warriors an assignment. It's how I operate. Everything they need to know for the assignment, and then there are no questions if something happens. They have written proof of what their objectives and obligations are. Hyde and Mateo will be ready when you are. Whenever you return back to D.C., let me know if you want Mateo to stay on duty with you, or whether he can return to Bel Rosso. Anything else you need?"

Alec stood and slapped Shade on the back. "I think that covers it, brother. Now, wish me luck that I can win the vote. Otherwise, all this was for nothing."

Shade looked at him and shook his head, laughing. "Your ass better win this, brother, I have a camp of young punks I'm whipping into shape to take on the White House. Get busy and do what you do best."

They fist bumped and Shade turned to leave the study. "No need to see me out, I can manage." As he walked to the front door, he stopped at the staircase and yelled loudly, knowing Rissa would hear him. "Have a lovely evening, Mrs. Canton."

As he headed for the door, he laughed like hell when he heard a shrill angry voice floating down the stairway. "Get out, you big mongrel!"

Shade shut the door behind him. "Bitch!"

41

Shade sat in his office having summoned Hyde and Mateo, two folders in front of him for the warriors who'd receive their assignment for Alec. This wasn't going to be an easy assignment for either of them. Hyde was already in the thick of it and Shade was certain he knew what lay ahead, but for Mateo, this would be a different ball game. Mateo had been with Shade a long time, raised in the camp at Castello, and one of the best. He'd been in the States a few years now, and was no stranger to the culture. He'd been Marco's right hand man before he was assigned to Bel Rosso, but he'd soon be on the road with Alec and Rissa.

Shade heard the soft knock on the door and knew his two warriors had arrived for the meeting. "Enter."

Hyde strolled in first, dressed casually, and clean cut. Shade was amazed that Hyde had stuck it out this long as Rissa's personal protector. It took more patience than any man should have to endure to put up with that wicked bitch's antics and attitude, but Hyde and Rissa seemed to have formed a bond.

Mateo entered behind Hyde and closed the door. He took the leather chair beside Hyde positioned to face the large desk. Shade looked across the desk at both of them and almost laughed out loud at the differences between the two. Mateo was still in leathers, and a complete contrast to Hyde in every aspect. His dark brown hair was long, hanging well past his shoulders. His facial hair made him look even more intimidating, and his brows heavy over intense brown eyes. Shade had seen him clean shaven a few times, but he almost always sported some type of facial hair or at the very least, a five o'clock shadow. His 6'2" frame was muscular. He wasn't meant to blend in with a crowd. There was no mistaking his presence, wherever he went. Mateo was the quiet type, but never misjudge his quiet demeanor.

Shade stood from behind the desk and went to the bar,

pouring out three large tumblers of Midnight. "I don't suppose my calling you here tonight is of any great surprise to either of you. I appreciate you coming and I won't hold you up too long."

Handing the two warriors their drinks, he grabbed his own glass and returned to the desk. He pushed two large folders across to them, filled with details on everything they'd need to accomplish on this assignment. "Inside are the details. Senator Alec Canton and his wife, Rissa, are going on the campaign trail. Of course, they must appear as mortal at all times. He has made the announcement he will be running for President of the United States this coming election. With that being said, this is going to be a circus."

Shade's eyes went to Hyde. "Hyde, as Rissa's protector, your assignment doesn't change. As always, you take all direction from Master Alec. Keep her out of Alec's hair as much as possible. We clear?"

Hyde knew this was coming and had been prepared. He knew this would be a challenge and he was ready for anything she could throw at him. Hyde could handle her. "Clear. Leave her to me, master. She responds to me well, most of the time."

Shade lit up a cigarette and nodded to Mateo. "Master Canton was very specific on what he wanted for his personal security, so I chose the warrior I thought would fit the bill. You are one of my best. Alec will be entering other masters' territory and he has made all the arrangements, but I don't have to tell you, none of them like him appearing as a mortal in such a public way. Our community feels he risks exposing us all by his antics to appear mortal. He expects no trouble, but if there is, you'll know what to do."

Shade emptied his glass of Midnight as Mateo nodded, scanning the documents in his folder. "There is one problem we will have to address, and that is your appearance. There is no delicate way to put this. You need to lop off that head of hair, as well as get rid of your facial hair. I could give a damn about it, but this assignment calls for brawn without beast. Your face could appear in papers, on news channels, so appearance is everything. You go everywhere they go. You are his personal warrior. I expect you to show him the respect he deserves. We clear?"

Mateo sat listening as his master gave him the details of the assignment. He wasn't surprised by anything he had to say. Cutting his hair and shaving his beard was no problem for him, it was part of the assignment. Mateo knew Canton was nothing to sneeze at, he knew his reputation. He had no opinion one way or another about Canton's life or his campaign, but he did know how to protect a great master. "Everything's clear, master. When do we report for our assignment?"

Shade nodded at Mateo's acceptance. He didn't think he'd give him any grief. "Just a few basic details. You both will be given a large clothing allowance. No leathers on this trip. So you need to be kitted out with proper clothing before you leave. Alec will expect his security detail to be in suits. You will take whatever weapons you feel necessary from Bel Rosso. You report in one week to Canton. Time, date and place are in your folder. You will be on the road for much of the time, with short trips back to D.C. Report back to Bel Rosso whenever you return. You will need to feed here. No hunting while on the road. You have to appear mortal, never forget that. Even if something goes down, remember he will be surrounded by the press. Never expose your skills to the mortals. Can't stress that shit enough. Unless you have any questions, I think that is it."

Hyde answered for them both. "We've got this." As they stood both warriors fist bumped him. "Medici *per sempre*."

Hyde and Mateo left the office together. As they got outside the door, they looked at each other. Hyde laughed and slapped Mateo on the back. "Don't worry, brother. I have the hard part of this one."

42

Madison stood in front of her closet, trying to decide what to wear. She'd been asking Cory for some time now about his family and where he lived. Cory always came to her place, but she'd never seen where he lived. Cory referred to his family frequently but didn't really reveal much. She knew he was living with his biological dad and his stepmom, but other than that, she didn't know anything about them.

She pulled things from her closet and tossed them on her bed. She felt pressure to make a good impression and she bit at a nail. Looking back at her closet, she sighed. She didn't have anything very traditional in her wardrobe. Putting her hands on her hips, she shrugged. "Oh well, this is who I am. They might as well get used to me from the start."

She selected an old ivory lace dress she'd bought in a thrift shop and paired it with a western belt and an old pair of cowboy boots. She layered on some silver jewelry and checked her hair in the mirror. Her dark blond locks hung in loose tendrils past her shoulders, and no matter how much she brushed it, her hair always looked a little wind-blown. She grabbed the leather bag Cory made for her and slung it over her shoulder just as she heard his truck pull into the driveway.

Cory made his way to Madison's apartment, the gravel making a crunching sound under his feet, his nerves on edge. This was a big step for both of them. He knew his dad wouldn't meet her during this visit as he'd be in his death slumber, and Cory was never more thankful. He still had the rest of the household to deal with, though. Both his dad and Kate had assured him, they were used to dealing with mortals, and they'd support him in every way possible.

As he approached her door, he took a deep breath before knocking lightly and heard her yell the door was open. Walking in, he looked around for her and saw her coming from her bedroom, dressed in a feminine ivory lace dress with cowboy boots. He loved her style and the unique way she put things together. "You look awesome."

Looking down at his own garb, he wondered what the hell she saw in him, and hoped whatever it was, she still liked it after today.

Madison flashed him a smile. "I'm ready if you are. I can't wait to meet your family. Do I look okay?"

Cory kissed her softly and looked into her eyes. "You look great, relax, it's just my family, nothing special. Come on, let's get on the road, it's a beautiful day outside."

He grabbed her hand to walk out to the truck, wishing he believed what he'd just said. This family was far from nothing special.

He helped her into the truck as she tossed her bag on the floor. She felt his hands on her backside, as he gave her a boost into the seat and she laughed. Cory climbed into the driver's seat and started up the truck, backing out of the driveway. She could sense his nerves as well. "Do they know about me, Cory? Have you told them anything about me?"

Cory headed through town going west toward White Hall. "Of course, I've told them. They know a lot about you, about your school and your pottery. I talk about you all the time. We have a close family."

Reaching over, taking her hand as he drove, he squeezed it gently. "Are you nervous?"

She nodded. "Yes, I am. I'm not usually nervous around people. I don't always fit it, but that never bothers me. I just hope, you know, they like me. I can tell you're close, especially to your dad. I guess I worry if they're not impressed with me, well, maybe it will come between us."

She looked out the window as they left the city limits and drove down Garth Road out to the countryside. "Neither of us speaks much about our feelings, but I like you a lot, Cory, maybe more than I even want to acknowledge sometimes."

"Madison, please don't worry. My family will accept you because..."

Cory stumbled on his words but Madison was being honest

about her feelings and he knew they were moving toward a serious relationship. "Well because, I like you a lot, more than a lot. I've never brought another girl to the house before. To be honest, I'm nervous too. But my stepmom, Kate, she'll make you feel welcome."

Cory wove his way through the winding country roads, as they were soon approaching Bel Rosso and the long private drive.

Madison whipped her head around to look at him as he drove. "You've never brought another girl home to meet your family? I'm the first?"

Cory could feel his face turning red in embarrassment. With a grin, he looked at her. "Yep, first one. So, if they fall over their feet trying to impress you, that's why."

As they both laughed, his face became serious. "Madison, I really want to be with you, not just as friends. I never really had a girlfriend if that's what you want to call it. I've had friends, but never one I wanted my family to meet. You're very special to me."

As Cory pulled the truck into the long lane, he took a deep breath and slowed down to a crawl, allowing her time to see the surrounding property. "Well, here it is, home."

Madison looked about as he pulled into a private drive along an estate bordered by miles of white rail fence. She could see the sign just inside the entrance that read "Bel Rosso Vineyards." She looked at him with surprise. "Your family owns a vineyard? You never mentioned that."

Cory drove down the lane to the house, a good mile. "It's my dad's business, he makes wine. He has vineyards all over the world. I think I mentioned he was from Italy, so he began with his first vineyards in Tuscany. There are other vineyards. I haven't been to all of them. I know there are some in California where I'm from, but also Greece, and some in France, I think. It's the family business. My stepmom actually has an inn in California located in the vineyards in Napa Valley."

As the truck moved down the private driveway, Madison could see where the road split off in the direction of the vineyards. They passed fields where thoroughbred horses grazed in the sun, their coats glistening. She could see the rolling hills, planted with the grape vines, and fields dedicated to other plants. She recognized the early growth of the lavender plants but wasn't sure of the other. The property was massive, and she squirmed in her seat, suddenly feeling under dressed for the occasion. "Cory, you never told me you came from money. This place..."

Before she could finish her sentence, he'd taken the right fork in the drive that led to the large Tuscan style house, its stucco facade a soft butter yellow, with a red tiled roof, and surrounded by lush landscape. "Oh my god...Cory, I should have worn...something else."

Cory could feel her nervousness building. "Madison, my dad has money, not me. I work for what I have. And he expects me to earn everything I have, trust me. And you look great, it's laid back here, don't judge the people based on the surroundings."

He pulled up to the front door and turned the engine off. Turning to Madison, he could see her eyes were wide, and read the trepidation on her face. "If you don't want to do this, I'll understand. I can take you back home if you like."

"No! I don't want to go home, I was just caught off-guard, I guess. It wasn't what I was expecting. Are you sure I look okay?"

As Cory helped her down from the truck, the front door of the house opened, and Madison looked up to see a young woman, not much older than herself, emerge. She was petite and delicate, with pale skin and bright red hair. She knew Cory had a stepmom, and her first thought was trophy wife. Cory's very rich dad ditched the first wife and married a much younger one. *Typical male.* She brushed the thought from her head, trying hard not to pre-judge Cory's father, but the impression was already made.

***

Kate heard the truck as it rumbled up the driveway and remembered Cory was bringing his girlfriend out to the house today. She scrambled to the front door and exited quickly, signaling to Aegis to stay hidden. She saw both Aegis and Night-Stalker slink back into the tree line. Kate brushed the hair back from her face and looked down at her jeans and sandals, wondering if she should have worn something nicer for this first meeting. She watched as Cory hurried around the truck and opened the door for his girlfriend. Kate saw the young woman emerge, her dark blonde hair caught immediately by the breeze. Kate approached her with both arms extended.

"Welcome to Bel Rosso. My name is Kate. Cory has told us so much about you. We've been looking forward to meeting you finally." She embraced the girl who seemed a bit surprised by the gesture. "Come on inside."

Madison felt a little reassured that Kate was dressed casually in jeans. She was less concerned about her dress now, and although she was surprised at how young this woman was, she felt her genuine warmth in welcoming her here.

Cory slid his hand around her waist as he beamed at his stepmom. "This is Madison. But I guess you figured that out already."

Kate took in the couple and could see in Cory's eyes how much this girl meant to him. She took Madison by the hand and led her toward the house when Lorenzo came blasting through the door at full speed, heading straight for Cory.

Lorenzo launched himself in Cory's direction. "Cory!"

"Hey, little dude. How's that pool going, have you done your inspections today?"

Lorenzo planted a wet kiss on Cory's cheek. "The outside pool is done, but inside is not ready. Who's that?" Lorenzo pointed to Madison.

Cory placed his hand over Lorenzo's out-stretched hand. "It's not polite to point, Lorenzo, and she's my girlfriend, her name is Madison."

Cory turned with Lorenzo in his arms, and winked at Madison. "Madison, this is my little brother, Lorenzo."

Madison looked at the beautiful child in Cory's arms, with piercing blue eyes and a tumble of coal black curls, and instinctively knew she was getting a preview of the father. She extended her hand to Lorenzo. "It's so nice to meet you, Lorenzo."

Lorenzo took her hand, and Madison bit her lip to suppress the giggle as she noticed the dirt on his hand, and on the knees of his jeans. Lorenzo responded, "Nice to meet you. I'm a prince."

Kate gave him a stern look as she lifted him from Cory's grip. "Oh, you're a prince all right, the prince of making big messes in the house. Come on. Let's take our guest in the house."

Lorenzo squirmed to get down as Warrior bounded from the house, and danced around Lorenzo's feet. Kate led the small boy and the dog back toward the house as Madison turned to Cory. "A prince?"

Cory grinned and shrugged, trying to cover for Lorenzo. "Yeah, one day he's a prince, the next day a pirate or a dragon. Oh, and the dog, that's Warrior. He's really friendly. Come on. I'll give you the tour."

Taking Madison's hand, Cory led her into the house and directed her into the living room. "Would you like something to drink? We have just about everything."

Madison entered the house and tried to take it all in. The house was magnificent, and she recognized some art pieces on the wall that looked like originals, but thought that couldn't be. Cory directed her to the living room, which was both opulent and yet welcoming and homey. The dog continued to follow her, and Madison absently reached down and scratched his head as she took in the room.

Lorenzo appeared again, having escaped from his mother who was close on his heels. "Are you Cory's girlfriend?"

Madison smiled at the boy and nodded yes.

"Does that mean you kiss and stuff?"

Kate laughed as she caught up to the child and pulled him closer to her side. "Lorenzo, it's not polite to ask."

Lorenzo shrugged and persisted with his commentary. "Uncle Luca kisses Shannon, and she's his girlfriend."

Kate looked at Madison and smiled. "Please ignore him.

Lorenzo has no filter."

Madison smiled at the precocious child, when an elderly gentleman in a formal suit and bow tie entered the room. "May I serve refreshments to our guest?"

Kate looked to Madison. "Madison, this is Gi. Would you like something to drink?"

Madison felt momentarily overwhelmed and shook her head no. She eyed the old gentleman and had a sense of someone who'd stepped through time. "Not right now, thank you."

Kate looked to Cory and suggested he give her a full tour of the house before they retreated to his room.

Lorenzo piped up again, "Are you a day-walker?"

Kate saw the panicked expression in Cory's eyes as Madison looked at the child quizzically. "A what?"

Kate picked him up, with intentions of leaving the room as Lorenzo kept talking. "A day-walker, like me, and Mommy and Cory. We can all go in the sun."

Kate shook her head. "Don't pay any attention. I'm reading him books at night and he has a vivid imagination."

Madison laughed. "Nothing wrong with a vivid imagination. He's just an artist in training."

Lorenzo shook his head no. "I'm not an artist. I'm a warrior!"

Madison made a look of surprise. "Oh! A warrior. I thought you were a prince."

Lorenzo nodded yes. "I am! A warrior and a prince. My dad is the king."

Kate laughed as she tried to cover Lorenzo's non-stop chatter. "Well, I guess that makes me a queen." Lorenzo nodded his head as Kate held the child on her hip and scurried from the room.

Madison turned to Cory. "Your little brother is a handful."

Cory breathed a sigh of relief when Kate escaped the room with Lorenzo. "He wakes up like that and never stops. He's one big ball of energy, but I love him. I wouldn't change him for anything. So, uh, I guess I should give you a tour of the house.

The bottom level is pretty simple, just a normal house. So, what do you think so far?"

"Cory, this is not a simple house. This is a grand house, and you have a butler, for Pete's sake. It's breathtaking. I love it. I had no idea you lived like this."

Cory looked down at his feet, shuffling them a bit. He felt like he should say something, make her understand, this changed nothing about him, this wasn't where he came from. "Madison, I lived in California and was raised there my whole life by my mom. We didn't live anything like this. I didn't know my dad then, we've only recently met in the last few years and he offered me a place to live. My mom and I both agreed this was better for me, a better environment and my dad could provide me with the opportunity to promote my craft. I wasn't used to anything like this. So, please don't judge me by the house or the money. It's not mine. It belongs to my dad and Kate. But this is where I live now. And yes, I do have money, but not like this, believe me, my dad is a self-made man in a manner of speaking. He works hard for all of this, and to maintain it. And he expects the same from me."

Hugging Madison tightly, he whispered softly in her ear, "I'm glad you're here."

Taking her hand, he showed her around the lower level of the house, letting her take it all in. Madison followed him on the house tour, taking in the beautifully restored antiques, as they walked through the dining room and into a large, well-appointed kitchen. He led her through a sunroom on the back of the house where she caught a glimpse of the patio and large in-ground pool.

"Thank you for telling me. I knew Kate was your stepmom, but you haven't spoken much about your life with your biological mom. So, your parents divorced when you were young?"

Cory grimaced. He knew he had to tell her the truth, or as close as he could without revealing too much. He retraced his steps, taking her back to the front of the house and Shade's office and found the door was open. He pointed inside but didn't take her in. "This is my dad's office."

Madison looked inside at the masculine room with the leather furniture and dark wood as Cory kept talking to her.

"Well, I'm the result of what you might call a one-night stand. It was more than one night, but not much more. My mom, Rachael, met my dad at a club in San Francisco when she was young, and they hooked up. He was here visiting the States for a short time on business. He left and went back to Italy. My mom didn't really have any information about where he lived or how to contact him after he left, so he never knew she was pregnant with me. They met up again when...well, when I met my dad in California when he was back there again. He didn't know I existed, and I had no idea who he was. It was all a little weird."

Cory wanted desperately to change the subject before he ended up screwing up this tale of half ass truths. "This room holds the security system that monitors the property, its real high tech." Taking her hand, he led her away from the office and down the hall in the direction of Luca's living quarters.

Madison gripped his hand. "Wait! Your father didn't know your mom was pregnant? So, you never knew him growing up?"

"No, I didn't know him at all growing up. So, you see, Madison, all of the money and fancy things are new to me as well. I didn't grow up like this. And I'd really like for you to meet my mom in California. Would you like to meet my mom, maybe spend a week in California?"

"Of course! I'd love to meet your mom. So,...your dad didn't leave your mom for Kate. I was painting this picture in my head, you know. The middle-aged man who strikes it rich, then dumps his first wife for a younger, prettier one. I'm glad you told me. I mean, a lot of men wouldn't have owned up to their responsibility, especially after so many years. I guess I had him pegged wrong."

Cory bent over laughing, it struck him funny. If she only knew the rep his dad actually had. "Sorry, but that's not how it went down at all. My dad's first and only wife is Kate. And trust me when I tell you, they're very much in love. You'll see for yourself whenever you see them together. They're a good example of what I hope I have with my wife, if I ever have one."

Cory smiled at her when he heard Luca's door open and he walked out in his sweat pants, hanging off his hips, bare feet, and no shirt.

Madison turned her head, as she heard the door open and saw a man unlike any she'd seen before. She stared unabashedly at the tall, dark skinned male, with the bare muscled chest and the sweats hanging low on his hips. His dark brown hair hung loose around his face as his pale, hazel eyes took her in. *Is this Cory's father?*

"Oh, hi, I'm Madison." She extended her hand as he had her locked in his gaze. She felt almost pinned in place, unable to move. His voice was a soft purr as he responded to her, his Italian accent evident.

"So happy to meet you, Madison. I'm Luca."

Madison's head was swimming. *Luca? Cory never mentioned anyone named Luca!*

Cory saw Madison's reaction to Luca and knew Luca had her locked in his gaze as he assessed her. Most mortals would feel the lure of the vampire, and find it hard to resist, not understanding the reason for why they felt so drawn but recognizing it instantly as something very different. Cory knew he'd never have the powers of a warrior. He wasn't jealous of Luca. He understood Luca was taking her measure, assessing any threat. "Luca works for my dad. He lives here, this is his suite. He's responsible for security around here, like a body guard type thing."

Madison heard Cory explain that Luca provided security for the house, and she had no doubt. He was an imposing figure and couldn't imagine who'd be dumb enough to challenge him. He could easily intimidate, but his greeting toward her was warm and welcoming. He released her hand, but maintained eye contact and she felt unable to move, as if her feet were encased in cement. She blinked her eyes a few times as he broke eye contact and she finally felt released. She stumbled over her words as she responded to his greeting. "I'm pleased to meet you. I, uh, Cory never mentioned you, so I think I was just expecting to meet his parents and his brother." She turned to Cory. "I had no idea other people lived here."

"Well, there are a few people who live here. Gi, you met, and Emma is our maid and Theresa is Lorenzo's nanny. It's a very busy household, but my room is really private like Luca's." Cory fist bumped Luca and smiled. "So, this is the lower level, we should go upstairs to my room now. See you later, Luca."

Luca smiled at Cory as he led his new girlfriend on the tour, teasing him as he walked away. "Let me know if you need any help, young blood."

Cory looked over his shoulder at Luca, as he and Madison started up the stairs. "Right, thanks. I think I can manage from this point."

Luca winked at him as Cory turned his attentions back to Madison. "I guess this is a lot to take in. I never realized how much I take for granted living here. I pretty much do my own thing."

Madison blushed at Luca's comment and giggled as Cory started to lead her up the stairs. "I don't know how you could ever take this for granted. You live in a house with staff, and a security guard, in the middle of a vineyard. You surprise me, Cory. This isn't at all what I was expecting."

"I got used to being here, I guess. At first, it was very overwhelming, but after you're here a few times, you'll be okay. Everyone is cool."

As they got to the second floor, Cory didn't take her on a tour of the bedrooms, and he didn't want her anywhere close to his parents' bedroom, where Shade was in his death slumber. "Some of the staff have bedrooms up here, the rest live in the staff quarters. My parents' room and Lorenzo's are up here. I don't want to bother anyone, so I think we can do that another time. My room is on the third floor."

They could both hear the sound of Lorenzo jabbering from his bedroom, as Cory quickly led Madison to another flight of stairs and up to his rooms. Opening the door, he held out his hand gallantly for her to enter. "This is it, my pad." He and

Emma had spent two days cleaning in preparation for her arrival.

Madison stepped into the massive suite of rooms that was Cory's space. She was expecting a bedroom, but he had his own apartment on the top floor of the house. "Are you kidding me?"

She walked over to the windows and looked out over the expansive property. The scope of the vineyards was clearly visible from this height, as was the winery and the stables. "What are those fields over there? One looks like lavender, but the other plants aren't full enough for me to tell what they are."

"That would be sunflowers. Kate has her own business. She does things with the lavender and sunflowers." Walking up behind her, he wrapped his arms around her waist, glancing out at the view. "I have the best view in the whole estate. The property goes all the way to the base of the mountains. It's pretty huge. Dad has stables here as well, and horses. He and Kate ride together. He also boards horses for some of his friends. The vineyards and winery are the main business for my dad, but it was Kate's idea to plant these flower crops. I have no idea exactly what she does with those flowers, but we have people who do the harvesting. It's not something I pay much attention to. I just do my own thing, but it is very beautiful and peaceful here."

Madison turned in his arms, so she was facing him. "You live in paradise, Cory Medici. You've been holding out on me. Now show me the rest of your place."

Cory took Madison's hand and led her through the living room into his bedroom. "This is it, where I sleep. It's real open and roomy. Kate did all the decorating. The lighting in here is really amazing at sunset."

Madison's mouth was hanging open as he led her into his bedroom. The room was massive with vaulted ceilings and exposed beams, and a large stone fireplace. She'd never seen a room like this. Although it was very different from her personal style, the artist in her appreciated the blend of colors and textures. The room was warm and masculine, with the tartan plaids and the oriental carpet on the hardwood floors, in shades of brown. "Wow, Cory, I don't think I'd ever leave this room if I lived here. This is an awesome space! And you have a fireplace in your bedroom? How cool is that?"

Cory beamed at her appreciation of his space. "It's really nice when winter comes. I'm not used to the cold weather since I was raised in California. So, it's nice to lay here and look out over the vineyards with a warm fire going. Maybe we can do that sometime. It will be nice and cozy."

He wiggled his eyebrows at her as she giggled in response. He didn't want to push her to make love with him and today was definitely not the right time. "The bathroom is right in here, it's awesome. When I first saw my rooms, I couldn't believe I'd have all of this to myself."

Madison followed him to the bath, where the stone of the exterior wall was exposed, and the long counter for the double sink was made of roughhewn wood that had clearly been recycled from another structure. She loved how the natural elements of nature dominated the space. He had a large shower stall, also built from natural stone, and one of those rain forest shower heads. She shook her head in amazement.

"Kate designed all this? I guess I assumed she hired a decorator or something. This really suits you, Cory. It just feels so inviting."

She wandered back into his bedroom to one of the large windows, taking in a different view of the property. She could see the pool and the lush landscape, a tree swing in a massive oak, and an elaborate tree house built into the tree for Lorenzo and she smiled to herself, imagining that rambunctious child growing up here. She saw a large house behind the main house and pointed it out to Cory. "What's that building?"

Cory walked up behind her to see what exactly she was looking at. "Those are the staff quarters, for the people who work here, like Gi and Emma. Dad and Kate wanted all the buildings on the property to have the same architectural feel, so it doesn't look all mixed up. You can't tell what's new and what's old, and it all blends in with the landscape around us."

Madison nodded as she scanned the property. In the

distance was a high stone wall, covered in ivy. It was set apart from all the other buildings. "And over there? That walled area? What's behind there?"

Cory's got a little nervous as she pointed out the warrior camp. How could he explain that? "Oh, that's the uh, yeah part of the winery. Top secret stuff over there, that's why there's a wall. My dad has some special blends he makes, expensive ones that have come from Italy, old secret brewing stuff. He's really edgy about that."

Taking her hand, he dragged her back into the living room and to the couch before she could ask more things he couldn't answer. "Are you hungry? We can order a pizza."

"Sure! I'd love a pizza. What about your family? Will they eat with us?"

Cory threw his arm over the back of the sofa, stalling for time. "Well, they eat really late usually, so no. Let me get Gi to order us a pizza. You want any meat on it or just veggies? We have a ton of things to drink. What's your poison?"

"Oh, whatever you order is fine. I like everything. And any kind of diet soda will be fine." Madison walked around the spacious living room, taking in the details.

Cory watched her as she casually strolled through the room. He loved the way the ivory lace dress draped over her curves. His eyes went to her neck where he saw her vein pulsing softly. He closed his eyes for a moment to get himself under control. "I'll be right back, let me tell Gi what we need and grab us some drinks. Make yourself at home."

Madison took in the massive TV. It must be a 72" screen. She noticed all the video gaming equipment and laughed to herself. She was exploring the gallery wall of art over the large sectional sofa when she recognized Kate in one of the paintings, and the very handsome man with the brilliant blue eyes and coal black hair. So, that was Cory's father. She was right about one thing, Lorenzo looked just like him. Cory had come back in the room, as Madison was examining a portrait of another woman who looked much older, but had a very kind face. "Cory, these paintings are beautiful! Who did these?"

Holding the drinks in his hands, he looked up. "These were done by Luca. You met him earlier. He's an artist and a really amazing one at that. He has mad skills. Do you like them?"

"Luca? Your security guy? He painted these? Cory, these are amazing! And this one, who's this?" Madison pointed to the painting of the older woman with the gentle eyes.

Reaching up, Cory slid his fingertips gently over the painting. "This is my mom."

Madison looked more closely at the picture, other than her brown eyes, she didn't see any real resemblance to Cory. "Your mom? Oh...."

She was confused as she looked back at the portrait of Kate and the dark haired man. He was clearly older than Kate but looked much too young for Cory's mom. "Well, I'm confused now. I assumed the man in the portrait with Kate was your father, but he looks much younger than your mom, so do you have a picture of your father?"

Cory could feel his palms sweating. "Well, actually my dad is younger than my biological mom. And to be honest, my mom and I had a really hard life, we didn't have very much, and I was a bit of a handful. She worked really hard her whole life. She looks older than her years."

Cory sat down on the couch, taking a drink for himself, he tried to change the conversation. "Everyone says I really don't look like my dad or my mom."

Madison looked back and forth between the two portraits, the strikingly handsome man who looked model perfect, and the woman with the kind but aging face. "You have her eyes, I think. There's sadness in her eyes, but there's gentleness too. She feels kind and good. She feels like a giving person. I see those things in you, Cory, those same character traits. So, no, you don't look like her, but I think she passed on that part of her."

She glanced back at Cory and his androgynous features, almost feminine in his beauty, and then back at the man in the portrait, a strong alpha male with chiseled cheek bones and a strong jaw, full sensual lips, and those eyes, there was something in those eyes. Like when she locked eyes with Luca. His eyes had a power to hold you in your place. She felt mesmerized even now, looking at the portrait. She looked away and back at Cory. "His hair maybe. His looks a little darker, but the soft waves, and the way it falls around your face."

Cory shook his head and laughed. "Yeah that would be my dad, Mr. World Traveler, head for business, always in control, ladies' man, handsome, suave, and educated. And all I got was his hair. He wasn't around when I was growing up. I didn't even know his name. But once he and my mom met up again, he made amends and paid all her debts, bought her a house and she doesn't have to work anymore. So, I have to give him props, he did everything right."

Madison sat down beside him on the sofa. She could hear the pain in his voice. It was clear he and his mom didn't have it easy growing up, and he still carried the burden of it. "But you have to really respect that, right? I mean, look at all the men who don't take care of their children. Your dad didn't know you existed for most of your life. He was married to Kate, and they have their own child, and then he finds out he has another son out there. I have to really respect him for that, and Kate too. She had to let another woman's son into her life. And then he takes care of your mom? I mean really, Cory, there's not a lot more you could ask. He loves you, right? I mean, it's clear Kate loves you, and I haven't met him yet, but I can feel warmth in your voice when you speak of him."

Gi entered as they talked and delivered the pizza, complete with plates, forks, and napkins. Cory thanked him as Gi nodded silently and left. Madison watched the elderly gentleman and wondered why he was still working. He must be a hundred years old!

Opening the box, Cory took out two slices for himself and one for Madison and handed it to her with a napkin. "Madison, I love my dad, he's allowed me to completely turn my life around. I was lost before he came along. He's given me opportunities I never even dreamed for myself. I work hard to live up to his expectations of me. To try to make sure he knows I appreciate what he's done. He was raised in a good family, they had a lot, but he's been through hell as well. It wasn't always easy for him, so he gets me. I guess what I'm saying is, I hope I grow up to be half the man he is."

Wolfing down his pizza quickly, he grinned at her as she took small bites and tried not to get anything on her dress. "I just hope now that you've seen where I live you don't feel differently about me."

Madison stopped mid-chew. "Why would you ever think I'd feel differently about you? We're two of a kind, you and me. Neither of us really fits in and we're struggling to find our place in this world. And something tells me your father isn't concerned about you following in his footsteps, but hoping you make your own path, follow your own heart. I mean, look at you now. Your dad owns and runs vineyards, but he's letting you pursue your own passion as an artist, and not trying to force you into running the family business. I think that speaks volumes."

Cory leaned in and kissed her softly. "Thanks for saying that, you do understand me."

Madison looked back at him and smiled. "You're not getting rid of me, Cory Medici. I plan on sticking around a long time, if you'll have me."

"Have you? Oh, Madison Barnes, I already have you, and I plan to keep you." Looking at her with a grin, he flipped his hair back.

He grabbed the remote and turned on the iPod nestled in a speaker as the music of The Black Keys filled the room. "You like the Keys?"

She leaned back against the sofa as the music washed over her. "I love The Black Keys. So, can you show me your leather studio while I'm here? I'd love to see where you work."

Damn! He couldn't take her there, it was at the camp! "Not today, if you don't mind. It's really a mess and it's a long walk. Maybe next time, okay?" He watched her closely to see if she was buying this excuse. "Listen, I'm glad you like the Black Keys, they're playing in Charlottesville in a few weeks, would you like to go?"

"Seriously? I'd love to go see the Keys!"

"Great! It's a date. I'll get the tickets."

He hugged her to him and kissed her softly, as her hands slide around his neck. Deepening the kiss, he could feel her heartbeat pick up. Her tongue probed into his mouth and he sucked it gently. She was the most beautiful perfect girl he'd met in his life and he never wanted to lose her.

Madison melted in to him. Despite her vow to not get romantically involved until she graduated, she knew she was falling hard for this man-child. She felt Cory's hands exploring her back, pulling her closer as he leaned into her, pushing her down on the sofa, and she let him.

They were both startled by the sound of a door banging open and tiny feet running across the floor, a second before Lorenzo launched himself on top of Cory.

"Cory! The inside pool is finished. You want to come see? Eww, were you kissing?"

Sitting up quickly, with Lorenzo still clinging to him, Cory struggled for a sense of normalcy as Madison suppressed a laugh. "Little dude, you need to learn some manners, you should always knock first. And yes, we were kissing, we like each other. Now, you need to apologize to Madison for being so rude."

Kate rushed into the room. "Lorenzo! Get back here! What is the rule about closed doors?"

Lorenzo slid off Cory onto the floor and looked at his feet as he answered softly. "Knock first, and wait for permission. But I got excited."

Kate apologized to Cory and his girlfriend, both of them looking a bit disheveled. "I'm so sorry for the interruption."

She took Lorenzo by the shoulders and turned him to face Cory and his guest. "Now, apologize, and when your father wakes, I'll tell him of this behavior. Be prepared for him to take away some of your cards."

Lorenzo pouted as he apologized, "Sorry, Cory. Sorry, Miss

Madison. I was just excited 'bout the pool."

Cory stood up and kissed Kate's cheek. "It's okay." Squatting down in front of Lorenzo, he gave him a hug. "Still love me?"

Lorenzo threw both arms around Cory's neck, planting another wet kiss on his cheek. "You're my best friend, Cory."

"I love you too, little dude. Can you give Madison a hug too?" Leaning into Lorenzo's ear he whispered, "It really helps when you say you're sorry."

Lorenzo immediately placed his arms around Madison and kissed her cheek. "You smell good."

Madison laughed and said, "Thanks."

Kate steered him away, apologizing again for the interruption as she led Lorenzo from the room, closing the door behind her. They could hear Kate lecturing Lorenzo as they walked down the stairs, and Lorenzo talking a mile a minute in his defense. Both Cory and Madison collapsed into giggles before Madison turned to him. "Your father is asleep? I thought he was working in the vineyards."

His heart raced and he concocted another story. "Oh, he was on a business trip and got home really late, so he's probably resting, jet lag and all. He travels a lot. We should probably get moving, it's getting late and I know you have school tomorrow. Are you about ready to head back?"

Madison seemed a little taken aback by his sudden offer to take her back home. The sun hadn't even set yet, but she did have some art history homework to finish. "Uh yeah, I guess I should be going. This was really nice, Cory. I'm glad I came. I like your family."

Smiling at her, he took her in his arms. "I'm glad. I was worried you wouldn't like it here, it can be hectic sometimes. I'm sure the next time you're here, my dad will be around. I'm sorry you didn't get to meet him."

Kissing her softly, he took her hand as she grabbed her bag and they walked down the flight of stairs and encountered Kate. "Mom, we're leaving now, I'll be back later." He hoped she got the message loud and clear she needed to keep Aegis at bay.

Kate was about to enter their bedroom when she heard Cory approach. Letting go of the doorknob, she turned and walked toward them, sending a message to Aegis once again to steer clear. "Madison, I'm so happy Cory brought you here. Please feel free to visit us any time. I apologize, but our house is usually in chaos." Kate gave her a warm hug. Looking over her shoulder at Cory, she said, "Be sure you schedule her next visit, so your father can meet her too."

Looking at Madison, she explained. "There was a new foal born in the stables last night, and Shade was up all night assisting our Stable Master with the delivery. He'll be so sorry he missed you."

Cory rolled his eyes at Kate. This couldn't be more of a disaster. He quickly tried to cover for his own story he'd told Madison. "Oh, I thought Dad was napping from jet lag from his trip. So, we have another new foal. Great." Cory felt like his heart was going to pound right out of his chest. Madison must think he was a moron.

Madison was pondering the various versions of the story as to why she wasn't meeting Cory's father, as he lead her down the second flight of stairs to the main floor where she caught a glimpse of Luca entering the office. Gi was standing at the door and opened it for them both. Madison frowned as she became aware she was listening to "The Addams Family" song in her head. She bit her lip and suppressed a giggle as Cory asked if she was okay. She nodded her head, she liked Cory's family, but things were definitely a little weird. "Yeah, of course."

As they got to the truck, he grabbed her in his arms and kissed her. "Thanks for coming today. I hope it wasn't too painfully weird for you."

Madison smiled back at him. "I liked them, no, I really loved them, Cory. Weird is good."

43

Alec had received notice from Shade both Hyde and the new warrior, Mateo, had been prepped and were ready to begin their assignment. He was surprised at how easily Ashton caved when confronted with the threat of releasing the video footage of him and Rissa together. He'd expected Ashton to put up more of a fight.

He met with the RNC after Ashton's announcement and they'd been very supportive of his decision to throw his hat in the ring. He'd had the press conference scheduled, and he'd announce to the nation he was officially in the running. Braden was setting up his campaign schedule, and they'd be making the rounds, starting first in Iowa. It was time to pull Rissa into the process and make sure she understood her role and what he expected from her.

Pouring another Midnight, he walked to the bottom of the stairs and called up to her. She'd worked from her home office most of the day, and he wanted to catch her before she went riding. "Rissa, could you join me in the study please?"

Rissa stood with hands on her hips, looking through her walk-in closet. She'd been preparing for the campaign and wanted to be well dressed and have everything organized before leaving. She desperately needed a drink and a cigarette when she heard Alec call. Sighing, she walked down the stairs and into his study. "Is something wrong?"

"Nothing wrong, darling, just some details we need to go over. Why don't you sit with me in the study?"

Eyeing him, she smiled and strolled over to the comfortable couch, sitting down, curling her legs beside her, and cocking her head to one side. "What kind of details?"

Alec lit up a cigarette as he sat. "I have the press conference scheduled two days from now where I will officially announce my candidacy. It will, of course, be televised and picked up by all the major networks and news organizations. I'll expect you to be at my side. I'll need you to dress professionally, nothing sexy. You'll need to present a fashionable, but highly respectable image to the public. Designer is okay, as long as you keep it on the conservative side. You probably won't be asked to speak, as it will just be me announcing my intentions, but Braden will counsel you on a few canned responses in case the press does start throwing questions at you."

Biting her lip with excitement, their time had finally come. "Oh Alec, this is so exciting. We've finally made it. Almost there! I promise, I won't let you down, I've been thinking about my wardrobe. I've chosen some very respectable but elegant outfits. I'll tone down the jewelry. Braden is so..." Wiggling in her seat, Rissa threw up her hands. "Well, he's so proper and standoffish with me, like I don't exist."

Alec took a sip from his glass before answering. "Braden knows what he's doing. He's managed several very successful campaigns before, including my own Senate campaigns. So, get used to him. He'll be calling a lot of the shots. Soon after the press conference, we'll be making our first campaign stop in Iowa. We'll make rounds to a number of functions where I'll be giving a canned speech, but we'll mingle with the people at the State Fair. Braden will advise you on your wardrobe, but you'll need something appropriate for the occasion. It's outdoors. A lot of emphasis on agriculture. Nothing fancy. You'll need to look good, but your clothing will need to be more off the rack than designer. You want to look fashionable, but not so rich people can't identify with you. You'll interact with the locals. Kiss babies. Provide photo ops with the locals, that sort of thing."

Rissa listened as her excitement waned. *Iowa? Who in the hell chose this place to begin?* She sat back and dropped her legs to the floor, her hands folded in her lap, her smile fading. *Mingle with farmers? A state fair? Oh no, she wasn't going to be stomping around some damn hay riding, cowboy roping fair in the mid-west, acting as though she was happy!* And Braden would advise on her wardrobe! She could feel her beast rising. Her face was scrunched tight as she stood up and started pacing. *Off the rack? Kiss babies? Oh, hell no!*

Saying nothing, she walked to the bar with a purpose and poured a tall Midnight, downed it in one throw and poured another. Slowly turning around, her eyes bored into Alec's. "Is this some kind of cruel joke, Alec, some scheme you cooked up with Braden?"

Alec drew on the cigarette before stubbing it out in the ashtray. "Rissa, you were mortal once. Didn't you pay attention to your own political process? Do you ever bother to watch the news? This is how campaigns are conducted. I have to win the vote of the people. That means we mingle with the people. Every hand we shake, and we will shake thousands, is a potential vote. How did you think this was going to go?"

Walking with a determined stride across the room, she crossed her arms over her chest, her Midnight still in hand. "Seriously Alec, Iowa? I don't give a fig about the poor, we've spent our lives mingling with the best, brightest and richest people in America and now you want me to mingle with some poor farmer and expect me to just jump in with both feet? I don't do Iowa. I do Boston, New York, L.A., and Chicago! I do D.C. and I handle some of the oldest money in this town, so let me dig in my closet and have Braden pull out my cotton dress and my grannie shoes and show them a good time!"

Throwing back her Midnight, she drained the glass and gritted her teeth. She wasn't going to do this without a fight.

Alec took a deep breath before he answered. "And just how would that look, my darling, if all the other candidates have their wives at their side, except me? All campaigns start in Iowa, and it will be the first of many state fairs we'll attend. And I suggest you climb off your high horse and learn to deal with the 'poor' as you call them, if you ever expect to live in the White House. You knew what you signed up for with me, so don't start pulling this shit now."

"Oh, I signed up all right. I signed up to be your mate, and do as you command, but this was never in the bargain. Off the rack? Alec, I'm a blue blood, I've never in my life owned anything off the rack. And let me assure you, I'll have a stylist and you can bet your vampire ass it won't be Braden Childs. This shit? Pulling this shit? In case you've forgotten, I fucked that old buzzard, so you could go on this campaign. Don't strangle me now, Alec, don't. Give me some space to do things my way and get you to the White House. Braden may have the brains, but you and I are a team. I won't do this."

Alec stood, towering over her. "Rissa, I'm not asking you to dress in rags, and there will be many fundraising dinners with the elite where you can dress as expensively as you want. But there is a time and place for everything, and you'll follow Braden's direction, and mine. And while we're on the subject, you'll need to make some decisions about your business."

He towered over her and she could feel his heat, smell him deep in her nostrils. Her business was her life line, hers alone. He had nothing to do with her success and now he was going to control that as well? She felt a line drawn in the sand. "Choose your words carefully, master."

Alec squinted, deepening his frown. "Excuse me? Are you giving me direction now?"

Slowly lifting her hand, softening her tone, she let it slide gently across his cheek, her eyes never leaving his. Her hand trailed down his neck. "Not direction, advice."

He grabbed her wrist, squeezing tightly, speaking through clenched teeth. "I don't take advice from my mate. It's the other way around, or have you forgotten?"

Rissa felt the pressure on her wrist, he could snap her bones in two, but he wouldn't, especially not now, he needed her. "I haven't forgotten. I just ask you to remember I built my business from the ground up, it's mine. It's who I am. Please Alec, remember that."

Alec released his grip and sighed heavily. "Rissa, be practical. For the next eighteen months we'll be on the road, traveling from state to state. You can leave one of your employees in charge in your absence, but that would only be a temporary solution. If I win the Presidency, you won't be able to continue with your business. Your best option is to sell the business now, while you still have the strong reputation attached to it."

Rissa felt her heart crack. *Sell?* She slowly backed away from him, her eyes wide with astonishment. She was speechless. Never did she consider she'd have to give up the one thing she excelled at. It was hers! She turned and walked to the large window, staring out at the lights of Georgetown. She had to take a chance on him; she had to believe in him. If she wasn't going to be the Darling of G-town, she'd have to be the First Lady of the White House. She turned her head and looked at him over her shoulder and for the first time, she wasn't sure of this anymore. "I'm scared."

He went to her and wrapped his arms around her, kissing the top of her head. "It's a risk, my darling. There's no guarantee. But if I should fail at the White House, I promise you, I'll do everything within my power to help you restart your business. If you have someone who you think can run it in your absence, then do that. Keep it. You'll have it to go back to in eight years when I've completed my Presidency. But without that, I don't see many options, do you?"

His arms felt like a safety net. His voice was softer, caring, and she was grateful he understood how much she was giving up. "I guess I never thought about this part of it. I know most mates don't have the advantages I do. I get to be my own person, have the freedom to make my own decisions in my business without consulting you on anything. Please never think I take that for granted, Alec. I know how fortunate I am being your mate. I need some time to think about this. My assistant can handle things until I make up my mind whether to sell it outright."

Spinning around in his arms, she laid her head on his chest. "Alec, tell me you can do this, assure me and I'll do whatever you want. I love you and I'll do what you need. I don't like being scared."

He uncharacteristically gave her comfort and allowed her to lean against his chest as he held her. "It's my intention to succeed. I wouldn't undertake this if I didn't think I could achieve it. It was the only reason for getting the Senate seat in the first place. I was bored with the immortal manipulations for land and power, and found the mortal struggles entertaining. Eternity can be both a blessing and a curse, my darling. I'm afraid one can become quite jaded with life. Take some time to decide what you want to do with the business, just understand you won't be here to run things on a day to day basis."

"I know you can do it, Alec. You're my wicked vampire, who else could tackle this chaos." As she laughed softly, he walked away from her and got himself another Midnight. "Alec, is there anything else?"

"I can't think of anything else for the moment, darling. The campaign will be exhausting. It's non-stop with speeches and fundraising. Putting on a good face regardless of what's happening behind the scenes. It's always about managing your image and controlling how the public sees you. That's where Braden comes in. He'll run the campaign, get us where we're supposed to be, manage the events. I just need you to play the role of dutiful and devoted wife until we're in the White House. Can you do that for me?"

"Before I answer, I have a question. Tell me, please, Hyde is going with us, it will help my attitude tremendously."

Alec was relieved he could give her something. "Yes, Hyde will be there every step of the way, as will a new warrior who'll be assigned to me. His name is Mateo. Alto will be along as well. We'll spend a lot of time on that campaign bus, traveling from town to town, and Alto will be my driver."

"Bus?" Closing her eyes, taking a deep breath, she tried to calm her anger. Opening her eyes, she walked slowly toward the door of the study.

Sighing heavily, she answered him. "Yes, Larissa Benneteau Canton, wife of Senator Alec Canton, will wear her conservative, off the rack clothes, disgustingly comfortable shoes, kiss slobbering babies, shake millions of filthy hands, live on a rickety ass bus while she smiles like a good little mortal wife while her handsome husband wins them over with his charm."

Getting to the door, she could almost feel him smirking. She turned with her arms crossed over her chest and her hip jutting out. "In case you've forgotten, Senator Canton, you have yet to fulfill your end of the bargain concerning Ashton."

He smiled to himself as he listened to her describe life on the campaign bus as he poured another Midnight. "Oh, I haven't forgotten. Shade is having his people at Castello crate everything and ship it here. Of course, we won't be here often, but we'll be coming back to D.C. in between campaign trips. I've arranged to have the basement finished and soundproofed while we're on the first leg of the campaign. Santos will bring someone in from one of the underground clubs to set everything up, and it will all be waiting for you when we get back home. So, you see, my darling, you do have something to look forward to."

The smile began at the corners of her mouth and lit up her entire face. She ran to him, throwing her arms around his neck and kissing him with unleashed abandon. "Thank you, Daddy, baby girl can bear anything if she comes home to that." Still grinning, she released him and strutted out of the room, a swivel in her hips. "There better be horses at these damn state fairs."

He laughed. "Oh, I'm sure you'll see horses, my darling, probably not up to your standards, but plenty of horses."

Rissa stopped at the stairs and smiled. "Good night, my wicked vampire. I love you, Alec, I'll always love you."

44

Shade left the house and took the long walk to the warrior camp. It was beginning to feel like summer, and the days were getting longer. The sun had set, but it was still light outside, allowing him to walk freely outdoors. He liked the color of the sky at sunset. He closed his eyes and took a deep breath, enjoying the scent of the lavender carried in the air.

Stepping inside the massive gate, he knew the warriors wouldn't be out yet. Their field activities didn't get hopping until about 10 p.m. He could hear the squeal of delight from his son as he worked with Skelk to practice his skill of throwing fire. It was a rare gift, but nothing as rare as animalism. Shade had met a few fire throwers but had never had one in the Medici camps before. Shade was grateful for Skelk and his offer to help. He was doing a great job with Lorenzo.

He stood back along the high wall, so he could watch Lorenzo's progress. It didn't take the child much effort to produce the fire, and he was learning control. This was a huge step for him. What pleased Shade even more was Lorenzo was no longer afraid of his gift.

Shade stepped forward and it didn't take long for Lorenzo to notice him. The child flashed him a smile as his feet went into motion, heading straight for him at full speed. Shade crouched down to accept him as Lorenzo hurled himself into his arms, already chattering away. "Daddy, did you see me? I can hold the fire in my hand. Skelk is teaching me. Did you see me, Daddy?"

Ruffling his hand through that mop of raven curls, Shade's smile was genuine. "I did see it. You are pretty amazing, little warrior. Do you like working with Skelk?"

Nodding his head, his curls bobbing with the motion, he replied, "Skelk is my third best friend. First is Cory, then Luca. Don't tell him he's third, okay, Daddy? It might hurt his feelings. Mommy says I have to be careful with my words to not hurt people's feelings."

Shade hugged him tight to his chest, rubbing his back. "You know, your Mommy is a pretty smart Mommy if you ask me, and she is correct. But it is always a good thing to have many friends, especially ones like Skelk who can protect and teach you. I have something to ask you, will you listen?"

Lorenzo cupped his tiny hands behind his ears and giggled. "I put my listening ears on."

Shade chuckled. "I think I might need to borrow those sometime. But here is my question. First of all, I am very impressed with your skill of fire throwing. You're doing a fine job as a warrior. As a reward, how would you like to go camping up on the mountain with me tonight? Just Daddy and his little warrior."

Lorenzo bounced up and down at the chance to have his father all to himself. "Yes, please! Can I stay up really late? Will we sleep in a tent? Can Warrior come?"

Skelk approached them, shaking his head and grinning. A man of little words, his next comment took Shade off guard. "He seems to get some of his traits from his mother, a million questions at once."

"Skelk, there are times that female drove me to distraction with her questions, but Lorenzo, I think he might give her a run for her money."

They both laughed and Shade slapped Skelk on the back. "Appreciate this more than I have words. It is obvious he is learning control. Take the night off, Skelk, it is the least I can do for you."

Lorenzo scrambled over to Skelk and wrapped both arms around one massive leg of the imposing warrior. "I love you, Skelk. Uncle Luca says you'll help me to be as good a warrior as my daddy."

Skelk ran his hand through the small boy's hair, feeling awkward and unaccustomed to the display of affection, his face turning red as he responded, "I love you too, little buddy."

Shade observed the interaction between his son and the fierce warrior, who had little contact with anyone before he joined Shade's coven. He could see the love for his son in the grizzled warrior's eyes, but he also saw the loneliness. Something Shade had been all too familiar with.

"*Grazie*, Skelk, you give much more than is asked of you. You have become a vital part of this camp, and my family. You are good for Lorenzo, and I am happy he has someone with your skills at his side always."

Skelk responded with his usual discomfort when shown words of praise. Turning back to Lorenzo, Shade took his hand. "Now, little warrior, we need to let Skelk get back to his own business and we need to head back to the house and gear up for our camping trip. I don't think your mommy would be pleased if either of us disappeared without her knowledge."

Lorenzo started running toward the house. "Come on, Daddy. We've got a lot to do!"

Aegis bound from the tree line as Lorenzo exited the large gates of the camp and stayed close on the boy's heels as he ran back toward the main house.

Shade shook his head as he watched his son take off. Fist bumping Skelk, he winked. "I may need to improve my running skills at this rate."

Shade took off after his son. He could easily teleport ahead of him, but that would be no fun. "Last one to the house loses, and I won't lose!"

Lorenzo hadn't yet learned to teleport and yelled out, "No flying, Daddy!" He ran twice as hard, trying to win the race as the wolf kept pace.

"No flying!" Shade slowed a bit, knowing he was still running way faster than he needed to. He waited until Lorenzo got closer to the house then sped up until he was right on his heels. Shade had no intentions of catching him but wanted to give Lorenzo the thrill of winning.

Lorenzo crashed hard against the back door, shouting, "I win!"

Aegis danced at his feet and they could hear Warrior barking from inside the house. Kate heard the commotion and rushed to the door, opening it suddenly and Lorenzo stumbled in face first. She caught him before he hit the floor as the boy, unfazed by his near fall, was still shouting, "I win! I win!"

Shade saw the door open, and before he could stop himself, ran straight into *bel*. The dog, the wolf, his mate, and son landed in a tumbled, tangled mess in the foyer. They were laughing as Warrior was jumping on him, and Aegis realized she was actually inside the house and tried to get herself back out the door.

Kate laughed as she lifted Lorenzo to his feet, as Aegis and Warrior both danced about the narrow hallway. Smiling back at Shade, she responded to her son, "And what exactly did you win, Lorenzo?"

He was bouncing in place as he answered her. "The race. I beat Daddy in the race. Now we're going camping in the woods, in a tent. I'm going to stay up really late. Can Warrior come too? I need my teddy bear, and my blanket, and my pillow too."

Kate looked at Shade and bit her lip. "Are you sure that's a good idea?"

Before Shade could answer, Lorenzo spoke up, "Course it's a good idea."

Shade nodded to Lorenzo. "Course it's a good idea, Mommy." He winked at *bel*. "Lorenzo has been practicing his gift with Skelk. I was impressed and thought we would go camping on the mountain just until sunrise. Give you some time to rest."

Grabbing Lorenzo, Shade let him climb on his back, his little arms clinging around his neck. "Come on, son, I have gear stored somewhere, a tent and a sleeping bag. You won't need a blanket or pillow. It will be warm tonight. As for Warrior, I am sure Aegis and Night-Stalker will be close by, so we probably won't need Warrior, but if you think you must have your teddy bear, we can take that along."

Lorenzo cast a worried look at his mother when he heard he wouldn't be taking his blanket and pillow. "But I might need my blanket, Daddy."

Kate shushed him and told him she'd gather up his blanket and pillow along with his teddy bear while he went with his father to get the tent and other camping supplies. She knew he wouldn't need the blanket for warmth in the tent, but for the comfort of the scent it carried. She followed them up the stairs and headed to Lorenzo's bedroom, letting Theresa know she could take the night off as she gathered the soft blanket from the bed and rolled the bear and pillow inside.

Carrying Lorenzo on his shoulders, Shade took him into the bedroom. Lowering him to the floor, he nodded to the closet where the tent and sleeping bag had been carefully rolled and stored in the duffle bag. Shade intended to teleport them both most of the distance.

Lorenzo squealed and ran for the gear.

"Everything we need is in that pack, Lorenzo, so I can sling it over my shoulder, hold you in my arms, and we can teleport up to the mountain and then set up the tent. How does that sound?"

"Good, Daddy. But don't forget my bear okay?"

Kate entered the bedroom with his blanket rolled tight and handed it to Shade. "Your bear and pillow are rolled inside."

Squatting down, she took him in her arms. "Now you be good, and look after Daddy while you're out there, okay? I need my two best warriors."

Lorenzo returned the hug and asked her. "Who will look after you, Mommy?"

She brushed his hair from his face and told him Uncle Luca was here and all the warriors in the camp. "I'll be fine, Lorenzo."

He nodded but looked skeptical. She felt his energy and knew he was both excited and nervous at the same time.

Shade watched them together. Lorenzo was so concerned for her. It made his heart leap in his chest. "We will be fine, we are warriors. As for your *madre*, Uncle Luca would never let anything happen to her, and Cory is here as well. So, you need not worry about your mommy. Now, I want you to go downstairs and wait for me, I will be right there, but I need to speak with Mommy before we leave. No misbehaving, sit on the couch and wait. I promise we will not be long."

Lorenzo hopped out of the room. "Okay, Daddy. Don't be

long!"

They could hear him as he hopped down the steps. Kate turned to Shade and slipped into his arms. "He's excited to be with you, but he's a little nervous about this too. Are you sure you want to do this? He's so young."

He snuggled into her crimson, breathing deeply. "*Si*, I want to do this, *mi amore*, but you don't sound too sure. Are you all right with this? Seriously, you are much too soft with him, *bel*, a pillow, and blanket? He is a warrior. He needs to learn comforts are not always something he will have."

"He's just a baby. He's never slept anywhere except his own bed here or at Castello, with Theresa in the same room, and both of us down the hall. Even then, he'll still climb in our bed when he's had a bad dream. He'll have all eternity to be a warrior. I don't want him to grow up so fast, or to feel like he has to put on a brave face just to make us proud. It's okay for him to be afraid sometimes."

Kissing her softly on the cheek, he could feel her angst, the worry deep inside her. "I would never let harm come to him. I will die protecting him. I am teleporting us up there, I will be with him every second. He has to feel fear to conquer it, master it."

Kissing her with more passion this time, she moaned in his arms, their lips locked, when a small but loud voice was heard from the lower level. They both broke the kiss and laughed.

"I think Lorenzo has lost his patience already. We will return before sunrise. If you need me, I am not far away. Luca is in the house. I want you to rest, take advantage of this time. *Ti amo*."

With reluctance, Kate let him go, knowing this was just the first of many times she'd have to relinquish any control over her child.

45

Shade teleported out to the mountain with the duffle bag slung across his back, and Lorenzo held tightly in his arms. Lorenzo held his small package of teddy bear, pillow and blanket cradled tightly against his chest. Shade landed softly on a mossy green clearing with trees surrounding them. Sitting Lorenzo down, the darkness was all encompassing. The only light provided for them was from the moon and stars. Lorenzo was excited but also a little intimated. Shade felt his son's emotions.

"Don't wander off, Lorenzo, it is dark out here, use your senses to help you. Listen for sounds and movement. There are many animals out here tonight. Can you hear or see Aegis or Night-Stalker?"

Lorenzo stood stock still, and that alone was a miracle. As he began to unpack, Shade quickly retrieved the flashlight.

Lorenzo picked up the scent of both Aegis and Night-Stalker and looked deep into the darkness and could see the glint of moonlight reflecting in their eyes. He pointed them out to his father. "Yep. They're here all right."

He watched as his father removed the camping gear from the pack and Lorenzo laid his blanket on the ground and unrolled it, retrieving his bear. Tucking the bear tightly under one arm, he slipped a thumb in his mouth, a habit he hadn't indulged in since he was one.

Shade didn't miss the gestures Lorenzo employed to soothe himself. Kneeling down beside him, he turned on the flashlight and handed it to him. "Lorenzo, are you scared of the dark?"

Lorenzo shook his head no as he removed his thumb, and a little drool ran down his chin. "I'm not scared, Daddy, but I think Ted is."

Shade smiled at his son. "Then hold him tightly, keep him safe. Aegis and Night-Stalker will let us know if anything is out there. They protect us both, so no worries. Let's set up the tent, and then we can put our things out to sleep. Always get your shelter set up first, that's vital. Then you can go about doing other things once that is done."

Standing, Shade unpacked the tent, laid it out, then lined up the metal poles to where they belonged. All the while, Lorenzo was watching him. "Okay, we have all the parts for the tent, so let's put the poles together and slide them in the proper slots and the tent will go up. Can you help me, little warrior?"

Lorenzo reluctantly laid the bear down, so he could help his father with the tent. He steadied the tent poles as directed, while his father pulled and secured the canvas. Shade unrolled the two sleeping bags inside the tent and Lorenzo gathered his own blanket and pillow and placed them on his sleeping bag. He laid the bear on the sleeping bag, gently tucking the blanket around him, just like his mommy did to him. He kissed the bear and said, "Good night, little warrior."

"You have good warrior skills. I am so proud of you, Lorenzo. It is not easy to be a warrior, you have to be brave and take care of others and tonight, you have done both already. I think we should take a walk. You can bring your flashlight. We need to collect some branches and wood for a campfire. It will give us light and also keep us warm."

Lorenzo looked unsure about leaving Ted behind when Aegis walked into the camp and nuzzled his hand before curling up in front of the tent. Lorenzo pet the wolf and told her, "You watch out for Ted while I'm gone."

He took his father's hand as they walked together through the low brush, looking for small branches and sticks on the ground.

As they wandered along, Shade tried not to laugh out loud at the bobbing light of Lorenzo's flashlight. His arms were full of branches from the trees that had taken a beating during the winter months. "I do believe, little warrior, we have a good amount of firewood to start this campfire. Let's head back, do you remember the way back?"

Lorenzo carried a small bundle of sticks under one arm as he held the flashlight in his other hand. "Yep. I paid attention like you told me. And I can follow Aegis' scent. Want me to show you the way?"

Shade grinned at him. "That would be a big help, because I think I might be lost. Lead the way, little warrior."

Lorenzo turned in the direction of their camp and honed in on the scent of the wolf. He made his way through the brush, trying to illuminate the path ahead of him. "Stay close to me, Daddy!"

He was pushing his way forward when he stumbled and dropped the flashlight. The light went out as it bounced on the ground and Lorenzo froze in panic. He stood still but could hear his father behind him. He calmed himself, taking a deep breath, and let his eyes adjust to the dark. His vision intensified, and he realized he could see in the dark just as well as he could in the day. He found the flashlight on the ground and picked it up but didn't turn it back on. He continued forward, letting his nose lead him to the wolf. As they reached the clearing, Aegis lifted her head and issued a soft chuffing sound. "See, Daddy. I told you I could find it."

Shade had a moment of panic himself as he watched Lorenzo drop the flashlight and it went out. He could feel Lorenzo's heart rate increase dramatically, but he watched with amazement as Lorenzo gained control of his fear and used his vampire sight. "Yes, you did, son! I am very happy you have such great skills. You are a fast learner. Okay, let's stack this wood into something that will light quickly and burn, shall we?"

As Lorenzo nodded, Shade showed him how to place the branches, starting with the smaller branches and kindling. Lorenzo helped stack and prop and then Shade spotted a large log only about five feet away.

"Lorenzo, there is a large log over there, let's roll it over here, and we can use that to sit on while we enjoy the campfire, *si*?"

Lorenzo rushed to the log and tried to lift it on his own, but it was too heavy for him. His father grabbed it up with one hand and Lorenzo hung on to the back as they dragged the log into their camp.

"Want me to start the fire, Daddy? I can do it!"

Shade knew deep in his heart this was exactly what Lorenzo needed to build his confidence with his gift. "It would be a good use of your gift, son. Do you need any help from me?"

Lorenzo knelt in front of the sticks and branches, and shook his head no. "I just need to concentrate."

He stared at the palm of his hand, his forehead furrowed as he focused his attention. A wisp of smoke appeared to hover just above his open palm and suddenly ignited into a small ball of flames that hovered in the air. Lorenzo made a fist, as if capturing the flame and threw it in the direction of the kindling, watching as the small sticks caught fire, hissing and snapping as the fire grew. Lorenzo looked up at his father, his face lit from the flames of the fire he created. "Pretty good, huh?"

Shade found himself entranced by this small boy of his own flesh and blood. He watched in amazement as he created fire, contained it and then, to his ultimate pride, aimed and threw the flame into the wood pile. He stared at Lorenzo and knew the child in front of him would rule the vampire world. "That is far beyond pretty good, son."

He gave Lorenzo a hug. "Lorenzo, I can't tell you how proud I am of you, how extraordinary you are. You fill my heart with pride and love. You are brave, smart, and your skills as a warrior are growing so fast." He held him for a long moment and then leaned back to look into his eyes. "Tell me something, can you see in the dark as you do in the day?"

Lorenzo looked around the camp and nodded his head. "It looks different than day, but I can see everything clearly, like it was day, only... it's dark. I know I have to be careful with the fire, Daddy. Skelk tells me every day. He reminds me the other vampires will die in the fire, and I must always control it when I use it. I don't have accidents anymore, like the stables, so you don't have to worry about me."

Shade sat down beside him on the huge log. "Well, Lorenzo, I will always worry about you, it's my job. Loving your family means you worry about them sometimes. And I know

Skelk reminds you every day, it is part of the learning process. But also, you need to play and have fun. Mommy wants you to be happy. I want you to be happy as well. Is there anything you want to talk to me about? Any questions you have about anything."

Lorenzo scuffed the toe of his shoe in the dirt as he looked at the ground. "Skelk says I will train some here, but when I'm ten you will send me to the camp at Castello, to train with the other boys my age. Is that true?"

Shade read his body language, and knew he'd probably heard way too much in the camp and around the warriors. He hadn't planned on discussing this with Lorenzo so soon, but Lorenzo needed to be prepared for his destiny.

"I grew up at Castello, it was my home when I was your age. All the warriors were trained there when I was boy. My daddy was the king then, and I was the prince. It was not so hard for me because I lived there, inside the castle. My camp was right there. Our camp here in Bel Rosso does not train children; we are not equipped to do so. When I was ten years old, I went to camp like all the other young warriors. I often lived in the barracks. It helped me to learn my skills to be the best warrior I could be. It is my wish that you go to Castello to train. But don't worry about it now. We will see what things are like once you turn ten. Until that time, you will be here at Bel Rosso and in this camp. Do you understand Castello is yours now? It will be yours when you grow up?"

Lorenzo looked up at him, the light from the fire reflecting in the brilliant blue of his eyes. "Will you and Mommy live there with me?"

Shade felt his heart crack a little. He couldn't lie to his son. "No, son, Mommy and I will always live here at Bel Rosso where we will be throughout eternity. This is ours, what we built and where we will raise you and your sisters when they arrive. Our heart is here, Lorenzo. Do you understand? Castello is our gift to you. It is the legacy of Medici. You are my legacy now."

"But who will take care of me, Daddy?"

He looked deep into his son's eyes. "Marco will take care of you. Nita will follow you there. When you grow up, you will become the strongest and most powerful vampire warrior. You are a prince. You will learn to take care of yourself, the coven, and your family, just like me. You will find your own mate and have your own children. But always remember everyone in our coven is your family, we take care of each other. That is what love and family is about. Mommy and Daddy will always be here for you. That will never ever change."

He nodded his head but found it hard to imagine himself as an adult, living in Castello, without his parents, without Theresa, without Gi or Uncle Luca. The thought of it made him feel lonely and he moved closer to his father. He knew Uncle Marco was at Castello, but Marco wasn't like his daddy. He wondered if he'd make new friends with the young warriors who trained there. He felt a lump in his throat, but he didn't want to cry. "That's where you trained to be a warrior, right?"

Shade could feel his thoughts cascading like water over a falls. Pulling him onto his lap, he wrapped his arms around him to keep him warm and calmed his feelings of abandonment.

"Yes, I did all my training at Castello. So did Luca, Marcello, Raven and so many warriors you know at Bel Rosso. Gi, Theresa and Emma were there since they were young as well. So, you see, a lot of people grew up at Castello. Lorenzo, the next time we go to Castello, your sister will be born there. I think it would be a great idea if we went to the camp together, so you can see what it is like there. There will be lots of warriors there your age. Marco and I were best friends growing up. We were warriors together and learned together. You will make great friends too." Shade kissed the top of his head. "Anything else you want to ask me?"

"I'll be a great warrior too. I'll train hard, and you and Mommy can come see me, okay?"

"Of course, we will, Lorenzo, we will be visiting a lot. Mommy will miss you so much, and so will I. You know, sometimes, I am afraid too, it is okay to be afraid. But the best thing to cure that is to have the skills to combat the fear. You will get those skills at Castello."

As the fire died down, he could feel Lorenzo relaxing heavily in his arms. It was very late for him to be up. Standing, Shade carried him inside the tent. "Let's get some sleep. We will have to get home to Mommy before the sun rises."

Lorenzo curled into his father's broad chest and allowed himself to be carried into the tent. His father laid him down and Lorenzo lifted the blanket and pulled the teddy close. "Tuck me in like Mommy does."

Shade smiled at his son as he tucked the blanket around his small frame and kissed his forehead. "I love you, my beautiful boy. You are my little warrior. And you did such a good job I am giving you cards for your work at camp with Skelk today and for your skills at starting the camp fire. Now, sleep, your dreams will be of slaying dragons."

Lorenzo's eyes were heavy, but he wanted to make sure his father stayed near. "You sleep right next to me, Daddy, and Aegis will guard the tent."

Shade stretched out on his sleeping bag and smiled. "I am right here, warrior, I have your back and Aegis has mine. If you feel cold or want to be with me, you can always get in the sleeping bag with me and we will sleep together, protecting each other."

Lorenzo pondered the option of moving to his father's sleeping bag and it was tempting, but he wanted to make his father proud. "I'm good."

He lifted his small fist toward his father, and Shade gave him a fist bump. Shade watched as his son pulled the bear close to his chest and nestled back under the covers.

Shade didn't sleep during the night hours. His slumber would come in the morning with the rising sun. He lay awake and listened to his son's soft breath. He reached over and laid his hand gently on his head and walked into his dreams, giving him visions of great dragons he slayed with ease, and running home to Bel Rosso to tell his mommy and daddy of his great victory. This was his life now. He'd dreamed of a son who ruled Medici stronger than he ever could. Shade closed his eyes and his thoughts went to *bel*, the only woman who'd ever held his heart and they were suddenly connected, her voice ringing like a beautiful angel in his head.

***

Kate found the house much too quiet with both her warriors gone. She knew Lorenzo would be fine, but she still worried about him. She'd sent Aegis to follow them both. **"Lover, I know I worry too much, but I miss him already. How will I ever let him go?"**

He answered her, **"He will grow up, *mi amore* and want to leave. I know you can't conceive of that right now, but our son will be a powerful warrior in his own right. Do you not miss me even a little?"**

She smiled at his response and sent him an image of the two of them, wrapped around each other inside his sleeping bag. **"Does that answer your question?"**

The pleasure washed over him in waves, her heat and scent. **"Damn woman, you are a wicked vixen. I miss you, and you already know how much I need you."**

He visualized his tongue sliding slowly up her inner thighs, and heard her gasps in response, as he smiled wickedly in the dark.

46

Cory stood in the shop downtown, waiting on Marcello. He'd found this small shop when he was out with Madison, and it had some great handmade beads and studs he could use for embellishment on his leather pieces. Marcello had asked him to make him a coat: a long, black leather duster and Cory had remembered this shop. They had some interesting studs, skulls and other gothic inspired buttons and beads.

He'd asked Marcello to meet him here, so he could take a look and pick out what he liked. Cory checked his watch as he browsed through the shop, expecting him to arrive any minute. Pacing the floor of the shop, he heard the chime over the door and looked up to see Marcello enter.

Marcello had teleported into the city and cruised over the shops in the area where he was to meet Cory. He found an alley a block away from the shop with no foot traffic and landed near some dumpsters. Exiting the alley, he blended into the crowd walking the open mall. His hair was down and flowed softly around his shoulders as he nodded at a few college females who giggled as they walked past him. His jeans were tight, and his booted feet clicked on the pavement.

He found the shop with no problem and saw Cory inside. "Hey, bro. Area is busy this early in the night."

Cory turned to greet him, exchanging a fist bump. "It's always busy down here." He walked Marcello over to the selection of studs and beads and asked him if he saw anything he liked.

Marcello glanced over the huge selection of colors and styles, when his eyes landed on some silver skull studs with black jewels for eyes. Picking them up, he held them up to the light. "I like these. They'll look good on the black. What do you think?"

Cory smiled. "Yeah they're the ones I thought you might like. I can do a pattern on the back using these studs. Come over here, there are some cool coat buttons, I think you might like those."

Marcello followed him to where they were displayed, right in front of the windows overlooking the street. After he picked out the ones he wanted, Cory took the items to pay for them, and the two of them left the shop and walked in the direction of the parking lot where Cory had left his truck. "You need a ride home?"

Marcello shook his head. "Nah, I'll teleport. But I'll walk with you to the truck, less people around to see me leave."

Marcello nodded and smiled at every young female they passed, and the girls returned his smile. Cory shook his head. "Man, you're like a chic magnet. That blonde almost fell on her face, as she passed us trying to look at you."

Marcello laughed and threw his arm over Cory's shoulder. "Ah, my young brother, I could teach you some tricks, but word has it you already have a female setting your hormones on fire."

Cory laughed. "Yeah and she's mine too, and I don't share, so don't use your tricks when she's around, bro."

They kept teasing each other as they approached the truck. Cory hit the remote button on his key fob, unlocking the truck. Opening the door, he put the packages inside as Marcello scanned the parking lot.

"The lot looks pretty empty. I can teleport from here, see you back at Bel Rosso. Thanks bro, looking forward to my new threads."

Marcello slapped Cory on the back, stepped back and instantly, he was gone. Climbing into his truck, Cory fired up the engine, pulled out and headed back to Bel Rosso. He had a lot of work to get done.

***

Madison grabbed up her new leather bag Cory had made for her and slung it over her shoulder. She had packed up several new pieces of pottery she'd recently completed and was ready to take them downtown to the shop. It had been a few days since Madison had been to Bel Rosso. She'd been entranced by the beauty of the place but surprised too. She would never have imagined Cory came from money. Not that it mattered, and Cory had made it clear it wasn't his money, that he was still expected to work for what he earned. She had loved meeting his family and they had all seemed to go out of their way to make her feel welcome there, but still, there was something she couldn't quite put her finger on.

Both Kate and Cory seemed eager to remove Lorenzo from her presence as quickly as possible, and the butler, she had this feeling when she was around him she couldn't explain. He looked ancient, and she wondered why anyone that old would still need to be working.

Then there was Luca, their security guard. He was extremely polite, but when he had looked at her she felt momentarily immobilized. His eyes locked into hers and she couldn't look away. She felt a shiver run up her spine just remembering it. It was like he could see right through her, read her thoughts. She shook it off as she picked up the box of pottery and headed out the door. "You're just imagining things."

Catching the bus at the corner outside her apartment, she rode with the box on her lap to the downtown mall. It was early evening and the crowds were just starting to gather on the mall for the people going out to dinner. Madison was walking slowly, checking out the shop windows when she saw Cory's truck parked on a side street near the parking lot. Smiling to herself, she headed in the direction of the truck when she saw Cory and his friend from the frat party approaching the truck. She picked up her pace, hoping to get to him before he drove away.

She was watching the exchange between the two men when Cory's friend disappeared before her eyes. Madison stopped in her tracks with her mouth open, and watched as Cory nonchalantly got into the truck and drove away. Madison stepped back, and leaned against the wall of the building, questioning what she'd just seen.

Maybe it was an optical illusion? Maybe he walked away at an angle that didn't allow her to see him? Or maybe she was losing her mind? She slowly lowered herself to the sidewalk, sitting down and laying her head back against the brick wall, clinging to the box of pottery, her eyes closed tight. She felt a hand on her shoulder and was startled. Her eyes flew open as she gasped.

A young man stood over her. "Are you okay? I saw you go down. You look really pale. Would you like some water?"

The stranger offered her his bottled water, and Madison gratefully took it. She poured a small amount onto the hem of her long skirt and held the cool cloth to her face. "Thank you. I think maybe I just got overheated."

He helped her to her feet and she thanked him again as he walked away. She continued on her way to the pottery shop, her mind in chaos. "Cory. Who are you?"

47

They arrived by private jet in Des Moines, and the campaign bus Braden had purchased for them was waiting on the tarmac. Braden had spent the entire flight with Alec, going over their schedule, and working with the speech-writer to put the final touches on the stump speech. Alec had practiced it several times until they were all pleased with the tone.

Braden was ushering them off the plane and onto the bus, which had been modified to include a small bathroom and a private room with two narrow built-in cots that would accommodate Alec and Rissa if they wished to rest between stops. Braden found the bus on sale from a rock band that used it for touring and did a few modifications to make it as elegant as possible, knowing already it would never be enough to suit Miss Prissy. He had to smile to himself. He'd overheard the campaign staff referring to Rissa as Miss Prissy and thought how appropriate it was. The problem was, she couldn't be perceived as Miss Prissy by the voters, and that was going to be Braden's problem.

Braden ushered them to the bus. "We'll transfer your luggage from the plane to the bus. Do you need any of the bags inside before we put them all in the storage compartment?"

Alec shook his head and said he was fine. He looked to Rissa. "Anything you need, darling?"

Staring at the bus in disgust, gritting her teeth slightly, she gave him a fake smile. "A limo, maybe?"

Alec shook his head. "The bus is larger, and has been modified to accommodate the staff, so they can work while we're on the road. Also, there may be times when we have press on the bus for short periods, while we give interviews. It's important we look like we can identify with the lives of the constituents, Rissa. They know I have money, but it's not smart to rub their noses in it. Now, come on, be a good girl and get on the bus."

Rissa rolled her eyes and sighed. "Right, the bus."

Alec took her hand and Braden gave them a tour of the tin can. Rissa had to bite her lip to keep from commenting. As Braden showed them the cots, her eyes widened, and she glared at Alec. "Cots?"

Alec sighed. "It's just a place to rest. You'll be on your feet a lot. If we have several events scheduled on consecutive days, we'll drive, and it will allow you to get some sleep. You'll survive it, my darling. Just think of the pay-off."

"Of course." Her eyes slid to Braden Childs. If she could have staked the vampire with her eyes, she would have. "Would you please direct me as to where I am to perch while we drive along the Iowa countryside on our way to charm the local voters." Turning to Alec, she inquired, "Where's Hyde?"

Braden caught the cold stare and shook his head. It was going to be a long campaign. He'd managed Alec's first Senate run, but Rissa wasn't part of the picture then. He was seeing her then, but it had not gotten serious, and Braden didn't have to deal with her on the campaign.

"Rissa, it's standard for the candidate's wife to introduce her husband. I've written out an introduction for you. I'd like you to practice it before we get there. Our first stop will be the VFW, so we'll have a lot of veterans in the crowd. I have emphasized Alec's record with veterans' issues in your intro. Once you introduce him, he'll come on the stage. You need to give him a warm but discreet kiss, and then leave the stage. Any questions?"

Rissa took the papers from his hands. "First of all, I'm well versed in public speaking. Secondly, Alec and I are both skilled in manipulating mortals, so consider it handled. Now, two things I need to be advised on. What is VFW? And do I exit the stage left or right, and where do I go from there. These may be small things to you, but vital information to me so I don't look like a fool."

Braden looked at her a moment, blinking his eyes. Was she joking? She was the only person on the bus who was born mortal and she was asking him about the VFW? He heard the snickering of the other campaign workers as they all grabbed up papers and laptops and tried to busy themselves and not make any eye contact.

"Uh, the VFW stands for Veterans of Foreign Wars. Most every town of any size will have a local VFW hall. As for the set-up, we'll have some time before the hall is opened to the public, so you can see how the stage is set up, and where to enter and exit. We'll do a sound check, and you can practice your intro at the podium."

Rissa heard the snickers and ignored them. She was no fool, and she'd show them, no one could do this better than her. "No one knows Alec as I do. Relax, Braden, I can do this." Rissa looked down at her speech and, within seconds, had it memorized. "So, these people are soldiers?" Sighing softly, she looked out the window of the bus. "Please send Hyde to me immediately, it's all I ask before we leave."

Braden looked about for her protector and saw him standing on the tarmac with Mateo, both of them having a smoke. "He'll be on the bus in a moment. But just to clarify, these people are mostly retired military, not active military, and they may be there with their spouses. There may be a few active military in the audience, and also just locals. The audience will be a mixture of people."

Both Hyde and Mateo stepped onto the bus as he finished his explanation. Their height barely gave them room to stand up straight, and they filled the space.

Braden welcomed them aboard. "Gentleman, please make yourselves comfortable, and let me know if there's anything you need. Hyde, I do believe Rissa is waiting for you."

Hyde removed his suit jacket and loosened his tie as he walked in her direction. "Got a problem, Rissa?"

Rissa saw him when he stepped on the bus, but he wasn't alone. The man with him was definitely vampire. Tall and muscular, his hair a dark brown, cut short but longer than Hyde's. He was clean shaven and smelled like heaven. He wore a suit that fit him perfectly. She imagined him dressed in leathers and no shirt. Shaking her head, licking her lips, she watched as Hyde removed his jacket and looked at her with those beautiful eyes. "Just sit beside me, please. Get me through this, Hyde, I'm a bit nervous. Where is my bracelet with the communication system? You have it, right?"

Hyde slid into the seat beside Rissa. He didn't miss her complete appraisal of Mateo. Taking her hand, he gave it a squeeze. "Relax, Rissa, you'll be fine. You're the Darling of G-town, remember? If you can handle that crowd, what you experience here will be nothing. And yes, I have your bracelet."

Lifting her hand, he took the security bracelet from his pocket and attached it to her wrist. They had designed the bracelet especially for Rissa. It was a narrow diamond cuff with a single charm. If she ever felt at risk, she could grasp the charm and it would transmit a signal through the tiny earpiece Hyde wore in his ear. She smiled at Hyde, enjoying the attention. She felt safer now. He calmed her just knowing he'd be with her. "Who's that man with you and what's his name?"

Hyde grinned. "That would be Mateo, Medici warrior, he's Alec's body guard for this campaign, so don't get yourself all worked up."

Rissa laughed and slapped him lightly on the arm. "I have you, Hyde, and I have Alec, and I sure don't need any more Medici's in my life."

Alec was talking with Braden but noticed the interplay between Hyde and Rissa. He was aware her attraction to her protector was real, but he also knew Hyde would never act on it. Hyde cared about Rissa's safety, but his allegiance to the Medici coven was unbreakable. Alec had to give Shade credit. The loyalty of his warriors was something every master envied. Wrapping up with Braden, he stepped over to Rissa and Hyde. "Any last questions, darling? You know what you have to do? There will be press there, I'm sure, since this is one of our first stops."

Beaming up at Alec, she responded. "Yes, I know what to do, have my speech memorized already. I'm glad to hear there will be press. That's where I do my best work, you know that,

Alec. Let's get this show on the road, shall we, Senator Canton? How long is our ride?"

"Not far. We'll be there in ten. You'll make your intro, then I'll give my speech. We'll mingle with the crowd afterward, and let them take photos, shake hands, then back on the bus for the next stop. We'll get in three stops today before we move on to the next town."

Rissa felt the bus lurch forward and she laid her head back on the seat, as Alec moved to a seat beside Braden. Rissa had continued to grip Hyde's hand and he knew she was more nervous than she let on.

"Take deep breaths, Rissa, you've got this, it will be a walk in the park. Keep a smile on your face, no matter what the hell you see or hear, never let them see you sweat."

Rissa took a long cleansing breath. "Thank you, Hyde, you always know the right thing to say."

As the bus pulled into the parking lot of the local VFW, the crowd had already started to gather. Braden stood up and told his team to look alive. Alec stood and checked his hair in the mirror. Hyde stood and put his suit jacket back on, and straightened his tie, nodding to Mateo. Braden stepped forward, taking charge.

"Mateo, you exit the bus first, coordinate with the local police and make sure we have a clear path. Alec, he'll signal to us when he's ready, then you'll exit and stand at the door. Rissa, you'll follow, and allow Alec to help you from the bus. Hyde, you can exit behind them, but keep a discreet distance. The focus needs to be on Alec and Rissa. Okay, people. Let's do this thing!"

48

Cory was feeling restless, he missed Madison. She'd wrapped up finals and was off now for the summer break and he knew she'd use the time to create a lot of pottery pieces to sell. He made a spur of the moment decision to ride into town and surprise her.

Taking one of the bikes from the garage, he headed into town. As he sat at a red light, he noticed a flower shop up ahead, with huge baskets of flowers sitting outside. As the light turned green, he pulled into the shop. He selected a beautiful bouquet of yellow daisies, with some small purple flowers he'd never heard of. The girl behind the counter wrapped the long stems in green tissue paper, and tied a wide purple satin ribbon around the stems. He tucked them carefully inside the side bags of the bike, making sure not to crush or damage them. His dad was always giving Kate flowers, and he hoped Madison would love these.

Pulling up to her house, he parked a few spaces down, so she wouldn't hear the roar of the engine. He wanted to surprise her. Taking off his helmet, he hung it over the handlebars and retrieved his bouquet. Ringing the bell, he waited but Madison didn't come to the door immediately, so he knocked loudly, hoping she was home.

Madison was working at the potter's wheel, her hands wet with the clay when she thought she heard the doorbell. She stopped the wheel and grabbed a rag to wipe her hands when she heard the knocking. "All right already. I'm coming!"

She headed for the door and peeked out the window to see Cory at her doorstep. Opening the door to him, she expressed her surprise. "Cory! I wasn't expecting you. Come in."

Cory was all smiles. Walking inside, he realized he must have interrupted her work. "Oh. Did I interrupt you? I'm sorry, Madison, but I was thinking of you, and thought I'd stop by. Um, these are for you." Holding out the bouquet to her, he kissed her softly on the cheek.

She was glad to see him. She hadn't spoken to him since the sighting on the mall, and she'd been plagued with questions. She accepted the flowers and returned his kiss. "Daisies! I love them. I'll put them in water."

She turned to walk to her kitchen and found an old Mason jar under the sink, filling it with water. She removed the purple ribbon from the flowers and tied it around the mouth of the jar. Placing the flowers on her small dining table, she turned to him. "Can I get you something to drink? I have green tea."

"Sure. Need any help?"

"Nope. I got it." She removed two bottles of green tea from her fridge and handed him one. "Let's sit on the sofa. It's more comfortable in there."

She led him to her small living room and took a seat on the secondhand sofa she'd purchased on Craigslist, and then updated with an off-white canvas slip-cover. The sofa was strewn with a collection of small throw pillows in bright colors, an assortment of designs and styles she'd collected over time from several thrift shops. She curled up in the corner of the sofa and placed her drink on the hand-painted coffee table, as Cory sat next to her. "I saw you in town a few days ago."

Cory was sipping his tea and snuggling into the pillows. "Oh yeah? I didn't see you. Where was I?"

She took a sip of her tea. "I was walking up Water Street, on my way to the mall and I saw your truck. I was about a block away, so I started in your direction and I saw you walk up to the truck with your friend....the guy that was at the frat party with you the night we met? I don't know his name."

Cory shifted uncomfortably on the couch, wondering how much she'd seen. "Oh, yeah, that was Marcello. He works for my dad. What were you doing down there?"

"Marcello." Madison repeated his name, and tried to erase the image in her head. "I was taking some new pottery pieces to the shops. I have a lot of time to create new stuff now school is out, and the summer draws a lot of tourists here, so I can sell a lot, and save up for the winter when I don't sell as much." How did she tell him what she'd seen? How did she approach this, when she wasn't sure herself what she'd seen?

Cory steered the conversation away from Marcello. "Sure, sounds like a great idea, saving up some cash. Hey, do you want to do something, go grab something to eat?" He was trying to think of anything to distract her from this conversation.

"Yeah, sure. I'm starving. Let me get my sandals." She stood up to head for the bedroom. "So, this Marcello, when he was at your truck. I mean, I saw the two of you talking, and then you got in the truck and he just sort of...you know. I mean, one minute I saw him talking to you, and then, like, he was gone or something. It sounds weird, right?"

She kept her back to him as she searched the floor for her sandals, finding them by her bed and slipping her feet into them.

Cory stood up, feeling panicked. *She saw it, she saw Marcello!* He was grateful she had her back to him because he knew his surprise was written all over his face. He felt like someone had punched him in the gut. "Yeah that sounds weird, must have been a play of light or something."

She spun around and stared at him and he kept his face neutral. At least, he hoped he did. "Marcello just walks fast, sometimes." He shrugged his shoulders, as if to imply it was nothing, but his voice sounded a bit squeaky even to him.

Madison studied him as he responded. "Yeah sure, that makes sense. I mean, I knew there had to be a logical explanation." She laughed. "But I have to admit, it kinda freaked me out at the time. So, when are you inviting me back to Bel Rosso? I still haven't met your dad."

Cory took a deep breath and tried to relax, sliding his hand through his hair, pushing it behind his ear. He smiled at her, stalling for time to think of answers. "You can come back anytime you want. But as for my dad, well I'll have to check with him on his schedule, he's so busy." Shrugging, he walked to her and laid his hands on her shoulders and began to play with her long hair. "So, what are you hungry for?" Leaning in, he nibbled softly on her neck and inhaled her gentle scent. "You smell like clay."

She laughed out loud, throwing her head back. "Well, let's hope you find the smell of clay erotic. I'm afraid I smell of clay quite frequently. Come on. Let's go for some Italian. Oh...unless you get that at home all the time. We can do Chinese if you want."

"Well, I happen to like the smell of clay, and on you, it does smell erotic." He slid his hands to her face and kissed her. It was no ordinary kiss, but one that held promise of what was to come, and communicated the urgency he felt to be inside her. Ending the kiss, he looked deep into her big eyes.

They both stood silent, taken aback by the unexpected kiss, and the desire it had created in both of them. Struggling to find normalcy, Cory returned to the topic of dinner. "I say Italian, to be honest, we don't eat a lot of it at home, so fresh pasta would be awesome."

Taking her hand, he led her out to his bike, glad the questions were over... for now.

49

Alec was pleased with their first round of campaign stops. Braden had done an excellent job of maximizing their schedule and working in as many stops as possible. The crowds had been impressive and his early poll rankings had him at the top of the potential candidates.

Still, he could tell there was friction between Braden and Rissa. She bristled at being told what to do. They'd come back home for a short break in the campaign and were scheduled to leave again tomorrow for New Hampshire. Alec expected to do well in the Northeast part of the country, since he was from Connecticut.

Hyde and Mateo had been given a few days off while they were home, and Rissa had temporarily turned over her business to one of her associates. He knew she was going to have to sell the business when he became President. But for now, he'd decided not to push the matter. Rissa had done well on the campaign when she was on stage, or when she was in front of the press, but she wasn't happy mingling with the voters.

Braden had pointed her behavior out to him, not that he needed to. Alec knew before they even got started Rissa would have an issue with all the glad-handing. At least coming home had appeased her to some degree, and all the equipment from the sex chamber at Castello had been shipped here. Santos was coordinating with a construction crew to finish out their basement, and make it sound-proof, and Rissa was at least excited about that.

Alec poured a glass of Midnight and walked out to the pool. He knew they wouldn't be home often with all the demands of the campaign, and once he was in the White House, there was no way they could move the dungeon playroom. He swallowed down the drink before he stepped back inside the house and called out to her. "Rissa!"

***

Rissa was glad to be home, sleeping in her own bed, enjoying the quiet of their house. Her associate had taken over the reins of her business and she'd had little time to check on things while they were on the campaign trail. But so far, her associate had done an excellent job.

She dumped out her luggage and sent her clothes to the cleaners, as she rummaged through her closet, deciding on what she should pack for the next round of the clown tour. She heard Alec call to her and she scrunched up her face. What in the hell could he possibly want now? She loved being with him, but they had little time alone. There was always some speech to prepare, or someone from the campaign approaching him with details of the next stop on the tour. If she didn't have Hyde, she would have quit this circus days ago.

Throwing the two designer dresses onto the bed, she took a deep breath, plastered the smile back on her face and headed downstairs. She found Alec standing in the open doors leading out to the pool. She wished he'd take the time to swim with her, but she knew better. "Alec, what could you possibly need me for? Seriously, I have no time to be lectured on what I did or didn't do on the circus bus charades."

Alec smirked at her. "Just wanted to make sure you were getting packed for the next round. We'll fly to New Hampshire early tomorrow morning. Alto said wheels up at six, so we'll need to leave the house by 5:00 a.m. at the latest. I've already let Shade know and his warriors will be here around 4:30. You've been doing a good job on the stage, darling, and you are expert at handling the press, I just need you to be a little more engaging when you're meeting with the people. They need to feel like you care about them."

She stared back at him. "Yes, my wicked vampire, I'll do all you ask." Opening the gold cigarette box, she pulled out a cigarette and lit it, then walked to the bar and poured herself a Midnight. Spinning in her bare feet, she leaned her back against the bar. "I was packing. I had fourteen new dresses and suits delivered. I can't be seen wearing the same outfit in any photos. I need to be prepared for that. I'm doing the best I can, Alec. You asked me to mingle with the peasants and pretend I give a shit when I don't."

Alec let the comment slide. "And one more thing. Braden says he thinks you should tone down the wardrobe. There will be fundraising events where I meet with rich donors where that attire will be appropriate. But when we're in these small town hall meetings, mingling with the mainstream voters, he thinks it's best if your clothing looks a little less, well, unattainable to the average consumer. He thinks you should dress more off the rack."

Sighing heavily, she looked up at the ceiling, taking a long drag on the cigarette. "You know, Alec, Braden has no idea about fashion and what the papers will do to me if I look like I walked out of some department store. I have designers already sending me sketches. The clothes are free. They just want me to wear them so their names are in the press. I refuse to look like some middle class cow when we have money. Besides, I don't see you toning down your wardrobe."

Alec sighed and lit up a cigarette. This was just the beginning of a very long campaign and he wondered how much energy he wanted to expend on this issue. "My suits are hand tailored. But if you notice, when I'm in the masses, I wear a button down shirt and a pair of khakis. When we make the rounds of the various outdoor events, you see me in jeans and a polo shirt. I dress appropriate for the occasion, Rissa, and I expect you to do the same. Once we're in the White House, I don't give a flying fuck if you wear a new designer gown every day. But while we're on the campaign trail, you'll do as I ask. I don't want to argue this point. It's not a request, understand?"

She slammed the glass down on the bar, her temper rising. "You don't want to argue the point? All we ever do is argue lately. Is all this truly worth it to you, Alec? Is getting there worth us?"

Alec turned his back on her and took a slow drag on the

cigarette before exhaling, taking time to get his temper under control. He turned to face her, speaking with control through gritted teeth. "Us? Are you saying to me your wardrobe is more important to you than our success? You've known from the beginning what I wanted, Rissa. I never hid my ambition or my goals. You knew what you were signing up for. Do you want me to release you? Is that what you want? If not, you'd do well to remember I'm your master."

With those two words her heart stopped beating. All her anger left her, replaced by fear. Release her? Alec had never spoken those words to her and suddenly, she felt her skin chill and her throat tighten as she lowered her head. "You'd release me? No, Alec, please, that's not what I meant at all." Her body trembled slightly, and she shook her head. "No." With more bravery than she felt, she raised her eyes to him. "I'm your mate, I'd never asked to be released. Please, Alec, tell me you wouldn't consider it."

He sat in the large leather chair and took her hand, pulling her into his lap. "You try my patience like no other. I swear to god, Rissa, you seem intent on making my life more difficult."

He kissed the top of her head. "I was drawn to your stubbornness. I guess I never anticipated just how much you'd use it against me. Can we please, just for once, have you agree to follow my instructions? We're only just beginning this campaign. We have a long road ahead, and we're both tired already. It will be tedious. I know that. And I know I'm asking a lot. But I don't want to go through this with you every few days."

Rissa lay against him, glad to have his touch. She didn't want to fight with him, but at least try to have something left of her dignity after this campaign. "I know you don't, Alec. I'm trying so hard, I truly am, I promise I'll do better."

Leaning into him, she kissed his neck softly, her lips brushing the pulsing vein that called to her constantly. "So, tell me, is our playroom completed? I think we both could use it."

He laid his head back against the chair, exposing his neck to her, signaling she could feed. "It isn't completed yet. Alto says all the shipments arrived, and he has them in storage while the basement in under construction. Soon, my darling."

There was no other thought in her head except his call to her to feed. Without another second wasted, her fangs punched through as she sank her teeth deep into his neck, absorbing his power as she swallowed. Every fiber of her body responded to him, as his blood eased her hunger but stirred her sexual desire. She drank her fill before slowly disengaging from him, licking her lips.

He swatted her bottom as she finished feeding. "Now go. Finish your packing. I have a call scheduled with Braden. I'll be up soon."

Closing her eyes, she knew he'd prefer something else besides the pleasures of her body. She stood and walked to the door. "Yes, master."

50

Cory drove the truck back to Madison's apartment after The Black Keys concert. It had been a perfect evening and Madison looked amazing tonight. Cory was proud to have her as his date. As he pulled up to her apartment and parked, he switched off the engine and walked around to open the door for her. "I had a great time, Maddie. I love the Keys."

Madison slipped from the passenger seat in the truck and kissed him. "That makes two of us. You want to come in? I don't have any summer classes tomorrow."

Cory was hoping she'd ask. "Yeah, sure, I'd love that, plus I need a drink. Give me your keys, I'll open the door."

Opening the door for her, he grabbed her hand and led her inside. She headed into the kitchen as he made his way to her bedroom and flopped down on her bed, covered with a blue Indian print spread, and surrounded by netting, hung from the ceiling. He loved this place. He called out to her. "Water will be fine."

Madison laughed. "I can do better than water. How about some wine? I have some white wine chilled in the fridge."

She pulled the bottle from the shelf and removed the cork, pouring two generous portions for them in some mismatched wine glasses she'd bought at a flea market. She carried the glass to him and stretched out on the bed next to him. She shook her head. "My ears are still ringing from the concert."

He loved her laugh, so carefree and easy. He took the glass of wine, watching her stretch across the bed. "Yeah, but it's a small sacrifice. The music was awesome."

Taking a large sip of the wine, he sat the glass on the side table and rolled onto his side, looking at her. "You look beautiful tonight."

Leaning over, he kissed her softly on the lips. Madison rolled toward him, returning the kiss and almost spilling her wine in the process. She let Cory take the glass from her hand

and set it aside, as she moved closer, feeling the heat of his body through her clothes. She ran her hand through his hair and kissed him again, slipping her tongue in his mouth.

Cory let her lead. He could feel her tongue as it explored his mouth. He felt a sharp tug in his gut. He knew he had to be careful to not let the beast emerge. He wanted so much more with Madison. His hand wandered slowly up her rib cage and cradled her breast as he massaged gently, and her kiss deepened. He felt her hand in his hair and he moaned through the kiss. He wanted her, but he must let her move at her own pace.

Madison pushed him onto his back and straddled him. The hem of her long skirt pushed up her thighs. She ran her hands down his chest. His build was slender but he was rock hard. He never mentioned working out, but she knew he must. Her hands sought out the snap closure on his jeans and she popped it open. "It's time, don't you think?"

Cory stared up at her as she was surrounded by a small halo of light from the ceiling. This was what he'd been waiting for, but he had to slow things down. She still had no idea what he was, and he wanted her to know before they had sex. He wanted her to come to him willingly, and with no regrets. He grabbed her hands to stop her.

"Madison, wait. I'm not sure it's the right time yet. I love you so much, but I don't want you to feel pressured. You don't have to do this just to keep my attention." Letting go of her hands, he slid them up her arms and through her hair, pulling her down for a kiss. She resisted and sat upright.

"I don't understand, Cory. I love you too, and I've been waiting to hear you say it. We've been together for months now. You've never pressured me. If anything, I have pressured you."

She slid off of him and picked up the wine, downing it. "I'm beginning to get a complex. I mean, I really appreciated that you took it slow in the beginning. Most guys don't." She turned her head and looked at him as the thought formulated in her head. "Are you a virgin, Cory?"

His laughter filled the room. He was so far from being a

virgin, having sold his body to both male and female vamps to do with what they will. "I'm sorry, Madison, I didn't mean to laugh. No, I'm not a virgin, and not gay." Sitting up, he got his laughter under control. "I love you." Slipping from the bed, he paced in her room. "It's not that I don't want you. It's the complete opposite. I want you so much. I care about you so much. I just want it to be special."

Madison watched him as he paced; his features so beautiful in the soft light of the bedroom. She had loved him for some time now, but never expressed how she felt. He always held back, never letting their passion take them very far and it had confused her.

"I don't understand, Cory. If you love me, and I love you, it will be special, wherever we are. You don't have to do anything to impress me. You have my heart already."

He stopped his pacing and knelt on the bed, kissing her gently on the lips. "Madison, having your heart means so much to me. It means the sex is not important at the moment, but what we have between us is real, it will last. You have all of me, heart and soul. I'm asking you to wait. It's important to me we spend more time together and develop a strong bond without sex. I know you think I'm crazy, but I do this for both of us. The sex can confuse things. Many couples confuse sex for love, and later, they find they have nothing. If our bond is strong and stable before we have sex, nothing will break it. Do you understand?"

She tilted her head and looked at him, pondering his words. "I'm trying to understand, Cory. I mean, I feel like I'm ready for us to move to the next step. But if you're asking me for more time..." She chuckled. "You know this sounds like role reversal, right? It's usually the girl saying we have to wait."

He smiled at her, knowing she understood. "Well, my dad has taught me to respect women. He says women are valued for their gift of giving life and loving us is never to be taken lightly. It sounds crazy, but when I see my dad and Kate, I want that for myself. I want this to be forever, Madison. My love for you is real, as is my respect."

Kissing her nose, he rolled off the bed and walked to the table, downing his wine. "I guess I should head back home. I don't want to leave here until I know you're okay with this though, okay with me."

Her head was spinning. He was talking about a real commitment, a forever commitment. She wasn't expecting him to be so open. "Wow. I don't know what to say. I mean, I fell in love with you quickly, but you never said how you felt, so I kept it to myself. I didn't want to scare you away. And when you never tried to make love to me, I thought it was just a *good friends* thing. And tonight, you not only say you love me, but you're talking about us being together forever. Being like your dad and stepmom. It's a lot to take in. I mean, don't get me wrong, I've thought about us being together too."

She stood and went to him. "Does your family know how you feel? I mean, I've only been there once, and I haven't even met your dad yet. Are you concerned about how they'll react?"

He took her into his arms. "They know I really care about you. I think Kate knows more than my dad. I'm not concerned how they'll react. If I love you, they'll accept that. My happiness is important to them, our family unit is tight. And to be honest, I don't want to be with anyone but you. I love you, Madison. It's simple but complicated, and I do want you to meet my dad. It's just his schedule. It's easier to have time with him in the late evening, when he's more likely to be home. Do you want to meet him?"

"Of course, I want to meet him. I know how close you are to him. You talk about him all the time, and besides, I already have so much respect for him. He stepped up and acknowledged you as his child, even after all these years, and the way he took care of your mom. A lot of men would have just walked away, not accepted responsibility. You set up the time. My schedule is pretty loose right now. I just have two summer classes, so whenever his schedule will accommodate us, just set it up."

Leaning his forehead against hers, he sighed. "Do you know

how special you are to put up with me? I've never been in love before. It's my first time, so please don't think I'm weird."

The pieces fell into place for her when he admitted he'd never been in love before. It made sense now why the love making needed to be special, something sacred, and not just another hook-up. "I don't think you're weird. Well, yeah, I do, but in a good way. But I'm weird too, and I've waited a long time to find someone who could appreciate my weirdness."

Cory nuzzled into her neck and laughed. Kissing her, he led her to the door. "I need to go. I'll set up a night to come out to Bel Rosso and meet my dad. I had a great time tonight." Kissing her again, he smiled down into her eyes. "I love you."

Walking out the door, he felt like a million bucks. Everything was going to be okay, he could feel it.

51

It was the big night. Madison would finally be meeting Shade! Cory was a bit nervous. His dad could be intimidating. As he drove down the private drive to Bel Rosso, Madison was fiddling with a long strand of her dark blonde hair. "Are you nervous? Because you don't need to be, he's expecting to meet you. Just be yourself, Madison, he'll appreciate that."

Madison anxiously wiped the palms of her hand across her skirt. She wasn't usually nervous about meeting people. She didn't usually care whether people liked her or not, but she knew this was different. She knew how close Cory was to his dad. What if he didn't like her? Would that change how Cory felt about her?

She looked out the window of the truck as the rolling hills of Bel Rosso slipped by. The sun was setting behind the mountain range, and the sky was a blend of pinks and purples. She thought this may be the most beautiful place she'd ever seen. She took a deep breath and placed her hand on Cory's thigh as he maneuvered the truck around the driveway, stopping in front of the house. She saw Kate standing in the doorway to greet them, and Madison released her breath, unaware, until now, that she'd been holding it.

Cory quickly slid out of the truck and walked around, opening the door for her, and helping her down from the cab. The lights were on in the house, and it looked welcoming as day turned to night.

As Madison stepped down from the truck, he wrapped his arm around her waist, kissing her cheek. "Remember, I love you. Just be yourself." With his arm still around her waist, they walked toward the door where Kate greeted them.

***

Kate had sent a message to Aegis to stay clear. She'd heard the rumble of the truck engine as it moved toward the house, and she hurried to the door to greet them. She knew how important this was to Cory, and she wanted this girl to feel comfortable here. Gaining her trust would be important to her accepting what they were when the time came to reveal that to her. She walked toward them as Cory helped his girlfriend from the truck. "Welcome back, Madison."

She wrapped her arms around the girl's shoulder. Madison was returning her hug when they all heard the scramble of small feet as a barefoot Lorenzo, clad in pajamas, ran out the door toward them.

Lifting his hands in the air to be picked up, Lorenzo called out. "Cory!"

Cory laughed as Lorenzo ran head long for him with his arms held open. Catching him in the air, he lifted Lorenzo over his head before settling the boy on his hip. "Hey, little dude, you should soon be in bed. Do you remember my girlfriend, Madison?"

Lorenzo squirmed until Cory put him on the ground and the child wrapped both arms around Madison's legs to hug her. "Hello, Miss Madison."

Kate saw Theresa at the door as she chased after Lorenzo and waved her back, letting her know it was okay. Madison laughed, and ran her hands through the toddler's coal black curls. Kate knelt down to Lorenzo and gave him a stern look. "I thought we understood it was bedtime."

Lorenzo looked back at her with a practiced innocence as he responded, "But I had to say hi to Miss Madison."

Kate shook her head and picked up her son, balancing him on her hip. "Come on inside, you two. Shade is still tied up in a meeting. He's running a little late. Cory, why don't you take Madison upstairs to your room, and I'll call you as soon as your dad is free."

"Sounds good, we can relax a bit before Dad sees us."

Following Kate up the stairs, as she held a wiggling Lorenzo, Cory shook his head. "Little dude, you need to get to bed, and listen to your mom. You need your rest."

Lorenzo looked over Kate's shoulder at Cory and Madison. "I know, Skelk says I need to rest so I can learn to be a better warrior. Are you coming to the camp tomorrow?"

Damn, Cory knew somehow Lorenzo would say something he'd have to later explain to Madison. "Oh yeah, little dude, see you tomorrow."

Cory quickly angled Madison down the hall to the next flight of stairs that led to his rooms. Shutting the door behind them, he apologized for Lorenzo's enthusiasm. "Sorry about Lorenzo, I think he was supposed to be in bed before we got here, but man, he never gives up. Let me get some music on."

Walking to the huge setup of electronics, he plugged his iPhone into the system and looked over at Madison. "Any preferences? I think I have just about everything on this thing."

She walked around the room again, looking at his things. "Nah, just hit shuffle. So, who was the other lady at the door? The one that looked like she was chasing after Lorenzo."

"Oh, that was Theresa, she's Lorenzo's nanny. She helps with him because seriously, you need a full-time runner for him. I'm sorry I didn't introduce you to her. That was rude." Walking to the large sectional sofa, he summoned her to join him. Madison curled up close to him.

"And what was that other name he mentioned? Skelk? Is that Scandinavian or something?"

Cory swallowed hard. He couldn't bring up the warriors and the camp. "Oh, Skelk? Don't pay any attention to Lorenzo, he has a wild imagination. I never saw anything like it, he's an only child and he lives in his own world here. Skelk is his imaginary friend. My dad built this pirate ship playhouse out back, and Lorenzo likes to play pirates and stuff like that. He pretends he's a warrior pirate and he has these imaginary friends he fights and plays with. Sometimes, Dad goes out there to play with him and I do too. It's fun."

Madison felt his nervousness, and it only fed her own. Was he worried his dad wouldn't like her too? "Lorenzo sounds like a handful. Didn't you say your step-mom was pregnant? I guess it's a good thing she has help. Sounds like she's going to need it."

"Yes, Kate's pregnant. Everyone is excited for the new

baby."

Madison picked up several books from his coffee table, all novels, and all about vampires. "Wow. You never mentioned you were interested in vampire mythology. I've read a few of these from Anne Rice."

"Oh, uh, yeah, I like vampires. It's pretty cool. So, you're into vampires too? I never knew that. What's your take on them?"

Madison scrunched up her face. "My take on them? I guess I never really thought about it. I mean, I believe there are supernatural elements in this world. I believe ghosts are real, and there are people who've had encounters with them, same with angels. I believe in angels. I know people who claim to be witches. But not, you know, flying around on a broom or anything. I think they're just connected to the energy of nature, somehow. I think their spells are more the power of suggestion. You know, if you believe it will happen, then it will, like a self-fulfilling prophecy sort of thing. But vampires? I don't think people rise up from the dead and walk around. I've read some stuff where people claim to be vampires, but I think it's just a lifestyle choice, like all those kids who dress goth. I don't know, what do you think?"

Cory watched her closely, trying to gage her reaction. She at least believed in some paranormal things. Maybe that would help her accept the reality of what they all were. His heart cracked a little then, because he didn't know how he'd ever explain this to her. He proceeded cautiously. "Vampires and their legends have been around for a very long time, so who knows. I find it interesting. You never know, we discover things all the time, maybe it's real. Maybe, someday, you could meet a vampire, not even know it's a vampire."

She laughed. "True. I mean, all legends are based on something, so who knows. I'm sure I don't have all the answers. And I like to think, as an artist, I keep an open mind to alternative viewpoints."

Cory sat forward on the sofa. "See, that's the whole point, keeping an open mind." Cory felt a bit of relief. At least she was open to the concept. He had to use the bathroom and excused himself. "Excuse me, but all that green tea you are constantly giving me has finished processing."

Madison laughed. "It's good for you. Flushes out the toxins. Is it all right if I go downstairs to the kitchen and get us some drinks? I think I remember where it is." She stood up and headed for the door to the stairs.

Walking into the bathroom, Cory looked back at her over his shoulder. "Sure, grab some snacks too. If you need help, Gi can help you. Someone's almost always in the kitchen."

Madison hurried down the first flight of stairs and could hear the voice of an angel singing a lullaby to Lorenzo. She wondered if that was Kate's voice. She headed down the second flight of stairs and stood in the hallway, disoriented now that she was here. Was the kitchen to the left or the right?

***

Shade sat in the office having a meeting with his top warriors. The meeting had gone well, for the most part. Mateo had filled him in on what was going down on the campaign trail with Alec and Rissa. No surprises there. Marcello and Aislynn had things under control at camp. There had been a few glitches here and there with some of the new recruits, but nothing out of the ordinary. Schedules were being met and the warriors were coming along as expected.

What he didn't expect was to see Theo nervous as hell, looking the worse for wear. Shade knew something had happened late last night, right before dawn. "So, now we come to the Dead House, and rumor has it, there was an incident. I don't do well with rumors, Theo. It's not good when word gets to me that you are out there in broad daylight still roaming around D.C. looking for something. What's going on?"

Shade lit up a smoke and waited for the details. Theo told him there was a group of rogues close to a busy tourist spot in D.C. He'd taken some warriors in, did what they could to discreetly kill and dispose of the rogues without being noticed, but one had gotten loose, and they'd lost the bastard.

Shade felt the beast sit up and take notice. This could not

be happening, not now with Alec's campaign in full speed. He lowered his eyes at Theo, his blood beginning to boil. The other warriors felt the tension rise and kept their traps shut.

Theo told him they spent the entire day scouring every grid in search of the bastard and came up emptyhanded. Shade had heard enough and slammed his fist down on the desk. "Theo, I gave you a hell of a lot of responsibility running the Dead House, *cazzo*! Alec and Rissa are in the middle of this campaign and you hand me a random fucking rogue roaming around! You spend all day with my warriors looking and can't find one rogue. What the hell is going on?"

Standing up, he paced across his office, running his hands through his hair. His temper flared the more he thought about it. His fangs punched and his eyes blazed red as he spun on Theo, his voice deep and threatening. "We are Medici, we don't make fucking mistakes. My ass is on the line with Alec, and now, your ass is on the line with me. If you want to go back to Florence, this is the way to do it. Now, get your ass back into D.C. and find that bastard tonight! Don't come back until this is handled. If I have to come out and do it myself, it will get real ugly and you, Theo, will pay the price. Move out, all of you. Go now!"

Madison thought the kitchen was to the left and headed down the hallway when she heard loud voices coming from the office. She knew immediately she'd made a wrong turn and was about to head back in the other direction when the door flew open and three very large men dressed in form-fitting leathers stalked out of the room, brushing past her. She stepped back in surprise as a woman emerged, her hair in a long braid down her back, but wearing the same leathers as the men. The woman barely took notice of her as she hurried after the men.

Madison looked into the open door to see an imposing figure of a man who stood taller than six feet, his dark hair falling around his face, his hands fisted at his side and his eyes casting a red glow in the room. She stumbled backward as he locked eyes with her.

Fangs! He had fangs! She knew instinctively who this was.

This was Shade. This was Cory's father. She turned to run, heading for the front door, her heart hammering in her chest. She saw the ancient butler hurrying to stop her as she pulled the door open and ran outside. Standing on the lawn, she wasn't sure what direction to take when she saw two wolves on the perimeter of the grounds, the moonlight reflecting in their eyes, as they slowly started to approach her. She wanted to scream for help, scream for Cory, but she opened her mouth, and nothing came out.

Shade saw the panicked mortal in the hallway outside the office as she turned and ran. He realized this was Cory's female, but he couldn't let her leave the property. Not now. He teleported outside and found her standing dead still in a panic of indecision. He landed in front of her and she took off again, but this time, she found herself surrounded as Aegis and Night-Stalker bounded toward her.

He scooped her up in his arms as she kicked and clawed at him, and he felt her terror. Pulling her into his body, he whispered into her ear. "Stop, relax, I am not going to hurt you. I am taking you back inside. There is no danger."

Teleporting back inside the living room, he didn't let her go, knowing she'd bolt again in her panic. He heard feet pounding toward them, the whole damn house was on alert and this wasn't what he needed right now.

Madison felt her feet touch the floor as he set her down, his hands still gripping her shoulders. She stared into those impossibly blue eyes. She could hear the chaos around her, as both Kate and Cory came stampeding down the stairs and into the living room. It was Cory's voice that broke through her fear first.

"Dad! Don't! It's Madison!"

Cory ran to her and slid his arms around her, calming her as his father released her and stepped back, but continued to hold her in his gaze, never looking away. Madison could tell it was his gaze that was keeping her immobile. She heard Kate, and then saw as she went to the man, watching as she reached for him, speaking to him in a soft voice. "Lover, release her. It's okay." Kate knew the animals had surrounded the house and Madison's fate was sealed. She'd either accept who and what they were, or she'd never live to see daylight.

Shade didn't let her go, he kept her locked down. His beast was still in charge, and he could hear Kate trying to calm him, bringing him back to her, speaking in her soft voice, reaching inside him. Shade continued to hold Madison in his locked gaze as he spoke to Kate. "Do you know what this means? I can't let her leave here, *mi amore*, not like this. This involves my entire *familia*, my warriors, my coven."

Shade could feel his heart racing, his blood pulsing, as he struggled to beat down the beast. He didn't want to harm this young female, but he couldn't let her go until they understood the risk. He heard Luca come rushing into the fray, Shannon with him. "I have this, Luca. But stay close."

Madison stared back at him, wild-eyed. What was he saying? They were talking about her like she wasn't even here. She was aware of others surrounding her. The man she'd met the last time she was here, Luca, and another girl, the ancient butler, and the nanny. She felt Cory's hands on her waist, but the man held her in place with his eyes. She watched as Kate stroked his arm and continued to talk to him in a quiet tone.

"Shade, let her go. You're scaring her more. Let me talk to her. I understand what's at stake. Let me talk to her alone."

Closing his eyes, he released Madison and turned to Kate, speaking to her with urgency. "This is a risk. We can't let her go until we understand, until she understands...take her, Kate. Take Shannon with you. I will keep Cory and Luca here with me. I need to understand how this happened and what we are going to do." Pulling her into his arms, he snuggled into her neck, kissing her. "*Grazie*, my queen. You know what you must do. "

Kate breathed a sigh of relief, as he released Madison from his immobilizing gaze. But she knew they weren't out of the woods yet.

Madison almost stumbled backward when he closed his eyes. It was almost as if he'd been holding her upright. She could hear the audible sigh from Cory, as his father backed away. She watched the tender exchange between Kate and Cory's father. The way the man held Kate and gently nuzzled his face into her hair, kissing her neck. She was confused by the contrast of the evil she'd seen standing in the office and this man who treated Kate with such devotion.

Luca stepped forward and nodded to him. "Master, let's go back in the office. Give Kate time to talk to her."

Luca looked at Cory and nodded his head, indicating he should follow. Reluctantly, Cory released Madison. "It's okay, Maddie. Everything will be okay. Go with Kate." The three men headed back to the office, as Cory cast one last glance over his shoulder at her.

Kate took her hand and led her to the stairs, motioning for Shannon to follow them. "Come on, Madison. We'll go back to Cory's rooms. We can talk there."

Madison was aware she was being led further into the house, but she knew running was out of the question. She felt resigned to accept whatever was about to happen to her, as she walked with the two women up the stairs and back into Cory's living room. Kate closed the door behind her and made her way to the sofa, patting the seat next to her. Madison sat down, keeping a little distance between them, and watched as the other woman sat across from her. Kate nodded toward the pretty girl with the long brown hair.

"This is Shannon. She's my best friend. We've been friends for over ten years now. She is...engaged to Luca. And she's mortal. Like you."

Kate sent Gi a message to bring up some wine and some Midnight. Madison blinked her eyes rapidly, looking back and forth between Shannon and Kate. "Mortal? I don't understand."

Kate gave her a sad smile. "I'm so sorry for this evening. I'm so sorry it unfolded this way."

There was a tap at the door and Gi entered with a tray of assorted bottles and three glasses. He nodded and left quietly. Shannon poured a white wine for herself and Madison, but then poured a thick, red wine for Kate.

Shannon handed her the glass, and said, "Drink up. It will

help, trust me."

Madison looked at the two women and then sipped at the wine. Shannon smiled at her and said, "Just chug it."

Madison looked back at her. "I think I might need a clear head."

Shannon shook her head. "I've been where you are now. Trust me, just chug it."

Madison tipped the glass up and drank, placing the empty glass on the table where Shannon refilled it. Madison looked at her. "What does that mean? I'm mortal like you. What does that mean?"

Shannon looked back at her and asked, "Do you love him?"

Madison nodded her head, looking back at Kate. "Yes, I do love him."

Kate smiled at her. "Good. That's the biggest hurdle. We can get past everything else."

Madison frowned. "I still don't understand. That man...his father...his eyes were glowing, and he had..." She left the words unspoken, questioning her own sanity now and wondering what she'd really seen.

Kate finished the sentence for her, "Fangs. He has fangs."

Madison was hoping she'd imagined it, but Kate only confirmed what she'd seen. Her eyes went to the novels scattered on the coffee table. "So, he's a vampire? Is that what you're saying?"

Kate nodded her head. "We're all vampires here, except Shannon. The staff, Lorenzo, Luca, they were all born vampire."

Madison looked at her with surprise. "Born?"

Kate nodded. "There's very little in the mythology of vampires that runs true. They're not the walking dead. They were never dead. They're born, like you. They're immortal, to a degree. They do require blood to live, but most don't attack mortals to feed. There are rogues among us, but they're rejected in our community. Most vampires mate with other vampires, but occasionally, they will sometimes fall in love and mate with a mortal."

Madison took another large gulp of the wine. Shannon

immediately refilled the glass and said, "Told ya."

Madison looked at Kate. "So, Cory's a vampire?"

Kate sighed and leaned back against the sofa. "Cory's a half-breed. His mother is mortal. Shade met her in a club. He was visiting in the States on business. She was about the age you are now, maybe a little younger. They stayed together for a few weeks while he was here. He fed from her, and, of course, had sex with her, and then he went back to Italy. She got pregnant. Shade had no idea about the baby, and Cory's mother had no way to get in touch with him. It's only coincidence that Shade and I ran into him in California a few years ago. Half-breeds are not accepted in the vampire community, because they can't sustain their race, and they don't fit into the mortal world either. Cory had a really hard time growing up. Shade offered him a job within his coven, making the leathers for the warriors. He still had no idea Cory was his son. It was only after Cory's mom came to visit, and she recognized Shade that we figured it all out."

Madison's hands were still shaking as she held her empty glass in Shannon's direction and Shannon filled it again to the rim. Madison looked hard at her.

Madison stared back and asked, "And you love Luca? You're going to marry him?"

Shannon smiled at her. "Well, yes, only they don't call it a marriage. They call it mating. And since I'm mortal, it gets complicated. But I have Kate to lead me through, and you have both of us, if it's what you want."

Madison drank again from the glass before looking back at Kate. "You mean there's more?"

Kate brushed the hair back from the young girl's face, the fear still evident in her eyes. "Madison. You're safe here. And yes, there's more. I was mortal too. Like you. Like Shannon. I met Shade and we fell in love. We wanted to stay together, to be mated. For Shade, it was imperative. He's a master, a king over a very large coven, and having an heir was required. In order for us to be mated, I had to be turned."

Madison shook her head. "But you said they were born.

You said vampires were born."

Kate stroked her arm, calming her. "Most vampires are born. But it's possible for a vampire to turn a mortal. It was the only way to ensure his dynasty. To make sure Lorenzo was born a full-blooded vampire. Shannon has chosen to be turned as well, and in time, Luca will turn her."

Madison set down the glass and started pacing. "So, what are you saying? That Cory will have to turn me? That I will have to be a vampire too?"

Kate stood up to calm her and pull her back down to the sofa. "No. That's not possible for you. Cory is a half-breed. He's not able to turn a mortal. He lives with one foot in each world. He can drink blood, and it gives him strength, but he can also eat food. He's not immortal, although he'll most likely live longer than a mortal. Of course, none of us are guaranteed a long life. Vampires can be killed, just like mortals. But for you and Cory, you could live a life together very much like most mortals. If you had children, they'd be only a quarter vampire, and with each generation, their blood is diluted. A half-breed can only mate with a mortal. A vampire would not dilute their bloodline by mating with a half-breed."

For Madison, some of the puzzle pieces fell into place. It made sense now why Cory moved so slowly with her. Why he never had sex with her. He was protecting her. Waiting until she knew. Making sure it was her choice. A tear ran down her cheek and before she could wipe it away, she felt the gentle touch of Kate's hand.

Kate continued to talk to her. "Cory doesn't have his father's power. He can't inherit the coven. But he's loved. I promise you, Shade makes no distinction between his sons. Cory loves you. He's told us you're the one. He's never opened his heart before. I hope you won't shun him now. I hope you know him well enough to know his heart. Please don't let this change how you feel about him."

Madison nodded her head. "His father didn't seem very pleased with me."

Kate smiled. "You caught him at a bad moment. I promise

you, he'll love and protect you as much as he loves Cory."

Madison polished off the last of the wine. Shannon turned the bottle upside-down to show it was empty. "Do I need to summon Gi for another bottle?"

Madison laughed weakly. "No, I won't be able to walk."

Kate laid her hand on Madison's leg. "So, are you ready to start over? Return downstairs to Cory and meet his father."

Madison locked eyes with Kate. "I had my palm read once. The palm reader took my hand and ran her finger over my lifeline, then dropped my hand and pushed her chair back. I asked her what was wrong. She just said, 'You're going to lead an interesting life.' That was all she'd say. I tried to pay her, and she wouldn't take the money. My friends were all laughing, but that memory has stuck in my head for years. So, I guess I have my answer. Yes, let's go back downstairs."

52

Shade walked back to his office, his fists still balled tight at his sides. How in hell could this have happened? He could feel Cory's fear and knew this was a delicate situation, but his coven was at risk of being exposed. He had the utmost faith in *bel*, but he wasn't sure this was going to turn out in their favor.

But first things first, he needed to know how this mortal ended up unescorted outside his office. Walking to the bar, he poured a glass of Midnight, downed it, and poured another. "Don't say a word, either of you. Just sit the hell down and when I ask a question, give me an answer."

Pouring two more drinks, he handed one to Cory and one to Luca. He paced back and forth behind Cory's and Luca's chairs, not looking at either of them. He needed to get his head around this. "This is something I never expected in this house. I trusted you, Cory. Now, I have a mortal female upstairs, panic stricken, knowing everything. My house is in chaos. You brought her here to meet me, and you knew she hadn't been exposed yet. You knew! You also knew I was in a meeting with warriors under this same roof. She saw the warriors, she saw me in full-out beast. You have given me few choices as to what I do next."

The more he talked, the angrier he became. He tried to tap it down, so he could think clearly, and make the right choices. Walking to the window, he stared outside, his back to Cory and Luca. He could feel Cory's eyes burning a hole in his back, waiting for an answer. "So, let's begin with how she got to my office, alone."

Cory stared at his dad. Shade couldn't even look at him he was so angry, but Cory was angry too. He loved Madison, and no one was taking her away from him, not even his dad. Madison loved him, and for the first time in his life, he had something to fight for. "Kate told us to go upstairs when we came in, that you were running late. Madison came downstairs to get some drinks. I don't know how she ended up in your office."

Shade spun around swiftly. "You don't know? Right there is the problem. Why would you let her roam in this house alone? She's only been here once before. What the hell were you thinking? Oh wait, you were not thinking. Careless, irresponsible!"

Cory stood to face his father and felt his fangs punch through as he growled low. His eyes locked with his father's. "I love her, and you told me this was my home as well. I'm none of those things...not careless nor irresponsible! You're the one who let things get out of control when you had the option to stop it. You scared the living hell out of her and now, I could lose her. Not all of this is my mistake. And if you hurt her, I swear I will..."

Shade growled, not letting Cory finish. "Don't threaten me. Tread carefully. I don't want this to go wrong, Cory, but I will protect my family to the death. You are part of this coven now, so if this does not go down well with Madison, she will be gone."

Luca stood and held up his hand. "Master, come on, relax. This isn't a fight. We need to come up with a solution. Both of you need to calm down."

Luca watched as neither of them unlocked their eyes. It was a battle of wills, and Luca was rather shocked at Cory's response. He never expected him to go up against Shade, and that's when Luca knew, Madison was the female for Cory. He touched Cory's arm and Cory turned to him, retracting his fangs and sitting back down. Luca watched as Shade closed his eyes and took a deep breath before sitting in his huge leather chair behind the desk.

Shade sighed and put his elbows on the desk, lowering his head, letting his hands slide through his hair. "Damn it, Cory, I love you. I can't always control my beast. It's who I am. I know you can't fully comprehend that feeling, but we could lose everything right now, that's my fear. I don't know shit about this female. I don't know how she is going to respond to being exposed to what we are. I'm relying on my mate to explain to her what the hell just happened. If Kate can't get through to her, nobody can."

Raising his head, he looked at Cory to see him staring back at him with determination. "You love her."

Cory nodded his head with confidence and pride. "I do love her, and she loves me."

Shade shook his head. "But you understand if she can't handle this, we have a problem. So, tell me, does this female love you enough to keep our secrets?"

Cory leaned into the desk, staring at his dad. "Maddie loves me. She knows my family is everything to me. And in my heart, I believe, once she knows and understands, she'll accept us."

Shade nodded. "Then let me meet the female who has stolen my son's heart, who claims to love him, and then we will decide how the rest of the night is going to go."

Cory stood, looking down at his father seated behind the desk. "She may be mortal, but she's no ordinary female."

Luca chuckled. "That sounds familiar, a theme that seems to repeat itself in this family quite often."

Shade spoke to Kate telepathically, **"*Mi amore*, tell me how this goes with you and Cory's female."**

* * *

Kate and Shannon were helping Madison from the sofa. The wine had gone to her head and they walked with her to Cory's bathroom where she could splash some cold water on her face. Shannon asked her if she wanted some coffee, but Madison shook her head.

"I'm fine. I just need to process this."

Kate heard Shade speak to her in her head and reassured him everything was under control. **"I'm bringing her back downstairs. For the love of all that is holy, please don't scare her again!"**

Shade heard *bel's* response in his head, and he almost chuckled out loud. At least someone still had some humor in the middle of this fiasco. **"Meet us in the family room. Let's see how this goes."** He stood from behind the desk. "Kate is meeting us in the family room, so let us go meet Madison."

As they all walked out together, Shade threw his arm over

Cory's shoulder. "Son, I am going to do everything I can to make this work, you need to help me with her as much as possible. This is a team effort here. I love you and I want this to work out. I am not the enemy."

Cory nodded, hoping for the best.

As they started down the stairs, Kate kept talking to Madison. "What you saw earlier was the vampire's beast. The beast rules when a vampire is angry or is in a battle to protect his life or the lives of those he loves. When you meet Shade now, he'll look like any other mortal to you."

Madison shook her head. "Not exactly. He looks mortal, but there's something...I don't know, I can't explain it, but I felt it when I met Luca for the first time too. There's something in their eyes that can hold you in place."

Kate laughed. "Yeah, there's that. Let's just take it slow, shall we? The most important thing for you to know, right now, is you're safe. No one means you harm here."

She was praying all went well, and her words were the truth. They all knew if Madison rejected them, she couldn't be allowed to leave. The three of them entered the living room to find the three men standing. They all turned to face them, and Madison was struck by their beauty, all three of them. Cory's androgynous beauty, his features almost delicate, his build slender yet toned. Luca with his bronze skin and pale hazel eyes, standing taller than Cory, broad shouldered and slender through the hips, and between them was Shade Medici. Standing taller than the other two, his coal black hair like that of Lorenzo's, hanging in loose curls framing his face, and touching the tops of his broad shoulders. His muscles defined and visible even through his shirt. His eyes were so blue it made her gasp, remembering how he'd held her immobile with a gaze. She paused in her footsteps and Kate and Shannon stopped with her.

Kate whispered, "It's okay."

Shannon nudged her forward slightly and laughed. "You never get used to it. They'll always take your breath away."

Madison flashed her a glance, surprised, as if Shannon had

read her mind. Shannon smiled at her. "Come on, they don't bite. Well, yeah, they do, but trust me, you won't complain."

Kate gave Shannon a stern look. "You're not helping!"

Leading Madison closer, they stopped before the three men. "Lover, allow me to properly introduce to you, Madison Barnes. Please try a little harder to make her feel welcome this time."

Shade got a look at Madison. She was slender, and quite beautiful. Her style was very different, like the young girls he used to see in San Francisco a few decades ago. He hoped her style reflected the same openness of spirit. He felt her trepidation, but the panic was gone. He smiled at *bel* and leaned in, kissing her on the cheek. "*Si, mi amore.*"

His eyes turned to Madison and he smiled. Holding out his hand to her, he watched as she carefully placed her hand in his. He brought her hand to his lips, kissing it very gently. "Welcome to Bel Rosso, Madison. I am Shade Medici, Master of the Medici Coven and Cory's *padre*. I apologize our first encounter was not a positive one. You are welcome here, safe here. I protect what is mine with my life. The people in this room are my *familia*, all that I have. I live and breathe to protect them, provide for them. It is my duty and my honor to protect you as well while in my home. So, please, will you sit with us and talk? I would very much like to talk with you."

Madison nodded. "I'd like that a lot."

She was mesmerized by his deep voice and the Italian accent, and, of course, those blue eyes. She glanced at Cory who nodded slightly to her, encouraging her to accept, as he reached his hand out to her. "Come sit next to me, Madison."

Cory guided her to the sofa and they sat together. Luca took a seat in another chair, and Shannon sat on the floor by his feet, her arm draped casually over his legs. Madison watched as Luca smiled at her and ran his hand through her hair. Shade took a seat in another chair and Kate climbed in his lap. What she saw between them was total love and devotion. These men, who could be very imposing, and she had no doubt, deadly, encircled these women with their protection.

Kate kissed Shade and ran her hand across his cheek. She whispered to him, "Talk to her, lover. Let her know she's okay."

Shade cleared his throat, a smile on his face, he looked to Madison. "I regret you have discovered the truth of us in this manner. I apologize for what you walked into this night. This is not how it ever should have occurred. But, you are in the company of the people who love Cory, and my understanding is you love him too. So, I know a few details about you that Cory has shared, but tell me about yourself, and why you love my son."

Madison looked at Cory and smiled as he squeezed her hand. She spoke with a slight tremble in her voice. "We're kindred spirits. We both don't quite fit in this world. We're both artists. We love to create. And Cory has gentleness, a kindness, a compassion that's rare. He's told me a little about his life, and how he came to live with you. I know how devoted he is to his family, and I can see how devoted everyone here is to each other. I can't say I completely understand it all, but I trust Cory. I know, now, he's been protecting me, even when I wasn't aware of it."

Shade watched them together, she was starting to relax a little and he found her intriguing. Her words struck a chord in him. She and Cory were like two odd ships passing in the night that had found each other. He knew how rare that could be. He'd led one lonely life until he met Kate and he knew Cory's would be even lonelier because of being a half-breed.

"Understanding it all takes much time, Madison. I do not expect you to do that immediately. But accepting it is another matter. We live in this mortal world. We have to adapt to it, stay safe in it. We are another culture that thrives amongst you, but our very existence has to be kept secret from the mortal world. If we were exposed, it would mean certain death for us. So, as you can see, I have much to lose if you do not wish to keep our secrets protected from your world. Once inside, you cannot leave our world, but you will be loved by all, respected, honored, and protected by all. Once here, you never leave us. It is a hard decision. I have an offer to make to you. Would you wish to hear it?"

Madison swallowed hard. What was he saying? That she could never leave this house again? Was she a prisoner here? Her heart started pounding again, unsure of his meaning. "Yes, I'd like to hear it."

Shade felt her fear spike. Cory eyed him and put his arms around her. He too was a bit unsure about what was to come.

"Relax, son." Shade looked at Madison. " I wish for you to stay with us this night, with Cory, in his room. You are protected, nothing will harm you. But you can't leave this house right now. This is not a threat, just a chance for you to think about what you have learned, talk with Cory, be together, and decide, together, what you want. I am not a vampire that can be in the sun, and at sunrise, I will be pulled into my death slumber. But Luca, Kate and Cory are day-walkers, they can be in sun, and need little sleep. When I arise tomorrow evening, we will discuss your decision and go from there. Do you accept this offer?"

Her head was spinning again. Day-walkers, death slumber, what the hell? Then she remembered her first visit, when Lorenzo asked if she was a day-walker. She wasn't sure what that meant, but she and Cory could talk at length. "Yes, I'll stay. We have a lot to discuss."

Cory pulled her into his arms, knowing she must be so confused and scared. "Madison, I know it's a mess, but we'll talk, I'll tell you whatever you need to know, explain as much as possible. Come on, we'll go upstairs and talk."

As they left the room, Shade looked at *bel* and winked. "It is way too much for her to take in, but I cannot let her leave until we know her heart, so this is the best way. I think Cory can explain to her better than anyone what is at stake. I can see he loves her, and I want him to have that, *mi amore*."

53

Cory led Madison upstairs to his room as neither of them said a word. Closing the door behind him, he leaned against the door and took a deep breath. This would be a night neither of them would ever forget and he only hoped Madison could come to grips with what she'd learned, and could accept the situation they were in.

Cory was acutely aware Madison's fate was still in his father's hands, but he was at least glad his dad gave them some time to talk. Madison made her way to the sectional sofa and plopped down, looking exhausted. She turned her head and looked up at him with questioning eyes. She knew everything now about who and what he was. He hoped he could convince her he'd always love and protect her, and never hurt her.

"I'm sorry, Maddie. I wanted to tell you, but not like this. Not this way." She looked back at him, like she was seeing him for the first time. "Say something, please."

Madison was trying to absorb everything she'd learned. "I'm not afraid, Cory. I've felt your gentleness from the beginning. I'm just, you know, trying to sort all this out. My view of the world has just shifted. I'm trying to figure out where this fits. There are so many things in this world that some people believe, and others reject. You know what I mean? I know we talked about this a little, and I believe in ghosts. I believe spirits can stick around sometimes. And witches, people who feel a connection to the power of nature and call on those powers. I never really thought much about vampires. I had accepted them as myth, so it's just taking a bit to adjust. Kate said they weren't the undead, they were born, but they did have the power to turn mortals. That she was turned, and Shannon would be turned, eventually."

Cory pulled her into his arms, kissing her and holding her. "You're going to have so many questions, and I understand. Believe me; my mom didn't know what I was when I was born, so she had to figure it out by herself. I haven't been totally truthful with you about my life. I had to make up these white lies, so I didn't expose you to any of this until I thought you were ready. I'm so sorry."

Pulling back, he looked into her eyes and felt bereft of her already. He needed to help her make sense of all this and get them back to where they were. "I'll answer all of your questions. Do you want a drink or some food? Do you want to stay here on the sofa, or lay in bed? Maddie, please understand, I want to make this as easy as possible. You can borrow a pair of my sweats and a tee shirt if you want to get more comfortable."

Madison leaned back against the sofa. "Just sit next to me on the sofa for now. And I don't think I should drink anymore wine for a while. Kate and Shannon kept me pretty lubricated while they were talking to me. Can we do that? Just talk a while?"

Smiling, Cory curled up next to her. He'd wait for her to make the next move, indicating when she was comfortable and relaxed, if that was possible. "We can talk for as long as you like. I'll answer anything, and if I don't know the answer, we can ask Kate or my dad to help us once we go back downstairs."

Cory blew out a long breath, pushing his hair back from his face. "This isn't how I wanted this to happen, Maddie. I wanted to tell you on my own terms, to gradually expose you, test the waters. I'm so sorry you were frightened. Damn my dad."

Madison shook her head. "It wasn't his fault. I got turned around. I wasn't meant to see what I saw. Kate told me your story, about Shade and your mom, and a little about how you grew up, how Shade met you and brought you to work for him but didn't know you were his son. So, I get that part, I think, at least for now. Kate said some things I didn't quite understand, like day-walkers? What is that?"

Cory was glad to have some questions he could answer for her. "Every full-blooded vampire is born with a gift, something unique that helps with their survival, as well as the survival of the coven. Being born a day-walker is one of those gifts. It means you can be out in the day. The sunlight won't destroy you. They also don't need as much rest. They can choose when they want to sleep, unlike my dad. Does that make sense?"

Madison nodded slowly. "So, there are vampires who have to avoid the sunlight, just like in the stories?"

Cory nodded. "Yes. My dad doesn't have the gift of day-walking. Most vampires born in the past few hundred years do have this gift and everyone thinks it's just an evolutionary change. In centuries past, being able to only move around in the dark was an advantage. But in this more modern culture, in order to blend in with the mortals, day-walking is a valuable gift. My dad has lived for a very long time, and without this gift, he can't be exposed to direct sunlight. It also means he must sleep during the day. It's called a death slumber, even though he doesn't die, but the slumber is deep and pulls him under. He could be aroused from his slumber if there was an emergency, if Kate called to him or something, but otherwise, he must sleep. All the windows here have electronic blinds that are light sensitive. They are programmed to automatically close when daybreak begins and open again at dusk."

Madison nodded. "Yes, death slumber, that's what Kate called it. She said they were immortal, to a point. She said they age slowly, but could be killed. Does it take a stake through the heart? Like in the movies?"

Cory chuckled, how the hell did he explain this? "Sorry, I know this is serious, and I don't mean to laugh. The myths you've heard and read about for centuries were created by vampires to protect themselves from the mortals. It helped them survive. You can kill a vampire by all the same means you can kill a mortal, with a gun, a knife, a sword, a bow and arrow and with your bare hands. The vampires are stronger, and heal faster, so unless the first strike is a fatal blow, they can survive easier. Some of those things might just slow them down, but it would be enough to give you leverage to make another attempt to kill them. Pretty much any means that can be used to kill a mortal can be used to kill a vampire. I have seen some strange ways to kill vampires since meeting my dad."

Madison looked at him quizzically. "What do you mean?"

Cory stood up and paced the floor. She needed to know about his father, and there was no turning back. "Maddie, my dad is a warrior and the descendent of royal blood. He's known as the warrior's warrior. His father was a king, as well as a warrior and began a camp for young vampires in Florence. They would train other vampire warriors to protect the Medici coven. When Shade became king after his father was killed, he built this empire, and his reputation, on training warriors. There is a distinct hierarchy in the vampire community, and you're born into your role. So, just as my dad was born a warrior, so will Lorenzo be a warrior.

"Dad has acquired territory all over the world, and once he met Kate, he began expanding his territory here in the United States. Right now, on this property, there's a huge warrior camp where he trains young vampires to be deadly warriors. Medici warriors are known all over the world as the best. He supplies warriors to other masters who are allies to the Medici coven, as well as warriors to protect our own.

"Luca is a warrior. It's a job, and you get promoted like any other job. Luca is assigned as protector to Kate and to any children she and Shade have. I actually work for my dad, making custom leathers and weapon holders for all his warriors. That's why I couldn't show you my shop. It sits in the middle of the damn camp. Shannon and my biological mom are the only mortals who've ever been inside the walls of the camp.

"My dad is the Master of Virginia, he rules all the vampires in this state. He's also Master of California, where Kate has an inn. And yes, everywhere you go, there are warriors. Just about everyone you meet here, besides the house servants, are warriors."

Madison pulled her knees to her chest and watched him, as he paced and talked. "So, those...vampires, those people I saw coming out of his office, the ones dressed all in leather, they were some of his warriors?"

Cory nodded without looking at her. "Yeah. Those were

some of his top warriors. Right now, he's protecting the Master of D.C.'s territory. So, we need a lot of warriors who go out at night and take care of bad vampires."

He scratched his head, wondering how best to help her understand. "Let me explain. There are such things as rogue vampires. A rogue vampire is one who's broken away from his coven, who refuses to submit to his master. They'll feed indiscriminately on mortals, draining them, leaving their bodies behind. They risk exposing the rest of us. My dad provides warriors to other masters to combat the rogues, or in the case of the Master of D.C., he's hired to constantly survey and get rid of the rogues. The warriors will do whatever they must to protect their territory from being taken over by other vampires looking for a land grab. My dad and his warriors don't kill innocent people. Please understand that. A rogue vampire is someone gone bad. This must sound like some Halloween horror movie to you."

Madison listened to his explanation of bad vampires, warriors and killing. This didn't fit the picture she saw of the people in this house, but then, the memory of his father with glowing eyes and fangs flashed through her head, and she had no doubt he could kill. "I think I'd like a little more wine, please."

Cory quickly grabbed the corkscrew and opened the bottle, pouring her a glass of white wine. A half opened bottle of Midnight sat on the coffee table and he poured himself one. He crouched in front of her, laying his hands on her thighs, looking up at her through his long dark hair. "Maddie, please don't be afraid of me, or of anyone here. I'm not a warrior. As a half-breed, I don't have the same strength or agility. And you're in the safest place you could ever be in this house with all of us. No one would ever harm you here. You just startled my dad, he wasn't expecting to see you standing there and that was my fault. I should have never let you go anywhere alone in the house. All of this is my fault."

She could feel his desperation, his need to have her understand and accept him. She took the glass he offered and took a gulp of the wine, feeling it calm her nerves. "I'm not afraid. I'm really not. I can feel your father's intention, and Kate, she's so kind. It's not an act. I don't feel like I'm being duped or anything, Cory. It just takes some...processing. So, this immortal thing, how does that work? In the books, vampires live, well, forever. So, how old is your dad?"

Her words gave Cory hope. Most girls would be running for the hills by now. Flopping back down on the couch, he smiled over at her. "Vampires of full blood live for centuries, they age but extremely slowly. My dad is about 500 years old in human years. But he looks like he might be late 30's. I'm different. Because I'm a half-breed, I'll live longer than normal humans. There aren't many of us, so it's hard to say how long I'll live, but 120 to 150 is about it for me. If we're together, and I'm hoping after all of this we still are because that's what I really want, you'll die before me. I can't turn you. You won't become a vampire. You won't have fangs. You and I can live like normal people, for the most part. Work and have lives like everyone else."

She looked at him quizzically as she absorbed the information that his father was 500 years old. "So, how old are you then?"

"I'm twenty-three." Cory grinned and pulled on the shoestring of his sneakers, as he crossed his leg over his knee. "Yeah, I'm not going to look like my dad when I'm fifty. Sorry about that, but I'll look younger than you once we start to get older, does that bother you?"

Madison smiled back at him and shook her head. "Not unless you have a mid-life crisis and start chasing after younger girls. Is it going to bother you that I look older?"

Cory played with his shoestrings. "I don't chase girls, Maddie, just you. I have you, and I'm not letting you go unless you want to go. And nothing about age or looks will ever matter to me when it comes to us. I love you because of your heart and who you are. You're beautiful and you always will be to me."

Madison accepted the compliment and kissed his cheek.

Cory laid his head back on the cushions of the sofa and sighed. "They kept telling me, as a vampire, I'd know when I meet my mate, and they were right, because I knew when I met you that you were the one. Kate had a lot of trouble adapting in the beginning too. She had trouble accepting the female warriors, and the feeders."

Madison took another sip of the wine. "The what? What's a feeder?"

Cory closed his eyes and scrunched up his face. "Yeah, feeders. Okay, let me see if I can explain this so it makes sense to you."

He poured more Midnight and sipped at it while he tried to formulate a response that would make sense to her. "Vampires need to feed on blood. Now, we can hunt, which means, basically, we can go out and mingle with humans and use skills to sort of trick them, seduce them, so to speak, so they don't know we're going to feed from them. You saw a little bit of this with my dad. He used his power with his eyes to hold you, immobilize you, like stunning you. We also can use shadowing, which allows a vampire to cloak themselves from the view of humans. But most importantly, we use seduction, and if the mortal isn't willing, we don't force them. The experience of feeding will be very pleasurable for both the mortal and the vampire. The feeding is very sexual, and the mortal won't be hurt by the experience. Once the vampire feeds, they'll wipe the mortal's memory. The mortal will remember some of the encounter, just not all the details.

"But we can't always go out and feed on humans. It's not always practical, or safe. In the vampire world, there are females called feeders. They're born to this purpose, so vampires can feed from them. Because of the warrior camp, and the number of vampires that reside here, they can't be running around all the time trying to find food. So, we have a feeder compound here, where the females live. The warriors all go there to feed. And if a warrior gets hurt badly, in battle or training, they need blood to heal. Full-blood vamps don't eat or drink mortal food. They only consume blood. And the more they expend their energy, the less effective their skills are, so they need to feed often."

Madison emptied her glass and reached for a refill. There was nothing in the movies about feeders. This was new territory. "I've seen you eat, Cory. Do you have to, uh, feed as well?"

Cory raised his eyes to hers, gauging her response before he spoke. His heart was pounding like a drum, his whole body thumping to the beat. "Yes."

Madison put the glass on the table and stood to pace. What did this mean? That he'd feed from her? She'd seen the razor-sharp fangs in Shade's angry growl and couldn't imagine she'd ever want that. "So, that's where you go? To feed? You go to the feeders?"

He kept his eyes glued to her as she paced. "Yes. Because I'm a half-breed, I can do human food and drink, but I also need blood, and I can drink the Midnight."

Picking up his glass, he held it up. "My dad makes this special blend of wine and blood. He's the only vampire in the world who has patented this mixture. It looks like a thick red wine. They sell it all over the world. It will substitute for feeding for a while. It's like a hit to get you through until you get the real thing." Draining his glass, he sat it on the table. "And I know you're wondering, yes, I have fangs."

Madison walked over to a window and looked out at the night, seeing her own reflection in the glass. "Yeah, I was wondering. I don't think I'm ready to see them yet, though. Can you control it? The fangs, I mean?"

Walking to her, he slid his arms around her waist and she didn't flinch or reject him. "Yes, I can control it. Mine are actually easier to control than those of a full blooded vampire. We're all ruled by the beast. The beast is that part of us that is more vampire than human. I have a beast, but since I'm only half vampire it's much easier for me. You saw the beast when you saw my dad tonight. The beast emerges in anger, or when the vampire is in a fight for his life. I can adjust to both worlds, live in both, but I prefer living here. It's the first time I've felt loved and accepted. I know all this is more than any human is supposed to handle. But I need you to understand something. I want to feed from you, only you. I want to make love to you, and only you. I didn't make love to you because I wanted you to have the choice to love me and make love to me, only after you knew what I was. Now, you know. It's up to you now whether we'll be together."

Madison allowed herself to be comforted by his embrace as he stood behind her. "I'm not sure, Cory. I do love you, but the feeding thing. I don't know. I mean, does it have to be me? If you have feeders, can't we be together without you feeding from me? This is just a lot to take in right now."

Cory sighed softly, laying his head on her shoulder. "I can feed from the feeders, but you need to understand there's a sexual component to our feeding. It's instinctive and part of our survival. If I feed from you, you'll feel intense sexual pleasure. I know you're scared, so am I. To be honest, I've never been with a mortal girl before. Before my dad found me, I pretty much lived in an underground community of vampires and half-breeds.

"So, I think if you have questions about sex with a vampire, you should ask Kate or Shannon, or maybe my father. Kate was mortal once, and Shannon is still mortal. You don't need to be embarrassed with them, Maddie, they want us to be together, and they want us to be happy. They'll help us in everything. Does the feeding scare you? Are you afraid there will be pain or anything like that?"

Madison laughed nervously. "I seriously don't think I can discuss sex with your father. Kate and Shannon, maybe. But yes, the feeding scares me a little."

Cory laughed with her. "I can only imagine how scary it must seem to you." Spinning her around in his arms, he kissed her gently. He had to find a way to make this work. "Madison, I love you. I know you love me. This is all very complicated and insane. But it's who I am, nothing has changed about me, nothing has changed about you, we're still the same. We have some decisions to make, and they're life changing, but there's something much more serious we need to discuss."

She looked at him confused. "What could be more serious than this? There's more?"

Cory slid his hands along the side of her face, letting his fingers slide through her beautiful long blonde hair.

"Maddie, my dad is giving us time. But right now, he's in a precarious position. You know we exist, where we are, what we're capable of. That's a dangerous thing to my family. This isn't your fault, but fate put you here. He won't let you leave this property until he knows where you stand. You know everything, and that makes you a danger to us.

"He wants this to work, and he told me that. He gave us time to decide if you accept all of this. I know what I want, I want you. But if you choose not to keep these secrets..."

Cory laid his head on top of hers. "I don't know the outcome. You can never tell anyone, Madison, no one. Not your family or your friends. Do you understand the magnitude of this?"

Madison was stunned by the revelation and had no doubt Shade would never let her leave here if he thought for one moment she'd expose them. "Cory, regardless of what happens between us, I love you. I'd never do anything that would hurt you. I promise. I mean, I understand the risks to the family. I'd never..."

He pulled her to his chest, crushing her tight into him. "I love you so much, Maddie, so very much. I hate this, I hate that my life is so messed up. I never meant to put you at risk, to scare you, and I hate that." His voice was full of pain, full of all the agony his life had brought him. He had to be strong for her, but he could feel his body shaking with the fear of losing her.

"He needs to hear you accept this, accept all of us, and you'll never expose anything, not a word of this to anyone."

"Cory, this is a lot to digest. I know I love you, and I'd never betray you or your family. If your father needs to hear that from me, then I'll tell him. But I need some time to figure all this out. I feel overwhelmed with it right now. I want to be with you, but you've thrown a lot my way. Can we just take it slow, please?"

He nodded. "Yes, that's what we both need. I'm exhausted, this has been a crazy night and it's almost 4 a.m. Let's sleep, rest our brains, if that's possible. Tomorrow night, we'll meet with my dad again, say just what you said to me and I'll back you up, Maddie. Then we can see what he says. It's the best I can tell you, right now. My dad makes good decisions, he doesn't make rash judgments. Do you want to stay here on the sofa? Or do you want to snuggle in bed with me?"

Madison was emotionally exhausted, and the wine had made her eyes heavy. She allowed Cory to lead her to his huge bed. He pulled back the covers to down-filled pillows and soft sheets. He tossed her a tee shirt and she stripped down to her panties, pulling his shirt over her head. She climbed in bed beside him and allowed him to cradle her in his arms. She was asleep before her head hit the pillow.

54

Shade felt the heavy veil of the death slumber slip away, as he became aware of her head on his shoulder, and her silky hair spread across his bare chest. He slid his hand down the curve of her back and across the firm roundness of her ass. He squeezed softly and felt her respond with kisses on his shoulder and neck. As the baby inside her grew, he knew she wouldn't lie in this position with him much longer, and he'd spoon with her, instead. He opened his eyes and reveled in her beauty.

The electronic blinds went up as the lamps on the nightstands turned on, and he knew, tonight, he must face Cory and Madison, but for this moment, he was alone with his woman. "Sometimes, *mi amore*, the best part of my day is waking up because it is so quiet, we are alone, and I feel you next to me."

Kate stretched slowly as she lay next to him. "I love sleeping next to you. I feel like it's the only time we have alone anymore."

Chuckling, he rolled on his side and kissed her neck. "Mmm, it's only going to get worse. There will be two sets of feet following behind us soon. But don't worry, we will make time."

He breathed in the scent of her, relishing these last quiet minutes together. "I have to meet with Cory and Madison. I instructed Luca to make sure she didn't leave until I came out of my death slumber, and I have no idea her state of mind. I seriously think you need to be with me. Madison will be calmed by your presence, and we need to see what the outcome is going to be. Thoughts?"

Kate caressed his face. "Shade, be gentle with her. This girl loves your son, and she wasn't eased into this situation. Please don't harm her if she decides she can't follow this path. There must be a way. Can't you try to erase her memory?"

He shook his head. "Her exposure was too long. She's known Cory for month's now and erasing a memory only works for short encounters. I will do my best, *mi amore*. I don't want this to go badly for either of them. Cory loves her, and he would never forgive me if I hurt her. I can feel that. There is a lot at stake. I may have to take a chance and trust her, and I don't like taking chances when it comes to my *familia*. If she wants to leave, I can assign someone to her. She would know they are there and that would be a deterrent. Let's see what they have to say, how their night went.

"She is not just a pretty face, she is smart, and she thinks before she speaks. She is honest, I felt that too. She is strong-willed, and she is not going to do anything she doesn't want to. So, let us go see."

He kissed her as she slipped from the bed and grabbed her robe, knowing Lorenzo was well aware of their schedule and would come knocking at their door any minute.

Kate asked, "Is there anything specific you need from me?"

Sitting up in the bed, he watched as she wrapped the silk robe around her body, the fabric clinging to her curves, and he wished they had more time. He wanted to pull her back in the bed with him. "You know, *mi amore*, that is a loaded question. I always need you. But, it is already too late. I think I can hear someone running like their ass is on fire, heading straight for this door."

They heard the tapping on their bedroom door and both answered. "Who is it?" It was a game they played with him every morning, only Lorenzo answered in all seriousness, "It's me, Lorenzo!"

Shade winked at *bel* as he quickly grabbed his jeans and pulled them on. "Lorenzo who?"

"Daddy. Your son, Lorenzo Medici!"

Kate smiled as she pulled a sundress from the closet and stepped into a pair of sandals, listening to the game as it played out the same every morning. "I wonder how old he'll be before he figures this out?"

Shade threw back his head and laughed, as he grabbed her quickly, kissing her with enough passion to move mountains before their privacy was invaded. "Oh yes, that Lorenzo. Please, do come in."

Before he finished the sentence, his son bound through the door and leapt straight for the bed, catapulting himself in one huge bounce straight into his father's arms. Shade looked at Kate and shook his head. "So, tell me, little warrior, did you behave today, or did you drive Theresa crazy?"

Lorenzo spoke animatedly, "I played in the dirt, and Tressa made me take a bath, and I saw Cory and his girlfriend walking around. They went to the stables to ride. I was going to go too, but Tressa said no, not this time. I went to see Skelk, and he helped me some more with fire, and then I played in the tree house. Can you make me a bigger pirate sword? I broke the other sword when I dropped it out of the tree. Then I went swimming in the outside pool, and Uncle Luca and Aunt Shannon watched me swim under water. I can hold my breath a long time, Daddy. Then Tressa said that was enough and made me take a nap, and now, here I am."

"Well, you have already had a very busy day, little warrior. And we most certainly need to get you a new sword. A warrior always needs his sword. So, I have something to tell you, Mommy and I must speak with Cory and Madison tonight, alone. No interruptions. So, you need to listen to Theresa, if you do not, no new sword. Deal?"

Lorenzo looked crest-fallen. He hated not being able to be a part of whatever his father was working on. "Okay Daddy, but if you need me just call me, okay?"

Shade held him tight and kissed his cheek, running his hand through the ruffled mop of curls. "Well, let's go downstairs and see Cory and Madison together, they are probably eating dinner in the kitchen. And since your brother eats like a horse, let's hope there was enough food for Madison. Then you can come back up with Theresa, settle down and do some reading. Theresa tells me you are very advanced in your reading skills."

As Lorenzo clung to his father, he held out his tiny hand to Kate. "Mommy, are you ready to go downstairs?"

Kate took his hand in hers, as Shade lowered him to the floor, holding his other hand as they headed for the stairs. She reminded him, "Don't forget, Lorenzo, your tutor starts this week. His name in Enzo, and he used to teach your daddy when he was a little boy at Castello. I have your schoolroom all ready for you. You'll have some time set aside every day for classes, and Enzo will live in the staff quarters with Gi."

Shade smiled as the memories flooded through his head. "Enzo, haven't seen him in centuries. He is a great teacher, Lorenzo, you will learn much from him, but you must be as great a student as you are warrior. Education is very important, especially the Medici history and no one knows it better than Enzo."

As they reached the ground floor, Lorenzo took off for the kitchen screaming Cory's name. Shade took Kate in his arms, kissing her. "That boy asks more questions than you. You ready for this, my queen?"

Kate laughed. "I hope Enzo knows what he's getting into. Come, let's see what's going on with Cory."

As they walked into the kitchen, Lorenzo was sitting on top of the bar in between Cory and Madison, blabbering away about his day. Shade watched as Cory's eyes locked with his, and he knew his son was a ball of nerves. Madison quickly stood up from her bar stool when they entered. She looked nervous as well.

Shade tried to lighten the tone with some easy banter. "Well, sounds like you two had a good day. I hope everyone got some sleep."

Madison stared at him and said nothing. Cory nodded. "We got some sleep, talked a lot, then we went riding. I'm not so good at riding, Dad, but Maddie seems to be good at it."

Shade nodded to this young girl, who was in love with his son. "I hope you got to see more of Bel Rosso in the daylight. It is breathtaking, is it not? I'm glad you got to enjoy the horses. I ride when I have the time, it helps me relax. You have experience with riding?"

Madison stumbled over her words, remembering the sight of him with glowing red eyes. "I, uh, I used to ride a lot when I was in high school. My family lived near a farm, but I haven't had the opportunity since I've been here at the university. I don't have a lot of free time, and I didn't know anyone with horses until now."

Shade smiled at her, trying to relax her. "Madison, please relax. I know this is not easy, but I promise you I am a fair man. I am glad you can enjoy the horses. You are welcome here anytime."

Shade stepped up to Lorenzo and laid his forehead against his son's. "Little warrior, you need to go do some reading with Theresa now, please. Mommy and Daddy need to be alone, like we talked about earlier. No interruptions and we will be up to tuck you in later, *si*?"

Lorenzo was hoping his father had forgotten. He sighed loudly as he climbed down from the counter and shuffled out of the kitchen, stopping for a kiss from Kate as he left. He looked over his shoulder as he exited the door. "But you can call me if you need me."

His mother smiled at him and said, "I'll be up soon, Lorenzo."

Shade smiled and winked at Lorenzo. "You got my back, little warrior. I will call if I need you."

Turning his attention back to Cory and Madison, his smile was gone, his game face was on. "It is a beautiful evening, I think we shall have our talk on the patio, and Gi can bring us some drinks. Come."

Cory and Madison followed him outside to the patio, where they were seated around the pool and the lush landscape and rock overhang that masked the far edges of the pool. The water glinted in the moonlight, and Madison picked up the fragrance of all the flowers in the clay pots scattered around the seating area. Candles flickered in the soft summer breeze. Kate led them to the patio chairs and Madison and Cory sat close to each other, holding hands. Kate joined Shade on a chaise lounge.

Shade slid over as Kate scooted in beside him on the chaise, getting comfortable. "You know, I don't get much time to enjoy this. I am always working at this time of night. I do appreciate all the wonderful things you do, *mi amore*. It is beautiful out here. You did amazing landscaping with the pool. *Grazie*."

He planted a gentle kiss on her head, but he could feel two sets of nervous eyes on them. He turned his attention to the issue at hand. "I know last night was rough, it was a lot of information to take in. I regret things unfolded as they did. But we can't change the past. So, before we begin, are there any questions you need answered, any concerns before we continue on?"

Madison had no idea what this man expected from her. She looked nervously at Cory and then back at Shade. "I don't think I have any questions. Cory and I talked for a very long time last night, and again today. Do you have questions of me?"

Shade nodded in her direction. "I'm glad you talked. I know my son loves you. And I would guess, since you are still here, and not looking like you think the world is coming to an end, you love him. I do have one question for you, Madison. Tell me what you have decided about us, about Cory."

Madison's mouth felt so dry her tongue was stuck to the roof of her mouth. Gi exited to bring them wine, and she took the only glass of white wine on the tray, understanding now the red was a special blend just for them. She took a sip and caught Kate's eye. Kate gave her a sweet smile and nodded at her, encouraging her to speak her mind. She wondered how old Kate was. She knew she was mortal once, but she never asked Cory how long ago that was.

"I know you have concerns about your family, concerns about how much I know. But I love Cory, and I was just getting to know his family when all this happened. I'd never do anything that would put him or his family at risk."

Shade's eyes bored into her, as he took her measure, reading her intent and looking for any signs there was a disparity between what she spoke, and what she thought. "Kate is thirty-one years old, by the way. And I am around five-hundred; we don't keep an exact count. She likes older men." He grinned widely as the look of shock crossed her face, and he heard Kate chuckle.

"My family is always my primary concern. You may have a

hard time understanding, to me, every single person you see here is my *familia*, every single one. And I take that very seriously. I will go to my death protecting them. Just as they protect me and mine. Since our encounter last night, I have had my warriors research your background. I know you are from Oregon, Madison Barnes, and you are young and smart. I know where you live. I know every class you have taken at UVA. I also know you do a decent business with your pottery. You have a talent in the arts just like my son. Work well with your hands. I know you feel like you don't fit in on campus. But you fit my son. You are scared, not sure this is a life you can embrace and make your own. But when you look at my son, I see that you love him, you don't want to lose him and your belief in that love is much stronger than your fear of what you have seen in the last twenty-four hours. Am I correct?"

Madison's eyes got wider as he divulged everything he knew about her life, as well as his ability to read her thoughts. "Yes, I mean, you're correct. I don't want to lose him."

"Good. I'm glad to hear it. Don't lose him, Madison. I won't hold you here, but it will take time to understand our culture completely. In the meantime, no harm will come to you. But let me make something clear. I am the Master of Virginia. I know every damn thing that goes on in this state. And in a matter of moments, I can find out anything I need to know. I am not trying to frighten you, just making sure you understand you are now on my radar. I love and trust my son. Therefore, I trust his judgment of you. And I do believe you understand the capacity and depth of my love for this coven. From this moment on, there will be protection for you always, my warriors will always be near, you won't see them, but they'll see you. You have nothing to fear from them.

"Cory can take care of himself and you, but he is limited in his abilities, my warriors are not. You are welcome here, this is my coven and you, now, are part of that coven, in a manner of speaking. You come here whenever you like, everyone will be informed, including Aegis and Night-Stalker, Kate's warriors.

Any questions?"

Madison's brain was spinning again, as she absorbed what he was saying to her. He trusted her, but she'd be watched. He was saying she'd be protected, but she wasn't stupid. It was protection for them as well. To make sure she didn't say anything. She nodded her head, acknowledging his words. "Uh, who is Aegis and Night-Stalker?"

Kate sat up slightly. "The wolves. They approached you last night when you ran from the house. I'm sorry, did Cory tell you about my gift?"

Madison looked at Cory who shook his head. She looked back at Kate. "He told me about day-walking, and Shade has a death slumber, that he is not a day-walker."

Kate nodded. "Lorenzo and I have two gifts, and as far as we know, we're the only vampires that possess two. I have the gift of animalism. I'm able to communicate with all animals telepathically. Aegis is my go-between. She connects me with all the others. Aegis is the grey she-wolf, and Night-Stalker, the black wolf, is her mate. You'll always see them on the property.

"Lorenzo is a fire thrower, although he's still learning to control his gift. He can start fire with the power of his thought, and he's immune to the damage of flames. Shade is a dream-walker. He has the power to infiltrate a person's dreams and manipulate the outcome."

Madison was trying to keep an emotionless expression on her face, to look like this was just a normal conversation. But once again, she could feel her heart rate pick up.

Kate smiled at her. "I know this is a lot. Trust me. I've been where you are. It just takes time."

Shade chuckled. "I was not joking when I said it takes time, Madison. Now that you know about us, things you see and hear will make more sense. But you can always ask Cory or me or Kate if there is something you don't understand. That is vital. The more you understand, the less you fear. I hope we see more of you, because I, for one, enjoy your company."

Shade smiled at his son, and saw he was breathing a bit easier now. "I love you, Cory. I know you need time, both of you.

But you have a responsibility in this as well, you are Medici. You need to take care of her, protect her, treat her well, and help her learn and understand our culture. If this female is your mate, she is your greatest gift. She will bring you light and love and give meaning to your life. Show her you are deserving of her love."

Cory stood up to face his father. "Dad, I know Madison and I will be fine. We talked a lot, we love each other and if we can get through this, we can get through anything."

Shade got up from the chaise and hugged his son to his chest. "See your female home safely. Warriors will be around. We have her protected."

Cory felt a lump in his throat as he realized everything would be fine. "I love you, Dad, thanks."

Shade released Cory and turned to Madison, holding out his arms. "May I ask for a hug, Madison?"

Madison looked up at the man towering over her, she was drawn in by his power and intimidated at the same time, but she knew he was sincere. She stood, he embraced her, and her arms went around his shoulders. He felt rock solid under her hands, and she hoped she never had to see his full power unleashed. "You have my word. I'll never betray Cory, or his family."

Shade tipped her chin up with one finger. "I am sorry for my behavior, I hope you will forgive me, and get to know me."

As he released her, he turned to Kate, knowing, deep inside, this small female would bring no harm. "Come, *mi amore*, I do believe we have a little warrior to tuck into bed, we both know he will not go down until we do so. And besides, I think we have taken up enough of Madison and Cory's time. Drive safe and enjoy the rest of your evening."

They walked arm in arm back into the house and without looking back, he knew his son and Madison were enjoying a long kiss under the moon in the summer skies of Virginia. Love seemed to blossom here at Bel Rosso.

Hyde and Mateo were back on duty, on-board the private jet and waiting for Alto to arrive with Rissa and Alec. Mateo lit up a cigarette and offered the pack to Hyde. "Got to hand it to you, brother. The warriors all give you a hard time about having a cushy assignment as Rissa's protector, but there's not enough money in the world for me to be happy with that job. Better you than me."

Hyde took a cigarette and laughed. "It's not so bad. We butted heads a few times in the beginning. I had to take the upper hand with her, set some ground rules. Since then we've been okay. But if you notice, I'm not usually the target of her anger. If I were, it might be a different story."

Mateo nudged his friends shoulder. "Oh, I notice all right, and I'm pretty sure everyone else does as well. She's hot for you, brother."

Hyde took a deep draw on the cigarette. "I'm aware, trust me. But I value my balls too much to ever make a move on that one."

The two warriors were still laughing when the black Bentley pulled up next to the plane. Alto exited the driver's door, and opened the rear door for Alec, Rissa, and Braden. They could both hear Rissa grumbling from where they stood, as Alec appeared to be able to totally shut her out.

Mateo slapped Hyde on the back. "I'm not a fan of Alec either, but damn, you've got to give him credit. I would've throttled the bitch by now."

Alec and Rissa climbed the stairs to the jet and took their seats as Alto scrambled into the cockpit, their co-pilot already onboard and ready. Alec nodded to the two warriors, and Braden pulled out an itinerary and passed copies to everyone. Braden cleared his throat and asked for everyone's attention. "Okay, people, we have another full week. There's a minimum of three events a day, and every evening we have fundraiser dinners scheduled. Most of the events are indoors, and will involve the usual, Rissa giving an introduction followed by Alec giving his speech, then some press time and shaking hands with the public. We have one county fair type event in the middle of the week. I'll give you more details on that when we get to it. Any questions?"

The female attendant was already passing glasses filled with Midnight to Alec and Rissa. Alec took a long draw from the glass before shaking his head and answering. "I'm good. You have any questions, darling?"

Rissa had become used to this routine, and the boring events on the schedule. Sighing heavily, her sunglasses still on, her hair piled stylishly on her head, she put on her fake smile, which seemed to be a permanent expression lately. Her eyes showed the weariness of this campaign, however. "A few questions. Tell me the night events will let me get out of these ridiculous clothes! They itch and feel like burlap on my skin and I can finally wear something that makes me look like Rissa Canton. And a county fair? What the hell am I supposed to wear?"

Braden tried to keep a positive tone in his voice, knowing how volatile she'd become. Working with Rissa was like walking on eggshells. "You can dress however you chose for the fundraisers. These dinners will be $25,000 a plate minimum entries and Alec will be stumping for bigger contributions. There will be a lot of very rich people in those seats, so you can dress to impress. Now, the county fair, I'd think you could just wear some jeans and sneakers. It's outdoors; the ground isn't level, so definitely heels are out."

Rissa felt she had pretty much done as asked during this campaign, but there was one thing she refused to give up, her designer heels. She'd taken to wearing lower heels, even flats at some events, but only because it seemed they were always on their feet. Now, he was telling her to wear jeans and sneakers? She didn't even have sneakers with her. She only wore them in the gym or when she went running.

She pulled her sunglasses down her nose as she peered

over them in disgust at Braden. "Jeans, how charming." She pushed her glasses back up and spoke through gritted teeth. "No one in the press has ever seen me in jeans and sneakers. When we get to wherever this event is, someone will need to go purchase me a pair of tennis shoes and jeans. I'll wear them, but I'll be damned if I'll like it. I have a navy blazer. Perhaps that can dress it up a bit."

Alec swallowed the last of the Midnight. "Braden, have one of the campaign staffers pick her up a pair of jeans and some running shoes. Just leave them on the campaign bus."

Alto announced they were taking off and requested everyone in their seats. Braden took his files and found a seat on the plane as Hyde and Mateo each took a seat as well. The flight to New Hampshire would be a relatively short one. Rissa sighed, bored with this trip already, and laid her head on Alec's shoulder. He kissed the top of her head.

"Hang in there, Rissa. We've got a long road ahead of us."

She loved these few moments when he paid attention to her, when he made loving gestures without even realizing it. "I'm doing the best I can, Alec. This isn't easy for me, and I'm only doing this for you. I've made a decision about my business. It's a big step for me."

"And what is your decision?"

Lifting her head from his shoulder, she felt the plane take off, easy and smooth. She pushed her sunglasses up on her head and looked down at her hands in her lap. "I had an offer to sell, a good one. I didn't say anything to you, I didn't want another argument, and I knew this was something I needed to decide on my own. I'm selling my business, Alec. I'm selling everything I've worked so long to build and make successful. So, if we don't get to the White House, your darling Rissa is going to be one bitch on wheels, because right now, everything I am is tied up in being Mrs. Alec Canton, wife of the President."

He knew this was a big sacrifice for her. As much as she loved being mated, she'd also worked hard to maintain her independence from him, and he had allowed it up to a point. He put his arm around her shoulder and hugged her to him. "I know that was a hard decision, but a necessary one. I don't take it for granted. You know once we're in the White House you wouldn't be able to run your business. Besides, you'll have different projects. Every First Lady picks a cause they think will have a positive outcome on the country, like education, or eating healthy and getting exercise. You should think about what you'd like to do. The press will start asking you that question once I win the nomination."

Rissa smiled back at him, but the smile didn't reach her eyes. She felt alienated from the whole damn world. She was so tired of this campaign, and felt certain once he won, she'd still be in his shadow. She'd no longer be the Darling of G-town. What if the press didn't embrace her as First Lady? Her fate was in his hands now. "Just get us in the White House. Don't fuck this up, Alec. I need this." Her voice was weary. She'd play this game only so long, and her master had better come through.

Alec signaled for another drink and wondered again if he'd made the right choice. He had come too far now to turn back, but she was right about one thing. He'd better win. He'd never discussed with her what their life would be like if he failed to win the Presidency, and he didn't want to dwell on it now. They'd be forced underground in the vampire community, since both of their faces would be recognizable by every mortal on the planet. He wouldn't have a Senate seat to go back to, nor would he even want it. The Senate had just been a stepping stone to the White House.

They both dozed off during the flight and were jostled awake as the plane landed. Braden was on his feet immediately, taking charge. Their bus was waiting on the tarmac as requested, and Alto left the details of getting the plane in the hangar to the co-pilot, as he left the plane and got the bus ready. Their luggage was transferred, and both Hyde and Mateo went on high alert. Alec stood and helped Rissa from her seat as they disembarked.

"Watch your step, Rissa. We can't afford to have you tumble down these stairs."

She just stared at him with annoyance. "Why don't you let

Hyde take care of me, you go along and do whatever it is you and Braden do."

She sought out Hyde and signaled for him to come to her. She watched him as he approached her, his stride strong and sexy.

"Rissa, what's wrong?"

She touched his arm and beamed up at him. "Why do you think every time I need you, something's wrong? Nothing's wrong, I just want you to escort me to the circus bus. Alec is concerned I might take a tumble and that would be such a disgrace. Please?"

She cocked her head to the side, giving him a smile. "Besides, Alec has so much business to attend to before we get to our destination, I need a bus partner."

Turning back to face Alec, her face no longer held the smile. "Hyde will take care of me, you go do whatever it is you do with Braden. I'll be absolutely fine. Hyde will never let anything happen to me."

Alec looked at her with a frown. "No, I'm sure he wouldn't, but don't let it go to your head, my darling. He's doing his job, and he's paid well for it."

He let her be led away by Hyde as they got on the bus together. Turning his attention to Braden, he reviewed last minute details for this first stop with his campaign manager, before they all piled on the bus and headed for the next stop on the long road to the White House.

56

Shannon walked with Kate through the lavender fields as the fragrance from the newly blooming plants hung heavy in the air. "So, how are you feeling? You barely show during your pregnancies until the last couple of months."

Kate smiled back at her as her hand instinctively went to the small swell of her belly. "Great. I feel great. It will be a girl this time. Sophia. The pregnancies have been easy. I'm a little more tired, and need to feed more frequently, but other than that, I feel great. I just regret, you know, that Shade has to feed elsewhere."

Shannon looked down at her feet as they walked through the rows of plants. "Yeah, I know. I know it's not a big deal for Shade or Luca, or apparently, even for you, but I still try not to think about it too much."

Kate took her friend's hand. "Shannon, it's not that I don't think it's a big deal. I know what you feel. I remember how conflicted I was when I was pregnant as a mortal and Shade had to go to him. Once I was turned, my perspective did change, but it didn't mean I liked it. It just meant I accepted it. So, Luca came to Shade, to both of us really, to ask about moving forward with your blood covenant. Have you decided?"

Shannon walked in silence for a few steps, pondering her response. "You know I want to be with him more than anything, I mean, I can't imagine living without Luca now. He told me he'd asked Shade's permission to proceed and had received his blessing. I feel like we're both ready, but I still wonder about my future. He said I'd live here. And I'd love that, but I worry about losing myself. He reassures me there's plenty to do here to keep busy, but I don't just want to keep busy, you know? I worked hard to get where I am today, and after you left the agency, I got a promotion to Director of Marketing. Luca said I needed to talk with you, that you had some ideas, so here I am."

Kate held out her arms, and stepped in a slow circle. "You

see all this? The lavender? The sunflowers? Right now, we just harvest the crops and sell them to the factories who extract the oils for bath and beauty products. After the last review with our accountants, Shade suggested I develop it further. Create my own brand of products, like he's done with the wine and with the lemons from Luca's lemon groves. But honestly, Shannon, with Lorenzo, and another on the way, and the two inns, I just don't have the time. But you would. When you bond with Luca, you're not just becoming Luca's mate, you're taking the first step to becoming a member of this coven. Once you're turned, you're Medici too. You're family. I'm not suggesting you work for me, I'm suggesting a partnership, where you own half the business.

"It's the same arrangement Shade has with Luca and the lemon production. You could work directly with the manufacturers, develop the product line, and develop the marketing and business plan. It would be a full-time job, trust me. It allows you to use all the education and skills you developed at the agency and put them to work for yourself. Shade has lawyers, accountants, and a host of people from the coven who'd be at your disposal. What do you think?"

Shannon stopped in her tracks and looked across the acres of purple and yellow. "What about the fields in California?"

Kate took her arm as they continued to walk. "All included. And there's more property in Tuscany that hasn't been cultivated. It's perfect for olive production. Long term, I think we should plant olive groves, and develop our own brand of olive oil, as well as divert some of that production for bath and beauty products as well. Quite frankly, I've had the idea for some time now, but didn't have the time to move on it. Say yes, Shannon. Say yes to the blood covenant and Luca, say yes to moving to Bel Rosso, and say yes to the business. And later, if you and Luca have your own children and you want to live in your own house, you know Shade will build something right here on the property."

Shannon looked at her best friend. "You make it all sound

so easy."

Kate smiled back at her. "Not easy. Just worth it. You know we work well together, and you practically live at Bel Rosso anyway."

Shannon stopped and inhaled the soothing scent of lavender. "I'll have to lie to my family. I'll have to cut all ties with them. I've never been able to tell them about Luca all these years. My mom is always asking when I'm going to meet a nice guy and settle down. I just tell her I'm married to my work."

Kate looked across the horizon, remembering her life before Shade. "Yeah, that's hard. You know I told everyone I took a job in London. I'd call my parents from time to time, stretching out the time between calls, so they were less and less frequent. They'd ask when I was coming home to visit, and I'd always say I was too busy. Eventually, they quit asking. It's a choice, Shannon, and you can't go back. I don't regret my decision, if that's any consolation."

Shannon stepped up behind her friend, placing her arms around her and resting her chin on her shoulder. "How did we get here, Kate?"

Kate placed her hands over Shannon's and shook her head. "I don't know, Shan. Everything about my life now is so improbable, so unimaginable. There's no way I saw any of this coming. All I can tell you is I need Shade as much as I need the air I breathe. There's no life without him. His blood is in my veins, our souls are one, and I'd change nothing. My heart tells me you want the same with Luca. You love him now, but you'll be bound to him in a completely different way once you feed from him and seal the covenant. And when he turns you, when that day comes, you live and breathe as one."

A tear ran down Shannon's cheek. Her love for Luca felt almost overwhelming. It was hard to imagine she could love him more. But she knew, without question, she could never walk away. "Yes. Yes, to all of it. I'll tell him I'm ready."

Kate turned and embraced her dearest friend. "Welcome, sister."

57

Max was practically living in exile in Bangkok. He'd shamed his wife, Lein, and her father, Fan Chen. The loss of his Virginia territory to Shade, and the massive loss of life at the Battle of Bel Rosso had been a huge embarrassment to the Chen Dynasty. Fan Chen ignored him, and Max knew if an opportunity presented itself, Fan wouldn't hesitate to have him killed, and have Lein mated to someone else. Fan had made it clear he didn't see Max as a capable successor to his coven.

Lein fed from him, because she must, but she came to him to survive, not out of passion and desire. He sought out feeders to avoid her, and her cold reception when he approached her to feed.

Fan's warriors ignored Max and took their orders directly from Fan. He'd been stripped of any power, and he knew his future here was limited.

He flipped on the TV to an international news network. It was one of the few programs broadcast in English. The large screen TV was projecting an image of Alec and Rissa, smiling for the camera, as they worked the campaign crowds and the newscaster's voice talked about the handsome couple and Alec's bid for the White House.

Max felt like someone was rubbing salt in his wounds. This all started with her, his obsession with Rissa. He remembered how she toyed with him and led him on, only to throw his love for her back in his face. He had destroyed everything in the States and came to Thailand to escape her. Why should she get everything? Why was he the only one paying the price? He grabbed the remote and turned the TV off as he stormed out of the room. "I'll make them pay. I'll make them all pay!"

He didn't have a plan, at least not yet. He had no warriors he could call upon, so whatever action he took, he'd have to pull off on his own. But he vowed to bring them all down.

58

Braden had them all checked in to a mid-quality hotel in Florida. He knew Alec had the personal wealth to stay anywhere he liked, but they were spending the campaign funds donated by their supporters, and they needed to appear fiscally responsible, not to mention, it made them appear more approachable to the mainstream voter.

They'd been doing well in the polls, and Braden made a point of checking the local news coverage, as well as local newspapers of every city they visited. He wanted to make sure he had his finger on the pulse of the voter's reaction, so he could coach Alec accordingly.

Alec wasn't his problem, though. Alec was doing well with the voters, and not surprisingly, had been especially strong with the women voters. The crowds tended to be about 60% female. His problem was with Rissa. The voters saw her as cold and aloof. He'd spoken to her several times about it, asking her to engage more, but she just rolled her eyes at him.

So far, Alec's charm had outweighed her dismissive attitude, but he was hoping she wouldn't become a liability in the future. He'd gathered everyone in one of the hotel conference rooms to go over the day's itinerary. He was passing out a cheat sheet that showed each venue and the key people in attendance that Alec and Rissa would need to schmooze. Getting the support and endorsement of these key VIP's would be important to maintaining their momentum in the campaign.

"Okay, people, here's our schedule for the day. As you can see, it's jam packed, so we'll need to keep on time. Rissa, the local newspapers are still describing you as aloof, can you at least try to be a little more engaging?"

Rissa was already miserable in this heat and humidity, and was worried about how it would make her hair look. Now, Braden was handing her their schedule for the day, with another round of sweaty people shaking her hand. All the while, the women were constantly trying to get close to Alec. They pushed and shoved past her, while she was ignored totally.

Sitting in the conference room, she tried to keep her face expressionless. Checking her hair in her compact, she heard Braden's request for her to be less aloof. Snapping her compact shut, she glared at him. He was such an ass kissing bore. "What the hell do you expect me to do? I feel like I'm wearing clothes from a thrift shop, and my hair is a mess. No one is interested in me, so why should I bother. It takes all my energy to even try to look human in these places."

Alec sighed, wishing he had a glass of Midnight. "Rissa, calm down, please. You look lovely in that outfit. Just because it didn't cost an arm and a leg doesn't mean you don't wear it well. Braden is just asking you appear friendlier. Smile more. Look like you're happy to be there. You're an accomplished actress. I've watched you manipulate people for years. This is no different. So just pretend you're enjoying yourself. Can you do that, please?"

The campaign staff squirmed in their seats uncomfortably. They all sensed the rising tension between these two with each new stop on the campaign trail. Mateo elbowed Hyde who was biting back a smile.

Rissa looked straight ahead, not making eye contact with Alec. "Why don't you just sigh a bit louder, I don't think everyone heard you. Pretending seems so simple for you. And it's not as if anyone is paying any attention to me, this is all about Senator Alec Canton. Please correct me if I'm wrong."

She heard the snicker coming from behind her and turned her head quickly to see Hyde and Mateo, not sure which of them was laughing at her behind her back, but she sneered and hissed. "Shut up!"

Alec knew better than to provoke her when she was in one of her moods, and lately, the mood never ended. Hyde looked surprised when she turned on him and told him to shut up. He hadn't spoken a word, and now, Mateo was trying hard to hold back his laughter. Hyde gave her a look that said, 'calm down.'

Braden decided to cut the briefing short before tempers

rose. "Okay, people, let's get on the bus. I know it's hot outside, so I scheduled this outdoor event first before it gets unbearable out there. It's a county fair, showcasing their agricultural heritage. Let's get busy!"

The crowd filed from the room, leaving Alec and Rissa alone for a moment. Hyde and Mateo stepped just outside the door, giving them some privacy.

Alec turned to her. "Rissa, of course, it's about me. I'm the one they'll be voting for. But we're a package deal. You'll be their First Lady. You have to make them want to see more of you."

Rissa huffed. "Make them? You know, Alec, all I see are hordes of women trying to get close to you. I've given up my business, I'm trying my best and still, every single day, you're at me to do something else to make this work better. Now, I'm being dragged into the heat, to see what? Farm animals? How do I become engaging while treading through cow shit? Right now, I want to engage my hand across someone's face. This has become one big boring affair. I want to go home, I want to fuck you, feed, and relax. But here I am, Alec, I'm here for you."

Marching to the door, she took a deep breath, getting her composure before exiting.

Alec watched her storm out of the room and saw Hyde drop in behind her. Mateo had heard more intimate conversations between these two to last him a lifetime. He couldn't imagine Kate ever speaking to Shade in that tone. These two seemed to go at each other on a regular basis. He leaned against the doorjamb and looked at Alec. "Anything I can do for you, boss?"

Alec just shook his head. "Track down some Midnight. Make sure we have plenty of it on the bus."

Mateo nodded. "Will do. You have your hands full with that one. Not being nosey, but we can't be in these close quarters and not hear everything that's going on."

Alec checked his cellphone for messages as he answered. "Yeah, well, it's not like I didn't know what I was getting into. Rissa is predictable if nothing else. Come on. Let's get this over with."

Leaving the room, Mateo followed as they climbed onto the crowded bus. Braden intercepted him immediately.

"Alec, this gentleman is from the local newspaper. He's asked to follow along today, get a feel for what happens on a campaign."

Alec immediately shifted gears, shaking the reporter's hand, and welcoming him on board. "Rissa, did you meet the reporter."

Rissa was about to take her seat when she heard Alec asking her if she'd met the reporter. *There's a reporter on this damn circus bus? Great, just great.* "Oh, no Alec, I didn't." She plastered her fake smile from ear to ear.

Alec introduced her and was keeping his fingers crossed. Rissa hadn't done well at hiding her dislike of this process in public, and she never held back her opinions when she was on the bus, away from the press and the public. Rissa shook his hand as Alec welcomed him. "We're happy to have you with us. I'll warn you, it's a pretty hectic schedule."

The reporter smiled back at him before Braden steered him away to an open seat.

Alec whispered to Rissa under his breath, "Please try to rein it in today."

Rissa heard the threat in Alec's tone as she answered bitterly, "Oh, don't worry, I'll rein in it. I'm sure Braden has a pair of overalls and boots for me to wear. Go impress whomever, Alec. I'm just going to sit here, smile and give the fucking performance of my life."

He'd had about enough of her attitude today, and the day was just beginning. He couldn't afford to let the reporter see anything between them other than a loving couple, though. He squeezed her arm tight enough to show his displeasure as he guided her into a seat. "Sit down, darling. I feel safer when you're seated when the bus is in motion."

He felt her jerk her arm away, as she took a seat and gave him a look that could melt steel. Alec drifted away from her and whispered to Hyde. "Stay on her today."

He moved in the direction of the reporter, and engaged him in a conversation, answering the predictable questions Alec knew he'd see printed in tomorrow's paper. The bus pulled into the fairgrounds, already crowded with the locals. There were a lot of kids around and Alec sighed inwardly. He knew this wouldn't be a good day.

Braden jumped into his role, ushering everyone off the bus and into the crowd. Alec excused himself from the reporter and went to Rissa's side, extending his arm for her to hold as they exited the bus together.

"There are a lot of kids here, Rissa. Please try to pretend you aren't annoyed."

Taking his arm, she gritted her teeth as she answered, "Just look, brats everywhere. How enchanting. Feels like I am at Bel Rosso."

Mateo overheard her dig and spoke to Hyde under his breath, "She should be so lucky to live at Bel Rosso. Seriously, dude, what is wrong with this bitch?"

Hyde shrugged. "She's having a bad day."

Mateo chuffed. "Really? Let me know when she's having a good day, will you? I feel for you, brother."

Hyde shook his head. "She's not like this all the time. I mean, don't get me wrong, she's a diva with an attitude, and she's used to getting her way. But she has a soft side."

Mateo laughed. "You've been brainwashed, dude. There's nothing soft about that bitch."

Braden rushed up behind them, breaking up their conversation. "Enough, you two, I need you to follow them in the crowd, but not too close. They need to look accessible."

Alec led her through the throng of people, as everyone pulled out their cell phones and started taking candid shots. The women were clamoring for a selfie with Alec, and he obliged, leaning in to each of them as they took the picture. Rissa was left hanging on his arm, as if she didn't exist.

Rissa tried her best to ignore it, her smile a cover for her disgust. She felt surrounded and wanted to scream at the top of her lungs. Closing her eyes for a brief moment, she took several deep breaths as she clutched Alec's arm. How she loathed all the attention he was getting. She was usually the one directing the show, smiling for the press, and having everyone clamor for her attention. The tables had been turned and she didn't like it.

A young woman, pretty in a rural sort of way, was coming towards them. She brushed past Rissa, almost knocking her from Alec's side and was begging for a picture with him. Rissa could feel her heart racing and her breathing accelerated as two knee-high children were at her legs, touching her. She was surrounded, and she couldn't breathe. She felt panic take over and she started looking for Hyde. Where was he? She quickly pressed the charm on her bracelet several times in rapid fire, alerting him to her danger.

Hyde saw the crowd encircling them both. Responding to her call, he moved in, so he can get closer and jostled people aside to step as close behind her as he could. He could see she was uneasy, but not in danger. He softly touched her back, low on her spine where no one could see and spoke to her, "Relax, right here, just breathe."

Just as Hyde spoke to her, she was jostled by the crowd, and let go of Alec's arm, where the crowd quickly stepped in to fill the void. Her face reflected her panic, as she was separated from Alec and she cast a glance over her shoulder at Hyde.

Hyde instantly stepped up, placing his hand at her back, as he led her through the crowd. "Relax, Rissa, nothing will hurt you, I'm right here. Keep smiling. I'm going to lead you through this throng of people. Shake hands, smile, and keep moving."

Rissa let him lead her through the crowd as she tried to take a few deep breaths and calm herself. She had lost sight of Alec now, and wondered if he was even aware she was no longer on his arm. A little girl with messy hair and a hand-me-down dress approached Rissa. She carried a bundle of hand-picked wild flowers that were wilting in the heat. Rissa stopped in her tracks. *Why me? Why the fuck am I always attracting these brats?*

The little girl smiled up at Rissa and handed her the small

bouquet, as she welcomed Rissa to the fair and wanted to know if she could have a picture because she was so pretty. Hyde spoke to her softly through her earpiece. "Take the flowers and smile for the camera."

Rissa gritted her teeth through her smile as she accepted the flowers. "Thank you so much, of course, you can have a picture."

Rissa watched in horror as a huge woman, the size of a tank, stepped forward in shorts and flip flops with a cell phone to take the picture. Reluctantly, Rissa squatted down next to the sweaty child, as the woman clicked away. Rissa was wondering if this would be the picture on their damn Christmas cards.

Hyde stepped in and said they needed to keep moving, and Rissa couldn't wait for this to all be over and she could meet up with Alec again.

59

Braden woke early, showered, and wrapped a towel around his waist before retrieving the morning paper left outside his hotel room door. He turned on the TV to the local news coverage as he opened the paper to scour for any news. He's pretty sure the reporter that was with them all day yesterday would have something.

As the local TV news focused on weather and traffic, Braden flipped through the pages of the paper until he saw the large photo of Rissa, squatting down next to a child who was presenting her with some wilted flowers. The child was looking up at Rissa with a giant smile on her face, as Rissa was caught with a look of disgust, trying to remove the child's hand from her skirt.

Braden cringed at the image. He started to read the article which gave a glowing view of Alec, and how he charmed the crowd with his rock star good looks, but went on to state, 'While the Senator seems in his element working the people, Mrs. Canton would clearly like to be anywhere else but here. Her disdain for the people is evident in her reluctance to touch or be touched, and the plastic smile never reaches her eyes.'

Braden tossed the paper aside just as the local news coverage swung to the county fair. There was footage of Alec working the crowd, smiling, posing with his potential voters, shaking hands, accepting hugs, and lifting babies in the air and making them laugh, and their mothers smile.

In contrast, they showed footage of Rissa, stepping gingerly through the fairgrounds, trying hard not to dirty her shoes, and constantly patting her hair into place. She reluctantly bent in close to people requesting selfies, careful not to make contact. And then, there it was again, the child running up to her with the flowers and the look of horror on her face. Hyde could be seen leaning in, whispering something to her, and she responded with her fixed, plastic smile. Rissa was seen kneeling down to the child but was more concerned with controlling the child's hands than accepting her gift of flowers. Her body language would tell the viewers everything they needed to know about Mrs. Canton, and how much she wanted to be with the people.

The news anchors were making a joke of the encounter, noting the Canton's didn't have children of their own, when one of the female newscasters laughed and said, "No wonder!"

Braden turned off the TV and pulled on a robe, not bothering to dress, when he grabbed up the paper and stormed out of his room and down the hall to Alec's suite, where Mateo was on guard. Brushing past the warrior, he was banging on the door, not caring any more whether they were awake yet or not.

Alec rolled over in bed, awakened by the pounding at the door. As he was grabbing a robe, he shook Rissa. "Wake up, darling. That sounds like Braden. You'll need to get dressed."

Rissa begrudgingly rolled from bed and headed for the bathroom to shower as Alec opened the door.

Braden stormed in. "Have you seen this?"

Alec shook his head, and looked for his cigarettes, lighting up and taking a deep drag. "No, Braden, I haven't seen anything. I'm standing here in a robe and the sun hasn't even come up yet. What the hell has you so worked up now?"

Braden shook the newspaper in his face. "Her! She has me worked up. Alec, the last time I ran a campaign for you, she wasn't in the picture. If I'd known what a liability she was going to be, I'd never agreed to run this campaign for you. She's a disaster! And she won't listen to me. So, you better get this female under control or you can kiss the election good-bye."

Alec growled back at him. "Calm down. The sky isn't falling, Braden. Let me see the paper."

Braden handed him the article with the photo. As Alec read, Braden looked for the remote to turn the TV on, hoping for a replay of the coverage at the fair. Alec read his own glowing reviews, and then read the negative impression Rissa made on the reporter, supported by the damning photo. He took a deep drag on his cigarette and exhaled, trying hard to control his anger. He'd given her everything she'd ever asked for, and all he needed from her now was a little play acting, but she was digging in her heels.

Braden was pointing at the TV. "Listen!"

Alec's attention was drawn to the video footage of him at the campaign, and the crowds fawning over him, compared to the footage of Rissa looking like she was walking through a leper colony. Alec had seen enough. "Rissa!"

Rissa was stepping out of the shower when she heard him yelling for her and she could feel Alec was about to go beast level. Biting her lip, she tried to think what in the hell she'd done to make them both so damn pissed off.

Wrapping a towel around her hair, she slipped back into her robe before she flung open the bathroom door. She saw Alec was in no mood for a conversation when her attention was drawn to the television and the images of her at the fair. She balled her fists at her side. "You bellowed, master?"

Alec shook the newspaper in front of her face. "Don't cop an attitude with me, we both know who'll win that battle. I've asked one thing of you for this campaign, Rissa, just one. And that's to at least pretend like you give a damn. Can you for once get your nose out of the air and realize you aren't any better than the rest of us? I won't lose this campaign. Do you hear me? I'll do whatever it takes to come out on top. You use the term master so glibly, but don't ever forget I *am* your master. Don't push me in a corner. I won't hesitate to make whatever changes I need to make to achieve my goal. Is that clear enough for you? Or do I need to spell it out?"

Rissa didn't flinch as he ranted on. She stared straight ahead at the middle of his forehead, as his hot breath brushed the bangs of her blond hair. She remained still, but her blood was boiling, and her fangs were about ready to punch through. The sound that came from her lips was a hiss, low and soft

"A change. That would be different. You making a change instead of me. Your point is very clear, master. This is a game. Your whole life with me has been a game, and I'm just a piece on the game board you use to get whatever you need. Your point is made. If this game piece doesn't play by your rules, a new game piece will replace her."

Alec swiped his hand across the top of the dresser, knocking bottles and glasses to the floor. Mateo heard the crash and quickly teleported inside the room, seeing only the three of them. He stood still and waited for direction. Braden was pacing, clearly agitated and Alec looked like he was ready to kill.

"Don't make me do this, Rissa. That isn't what I want. I want you beside me. I picked you for my mate. And I've been honest with you about my plans. You know what I want, and I want you beside me when I get there. But don't stand in my way."

Braden continued pacing as he talked, "Okay, let's just calm down. This doesn't solve anything. We know what we need to do. This is fixable. We just need full cooperation going forward."

Rissa remained defiant, standing stiffly and looking straight ahead. She was aware of Mateo entering the room, and wondered where her warrior was. But she knew Hyde would never interfere or come between a master and his mate. She listened to Alec's words, as the sound of his voice vibrated through her bones, and she heard the words speak to her soul...he picked her for his mate, he wanted her beside him.

She let out a gasping, ragged breath, as if someone had punched her in the stomach. Closing her eyes, a small blood tear ran down her cheek, and she knew somewhere in all this chaos, he still loved her. He still needed her and she had to oblige him.

Alec saw the tears but was too angry to comfort her right now. He sat down on the side of the bed and put his head in his hands. In a calmer voice, he spoke to her, "Rissa, I know you can do this. I've seen you manipulate people when there was something you wanted. All I'm asking now is you manipulate people for what I want. Listen to Braden. This is his job. He does this for a living. He knows what the public will respond to, and what they'll reject. Have you changed your mind? Do you want me to release you? I need to know if you can do this."

Rissa could feel his defeat and disappointment in her. But she also felt his belief that she could do this, if she'd just try. When he spoke of releasing her, the blood drained from her face, leaving her pale and she caught her breath. She rushed to him. Her heart was breaking as she stood before him. He was giving her a choice to remain with him or walk away forever and never look back. She had this choice once before with Max, and she chose Alec. Nothing had changed for her.

Dropping to her knees in front of him, she sobbed as she tried to speak. He sat before her with his head still in his hands. She removed his hands and took his face into hers. She stared into eyes that were tired and frustrated. "I don't want to be released from my master. I want you." Her lip quivered as her voice cracked. "I'll do this because you want me to, but only because you want me to, no other reason. I'm sorry, master, I love you."

Sliding her hands from his face, she bowed her head as she remained on her knees before him.

Braden watched the dynamics of their relationship play out before him. He had no doubt Rissa was sincere in her love for her master. But he'd seen this before. Rissa believed what she said when she spoke to him, she believed she could change. But Braden had his doubts. He moved across the room to Mateo and placed his hand on the warrior's elbow. "Come on. Let's give them some privacy."

Braden led the warrior from the room, closing the door behind them. "Stand guard, I'm going back to my room."

Leaving the massive warrior at their door, Braden walked back down the hall to his own room. They'd either work this out, or they wouldn't. He knew it was out of his hands.

60

The camp was a little quieter this evening as half of the warriors were out on a night expedition under Marcello's supervision. Shade noticed the light on in Cory's workshop and decided to walk over and see how things were going with Madison. Cory had been quiet in the last weeks since Madison had found out the truth of what they were. He'd kept a warrior on watch over Madison's apartment, and knew she posed no risk, but he was curious as to how their relationship was going.

Cory was carefully unrolling a bolt of the finest black Italian leather when he heard the door of the shop open and in walked his dad. He was grateful for the visit as there was something on his mind, and he hadn't found the right time to approach Shade with it. Madison had asked him about seeing his shop and she couldn't understand why he always refused, but now that the proverbial vampire was out of the coffin, so to speak, he could think of no reason she couldn't come here. Cory knew better than to just waltz her into camp, though. He needed to get his dad's permission to bring a mortal into this space.

Shade breathed deep and closed his eyes as he entered the workshop. He loved the smell of the leather. Walking to the large table, he slid his hand over the leather and nodded at this son. "Italian leather, the best, *si*? I love the smell of this place every time I come in here. Brings out the warrior in me. Any special plans for this?"

Cory grinned at his dad. "Just some pants for Rebecca. Why, did you want me to make something?"

His dad sat on the stool next to the table and kept sliding his hand over the leather. "Just thinking about something for Kate. Something unique for her, a skirt, perhaps, for after the baby is born. You have enough leather for that?"

Cory nodded. "I have plenty and if I don't, there's more I can order. Are you busy, Dad? I mean, like, right now? I wanted to talk to you about something."

Shade slid his hands through his hair. "Cory, I always have time for you. You know that, so talk."

Cory took a seat across the table from his dad and fiddled with the edge of the leather material. "Well, it's like this, you know Maddie has known for a while now about us, she's been to the house a few times, and she wants to see my shop. She's an artist like me, we both work with our hands, and I see her stuff all the time. So, I was wondering..."

Shade chuckled as Cory struggled with his request. "Wondering what, son?"

Cory raised his eyes to his father. "Can she come here and see my shop? I can bring her in the daytime when there are fewer warriors around, and I won't take her anyplace but here and I won't let her out of my sight, I promise."

Shade liked that Cory looked him straight in the eyes when he asked. "Cory, I know everything about this girl. I know every detail of her life since that night she walked into my office. So, yes, I know she hasn't revealed anything about us. I like Madison, and I think you should bring her here at night when the warriors are out."

He watched as Cory's eyes got wide with surprise and Shade laughed out loud. "Relax. She might as well see the rest of it. Better to know now if she can handle this life. Besides, I learned the hard way with Kate, keeping secrets only creates more questions."

Cory was in shock, he couldn't believe his dad was making this easy, letting him take Maddie wherever he wanted. "Thanks, Dad, it means a lot to me. This will help her to understand what a warrior is."

Shade nodded. "*Si*, but this is not a free pass to go exploring the whole damn camp. It is dangerous being around the warriors, especially ones learning to control weapons and their attitudes. "

Shade stood and wandered around, looking at all the tools hanging from the wall. "So, how are things going with

Madison?"

Cory followed his father's movement around the shop. "If you're asking if I've fed from her, the answer is no." His face turned red and he could feel the heat creeping up his cheeks. "And no, I haven't slept with her yet, either. She seems to be undecided about all of it. I know she loves me, but Luca said to let her set the pace. I'm not pushing her, Dad. I need her to make that decision on her own. It has to be hers to make, so when she comes to me, she comes knowing all there is to know."

Shade turned around and winked at Cory. "When the hell did you get so smart? Waiting is a good thing. You have time, both of you. She is special, and I can tell she loves you, and letting her decide is good."

Their conversation was interrupted by a loud ruckus outside. Shade looked in the direction of the door. "Well, son, it sounds like the warriors are back from their expedition. Damn good thing we live in the county, *cazzo*, that rowdy bunch could wake up a small country!"

Walking to the door, Shade turned before going out. "Protect her while she is in this camp, it is dangerous. Don't hang around too long with her here. Let her see the shop, and what you do for the warriors, and how valuable you are to the coven. How valuable you are to me, because I have no idea what I ever did without you."

Cory stood and walked to him, giving him a hug. "I feel the same, and thanks, I'll make sure she's safe here."

Shade walked out the door, yelling in his booming voice at the warriors and Cory smirked. "Yep, that's my dad. Kicking ass and taking names."

61

It had been a few weeks since Madison had learned the truth about Cory's family. His father said she'd be under their protection, and a warrior would be assigned to her at all times. Madison wasn't certain how she felt about that, and she wondered if Shade had assigned the warriors to protect her or to make sure she didn't talk about what she knew. Either way, it made her a little nervous to know she was under constant surveillance.

Cory still came and went, their relationship developing its own routine. They saw each other almost daily. She loved him, and even though he'd slept over a few times, he wasn't putting any pressure on her to move the relationship to the next step. She felt both relieved and disappointed at the same time.

She was working at the potter's wheel, enjoying the feel of the wet clay as it spun in her hands, almost lost in meditative thought as the vase took shape beneath her experienced hands, when she heard a knock at the door. She paused the wheel and wiped her hands dry on a cloth, wondering who might be visiting. Cory had said he had some work to catch up on in his shop and he wouldn't be by tonight. Walking to the door, she peered out the window before opening the lock to see Shannon.

Madison's heart was pounding, her first thought being something must be wrong. Why would Shannon come here? She wasn't even aware Shannon knew where she lived. Opening the door quickly, Shannon gave her a bright smile and held up two bottles of wine.

"Hey! Sorry to barge in on you. Cory said he had to work tonight, and I thought you might like some company."

Madison was surprised to see her but swung the door open, welcoming her into the space. "Come on in. I was at the potter's wheel, but I'm happy for some company."

In the back of her mind, Madison wondered if this was part of the surveillance. Shannon stepped into the living room, made cozy with an eclectic collection of pillows, all in different colors and fabrics and a lot of plants. Her apartment was very organic, and reflected her personality to a tee.

Madison waved her in the direction of the long bench sofa, piled high with pillows, which sat against the large window. "Have a seat. I'll get us some glasses."

Shannon set the wine bottles down on the coffee table and curled up on the old but very comfortable sofa, as Madison returned to the room with two wine glasses and a corkscrew. She opened a bottle and poured the wine, sitting down next to Shannon. Madison had spent very little time with Shannon, and always in the company of others. She found this sudden visit curious. "So, what brings you here? I wasn't aware you even knew where I lived."

Shannon took a glass from the table, sipping at the white wine. "We all know where you live now. Shade gave strict instructions, as you're aware, you're to be protected at all times. Luca and Marcello coordinate as to which warrior will be assigned to provide coverage."

Madison took a sip of her own wine. "I'm sorry, Marcello?"

Shannon shrugged. "He was one of the warriors you bumped into the night you accidentally wandered in the direction of Shade's office. He oversees the camp. You know about the camp, right?"

Madison shook her head yes, then no. "Uh, sort of. I mean, I hear them refer to the camp, and warriors, but no. I guess I don't really understand the camp."

Shannon gave her a long look before answering. Reaching over, she placed her hand on Madison's knee. "Do you love him?"

Madison nodded. "I think I've always loved him, even before I was ready to admit it. Cory was able to just, you know, meet me where I am. He didn't expect anything from me, didn't want to change me."

Madison smiled at her. "I know this is hard, Madison. I know this feels overwhelming, and confusing. I know you wake up in the middle of the night sometimes and think, 'what have I gotten myself into?' Am I right?"

"Yes, I do. It feels more than a little surreal. But I hope everyone knows I'd never say anything. Is that why you're here?"

Shannon laughed. "Madison, I'm not your keeper. Trust me, if Shade felt, for one minute, you were a threat to his coven, we wouldn't be having this conversation."

Madison swirled the wine in her glass, watching the liquid as it created a small vortex of energy in the center of her glass. "But there is surveillance?"

Shannon nodded. "I know, it's overkill. You're in no danger, but Shade is a master, he protects what's his, and right now, like it or not, you're a part of his coven. And since you're not a vampire yourself, he'll provide you with the protection of his warriors."

Madison nodded slowly. "Do you have warriors who protect you?"

Shannon smiled. "I have Luca. And if Luca isn't accessible to me, then someone is assigned. But I spend more and more time at Bel Rosso. Shade will be happy when I just move in permanently, and Luca and I are moving toward that."

Madison relaxed a little as she realized this would be an evening of girl talk, and Shannon was the one person in this madness who she could relate to. "So, how long have you been with Luca?"

Shannon's smile lit up the room. "Almost four years now. And they've been the best years of my life. We'll seal the blood covenant soon, and I'll move in. Of course, I could have moved in anytime. The invitation has always been there. But I had my own job, and I needed to hang on to it. I needed time to figure out where I fit, so I understand what you're going through."

Madison leaned back against the mound of pillows. "What changed that made you feel ready now?"

Shannon curled her long legs underneath her on the sofa. "It was partly me, but also Luca. You'll see, once you're exposed more, their community is a hierarchy. I struggled with it at first, but what you need to understand is, they don't...struggle with it, I mean. They're born to a station, and they all accept their place. I'm sure Cory has told you Shade is royalty, one of few remaining royal families. He's a king, although it doesn't carry much weight in the States, you'll see it's very important when he's in Europe, Italy especially, where he has more of his coven. All the vampires born in his coven have an unwavering loyalty to him as their master. I used to feel weird about that, like it was a slave thing, but it isn't. I can't really explain it very well, but you'll see it for yourself. They're like a family, a really large family, and they all rely on each other for their survival. They all have a role to play, and in doing so, they make the coven stronger, and safer. Does that make sense?"

Madison nodded. "Yeah, I can see that part."

Shannon took another sip of her wine before continuing. "Luca is Kate's protector. He was assigned to her when she was still mortal, but he'll remain with her, and her children, until they're grown and on their own. His primary responsibility is her safety. I had to come to terms with it, you know. I mean, I wasn't jealous. I just had to get over the feeling I was second place. His job and loyalty to Shade would always come first. But you'll see, with time, they don't see their relationships with their mates in the same way mortals do. They have an inner beast. You saw it in Shade. The beast emerges when they are angry or threatened. The beast represents the side of them that is vampire. They struggle to control the beast, but the beast also serves them in many ways. The beast senses danger, but it also helps them find their mate. And once they make that selection, it will remain unbroken. Their love and loyalty is for all eternity."

Madison had a flash of memory, Shade with exposed fangs and glowing red eyes, and shivered. "Does Luca have a beast?"

Shannon chuckled. "Oh, yes."

Madison hesitated before asking the next question. "Does Cory?"

Shannon looked at her sympathetically. "Yes, he does. But Cory is a half-breed, so his beast is not as powerful. None of his skills as a vampire are as strong. It's why he can eat human food, as well as drink blood. It's why he's smaller than the others. He'll never have their strength or be able to teleport as far or as fast. He's not immortal, and he can't inherit the throne from Shade. Most half-breeds aren't even recognized in the vampire community. They remain outcasts, rejected by both worlds, living among the homeless. Shade really turned the vampire community on its ear by insisting Cory be recognized as his son. Most half-breeds are used and abused by the vampire counter-culture, until they are bled dry and discarded. They don't usually live very long."

Madison pulled her knees to her chest and put her head down. Cory had hinted at the kind of life he'd led before his father found him, but he'd never go into detail, and Madison had vowed not to ask as it appeared to be a painful subject for him. "I had no idea."

Shannon finished off her glass and poured a refill for the two of them. "Madison, I don't want to paint a rosy picture here. There's much violence in their world. They aren't called warriors for nothing. And not all of them are good. Shade's coven is good, but there are rogue vampires out there. They are bands of vampires that don't belong to a coven, who have broken away, and live a very hedonistic lifestyle. They kill mortals indiscriminately, feeding from them, draining them dry and leaving them to die. That kind of behavior threatens the exposure of them all, and masters, like Shade, fight against them. All I can tell you is, as a mortal girl, I found myself pulled into their world, into Luca's life, and I wouldn't change any of it. I know you must have questions, so I just wanted you to know you can talk to me any time."

Madison accepted the refilled glass and took another sip. "I really appreciate that. Kate had said she'd answer any questions I had, but there are things I felt, well, uncomfortable asking. Some of it is just so intimate, you know? And she's his mom. Well, his step-mom, but still."

Shannon giggled. "No, I get it, Kate is my best friend. We've known each other for years. She was my go to person for everything. But I can see where you might not want to ask Kate everything. May I ask a personal question? You can tell me if it's none of my business."

Madison was pretty sure she knew where this conversation was going, but Shannon might be her only place to get answers. "Yeah sure, ask me anything."

Shannon fiddled with the broad leaf of the plant in the window, looking away from Madison as she asked, "So, have you had sex yet?"

Madison could feel her face turning red, as the heat rose up her neck and across her cheeks. Looking down at her hands, she answered softly, "Not yet. At first, I thought he was just being respectful, or maybe wasn't even interested, and then I realized he needed for me to know the truth, and I really appreciate it, you know? He didn't try to trap me or trick me into anything. But even since I've discovered that he's, wow, it sounds weird to even say it, but finding out what he is, we still seem to be dancing around it. Like neither one of us really knows what to do next."

Shannon knocked off the last of her wine. "He's never been with a mortal girl. You need to understand that. He's never been in love before. He was used for sex in the underground clubs, by both men and women. It was his only means to survive. Lead him there, when you're ready. Show him the way. Show him love is pleasure not pain, that it's gentleness not brutality. Don't be alarmed if his beast emerges during sex. He may or may not, but regardless, Cory's beast will never harm you."

Madison stood up suddenly, knocking over her half-filled glass. She'd never even thought about the beast in Cory, and now, Shannon was telling her he might show up while they had sex!

Shannon could see her anxiety level rise. "I'm not telling you to scare you, Madison. I'm telling you to prepare you. It's probably another reason Cory hasn't tried to have sex with you. The last thing he'd want is to scare you. But the beast will protect what is his, and as far as the beast is concerned, you're his too."

Madison paced nervously. "But, what do I do?"

Shannon smiled. "You won't need to do anything. The beast

will know what to do. The beast will want to feed from you, and although you'll find it hard to believe now, I promise you, when it happens, you'll want him to feed. Trust me. It's very primal, and instinctive. Your body will respond to him."

Madison's hands moved protectively to her throat. She was having a hard time imaging having his fangs in her flesh was something she'd want. The memory of Shade standing in the office, his fangs exposed, and that split second, when they made eye contact. She was frozen in place. Yes, she did feel fear, but if she's honest with herself, there was something else. It was desire, building in her belly like a smoldering coal, even as the rest of her broke out in a cold sweat. She was wondering if she'd feel that same pull of desire to Cory's beast, when her body shivered uncontrollably. She knew the answer already.

Shannon finished off her wine before standing and going to Madison, giving her a hug. "Don't be afraid, Maddie. Just enjoy the ride. Call me if you need me." Grabbing her purse, she headed for the door. "I'll let myself out."

Shannon looked over her shoulder at Madison who was staring at her wide-eyed, Shannon laughed. "Trust me, Maddie. Just take the leap."

62

Cory drove into Charlottesville to pick up Maddie. He was taking her back to Bel Rosso and hoping she'd spend the night. He had a surprise for her. He'd received permission from Shade to allow her to see his shop and he was feeling conflicted. He was excited and proud to show her his work, but also concerned about her response to the camp. She'd be seeing the warriors in their element for the first time and he knew how intimidating it could be. Hell, he couldn't believe his own eyes when he saw them the first time.

Knocking on her door, he heard her yell, "It's open," and walked inside. He found her in the bedroom, sitting at her small vanity and he leaned in, kissing her cheek. "You ready to go back to Bel Rosso? I think you should plan to spend the night. What do you think?"

She caught his eyes in the mirror as she brushed out her hair. He'd spent the night here on many occasions, but she'd only spent the night at his place once before, and that wasn't planned. "Sure, let me throw some things in a tote bag."

She grabbed up a few things from her dresser and pulled some clean underwear and a big t-shirt out of the drawer, stuffing them in the bag. Walking to the closet, she pulled a tie-dyed sundress off a hanger and rolled it into a ball before tossing it in the tote. "Ready?"

Cory seemed amazed at how little she packed and was laughing at the comparison to Kate who packed up half the house whenever they traveled anywhere. "You know, if Kate ever packed that fast, I think my Dad would stroke out."

Taking her tote bag from her arm, he led her out the door, locking it behind him. Opening the truck door, he helped her inside and handed her the bag and then climbed in the driver's seat and fired up the truck. "Do you want to stop and eat or just wait until we get back to Bel Rosso?"

"I'm good. We can eat later."

She stored her stuff on the floor by her feet, as she fastened her seat belt. He usually took her to Bel Rosso during day hours, which meant she rarely encountered his father. She was always acutely aware when she was in their house that Shade was in a death slumber, although no one seemed to feel the need to be quiet, especially Lorenzo.

She'd grown attached to the precocious child who talked non-stop. He was sometimes in class with his tutor when they arrived and had a burst of unspent energy when he was finally set free. Madison had been told about Kate's pregnancy, and its duration, and her ability to see her children before they were born. Kate spoke about Sophia, and what she'd look like, and that she'd be willful and stubborn. She continued to be amazed at what she learned about them with every visit. She hadn't told Cory about Shannon's visit, and was thinking she might keep that piece of information to herself.

Their ride to Bel Rosso was accompanied by music blasting from the radio, as they rode with the windows down. The sun was almost setting when they arrived, and Cory saw Aegis and Night-Stalker along the edge of the woods, surrounded by a new litter of pups. Cory pulled up in the drive and shut down the engine. "Well, here we are, my dad is probably going to be up and about. I hope that doesn't make you feel uncomfortable. He really does like you, Maddie."

He helped her from the truck as she grabbed up her things. "Oh, he doesn't make me nervous." *What am I talking about? He makes me very nervous!*

Madison saw the wolves at the tree line. She knew about Kate's gifts, but she didn't understand how it worked or exactly what she did with the animals. She saw the small pups following on their mother's heels. "Oh, look at the babies. Can we pet them?"

Cory wasn't exactly sure how Aegis would react to them petting her pups. But then he watched as Aegis casually moved toward them, her pups jumping and playing as they followed her. The wolf nudged Cory's hand. "Don't make any quick moves, Maddie, let Aegis lead. She knows us, but I don't have what Kate has, and they're wild animals."

Aegis slithered around Cory's legs and went to Madison and nudged her hand, begging for attention. Madison obliged and Cory crouched down and the pups were all over him. "I think she trusts you, Maddie."

Madison allowed the she-wolf to sniff her hand before she scratched her head. She kept a watchful eye on the male who was pacing nearby. Madison squatted down next to Cory and the pups were licking and nipping at her, issuing little barks as Aegis circled. Madison couldn't help but laugh, as she was buried under the pile of pups. Night-Stalker moved closer, as one of the pups took a mouthful of her long blonde hair and tugged hard, earning him a cuff on the head by his father.

Madison was suddenly aware the two adult wolves were standing over her and she felt vulnerable being in a submissive position, so she quickly stood, as the pups tumbled to the ground.

Kate emerged, clapped her hands, and told Aegis to stop harassing their guests. Aegis responded with a soft whine, as she led the pups and her mate back into the tree line.

Cory was still laughing at the pups' antics when Kate came outside. Smiling at her, he took Maddie's hand. "Hi, Kate. The pups are worse than Lorenzo. At least we only have one Lorenzo. Is Dad up yet?"

Kate gave Madison a hug before answering Cory. "He's up. He's with Raven right now, but he said it wouldn't take long. Lorenzo's in the pool in the backyard. I can't get him out. He lives there now. Luca and Shannon are watching him while Theresa takes a break."

Cory's face broke out into a huge grin. "Wow, Raven's here!"

Just then, there was loud laughter and Shade and Raven came spilling out the door. Raven took one look at Cory and grinned. "Hey little brother, what's shaking?"

Raven grasped Cory in a huge hug, slapping him on the back

as Cory answered, "A lot! Oh, this is my girlfriend, Madison."

Raven bowed slightly to the blonde girl as Shade shook his head. "Don't overdue the show, Raven, she's new to our coven."

Raven looked over his shoulder at Shade. "I have no idea what you mean, boss man." Turning back to Madison, he smiled into her eyes. "It is nice to meet you, welcome to the gang."

Cory grinned at the look on Madison's face but she didn't say a word. Raven had that effect on people the first time they met him. Cory was happy to have the visit from the person who befriended him when he lived in Florence. "So, how is mated life?"

Raven slid his arm around Cory's shoulder and gave him a cheesy grin. "Nothing to complain about, believe me, and I love California. Life's a breeze, brother." Raven turned to Kate and bowed low to the ground, a dramatic bow worthy of a Oscar. "My Queen, I'm humbled by your beauty, which surpasses my own."

Kate laughed. "I'm afraid my beauty pales in comparison to yours. Now, stand up and behave yourself before I call Lorenzo."

Madison was fascinated by the vampire before her, his long hair hanging to his waist. Like Cory, he was more androgynous than the other men she'd seen here, and Kate was right, he was beautiful, even exotic looking. She was drawn into the comfortable banter between them but didn't feel like she should add to the conversation. She was aware she was on the inside, but not an insider, and there was a difference.

Raven stood and hugged Kate, kissing her cheek. "I love coming back to Bel Rosso. Even though my heart is in California, coming here is like coming home. Mica sends his love."

Placing his ring covered hand over her belly, he smiled at Shade. "Oh, this feels like a princess." Raven looked at Kate. "Fun times with this one. Boss man will be in a mood when she arrives. I need to be getting back, can't stay away too long, miss Mica already."

Kate laughed as he described the baby she carried. "Oh you have no idea. Shade doesn't know it yet, but this one will require reinforcements. Give our love to Mica."

The words were barely out of her mouth when Raven teleported out, disappearing in an instant. Madison stepped back, blinking her eyes rapidly, shocked by how quickly he was gone.

Kate laughed at her expression. "You'll get used to it, I promise. Come inside." She slid her arm around Shade's waist as they walked back toward the house, with Cory and Madison behind them.

Getting inside the house, Cory looked at his dad and nodded, letting Shade know tonight was the night he'd be going over to the camp.

Shade smiled at Madison. "I apologize, Madison, for not greeting you properly. Raven tends to steal the show whenever he is around. Welcome back to Bel Rosso, it is good to see you again. I seem to be always apologizing to you."

Madison looked at him before looking away, finding it hard to maintain eye contact. He still made her so nervous. "No, no need to apologize. I'm uh, happy to be here."

Kate smiled at her, recognizing how ill at ease Madison was around him. She took Madison's hand and pulled her close as she whispered, "You'll get used to him too. He left me tongue-tied in the beginning as well."

Madison smiled back at her, disconcerted her nervousness was so apparent, but glad for the reassurance.

Shade noticed he intimidated her and knew it would take her a while to feel comfortable here. "*Mi amore*, I am heading over to camp. I will be back in time to tuck our son into bed, but he is not allowed in the camp tonight. I have already told him, but that does not mean he will not try like hell to convince you otherwise." Taking her in his arms, he kissed her. "I love you *bel*, always and forever."

Turning, he hugged Madison and she stiffened in his arms. "Have a good night, enjoy your stay, you are always welcome here." He hugged his son and telepathically sent him a message. **"Don't let her get overwhelmed at camp, if she gets too nervous, bring her back to the house. Kate and Shannon can**

calm her down." "Love you, son, see you later."

As Shade headed out, Cory grabbed Madison's hand. "Come on, let's go up to my room and you can put your things away. Kate, Maddie is spending the night. She can stay in my room, if that is okay."

Kate smiled at her. "Of course, you're always welcome here. Let Gi know if you need anything. I'm going back to the pool to keep an eye on Lorenzo. You two have fun."

Cory grabbed her hand and led her to his rooms. Taking her bag, he put it in his bedroom before he flopped down on the couch and pulled her down to his lap. "Sorry about all that, it's always a circus here this time of night. I'm so glad you got to meet Raven. He's like a brother to me. He was my first real friend when Shade hired me and sent me to live in Florence. We have a lot in common. He's a great warrior, and he's funny too. Are you okay?"

Madison nodded her head. "Do I look okay? I try not to let my nervousness show, but your dad still makes me a little anxious. I tell myself you're all just people, and then something happens, like Raven disappearing and it reminds me I'm out of my element."

"I understand why you're nervous around my dad, he takes some getting used to, but it will come with time. I know you're still struggling with all of this, but I think spending more time here will help you to feel more comfortable. If you're not ready, I can take you back home later. I can always just stay at your place."

"No. I want to be here. I really do. I love Kate and Shannon, and Lorenzo. And I can't learn if I'm not exposed."

Cory smiled back at her. "Then let's work on that exposure." He was relieved she wanted to stay. "I have a surprise for you tonight."

"Really? What's the surprise?" She was wondering how many more surprises there could be with Cory.

He kissed her cheek quickly and took a deep breath. "I want to take you into the warrior camp and show you my shop. Show you what I do for a living, but you'll be exposed to the warriors.

Interested?"

Madison beamed. "Yeah, of course. I've been asking to see your leather shop. And I saw some of the warriors here, remember?"

He shook his head and grinned. "Seeing a few warriors in the house is not the same as seeing a lot of them together training. I just want you to be prepared. I really do want to show you my shop. It's important to me."

"Lead the way. I'm ready."

He lifted her off his lap and took her hand. Leading her outside, they walked along the road that led to the camp when Cory heard Lorenzo yelling at the top of his lungs. Cory smiled but was a bit frustrated. He wanted this time alone with Maddie. Looking at Madison, they both stopped in their tracks. "He won't give up until he talks to me. Sorry about that."

Turning around, he saw a dripping wet Lorenzo running as fast as he could, with Luca and Shannon on the chase. As Cory crouched down, Lorenzo ran straight into his arms. "Lorenzo, are you racing Uncle Luca?"

Lorenzo landed, dripping wet, in Cory's arms. He'd been playing in the pool when he saw Cory heading toward the camp. "I saw you, Cory! You wanna come swim with me?"

Luca and Shannon arrived behind him, Shannon doubled over, catching her breath. "This kid is going to kill me."

Luca chuckled and rubbed her back as he addressed Lorenzo. "I think Cory has other plans, Lorenzo."

Cory laughed. "You know, little dude, I have some things to do tonight at camp. But maybe tomorrow we can go swimming. Madison is going to spend the night and we can all go swimming. So, you need to go inside with Luca and Shannon and get ready for bed. Theresa needs to give you a bath and I know Dad will come to tuck you in. I promise, I'll see you tomorrow, okay?"

Lorenzo flashed his eyes at Madison. "Are you sleeping in the guest bedroom next to my room?"

Madison was caught off guard. "Uh..." she looked at Cory, unsure how to answer this child. "I'm not sure, yet, where I will be sleeping."

Luca picked him up to carry him back to the house before this conversation got more complicated, as Lorenzo kept talking. "I have a sword. You can sleep in my room if you get scared."

Madison laughed and said, "Good to know."

Shannon laughed and shouted over her shoulder, "I'm pretty sure Cory has a sword too."

Cory blushed from his toes to his eyebrows and shouted at her, "Shannon!"

He could hear her and Luca laughing as Lorenzo was still gabbing on. "Sorry, Shannon has no filter."

Taking her hand, he shuffled his feet and continued to walk toward the camp. The closer they got the louder the noise level. The sound of swords clashing, and orders being shouted out above the fray was all part of the routine here. Cory stopped before he opened the gate. "Are you sure about this?"

"Cory, for Pete's sake. I'm not a china doll on a shelf. I'm not going to break. Take me to your shop already!"

Cory held up both hands. "Okay, okay."

Opening the gate, the sound hit them like a wave crashing over the shoreline. Cory pulled her inside and shut the gate tightly. Leaning in close to her, he was almost yelling, "Stay close to me, hold my hand. Follow me."

She held onto his hand, as he led her around the edges of the field toward the barracks that housed the warriors, and where he had his shop. It didn't take long before the warriors picked up the scent of a mortal and cast a glance in their direction. He knew Shade would have informed the warriors of her presence here tonight, but she was still a curiosity, and they'd keep their eyes on her. Cory saw a group of female warriors led by Aislynn in their path. Some of the females stopped their sword practice and turned to look at Madison, and Cory kept moving. Aislynn moved the group farther into the middle of the field, firing orders at them to get back to work.

Striding over to Cory, her long braid swinging on her back, she came to a stop in front of them. "Sorry, brother, I had no idea when you'd be arriving."

"Not a problem, Aislynn, thanks. This is my girlfriend, Madison. Maddie, this is Aislynn, she's Lieutenant here at the camp. She's in charge of the female warriors."

Aislynn reached out to shake Madison's hand.

Madison had to look up at the tall, statuesque female; her muscles toned and visible through the form fitting leathers, her coal black hair pulled back tight in a single braid that hung down her back. Madison extended her hand and felt the bone crushing strength in the woman's grip. Madison remembered seeing her when she stumbled upon them in Shade's office, but there had been a number of warriors present and she'd been too shocked to really take any of them in. "It's very nice to meet you. Aislynn, that's a beautiful name."

"Thank you. It's very nice to meet you, Cory's a good guy. You're a lucky girl."

Just then, Shade's voice boomed like thunder across the field and everyone stopped and turned in his direction. "*Cazzo*, one damn mortal walks in your midst and you suddenly think this is a damn social hour. Stop your gawking and get your asses back to work. Now!"

Aislynn rolled her eyes. "The master has spoken. Enjoy your night, Madison."

As she strolled off, yelling at the females in her group, Cory led Madison quickly to the barracks. He could still feel their eyes on them. "This is the warriors' quarters. They live here, everyone has their own bunk, there are some recreation rooms, and Dad has a lot of meetings in here as well. I used to live here until I found out Shade was my dad."

Marcello casually strolled out and smiled. "Cory, so this must be Madison. You can give her a tour if you want. Everyone's out on the field. Just stay out of the living quarters, ground floor is fine."

Madison remembered this guy from the frat party where she first met Cory. He had rock star good looks with his long hair, and longer eye lashes. She was certain while he might arrive at a party alone, he never left alone. She stood a little closer to

Cory, although Cory was clearly no match for any of these warriors if they decided to turn on her.

Cory felt Madison step in closer. "Thanks, Marcello, and may I officially introduce you to Madison. Madison, this is Marcello, he's Second-In-Command here at the camp. Pretty much the boss."

Marcello grinned and shook his head. "The warrior that stands heads above everyone on the field is the boss, but I'm honored to meet you, Madison." Turning back to Cory, he excused himself. "I need to get to work, keep her safe here, brother. I can only control these warriors for so long."

Fist bumping Marcello, Cory watched him walk into the fray. "Come on, let me show you inside the living quarters really quick, then we can head to my shop, it will be quieter."

Madison followed him into the living quarters for the warriors, full of large open spaces designed to accommodate their size. Despite the masculine decor, Madison recognized Kate's touch in the design. The wood floors shined, and there was a huge fireplace on one wall. Madison could easily envision the warriors all huddled here around a large fire in the winter. A glint of light on steel caught her eye as she was drawn to a large sword mounted on the wall behind glass. She walked in the direction of the sword and read a simple brass plaque mounted beneath it that read: Fiamma. She touched the plaque and turned to Cory. "Fiamma? Is that Italian for something?"

Cory stepped up behind her. "Fiamma means fiery in Italian. She was a warrior from our coven. She was killed here at the Battle of Bel Rosso. She's the only female I think Kate ever trusted around my dad. She spent most of her life fighting beside my dad and when she died, this place was like a tomb. Everyone loved her so much."

Reaching out, he placed his hand on the case and traced the line of the sword. "She always wore red. You could spot her anywhere in the field."

Madison looked at him quizzically. "The Battle of Bel Rosso? Am I in danger here, Cory? I don't understand."

"No. I'd never bring you here if you were in danger.

Everything's quiet now. This happened a few years ago when my dad had to fight for this territory. Bel Rosso used to sit in the middle of another master's territory. His name was Maximus, and he was a warrior, like my dad. Dad tried to negotiate with him, but they ended up going to battle over the land. We were attacked right here at Bel Rosso. We won, of course, but we lost warriors in the battle, one of them was Fiamma. Dad has been rebuilding the ranks and is just now getting our warriors back up in numbers. But he defeated Max, and now, he's the Master of Virginia."

Madison listened to the loud clashing sound of metal against metal that could be heard inside the living quarters, as the reality for why the warriors practiced sunk in. She was still having a hard time imagining a battle here in this peaceful paradise. "Can we see your shop now?" She wanted to move to something where she'd be more familiar.

"Definitely." Taking her hand, they walked back outside, and he rushed them into his shop. "Well, here it is, this is where I spend a lot of my nights."

He opened the door, flipped on the light, and gallantly held out his hand for her to enter. "I make all the leathers the warriors wear. I design everything myself, cut the patterns, select the materials, and put them together. Each piece is custom fit to the warriors needs. I can make anything. When I met Kate, she was with my dad at a club in California. I didn't know he was my dad then, and well, long story, but he wanted to give me a new life, get me out of the clubs. Kate noticed the leather jacket I was wearing and asked me about it. When I told her I'd taken several secondhand pieces and remade them into my own jacket, she was the one that actually had the idea of letting me try to make the leathers for the warriors. Dad agreed, and this is the end result. I think I was born to end up here doing all of this, almost like fate."

Madison could smell the leather as soon as he opened the door, and she inhaled deep, taking in the scent. She knew how the smell of the wet clay inspired her as she worked the clay into shape on the potter's wheel, and she imagined Cory felt the same, working around these large bolts of leather. Most of the leather was in brown or black, but she saw occasional patches of color. He had huge work tables in the space, well-worn and scarred by the blade of a knife, where he cut the leather into the patterned shapes. She ran her hands over the well-used tools, the blades, awls, and small tack hammers. He had a large industrial sewing machine to accommodate the tough leather, and a wall full of spools of a very course thread, again mostly in shades or black or brown. She saw finished pieces hanging and pieces in various stages of production stacked on a bench. It was easy to imagine him here, working late into the night. "This is perfect, Cory. I love it."

Cory watched her as she took in his work space and tools. She was an artisan herself and it showed in how she admired everything in his space. "I'm so glad you like it. I love it here, Maddie. This is what I love to do, it makes me feel like part of the family, my contribution to my family, the only real family I've ever had. I fit in here. It's hard work, takes a lot of time and patience, but with every piece I finish, I know it will be used in a way to protect and serve my family."

The door burst open and Rebecca rushed in. "Oh, sorry Cory, we had a break and I didn't know your friend was still here. I just came to see if my leathers were done yet."

Rushing to Madison, Rebecca was bubbly and energetic, as she grabbed her hand. "Hi, I'm Rebecca. I think I've seen you in town. Do you live around here?"

Madison was caught off guard by the sudden intrusion, but the girl seemed warm and welcoming to her presence. "Uh, I live in town, yes."

"That's great. I live close by with my family too. It's nice to meet you. Cory's the best ever, isn't he? He makes the best leathers for us. He's our hero."

Cory laughed. "I am not quite done yet, Rebecca, I won't be finishing anything tonight, so I'll try to have them ready tomorrow night."

Rebecca flashed a smile and gave Cory a hug. "Thanks,

Cory, I can't wait to wear them."

As she rushed out the door, Cory apologized. "Never a dull moment around here. Sorry, the warriors have little down time, so when they see my light on, they're trying to catch up with me. Dad's really strict with them."

Madison looked out the window as the warriors practiced their weapons skills. She could see the warriors divided into groups, some led by Aislynn, and some by Marcello. The largest group was with Shade, and they were giving him their undivided attention. She had no trouble imagining Shade was strict. In fact, she had trouble imagining him in any other light.

Cory walked up behind her and put his arms around her waist. "Let's go back to the house, grab something to eat and relax. But instead of walking back, would you let me teleport you?"

She turned with a gasp. "You can do that? Take me with you?"

Grinning down at her, he kissed her nose. "Yes, I can, not for long distances, though."

Lifting her up, she wrapped her legs around his waist and he walked to the light switch and flipped it off. "Don't be scared. I can do this short distance easily."

Madison had no idea what to expect as she clung to him. "I'm not scared. Just don't drop me!"

He lifted them quickly and they moved effortlessly through the night sky. She felt weightless in his arms, and he knew she was excited. "Just hang on. Let's take a spin."

He guided them easily across the stables, and the open pastures. Even at night, it was easy to see the mountains and rolling hills of Bel Rosso. Her hair blew in his face and he felt alive and happy. She was the one for him, the one who could make his life worth living and he'd do anything to keep her. Taking them back to the house, he landed easily inside his bedroom, as she still clung to him. Kissing her, he could feel her heart racing. "Told you I wouldn't drop you."

She returned the kiss. "Don't ever drop me, Cory Medici."

"Never. I love you, Madison Barnes."

63

Braden was reviewing the latest poll numbers, and Alec was ahead by a slight margin. The press had been referring to the young couple as *the new Camelot*, envisioning the young, handsome couple in the White House. Now, all Braden had to do was keep the illusion going until the election.

Alec had been easy to control, but Rissa had resisted him at every turn. Tonight, they'd attend a fundraising dinner with a lot of wealthy CEO's, so Rissa would be able to pull out all the stops and dress however she wanted. He hoped that would at least put her in a good mood.

He was heading to the conference room for their daily briefing, as the campaign workers all gathered around the table and Alec and Rissa joined him, followed closely by Hyde and Mateo. "Okay, people, everyone take a seat. We have another big day. The fundraising dinner is tonight, and this is key. These are big donors, so we'll be in a private ballroom in the hotel. I'll need for the staff to dress formally, for those of you who'll be working the room. Rissa, this means you can pull out your designer wardrobe. That should make you happy."

Rissa looked around the room at the campaign robots. They were all so boring, and she was tired of the same routine, pretending to be interested, smiling, and shaking hands. She sighed and answered him mechanically, "Yes, Braden."

Alec nodded. "What time do you want us there?"

Braden gave him the details and introduced him to one of the staffers named Kelsey. "Be there by nine. Kelsey will stay at your elbow most of the evening. She's studied the profiles of every attendee. She'll be able to prompt you on their names, their kids' names, where they work, what position they hold, anything that may be relevant. That will help you to connect on a personal level with these people. Make them feel important. The happier they are, the more money they give."

Kelsey gave him a broad smile, happy to have this

assignment, and the chance to work so closely with Alec. "I'm looking forward to helping you, Senator, in whatever way possible."

Alec didn't miss the subtle undertones in her message, as he took her outstretched hand.

Rissa raised her eyes to the vixen bitch and leveled her with a deadly stare. She wanted desperately to grab the bitch by the hair when she felt Hyde's hand on her back.

"Settle down, Rissa. This isn't the place."

Rissa sneered at Hyde before returning her attentions to the female staffer. She leaned close to her ear and hissed low and deadly, "That's my master and I'll rip your heart right out of your useless chest, bitch."

Brushing past the staffer, Rissa walked to the other side of the room and took a seat.

Kelsey had watched the dynamic between Alec, the charming politician, and that cold fish he called his mate for the last month and a half now. All the females on the campaign staff had their eye on him and looked for any opportunity to get close to him. She was excited to get this assignment, and not the least bit surprised at Rissa's response. She felt Rissa slither up behind her whispering her threat as Kelsey turned slowly, issuing a slow hiss. She wasn't intimidated by this cold bitch. Alec looked up to see the interplay between the two females and shook his head, ignoring the responses of both women as he finalized plans with Braden.

When they were done, he looked for Rissa and barked. "Let's go. Now!"

Rissa felt alienated from this whole process. He had the whole campaign staff now, and they took care of everything. She missed the days of doing dirty deeds for him, being sent on her own assignments, pulling them off and pleasing him, getting her master's reward for a job well done. Now, he didn't even notice her, except as an accessory on his arm. She wasn't a part of this, and she realized, she never really was. As he barked, she stood. Holding her head up, there was no expression on her face as she walked to him, Hyde pulling up behind her. "Yes, Alec."

They headed back to their hotel room, and Alec gripped her arm firmly. "What the hell is wrong with you? Cut the crap, Rissa, and at least pretend like you want to be here. I've had about enough!"

Rissa looked down at his hand as it sank deep into her flesh, biting into her with pain. She began to laugh, throwing her head back, her laughter almost hysterical.

Her laughter enraged him. Mateo walked ahead of them and unlocked the door to their hotel suite, checking inside and then holding the door open for them to enter. Both he and Hyde remained emotionless as the drama played out in front of them.

Alec led her through the door and gave Mateo a look that indicated he was to stand guard outside the door. Both Mateo and Hyde took their stations on either side of the hotel room door, as Alec closed and locked it behind them. Alec spoke to her through gritted teeth, holding his beast at bay. "What the fuck is going on here?"

Rissa hissed, holding her own beast down. "I should be asking you the same? Wait, is my master actually showing me some attention. I almost missed it. Or didn't recognize it, it's been so damn long."

Rissa knew she was walking a fine line and she didn't care. Stepping into his face, she locked eyes with him. "You can't win this without me. I've done all you've asked. You think I don't notice how you look at the female staffers? And you expect me to sit back and smile like I don't care. Why don't you rip my heart out and feed it to the bitches waiting in line to fuck you? They whimper when you look at them. You're so ridiculous in your attempts to charm them. What about me?"

Alec bared his teeth at her, issuing a low growl as his hand encircled her throat. "What about you? Can you stand to not be in the spotlight for one fucking minute? It's always about you, Rissa, always, the Darling of G-town, always on the front page of the society section. Well, now you have national attention, so fucking act like it. Don't screw this up for me!"

Her rage went into full swing. She clawed at his hand and

broke free of him. Lowering her head, her eyes blazing red, she growled out each word, "You want a show? Oh, I'll give them a show like never before."

In one quick move, he slammed her against the wall, holding her there immobilized, speaking through gritted teeth. "There will be no show. If you aren't capable of doing your job, I'll gladly make excuses for your absence. I'm sure you won't be missed if I have to tell everyone the Darling of G-town isn't feeling well this evening. She regrets she'll have to spend the night alone in the hotel room, sipping a light broth to sooth her delicate stomach. Don't think for one minute I won't post Hyde and Mateo both on your ass, and you won't be going anywhere. And if you think, for one minute, your precious Hyde will come to your rescue, think again.

"And you...you dare to accuse me of *my* wanton thoughts? You think I don't see what goes down between you two? I allow it because it amuses me, and I know the warrior won't act on your desires. So, let's not act so sweet and innocent, shall we? I'm sure Kelsey can fill your shoes for the evening quite nicely, in more ways than one."

Rissa understood his threat to abandon her here and replace her with that bitch. Defeated, she lowered her eyes, her voice soft and pleading. "Hyde has never touched me. I've never touched another without your consent. No one can fill my shoes, no one can love you like I can, because I know you. I know you, Alec, and I feed and heal all that haunts you. I don't mean to disappoint you. I don't know what else to do to please you. I keep failing."

Alec slowly released the hold on her neck as she slid to the floor on her knees.

"I beg you, let me attend with you, Alec. Don't leave me here alone. I don't want to be alone."

Alec paced the floor. "Empty promises, Rissa. You keep saying you'll do better, then as soon as you don't get your way, I have to go through this crap all over again."

He walked to the window, looking out over the city, debating whether to take her with him today, or give her some cooling off time. He shook his head. He couldn't afford to have her screw up in front of the press. Turning back to her, he barked, "Give me your phone."

Rissa raised her head and looked at him in complete puzzlement. "What? My phone?"

He grabbed her handbag and rummaged through it, extracting her phone and sliding it in his jacket pocket. "You're staying here today. Calm yourself down. Take a long bath or whatever the hell you do. Don't leave this room. Do you understand? I'm leaving Hyde here, stationed outside. You're to be ready for the fund-raising dinner when I return at seven. I'll decide, then, if you're calm enough to go."

Rissa watched in shock as he took her phone and gave her his orders. Clutching her chest, she called out to him in a strangled cry, "No, Alec, no."

She scrambled on hands and knees, trying to get to his ankles, like a beggar. He rushed out the door, and she stopped and hung her head. She'd been abandoned by her master. He'd leave her as he went out without his darling Rissa. She fell to the floor in tears. They'd all laugh at her now. She was a joke, his failure. The Darling of G-town confined to a hotel room, alone.

Hyde and Mateo snapped to attention as he exited. Alec told Mateo to come with him and told Hyde he was to stand guard outside the door until he returned. "Do you understand me? Outside. No visiting. And if she asks for your phone, the answer is no."

Hyde looked straight ahead and answered. "Yes, sir."

Hyde and Mateo made brief eye contact as Mateo fell in line behind Alec.

Rissa spent the day with nothing to do, no company, no phone, alone with no contact. She tried to talk to him telepathically, but he'd blocked her. She lay in the bed for hours, crying. He'd never abandoned her before, and she couldn't bear the loneliness. This was how it would feel if he released her. She'd be shunned by any other master, and she'd never fit in back in the mortal world. She wondered if he could win this election without her, and she felt a stabbing pain to think of him reaching his goals without her. He'd stop at nothing, with or without her. Rissa was a fighter, but she couldn't fight Alec. He always got what he wanted in the end, and what he wanted was to be the President.

With sudden clarity, she realized no matter what happened, win or lose this campaign, if she didn't have Alec, she didn't have anything. With heaviness in her heart, she went to the bathroom and stared at herself in the mirror. She looked a mess, and she knew if he was going to take her with him this evening she'd better pull herself together.

She showered and washed her hair, brushing it until it glowed. Looking through the closet, she chose a blue cocktail dress that was simply cut and accented her eyes. She picked out shoes of black and blue that has been designed for her, the perfect height to compliment his stature. She selected several expensive but tasteful pieces of diamond jewelry. The look was elegant, and classic.

She braided her hair in a French braid on the back of her head, secured it with a diamond clip, leaving a few soft tendrils around her face. Her makeup was applied modestly. Rissa stood before the mirror and was pleased with the look. Classic, elegant, and understated, it's what he'd asked for. She sat for the longest time, her hands clasped in her lap, waiting for his return.

Alec hurried back to the hotel after a full day of campaigning. He hated to admit it, but the day had gone much smoother without her. As he and Mateo approached the hotel suite door, Alec addressed Hyde. "Any problems?"

Hyde shook his head. "No, sir. No problems."

Alec entered the suite to find her dressed and ready. She looked beautiful, and her demeanor was calm. "So, what's it going to be Rissa? Are you ready to go to this dinner and charm the donors?"

She turned to face him, and gave him a smile. "I'm prepared to do as you wish. It's your decision to make."

He sighed loudly. "I'm counting on you, Rissa. Please try to hold it together."

He extended his arm to her and she slipped her hand around his elbow. He kissed her lightly on top of her head, getting little response. He placed his forefinger under her chin and lifted her face to his. "We're good here, right?"

Rissa felt giddy. He wasn't going to leave her behind. She'd give him whatever he needed. "Of course, we are."

Alec freshened up, changing to a fresh shirt and tie before he exited the room with Rissa on his arm, as Mateo and Hyde fell in behind them. Alec instructed them over his shoulder.

"Keep a low profile tonight. Stay on the perimeter of the room. All the guests are invited, and Braden will make sure there's no one here who wasn't on the list."

The two warriors nodded as they received their instructions. They entered the grand ballroom with much fanfare and applause, as Alec immediately turned on the charm, shaking hands, and greeting potential donors to his campaign, and Rissa stood quietly beside him.

Kelsey saw him come in and moved to stand on the other side of him, efficiently whispering to him the names and information she'd stored away on each of the guests, helping him to personalize each greeting.

Rissa placed the mechanical smile on her face, but it already felt like a chore. The crowd was there for him, and no one was looking at her. She noticed immediately when Kelsey stepped in close to him and held his attention, as she supplied him with information. Her eyes glazed over as she mentally checked out, the endless line of greeters, the speeches, and the meal she must push around on her plate.

As the evening progressed, she broke away and found a seat at a vacant table. Alec hardly noticed her absence and she wished the evening would move along faster.

Alec worked the room like a pro, shaking the hands of his rich and powerful donors, people who'd expect to see a return on their investment once he was in office. The men wanted to be him, the women just wanted him, and he never missed an opportunity to impress, to make the promises they wanted to hear. At some point, he felt Rissa slip away from him and he surreptitiously watched her as she walked aimlessly through the crowd, and finally settled at a table by herself. He wished she'd play along with this charade, but he should have realized she'd sulk over not being the center of everyone's attention.

Kelsey remained at his side, whispering names and info on the people who approached him. He allowed the women to stand close, closer than decorum dictated, as they found a way to lay their hand against his chest or stroke his biceps through his suit. He felt a few hands as they slipped a folded piece of paper in his suit pocket, holding a scribbled cell phone number, no doubt, or perhaps information on a local hotel and room number.

Like most vamps, he had no trouble attracting mortal women, or even mortal men for that matter, but normally, a vamp wouldn't put themselves out front and center in the mortal world.

He continued to work the crowd as Braden approached, and with a smile fixed on his face, he heard the campaign manager complain about Rissa. Alec turned to him, leaned in, and clapped Braden's back like they were having a friendly exchange as he answered him under his breath, "At least she's quiet. That's better than having her on my arm and making a scene or rolling her eyes."

Braden sighed and walked away. Alec had a point, but still, Rissa's aloofness wouldn't go unnoticed either.

Rissa looked down at her hands, clasped in her lap, and rolled the large diamond around her finger. She reached for the glass of white wine some waiter had placed before her, and pretended to sip slowly, holding the glass in her hand. She looked up every now and again, searching for Alec in the crowd. She had no idea how long she sat there, it seemed like hours.

She stood to go to the ladies' room and grabbed her clutch when she realized Hyde was beside her. "You're very quiet this evening, Rissa, I'd have thought this would have pleased you to be here. You look beautiful, by the way."

Rissa stopped and raised her eyes to him. He was so

handsome in a suit, classically rugged no matter how he dressed. "I'm just being the good little mate Alec requires tonight, nothing more, following my orders, just as you are, Hyde."

Sighing heavily, she laid her hand on his arm. "To be honest, I wish you could just take me back to the hotel room. I'm tired of playing this game."

Hyde placed his hand over hers. "Try to at least smile and look as though you want to be here. This is for both of you, not just Alec. Where are you going?"

Rissa shrugged at his comment. "The ladies' room, if you must know."

"I'll escort you and wait outside. Do us both a favor. Don't do anything I'll need to report to your master."

Rissa looked at him and wondered when he'd decided to be on Alec's side. She walked ahead of him to the ladies' room. Once done, she returned to find Hyde right outside the door. No one trusted her anymore. She smiled half-heartedly at him. "Let's go back to the circus and be clowns."

Hyde escorted her back into the ballroom and she, once again, took her seat at a table, alone.

64

Madison had spent the day cleaning her apartment. She'd shopped at the downtown farmer's market in the morning for fresh produce and herbs and was preparing an Italian dish for dinner. She loved to cook, but didn't get the opportunity very often. Cooking for one wasn't much fun. She'd bought some fresh flowers while she was there and was placing them in vases in both the living room and on the dining table. After a quick shower, she brushed out her hair and slipped a tie-dyed sundress over her head. Making a last minute inspection of her place, she lit the candles, giving the rooms a soft glow. It didn't look anything like Bel Rosso, but it did reflect her style. She scurried about, fluffing pillows, checking the moisture in the potted plants, and making last minute adjustments, as she waited for Cory's arrival.

Cory was relaxed driving into Charlottesville. As he drove up and parked outside her apartment, the sun was slowly setting, and the sky was alight with a beautiful sunset. He retrieved the case of white wine from the Bel Rosso Vineyards Kate had insisted he bring for Maddie. With his hands full, he used his foot to rap on the door several times.

Madison rushed to the door to find him struggling to juggle a whole case of wine in his arms. She laughed as she swung the door open for him. "You know, a bottle would have been sufficient. Hurry! You can put it down on the kitchen counter."

Laughing, he answered her. "It wasn't my idea, it was Kate's, and I think Shannon probably had something to do with it as well."

As he headed to the kitchen, setting the case of wine down on the counter, he could smell the aroma of something delicious in the air. "Man, that smells amazing! I never get to smell food being cooked at home."

Turning, he took her in his arms and kissed her softly, just as his stomach made a gurgling sound that announced his hunger. "Sorry, I haven't had home cooked food in a while. Did you do all of this for us?" His eyes scanned the candles and flowers, and he smiled at her.

"For us, for you. I hope you like my cooking. It's just a pasta dish, with vegetables and some chicken, fresh herbs. It will go great with the wine. I figured you might be tired of pizza."

Cory laughed. "Yeah, well, pizza is easy and quick. I don't know how to cook, but by the smell of that stuff, it is going to taste awesome."

Pulling out a bottle of wine, he removed the cork easily and poured them each a glass. Looking over his shoulder, he asked, "Need any help? Not sure what I can manage, but I take direction well."

Madison checked the progress on her dish and thought it would need a few more minutes of cooking time. She popped the Italian bread, slavered in butter and garlic, into the oven. "I think everything's under control. Let's have a glass of wine and by then, I'll be ready to serve dinner."

She took the glass from him and walked back into the living room, sitting down on the old sofa, made comfortable by the piles of throw pillows. She took a deep sip of the wine before laying her head back against the cushions, as she felt the liquid course through her system, warming and relaxing her.

Cory carried his own glass of wine into the living room, following behind her, watching as her hair swayed across her back with the timing of her hips. She did a soft flop on the couch, as she sunk into the cushions. He sat next to her, as she laid her head back, closing her eyes. She was so beautiful. There was a glow about her he'd never seen in anyone else. Taking a sip of wine, he softly brushed a loose tendril of her hair from her face. "Tired? It looks like you had a busy day. You didn't have to do this for me, Maddie. I thought, maybe after dinner, we'd go for a walk or catch a movie tonight, but maybe just hanging out here is a better idea."

With her eyes still closed, she enjoyed the gentle touch of his hand. "I never cooked for you before, and I like to cook. I just never have much reason to make the effort. I just hope you like it. So, maybe you should save your praise until after you eat. You may feel differently."

She laughed, but knew she was as skilled in the kitchen, as she was at the potter's wheel. Preparing food from scratch was soothing to her. She saw it in the same way she saw her art, creating something from nothing. She took another sip of the wine and leaned her head on his shoulder as the rich aroma of the bread and garlic permeated the room. She giggled as the wine performed its magic. "I forgot to ask about the garlic thing. You're safe, right?"

Cory chuckled and kissed her forehead as she lay on his shoulder. "Yes, I'm safe. The cross, holy water, garlic and all that stuff is nothing more than myth that was created by the vampires to make you feel safe around us. And some of the stuff, to be honest, we have no idea where it came from. Like the coffin thing. We think a lot of it was created for the movies. We have this old vampire at the house now tutoring Lorenzo. I swear, Maddie, I think he's older than Gi! He taught my dad when he was a kid. I talk to him sometimes, because he knows so much about vampire history and the Medici reign. He's like an encyclopedia of Medici family history. He gave me a few things to read, and I like that because, even though I'm not completely vampire, I'm part of that history, and I want to learn as much as I can."

Taking a large gulp of wine, he felt it soothe him, giving him a light buzz, but nothing like the Midnight. His stomach made another grumbling response to the smells permeating the house. "Is it done yet? I can't stand this much longer, I want to taste your cooking."

Madison polished off the rest of her wine before getting up. "It should be ready. Let me get it on the table. You want to take a seat?"

Madison pulled the hot bread from the oven and placed it in a basket, covering the bread with a cloth napkin. She placed the bread on the table, as Cory brought their wine glasses and refilled them both before taking his seat. Madison took two fresh green salads from the fridge and placed one in front of him, as she sat down with her own. "Dig in. Salad first, and then I'll serve the main course."

Cory sat down after pouring more wine, and grinned. "Yes, food! Man, you're worse than Kate, making me eat rabbit food. Shannon made me eat some weird vegetable thing the other day too. I'm only eating this so I can get to the good stuff."

Taking huge forks full of salad, he gobbled it up quickly, as he realized Maddie was staring at him. "What? Sorry, I'm starving."

Madison shook her head as he wolfed down the salad. "I made the salad dressing from scratch, and I made the bread. Try some."

She cut into the crusty goodness of the bread, as the steam escaped, releasing the strong doughy fragrance mixed with garlic into the air. She handed him the bread and he devoured it.

"So, what kind of stuff are you learning from Lorenzo's tutor? I learned a lot about the Medici's role during the Italian Renaissance. Is your father connected to that branch of the Medici's? A lot of the artists of that era wouldn't have been so prolific without the sponsorship of the Medici's. Michelangelo, Da Vinci, Botticelli, to name a few."

Grabbing more bread, Cory's appetite was out of control. He knew Maddie cooked all of this especially for him tonight, and he needed to slow down and enjoy her hard work. He pulled apart some of the bread and took small bites as he talked with her. "Yes, we're related to the mortal branch of the Medici's. My dad was born during the Renaissance period, and his parents, Christofano and Portia, were also patrons to the artists. Inside their home in Florence are many paintings and pieces of sculpture that are originals of some of the famous artists. My grandparents were killed during the Bonfire of the Vanities. Some of the vampires, like Gi, survived and actually stole away some of the art, hiding it to preserve it. My dad had finished his training in the camps and was traveling the world when it happened. When he got back, it was all over, and his parents were dead, burned alive. He doesn't really talk about it a lot."

Madison looked at him in amazement. "Your grandparents? Wow, I have to get my head around this. That was in the 15th century. Your dad's parents were killed during the upheaval of the bonfires? That means your dad probably knew some of these artists. This is blowing my mind right now." She took another drink from her wine glass, as she moved to the kitchen and returned with their plates piled high with the pasta dish. "I assumed you'd like Italian, but to be honest, I just sort of threw this together myself without a recipe. I like to experiment in the kitchen." She put the plate in front of him, as she sat down with her own.

Cory's eyes lit up as she sat the heaping plate in front of him. "Maddie, this looks incredible!"

Taking his fork, he plunged it into the steaming pasta and then placed it in his mouth. He moaned as the flavors exploded on his tongue, the herbs and garlic not overpowering the pasta and the tender chicken. Closing his eyes, he sighed as he chewed. "Babe, this is like heaven in my mouth."

She grinned and dug in.

"Look, Maddie, I have no college education, I didn't even finish school. I'm not really educated on all the arts. That would be Kate and Luca's thing. Luca's an artist and he's really talented. But I do know there's a portrait of my dad and his parents when he was younger that was painted by Michelangelo. So, yeah, he did know some famous artists. My dad has lived through a lot, come to think about it, he probably knew a lot of famous people."

Madison stopped mid chew. "Michelangelo painted a portrait of your dad? Seriously?" She took another gulp from her wine glass, as she processed the information. "Is it in a museum somewhere? What's the name of the piece? Maybe I can look it up in my art history books. Oh my god, that's amazing!"

Cory was enjoying every bite, as well as her excitement and interest in his family's history. Shaking his head, he said, "No, it's at Castello, my dad's home in Florence. Well, more like a castle than a home really. It sits on the River Arno. I just had a really great idea. When Kate has the baby, we'll all go to Florence for the delivery. I'm sure Dad won't mind if you come along. You can see everything then, at least you'd appreciate all the stuff in there. The place is like a museum. It's way old. Would you like to go with us? It's huge and has plenty of room."

Madison almost choked. "Go to Florence? Are you kidding me? I'd love to go! Could we go to the Ufizzi and see the statue of David? Cory, this is an art major's dream come true!"

Cory looked at her and laughed. "The Ufizz what?"

"It's an art gallery today, but it was built by the Medici's to hold the offices of the local magistrates. There's art there from all the Renaissance artists, and a lot of murals painted by Vasari."

Cory held up his hand. "Hey, that name sounds familiar. I heard Kate talking to Theresa once about Vasari and they were looking at this huge mural inside Castello. It was beautiful. I can't believe someone has talent like that."

He watched as her face blossomed into more amazement. He remembered his dad talking about the first time he took Kate to Castello and her excitement at the treasures it held inside. He said it was the happiest time for him as he was looking at the world through her eyes, like seeing it for the first time. "You don't mind flying, do you?"

Madison shrugged. "I haven't flown much, other than across country for school and when I get to go home. I don't fly home too often because it's so expensive, but I'm okay with flying."

Cory stood to help clean up the dishes. "Good, because I can't teleport us that far. Everyone will take my dad's private jet because Kate can't teleport being pregnant. Everyone will come with us. It's like this huge celebration. I think we actually stay about a month, until the baby is okay. If you wash, I will dry, and I promise not to drop anything."

They worked side by side in the kitchen cleaning up. Madison's apartment didn't have a dish washer, so everything was done by hand. They laughed and talked through the chore as the time passed quickly. Wiping her hands dry on a towel, she turned to him before leaving the kitchen. "Why don't you get another bottle of wine and join me back in the living room?"

Cory was enjoying the simple pleasure of being with her and performing these domestic chores. Opening another bottle of wine, he grabbed the two clean wine glasses and headed into the living room. Sitting down the glasses, he filled them halfway with the sweet white wine. They were down one bottle and he liked how it made him relax. Taking Maddie in his arms, he kissed her with love and passion. "Thank you, that was delicious and now, we can relax without my stomach complaining."

"You're welcome. I'm glad you enjoyed it."

She laid her head back against the sofa and closed her eyes, letting the wine relax her. She absentmindedly ran her hand up and down his thigh as he sat next to her.

Cory could feel his heart beat go up a notch, her fingers innocently sliding across his thigh. He wanted so much to be with her, be inside her, and make her his own. She had to make that choice, though, and he had to have patience. It would be another long night of kissing, caressing and then they'd sleep. It was becoming hard to resist not having her, but he was determined to wait for her to come to him on her terms. "Is there anything you want to do tonight?"

With her eyes still closed, her tummy filled, and her body relaxed, she answered, "We're doing it. I just want to stay in, if that's all right. Unless you had something planned?"

"Nothing planned at all, just want to be with my girl. That's all I ever need." Throwing his arm around the back of the couch, he snuggled softly into her hair, close to her neck. "You smell beautiful, like bread warm from the oven."

She chuckled. "Well then, I should be hard to resist." She nestled into him, sliding her hand across his chest. She left soft kisses along his jawline. "Who doesn't love hot bread?"

Feeling her soft lips along his jaw, his hand slid into her hair and he smiled. "I love hot bread."

Letting his other hand slide across her hip, he kissed her neck, and felt the soft pulse of the blood through her veins. He didn't want to scare her, but he couldn't resist the feeling of her heart beating, as his lips were pressed against her delicate throat. He wanted everything about her.

Madison felt the goose bumps rise on her skin as his lips brushed her neck, and she could feel the heat of his breath. She slid her hand into his hair, pulling him close as she lay down on the sofa, and encouraged him to follow. "Lay next to me," she whispered.

Her whispered tone excited him, and he took a quick intake of breath. Trying to relax his body, he knew they'd been here before, but she always stopped. He was struggling to control himself once again, trying to shut off his feelings in anticipation of that moment when she felt things had gone too far. "Maddie..." Sliding beside her, they were tangled in each other's arms.

She kissed him, letting her arms slide easily around his shoulders, as she felt the weight of him on top of her. His hand was on her bare thigh, as he pushed her skirt up higher. Her skin burned under his touch. She slid her tongue inside his mouth, tasting the wine on his lips. "Don't stop, Cory."

Cory didn't think twice and didn't give her time to change her mind. Those were the words he'd been waiting for. Her kiss told him this was the time, here and now. Her words fired his blood into overdrive. Picking her up, he carried her to the bedroom and laid her down gently on the coverlet, the pillows making a sweet nest for them.

He pulled the shirt over his head and flung it to an overstuffed chair. Kicking off his trainers, he was standing in ripped jeans that hung off his slender hips. Climbing onto the bed on his knees, he wiggled the sundress up her body, lifting it over her head and threw it carelessly aside. His lips left small kisses in a trail that began high on her neck, down her throat and onto her shoulders and breasts, his tongue making intimate, delicate swirls on her soft skin. She was small breasted, and Cory found her perfect. She wasn't muscle bound like the female warriors, but all softness and gentle curves. He could feel her body lurch softly upwards, arching her back, as she responded to his delicate touch.

Madison let go of her reservations. She'd kept him at bay for a long time. First, it was to avoid the complications of a serious relationship, and then, it was to give herself time to adjust to this new reality, but it was never easy. She'd been attracted to him the moment she saw him. Her breath caught in her throat and she issued a small gasp as his mouth sought out her breast. She ran her hand along his lean and muscled back, relishing in the feeling of skin on skin. Her body responded to him of its own accord, her back arching to meet his mouth as it surrounded a nipple, his tongue hot and wet against her skin.

Cory knew he must go slowly, but his body was pushed by an urgency he couldn't explain. He wanted desperately to claim her, make her his own. He knew he must control his beast, even though his beast was a mere fraction of that of a full-blooded vampire. He'd never made love to a mortal woman, or to someone he loved. He continued to spread kisses slowly down her tummy, swirling his tongue around her belly button. He kissed each hip and he could smell her sex, it called to him. He could barely breathe and lifted his head to look at her. "Maddie, please, I want you. Tell me you're not afraid, and you want me too."

Madison lay with her eyes closed, reveling in the sensations when she heard his plea. "I'm not afraid, Cory, and I've always wanted you."

Her hand was tangled in his hair, as he kissed her belly, tongue circling and teasing. Her breathing was ragged when she told him. "Take off your jeans."

Cory had never moved so fast in his life. Scrambling, he wiggled out of his jeans. Crawling back up the bed, he lay between her legs, looking up at her. He experienced a sudden moment of panic, not sure if he should slide off her panties or if she wanted to take control.

Madison started to shimmy out of her panties when he helped her, pulling them down her hips and low on her legs where she could kick them free, as they both giggled like teenagers. She quickly kissed him again. She could sense his nervousness, and she was nervous too. She wasn't sure what to expect with him. Would it be different? She quickly kissed him again, blotting out the thoughts in her head. She just wanted to feel.

Snuggling on top of her, holding the weight of his body off of her, they were skin to skin. The candlelight created a soft erotic glow to their surroundings. Sliding his hands on either side of her face, he pushed her hair back as his mouth slowly assaulted hers. They battled with tongues, and he moaned softly, wanting more. He could feel his cock grow hard against her thigh and he loved how warm and soft her skin felt against him. He tried to embrace every sensation, it was the first time he'd opened himself up to the experience, as he was always blocking out what was happening to him when he'd been with the others.

"You're so beautiful, Maddie."

Sliding slowly down her body, he wanted to make love to every part of her. Kissing the inside of her thighs, she opened her legs to him and his heart hammered hard inside his chest. His tongue slid hot and wet along the inside of her thigh, as he worked his way to her sex, swirling his tongue slowly around her clit before quickly plunging his tongue inside of her, wanting to taste her. He'd waited so damn long to just taste her sweetness and he didn't stop. He felt her hands in his hair, as her hips rose to each stroke of his tongue.

Madison threw her head back on the pillow, as his tongue explored her depths, and a moan escaped her lips. She could feel how wet she was, how wet he made her as he expertly teased, his teeth nibbling softly at the tender flesh on the inside of her thighs. He worked his way back to her sex. His hands stroked her legs, his tongue continued to stroke her clit. She was gripping his hair more tightly, as he brought her to a climax and she cried out his name.

Her climax took him to another level and he wanted more. He softly kissed the swollen lips of her sex and slid up her body, his cock sliding over her sensitive sex and she moaned and shuddered. He rolled to his side and pulled her into his arms, letting her recover her breath.

Her heart pounding, she rolled on top of him, straddling him as she sat upright. He was beautiful in the candlelight, and she ran her hands over the smooth skin of his chest, as she slid her hips down his body until she was sitting on his hard dick. She could see his chest rise and fall as his breathing picked up. She placed her hand between her legs, positioning his cock to penetrate her as she lifted her hips, and slid him in, slowly lowering herself onto his thick shaft. Her head dropped forward as the moan escaped her.

Cory lay back as she straddled him. He looked up into her face. She easily slid his cock inside her and he felt her tightness and her heat. She was so wet and soft, like a silken cocoon. Gripping her hips, he loved watching her face, how every move he made brought her a different sensation. He lifted his hips, pushing deeper, feeling her body clench him tightly, and he let out a growl.

He instantly stopped, the sound surprising him. His beast was on the edge. Blinking his eyes quickly, he hoped they weren't changing to red. He didn't feel his fangs emerging, but he wasn't sure what to expect once he got closer to orgasm. Maddie continued to ride him slow and easy, and he got lost in the feeling. It was worth every moment he'd had to wait for her.

Madison lay down on top of him, wanting to feel all of him. His arms encircled her. He rolled with her in one swift motion, so now she was on the bottom and he was on top, and in control. She was somewhat taken aback by his strength and speed, but her desire for him now felt primal. She wrapped her legs around his hips and clung to him.

Cory pushed deep inside her. He'd taken it slow at first and then felt her body urging him on. He took long, deep strokes, as his pleasure built and his need to explode and claim her took over. He held off until he could barely breathe, both of them moving together perfectly. It felt right, everything she did felt right to him and then she arched her hips forward and issued a soft little scream and pulsed around him hard and fast and he let go, cumming hard inside her.

Throwing his head back, his chest heaving, she was his now, all his. His voice was deep and low as he moaned, "Maddie. Mine."

Madison lay quietly beside him, letting her breathing find its normal rhythm. She'd heard his voice deepen as he claimed her, called her name in a soft growl. It had thrilled her, sent a chill through her. "Yours," she whispered.

65

Shade not only heard the soft electronic hum of the blinds as they went up, he felt the sun sinking down behind the mountain range. His death slumber had been troubled. Cory had gone to visit Madison and hadn't returned home. Shade was aware he'd spent the night with her, and the relationship had been consummated. He knew Cory had been able to control his beast, and both Cory and Madison were fine, but this changed everything. His son would not be able to continue to have sex with this mortal and not feed from her. He wanted to talk to Cory, to make sure his son understood what this now entailed.

He reached across the bed, into the empty space beside him, already knowing *bel* wasn't there. He'd felt her leave their bed a good hour before, which was unusual. She slept with him as much as possible, trying to keep her schedule aligned with his. He closed his eyes and knew she was close, just as she re-entered their bedroom. Her pregnancy was visible now, no doubting her condition. He turned his head and smiled at her. She always looked radiant when she was pregnant. "Who took you from my bed, *mi amore*?"

Kate climbed across the bed to him, covering his face with kisses before she answered. "Your son. Lorenzo woke me with a tap on the door. When I answered, he said he had something important to show me. He'd just finished class with Enzo, so I thought maybe it had something to do with that, but no, he needed to show me his plastic dinosaur was at the bottom of the pool. He was teaching the dinosaur to swim and it apparently didn't go well."

Kate laughed but continued, "And then I saw Cory come home. He didn't come home last night, and he still wasn't home when we went to sleep this morning. I knew he was going in to town to see Madison, and this wasn't the first time he's spent the night with her, so I wasn't concerned. He was wearing a smile bigger than his face, so I didn't have to ask if he was okay. He said he was going to his room to take a nap, but he wanted to talk to you as soon as you were awake."

Shade nodded. "He was with her all night, and I don't need to tell you why he had a smile on his face. But I am a bit concerned. He will need to feed from her soon. It is not a desire he will be able to control, and I want to make sure they are both prepared. I'm glad he wants to talk."

He brushed her crimson hair away from her face and kissed her neck, releasing a low moan. "I will soon need to go to Luca to feed, and although we have been through this process before, I will never like it."

Her face turned solemn. It was a reality she'd come to accept. His need to feed from Luca as her pregnancy advanced, and all that went with it. It was a necessity to protect the life she carried, but she still didn't like it, and she didn't like the turmoil it created for Shannon. "I don't want to think about that now. Go to Cory. Your son needs you, I think."

She watched him from their bed as he slid from beneath the sheets, his skin a dark bronze against the white linens. He dressed in jeans, hung low on his hips, as he pulled a clean t-shirt from the drawer. He gave her a final kiss before leaving the room.

Closing the bedroom door behind him, he leaned his broad back against it and closed his eyes. Taking a deep breath, he headed to Cory's room. Standing outside the closed door, he tapped lightly as he heard the music playing inside.

Cory was lying across his bed listening to music and remembering his night with Madison. They had slept after making love, and then would wake, make love again, and fall back asleep. They slept late and when he woke, he could smell the strong coffee brewing and the smell of bacon frying as Madison prepared a breakfast for them. When he climbed out of her bed, he pulled on his jeans and found her in the kitchen, wearing a white cotton robe, her hair tossed from a night of love making, her lips still swollen from their kisses.

She smiled at him when he entered the kitchen, as he took

a seat at the table and she slid a large cup of coffee in front of him. They ate a huge breakfast, and then made love again before taking a shower together. He'd spent the rest of the day with her before he knew he had to get back home. There would be a backlog of work in the camp, and they hadn't slept much the night before. He was hoping to catch a quick nap, and also, he wanted to talk to his dad. He heard the tap at his door and rolled off the bed, rushing to open it. "Dad! Did Kate tell you I wanted to talk?"

As the door whipped open, Cory was already firing questions at him. "Yes, son, she did. Damn, let me get inside the door, will you? Relax." Shade took a seat in the living room and waited for Cory to get situated. "Sit down, son. Tell me what is going on."

Cory dropped down on the large sectional sofa, not sure where to start. "It's about Madison. Last night, I, uh, I spent the night with her. I mean, I didn't just spend the night. We made love. I waited a long time, Dad, and I let her make the first move. I didn't want to do anything until she knew what we were, and I knew she could accept that, so I waited. I love her, but I really needed her to come to me of her own free will. And now, I need to know you're okay with this. I really love her, Dad."

Shade sat back on the sofa, his huge frame filling the space. He crossed his arms over his chest. "I'm glad you came to me, and I'm glad you let Madison set the pace. Did you struggle with the beast?"

Cory nodded. "I can feel the beast. He pushes for release when we make love, but he was easy to control. I could feel myself lose control of him slightly when I would, uh, you know, whenever I'd cum. But I never exposed my fangs with her, and my eyes didn't turn. I didn't feed from her either. I feel the desire to feed, but I didn't want to scare her, or push her too far. I wanted this to be normal. For once, I just wanted to feel normal. To feel what other people feel. To not just have sex, but to make love to her, and have that returned. I've never had that before."

Shade smiled and nodded his head. "Well, the beast is

going to start pressuring you harder, Cory. He will not be satisfied until he gets her blood. Blood is the only thing that will satisfy him. Being half-breed, I know your beast is not as strong, and his blood lust will not be as great, but it is there. It is important to understand that eventually, you will not be able to control that urge. Madison needs to know that, son. It will give her time to prepare."

Shade stood up and walked to the paintings on the wall, admiring them once again. "Cory, I know the life you had on the streets was not something you chose, and sex was a way to survive. I want you to have as normal a life as possible. You will live a different life than anyone here because you are not a full-blooded vampire. But love is something not to be taken lightly. This is serious stuff. You now have a responsibility to her."

"She loves me, Dad. I can feel her love for me. And she doesn't indulge in casual relationships. She doesn't sleep around. We've talked about this a lot. She wasn't a virgin or anything, but she has been selective, and only slept with guys she developed a relationship with. Since she's been in college here, she said she didn't want to get side-tracked. She wanted to finish her education. But we were both attracted to each other from the beginning. I know I won't be exactly normal, but Madison makes me feel normal. And I know she loves me. I wish I could be with her all the time. It's what I want."

Shade walked back to the sofa and sat down beside his son, throwing his arm around the back of the sofa. "Be sure the two of you are ready to commit for life, the span of yours and hers, for however long that will be, Cory. I understand that need. Mating, in the traditional sense, is not an option for you, but once you feed from her, trust me, she is not going to ever go back to any mortal man. Until that time, you will still need to use the feeders. No outside hunting, keep your blood clean. So, be mindful of things, your life is about to change."

He hugged Cory tight to his chest. "It will be all right, son. She will be worth the wait. Anything else you want to ask?"

Cory accepted the hug, leaning in to his father. He sometimes found it hard, after all this time, to accept this was his life now. It was such a dramatic change from his life on the streets, and he never dared to dream of anything different for himself. But now he had it, he knew he'd kill to keep it. He swallowed hard at his father's advice. It wasn't the feeders' blood he wanted but hers. He knew he must move slowly though, and he was right, Madison was worth the wait.

"I don't know how to prepare her for the next step. When I was living on the streets, and in the clubs, I rarely fed from mortals, and when I did, I would erase their memory. I don't want to hurt her. It would destroy me to hurt her. I don't know what a mortal feels when we feed."

Shade smiled. "If you are gentle with her, and feed from her during your passionate encounters, the feeding will be pleasurable for her. She will feel claimed. Talk to her about it. Let her lead, just as you let her lead with letting you know when she was ready to make love with you. She will let you know. Madison already knows we feed, it is not news to her, so she has had time to think about it. If her love for you is as you say, her curiosity about the experience, and her love and trust in you, will help her get there. Trust your instincts. Trust her. Don't be afraid, you won't hurt her. Let her experience what only you can give her."

Cory nodded as he pushed back from his father, breaking free from the hug. "Thanks, Dad, for finding me, for giving me this life. I'd never have found her. I'd never have been able to love a mortal girl until I was healed myself, and knew what love felt like. You healed me, and you healed my mom. I can never repay you for that. Whatever I have with Madison, whatever path we choose to follow together, I owe that to you. I don't tell you enough, but I love you."

Shade felt an immense wave of love fill him. "Cory, the healing was mutual. You healed me in a way I wasn't sure could happen. You have already repaid me. You love me. And I can ask for no greater gift from you. I will always love you, son."

Shade walked to the door, his hand around the doorknob and he stopped without turning around. "Just love her, son, it is the best thing you will have in your life, to have that love returned to you."

Walking out the door, he headed downstairs when he heard a small voice screaming with glee. "Daddy!" He was a father now, and he loved every second of it, even knowing his ass was about to go diving into a pool to retrieve a dinosaur.

66

Braden angrily tossed the *Washington Post* aside as he picked up the newspapers from Iowa and Florida, reading the very negative reviews from the press. Alec was starting to slip in the polls and it had nothing to do with Alec. The reporters all took note of his good looks and charm, and how his constituents seemed to flock to him, but then the focus always turned to Rissa, and never failed to include a photo of her, looking sullen or bored.

Kelsey entered his hotel room with another stack of newspapers, and tossed him the latest issue of People magazine. It featured a cover photo of Alec, all smiles, with Rissa standing off to the side, eyes glaring at him. The headline read, "THE NEW CAMELOT IS CRUMBLING!"

Braden grabbed up the magazine, which had provided such great coverage of their wedding, and now seemed only too eager to showcase this riff. But then again, how could they not? Even Braden knew the divide between them was obvious for all to see. Despite the number of times Alec had lectured her, and how many times she promised to do better, as soon as she wasn't the focus of everyone's attention, she pouted like a spoiled two-year-old.

Braden flipped through the magazine, looking at picture after picture of the couple, Alec smiling and Rissa looking sullen. "Fuck!" He tossed the magazine across the room.

Kelsey handed him a Midnight, which he downed in a gulp. "Don't even bother looking at the rest of these newspapers. It's just more of the same. What are you going to do, Braden?"

Braden slammed the glass down on the table. He'd never lost a campaign before, and now, this bitch was going to destroy his perfect record. "It's time for a showdown. Alec needs a reality check."

Braden stormed out of the room, and headed for the Canton's suite, as Kelsey plopped down on his unmade bed, thinking to herself, *he needs more than that.*

Reaching the large double doors that lead to the suite, Braden banged on the door. Mateo answered and let him in. "The boss is in the living room. He's watching the morning news coverage, and he's not very happy."

Braden snapped at him, "Yeah? Well, that makes two of us!"

Braden pushed past Mateo and into the separate living room of the Presidential suite to see Alec standing with his hands on his hips, as the morning news gave a recap of the campaign. "Camelot is crumbling" seemed to be the catch phrase on every reporter's lips, no matter which channel they turned to. Braden's face was red with anger as he paced.

"We're going to lose, Alec, *you* are going to lose, and it's all because of her. You better find a way to get her under control. I've done everything I can, and she ignores me at every turn!"

Alec poured himself a Midnight and offered a glass to Braden. "I'll talk to her."

Braden shook his head. "You've *been* talking to her, Alec! She needs more than talk. She's going to destroy your campaign! The American people have to see two things. They have to envision you as their President, trust you will keep them safe, and feel that. But they also have to envision her as their First Lady, even though she doesn't make any policy decisions, she represents this country, and right now, they're not buying it!"

Alec paced as he drank. "All right, Braden. I get it. Let me handle it."

Braden stormed out of the room, shouting as he left, "You better fucking handle it, or plan on spending your retirement years in Connecticut, because you won't have your Senate seat to go back to."

He slammed the door behind him as he left. Alec went to the bedroom door and tapped lightly, but didn't get an answer. He'd told Rissa they'd need to leave by eight this morning and it was now a quarter till. When he opened the door, he found her still in bed asleep. "Rissa!"

Rissa had heard the alarm when it went off, but ignored it and fell back to sleep. Sleep was a wonderful escape from the nightmare that was her life right now. She'd drank too much Midnight the night before to take the edge off her hunger, but now the alcohol had left her feeling sluggish. She rolled over when she heard Alec calling to her. "Why do you have to be so loud, I'm trying to rest." Rolling back onto her stomach, she moaned, her head pounding.

Alec grabbed a handful of her blonde hair and dragged her from the bed to her feet. Controlling his beast, he spoke through gritted teeth, "I told you be ready to leave at eight. You're screwing up this campaign, Rissa. Do you even care?"

He pushed her back onto the bed. "You know what? Stay home today. Get some sleep. I'm better off without you anyway. You're not going to pull me down."

He turned on his heels and stormed out of their bedroom to encounter Mateo. "Where's Hyde?"

Mateo told him he'd gone out to pick up more cigarettes and would be back momentarily. Alec slipped his phone into his pocket and grabbed his laptop just as Hyde returned. Alec barked at him, "She's not to leave the suite today, understood? The last thing I need is more bad press."

Hyde dropped the cigarettes on the table as he responded, "Yes, boss."

Alec stuffed a pack of the cigarettes in his pocket and nodded to Mateo. "Let's go."

Mateo gave Hyde a look, warning him not to make further inquiries. **"I'll fill you in later, brother."**

Hyde nodded and sighed. He'd seen the news already, and he didn't need Mateo to tell him what was going wrong.

Rissa was stunned and then angered, as she realized he was going to leave her here alone. She jumped up from the bed, as the door slammed and could hear him barking at Hyde. Wrapping the sheet around her, she rushed out of the bedroom in time to see him preparing to leave the suite with Mateo. "Oh, no you don't!" She screamed at his back.

From the corner of her eye, she saw Hyde reaching for her, blocking her from following Alec. She turned on him like a caged animal and came at him clawing and screaming. "Get off of me. Now!"

Alec turned to look at her and she ran to him, clutching the sheet to her chest, her voice rising, "So, this is all my fault? I don't think so. I've done everything you've asked! I feel like a pawn in your game for power. This is all about you. So, tell me, master, have I always been a pawn? This won't change, will it? It will be the same in the White House."

She felt her body shaking from the anger. "Can you not feel me, Alec? Just try to feel what I feel. I gave up everything for you, and this is what I get in return?"

Hyde and Mateo slipped quickly into the foyer, to give them as much privacy as possible in this confined space.

Alec gripped her shoulders, shaking her. "You've not done everything I asked, my darling, and if you're a pawn, you're a poor one at best. Turn on any TV, pick up any newspaper, and your sad, pouting face is there for all to see, the poor little rich girl, no longer the center of everyone's attention. And what exactly have you given up? You live like a fucking queen, you have unlimited access to my money, you have cars, jewels, whatever you've asked for. You knew what you were getting into when you mated with me, so don't play the fucking victim now. Stay here, and behave yourself, and the next time I say be ready by a certain time, perhaps, my darling, you'll learn I mean what I say. I'm tired of this shit, Rissa. Stay here and Hyde will make sure you don't encounter any press today."

Rissa lowered her head, her voice was soft, almost a whisper, "I don't have you."

She had no idea if he heard her, as he'd turned and stomped out of their room. She felt Hyde put his arm around her shoulder and lead her back toward the bedroom. As they got to the door, she pushed him away. She couldn't stand to look at him. "Even you. Even you've fallen under his ridiculous charms. If you care at all about me, you'd just take me home."

Rissa walked inside the bedroom and closed the door behind her. Hyde stood at the door, questioning whether to follow. He was worried about her and what she might do alone. He tapped on the door and waited, but the only sounds he heard were her sobs. He knew she was hurting, but she kept bringing it on herself.

Hyde laid his forehead on the door. How in the hell did he get into this mess? It was like dealing with a child. He was getting tired of this as well.

67

Rissa was, once again, stuck in a hotel room alone, as her mind started working in overdrive. Alec had forgotten to take her cell phone this time, and that was her ticket for payback. She immediately blocked Alec from her thoughts. What's good for the goose was good for the gander. He'd find out her plans soon enough. She wasn't about to go down without a fight. After all, she was still the Darling of G-town and her connections were worldwide.

The winter fashions were coming out, and she began dialing as fast as she could. She ordered every new line from every designer and requested they ship everything to their home in Georgetown. She engaged the stylists to select coordinating shoes and bags to go with the new clothes, and to have them shipped as well. She was spending money like it was water. Everyone who was anyone wanted her as their client, after all, she was going to be the First Lady and getting her to promote and wear their clothing was money in their pocket.

Then she began to call for Alec's new wardrobe as well, including only the best designer suits, silk shirts, ties, cufflinks, and shoes. She had no doubt someone would leak this expensive little shopping venture to the press.

When she was finished with her shopping spree, she tossed her phone aside, already calculating her next move. She rinsed her face in cold water and touched up her make-up. There would be no more tears today. She'd been on the phone for hours, and she knew Hyde would be antsy for a smoke break. She was sure he hadn't left his post outside her door. Picking up her phone, she made one last call to a reporter.

Going to the door, she opened it slightly to find Hyde leaning against the wall.

Hyde jumped to attention when she peeped out, and he was relieved she appeared to be calm. He'd heard her talking all morning, and knew she was on her phone. "Rissa, is everything all right?"

Displaying her trademark pout, she inquired, "Hyde, do you have any cigarettes? I could seriously use a smoke."

Hyde was immediately suspicious of her motives, but he could sure use a smoke break. "I'm not taking you outside to smoke, Rissa, so don't even think about it."

Rissa had anticipated that response. She knew he wouldn't let her leave the hotel. She sidled up close to him, her head down and laid her hand on his broad chest. "Hyde, I know I can't leave, but we can go outside on the balcony and have a quick smoke." She lifted her face to his, her eyes sad, and she knew instantly he was considering it.

"Okay, but you better behave, or I swear I'll do something I might regret."

Rissa smiled and turned to re-enter the bedroom as Hyde followed her. "It's a balcony, Hyde. There's not much I can do on a balcony."

He looked at her cautiously. "Okay, well, here's the deal. I want you to stand behind me. The press knows we're here, but they have no idea which room. We can't take any chances of them seeing you, are we clear?"

Rissa had to control her sense of glee. She'd alerted the press, letting them know where they were staying, and which room they occupied, and if they were discreet and paid attention, there might be a great photo op.

Hyde opened the sliding doors and steps outside, checking in every direction. He quickly pulled out his smokes and lit up, taking a long, deep drag on the cigarette. It felt good to get some fresh air and sun after standing in the hotel suite all day. He didn't notice any unusual activity around the hotel, so he beckoned for Rissa to join him. "Stand directly behind me. If I say move it, then back your ass back into the room."

Rissa bit her lip and agreed, as he handed her the pack of cigarettes and the lighter. She stood directly behind him. "It really is a beautiful day outside, isn't it? I wish I was riding Biondo, this would be a perfect day for it."

Hyde stood with his back to her, keeping his eyes and ears

peeled. "Well, that's not going to happen. Alec has begged you to do as he asks, and you keep refusing him, so I think you best get used to being alone in hotel suites if you don't start to listen."

Rissa stared at his strong, broad back. He'd taken off his suit jacket, rolled up his shirt sleeves, but still had on his tie. Even dressed like this, he looked rugged and all male. Rissa leaned her weight against his back, gently resting her head on his shoulder. "I wish I had a drink, a nice Midnight. I'm sure there's still some left."

Hyde was used to Rissa using her body to try and manipulate him and ignored her closeness. "Are you finished with your smoke? I'll get us both a Midnight if you want. But move back inside."

She did as he requested and returned to the bedroom. He left the balcony and closed the door, pulling the drapes closed behind him. He left her there while he went to pour the Midnight and returned with the filled glasses.

She curled up on the couch, tucking her feet under her, as she accepted the glass, and sipped her Midnight. "Thank you, Hyde. That was kind of you. I know I haven't made this easy, but without you, I'd be lost. I just want to get the hell out of this room. Can I make a suggestion?"

Hyde stood eyeing her, wondering what she was up to. "Rissa, you aren't going anywhere, so don't even think about it."

She sighed heavily. "They have a beautiful spa downstairs. I won't have to leave the hotel. You can escort me there, and I could at least get a massage, get my nails done, just something to help me relax. You can stay with me. It's not like I can escape."

Hyde sat down beside her and looked directly at her, trying to think if there were any ulterior motives to her request. He knew she wouldn't be able to leave if he went with her and decided to cut her some slack. "Here's the deal, Rissa, I'll go along, but you make one false move, and it's over! Your ass will be coming right back to this suite. Understood?"

Rissa gave him a hug, as her face broke into a smile. "Oh

Hyde, I promise I won't make any trouble. I just want to relax and look good for Alec when he returns tonight."

Standing up, she grabbed her purse. She'd already perused the spa treatments, and planned on getting the 24K gold-leaf facial, for the nominal fee of $10,000, along with every other expensive treatment they could work in before Alec returned. It would be hours before she walked out, and she couldn't wait to see Alec's face when they checked out of the hotel and he saw the spa bill. She'd have to wait for the pleasure of seeing his face over the credit card charges from her earlier shopping spree.

68

Shade was working in his office, going over assignments for their upcoming absence, as the family would need to go to Castello soon. Sophia would arrive before they knew it. He pushed the papers around his desk, unable to focus his attention, and he knew why. He picked up the faint scent of roses and his beast rumbled. Standing quickly, he knocked over the tumbler of Midnight, as papers floated to the floor. He took a few deep breaths, getting his beast under control. He'd waited much too long to feed, and the time to go to Luca was now.

Walking quickly to Luca's suite, he was ready to barge in when he remembered Shannon was with him. He impatiently tapped at the door, waiting, his body aching in need.

Shannon was with Luca in his suite. She spent more time at Bel Rosso now than she did at her condo. She'd been curled up with a book on the sofa, while Luca was standing at his easel painting. She looked up from time to time to watch him, standing in his low slung jeans, torn at the knees. His feet were bare on the painter's tarp stretched on the floor beneath the easel. He was shirtless, and she watched the play of muscles in his back, as he stood facing the easel, backing up from time to time to look at his painting from a different perspective. They heard the tap at the door and Luca looked up, his concentration broken. He told her he'd get it as he lay down his brush and pallet and made his way to the door.

He could already pick up his master's scent and felt his desire. Luca had been wondering when Shade would seek him out. As with the last pregnancies, he delayed coming to Luca as long as possible. Luca opened the door and the two men exchanged a knowing look, no words spoken. Luca held the door open for Shade to enter.

Shade entered the room, his presence seeming to dominate the space. Luca stood at the door and spoke to Shannon. "*Mia belleza*, we need some privacy. Perhaps you could visit with Kate for a while."

Shannon looked caught off guard. She knew from the last pregnancy Shade fed from him, and they had sex, but she'd never been present when it happened. Seeing the two of them together, feeling the sexual energy build between them, brought a lump in her throat, making it hard to swallow. "Of course."

She laid her book on the table and stood up, rushing past Shade, not making eye contact with him, as she moved toward the door. Luca grabbed her arm as she exited and pulled her close, his lips close to her ear, his breath hot against her neck. "It's you I love, *mia belleza*."

Shannon looked at him and nodded, giving him a smile that didn't reach her eyes. He kissed her lips lightly, as she pulled away and he closed the door behind her.

Shade observed the interplay between them, and he knew he put Luca in an awkward position. But Shannon must learn to accept that this was their lifestyle. Shade felt her anxiety, her feeling of betrayal, as she brushed past him, and he kept his eyes straight ahead. As she left, he heard the door shut softly behind her, and felt Luca's hands slide up his back and massage his neck and shoulders.

His moan was one of both a strangled need of hunger and sex. "Luca, my timing is horrible, I apologize, but I need you. She will be okay with Kate."

Luca stepped in front of him and softly kissed his cheek, his lips trailing down Shade's neck, across the pulsing vein, and Shade pulled him in closer. From now until after Sophia's birth, he'd feed only from Luca.

***

Shannon rushed up the stairs, looking for Kate. Heading into Lorenzo's bedroom, she found Theresa chatting with Emma, as they stripped his bed. Both women looked up as she entered with a questioning look on her face. She scanned the room.

Theresa answered her unasked question, "Kate's in the new baby's bedroom and Lorenzo is with her."

Shannon nodded and backed out of the room, walking

further down the hall past the bedroom Kate had set up for Lorenzo's home schooling in search of the nursery. The door was open, and she could hear Lorenzo's chatter, as she neared the door. Stepping into the doorway, she saw the soft pink and ivory colors, and the antique crib that adorned the room. Kate looked up at her as she worked in the room, seeing the stricken look on her friend's face.

Kate paused, cleared her head, and tuned out the endless chatter from Lorenzo, letting herself feel the sexual energy from her mate. She knew Shade was with Luca now, and Shannon was struggling with the visions that must be playing out in her head. Kate went to her friend and took her hand but spoke to her son, "Lorenzo, I need you to go find Theresa. Play with Theresa now, okay?"

Lorenzo gathered up an arm full of dinosaurs and marched out of the room. "Okay, Mommy."

Kate led her friend back down the long hallway to the master bedroom, closing the door behind them. Even from here on the second floor, behind closed doors, Kate knew the sounds of their pleasure would reach them both. She remembered all too well the nights she lay in this bed alone, listening to him find his release in Luca's arms, not hers. She understood Shannon's pain.

Kate climbed onto their bed and slid across, patting the bed for Shannon. "Come on, sit next to me."

Shannon crawled across the bed, sitting next to Kate as the sounds reached them both. Shannon fought back her tears and Kate could hear the straggled cry caught in her throat. She placed her arms around her friend, as Shannon laid her head on Kate's shoulder.

"Shh. It's you he loves, Shannon. This is just biology. They'd both avoid it if they could. He'll never betray you, you know that."

Shannon answered in a whisper, "I know. I keep telling myself that. But this is the first time I've been present. I didn't know it would hurt so much."

Kate stroked her hair, soothing her in the same way she

soothed Lorenzo after a bad dream. "He loves you, Shannon. If he could take your pain away, he would. Shade waits too long as it is, to spare us both. They can't change what they are. It's been easier for me since I was turned, but I remember it all too well. Does it make you regret your choice?"

Shannon lifted her head; her cheeks stained with tears and looked into Kate's eyes. "No. I'll never regret choosing Luca, no matter what the future holds for us."

Kate smiled at her, wiping the tears from her cheeks. "When will you take the next step? The blood covenant? Have you decided?"

Shannon sat up, happy for the distraction. "Luca said he wants it to be special. He wants us to be in his home in Empoli, so he was thinking when we all go to Florence for Sophia to be born. He could take me back to his home then."

Kate beamed at her. "Then we'll have much to celebrate in Florence! I'm so happy for you, Shannon, and selfishly, happy for me. I love knowing you'll be with me on this journey."

The two women hugged as the sounds of pleasure echoed through the house.

69

Braden woke up early, as usual. They'd had a really good day on the campaign trail without Rissa. Alec had explained her absence to the press and the supporters, as being related to her being a little under the weather. He'd said she was so sorry she couldn't be with him today and sent her regrets. They made good time, and Braden didn't have to worry about her sulking, or ignoring the mass of people trying to shake her hand or get a photo with her.

Braden missed the last campaign he ran for Alec when he was still single. He wasn't prepared for the level of complications Rissa had brought to the table. He'd spent some time with a feeder the night before, and after a hot shower, felt ready to tackle another day. He was hoping Rissa's day in exile might improve her demeanor, at least for a few days.

He flipped on the TV to the twenty-four-hour news channels and was smacked with a photo of Rissa on the hotel balcony with Hyde, standing behind him, her head resting intimately against his back as they both enjoyed a cigarette. The news reporters were speculating on who was the mysterious handsome man in her suite, when she was supposedly under the weather. One of the male anchors thought he recognized him as her "bodyguard", as he made air quotes when he spoke the words, while the female newscaster giggled and said, "Maybe that's her doctor."

The news went on to report they'd received an anonymous tip that Mrs. Canton had spent hours in the spa, even indulging in a 24K gold facial that cost $10,000. The coverage kept flashing back and forth between shots of Alec campaigning yesterday, and a number of still shots of Rissa on the balcony with the *unidentified man*.

Braden picked up an empty glass and threw it through the TV screen, as the glass broke and the screen crackled and hissed. His roar could he heard across the entire floor of the hotel. "That fucking bitch!"

He dressed quickly and stormed down the hallway to the Canton's suite. As he approached the door, he saw both Mateo and Hyde standing guard, talking with each other. Braden was no match for either warrior, but if he could, he'd choke the life out of Hyde right now. Pushing past him, he gruffly shouted, "Get out of my way!"

Barging into their suite, he found Alec getting dressed and Rissa still in bed, the blankets pulled over her head. Storming over to their TV, he grabbed the remote and turned it on. "You better see this before we go out there today!"

Alec continued to dress as the news came into focus on the TV. It was showing images of him on the campaign trail yesterday, smiling and shaking hands, signing autographs, and stopping to pose for photos. He was wondering what had Braden in such an uproar when the images switched to grainy photographs of Rissa on their hotel balcony, with her head against Hyde's back. His blood was already boiling when he heard the newscaster speculating on the identity of the man, and exactly what it was he was doing in Mrs. Canton's hotel suite.

Alec wasn't sure who he wanted to kill first, Hyde, for his poor judgment, or Rissa, for her clear manipulation of the situation. He turned toward the bed, his eyes glowing as he ripped the blankets off the bed, screaming her name. "Rissa! Get the fuck out of bed and explain this!"

Rissa was still in a deep sleep when she heard Alec shouting. She started to sit up when he ripped the blankets from the bed, baring his fangs and eyes glowing red. She backed up against the headboard, as her own beast emerged in response to her master. She scanned the room and saw Braden who looked like he was ready to rip her apart as well. She tried desperately to de-escalate the situation. "Back up, tell me what's going on. Just tell me, Alec!"

He growled at her, as he heard the newscaster giving details of her extravagant spa day and the $10,000 facial. "Listen to it. Don't tell me you didn't know this would get out. Look at it, Rissa! Look at the picture of you and Hyde, all cozy on the balcony. You're too smart not to know the press wouldn't catch that. You've been using the media to serve your purposes for years!"

He grabbed her and dragged her from the bed, holding her in front of the TV, clutching her by the hair, forcing her to see the images flashing across the screen. He screamed, "Hyde! Get in here!"

Hyde and Mateo had both already heard the angry exchange, and although they couldn't see the TV, they could hear the commentary through the door. Hyde already knew she'd tricked him, and he'd made a big mistake taking her out on the balcony.

Mateo flashed him a look. "Be careful, brother. He's a master. Don't antagonize him."

Hyde sighed and nodded, as he entered the suite, preparing to face Alec's anger. Braden stepped back against the wall, as the warrior entered. Alec still had a firm grip on Rissa as he screamed at Hyde, "What the fuck were you thinking? I asked you to keep her inside!"

Rissa was struggling to free herself, but he wasn't going to let go. She tried to defend him. "Hyde was consoling me and..."

Hyde interrupted her, "Rissa, your master speaks to me, be quiet. She was distraught. She'd been locked in her room for hours. When she asked for a smoke, I obliged her. I did check the area before she came out and didn't see any activity. I didn't think about a reporter with a telescopic lens. I was more focused on someone who could impose physical harm. The mistake is mine. My intention was to provide a presence that would offer protection."

Alec growled back at him deep in his throat, a low rumble that could be felt. "Oh, your presence is clear for everyone to see."

Alec nodded toward the TV where the image of Rissa with her head nestled against Hyde's back was being flashed across the screen again, and Hyde heard the speculation from the newscasters about the *unidentified man* in Mrs. Canton's hotel suite who appeared to be providing her with great comfort in her husband's absence.

Hyde cringed at the photos, and the speculation. Alec snapped at him, "The damage is done! She wasn't in any physical danger, but the press got what they wanted. And now, we have another mess to clean up, thanks to you two. I'm sick of the both of you!"

He released Rissa with a shove, letting her stumble to the floor. Hyde started to make a move to help her when Alec growled at him again and he backed off, knowing the limits of his authority with this master.

"I can't look at either one of you right now. Braden, take care of this!" Alec grabbed his phone and slid it in his pocket, as he stormed from the room, intentionally brushing past Hyde, bumping his shoulder hard as he exited. Once outside the room, he slammed the door behind him and looked at Mateo. "Follow me!"

Hyde moved to help Rissa from the floor as she screamed at Braden. "Get the fuck out, now." Braden snarled and looked at Rissa with disdain. "Fucking bitch." Walking out, he also slammed the door.

Hyde crouched down and lifted Rissa's chin, staring at her a long time. He watched as a small tear rolled down her face. "You broke my trust. I offered you consolation, and you betrayed me. It will never be the same between us, Mrs. Canton."

Standing up, he exited the door, closing it quietly behind him and standing his post in the hallway outside the suite.

Braden was standing in the hallway when the warrior exited. "Needless to say, Alec doesn't want her on the campaign with him today. I'm begging you to keep her in her room, and off the balcony, and out of the spa. Take her damn phone and laptop, and keep her invisible please. I'll do what I can for damage control with the press. Make sure they know the man on the balcony was her bodyguard who was trying to shield her from view while she smoked a cigarette. Then tomorrow, she'll need to be back in front of people with Alec. I'll deal with Alec and the press, you just manage her."

Hyde nodded to him, silently acknowledging the order, as Braden scurried off to catch up with Alec.

70

Max's anger grew with each passing day. He couldn't turn on the fucking TV or pick up a newspaper or magazine without seeing pictures of Alec's face, and Rissa right behind him. He'd heard the rumors about trouble in paradise, or as the press liked to call it, the crumbling of Camelot. Alec was down in the polls, and it was clear Rissa was the cause.

That bitch had ruined everything for him. He'd lost everything. At least now she was making Alec as miserable as she'd made him. Max paced the floor. Alec was smart, and he could still pull off this bid for the Presidency, despite Rissa.

Max let the seeds of anger grow inside his head. He knew the one thing Alec could never forgive her for, the one thing no master would forgive. He went to the safe in his bedroom, the one where he now slept alone, Lein having retreated to separate living quarters in the palace. Entering the combination, he opened the safe and withdrew the package. He dumped the contents out on the bed. Spilling out across the sheets of the unmade bed were photos of Rissa, splashing in the waves, the date stamp clear on the photograph. They were taken the day he took her to his private island in the Caribbean, the day he'd asked her to stay with him and she threw his love back in his face. He shook the envelope and the DVD slid onto the bed. It was the feed from the security camera mounted in the cabana. Max had watched it over and over when he first came to Thailand to escape her, and then had locked it away in the safe.

He slipped the disc into the laptop and watched as the images of their love making were displayed on the screen. Rissa writhing in pleasure beneath him, her legs wrapped around his hips, and her hands clutching his back, pulling him closer, deeper. He fed from her, hungrily drinking her blood as she threw her head back, welcoming him. He made her cum, and as she did, the ultimate betrayal, her fangs sunk into his flesh, and she took his blood, re-sealing her earlier bond with him.

Max smirked, as if a bond meant anything to Rissa. He retrieved a padded mailing envelope from the desk drawer and quickly scrawled the name and address across the front, stuffing the photos and flash drive inside before sealing it up. Calling for his butler, he handed him the envelope. "Make sure this goes out, express mail, today."

The butler nodded and took the package.

71

Braden had worked his magic with the press and smoothed over the controversy over the unidentified man. The press had even dug up old photos of the campaign where Hyde was clearly visible in the background of many shots. He assured everyone Rissa had indeed been under the weather, and she had simply wanted to step outside for some fresh air. With her bodyguard protecting her, she stood close to his back, thinking it would conceal her from view.

They spent several more days on the campaign, with a compliant Rissa at Alec's side. She wasn't happy, but at least she wasn't looking like a petulant child, and she managed to put a fake smile on her face when the cameras flashed.

As they wrapped up the week, Braden suggested this would be a good time to take a break. "We don't have anything else on the schedule until we go back to New Hampshire next week. Why don't you go home, keep a low profile, and get some rest? Stay out of the press completely. We have some debates coming up. Let's not give the press any ammunition to throw at you during the debate."

Alec was more than ready for a break. He was tired of the campaign, and even more tired of her. There was no escaping her as they were living in such close quarters on the bus or in a hotel. "You don't have to tell me twice. We'll fly home tonight. I'll have Alto get the jet here."

Braden nodded. "Remember, low profile. That means you need to keep Rissa home and out of sight."

He nodded his understanding, as he headed for the hotel room, directing her as he entered. "Get your stuff packed up. We're going home for a few days. Alto is filing a flight plan and then we'll be ready to leave."

Rissa had played the role of obedient wife over the past few days, but she didn't like it. When Alec walked in the door and started giving her orders to pack, she didn't hesitate. She'd do anything to get back home and have him all to herself.

"Finally, home. I just want to be alone with you, Alec. No crowds, no press, no campaign staff, just us. Please, is that possible?"

He glared at her. "Oh, it's possible, my darling. We won't be leaving the house, either one of us. Is that understood?"

Rissa nodded. Her head was down, but her heart was taking flight. She stuffed her clothes carelessly into her suitcases, in a rush to be ready to leave. "I'm assuming the sex chamber is completed?"

Alec nodded his head and ran his hand through his hair. Was she completely oblivious to his mood? "I'm sure it's done by now, Rissa, but I hope you don't think that's my reason for taking you home."

She sighed loudly. "Alec, please listen to me. I just want to be with you. You have nothing left for me when you're done campaigning every day. I need you. I need to feed. I need you to make love to me. Why can't you just see that?" Her voice was pleading, hoping for any attention.

He ignored her pleas as Braden tapped at the door before opening it. "The car is ready to take you to the airport any time you're ready."

Alec nodded and said his bags were packed and headed for the door, motioning for Mateo to follow. Braden ushered in the bellhop to carry out their luggage. "Rissa, are your bags ready, or do you still need a few minutes."

She watched as Alec ignored her, leaving her standing in the middle of the suite with her luggage. She stared at the empty space where he'd just stood. Looking up at Braden, she stared blankly at him a few seconds before answering, "No, I'm ready. I just want to go home."

As she walked out the door, Hyde was in position in the hallway, his hands clasped behind his back. He no longer spoke to her, just nodded as she walked to the lobby, and he dropped in behind her.

The flight home felt long and silent, the tension so thick it could be cut with a knife. As they landed in D.C., their limo was brought around on the tarmac. Both Mateo and Hyde exited first and inspected the car, even though Hyde knew the warriors at the Dead House had had it in their possession ever since they left. The luggage was moved from the plane to the car, and then Rissa and Alec exited down the stairs and into the waiting limo.

Alto climbed behind the wheel and started the engine as soon as the doors were closed, carrying them back home to Georgetown. Alec was looking out the window at the lights of D.C., the Washington Monument and the Capital Building lit up in the night sky. He was wondering, now, if he'd ever call the White House home, or if she'd find a way to crush his dream. He understood her well. She meant it when she said she'd behave, she meant it when she said she'd try harder, but Rissa was much like him, maybe too much like him. Rissa only cared about Rissa, and he'd always known it. She was an attribute when their goals were shared, and she was in the spotlight. But now, she didn't like being second-fiddle. He tried to envision her as the First Lady, pretending to care, smiling for the camera as he rose to glory, and he knew in his heart she wouldn't be happy. It was a role she'd ultimately reject. He sighed, unsure of this path he'd chosen, unsure of its outcome and whether he could succeed.

He'd watched his poll numbers continue to drop, as the voters said they accepted him, but they rejected her. Alto pulled up in front of their Georgetown home and Alec had never been so glad to be home in his life. Mateo exited the limo, followed by Hyde, and then allowed Alec and Rissa to get out of the car.

Alec turned to the warriors. "You two can take off. We're not going back out tonight, and we'll be home tomorrow. I'll let you know when we need you."

Rissa walked briskly to the front door, as Santos swung it open. She stood in the foyer and took a deep breath, her head falling back. "Home."

Alec brushed past her and headed straight to his office. She called after him. "I'm going down to see the chamber, want to join me? First look together?"

Alec was already pouring himself a glass of Midnight when he heard her invitation. He looked over his shoulder at her as she stood there, looking at him as if nothing had changed in their life.

He shook his head. "You go without me." He downed the drink and quickly poured another glass.

She nodded. "I see. Well, I'm going to investigate by myself then."

Turning her back on him, she sighed as she walked down the stairs to the newly renovated underground room. She wandered through the huge open space, looking at all the elaborate torture gadgets of whips, chains, and prods, all to make her scream in ecstasy. "How delicious. Now I just need to figure out how the hell to get Alec down here. That shouldn't be difficult, just piss him off."

Letting her hands slide through the floggers, she was so giddy she spun around in the middle of the floor. "You won't be able to deny me long, Alec Canton. I know you. I know what you lust for."

She felt aroused just standing in this room. Everything she remembered from the chamber in Castello was now here. How she wanted him, fucking her, torturing her, feeding from her. She picked through the long, thick dildos, choosing the one she wanted and climbed onto the table. She stripped naked and began to fuck herself, slow and easy, until the pace was making her insane with need. She made herself cum hard the first time and then began the ritual, over and over, feeling the delicious toys do what her own mate refused her this night.

She knew he'd feel her own passion and desire, and at some point, he'd have to succumb.

72

Santos entered the study with a stack of mail. "Master, do you want the mail now? If not, I can bring it to you tomorrow. I know you must be tired."

Alec dropped down in the chair behind the desk and waved Santos in. "No, bring it now. I need to unwind a bit before I sleep anyway. How did things go while we were gone?"

Santos bowed slightly, as he laid the stack of mail on the desk. "Fine, master. No problems here. The chamber has been completed just as you asked."

Alec grunted as he picked up some envelopes and started to shuffle through them, discarding some to the trash, and opening others. He made a chuffing sound. "Yes, I'm sure Rissa will be pleased. She couldn't wait to check it out. She's there now. That will be all, Santos."

The old butler bowed to him again, as he left the room. "Yes, master." Alec sipped at the Midnight, and propped his feet up on the desk, continuing to work his way through a week's worth of mail. He made his way halfway through the stack when he picked up a FedEx envelope. He checked the return address to find no name, but it was postmarked Thailand. He opened the envelope and a note slipped out onto his lap. Placing the envelope down on the desk, he picked up the note.

Alec, In case this date doesn't ring a bell,
it was the day she told you she was in NYC for
a fitting for her wedding dress.

Sincere Regards, Max.

Alec creased his brow as his feet hit the floor. *What the fuck?* He slid the contents of the envelope onto the desk to find several photos and a flash drive. The photos were all of Rissa, her back to the camera. She was romping nude and with complete abandon in the waves of the surf, her blonde hair tossed by the wind, soaking up the rays of the sun. In another shot, she sat on the end of a pier or boat dock, still nude, looking out over the water. If she was aware of being photographed, she didn't show it.

Alec looked at the water in the photo, the clear blue turquoise color, and knew she was somewhere exotic. He could see the date stamp on the photos. He ran the timeline through his memory and recalled her request to travel to NYC without him, to meet with her dress designer for a fitting and complete some other shopping. His heart started to pound. So, what was this? She was with Max instead?

He calmed himself down, taking another long drink from the glass of Midnight, telling himself not to jump to conclusions. Falsifying a date stamp would be easy enough to do. And a lot of people would like to bring down his bid for the Presidency right now. These photos could have been taken anytime. Alec wasn't ignorant of Rissa's relationship with Max before she met him. He picked up the flash drive and, opening his laptop, inserted it into the USB port. The images immediately played across the screen of Rissa, lying beneath him, writhing in obvious pleasure. Alec jumped to his feet, the photos falling to the floor as he watched her throw back her head, freely giving him access to her neck as he drank from her. Alec's eyes glowed red, casting a glow in the dimly lit study. He saw Rissa's hands clawing at his back, leaving the deep scratch marks she always left on Alex's back, and he couldn't miss the large diamond on her hand, the one he'd given her. There was no playing with the date stamp. He knew exactly when he gave her that ring. As the reality of her deceit sank in, he watched the unthinkable as she turned to him, sinking her fangs into his flesh, and drinking from him.

She shared the blood covenant with him! She'd sealed herself to him once before, but he refused to make her immortal. That was when Alec had stolen her away, making her his mate. How could she betray him like this? He remembered all the late nights she spent at the gym when she'd blocked him and wondered if that was where she really was. He wondered how long this betrayal had been going on, how many times she'd laid beneath him, and then came home to him! With a single swipe of the hand, he knocked the laptop, the glass, and the lamp from the desk as they all crashed to the floor. His fangs punched through and his breathing was ragged. The bitch played him, humiliated him!

Santos quickly appeared at the door, responding to the commotion. "Master?"

Alec picked up the photos and stuck them in his pocket before he brushed past the butler, as he headed for the newly built chamber. "Get out of my way, Santos."

Alec made his way down the stairs to the underground chamber. He stood at the door and calmed himself, retracting his fangs. She'd not see his anger, at least, not yet. He opened the door and could hear the sounds of her pleasuring herself. As he closed the door in the dimly lit room, he saw her on the table, lying on her back, knees bent and legs spread, as she artfully slid the dildo in and out. "Does it feel good, my darling?"

Rissa snapped her head to the side, as the wicked grin spread across her face. She knew she could lure him down here. Sliding the dildo deep inside her, she moaned and licked her lips while staring at his face. "Yes, but nothing feels as good as you, daddy."

She pouted and moaned as she worked the dildo, coming hard for him, exaggerating the feeling it gave her just for his pleasure. Sitting up, swinging her legs over the side of the table facing him, she threw back her head, her blonde tresses falling across her shoulders. "Want to come play with your baby girl?"

Alec walked slowly around the chamber, ignoring her question as he examined the installation of the equipment transported here from Castello. He ran his hands over floggers and whips, leaving them swaying, as he walked past them. His brain was flooded with the memories of the chamber in Florence, and the nights of debauchery, with both willing and unwilling participants. He turned to her with a wicked grin. "Oh, we're going to play, baby girl. We're going to play like we've never played before."

Walking to the stockade, he lifted the top portion, and ran

his hand inside the carved opening for hands and head, the wood worn smooth by the struggles of the men and women trapped in it. "Get over here, baby girl."

She slithered off the table, and strolled naked toward him, her hips swaying seductively, as she locked eyes with him.

He watched as she walked toward him, proudly displaying her body. *Did she parade herself in front of Max like that? Did she revel in her sexuality?* He already knew the answer and swallowed down his anger. As she got closer, he positioned her in the stockade, as she laid her head and hands in the openings carved into the wood, and he closed the top, securing her in place, locking the latch on the side. She was his now. He stood behind her, and gently ran his hand down her spine, from her neck to the lower back, and watched as the goose bumps rose on her skin. "Is this what my baby girl wants?"

The touch of his fingers down her spine made her wet. She'd waited so long for this moment. Being on the campaign had felt like years to her, and they never had time to be alone. Alec was a master in the art of creating erotic pleasure through pain. "Yes, daddy, please more."

Alec removed one of the leather floggers from the wall, and snapped it across his hand, and watched her startle at the sound. "Oh, there will be more, my darling."

Standing behind her, her bare ass exposed to him, as she was bent over in the stockade, he swung the flogger with a snap of the wrist across the plump rounded flesh.

Rissa kept her head down. She could only raise it so much locked in the stockade. She jumped as she felt the leather tendrils bite into her skin. Alec gave no commands for her not to speak. He gave no commands at all, which was unusual. Rissa moaned, no commands meant she had free reign. "More daddy, please more."

Alec answered, "Yes, I think more is called for tonight, baby girl."

He hung the flogger back on the wall and chose another one with small metal stars, sharpened to cut the flesh, sewn into the tips of the leather strips. Turning to stand behind her, he snapped the flogger hard, watching the metal bite into her flesh, drawing blood.

Rissa waited as she heard him walking away, she couldn't see what toy he'd selected, and the anticipation of what he might choose to do next made her even wetter. He stepped behind her again and she heard the whistle of the flogger as he snapped it against her flesh, and the burning pain made her scream. She squeezed her eyes shut. It felt like shards of glass cutting into her tender flesh. She could feel the blood trickle down the backs of her legs.

Alec was aroused despite himself, her blood ran down the back of her long shapely legs and he'd denied himself too long, the scent of her sex and her blood called to him. He unbuttoned his shirt and tossed it aside, then kicked off his shoes and stepped out of his pants. No reason why he shouldn't take advantage of her...his whore. Squatting behind her, his tongue snaked out, licking the blood from her calves. His tongue followed the blood trail up her thighs and onto her ass, his tongue healing the wounds. He slid his hand between her legs, inserting his fingers into that pool of wetness. "How many, my darling?"

Moaning as he licked her blood, his tongue hot and wet against her skin, she didn't understand his inquiry and cried out breathlessly, "Daddy." She felt his fingers slip deep inside her, teasing her. "Baby girl wants you to fist her, please daddy, now."

Alec chuckled at her response. "You don't tell me what to do. I decide. I'm master. At what point did you forget that, baby girl?" He gripped her hips as he slid his cock into her, pounding her hard.

Rissa smiled as he called her baby girl. She felt him slam into her and her growl of pleasure was animalistic. Her body was being slammed hard, back and forth against the stockade, as he drove hard and deep inside her. "Master, no one ever fucked me like this. I belong to you and only you. Fuck me, master."

Alec rode her hard, oblivious as to whether his actions brought her pleasure but seeking his own release. He gripped her hard as he bent over her, lying over her back, his legs spread wide as he thrust into her. His fangs emerged as he sank his teeth deep into the flesh of her shoulder and drank, swallowing mouthfuls. His body was on fire with the primal need to feed and fuck, and he succumbed to both.

She felt him sink his fangs deep into her shoulder, and she screamed from the sweet sensation. She'd held back as long as possible, but he hadn't commanded her to withhold her orgasm.

Alec continued to feed, to draw deep from her, like she was a bottomless well. Her blood in his veins fed his hunger, but it also fed his desire and he rammed harder inside her until he reached his climax. Spilling his seed deep inside her, he growled deep in his throat, but never broke his hold on her, and he continued to drink.

Rissa came as he released inside her, filling her. She tried to move but she was constricted by the stockade. He maintained his tight grip on her and continued to drink as she felt the lightheadedness wash over her. He took her blood in large gulps, indulging his appetite, and it sounded like an animal ravaging its prey.

"Daddy." Her voice was a soft plea as fear started to creep in, but he continued to drain her. "Master!"

She felt her world darken, as her vision blurred. He was going to drain her and didn't realize he was doing it. He'd waited too long to feed from her. "Alec, stop. Alec!"

Alec broke his grip on her, licked her wounds and watched as they healed. Still breathing heavily and covered in sweat, he stepped back, looking at her, helpless in the stockades. "Stop? Of course, my darling, if only *you* knew the meaning of those words."

He bent down to the shirt he'd tossed on the floor and retrieved the photographs and walked slowly to stand before her in front of the stockade. He gently lifted her chin and brushed the hair away from her face before he bent down and kissed her forehead. "My Rissa, my beautiful Rissa. Why did you betray me?"

Rissa looked at him quizzically. Betray? His eyes were still soft but there was sadness in them, a deep sadness. "Alec, what do you mean betray you? I've never betrayed you? Is this about Hyde? He never touched me, never No one has ever touched me. Not once!"

Alec shook his head. "Hyde? I have no concerns about Hyde and his antiquated warrior code, my darling. He'd never touch you, no matter how much he desired you, or how hard you tried to seduce him. And yes, my darling, I know you tried. No, it's not Hyde."

He held up the photos in front of her face, showing her nude and running through the surf. "Tell me now," he hissed at her through clenched teeth.

Rissa looked at the photos. She was running through the water naked. She'd spent only one day on the beach in recent years and her heart pounded. *Max! No, he couldn't have, why would he do this to them? No, no, no!*

Rissa shook her head. "Alec, I went on a day trip, I needed to be free in the surf and feel the sun. I was stressed about the wedding, everything was building up and when I went to New York for my dress fitting, my friend was with me. Please remember, Alec, please. She took the photos so we'd remember that day. The press must have gotten these photos. Are they trying to blackmail you?"

Rissa felt her breathing increase as she tried to pull her hands free. If she could only touch him, convince him.

Alec smiled at her as she struggled and he eyed her coldly. "Your girlfriend? Really? Was she there when you fucked Max? When you let him feed from you? When you fed from him?"

Rissa took in a breath so fast, she squeaked. Her eyes opened wide in fear. She could hear her own panicked breathing and the room started to spin. She knew if she was going to get out of this, it would be the performance of her life. Her head spun with the consequences. Her mouth was dry, her heart hammering inside her chest and she was trapped, she couldn't break free of the stockade.

She looked at him, her voice calm. "I did it for you. All of it was for you. It was only once, Alec. I promise you. The potion,

Max had the potion. I had to get it from him. He wanted to kill you, take D.C. from you. He wanted me to leave with him, but I didn't want him. Alec, please, I did this for you."

Her sobs racked her body, as the blood tears spilled from her eyes, but this was no performance. Her heart was breaking. "I love you. I love you Alec, please, please."

Alec let the photos drop from his hands as they fluttered to the floor. "You do nothing for me, Rissa. You do what serves you, and if it also serves me, you take credit for it."

He knelt down until his face was close to hers, looking into her tear-filled eyes. He saw fear but no remorse. "I did love you, Rissa, in my own way, as much as it is possible for a man like me to love. You should at least know that."

He reached up and placed both hands on either side of her face, and planted one last kiss on her lips. Looking into her eyes, he snapped her neck, hearing the sharp crack and one last straggled cry cut short in her throat, as he watched the life fade from her eyes. Her head dropped lifeless, and her legs collapsed, her body dangling limp from the stockade. He stood up and stared at her, feeling nothing, not even the satisfaction of exacting his revenge.

73

Alec turned and walked out of the chamber, slowly climbing the stairs to the main floor. He walked into the study to find Santos cleaning up the mess of broken glass. He poured himself another glass of Midnight and downed it in one gulp. Picking up his cellphone, he dialed Braden. As always, Braden picked up on the first ring. "What's up, boss? You get home okay?"

Alec paused for a second before he answered, "I think you need to get over here."

Braden looked at his watch. It was after midnight and he'd been looking forward to a good night's sleep away from the campaign. "Yeah, sure. Drive or teleport?"

Alec took a cigarette from the elaborate box on the desk and lit up, his hands shaking slightly. "Better drive. Just in case we have paparazzi."

Braden told him he'd be there in thirty minutes tops. Alec tossed the phone back on the desk before collapsing in the chair. Santos looked at him as he replaced the broken lamp back on the desk. "Is there anything I can do for you, master?"

Alec looked at him with blank eyes. "What?"

Santos had never seen him this distracted. "I said, is there anything I can do for you?"

Alec shook his head and dismissed him with a wave of his hand. "No, thank you, Santos, not yet. Stay close, though. I may need you."

Alec sat, almost immobile, in the dimly lit office, smoking one cigarette after another, the red glow of the cigarette's tip visible in the darkened room. He had no concept of time passing, when he heard the knock at the door, and Santos rushing to answer it. Within minutes, Braden was in his study, turning on a few other lamps.

"What the hell is going on, Alec. Why are you sitting here

in the dark?"

Alec stared back at him before standing. "Follow me."

Braden shrugged and followed Alec to a door beneath the main staircase that led to a basement. "I didn't know you had a basement."

Alec didn't answer him, as he led the way down the stairs. Opening the heavy, reinforced door to the chamber, he stepped back to let Braden enter. Braden stepped into the room, his eyes scanning the walls and the various contraptions, all specifically designed for the BDSM set. He wasn't surprised. Then his eyes landed on her. It was Rissa, her lifeless nude body hanging limply from the stockades. Braden stopped in his tracks. "Christ, Alec, what have you done?"

Alec stood still in the deadly quiet room, staring at her lifeless form. "Doesn't matter now. Just tell me what to do."

Braden walked over to her, looking at her body, checking for any visible marks or injuries. "How did you do it?"

Alec stepped closer and stroked her shoulder, already cold to the touch. "I snapped her neck. One quick twist and it was over."

Braden ran both hands through his hair. "On purpose? Or did things get out of control?"

Alec closed his eyes. "On purpose. She betrayed me, in a way I couldn't forgive. I had no choice."

Braden paced the room as he started to consider his options. "Okay, let me think. There's no way to hide this, Alec. She was too high-profile. I have people on the payroll. It will cost you, but we can bring in our own doctor who will oversee everything. We're going to have to move her, get her dressed in a robe or something long. We've already established she wasn't feeling well on the campaign. We can say you guys came home, and she took something to help her sleep. She got up to get something to drink from the kitchen and she fell down the stairs, tripping on her robe. We need to move quickly. We'll have to call 911. People would expect you to do that. This means mortals will come. They'll have to see her body at the foot of the stairs. Once they take her away, I can have my doctor take over. He can oversee the autopsy. The broken neck will fit the story."

Braden started to unlatch the stockade. "Come on, Alec. A little help here, buddy."

Alec stepped forward, catching her limp body as Braden released the stockade.

"Come on, Alec, follow me."

Braden rushed up the stairs as Alec followed him. He called for Santos as they re-entered the foyer on the main floor. "Santos, run upstairs and grab one of Rissa's robes, something floor length, and silky."

Santos stared at Braden, then saw his master come through the door holding Rissa's nude lifeless body in his arms. His mouth dropped open, but he didn't question. Turning, he ran up the stairs, rummaging through her closet until he found one of her long robes. When he returned, he found Alec and Braden standing at the halfway point on the staircase. Alec was holding Rissa's body upright and Braden grabbed the robe from his hands, and slipped it on her, untied. Stepping to the side, he instructed Alec. "Okay, now push her forward gently, let her fall naturally."

Alec did as he was instructed, as the three men watch her body crumble and fall in a contorted heap at the bottom of the stairs. Braden was satisfied with the result. He turned to Alec and told him he was to say he'd been in his study when he heard her fall. "Now, call 911. And keep your fingers crossed."

As Alec left to call 911, Braden pulled out his phone and called the doctor. "Got a situation here." Braden relayed the details of what he needed, and the doctor responded, letting him know everything was under control.

74

Kate was putting the finishing touches on the nursery that would soon be occupied by their daughter. Sophia was the first child to present herself to Kate, shortly after she was turned. The room was painted the palest pink, and Kate had found an antique crib in an ivory color, along with a large armoire, also in ivory, both worn with age. The sofa bed had been reupholstered and moved from Lorenzo's room to Sophia's room, and Kate added a rocking chair, a toy chest, and plush rug to cover the hardwood floors. She was putting baby clothes into the armoire when Theresa rushed in. "My lady! You need to come see this."

Kate stopped what she was doing and followed Theresa to her bedroom where the TV was blaring out news about the sudden accidental death of the wife of Senator Canton. Kate's hand covered her mouth.

"Oh my god!" She sat down on Theresa's bed as Theresa sat next to her. They listened to the details, as the newscaster described the urgent 911 call in the middle of the night, and the EMT's finding Rissa's body at the bottom of the stairs where she fell, breaking her neck. Kate leapt up from the bed and ran to their bedroom, opening the door to where Shade lay deep in his death slumber. She crawled across the bed, shaking him awake. "Shade. Wake up. Please! I need you."

Shade heard her voice, as if it were coming from the bottom of a deep well, and he fought the pull of his slumber, pulling himself from the deep sleep to respond to her. Opening his eyes, he saw and felt her panic. "*Bel*, what's wrong? The baby?"

She shook her head and pulled at his hand to follow her. Grabbing the sheet and tying it around his waist he followed her back to Theresa's room where the images of a covered body being carried on a stretcher from the Canton residence and loaded in an ambulance flashed across the screen. The reporter's voice relayed the sad news about the young, handsome couple who were destined for greatness, and the Senator, whose future path was now in question. Would he continue his bid for the White House?

Shade's mind was in over-drive. The reporter was saying she fell to her death, but until he knew what was going on his first responsibility was to protect Alec. He hoped like hell nothing happened to Rissa while his warriors were on duty. He hurried back to the bedroom with Kate on his heels, and pulled on a pair of jeans before heading down the stairs to his office.

Kate rushed behind him. "What should we do?"

Shade called out to Mateo telepathically and told him to get to the Canton residence now. He heard the warrior respond and knew he'd be there in seconds. He grabbed his phone and called Theo in the Dead House. "Have you heard the news?"

Theo told him he was watching it now on his laptop. Shade told him to call in all warriors assigned to the Dead House and to stay on high alert, with special attention to the Georgetown grid. Theo said he was on it.

Marcello appeared in the doorway of his office, having heard the news through Mateo. "Master?"

Shade told him to keep the camp on high alert until further notice. Marcello nodded and said, "Taken care of."

Kate sat of the sofa, her feet curled under her watching as he gave out orders, and his warriors swung into action. "Lover, are we in danger?"

He sat down beside her, kissing the top of her head. "I do not think so *bel*, but until I know what is going on, we take no chances, si? I do not want Lorenzo outside until we have answers."

Kate nodded. "He's with Enzo in class. I'll make sure he doesn't go out."

Luca stepped into the doorway, drawn by all the activity. Shade waved him into the room. "Rissa is dead."

Luca took a step back. "What? How?"

Shade shook his head and called for Hyde who teleported into the office. The warrior looked pale, his face drawn. He'd heard the news. Shade poured him a large Midnight and handed him the glass. "Sit down Hyde. Tell me what you know."

The warrior took a long swallow of the thick elixir. "Nothing you don't know already. They haven't been getting along. Rissa wasn't happy on the campaign, and she seemed to go out of her way to antagonize him. Braden has been pissed off for some time now because Alec is down in the polls, and it's all because of her. There was definitely a lot of tension on the flight home last night, but Mateo and I were with them when Alto drove them home, and Alec told us we could both take off a few days."

Shade lit up a cigarette, trying to get as much information as possible before he put a call in to Alec. "So any chance this came from the outside?"

Hyde ran his hand over his face. "I mean, we can't rule it out, but it doesn't fit. Alto was near, he's not a warrior, but he's pretty formidable. Plus whoever got in would have to get past Alec. Santos wouldn't be much help in a battle, but he could at least call out, and I heard nothing. And Rissa, if she was in danger, she didn't call out to me." He shook his head. "It doesn't make sense."

Shade sat down on the desk, taking another drag on the cigarette. "No, it doesn't"

Picking up his cellphone he dialed Alec's number and listened as the familiar voice answered in a flat tone. "Brother, Shade here. I've sent Mateo, and the Dead House is on full alert, as is the camp."

Alec answered him, "Thanks, but no need. We're in no danger. It was just an accident. Just like what's being reported. Braden is dealing with the press, and he's called in a doctor, one of our own, who will oversee the autopsy, and make sure the report is consistent with the story. There won't be any questions."

Shade let his words sink in. "Why would there be questions Alec?" There was a silence on the other end of the phone as Shade waited for an answer.

After a long pause, Alec answered. "Aren't there always questions? Don't worry brother. What's done is done. Braden is coordinating the funeral arrangements. I'm sure it will be a circus. I don't anticipate any problems but you should probably have some security there just in case."

Shade looked at Kate who was watching him closely. He tried to imagine his own pain if he ever lost her. He knew he'd have to end his own life and follow her in death. A life without his *bel rosso* would be a living hell. Alec didn't sound like a man who'd just lost his eternal mate. "Is there anything you need to tell me brother?"

Alec sighed heavily. "We've know each other a long time old friend. Do me a favor and don't ask questions, okay? Let it go, Shade."

Shade was silent as the words sank in. "Okay, brother." He laid the phone down on the desk and stared blankly across the room.

Hyde stared at him. "He did it, didn't he?"

Shade looked back at him without answering, and the two warriors locked eyes.

Kate sat upright on the sofa. "What? What are you saying?"

Shade looked at her and said, "It is not our problem *bel*. He is her master. We do not intervene."

She was staring at him with an open mouth when Lorenzo came crashing through the doorway. "I finished my class. Enzo was teaching me algebra, and then we studied Plato. Hey, why are you sad Mommy?"

Kate scooped him up in her arms, holding him close. "Miss Rissa died. She fell down some stairs. We're all sad for Miss Rissa."

Lorenzo consoled her. "Don't cry Mommy. She was bad."

Kate shushed him. "Don't say that Lorenzo. I know she didn't appreciate being around children, but that doesn't mean she was bad."

Lorenzo looked back at her with wide, innocent eyes. "That's not what sleeping warrior says."

Kate flashed a look in Shade's direction, as he moved to join them on the couch. "What do you mean Lorenzo?"

The child continued, "He talks to me, when I visit the garden. The sleeping warrior talks to me. He says he died because she gave him poison pills."

Kate's mouth dropped open, as she shook her head no. How could Lorenzo know anything about the pills she'd taken? They'd never discussed her first pregnancy around him. Shade lifted his son from Kate's lap, and placed him in his own. "Tell me Lorenzo."

The child shrugged. "That's all. The sleeping warrior says when he was in mommy's tummy that Miss Rissa brought pills that were poison for her to take. She said they would make her stronger, but they were supposed to kill the baby and maybe mommy too."

Shade stood up so suddenly that Lorenzo tumbled from his lap, and Kate grabbed to catch him. Hyde and Luca saw the beast emerge in their master, his eyes glowing and his fangs elongated. They heard Kate's soft cries, as she bent her head over her child and whispered, "My baby."

Luca stood and cautiously approached his master. "She's dead now master."

Shade gained control, pulling hard against the beast who wanted to extract revenge. "It is a good thing, because I would have to kill her myself."

75

Kate walked barefoot down the winding path that led to the baby's garden, lush with roses and lavender. She came here often, and she knew Lorenzo came here to play, and talk to the brother he never knew. Lorenzo said the sleeping warrior talked to him, and Kate wondered if it was his imagination. She felt close to this lost child, emotionally connected, but he didn't appear to her like *Madre* and *Padre*. He didn't speak to her.

She reached the small statue of the angel just as the sun was setting. The moss was growing at its base and she sat on the ground. They never named this baby, and Shade had always called him his sleeping warrior. Since he was a half-breed, they had known his birth was always in question from the beginning. The tears flowed down her cheeks, as she laid her head on the ground. If not for the pills, this baby might have lived. Look at Cory. They both knew so little at the time. She was still mortal, and they'd sought out the advice of Alec and Rissa. Rissa had seemed so helpful, so eager for her to take those pills. But why? Kate sobbed, consumed with guilt. "I'm so sorry, baby. I fought to protect you, and I placed you in harm's way."

Shade woke from his death slumber and found the bed empty, the house strangely quiet. He sat up, running his hands through his hair. He felt a sudden rush of sadness and regret wash over him like a blanket of pain, and knew it was Kate's emotions he felt.

There was a soft tapping on the door and he knew it was Lorenzo. "Come in."

The door opened slowly, and Shade saw the tousled curls and the huge blue eyes, just as Lorenzo pushed through the door and hurled himself onto the bed, curling into his father's arms. "Daddy, I'm sorry to make Mommy sad, I didn't mean to make her cry."

Shade held him tight to his chest. "It is not your fault, my little warrior. It was fine that you told her, you spoke the truth, which is what you have been taught. Where is your *madre*?"

Lorenzo looked up at his father. "She's with the sleeping warrior."

Shade kissed the top of his head. "I need to go talk to Mommy. Will you please go to Theresa, stay there until we come back, *si*?"

Lorenzo agreed and scurried off the bed, his bare feet making a slapping sound on the hardwood floors, as he raced back to Theresa. Shade got dressed and walked to the garden, his mind filled. He'd carried this guilt for so long and now he had to confess. With the help of Gi, they'd replaced some of the pills after Kate became so gravely ill. Shade had chosen to let their unborn son die to save his mate, and a day never passed that he didn't feel the weight of that choice. He knew now his decision didn't kill their son. Maybe without Rissa's pills the baby would have lived, although the odds were always against him. They'd never know.

He approached the garden and found her lying next to the angelic grave marker, her heart aching for the *bambino* she'd lost. Walking up behind her, he sat down on the ground and cuddled her into his arms, stroking her hair, his body a shield to protect her. "I know the pain feels fresh *bel*, like it just happened. But there is something about our sleeping warrior I never told you. I have carried this guilt since the day he died, and I need to unburden this from my heart, *mi amore*."

Kate welcomed his embrace as he leaned over her, surrounding her, as if he could somehow block the pain. "We both feel guilt. I look at Cory now, and I think this baby could've had a chance. Why would she do it? I don't understand!"

Shade shook his head. "Rissa was just an evil bitch. I have gone over this in my head so many times. I cannot imagine why she would do this. Maybe she was jealous of our happiness. But the bitch is dead now, and to be honest, I am glad. "He held her tightly in his arms and stared at the grave of their child. "There isn't a night that goes by I do not think of our warrior, so small."

Kate let the grief wash over her, feeling as raw as the day she'd lost the child, almost five years ago now. "That doctor. He brought the first pills. I don't understand how they were poison. Then, later, Rissa brought me extra pills, and I took them. Were they all poison? Or just hers? Did our baby feel pain? I have so many questions in my head, and so many regrets. It's my fault." Kate sobbed uncontrollably, as he held her tight against his chest.

He rocked her gently in his arms. "We must leave these questions behind, as well as the pain. We must go on, for we have another *bambino* now who needs us. We will never forget this lost one, *mi amore*, he lives in our hearts."

Shade felt the tightening in his throat from the pent up emotions. "Kate, please listen to me." He lifted her face to his. "I have my own confessions, my own guilt. I was so confused, so hurt that I had done this to you while you were mortal, and then you became so sick. I feared I would lose you both and I couldn't bear it. It was killing me inside. The pills were killing you, and I had to make a choice. I switched out the pills. I gave placebos instead of the pills the doctor prescribed for you. I have thought all this time it was my actions that killed our son, but I had to save you." His pain was visible in his face, and his voice was wracked with his emotions, as his tears flowed. "I am so sorry, please understand and forgive."

"Lover, there's nothing to forgive." She kissed his tear-stained cheeks. "Why was I so blind to her? When I look back on it now, it all seems so intentional. Lorenzo has always said she was bad and I'd correct him, but in his innocence, he saw something she managed to keep hidden from the rest of us. Lorenzo says the baby talks to him. Does he talk to you?"

"No." Shade clenched his eyes shut. "I wish he would. He was only a half-breed, *bel,* and not fully formed, so I don't think he dwells in the spirit realm like *Madre* and *Padre*. His spirit would not have been strong enough. But somehow our sleeping warrior connected with Lorenzo, though. He found his brother."

Shade reached over and touched the angelic statue. "Rissa had a black heart. I always knew it. She did nothing that was not to advance her own agenda."

Kate placed her hand over his. "Rissa's heart was always

black. I knew her as a mortal, and she was manipulative even then. She looked down on people, and was always jealous of others, hating their success, as if it somehow took away from her own. I leaned on her, when I should have known better. I trusted her, and she'd already shown me her true self. I was foolish, in getting pregnant, and in trusting her. I need your forgiveness."

"You don't need my forgiveness, *bel*. This is not your fault."

Taking her hand, they stood together. His hands encircled her waist, as he pulled her close. "*Bel,* we both have carried the guilt of his loss too long. No one can hurt him now. If he can speak with Lorenzo, then he resides in some form in the spirit realm, and perhaps *Madre* takes care of our little one. He knows we love him. You have to believe that, *mi amore.*"

He lifted her in his arms and carried her back to the house, the lights glowing in the windows. Kate lay against his chest, safe in his arms. As he walked back toward the house, Kate looked skyward at the clear, black night and the star-filled sky, and watched as a single star shot across the horizon.

76

Braden had called in his staffers to help manage this debacle. Alec's public persona was larger than life, so there was no way to sweep Rissa's death under the proverbial rug. Braden quickly crafted the story they'd tell, sending Santos back upstairs to unmake the couple's bed, and make it look like Rissa had been sleeping there. They'd called the EMT's, who then called in the police before they removed the body.

Braden had cut out all the lights in the downstairs chamber, closed and locked the door, and hoped like hell the police didn't ask too many questions. The police had questioned Alec and Santos, as well as him. They'd all repeated the same story. Everyone was aware of how much the Senator and his wife had been traveling, and they were both exhausted from the campaign. Rissa hadn't been feeling well over the last week, and they'd come home to take a break. Alec had said he was in his study with Braden, trying to catch up on the mail, and planning the next stage of the campaign.

Rissa had gone to bed early. Alec said she might have taken something to help her sleep, and that could have made her unsteady. They heard the fall, but when Alec got to her, it was already too late. The police made the report, did a quick walk-through, and found no disturbance in the house. They'd taken photos of the scene before allowing the EMT's to remove the body.

Braden had their own doctor waiting at the coroner's office to officially pronounce her dead, and to perform the autopsy, at the Senator's request. Everything had gone according to plan, and the morning newspapers all carried the headline of Rissa's death. In fact, every paper and every TV news program opened with an update on Rissa's life. They showed news footage of Rissa on the campaign, at her wedding, attending fundraising events and spoke of her status as event planner for the socially elite. And now, they outlined the plans for her funeral and how many would attend.

The newscasters reported that Senator Canton had decided to hold the service in the National Cathedral, where, only a short four years ago, she'd married the handsome Senator.

Braden had remained at their Georgetown home for several days following her death, answering the phone calls from press and concerned friends and clients and trying to control the message. He also wanted to keep Alec as low-key and out of the limelight as possible. He tossed the latest stack of papers aside. "Well, Rissa, looks like you got your wish. You wanted to be the center of attention."

Today was the big day of the funeral, and there would be as many, if not more, in attendance for this service as there were for the wedding. Most of the attendees would be mortal. Hell, the mortals were the only reason they had to hold this service. No vampire was ever buried in a coffin.

Braden entered the study to find Alec already dressed in a black suit, pacing, and drinking Midnight. "Everything is under control. I've coordinated with Shade, and we'll have some security from his warriors, but I don't think we have anything to worry about. This event will be mostly comprised of mortals. Alto is bringing the car around, and we'll drive to the funeral home, where we'll follow the hearse to the cathedral. Are you ready? Is there anything else you need me to do?"

Alec stood with his back to him, as he looked out the window, sipping at the Midnight. He was barely aware of Braden's presence. The images of Rissa lying beneath Max continued to play across his brain. *Why did she do it? She knew the consequences of betrayal.* He missed her, the smell of her perfume, her never-ending attempts to manipulate him into bed, her scheming, even her tantrums and door slamming. His house felt empty now, and he'd meant what he'd said to her. He loved her, in his own way. He'd need to feed soon, but he didn't have time to think about that. Braden's words finally broke through, as Alec finally turned to him. "What? Oh, uh, no,

I don't need anything."

Braden looked at him and was pleased. He looked broken and distracted. He wouldn't need to perform during this service. No one would see him shed a tear, but the stoic Senator looked like he'd lost a battle and that would do. Braden motioned to him. "Come on, Alec, the car is here. Let's go."

Braden accompanied Alec to the car and slipped into the passenger seat as Alec sat in the back. They drove to the funeral home where the hearse was waiting, with Rissa's casket inside, covered in white lilies. The funeral director came to the car to offer his condolences and provide instructions to Alto, who nodded in silence. The two cars pulled out and drove slowly through the streets of D.C. to the cathedral.

The massive stone church was already filled to capacity as all of Alec's fellow congressmen and women, and their spouses, along with all of Rissa's elite clientele filled the seats. The press was everywhere, and Alec was met with a wall of flashing lights as he emerged from the car.

Shade, Kate, and Cory had arrived at the Cathedral and taken their seats, along with Hyde and Mateo. Shade had warriors stationed strategically throughout the crowd, although he didn't expect any trouble. Reaching over, he took Kate's hand and held it in his lap. He looked toward Hyde. He knew Hyde had developed a relationship of sorts with Rissa. He leaned over and whispered, "You okay, warrior?"

Hyde turned to look at his master and shrugged. "Fine, I'm fine, believe me. My last experience with Rissa didn't leave us on the best of terms."

Shade smirked. "Sounds typical."

His eyes scanned every corner of the massive cathedral as he sat quietly. He couldn't say he felt any remorse over her death, and his presence here was more a show of respect for Alec. Taking in the crowd, he didn't notice any other masters present. Alec's choice to live in the mortal world had alienated him in the vampire community, and they showed their displeasure through their absence.

Kate looked up at the height of the cathedral ceiling before glancing around at the many stained-glass windows, constructed in the traditional style. Her eyes sought out the window that held the moon rock and designed in a very modernistic style. It was her favorite. They all stood as the pall bearers carried the solid mahogany casket, covered with the spray of white lilies, down the center aisle, as a choir sang, accompanied by the massive pipe organ. Kate scanned the faces of the crowd. They all looked appropriately somber, but she didn't see any tears.

Cory fidgeted as he stood next to her. He really didn't want to come, but his father said it was their duty to be here. Kate was glad, at least, that they had left Lorenzo with Shannon and Luca. He'd never have remained still or quiet through this whole service.

Alec walked behind the casket as it was carried to the front of the cathedral, and then took the seat left vacant for him on the front row. He glanced across the aisle to see President Ashton glowering at him. Alec stared back until the President looked away. The service was elaborate but not overly long, and when it was over, the pall bearers, once again, hoisted the casket up and carried it back down the aisle, as Alec followed. He stood as they loaded the casket back into the hearse, then got back in the car, as Alto held the door for him. Braden slipped back into the passenger seat.

Braden turned to Alec. "Okay, that went very well. The graveside will be very short, then we have the reception at your house. My staffers are setting everything up. There will be finger foods and drinks for the mortals. You'll just need to greet people, let them offer their condolences, and then we'll be done. How are you holding up?"

The car pulled out as it followed the hearse graveside. Alec looked blankly out the window, not seeing the stately embassies along Embassy Row. They slowly drove to the Virginia countryside for the burial. "I'm going to need to feed soon, Braden."

Braden nodded at him, noting how pale he was, which had been good to facilitate the image of Alec's mourning. "I'm aware. Just hold on until tonight, and I'll take care of it."

Alec nodded as the stream of cars pulled into the cemetery and he exited the car, watching, once again, as the casket was removed from the hearse, and carried graveside.

Shade and Kate were chauffeured by Dante, who followed behind Alec's car. As they pulled into the cemetery, everyone exited. They stood along beside Alec as the only family. Shade looked at his longtime friend and noticed his pale skin. His need to feed was evident. Shade only hoped his beast could hold out. Alec appeared more distracted than mournful, and Shade wasn't buying the accident story. He hadn't had time to speak with Alec privately, and wasn't sure what he'd divulge when he did. Not that it mattered, at least not in the vampire community. A mate was considered a master's property, and if things went south, it was a master's prerogative to release her, or in rare circumstances, destroy her. But, regardless of the outcome, it was off limits to question a master's treatment of his mate.

Alec stared blankly ahead as the priest said his final words over Rissa's casket and the spray of lilies was removed. They stood silent as the casket was slowly lowered into the ground. Alec stepped forward and scooped up a handful of dirt and tossed it into the grave, as Shade, Kate, Cory, Mateo, and Hyde followed suit.

Max watched the proceedings from a distance, remaining shadowed from view. He knew there would be consequences for Rissa once Alec knew the truth, and he couldn't help but gloat at the outcome. The bitch finally got what she deserved, but he knew it was still no easy task. For a master to destroy his mate, he must destroy a part of his own soul. For the first time since the Battle of Bel Rosso, Max felt a measure of justice.

Max took note of Shade standing alongside Alec, along with his mate and a young half-breed. The half-breed looked uncomfortable and out of his element, and Max zeroed in on him, watching his every move. They all left the graveside and returned to their cars, and Max teleported out, formulating the next idea in his head.

The crowd dispersed, as they all moved back to their cars.

Some of them would return home now, while others would continue on to the Canton's home in Georgetown, to shake his hand, and offer their personal condolences to the Senator, and to glean any gossip. There was the question on everyone's mind now as to whether Alec would continue his bid for the Presidency, and everyone wanted to be the first to know the answer. This was Washington D.C., after all, and politics always came first.

77

Once back at the Canton residence, the long line of guests followed Alec inside the house. Shade instructed Mateo and Hyde to keep an eye on the crowd. Alec took a stand near the door and greeted people as they came in, offering their condolences. The mourners then moved through the room, seeking out the table filled with food and fine wine for the mortals.

Shade turned to Cory. "Look after Kate for a minute. I need to get inside Alec's study and get us some Midnight. I won't be long, just stay by her side."

Shade made his way to the empty study and found it locked. "Cazzo!"

As he spun on his heels, he bumped into Santos, who quickly unlocked the door for him. "Thanks, old man. I think Alec is in desperate need of some Midnight, and I know I sure as hell could use a drink myself."

As Shade started to fill three wine glasses, Santos interceded and told him he'd take it from here. Shade nodded and returned to Kate, kissing her on the cheek. "Santos is coming around with our drinks. How are you holding up being on your feet?"

Kate took his arm and leaned into him. "I'm okay."

She wasn't used to wearing heels anymore, despite the closet full of designer shoes. Around Bel Rosso, she was in sandals or boots. Santos appeared with wine for them, and they each took the offered glass, sipping discreetly as the crowd filed past them offering weak smiles to these strangers. Kate recognized many of the faces from the news, as she scanned the crowd, and then saw one face that stood out over all the others.

Jacks stood patiently in line, wearing a black dress, black hose, and black heels. The color was appropriate, but the style wasn't. The dress was a little too tight, and a touch too revealing, and Kate huffed, thinking that was probably as discreet as Jacks ever got. She nudged Shade and nodded in Jacks' direction as she spoke softly, "Well, look who showed up."

He looked in the direction Kate indicated and saw Jacks. He wondered where she was working now. He knew she wasn't in the States. Jacks caught his eye when she felt him starring at her and gave him a slight smile. "She was Rissa's protector for a time, Kate. She is just paying her respects to Alec. Pay her no mind."

Kate thought to herself the visit had little if anything to do with respect.

Shade chuckled softly as he picked up on her thoughts, and watched as Jacks approached Alec.

Jacks took Alec's hands, and offered her sincere sympathy. She'd come to let him know she was here for him, but she wasn't the least bit sorry for the loss of that blonde bitch. Jacks never did see what he saw in her, he deserved so much more in a mate.

Alec looked up from the line of faceless people as he shook their hands, or accepted the kisses of the female mourners, some of them whispering to him, "Call me." He chuckled to himself, if these mortals only knew. Jacks approached him and offered her hand, which he gratefully accepted, locking eyes with her. He felt his mouth water, as he remembered the taste of her blood across his tongue, and his body was calling out for nourishment.

"Jacks, how very good to see you." He was well aware of the eyes on them, so he kept his greeting formal.

Jacks looked at Alec, he looked worn down, tired. She had followed the news reports of his campaign and was aware of the conflicts between him and Rissa hinted at by the papers. From her short stint at living here, she knew all was not well between them. There was already a lot of speculation in the vampire community that Rissa's death wasn't an accident. "Alec. I'm sorry to hear about Rissa. I came to give my support."

She could feel the sparks rise up through her arm as she shook his hand, slipping him one of her cards with her newest contact number. "If you need anything, please don't hesitate to call."

Laying her hand on his shoulder, she pressed her cheek slightly against his and hugged him gently. It was a gesture that wouldn't draw any attention from the crowd.

Alec inhaled her scent and could feel the pulse in her neck, as she laid her head next to his. He closed his eyes and took a deep breath, resisting the urge to feed. "Thank you, Jacks. Thank you for coming. It means a lot to me. Perhaps, I'll see you soon, under better circumstances."

He dare not make the conversation any more intimate than that. He knew every damn move he made would end up on the cover of the newspapers or played over and over on the news channel. He greeted the last of the well-wishers, and moved through the crowd, as they ate and drank and slowly began to take their leave.

Jacks proceeded to move through the crowd, making eye contact again with Shade. He was one handsome master, but one she'd never been able to seduce. He'd always remained aloof to her advances, even long before he was mated. She knew his reputation with women, so it had always stuck in her craw to be rebuffed by him. The crowd moved slowly until Jacks found herself close enough to speak to Shade. She smiled, nodding, her head held high. She was the tallest woman in the room.

"Shade, it's good to see you again. So sorry it had to be under such unfortunate circumstances." Jacks turned to Kate. "It's a pleasure to see you again, Kate. Congratulations on your pregnancy."

Kate stared back at her and nodded slightly. She thought Jacks was as manipulative as Rissa, she was just more subtle and used different tactics. "It's good to see you as well." She spoke the words, but let her eyes convey something quite different. "And thank you, we look forward to adding to our family. Have you met our son, Cory?" Kate introduced her step-son who looked very uncomfortable in these surroundings.

Jacks eyed the young man standing beside Shade. She'd

heard the stories of his half-breed son. Reaching out, she shook the young boy's hand. She noted some resemblance to Shade, although the boy's features were softer, more delicate. "It's a pleasure to meet the son of such a respectable master as Shade. I'm Jacks, and although I wasn't raised in the Medici camps, I've had the distinct honor of being trained at your father's hand."

Cory listened to their conversation and picked up on the tension between Kate and Jacks. As he shook her hand, he couldn't help but notice her beauty. She was tall and exotic looking, and clearly, a warrior. He just wanted to get the hell out of here and be with Madison. He got nervous around crowds and this woman made him even more uncomfortable for some reason. "Oh uh, nice to meet you."

Shade could feel Kate's animosity and his son's discomfort and took control of the conversation. "So, Jacks, it is good of you to come to support Alec. You can see from the crowd the other masters have snubbed him. I haven't heard from you in a while, I take it you are keeping yourself busy?"

Jacks smiled. "Yes, I've just come in from Norway, actually. As soon as I heard the horrible news, I wanted to at least make an appearance. I didn't know Rissa for very long. Our time together didn't go well, but Alec and I go way back. I owe him the respect. Congratulations to you, by the way. The Council is pleased, I'm sure, that you are expanding the Medici legacy with your progeny. I wish you the best, as always." Leaning in, she kissed him gently on the cheek.

Kate bristled as Jacks kissed him, like the bitch was marking her territory. She listened to the conversation between them before she interjected. "So, you're in Norway. Good. When are you returning?"

Jacks didn't miss the look she shot her, even though her words were smooth as silk. "As soon as possible. I have an assignment there and was graciously allowed to return to give my support to Alec. I'll let you get back to your evening. Good night." Jacks disappeared into the throng of well-wishers crowded into the Canton residence.

Shade saw Cory's quizzical stare and shook his head. "Don't

ask." Turning to Kate, he chuckled. "Settle down, *bel*. She is gone, no threat to you. Never was."

After an hour, people began drifting away, slowly taking their leave, extending their condolences one last time to Alec, always with the words, "Call me if you need anything." Jacks was the last to exit, casting one last glance at Alec, waiting for the invitation that never came.

Braden stood at the door, shaking everyone's hand as they left. Alec approached Shade as the crowd thinned down to a few. "Thank you for coming, brother, and thanks for the security detail. I didn't expect there to be any problems, but better safe than sorry."

Shade shook his hand. "Look, brother, I know this was not easy. We are here for you. I am taking Hyde off the campaign detail, unless you still wish to have him, and, of course, Mateo will be at your disposal. We have everything under control, so do what you have to do. I assume you are still going forward with this?"

Alec nodded his head. "I have to go forward, or it was all for nothing. So yes, I'll still need Mateo. I won't get back on the campaign trail right away, so he can rest up. We'll need to wait a short period of time for mourning. I'll take Braden's lead on that. He'll give you a call when we plan to start campaigning again."

"Okay, brother." Shade put his arm around Alec's shoulder and led him away from Kate and Cory. "Look, you need to take care of yourself. You need to feed, take care of it soon. Do you want me to send you a feeder? Just let me know. I got you. But, right now, we are going to head out. I want to get Kate back home."

Alec thanked him but assured him Braden was taking care of the feeder. As they pounded each other on the back, Shade took his leave and returned to Kate and Cory. He slid his arm around Kate's waist and they headed out, being the last to leave. It felt odd to Shade, not having Rissa making some smart ass remark as he exited.

Braden closed the door behind them. Santos was already

hard at work cleaning up the abandoned glassware and plates. Turning to Alec, he grasped his arm and led him to the stairs. "Now, my friend, we need to take care of you. Kelsey is waiting in your bedroom. Feed. Rest. And tomorrow, we'll talk strategy."

78

Lorenzo had been waiting for his parents to return. Luca and Shannon were sitting outside on the patio by the pool, and he was climbing up to his tree house. Once inside, he climbed out the window and onto the roof, and proceeded to climb even higher in the tree. From there, he could see the private drive that led to the house.

Luca shouted up at him, "Lorenzo, what are you doing?"

Lorenzo yelled out, "I'm waiting for Mommy and Daddy! I can see when their car pulls in!"

Luca laughed at the precocious child. "Don't fall."

Lorenzo deftly jumped from branch to branch. "I won't!"

Shannon looked up nervously. "Should he be doing that?"

Luca ran his hand along her thigh. "He's fine. If he falls, he can start to teleport."

Shannon looked at Luca with concern. "Does he know how to teleport?"

"He hasn't been taught how to use the skill, but instinctively, yes, he does know. If he were on the ground, and he just stumbled and fell, his gift to teleport wouldn't manifest. But if he were to fall a great distance, it would kick in. It might not be graceful, but he could land safely."

Shannon leaned back in her chair, kicking off her sandals and dipping her feet in the cooling water of the pool. "I have so much to learn."

He smiled at her. "In time, *mia belleza*."

Luca playfully dipped his hand in the pool and splashed her as she squealed. Lorenzo called out from the tree-tops, "They're here!"

He started to scramble down from the tree. As his feet hit the ground, he ran across the lawn to the front yard to greet his parents. Cory had exited the car, and Shade was helping Kate from the car when Lorenzo appeared from around the side of the house, running at top speed. "Daddy!" He catapulted himself into his father's arms, almost knocking him over in his exuberance.

Shade caught his son and hugged him tight, his heart overflowing with love. He knew how quickly the time would pass, and this child would be a full-grown warrior. "Tell me you are not out here by yourself."

Lorenzo planted a wet kiss on his father's cheek. "Nope. Uncle Luca and Aunt Shannon were supervising me. I was in the tree house. I climbed out on the roof and all the way to the top of the tree."

Kate looked at Shade and rolled her eyes. Lorenzo was unconsciously discovering his own strength and there was no stopping him now. She cringed when Shade took him to the camp, but she knew it was an environment he must get used to, and Skelk continued to work with him on his skills with fire. Kate gave the boy a kiss. "I hope you behaved for them."

Lorenzo nodded, as his black curls bobbed. "I was good, Mommy. You can ask Uncle Luca. Does that mean I get another card?"

Cory stepped up behind him, as Lorenzo clung to his father, and tickled his sides. Lorenzo collapsed into giggles, as he turned and fell into Cory's arms. Cory lifted him onto his shoulders. "Where to, little brother?"

Lorenzo wrapped his hands around Cory's chin. "The stables, please. If I get another card, I have enough for a pony. Do I get another card, Daddy?"

Shade smiled at him. "Well, since you have been such a good warrior today for Uncle Luca, I think perhaps that is manageable." Shade looked at Kate and grinned. "So what does Mommy think about this?"

Kate laughed. "I can't keep up with him now. I don't think the pony will make much difference."

Shade threw back his head and laughed, as he pulled her close. "Go inside, woman, and get out of those heels and that dress, you look stunningly beautiful, but I can feel your misery. Have Emma draw you a nice hot bath. We're going to head down to the stables. I want to check on Biondo. Rissa had spent little time riding since the campaign, and now, Alec will need to decide what to do with her."

Kissing her softly, he looked into her eyes. "It will not be long before we have another one to chase after. Our life is changing again, *mi amore*."

Kate returned his kiss before heading for the house. She kicked off the heels the moment she was inside. Emma greeted her and picked up the shoes, following her upstairs.

"I'm going to take a hot bath, Emma, and then lay down for a while. Lorenzo won't stay occupied in the stables for very long and I need to take advantage of it."

Cory walked toward the stables with Lorenzo on his shoulders. He'd gone to the funeral because his father had requested him to, saying it was the proper show of respect to another master, but Cory didn't really know much about Alec, and he was glad to be back home. Shade walked along beside him, as Lorenzo talked non-stop and Aegis fell in step behind them.

Cory looked over at his father. "I've been thinking about going out to California to see my mom. I know you want me to be at Castello when Kate has the new baby, so I was thinking this would be a good time to go. What do you think, Dad?"

"You want to go see your mother? You are still calling her regularly, I hope?"

"Oh yeah, I call her about once a week to check in and see how she's doing. She asks me, every week, when I'm coming to see her. I told her about Madison, and she was really happy for me. I was thinking maybe I could take Madison with me, to, you know, meet my other mom."

Shade smiled as they approached the stables and Cory lifted Lorenzo off his shoulders. The child scampered away ahead of them to find Angelo. "Do you think Madison is ready for all of this? We haven't spoken lately about the two of you. How are things going?"

Cory stepped up on the gate to the stall that held Meile. Kate let him ride the Arabian horse whenever he wanted to. He stroked the white horse's nose and fed her an apple. "We're good. Really good. She's the one. You said the beast would know, and she's the one. I'd like to take her back to Castello with us when we go. What do you think?"

"Let's tackle one thing at a time, son. First of all, right now, there is too much going on around here, especially with the *bambino* on the way. It's too much for me to be worrying about you. I don't know what Alec is planning on doing, so I need to let that situation settle down as well." Shade could hear Impavido snorting and kicking at the stall. "Settle down, Pavi, I will be there shortly."

Shade shook his head. "Damn horse is like one of my *bambinos*. Cory, it will be a lot for Madison to take in going to Castello, but in the long run, if she's the one, then the exposure will be good for her. It will help her integrate into our family. Let's see how that goes and once we get back after the baby is born, then you can head out to see Rachael."

Shade reached out to Meile, as she snuffed into his hand. "Have you fed from her yet?"

Cory blushed. "Not yet, but we've, you know, made love. Luca told me to go slowly and sort of let her lead. He said she'd let me know when she was ready for the next step. So, that's what I've been doing."

Shade headed toward the stall that held Biondo as Cory followed. Shade stroked the mare's mane, easing the animal. "Good advice. Let's take her to Castello, you two will have time to sightsee, with a protector, of course. I can assign Hyde, and don't give me argument, my orders. And I assume she will share your room at Castello?" Shade looked at him and winked.

Cory laughed and punched his dad in the arm. "Come on, Dad. I'm not a kid anymore. I'll tell her about going to Florence. I mentioned it once before, but we didn't have a date. She'll be excited. She wants to see the art gallery there. She doesn't know yet there is more art inside Castello than there is hanging in the Ufizzi. It will blow her mind! I'll tell Mom we'll come to California after the baby is born, so at least she knows I'm planning something."

"Sounds good. Once Sophia is born it will be a great relief.

It is always a stressful time for a coven until the *bambinos* are born."

Angelo approached with Lorenzo on his heels. Shade nodded toward Lorenzo. "And that one will receive his usual grand welcome at Castello. They haven't seen their prince in a while."

Lorenzo sauntered up to the two of them. "So, do I get my pony or what?"

Shade crouched down with a stern face and stared into Lorenzo's eyes. "For someone getting a very big and expensive present, you do not appear too gracious. Want to try that again, little warrior?"

Lorenzo looked back at Angelo who was biting his lip, trying not to laugh. Lorenzo tucked his head and looked up at his father, as he knelt in front of him.

"Sorry, Daddy. I earned enough cards, just like you asked me to. May I have a pony, now, please? I promise to help Angelo take care of him."

"Much better, son. A warrior must always show respect, even when that warrior is in charge. Be mindful of your words." Picking up Lorenzo, he hugged him tightly. "When it is near time for Sophia to be born, we will return to our homeland, in Florence. We shall go to the breeding stables, and we will choose a pony just for my little warrior. We will also have a saddle fitted and made for you. Then your pony will be shipped here over the water. It will be here before we return, since we must let Mommy and Sophia rest a bit before coming home. So, now, you must choose a name for your first warhorse."

Lorenzo nodded. "I'll think about it. It has to be a good name."

"Of course, we will wait and see the pony, sometimes the name comes to you once you see the horse, *si*? Now, I think I am going to take Pavi out for a nice ride. Do you wish to come along and ride on Impavido with me?"

His eyes lit up as he threw his arms around his father's neck. "Yes, Daddy, please! And Cory too."

Cory laughed. "Not this time, little buddy. I promised

Madison I'd call her when I got home. We have plans for the night. But I'll let Kate know you're going out for a ride with Dad."

Shade put Lorenzo down and he took off for the wooden crate of carrots and grabbed several, heading in Pavi's direction. Shade shook his head, but his grin was wide. This was the life he had tried to put off, the life he had tried to avoid, not because he didn't want it, but because it would be too painful to lose it. He hoped, one day, to repeat this same scene with his grandchildren, when he would have much more time to spoil them.

79

Mateo gathered his things. He was heading back to the Canton residence in G-town. Shade informed him that Alec and Braden were ready to get back on the campaign trail, and he'd still be assigned to Alec. He felt weird leaving for this assignment without Hyde, but clearly, his fellow warrior was no longer needed.

Mateo knew this campaign would go much smoother now without Rissa, and both Alec and Braden would be in a better frame of mind without her. He and all the other warriors had no doubts that Rissa's death wasn't an accident, but in their culture, he also knew no one would intervene. A male and his mate shared an eternal bond, and although the male could release the female, there was really only one way to break the blood bond.

He stopped in on Hyde before leaving the barracks and saw him sitting in his room with a laptop in front of him, but he was staring blankly out the window. Mateo knew he was taking Rissa's death harder than most, but he'd never share those feelings. "Heading out, brother, just stopping in to say goodbye."

Hyde looked up to see Mateo standing in his doorway with his bags in hand. "Where you going?"

Mateo dropped his bags outside the door and strolled in, taking a seat. "Canton residence, they're restarting the campaign."

Mateo eyed him carefully, not sure how he'd respond. Hyde put his head in his hands and sighed, feeling a great heaviness inside him. "Great. Guess I'm heading back to the Dead House."

Mateo leaned forward in the chair, his elbows on his knees, his hands intertwined. "Look, Hyde, I know this isn't easy, but you can't seriously miss that bitch. She was a hot mess, brother."

Hyde shook his head. "You didn't know her like I did. She had a soft side. I tried to coach her, but she seemed intent on self-destruction. She didn't deserve this."

Mateo laid his hand on his brother's shoulder. "She got to you, brother. I get it. It's hard, when you're a protector, not to develop a bond. But you've got to let it go. There was nothing you could do. Your job was to protect her from danger from the outside. What goes on between a master and his mate is none of our business."

Hyde nodded but couldn't stem his anger. "He killed her, you know he did. We all know he did. Why didn't he just fucking release her?"

Mateo stood and walked to the small table holding the Midnight, he poured them a drink and walked back, handing Hyde one of the glasses. "We both heard that fight not long before her death. He asked her straight out if she wanted to be released. She caved at his feet. Being released was a scare tactic and I think Canton was running out of options, to be honest. She was out of control. Besides, if Canton released her, he'd have to think about how that would look to his voters. They would have to play out the whole mortal divorce thing, right in the middle of his campaign. But you're too close to see the big picture, you're not thinking straight, warrior. There are rumors she was with another master. Think about all the crap she pulled, no other master would put up with that bullshit. But if she fucked another master, fed from him, he'd have no choice. They did some kinky stuff, brother, but you know as well as I do, she belonged to him and he'd never share her blood with anyone."

Hyde downed the Midnight and listened to Mateo. *What the hell had Rissa done? Slept and fed from another master? Who?* Hyde looked up at him. "She wasn't around any masters I was aware of. Hell, I was with her everyplace she went, brother. She was never out of my sight."

Mateo shrugged. "Maybe it was before you. She did what she wanted, when she wanted. Hell, she manipulated your ass with that balcony ordeal. Let it go, brother."

Hyde sighed. "That's probably what bothers me the most. I hardly spoke another word to her after that incident. She broke my trust. We left things unfinished between us."

Mateo laid his hand on his brother's shoulder and squeezed hard. "She knew you cared about her beyond your duty, she was lost without you half the damn time. But this is how she repaid you, breaking trust and manipulating you. She cared about one thing, Hyde, herself. No matter what you think, that's the bottom line, and Master Canton knew that as well. He's no fool. Get back to the Dead House, it's a change from being a high-profile protector, but you're a Medici warrior, you did your job, and Shade won't let that go unnoticed."

Hyde knew Mateo is right, and although Rissa was gone, he'd never forget her. Standing up, he fist bumped his brother. "*Per sempre*, brother. Get your ass over to Canton's before he decides he wants me back."

As they both laughed, Mateo knew Hyde would be fine in time. Sometimes, even warriors got too involved in their job.

80

Madison and Cory lay stretched across her bed. She'd been reading and he was watching a soccer game on TV. It had been a dark, rainy day that made them postpone their plans of taking a long ride through the countryside on Cory's motorcycle for another day.

She dropped the book by her side and stretched out, reaching her hands above her head, as she yawned. She couldn't remember the last time she'd read for pleasure, and not for homework. This had been such a beautiful, lazy day. Cory spent as much time here with her now, as he spent at Bel Rosso. She rolled over on her side and looked at him, propped up against a mound of pillows, with one hand behind his head.

He'd told her a little earlier about the funeral he'd attended. Madison had watched the news coverage of it on TV. The death of the Presidential candidate's wife was the only thing the news was covering lately. Madison had asked how they knew the Senator, and Cory had said his dad did some work for him. Madison wondered if the Senator knew Shade was a vampire but decided not to ask. She looked at his delicate profile as he watched the TV when he became aware of her staring at him and turned his head, smiling at her. "Did you ask your parents about taking me to California to meet your mom?"

"I talked to my dad, he wants us to wait until after the baby is born and we come back from Florence." He rolled toward her, throwing his arm over her hip. "But he has no objections to us going to visit my mom. He likes the idea. You still want to go, right?"

"Yeah, of course! But you said we, when *we* come back from Florence. Does that mean I'm going to go to Florence for sure?"

Cory grinned at her, kissing her softly on the lips. "Yes, Dad said definitely, you're coming, and we'll be there a while, a few weeks, actually. So, you better pack enough to last. We have to go early, just to make sure Kate's at Castello when the baby comes. Once the baby is born, there are a lot of celebrations to introduce her to the coven. We might need to go shopping for a gown or something. It's a really big deal."

Madison sat forward, as her hair swung free. "A gown? Like an evening gown? I'll need to check the thrift shops, see what I can find. I'm pretty sure my budget won't accommodate the purchase of an evening gown, especially for something I'll probably only wear once. What kind of celebration for a new baby requires an evening gown?"

Cory reached out and caressed her cheek. "Dad and Kate are the King and Queen of the Tuscan coven. My dad is royal blood. Not all masters are royal. I don't think there's a royal line in the States, but there are a few still in Europe. My dad's coven is really large, all of Tuscany, with branches in France and Greece, and of course, here and California. Dad provides protection for them, jobs for them, he takes care of them in a way, and they provide protection to the family. The Medici line is really long, Maddie, they go back centuries. Lorenzo is my dad's first born full-blooded son, and he'll inherit much of my father's responsibilities to the coven, but the birth of another child is more assurance the blood-line continues, and the legacy is secure. Each of his full-blooded children will have responsibilities to the coven. When a new baby is born, it's sort of like a coronation. And don't worry about a dress. We can shop in Italy and I'll pay for whatever you want. You don't have to worry about money. We can go to the museums in Florence, shop, eat, I'm paying for it. This is a trip of a lifetime, but I hope it will be the first of many."

Madison listened to him with a furrowed brow. A royal birth? She'd heard him reference his father as a king before, and Lorenzo had referred to himself as a prince, but the significance hadn't struck home. "Wow, so this is a really big deal then." Madison laughed. "Sorry, but I'm still trying to process all this. Every time I talk with you, it's like peeling back an onion layer. I never know what you're going to share with me next. I fall in love with a half-breed vampire, whose father is royal blood, and rules over a large coven that covers two continents. He'll sweep me away to Florence where I'll dine on champagne and strawberries, while wearing a designer ball gown."

Madison rolled over in his direction and draped her arm across his chest. "You know that sounds like a fairy tale, right? People don't really get to do that in real life."

Pulling her on top of him, he cupped her face. "I know very well, more than you can imagine that it sounds like a fairy tale because I'm living it. Just don't forget that we're the monsters."

Snuggling into her neck, he breathed in her scent as his lips lay on her vein as it pulsed. He moaned softly. He hadn't fed in a long while. He didn't need to feed as often from the feeders as a true vampire did, because he could eat human food, but he hoped Maddie would eventually invite him to feed.

She stroked his face, letting her hand tangle in his hair. Her lips close to his ear, she whispered, "You're not a monster, Cory. You're my knight in shining armor, come to rescue me from a life of boring normalcy." She kissed his ear, her tongue gently teasing.

Cory could hardly breathe he wanted her so much, to feed and claim her as his own. But he wouldn't make a move until she was ready. "Maddie, I love you. Please tell me you're thinking about letting me feed from you, because every time we're together, it's harder for me to hold off." His breath was ragged, and his voice was hoarse.

She'd felt the pull, every time they made love. She felt her own body's need for him, and her desire to have him feed. She knew he was holding back, waiting for her to let him know she was ready. She'd struggled with the idea of it, as well as the implications. "Will it hurt?"

He pulled her close and looked at her, his love for her evident in his eyes. "You'll feel a sharp sting, but there's also pleasure. I only feed from you in the midst of making love. I don't know exactly what you'll feel. I have never done this with a mortal before, but both Dad and Luca have told me it won't hurt you, the experience will bring pleasure to us both."

She knew he'd never intentionally hurt her. Cory might be

the kindest person she'd ever known. "If I say yes, and you start, and I don't like it, can you stop? If I ask you to stop, will you stop?"

"Of course, I'll stop. I love you, and if you're not ready, I'll wait. I want this to be special between us. I know it seems strange to you, but I'm asking you to trust me."

She looked at him, his eyes filled with love for her. No one had ever looked at her like that before. "Then just do it. Don't tell me. Just let it happen naturally. I don't want to anticipate it. That will make me nervous."

Cory couldn't believe what he was hearing. His heart was bursting with love for her. Rolling her over, he nuzzled into her breasts, moaning. "You smell so good."

She wore a soft sundress, and he sat up on his knees, lifting the dress above her head. His fingers slid down her neck, across her shoulders and across her breasts. She was braless, and he loved that. His fingers followed a soft trail down her body until he reached her panties. He pulled them down and tossed them to the side.

Standing beside the bed, he stripped off his clothes as her eyes devoured him. Crawling back between her legs, they lay now, skin to skin, their bodies warm from the summer heat. His kisses were passionate and their tongues tangled as if they were somehow linking them together. He felt her hands as they explored his body, his back, and his hair. He could feel her slight nervousness, and he tried to let the kisses and his touch relax her, make her forget what he was about to do.

Madison gave herself up to him. Cory was so gentle out of bed, but there was another side to him when they made love. Something more primal emerged, and her sweet, androgynous boy became a man. He re-positioned her with such ease, as if she weighed nothing. His strength more on display when he was locked in the throes of passion, his voice deeper, gruffer, almost a growl. And yet, he took care to never hurt her.

She wrapped her legs around his hips as he thrust deep, and she clung tightly to him, feeling the need to be closer still. His mouth covered hers, and she broke free, letting her head fall back on the pillow, her mouth open, gasping for air when she felt his hot breath on her neck, followed by his hot, wet tongue. She started to tense up when she felt his lips on the soft skin of her throat, followed by the slightest sensation of pain as his sharp fangs sink into flesh.

She cried out as the sensation of heat exploded between her legs and she felt him thrust even deeper. The orgasm was intense. She slid her hands down his back, gripping his hips as she thrust upwards to meet him. His growl was deep in his throat as he drank from her, and his hot seed spilled inside her. He'd claimed her now, taken her blood, which she gave freely. And she knew her life would never be the same.

81

Kate was walking back from the flower fields with Shannon. Both the lavender and sunflowers had been harvested for the season, and Kate wanted Shannon to meet with the foreman who oversaw these crops. It had been a good summer with a good yield. The two women were discussing plans for developing the business and Shannon was getting excited about the opportunity to take things to the next level, developing their own product line.

The sun was setting over the mountain range as they approached the main house, and Kate could see Luca climbing down from the tree house, Lorenzo still perched high in the tree. As they got closer to the house, she saw Shade exit the door onto the patio, and the two men were laughing and talking together. It made Kate smile to see them. She knew the plan was to take Shannon to Florence with them when the baby was born, and Luca would have her feed from him there, completing their blood covenant.

Kate reached out and took her hand. "We'll be going to Florence soon. Are you ready?"

Shannon looked at her best friend and smiled. "Yeah, I am. Will I feel different?"

Kate nodded. "It's gradual but yes. His blood will make you stronger, to prepare you for the turning, whenever you two get ready for that. And the sex is more intense."

Shannon's laugh could be heard by the two men as they looked up to see the women approaching. "Heaven help us!"

Shade heard the familiar laugh and his head snapped up to see his *bel* and Shannon approaching. Kate moved a bit slower, holding her well-rounded tummy. She looked amazing in the light of the sunset, her red hair glowing, like a fiery Goddess sent from a foreign land. "Never have I seen two more beautiful females in my life, Luca. And they are both ours. How in the hell did we pull that off?"

Before Luca could answer, they heard the sound of cracking wood and Shade looked up to see a branch giving way and falling to the ground. Shade called out to Lorenzo as he ran beneath the tree to catch his son. "Teleport, little warrior, go up, up!"

He heard Kate scream, but Lorenzo gained control of his fall and gently slowed his descent. The boy's laughter echoed across the fields, and Shade sighed in relief. "Come to me, Lorenzo." Shade held his arms out to his son.

Laughing as he landing on his feet, Lorenzo ran straight into his father's arms.

"You, my little warrior, are going to be the best warrior Medici ever saw."

Kate rushed up behind Shade. "Lorenzo! Are you all right?"

Lorenzo had a huge grin on his face as he turned to his mother. "Mommy! Did you see me?"

Kate pinched his cheek. "Lorenzo, you're going to send me into early labor if you keep falling out of trees. Please be careful."

Lorenzo nodded his head. "I am careful, Mommy. Did you see me fly?"

Kate caught Shade's eye as she answered her son. "I did see that. You landed much better than I did on my first try."

Shannon stepped into Luca's arms. He pulled her to his chest and buried his nose in her hair. She smelled like the sun. "I love you, *mia belleza*."

Shannon looked up at him. "Love you more."

Shade gave his son a kiss before putting him down. "Now, little warrior, you need to go inside and find Theresa, it is your bath and bed time."

Lorenzo skipped into the house as if on a mission, the dog trailing behind him. Shade took *bel's* hand. "Come, all of you, let's sit down on the patio and talk. We have some things to discuss. I have already asked Gi to bring us some refreshment. Now is as good a time as any since we are all gathered."

They gathered in the seating near the pool, as they felt the temperature dropping. Shade stretched out on a chaise lounge and pulled *bel* into the space next to him and helped her get comfortable. Placing his arms around her, he kissed the top of her head and placed his hand on her rounded tummy. "She comes soon, *si*?"

Kate placed her hand on top of his. "Dr. Bonutti said by the end of September. So, we'll need to go to Florence in about two weeks, I'd think. It took Lorenzo another two weeks to arrive when we went to Florence for his birth, but I think this one is much more eager to get here. I've already met with the feeders, and I selected Gita. She is Nita's sister and they have a very similar temperament. You can meet her when we go back to Castello."

"*Si*." Shade rubbed gently and felt a strong kick under his hand. "She is strong, *mi amore*. I am sure Gita will do fine. Lorenzo adores Nita and I am sure Sophia will be the same with Gita."

Shade looked up at Luca, who was seated in a patio chair, with Shannon seated between his splayed legs. "Madison will be joining Cory on this trip to Florence. We need to assign a warrior for them. Not letting those two roam around Italy. Neither of them has ever been there before. Any thoughts on that, Luca?"

Luca sat forward in the deck chair. "Yeah, actually, I think Hyde could use a special assignment. He's getting used to being just another warrior in the Dead House. Being assigned to your son would be a promotion. Not only that, it will give me some free time to take Shannon to Empoli for a few days."

Shade nodded. "I have kept an eye on Hyde, and Mateo also gave me a heads up, so I think you might be right. It would do him good to be back in Florence a while as well. He needs a distraction."

He looked at Shannon. "Are you ready for the covenant? Ready for the changes you will feel and to take this relationship to the next level?"

Shannon nodded at him. "I'm ready. Besides, Kate says the sex is better." She turned her head and bit at Luca's thigh. "And, you know, Luca needs all the help he can get."

Shade laughed hard and loud. "And now, you challenge his beast? Be careful what you wish for, mortal."

Luca gave Shannon a look that said the beast was more than willing to take her up on her challenge and she giggled.

Shade laid his head back on the chaise, breathing in the night air. "Everything is underway in Florence. The Council knows to expect us. We have the plane and the house staff on alert, as Castello is made ready for the celebrations. Security is well in hand, so Marco informs me, and we must make sure Theresa has some time to spend with Marco."

Kate laid her head back against his chest. "Lorenzo has so many people taking care of him at Castello, I'm sure Theresa could take off for a few days and Lorenzo would hardly notice. Castello will be a nice break for everyone, I think, and I'll be glad to deliver this baby."

"You are not the only one. I am anxious to hold my princess in my arms. All our lives are about to change in one fashion or another. Our coven and family grows. I only hope my *madre* and *padre* know all they desired for me has come to fruition a hundred fold."

Kissing Kate on the top of her head, he sighed heavily. "We must go inside, get our son to bed and then, I must get to the camp." Helping her up, he smiled down at her. "Soon, *mi amore*, we become five instead of four."

82

It took a while to get everyone on the plane and settled, the luggage loaded and then they were off to Florence. Shade spent some of the flight with Lorenzo, but his death slumber pulled at him and he moved to the back of the cabin and the enclosed bedroom where he slept the rest of the flight.

Once they arrived on Italian soil, they were all escorted into two limousines and transported to Castello.

Madison had tried to sleep on the flight over, and managed to doze on and off, but this was her first trip to Italy, and her first flight on a private jet. She was trying to keep her excitement under wraps, as everyone else on board was responding as if this was no big deal.

There were cars waiting for them on their arrival at the airport in Florence. They never entered the airport terminal but were taken straight from the plane to the waiting cars. Cory made sure she sat by the window, so she could look out at the countryside as they drove. It didn't take long before she saw the red-tiled rooftops of old Florence, dominated by the Ufizzi tower and the Duomo. She squealed out loud and squeezed Cory's hand, as they drove through the city and along the banks of the Arno, on the streets where Da Vinci and Michelangelo once walked. They continued past the city and the Boboli Gardens, as the road meandered back into the hillside where the massive estate sat on a small rise right next to the river Arno.

Cory pointed it out to her. "That's it. Medici Castello."

Madison's mouth dropped open, as the impressive house at Bel Rosso was dwarfed in comparison to this grand castle. They all exited the cars and Shade issued instructions about being greeted. She clung to Cory's hand, as she tried to look around the estate and followed his lead as they approached the entrance.

Shade took Kate by the arm, and held Lorenzo's hand. He

issued instructions to the crowd. "Listen up. Kate and I will enter first with Lorenzo, followed by Cory and Madison, then Luca and Shannon. All of your luggage will be taken to your respective rooms. We are home now, and I want everyone to have a wonderful trip. We shall have a princess when we return."

Turning to look at Madison, he smiled. "Welcome to Castello, Madison. Cory is familiar with the routine. He will walk you through the protocol and introduce you to the staff. Now, let's get inside before they break down the front door and drag us in."

Antonio, the newly appointed majordomo who'd replaced Gi when he moved to the States, swung the massive door open to greet them. He bowed reverently to Shade and Kate. "Master, my lady."

Shade slapped him on the back. "Antonio. Good to see you. We will have a house full, *si*? Two mortals, so make sure we have plenty of food in the kitchen."

Shade led the group into the massive grand foyer, where the house staff was lined up in their uniforms to greet them. Lorenzo squirmed free so he could run ahead. He loved coming to Castello and greeting the staff, where he became the center of everyone's attention.

Madison was overwhelmed by the size of the greeting hall, the height of the ceilings, the massive chandeliers, and the grand staircase in marble. The staff all responded to Shade, as they each bowed and called him master, and they kissed Kate's hand. She knew they were a king and queen, but in Virginia she'd seen no evidence of any royal protocol. Cory was introducing her, but the faces became a blur as they each shook her hand and welcomed her. She noticed they were all very tall, even the women.

Lorenzo was being picked up and told how much he'd grown, as he was passed from staff member to staff member. It was a whirlwind of greetings that was making Madison's head spin.

Shade suddenly spoke up, commanding attention, as he called select staff from the line. "Carlos, you will be assigned to see to the needs of Luca and Shannon. I know Luca will not need much from you, but Shannon is mortal, so be sure she is taken care of, *si*?"

Carlos stepped forward, letting them know their luggage would be brought to their room and scurried off.

"Cezare, you will resume your responsibilities to my son, Cory, and Rosa, I am assigning you to Madison. She is also mortal, and this is her first trip here. They will have Hyde as their protector, but make sure she wants for nothing, *si*?"

Rosa bowed to Madison and hurried off up the stairs. Madison turned to Cory. "I'll have my own maid?"

Cory laughed and said, "Get used to it."

Shade made his way through the house staff, each of them important in his life. As they finally made their way to the end of the line, Marco stepped forward as they hugged and beat each other on the back. Shade greeted his friend. "Good to see you, brother. We have a full house this time around."

Marco laughed. "I can't believe that old leather ass of yours can still manage to make *bambinos*. Everything here is under control. But don't expect to see much of me. Terri is here, and we have some time to make up for."

Shade slapped his back. "Well, I am going to need Theresa for the birthing, so you better get in your time while you can."

Marco turned to Kate. "My Queen, you look beautiful as ever. Congratulations on the coming birth of our princess. As always, I am at your disposal for any of your needs." He bowed slightly and raised his eyes, grinning at her, his voice a bit softer. "*Grazie* for not killing my oldest and dearest brother yet."

Kate returned his smile. "Oh, I think he has a few good years left yet." She turned and pulled Cory and Madison close as she addressed Marco once more. "Please welcome Madison. This is her first visit to Castello, please try not to scare her."

Turning to Madison, Kate slid her arm around the young girl's waist and she could feel that she trembled with excitement. "Madison, this grizzly old warrior is Marco. Now, he's going to try to come off like a bad-ass, but trust me, he's easily tamed."

Shade laughed in the background at Kate's introduction.

Marco scrunched up his rugged, worn face. "Ah yes, our beloved queen is home once again. I think I have missed that ribbing."

He turned to Shade and growled before turning back to Madison and bowing slightly. "It is an honor to meet you, Lady Madison. I am Second-in-Command of all Medici warriors here in Florence. I am at your service, and I've been instructed that Hyde is to be your personal protector. Hyde is one of our best."

He looked at the young girl, feeling her excitement and slight trepidation, and watched as Cory hovered close, protecting her. Greeting Cory, he pulled him into a tight hug and slapped him on the back. Turning to leave, Marco called out to Shade, "I'll catch up with you later, but if you think your ass can handle a real warrior workout, come on out to the field later."

Shade stood with his hands on his hips, his chest puffed out, his legs spread. "You are on, you old goat."

Kate looked at Madison and spoke softly, "Some things never change."

Madison was amused by the verbal sparring between the two men as Kate put her at ease.

Kate placed her hand on the young girl's back. "Now, go with Rosa and Cezare. They'll get you settled. I told them to put you in Cory's room, but if you'd like your own room, I can have your things moved."

Madison shook her head. "No, Cory's room will be fine. I think I'd feel lost in here if I were by myself."

Kate nodded. "I know this is surreal. Just get settled, take a bath, let the staff know what you'd like to eat, and get some sleep. Tomorrow, Cory can show you the rest of Castello, and you have a few weeks to sightsee in Florence and all of Tuscany. Shade controls Tuscany, and in Europe, the territories of the vampires are more strictly guarded, so unfortunately, you won't be able to visit other parts of Italy while you're here, unless specifically invited by that master. Cory understands the protocol, so just follow his lead. Be sure to pick out a gown for the celebration of Sophia's birth. Cory can take you to the proper shops, and the bills will be sent here."

Kate kissed the young girl on the forehead. "Have fun, Madison. You and Cory will be on your own schedule while you're here. Luca and Shannon have their own agenda, and I'll be sequestered here until the birth. Shade will take Lorenzo to the camp as much as possible, to prepare him for when he'll come here permanently to train. So, just enjoy your time. When the baby is ready to be born, everyone will come back to Castello. Until then, enjoy yourselves."

Rosa stepped up behind Madison and Cory, and with a slight curtsy, she announced, "Your room is ready."

Cory placed his arm protectively around Madison's shoulder as they followed Rosa back up the grand stairs. Madison looked over her shoulder at the crowd of people still assembled in the foyer, all laughing and talking. She leaned in to Cory as he guided her up the steps. "Oh my god, Cory. This is crazy!"

Cory smiled at her; he was seeing Castello all over again through her eyes. He loved how the staff treated her with great respect. "This is the Medici fairy tale, remember?"

As Rosa led them through the great hall, he chuckled as Madison swung her head from left to right, trying to take in everything she saw. He heard her squeal as she stopped in her tracks in front of a painting.

"What's wrong?"

"That painting. It's Da Vinci's Leda and the Swan! It looks like an original. He painted several versions, and most of them have been lost. There's supposed to be one remaining at the Ufizzi I'd hoped to see. Is this a copy?"

Cory shrugged. "Not sure, there's art all over this house. I'm afraid I don't know much about it."

Rosa turned to see which painting Madison was referring to and nodded slightly. "Excuse me, mistress, but that is indeed an original painting from Leonardo. The Medici's were great patrons to the Masters of the Renaissance, and this painting was given to Shade's father, Christofano, as a gift. It has hung here since 1507 and has never been viewed by the mortal world. You will find many such pieces, both paintings and sculptures, throughout Castello. You may inspect it if you wish."

Madison was dumbstruck. An original? Never seen by mortals? She was looking at a piece of art touched by the hand of Leonardo Da Vinci, and she wouldn't be able to tell anyone what she'd seen. "This is unreal! Can I try to sketch it while I'm here?"

Rosa shook her head. "That will be up to our master, but I would think not. If the outside world were to see it, then it would raise questions as to the location of the art. It would risk our exposure, *si*?"

Madison nodded, understanding the ramifications, as she stared in awe at the painting. "No, I understand."

Cory drew her away. "Come on. I'll give you a full tour tomorrow, and Rosa can come along to explain where the pieces came from."

Madison reluctantly allowed herself to be drawn away from the painting and led to the opulent room she and Cory would share.

***

Shade helped Kate up the grand staircase to their bedroom. Emma was already inside unpacking their belongings. Shade addressed her. "Emma, slow down, we are not going anywhere."

She stopped and looked at him, blinking her eyes a few times. "But, master, my lady needs her things to be put away as soon as possible, she will need a bath and some rest after our long journey."

Shade spoke to her softly, "Now, you go on ahead and leave. Get yourself settled. I will handle getting her bath and tucking her in, *si*."

Emma's eyes shot from Shade to Kate and back to Shade. She seemed unsure about leaving her post. Kate caught Emma's eyes. "Go ahead, Emma. I'll call if I need you."

Emma scurried from the room as Kate sat down on the bed, kicking off her shoes. "So, you're to be at my beck and call this evening, are you?"

Shade knelt beside the bed, massaging her feet with his strong hands. "*Si*, my lady, I am at your service. What is it you wish your master to do for you?" He smiled at her, his blue eyes flashing, and his dark curls hanging over his forehead.

Kate looked at him as he knelt at her feet, looking up at her with those steely blue eyes. "Oh, I think you have done quite enough, mister." She laughed as she ran her hand over the swell of her belly. His powers to seduce with a single glance were no less intense this night than the night she'd first laid eyes on him.

"Oh, my lady, I am just beginning." Standing, he leaned over her as she lay back on the bed. He kissed her belly, holding his weight off her body and gazed deep into her eyes. "I miss my lily white. Our life is not as it was before our son, but I would never trade it for anything. Speaking of which, where is Lorenzo?"

"Theresa has him in the room next to ours. And please, as much as I love him, I need a little peace and quiet. He was so rambunctious on the flight over. I'm trying to imagine juggling two of them and it makes me tired just thinking about it."

"*Si*, I will keep him occupied, as much as possible. Now, I think you need a bath with your master."

As the words left his mouth, the sound of the water running in the tub could be heard, as he willed it. Lifting her up gently, he undressed her, leaving small kisses across her delicate white skin. "You are so beautiful, *mi amore*. I love when your body is round with our *bambino*."

Lifting her into his arms, he carried her to the bathroom, sitting her gently down in the water of the large marble tub. He stripped away his own clothes and slid in carefully behind her, pulling her back to his chest. Pouring some aromatic salts into the bath, he slowly stirred the water with his hands, watching the water lap at her breasts. The scent of roses rose from the steaming water and filled the air around them. "Are you comfortable?"

Kate laid her head back against his chest, as the steam rose from the tub and the hot water soothed her tired muscles. "I can't remember the last time we were able to take a bath together like this." She closed her eyes and enjoyed this rare moment of alone time. Even the hours she spent sleeping next to him in his death slumber were interrupted daily to spend time with Lorenzo.

Grabbing the bath sponge, he proceeded to wash her. He could feel her body relax into him, and her thoughts rambled through his mind. "You give much to the men in your life, *mi amore*. Do not think I ever take that for granted. There are times I am jealous of my own son, because he needs you as much as I do, and I have to wait for your attentions. It feels good to be here, at Castello. It is filled with memories of my past, but we will be making so many more memories in the future, *si*. Do you feel our Sophia? Does she speak to you?"

Kate felt the tight muscles relax as he tended to her. "Hmm, she does from time to time. She refers to herself as Princess, not as Sophia. So, I don't think she'll have any problems accepting her role." Kate felt a hard kick from the baby and laughed, placing her hand over her belly. "Yes, I know you're an eager one, princess. It won't be long now."

Shade lathered her hair with shampoo and massaged her head while washing her crimson tresses. "She is anxious to be here, *si*. She knows what awaits her, so much love."

He rinsed the shampoo from her hair until all the soap was gone. "She will have red curls, I think, *si*?"

Kate nodded, her eyes closed as he washed her hair, his strong fingers massaging her scalp. When they were first together, without Lorenzo, he often washed her hair. Now, it was a luxury she rarely got to enjoy. "Yes, she shows me red hair like mine, and blue eyes, like yours. And a crown, she must have her crown."

Kate smiled at the image projected in her head. She also knew this would be a willful and stubborn child, not like their easy-going Lorenzo.

"A princess must always have her crown. She is Medici. Come, let us get out of this water, it is beginning to chill."

Standing, he stepped out of the tub and helped her get out.

Grabbing the large, thick white towels, he rubbed her body down until her skin was a soft pink, and then carried her to the bed. As they got into the main room, the fireplace was blazing, and the bed had been turned down.

He smiled. His staff knew their jobs and did them well. He was a fortunate master. Laying her down gently on the large bed, he climbed in beside her, holding her close. "You must feed, *mi amore*. You will need my strength to help you through the birth. Take from me."

Kate enjoyed being pampered. She knew their time alone together was a rare gift anymore. His responsibilities to the camp and training the new warriors, managing the Dead House, and overseeing the expanding coven and his business concerns consumed his waking hours. He always carved out time to spend with Lorenzo every night, and soon, he'd have two children to help raise.

During her pregnancy, she fed from him with more frequency, and he still made love to her, but with restraint. He must control his beast and not feed from her and she missed the intimacy. Her eyes were heavy as she fought the need to sleep. She'd slept only a short time next to him on the flight before Lorenzo had demanded her attention.

She stroked his face and his strong jawline, and nibbled at his lips before sliding her tongue down his jaw and neck. She could feel the pulse of the blood that ran through his veins and her body responded to her need to feed both her and the child she carried.

Closing her eyes, her hand sought the back of his head as her fangs emerged and she sunk her teeth into his neck. The first taste of his blood across her tongue was electric. The power of his blood, of feeding from him, never lessened with time. Its impact on her was immediate as she moaned and felt the familiar explosion of heat between her legs. She felt his hands slide around her, pulling her closer, as he rolled onto his back and she straddled him. They'd make love, and then he'd hold her while she slept, and the embers in the fireplace faded.

83

Cory and Madison woke early, still a little jet lagged and adjusting to the time zone changes. Cezare had arranged to have their breakfast served to them in their room, and Cory laughed as Madison checked out every single dish, astounded that someone had made this much food for two people. Cory heard the light tap on the door and answered it, finding Hyde on the other side.

"Sorry to interrupt, Cory, but will you need me today? I haven't received an itinerary of your schedule since we just arrived."

Cory looked back at Madison. "Maddie, did you want to go somewhere today?"

Madison was sitting at the table set up for them by the window, sipping at the strong coffee. "Well, I'd like to see more of the castle, if it's okay, and then I'd love to drive back into Florence."

Hyde chuckled. He was going to enjoy being Madison and Cory's protector while here. Being surrounded by their youth and joyful enthusiasm would be a big change from Rissa and her constant pouting and manipulative behavior. "I'm going down to the camp, catch up with some of the warriors. Let me know whenever you're ready. Don't leave these grounds without me."

Cory nodded. "No problem, Hyde."

As he closed the door, he walked over to Maddie and kissed her cheek, nuzzling into her neck. "As soon as you're done eating, get dressed, and we can explore Castello. I probably haven't seen it all myself."

"Sure. That coffee was strong enough to keep me going all day. Let me get dressed really quick. Can I just wear jeans? I mean, is it formal in the house?"

Cory shrugged with a grin. "Nah, you can wear whatever you like. Wear comfortable shoes. Do you need Rosa to help you?"

Madison shook out her long hair as she stood and shed her robe. "Uh, no. She already unpacked all my stuff. I think I can dress myself."

She rummaged through the dresser and pulled out a pair of jeans, and a long sleeve ivory tunic top. She found her running shoes in the wardrobe and pulled on socks and shoes. "You think I might need a jacket? It's cool inside this house, but it is probably warm in the sun."

"Bring it along. I'll carry it for you if you don't need it."

When she was ready, he took her hand and, together, they made their way through the winding halls of Castello. He laughed every time she gasped and had to stop to check out some bust or painting. She knew so much about the pieces and explained the history of the art or the artist as they went. Cory felt like he was completely inept. He didn't know anything about art.

They meandered everywhere inside the massive castle, and finally took a stroll down the Hall of Ancestors. Madison inspected everything up close, with wonder and excitement. He stopped in front of the painting of Shade as a young boy with his parents.

"This is my dad when he was about ten. He'd just started in the warrior camp. I think Lorenzo looks a lot like him."

Madison stared up at the massive portrait painted in oils. "Oh my god, Lorenzo is going to look so much like him!" Madison examined the portrait and saw it was signed by Michelangelo. "Seriously? This is crazy!"

"I know, right? I don't know anything about art, but I know enough to know this is unique and valuable. Michelangelo lived with the Medici's when he was a boy. This painting was a gift to Christofano, my grandfather. Dad looks a lot like him. You can really see the resemblance from one generation to the next. I've heard that my grandfather didn't like half-breeds. I doubt he would have approved of me being accepted into the family. Dad says it was just a different time. Still, it makes me wonder if he was alive today, would he throw me out. You know, Maddie, we can go to Michelangelo's tomb in Florence. Hyde grew up here too, he knows where everything is."

"I'd forgotten that. I know from art history class the Medici's were patrons of Michelangelo and many other Renaissance artists, but I'd forgotten he'd lived with them when he was a child. And I'd love to see his tomb. It's in the Basilica of Santa Croce, I think. And the Ufizzi. And the Galleria, to see the statue of David. So much to see! Can we go now?"

Cory laughed. "We have a lot of time to go see everything. We don't need to see it all in one day. Plus, you have to shop for a gown. But let's take a stroll outside. I want to show you the gardens. I think you'll really like it."

He led her through more halls and they passed the house staff, who nodded and greeted them. Once outside, Cory took her hand and led her through the meticulously maintained gardens of Castello. They ended up in the rose garden, which was still in full bloom.

Madison followed him through the formal low-hedge maze, and then into a large rose garden rich with blooms, even though it was late in the season. "Wow. They must have really mild winter's here. This garden is really lush. I've never seen so many roses."

Cory stopped and put his arms around her waist. "There's a story behind all the roses. My grandparents were killed here, right here in this spot, during the bonfires. My dad had completed training in the camp, and was off exploring the world, learning how to integrate into the mortal culture. They were dragged from the castle in the daylight, and burned at the stake, although the sun would have killed them both anyway. My dad could not save them. And when he finally got back here, all that was left was a pile of ash. He found my grandmothers ring in the ashes, a ring he'd given to her. He retrieved it, and eventually, gave it to Kate. There was one rose bush that survived the fire and my dad had them take cuttings from that surviving rose and plant all the roses you see now."

Cory picked a rose from a climbing vine and handed it to Madison. She inhaled deeply of the lush, fragrant bloom. "That's such a sad story. But I love how your father found a way to honor their memory. Hmm, smells heavenly. No wonder Kate wears this scent all the time. And what's over there?" Madison pointed in the direction of the camp.

"Well, uh, that's the warrior camp, where my dad trained, and where Lorenzo will come to be trained as well. Many of the warriors you see at Bel Rosso came from this camp. This camp is much bigger than the one at home. This is where Dad sent me when he first pulled me off the streets, before we discovered I was his son. I'm afraid it's off limits. Marco would have my head if I brought a mortal into the camp." He gave her a quick kiss on the lips. "I really love having you here with me, Maddie."

"And I love being here. I thought Bel Rosso was a fairy tale, but this place is magical. Come on, let's find Hyde and start exploring, shall we?"

"Yes, the sun is feeling warm now."

Taking her hand, they strolled back into Castello. Cory was wondering if they could pack in everything they wanted to see in the time they'd be here. He wanted this to be the trip of a lifetime for Maddie.

84

They had been at Castello for several days now, and Lorenzo was constantly on the move as he explored every inch of the massive castle. Shade tried hard to keep Lorenzo occupied and out of Kate's hair as much as possible. He wanted her to rest before the delivery.

Lorenzo tracked him down, asking if they could go to the camp. Lorenzo was well aware he'd be moving here on a somewhat permanent basis when he turned ten, and he had mixed feelings about the move. On the one hand, he couldn't wait to follow in his father's footsteps, to make him proud, but on the other hand, it meant moving away from his family, and living under Marco's rule. Lorenzo still felt a tinge of intimidation around Marco, who seemed to have little time for playfulness.

Shade lifted Lorenzo up onto his shoulders, as they trudged to the camp. The camp in Florence was more than twice the size of the camp at Bel Rosso. Shade headed into the section of the camp that housed the newest and youngest of their warrior trainees.

Lorenzo sat up, his attention focused the moment he heard the sound of clanging metal and the shouts of victory. Lorenzo knew these sounds well from the time he spent in the camp at Bel Rosso, and it spoke to his heart.

Entering the training field, Shade could feel the boy squirming to get down. "Lorenzo, you are too young to train with these boys. You must watch and learn. Be observant and keep your wits about you. Hone in on the sounds of the arrows, the shuriken's and swords. You will learn to sense their approach, long before they touch you, if you truly concentrate."

Lorenzo became still, and Shade knew he was doing just as he'd been instructed. "Okay, Daddy, I can do it."

Shade smiled. "That's my little warrior."

Shade stood for a while with Lorenzo on his shoulders,

watching the young recruits who ranged from ages ten to fifteen. He noticed there were no females, and he was displeased. He and Marco had very different views on the skills of female warriors. Shade felt strongly about expanding their ranks to include the female warriors if they were going to be effective in the future. He vowed to have a few words with Marco about his selections.

Suddenly, they were interrupted by a loud whistle, one Shade was familiar with. He watched as all the warriors on the field dropped their weapons to the ground, and everything came to a grinding halt. Every warrior turned his head in their direction and instantly dropped to one knee, their heads bowed.

Shade smiled and raised his hand to Marco, who appeared from one of the bunkers. Shade walked slowly across the field, Lorenzo still on his shoulders, as Marco walked to meet him halfway. The warriors remained on one knee. Some of them tilted their heads up slightly to get a glimpse of their master and the young prince.

"About time your old ass got out here to see the new blood." Shade took his outstretched hand.

"Show some respect, brother, or I will never get anything out of this pack of warriors."

Marco made eye contact with Lorenzo, who looked away, wilting under his cold stare. Marco made a sweeping gesture with his arm, encompassing the training field and the many warriors. "Your warriors await you."

Shade slapped him on the back and pulled Lorenzo down from his shoulders, setting him on his feet. "It is time to greet our new warriors, and release them from their stance of respect."

As Lorenzo's feet hit the ground, he was approached slowly and respectfully by a brigade of young boys. The boys were all older than him, and though not as tall as their adult counterparts, they stood strong and tall. Lorenzo had been taught, since birth, that he was a prince, a vampire of royal blood, who must rise to rule the coven. It was his birthright. But until today, he'd never been faced with the reality of his destiny. He'd been held safe and protected in the confines of Bel Rosso, and even though he visited the camp there many times, the warriors at home stopped and played with him, holding mock battles. The boys that approached him now were looking at him expectantly, and with reverence, and Lorenzo felt overwhelmed. He stood close to his father and slid his arm around his father's leg.

Shade pulled Lorenzo from his leg and crouched next to him. "Lorenzo, these are your warriors, you must not be timid. You are expected to lead. They will train to protect us and everyone we love, and they will follow your command, even now. Be strong, little warrior, but show respect."

Shade stood and smiled back at the young recruits. "Welcome to Castello. From what I have seen, you look as though you will all grow to be fine and strong warriors, worthy of the Medici. I am your master and King, this is your Prince. He will lead all of you one day. We are honored to have you with us."

Shade took Lorenzo's hand and led him through the ranks of the young boys who stood proud. He shook a few hands, nodded, and answered questions. They weren't shy but eager to have the attention of their master. They asked questions about their weapons, and any tips he had for their improvement.

Lorenzo remained silent and Shade could feel his curiosity mixed with intimidation of these older boys. One of the smallest warriors approached. He had dark blonde hair, and blue eyes.

Shade fist bumped the young vampire warrior. "Your name, son?"

The boy lowered his head in respect and raised his eyes, looking directly at Shade. "My name is Alfie, short for Alphonzo."

Shade smiled. "I would like to introduce you to your Prince." Shade nudged Lorenzo forward, encouraging him to take control.

Lorenzo stepped forward at his father's urging. There were

no children at Bel Rosso. All of Lorenzo's interactions had been with adult vampires, and his limited exposure to the two mortal women who visited there. The young vampire introduced himself and Lorenzo had been taught how to respond. He was the Prince, he didn't bow. The others would always bow to him. He must show respect to those who served him but remember he ruled them.

"Alfie, I'm Lorenzo, your Prince. Are you learning about swords? I like swords best. My daddy likes swords best too."

Shade felt everything inside Lorenzo and knew he didn't see this young boy as a warrior but a playmate. "Alfie, would you do your master a great favor? I would be most honored if you would take your Prince inside the barracks, show him where you live, and give him an idea of what is in store for him once he comes to join you."

Alfie's eyes lit up as he nodded eagerly.

Shade turned to his son. "Lorenzo, go with Alfie. Marco and I will be right outside talking."

The two boys walked quickly to the barracks, as Marco shouted out orders for the other warriors to continue their training. Shade and Marco stood together as they watched the two young boys head for the barracks.

It brought back memories for both of them, when they trained together as children in this same camp. Shade threw his arm around his oldest friend's shoulder. "Reminds me of the old days. There's nothing like working your ass off all night, then being too damn tired to even bathe, just dropping on your bunk and falling asleep."

Marco laughed. "Hell, brother, it's still like that for me. You are getting soft in your old age. But you always had the castle to go to if you wanted."

Shade smiled, remembering how he'd sneak away to Castello, and the comfort his mother provided, but with time, he preferred being here with his brothers. Changing the subject, he turned to Marco. "Not liking what I see here, Marco, no females. I know damn well they apply. Want to explain that?"

Marco stood with his hands on his hips, scowling. "Look,

you gave me this fucking job and I've done it well. What I get and what I can work with is two different things. But as soon as I find one who can perform to the likes of Fiamma, she will be inside these walls. So, deal with it."

***

Lorenzo had to walk twice as fast to keep up with Alfie's long stride. They entered the barracks to find rows of beds lined up side by side. Alfie walked halfway down the row and plopped down on a bed. "This one is mine."

Lorenzo looked around the sparse quarters. He'd seen the bunkers at Bel Rosso, and they looked nothing like this. He knew the warriors all shared a space, and Marcello had told him it built the camaraderie and sense of brotherhood between the warriors, but Lorenzo was wondering if he'd have his own room, like Marcello and Marco. He was the prince, after all. He'd ask his dad about that.

Lorenzo sat down on the bed next to the boy. "Do you like it here? Do you miss your mommy?"

"Yes, I love it here. I'm very proud to be here, so is my family. It's a big honor to be a Medici warrior. I miss my family a little, but I get to visit. Are you coming here soon to train with us?"

Lorenzo looked back at the boy. He had a wide grin on his face and seemed genuinely happy to be living here. "My daddy says I'll come here for short periods until I am ten, and when I'm ten, I'll come here to live and train under Marco. I train now at the camp in Virginia, but I don't live in the camp. Do you know Marcello? Or Skelk? And Uncle Luca? They all teach me stuff, along with my daddy."

Alfie nodded. "I know Marcello, and I've heard of Luca. He's one of the best warriors around. Our King, I know of his legend. Your father is the best warrior there ever was. They call him the Warrior's Warrior. Are you excited to come here with us? I wish I could visit your new camp in Virginia. They say it's the finest camp in the world. It's my dream to go there, and one day be like Marcello."

Lorenzo perked up. "You want to come to Virginia? You

could live in the camp there. We have bunkers there too, only..." He looked around the bare room. "Only nicer. We could train together, and you could come play in my tree house. We have a pool and we could swim. Do you have a dog? I have a dog named Warrior, and my mommy has lots of animals that must do what she says. I have a teepee in my room. You want to come? I'll ask my daddy!"

Alfie sat back on his bed as his Prince went on about the luxuries of his life. Alfie had dreamed, all his life, of getting into this camp, and training to be a Medici warrior. Standing up, he stretched his legs and looked at Lorenzo. "I don't think you understand. You're royalty, a prince. I'm just a warrior. I don't wish to disrespect you, but the camp in Virginia doesn't have the means to train the young warriors like me. I don't play in tree houses or teepees. I use swords, bows and arrows, and shuriken's. I attend class every day. We don't play or have time for such things. We don't have pets. That's not allowed. I want to be here, I want to learn and be the best warrior I can be, so I can be SIC someday. You can't do that if you play so much."

Lorenzo blinked his eyes at him, taken aback by the boy's response. He felt tears sting his eyes, but he knew his father wouldn't want him to cry. Lorenzo nodded. "Yeah, I knew that. I was just testing you."

He swallowed his disappointment and puffed out his chest. "I train too. I train every day. Just because I don't live inside the camp doesn't mean I'm not a warrior. And I have classes too. My teacher is Enzo. He lives at Bel Rosso and I have a classroom in our house. I have to go to class every day. My daddy says I'll be as great a warrior as he is, and he and Marco will make sure of it."

Alfie could see he'd hurt the prince's feelings, but he was here for one reason. If he could be the best, if he could earn the respect of his master, then maybe, one day, he could be a protector or SIC. It was the job they all strived for, and it would bring honor and respect for his family.

"I'm sure you train really hard, Prince Lorenzo. I didn't mean to imply otherwise. You're very fortunate to have such great warriors around to train you. Maybe someday I'll be able to come to your home in Virginia and then we can train together, but it will be a long time yet. We should be getting back outside. I have a lot to do tonight. Thank you for coming inside and meeting me. I'm honored."

Alfie bowed his head in respect and went down on one knee. "You will be a great warrior, Lorenzo of Medici."

Lorenzo had seen the warriors kneel before his father, but this was the first warrior to kneel before him. The seriousness of the responsibility he'd someday carry settled over his young shoulders as he started to realize all these warriors would, someday, look to him for guidance, and he must be ready to lead.

"Rise, Alfie. I am honored to lead you. You'll be a fierce Medici warrior one day, and I hope you'll come visit me. But Florence is where I'll eventually live and rule. Castello will be my home, not Bel Rosso. That's what my father has told me."

He slid off the bed and tapped Alfie on the shoulder. "Come on. We can go outside. Maybe we can train with swords."

As Lorenzo ran back to his father, Shade crouched down to greet him. "It is a little different than Bel Rosso camp, *si*?"

Lorenzo nodded and Marco spoke up. "Alfie, rejoin your warriors, get your ass back to work."

As Alfie ran off, he waved to Lorenzo, then picked up his sword and jumped back into the fray.

Marco redirected his attention to Shade. "Hey, old man, come back to my bunk, need to show you and Lorenzo something."

As the three walked together toward Marco's bunk, Lorenzo didn't take his eyes off the field of warriors. Shade knew the feel of that pull calling to his son even now, and he knew his son wanted to join this life. As they entered the bunker, Marco walked to his bed and knelt down. Reaching beneath the bunk, he pulled out something wrapped in a blanket. He laid the bundle on the bed and unwrapped the burlap, revealing a short sword.

Shade gasped and his mouth hung open. Marco walked

forward, holding the sword as if it were the most precious thing he'd ever held. "Prince Lorenzo, your *padre* didn't know I kept this, but it was his first sword, when he was just a boy. Your grandfather had this made especially for him."

Marco looked at Shade, his face filled with memories. "This was hidden during the bonfires. I've kept it safe all these years. I knew, someday, you'd give us a prince. I am honored to now pass this along to your son."

Marco bent down and handed Lorenzo the sword. "May you grow to be the warrior that will make your *padre* proud."

Lorenzo's eyes glistened as he looked at the sword his father once carried as a boy. He stepped forward to take the sword from Marco. "I'll make you and my father proud, Marco. You'll help train me, and we'll rule here together."

He was wondering now if he must wait until he was ten. He was a prince, after all. Maybe he should get started even younger.

Shade embraced Marco in a bear hug. "How will I ever repay you, brother?"

Marco released the hug, clearing his own throat, and spoke gruffly. "You can repay me," he looked down at Lorenzo, "by making him the King you are."

Shade looked down at his son. "Well, little warrior, you have had a great night, so I suggest we head back to Castello. I promised your *madre* I would not keep you here the entire night."

Lorenzo was bubbling over with excitement over the gift of a real sword, and Shade could only imagine *bel's* reaction. As they walked outside, he lifted Lorenzo on his shoulders as they took the long stroll back to Castello. "So, I guess this means you are a real warrior now, a real weapon in your hands. I practiced a lot with that sword. Tell me your thoughts, son."

Lorenzo clung to the sword, holding it against his chest. "I like Alfie, Daddy. He's going to be a great warrior, I can tell. These warriors will depend on me, won't they? Do you think I should train more with Marcello and Skelk? Do you think I should move here earlier?"

Shade chuckled to himself, the seed has been planted. "Lorenzo, I think Alfie will be a great warrior too. They will need you to lead them in time, show them how to be great warriors. You are young still, with much to learn before you join the camp. You lead by example. If you won't fight and lead yourself, how can you expect them to follow?"

Shade kept walking, letting that information sink in. "You know, Lorenzo, your *madre* and I made a deal. She wanted you to be able to have a childhood, to play without carrying the burden of responsibility you must eventually assume. I want you to grow up to be a great warrior, learn all you can, become a master and king. We have compromised, to give you a world where you get to do both. But your *madre* loves you so much, it is hard for her to let go of her little boy. She is not ready for the day when her child becomes a man and leaves her. She fears you will not need her, but we both know that will never happen, *si*?"

Lorenzo shook his head as he sat atop his father's shoulder. "I'll always need Mommy! I love her, and we have to protect her, right, Daddy? And Sophia too. That's what we do."

Shade beamed with pride. "Damn straight, little warrior. You have to do your studies. Prepare for the day when you move to the camp. But listen to me." He pulled Lorenzo from his shoulders, as the boy clung to the sword. "This is not a toy sword. It is a weapon and it can kill. This is no game, Lorenzo. This sword is not for play. This is for training."

Shade slid his hand along the hilt. "My *padre* had this made for me. I used to dream of slaying dragons just like you. That is why the hilt is made like a dragon. The dragon's long tail wraps around your hand to protect it."

Taking his hand, they walked the rest of the distance to Castello. Shade paused before going in. "I know you really like Alfie. He is about the same age as Marco was when I first came to the camp. Perhaps you could write to him. Enzo can help you with that. Then, when you move here to live, you will already have a brother. What do you think?"

Lorenzo nodded. "Yep. I can do that. And I can visit him when we come here, right? Maybe we can practice together."

"You get good with that sword, and you can do that when we come to visit. I will train you personally. Now, let us get inside to your *madre*. She will be fretting over both of us."

Once Shade opened the door, Lorenzo took off like his ass was on fire and he could only imagine the look on Kate's face when she saw the sword.

Lorenzo ran up the wide marble staircase that led to the second floor. He knew his mother remained sequestered in the master bedroom, with Emma and Theresa always close by. He came to a halt in front of the closed bedroom door. He'd been instructed to never enter his parents' bedroom when the door was closed. He tapped at the door as he heard his father's footsteps on the marble staircase behind him.

Emma opened the door and gave him a big smile. "Lorenzo! To what do we owe the pleasure of this visit today?"

Lorenzo held up the sword. "Is my mommy here? I have to show her something."

Emma stepped back from the door, swinging it open for Lorenzo to enter, just as her master appeared behind him. She nodded her head in deference to him. Lorenzo ran for the massive bed where his mother was resting, sitting up in the bed with pillows at her back.

"Mommy, look! Look what Marco gave me. A sword. A real one. It was Daddy's sword when he trained here. I'm going to train extra hard, so I can come here too, and learn from Marco. I met Alfie today, and he showed me his bed in the bunkers."

Kate locked eyes with Shade over the top of their son's head as he carried the real sword in the air. She was less than pleased to see the child with a real weapon. "Lorenzo, be careful with that. It's not a toy."

Lorenzo climbed up on the bed, pushing the sword ahead of him. "I know, Mommy. It's real. I'm a warrior and I have to learn to use it properly."

Kate gave Shade a stern look and asked him in her head,

"What were you thinking?"

Shade didn't back down, their son was warrior. **"Marco gave it to him. He kept my sword from childhood to give to my son. He is born to be a warrior. It is in his blood. I will train him myself."**

He focused his attention on Lorenzo. "Lorenzo, you need to hold your weapon properly so as not to injure anyone by mistake. No swords in the house, only on the training field. I know you are excited, but let's put the sword away for now. We can use it when we get back to Bel Rosso. Training begins then, *si*?"

Lorenzo reluctantly surrendered the sword to his father. "Okay, Daddy. But as soon as we get home, okay? And you'll tell Marcello too, right? So, he knows I can train with my real sword."

Kate hadn't acknowledged her son's enthusiasm for the sword that had been passed down now from father to son. She'd always known the day would come when Lorenzo would have to step into his legacy, but she'd hoped to delay it as long as possible. She ran her hand through the child's tangled locks, so much like his father's. "There will be time to train, Lorenzo. Right now, we have to get ready for your sister. She'll be arriving any day now. Aren't you excited?"

As Shade removed the sword from the bed, Lorenzo proceeded to jump across the wide mattress like it was a trampoline, returning quickly to the antics of a four-year-old, and forgetting the burdens of being a warrior. "Yep. I'm excited. Nita said there will be a big party and lots of people will come."

Shade placed the sword inside a chest of drawers. As he turned, he saw his little warrior reverting to his child's play, full of energy. "Lorenzo, please stop jumping on the bed, you will jiggle your sister out if you keep that up. I think it is time you go with Theresa, get your bath, and get some sleep. I need to spend some time alone with *Madre*, *si*? Give her your kisses and love. And if I were you, I would thank her for letting you join the warriors this night as well."

Lorenzo dropped to all fours and crawled toward his

mother. She leaned over and kissed him, and he placed wet kisses on her cheeks. "Good night, Mommy."

Theresa lifted him from the bed. "Come along, little warrior, let's get you in the bath."

Lorenzo waved at his parents and giggled as Theresa carried him from the room, and Emma followed, closing the door behind her to give the couple privacy.

Kate sighed and lay back against the mound of pillows, her hands surrounding the swell of her belly. She had felt mild contractions all day and knew it wouldn't be long now before Shade carried her to the chamber below the castle. "I know you'll always do what's best for him, I just hate to see him grow up. If I could protect him from the violence of this world, I would. I'd take him away from all of this, but I know that's not his fate."

Shade stripped down naked, as he prepared to take a shower. "There is violence in the mortal world as well, *mi amore*. It is not something we can escape, and as a warrior, he will learn to handle it. You can't protect him forever." He leaned over the bed and kissed her belly. "Come out, you wee vixen, I am anxious to meet my *figlia*!"

Looking up at Kate, he grinned and kissed her. "Don't fret, *bel*. Your son will be our salvation."

85

Kate sighed as she tried to get comfortable in the bed. She lay on her side, with Shade against her back, his arm draped protectively over her. He slept soundly still, and Kate was hoping the contractions would slow down. She knew he'd wake for her if she needed him, but she was hoping to hold off until sunset. She tried taking slow, deep breaths, relaxing into the contractions. Dr. Bonutti had visited her just days before. He was pleased and reminded her that the second birth would probably go much faster. She knew the chamber had already been set up in preparation for her, and the Council was on call. She felt the tightening of the muscles return, and she gripped the sheets, biting her lip, trying hard not to call out to him in pain.

From deep in his slumber, Shade felt her pain, and was immediately awake and alert. "*Mi amore*, she is close." He slipped from their bed, telepathically calling Theresa to come immediately. "It's time, *si*? What can I do to help you?"

Kate curled up in a ball, as both hands encircled her belly. He was standing beside her, asking how he could help, but she was in the middle of a contraction that took her breath away and she waited for the pain to subside before she could answer him. She reached out to him, taking his hand and nodded her head. "It's time. Your impatient daughter says she's waited long enough. Take me to the chamber, please."

Theresa arrived immediately, as he started giving her instructions. "Theresa, get to the chamber, get Gi, have him bring the Medici ledger and tell him to call the Council and Dr. Bonutti. Go now!"

Leaning down, he kissed *bel's* head. "Everyone will be here shortly. Do you need anything before I take you to the chamber?"

She shook her head as he lifted her in his arms. She had

another contraction and contorted in his arms.

"*Mi amore*, I think we need to teleport because she is coming faster than I anticipated."

As they teleported to the chamber beneath the castle, the Council members were already inside, setting up the ledgers and preparing to witness the birth. Shade eased Kate onto the stone altar Theresa had prepared with soft pillows and a comforting down coverlet.

Theresa returned to the chamber with Dr. Bonutti, who entered as if they had all the time in the world. Shade had laid Kate down on the altar, then eased himself down behind her, allowing her to rest her back against his chest, and let her get settled for the next wave of pain.

***

Lorenzo was playing with Nita in his room. He was waiting for sunset, so he could go to his parents' room. He was telling Nita about his new sword, and where his dad stored it in the wardrobe when a sensation washed over him, and he stopped talking mid-sentence.

Nita cocked her head to one side. "What's wrong, Lorenzo?"

The child took off running for the bedroom his parents shared. The door was already open, the lights were on and their bed was empty, the sheets hanging off the side of the bed. The blinds were still closed to the late evening sun, and the child felt a fleeting panic. "Mommy!"

Nita rushed up behind him and started to pick him up, but Lorenzo kicked free, fighting against her until she released him. "Lorenzo, your mommy is fine. She's been taken to the chamber where your sister will be born."

Lorenzo ran to the wardrobe in his parents' room and swung open the door, pulling the sword from behind the clothes hanging there.

Nita tried to take the sword from him. "Lorenzo, this is not a toy. Your father said it was not for play."

Lorenzo turned on her with a fierceness she'd never seen in this sweet child before, as he held the sword in front of him, daring her to take it from him. "My mommy needs me now."

He rushed past Nita as he headed for the marble staircase, and carefully navigated the stairs, trying to hold the sword in one hand as his other hand held to the massive banister. As his feet hit the floor in the grand foyer, he started to run down the long hallway, moving on instinct. He could feel his mother, feel her pain. "I'm coming, Mommy!"

He opened several doors until he found the one that led down to the chamber. He'd never been taken to the cavernous space that lay below the castle before. He'd never seen the chamber where he was born, but he could feel his mother and knew he was getting closer. He pushed the door open, and heard it creak on its hinges, and was hit by the musty smell. The stone steps were damp, and the tunnels were dark, lit only by torches hung high on the walls. The firelight cast weird shadows that flickered across the stone, and made his heart race faster. He stepped carefully down the uneven stairs, one small hand balancing him as he steadied himself against the stone wall, and his other hand dragging the sword as it clanked on the steps behind him. "Mommy?"

Rounding a corner, he saw the doctor that came to see his mommy and rushed to the entrance of the chamber. His mother was on the stone altar, lying with her back against his father's chest. Theresa was standing at the foot of the altar, administering to his mother. He stepped inside the chamber and saw the robed Council members who both looked up in surprise. He heard a cry from his mother, and saw his father soothe her, brush the hair back from her face as he whispered something in her ear. He approached the altar slowly and took her hand. "It's okay, Mommy. I'll protect you."

Kate felt her son's presence in the room, drawn to her because he felt her pain. She felt his tiny hand grip her, as he reassured her. The wave of pain passed as Kate caught her breath, preparing for the next contraction. "I'm fine, Lorenzo. Mommy is fine. It's time for your sister to come into this world. This is where you were born, and where your father was born and all the Medici Kings before him."

Lorenzo nodded as he looked around the room at the kind face of Theresa as she stood between his mother's legs, and the stern hooded faces of the Council. He looked back at his father, who cradled his mother in his arms protectively. "Don't worry, Daddy. I got this. I brought my sword, just in case."

Shade felt an overwhelming sense of pride for this child with the warrior's heart, overcoming his own fear and ready to face unknown danger to protect his mother. Malachi was about to object to the child's presence when Shade leveled him with a stare.

His eyes were pulled to a darkened corner of the chamber where he saw Christofano, standing with his *madre* to observe the birth of their next grandchild. Shade placed his hand atop Lorenzo's curls. "My son, my little warrior, you are brave this night. I'm so proud of you. I do not think you will need your sword, but you are a true Medici, coming prepared. Hold your *madre*'s hand, and together, we will help her, *si*?"

Shade kissed *bel's* neck, gently whispering in her ear, "You see, *mi amore*, your son is here to protect you."

Before the words were out, Kate screamed in pain and Theresa moved quickly between her legs to assist. Shade knew it wouldn't be long.

Kate felt the hot, wet gush between her legs as her water broke, and the contraction seized her in another grip of pain. Theresa's voice soothed her. "I can see the head, my lady. I need you to push now."

Unconsciously, she gripped Shade's thigh with one hand, pushing back hard against his chest. Her son's hand still clutched her other hand, and she squeezed hard out of reflex, and yet, he stood firm beside her, protecting her. She laid her head back on Shade's shoulder, her eyes closed to the pain, as she pushed hard to bring this new baby into the world.

She could hear Theresa's voice. "Just one more, my lady."

She was aware of Shade's lips, close to her ear, whispering soft words, encouraging her to breathe through the pain. Another contraction hit almost immediately and she bore down hard, feeling the baby slip from her body and into Theresa's capable hands.

Kate took a gasp of air as she relaxed back against Shade's chest. She opened her eyes to see Theresa holding the baby in the air, pink and squirming, her tiny fists fighting, her legs kicking, and a cry that filled the chamber. Kate laughed as tears streamed down her cheeks. Their daughter, their red-haired daughter had entered the world and was eager to let everyone know she was here. "Lorenzo, say hello to your sister, Sophia."

Lorenzo looked up at the baby Theresa held in the air. He wasn't impressed. "She looks icky."

Theresa laughed as she explained they must clean the baby up first. Lorenzo looked doubtful that anything could make this baby look presentable. "What's that rope for?" He pointed to the umbilical cord that still attached the baby to her mother. Theresa patiently explained.

"That is the umbilical cord. It is how the baby fed from your mother while she was still in the womb. But we will cut that now, and Sophia will be on her own for the first time."

Shade heaved a sigh of relief at the strong wail of his infant daughter, her small body squirming in rebellion. He laid his head atop Kate's as she rested against his shoulder. He chuckled softly at Lorenzo's reaction, clearly not impressed with his newborn sister.

As Theresa tied the thin hemp cord around the umbilicus, she handed the tiny infant to him. His daughter fit inside his two hands and was much smaller than Lorenzo was as a baby. Her head was covered in a thick mass of red curls. He bit through the umbilical cord, swallowing his infant daughter's blood, bonding them immediately. He looked at Sophia, who stopped squirming and stared back at him with huge blue eyes that looked too big for her face. She stared at him intently, as if taking his measure and his heart was filled. She was a tiny replica of Kate, with the exception of her blue eyes. She cooed loudly as her tiny fists beat at the air.

Dr. Bonutti approached and quickly inspected the baby and announced she was strong and healthy. He handed the baby to

Kate for her first feeding.

Kate took the infant in her arms and whispered. "Sophia, my impatient princess, we've waited a long time for you."

The baby stared up at her and blinked. Kate looked at her daughter, her head covered in ringlets of red hair, as red as her own, and eyes as blue as her father's. Her skin was fair, like Kate's. Kate lifted the baby to her shoulder where she rooted against her neck, her small hand grabbing a strand of Kate's hair. With her tiny feet still kicking, the baby sank tiny, sharp fangs into her mother's flesh, and drank for the first time. Kate felt the bond between mother and child, sealed for eternity.

Lorenzo watched wide-eyed. "I remember when I fed from you, Mommy."

Kate smiled at him. "Do you?"

He nodded his head vigorously. "Before Theresa, and Nita. I remember."

Shade supported his mate, letting her relax against him again and observed as mother and daughter bonded. The baby finally unlatched, and Theresa quickly took her and washed her body clean.

Shade moved from the altar and allowed Kate to lie back on the pillows as he adjusted them for her comfort. Kissing her on the lips, his heart was overwhelmed. "*Ti amo, mi amore*, you have given me a beautiful princess."

He heard Lorenzo gasp and he turned in time to see the boy lift his sword against Ivor as he approached Theresa to take the baby. "Lorenzo, lay down your weapon, little warrior. Ivor is from the Council, and they need to record the birth of your sister. Come."

Shade held out his hand and Lorenzo lowered the weapon and took his father's outstretched hand. They walked to the table where the open ledgers lie. Malachi recorded the date and name of the infant in the Council's records as he spoke out loud, "Princess Sophia of Medici, daughter of King Shade and Queen Katherine of Medici."

Malachi then scored Shade's wrist as Lorenzo intently watched. Ivor placed Sophia's foot in the blood and made the footprint in the ledger beside her name. Shade pulled Lorenzo close and flipped back the pages of the ancient ledger. "Lorenzo, look, here is your footprint on the day of your birth."

As Lorenzo looked up at him and grinned, Shade ruffled his curls. Shade then recorded the birth in the leather-bound Medici family ledger. Malachi stepped forward and initialed to witness the birth, then Shade handed the pen to Lorenzo.

"You have witnessed the birth of your sister. Your initials will be forever recorded in the history of Medici as a witness to her heritage. Will you sign now, as her brother and protector for eternity?"

Lorenzo proudly took the quill pen from his father. Enzo had taught him to write, both in print and cursive. Under the footprint made in blood, Lorenzo wrote on the ancient parchment. 'I love Sophia. Lorenzo Medici.'

Handing the pen back to his father, he looked up at him. "Is that good, Daddy?"

"That is perfect, my little warrior. She will always remember this."

Ivor returned the infant to Shade's arms, and the Council offered their congratulations as they gathered their ledger and exited the chamber, followed by Dr. Bonutti. Even in the bowels of the ancient castle, the reverberating sounds of the fireworks could be heard, along with the clanging of the church bells, announcing the arrival of the Medici Princess.

Theresa had attended to Kate, changing her gown, and replacing the soiled linens, and patiently waited for her master's instruction. "Do you wish me to take Lorenzo and leave you two alone?"

Shade looked to *bel*. "What do you wish, *mi amore*? This is your choice."

Lorenzo looked back at his mother imploringly. Kate knew the next few days would be chaos, and there would be almost no time for her to be alone with Shade, but she could see Lorenzo's need to be included in this moment of bonding. She held her hand out to Lorenzo, who scrambled up the stone altar, nestling in close to her, laying his head on his mother's shoulder and staring into the wide-open eyes of his new sister.

"We're good, Theresa. Lorenzo needs to be here to protect his sister."

Lorenzo beamed with pride as he looked up at his mother, and then to his father. "I promise to protect her, Daddy."

Shade sat beside *bel* on the stone altar as she held their two children. "I know you will, Lorenzo, but remember one thing, she is very fragile now, so we must handle her with the greatest of care."

Reaching out, he slid his finger across the infant's plump cheek, soft as velvet. Sophia turned her gaze on him. "Kate, she is so beautiful. I have never seen a *bambino* this tiny, it scares me a bit."

Kate looked at the tiny infant in her arms. "Her spirit is strong. I can feel her. She won't be a warrior like her brother, but she'll not be one to be taken lightly. She'll give Lorenzo a run for his money."

Kate chuckled as the images of her daughter's future flashed through her head, strong-willed and stubborn.

Shade threw back his head with a hearty, happy laugh. "So, she will be like her *madre*."

Shade took Sophia from Kate's arms and laid her between his knees. She immediately clutched his thumbs with a strength that startled him. "Ah, *si*, you know who your *padre* is. You also know he is warrior, and you are true Medici. *Cazzo*, you are so beautiful, Princess."

As she cooed, he lifted her gently to his shoulder. She gripped his long curls and yanked. "*Mi amore*, she is making a stand already."

Kate gave him a stern look. "Could we please not have her first word be *cazzo*?"

Lorenzo covered his mouth with his hand as he giggled. He'd heard the word used all the time in the camp and got scolded whenever he repeated it.

"*Si*, my apologies, but she is beautiful."

Shade felt a soft hand on his back and felt the spirit of his own *madre* surround him. His voice was soft, as he closed his eyes, "*Madre*."

Portia leaned over her son's shoulder, beaming as she stared into the eyes of her granddaughter. Shade heard a soft gasp and immediately looked at Lorenzo. "Lorenzo, tell me what is wrong."

"Who is that lady?"

Portia's voice was soft in his ear, as she spoke to Shade, "My *figlio*, he can see me, but only when you are with him. He can talk to me, but not hear me. I can hear him, though. He is a beautiful warrior. Tell him."

"Lorenzo, this is my *madre*, Portia. She is your *nonna*, your grandmother. She lives here, forever in the spirit realm. You may see her sometimes when we come here to Castello. You can talk to her, and she can hear you, but you can't hear her response. She loves you and she is very proud of you. Your *nonno* is here as well, his name is Christofano. You have seen their portraits here on the walls. Do you understand? There is nothing to be frightened about."

Lorenzo stared back at the lady with the blonde hair piled on her head and dressed in an elegant gown. Her face was kind and loving, and Lorenzo smiled back at her and nodded. "Your mommy? Did she take care of you like my mommy?"

"Oh, *si*, Lorenzo, she loved me and took care of me, just like your mommy. I will always love her, just like you will always love Mommy."

Shade smiled at Kate, as Portia laid her hand on Kate's shoulder.

Kate laid her cheek against Portia's hand. She could feel the love Portia had for her son, and for this new baby. Kate spoke to her. "I know you'd follow us home to Bel Rosso if you could, and I have a feeling I'll wish you were there. I'll have two to keep up with now."

Portia looked at the small babe. "I'm with you in spirit, daughter, but you are right. This one will be a handful. Do not let my son spoil her overly much. She is not a warrior, but she is Medici and she will have her own role to play. All of your children are vital to the legacy that is Medici."

Shade shook his head at her words. "I will always spoil my *bambinos*, *Madre*. It is my right as their *padre*."

She chuckled softly, kissing Kate on the cheek. Christofano stepped up behind her. "Come, *mi amore*, let them have their time as *familia*."

Lorenzo's eyes grew big as saucers, as he took in the imposing figure of his grandfather, as they disappeared together, arm in arm. Shade looked at his growing family, four of them now, five including his son, Cory. There was much to do in the next hours and days, and he knew they couldn't stay in the chamber forever.

"*Bel*, are you ready to return to our bedchamber? I think it is getting colder in here, and I know you would be much more comfortable. Are you ready for your warriors to escort their Queen and Princess back to the comforts of this great castle?"

Kate pulled the clean white sheets around her. "You lead, and I will follow."

"As it shall always be, *mi amore*. Come, we will have a short rest, and then, I fear, we must face the coven who will be clamoring to see their new princess."

Making sure Sophia was secure with Kate, he let Lorenzo climb on his back and he lifted Kate easily into his arms. "Everyone hold on tight. *Per sempre* Medici!"

As he teleported them all inside their huge bedchamber, he could already hear the ruckus of his warriors and his people as they heard the celebrations begin in Florence.

86

The household had been chaotic since Sophia's birth. They'd gotten through her presentation to the coven from the balcony, and now were preparing for the ball. Shade donned the suit that had been custom made for the occasion, as Emma helped Kate with her hair. Theresa had dressed Lorenzo in a suit that looked much like his father's and was now dressing Sophia. The infant was placed in a long white gown, before being wrapped in soft blankets.

The castle was already filling with the masters and mates of other European covens, as well as a few masters from other parts of the world. In the vampire community, there weren't many surviving lines of royal blood, so a birth from a royal family was something to be celebrated.

Shade checked himself in the full-length mirror one last time, and caught the reflection of his beautiful *bel,* as Emma assisted her with her dress. She wore a gown as black as the raven's wing, sharply contrasted against her lily white skin. The scoop of the neckline exposed the soft swell of her plump breasts, and her hair lay in perfect ringlets on her shoulders.

He swallowed hard and licked his lips. He hadn't fed from her in so long now, and the exposed skin of her neck and shoulders called to him. The Medici jewels lay shimmering around her neck, as the diamonds dangled from her ears, reflecting back the light. He looked at her from the tips of her heeled feet to the top of her crimson head. She was always beautiful to him, but it had been a long time since he'd seen her dressed in a gown, resplendent in her jewels, and she left him speechless.

Their eyes meet in the reflected image and his love for her was communicated through his gaze. She smiled back at him with a wicked grin, knowing full well the effect she had on him. He'd need to be patient. She'd let him know when he could return to her.

Emma zipped up the back of the long black gown as Kate inhaled, pulling in her waist. The beaded gown was cut low in front to display a discreet amount of cleavage, but was cut extremely low in the back, to the top of her derriere. Emma had assisted her in her bath, and once she was dried off, had covered her skin in a rose-scented lotion infused with crushed pearls. The lotion made Kate's pale skin glisten, and the light reflected off the pearls.

Emma smiled at her. "My lady, I have never seen you so beautiful."

Kate laughed. "Yeah, well, it's a step up from jeans, isn't it?"

Emma gave her a quick once over and added a few spritzes of Kate's perfume, when Kate waved her hand. "That's enough, Emma."

Shade turned from the mirror and couldn't take his eyes off of her.

He took her hand and spun her around slowly, as he suppressed a low growl, deep in his throat. He admired her exposed back, and the curve of her gorgeous ass. "Your master will be keeping a close eye on you tonight, for every vampire will be jealous of this gorgeous creature. *Cazzo*, you are beautiful, *mi amore*."

Kissing her on each cheek, he looked into those eyes. His love for her overwhelmed him.

"So, do you wish for your king to have his hair down or tied back? Not that a damn soul will notice me with you on my arm."

She smiled back at him and loved the mischievous glint in his eyes. "I like your hair down. I know it's probably not as formal looking when you're wearing a suit, but it reminds me of my warrior underneath all that finery." She ran her hand through his long hair, as it hung in loose waves around his face. "Is there time for a kiss? Or are you going to drag me out of here to stand in some boring ball all evening, and make me wait for a taste of you?"

"You tempt me, *mi amore*, you tempt my beast. What I would not give to remove you from the dress, and have you naked beneath me, as I make love to you all night long. But a kiss will have to do, unfortunately."

Emma had been clearing away things in the bedroom as things were heating up between her master and my lady, when she decided this would be a good time to slip out.

He nuzzled gently into her neck, his heart racing, as he felt her heart beating in her vein, her scent alone turned his cock to steel. He kissed her forehead, before he placed a soft kiss on each eyelid. His lips moved to hers, ravishing her with a deep kiss that would drop any female to her knees. Breaking the long kiss, he stared into her eyes. "I love you, Kate."

Kate succumbed to his kiss, melting into him, but before she could respond, Lorenzo came flying into the room, with Theresa on his heels.

"Daddy, look at me! I got a suit just like you."

Shade sighed and lowered his head. He was always glad to see his son, but there were times when he wondered if he'd ever lay with his mate again. He stooped down and lifted the boy up in his arms. "I do believe we will make your mommy proud tonight, two handsome, well-dressed warriors, *si*? Does not your mommy look beautiful?"

Lorenzo looked at his mother. "Mommy, you look sparkly!"

Kate laughed. "I'll take that as a compliment, Lorenzo."

Gita, the new feeder chosen for Sophia, appeared with the baby, wrapped in soft white blankets. Sophia was awake and wide-eyed, taking in her surroundings. Kate took the baby and looked around the room. "Where's Cory? We need everyone here before we go to the ballroom."

***

Cory and Madison made their way down the long hallway to the master suite. Cory was tugging at his tie. "I hate suits, they make me feel uncomfortable. But you look awesome, Maddie. Don't be nervous, it's just a big party."

Madison had felt like she'd been living in a fantasy world ever since they'd arrived. She and Cory had a private maid and butler, and she never left their bedroom without one of them, for fear of getting lost in this castle. They had toured all over

Florence and had been given access to private galleries that stored art pieces rarely seen by the public, not to mention, the art that had been kept from mortal view inside Castello. They had dined on the richest food, and drank expensive wine, and now she was wearing a one-of-a-kind Versace gown that was made just for her.

"How can I not be nervous, Cory? I have no idea what to expect. Everything's been so over the top, so far!"

Holding Cory's hand, they stepped into the master bedroom to find Shade holding onto Lorenzo's hand, both of them in matching suits, and Lorenzo looking like a miniature version of Shade. It made Madison smile in spite of herself. Kate looked radiant in her black gown as she held Sophia in her arms. "Wow. You guys would look great on a Christmas card."

Shade chuckled. "You look quite beautiful, yourself, Madison. I am honored to have you join us this evening. Now, let's get moving. We have about 400 guests awaiting our arrival and I am sure they are emptying barrels of Midnight by now."

As they approached the ballroom, they could hear the sound of laughter and conversation over the live band. The ballroom doors were closed, awaiting their entrance. Shade stopped outside the doors where they were joined by Luca, Shannon, Marco, and Hyde. Luca and Shannon were dressed formally, but the warriors were in their dress leathers, and armed. His warriors would be lining the walls of the ballroom. Although all the invited guests were allies and friends, he'd take no chances.

"Okay, we will be properly announced before we enter. Luca and Hyde, please escort Shannon and Madison inside, and take a seat at the family table. Go, now. I want the women seated before we enter."

The warriors entered, escorting the two mortal females, ahead of the royal family.

"Cory, I want you to stand next to Kate. Lorenzo, you hold my hand, and stand between me and Mommy, *si*?"

Everyone lined up, with Marco at their back. "Are you

ready, my queen?"

Kate smiled back at him as he took charge, orchestrating the events for the evening. "I'm ready. And your princess is ready to meet her following."

Shade nodded and heard the music stop. Antonio swung open the doors and the crowd grew silent, as Antonio announced their arrival. Shade led them inside the massive ballroom, as the crowd applauded loudly.

Shade scanned the room, seeing old, familiar faces, and a few new ones. He led his family to their table and Cory made his way to sit beside Madison. Hyde took up his position a few feet behind them. Luca was already seated next to Shannon, as Shade pulled out the seat for Kate, and Marco stood near.

The table was set with the finest of settings, each glass already filled with Midnight. Shade lifted his glass to the crowd.

"Your Queen and I are honored that you join us this night. It is with the greatest pride I present the first Princess born within the walls of Castello in more than a thousand years, giving us further assurance of the continuation of the Medici royal blood line. I have my queen, the love of my life, to thank for these gifts. Please raise your glasses to Princess Sophia Medici!"

Shade took *bel's* hand and lifted her from her seat as she held Sophia for all to see. The guests, all resplendent in their formal attire, stood and toasted the new princess.

Kate pushed the soft white blankets back from Sophia's face, as the baby looked wide-eyed at the crowd, as if she knew all this hoopla was just for her. Kate shook her head as she looked at her daughter. "You are quite something, aren't you? Don't get too used to it. Your life at Bel Rosso will not be so grand as this."

Sophia cooed and gurgled, lifting her small hands free of the confines of the blanket, as if she wanted to embrace the experience. Kate could feel her small feet kicking.

Kate laughed. "You know this is all about you, don't you?" She passed the baby to her father, where he could formally present her to the crowd.

Shade smiled down at his restless daughter. "*Si*, you are definitely my princess. Come; let us show you off, shall we?" He held her high in the air, so all could see her beautiful face and red hair. Their guests lifted their glasses in unison.

"Salute!" they shouted in a loud roar.

Shade held his daughter against his chest, puffed out with pride. "Please, let us all celebrate her arrival. Enjoy your evening."

As everyone began to chatter, the band began to play, and Shade sat down, holding his infant daughter. "They all think you are beautiful, *si*? But no one will love you like your *padre*."

Kate took a sip of Midnight. "Of that, I have no doubt. I pity the young man who comes to call on the daughter of the Medici."

Shannon laughed loudly. "Seriously? Who'd ever have the nerve?"

Luca smiled to himself but didn't speak. He knew any vampire who wanted the hand of the Medici Princess would have a challenging maze of obstacles to overcome. Turning to Shannon, who looked resplendent in her gown, Luca asked her to dance. She graciously accepted, and he led her to the dance floor.

Cory saw Luca make the first move and turned to ask Madison to dance.

"Cory, it's a waltz or something. I don't know how to dance like that!"

He laughed as he took her hand. "Just fake it. We'll just dance slowly, no one cares."

He helped her from the chair and led her to the dance floor, where others were starting to gather as well. Shade passed the warm bundle that was his daughter into the hands of Theresa, with Marco standing close by, as he turned his attention to Kate.

"And now, *mi amore*, before we are interrupted once again, may I have this dance?"

Kate smiled at him as they locked eyes, and he took her hand as she rose from the chair. He whisked her to the middle of the ballroom, where he held her close as they swayed to the music.

His hand slid down the bare skin of her back until it was resting at the base of her spine. Nuzzling into her neck, he breathed in the rose scent that had lured him from the beginning. "You are so beautiful, Kate. I am so proud of you. You are so loved by our coven. How did this happen?"

She looked back at those impossibly blue eyes and answered him. "You found me, as I recall, and stalked me, in fact, now that I think about it. You seduced me in my dreams and showered me with love. I think that's how it happened."

He laughed at her. "*Si*, you never stood a chance." He pulled her close, protecting the love he held most precious when he felt a hand on his shoulder. They stopped dancing as he turned to see who interrupted him and was momentarily left speechless.

Donatella stood before him, looking as exotic as he remembered. She was the vampire of royal blood his father had arranged for him to marry when he was still a child. "Donatella. Excuse me, I did not expect to see you here, but I am honored you have joined us to celebrate the birth of our Princess. Kate, this is Donatella, she is the female *Padre* had arranged for me to mate when I was young."

He could already feel the fires of jealously building inside of Kate. "Donatella, this is my mate, my queen, and the mother of my children, Katherine Medici."

Kate felt the smile leave her face as the woman stood close to Shade, her hand slipping around his arm. She was almost as tall as he was, her skin a golden bronze, her thick black hair tumbled around her shoulders, and her eyes so brown they were almost black. She looked exotic, with almond-shaped eyes, high cheekbones, and thick lashes. Her gown clung to her toned body, and her ample breasts were barely contained. The woman stared back at her with defiance, as if Kate was the intruder not her.

Kate felt her pulse race and tried to reel in her emotions. Making no attempt to hide her displeasure, she responded coldly, "Nice to meet you."

Donatella gave her a cold smile in return. "I'm sure it is. I've heard so much about you." Turning to Shade, she stroked his arm, feeling the familiar strength of him beneath the tailored suit. "And you. Who would have ever thought you would have been so domesticated. You were always such a proud warrior. Your father saw so much potential in our mating. I often wonder what my life would be like now had you not been so adamant about going against his will. You always fought him, you know? Resisting his direction when he only wanted what was best for you."

Shade felt the volcano boiling inside *bel as* Donatello stood proud beside him. She was the mistress of her own coven, a queen, the only child of a royal blood master, who was now dead and gone. She had always been conniving and sly in her younger days, and he saw not much had changed.

He removed her hand from his arm, where she had continued to stroke him. "You should not dwell on old times, Dona. That is ancient history for both of us. I am far from domesticated, still a warrior, master and king, you would do well to remember such. My *padre* knew nothing of my heart. He lived according to his times, but I chose a different path. This is my life."

He felt a sharp pull on his coat tail and looked down to find Lorenzo. "Daddy, can we go now?"

Donatella immediately knelt down to the boy and ruffled his hair with her hand. "And you must be Lorenzo. What a handsome prince you are, so like your father. Are you going to be a fierce warrior too?"

Lorenzo nodded with enthusiasm. "I am! I already have a sword and I go with Daddy to the camps."

Donatella looked at him with sad eyes, thinking this child should be hers. "And I assume you will be coming here to train as well? It is what all the young Medici warriors aspire to."

Lorenzo grinned. "When I'm ten! Daddy says I will train with Marco."

Donatella stroked his cheek. "You are a most handsome

boy, and I am sure you will live up to your father's legend, in more ways than one."

Lorenzo nodded as Donatella stood up and linked her arm through Shade's. Still looking at Lorenzo, she explained. "I have known your father for many years. Our families go way back. We share a lot of history together." Turning her attention to Shade, she whispered, "Don't we, Medici?"

Shade ignored her whisper. "Lorenzo, this is Donatella, she is the mistress of a coven that borders ours, in Umbria. I have known her since we were children." Turning back to Donatella, he once again disengaged from her clutches. "Now, if you will excuse us, I have a family and many guests to attend too."

Donatella nodded and leaned in, kissing him softly on the cheek, and he knew he was going to pay for that later.

Kate slipped her arm around Shade and gently pulled him away, indicating her desire to move away from this bitch. She took Lorenzo's hand and led him as well. "Come on, Lorenzo. We have a lot of people to meet tonight."

Kate was gritting her teeth, biting back her anger at the intrusion of the female. She'd known, for years, that Shade had been promised to another by his father, but Shade had never spoken her name. She was less than pleased to have this woman insert herself into their life.

Lorenzo walked with them. "She's a nice lady, isn't she?"

Kate looked down at her son's innocent face and closed her eyes. He shouldn't be tainted with her anger, which she knew was irrational. Whatever existed between Shade and Donatella was long over. "Of course, Lorenzo, I'm sure she's very nice." Turning to Shade, she gave him a look that said otherwise.

***

Marco watched closely as Donatello made her move on his oldest friend. He was well aware Dona was once promised to him, and everyone in the coven knew she'd never gotten over Shade's rejection of the mating contract. "There's going to be fireworks over this one, Terri. Look at our queen's face. *Cazzo*, she wants to rip her apart. I hope like hell she doesn't call in her wolves."

Theresa looked up to see Donatello, and she could feel Kate's anger from here. Moving closer to Marco, she slid her arm around his waist. "Donatella is well-known in Tuscany. Her territory of Umbria borders with Shade's. It's the reason Shade's father wanted them to mate."

Donatella had remained bitter at Shade's rejection of mating, and she had tried, for centuries, to lure him in. Theresa knew Shade had a history with her, as she had made herself more than available to him, as did every eligible female. But he'd never commit to her, and his rejection of committing to mating with her had made her a bitter and angry female, scaring off any suitable potential mates to share her bed, and rule her coven, producing heirs. She wasn't an enemy to the Medici. She'd never take up arms against their coven, but Theresa could see no good coming from this.

"Let's just keep our fingers crossed, Marco, that her visit is a short one."

87

Now that the grand ball to herald Sophia's entry into the coven had been held, Luca knew he'd have some free time before they all returned to Bel Rosso. After making rounds in the camp, and seeing a lot of new faces, he let Shade and Marco both know he'd be leaving for a few days to take Shannon to Empoli, and his ancestral home.

Returning to their bedroom, he found her packing. "You won't need to take much, *mia belleza*. Just a few days, and we'll probably stay on the grounds."

Shannon held up a thong, dangling from her forefinger. "Is this too much?"

He laughed and shook his head. "No, I think that will be just right. Are you ready? I'll have the luggage loaded in the car."

Shannon closed the suitcase and grabbed her handbag and a light jacket. "I'm ready when you are."

Luca had chosen a silver Alfa Romeo for their trip, and the car was brought around to the main entrance where the luggage was thrown into the trunk. Shannon slipped into the passenger's seat and locked her seat belt. She'd ridden with Luca before, and his foot didn't seem to know the car had a brake pedal.

They peeled out of the driveway and began the short drive to Empoli, across the Tuscan countryside. It was early fall, and the vineyards had been harvested, and the trees were starting to turn. The air was crisp, and the sky was a brilliant blue. Shannon was remembering her first and only visit to his home several years ago. They didn't often get this much time away from his responsibilities to Shade, but she knew since their last visit, the lemon groves had been expanded, and the Medici's had added a brand of Limoncello to their expansive wine selection. Luca was a very rich man, but still a man whose life was controlled by his master.

They approached the villa as they crested the hill, and it

was as beautiful as Shannon remembered. Luca pulled into the gravel driveway and parked the car. He exited the vehicle and rounded the car to open her door. Taking her hand, she stood and looked around at the house and surrounding grounds. Breathing in the fresh air with a hint of citrus, she looked back at him. "Do you think we'll ever live here, Luca?"

Luca turned to look at the house, his head flooded with the memories of his childhood. "It's not a promise I can make at this time, *mia belleza*. But who knows, *si*? My only wish is to have you in my life, wherever it leads me."

She took his hand as they walked to the front door of the villa. "Well then, let's make sure that happens, shall we?"

He led her into the house and up the stairs to his childhood bedroom. The house had electricity, but didn't have central heating, so Luca set to work building a fire in the bedroom fireplace, the firewood conveniently stacked by the hearth, no doubt by the staff from Castello. As the flames licked upward, Shannon slipped out of her clothes and into the large bed, pulling the blankets up over her shoulders. "Seriously, how did you sleep here in the winter?"

Luca laughed as he stoked the fire. "My mother would warm bricks in the fire, and then wrap them in towels and place them in my bed. It would warm the mattress and blankets and keep me warm until my own body heat could warm the bed. My father would get up during the night to stoke the fire in their bedroom, and then come to my room to do the same. He made sure the fires never went out. I can still see him in my head. I could see his silhouette against the flames as he laid more wood on the fire. He'd tiptoe in so as not to wake me, and I'd always pretend to be asleep. My father was not a demonstrative man. He didn't show his feelings. This act, of keeping me warm at night, I knew it was an act of love, a father protecting his child.

We live in very different times, do we not?"

Shannon stared back at him from the bed. "I really can't imagine it, Luca. I mean, I've been with you now for years, and I've heard you and Shade, and the others, make reference to events I've only read about in history books, and I still can't wrap my head around it, the idea that you lived through those times."

Luca undressed and joined her under the blankets, pulling her close. "I understand. But once you're turned, you'll live with me through eternity."

He kissed her, and she responded, feeling the warmth of his skin, and inhaling his masculine scent. He ran his tongue along her neck, and nipped at her skin as she lay her head back, offering herself up to him.

"Tonight, I'll feed from you, and then, *mia belleza*, for the first time, you'll feed from me. You'll be bonded to me then. I won't yet own you. That will only come with the turning. But you'll feel me in a way you haven't felt me in the past. You'll hear my thoughts as clearly as I hear yours. But this must be your choice. To be mated to me, you must come freely. Tell me now this is what you want."

Without words, she slid her hand behind his head, and drew him down to her neck to feed. He sank his teeth into her tender flesh and she felt the familiar flash of heat between her legs and gasped.

He rolled over on top of her, his cock already hard as he slid his hand between her legs, pushing them open to make way for him. As he plunged deep inside her, she gave in to the desire she'd fought since the first time he'd made love to her, and she bit hard into his shoulder, his blood hitting her tongue. She drank from him and felt the passion rise, the primal need to have him buried deep inside her, spilling his seed. She drank and wrapped her legs in a vice grip around his hips. As she fed from him, she heard his low growl.

She clung to him, her nails in his back as he rode her. Her lips broke free as her orgasm overtook her, and she cried out, her voice echoing through the house, until his mouth covered her, and she tasted her blood on his lips, mixing with his.

She was his. She was bonded to this man now, and she sighed as he collapsed on top of her.

Rolling off her, he asked, "Still cold?"

Shannon laughed as she rolled on top of him. "I think I still feel a chill in the air."

88

Kate was enjoying the quiet that followed the ceremony surrounding Sophia's birth, and her presentation to the coven. The castle had been a flurry of activity and excitement, and the staff had been as eager to see and welcome Sophia as they had with Lorenzo. The baby was still being fed exclusively by Kate but would start the process of being weaned to Theresa and Gita shortly.

Sophia fed well, but kicked and squirmed, as if she was already eager to be free of her mother's arms. Theresa took the baby from Kate. "Why don't you take a break, my lady? This one is a handful. I don't think she's going to be as cooperative as her brother."

Kate laughed as she stood from the rocker. "Thank you, Theresa. I don't know what I'd do without you. I'd love to get out of this castle and get some fresh air."

Theresa nodded her approval as Emma handed her a wrap for her shoulders. "It may be chilly in the night air, my lady, take a wrap please."

Kate accepted the lightweight cashmere wrap and draped it around her shoulders as she left the suite. Making her way down the marble stairs, she could hear Lorenzo's voice as it echoed through the halls. As she reached the grand foyer, she followed the sound down the Hall of Ancestors to the music room where Lorenzo was demonstrating his sword skills to Shade and Marco.

Kate sighed with exasperation as she'd spoken to Lorenzo many times about practicing with weapons in the house. "Lorenzo!"

The boy stopped the sword play and looked at her with innocent eyes. Kate nodded her head in the direction of the French doors that led outside. "Outside, please."

Lorenzo looked crestfallen but answered, "Yes, Mommy."

Kate joined Shade as he slipped his arm around her waist

and they followed Lorenzo and Marco outside. "Lover, you know I don't want him to play with that weapon in the house. He has a lot of space here, but not so much at Bel Rosso. And you're letting him use the real sword?"

Marco gave Shade a sideways glance. **"Busted, old man. That collar you're wearing looks pretty tight."**

Shade glared back at him as he led *bel* outside into the fresh crisp air. **"Fuck off, you old leather ass goat."** He returned his full attention to his mate and his son. "*Si*, I am, *mi amore*. He needs to get used to the weight of it, how it feels in his hand. He is warrior. On another note, how is Sophia? Is everything fine with our princess? I'm surprised to see you leave her."

Kate smiled in spite of herself. Leaning her head against his shoulder, she answered him. "Sophia is fine and in the capable hands of Theresa and Gita. And you, sir, are the master of redirection. I didn't miss how you shifted that conversation away from Lorenzo so deftly."

He walked with her through the gardens as Kate kept a close eye on their son sparring with Marco. "I never have envisioned Marco as being so good with children. He seems so crusty and grumpy sometimes. But Lorenzo clearly loves him."

Shade chuckled. "Lorenzo can be intimidated by Marco. But, let's face it. Marco can take some getting used to, *si*? Lorenzo has had a taste of the camp, met some of the young warriors, and saw what Marco has accomplished with them firsthand. The exposure was good for him. And Marco gave him the sword. Marco is not supposed to be his friend but his teacher. They will have a bond, for sure, and Lorenzo will grow to love him, but Marco will always try to keep the upper hand, as it should be. Lorenzo must grow into his role. He will rule here, and he already grasps the enormity of that responsibility. I hope I can guide him properly, teach him all he needs to learn to survive as king and warrior. On a separate note, he can't make a decision on what pony he wants. We visited every breeder in Tuscany. "

Kate squeezed his arm. "Lorenzo will rise to greatness. I see glimpses of his future. He'll be a powerful king, and the coven is loyal to him, as they are to you. But I'm surprised he can't find a pony to his liking. Lorenzo loves every animal he's ever seen. I would have thought he'd have picked the first one you showed him. He'd bring every creature from the woods home to live with us if he could. Did he say why he didn't like the ponies you've shown him?"

"No, *mi amore*, he didn't. Perhaps, you should ask him, if you can lure him away from his sword." He grabbed her softly around her waist, stealing a warm kiss under the full moon in Florence. "You are good at getting to the heart of a warrior."

Kate laid against his chest, listening to the beat of his heart. She was about to turn to address her son when Antonio interrupted them.

"Excuse me master, my lady, but Mistress Alizzi is here with a gift."

Kate looked up at Antonio. "Who?"

Antonio bowed his head to her. "Donatella Alizzi, the Mistress of Umbria. I believe you met her at Sophia's ball?"

Kate immediately stiffened in Shade's arms and spoke to him through gritted teeth, "What's she doing here? Did you invite her?"

"*Bel*, I would not invite her here without telling you."

As Marco and Lorenzo walked up beside them, Shade gave direction to the majordomo. "See her inside, Antonio. Exactly what kind of gift, can you be more specific?"

"Uh, it is not a gift I think you want inside Castello, master. She has brought a pony. Shall I escort her here around back?"

Shade didn't answer immediately. His mind was reeling. Leave it to Dona to bring such an extravagant gift without asking his permission. It hadn't taken the rumor mill long to spread the word he'd been searching for a pony. Lorenzo was already jumping up and down and squealing in excitement.

"*Si*, Antonio. Bring her here."

As Antonio left to escort Donatella to the gardens behind the castle, Kate turned to Shade. "Are you going to accept this gift from her? I'm not sure I want our son to be beholding to this woman. Can we talk about this please?"

Before he could answer, Donatella rounded the corner of the castle, leading a Frisian pony that looked like a miniature replica of Impavido. Lorenzo took off like a bullet, running and squealing in the direction of Donatella. "That's it! That's the pony I want. Look, Daddy. He looks just like Pavi."

Kate felt her heart sink. She wouldn't deny her son this gift, even if it meant the unwelcome intrusion of this woman in their lives.

Shade shared a look with Marco, who knew well the ancient history Shade shared with Donatella. He, too, would prefer not to have Dona too close. "I do believe, *mi amore*, that your son has left little time for talk. Come."

Grabbing her hand, he led her to Dona and the pony. Shade knew damn well Dona was aware of what she'd done. It was a well calculated move on her part. "Dona, we meet again. This is a very generous gift, but one we cannot accept."

Lorenzo wailed. "No, Daddy. I want this one. Please, he's just like Pavi. This is my pony!"

Donatella ruffled the boy's hair as she easily lifted him up and placed him on the back of the solid black pony, his coat brushed so clean he glistened even in the moonlight.

"Come on, Shade. You would not deny your child this gift, would you? Please don't let our history come between us. I know how you are attached to Impavido, and your son should have the same experience, *si*? A horse and the rider, they choose each other, do they not? And it looks like your son has chosen this pony."

Kate was gripping Shade's arm tightly. Her eyes never left Donatella's face. This one was a master manipulator and she'd keep a watchful eye on her.

Shade looked into his son's pleading eyes. Lorenzo sat atop the pony, his small face buried in the long wavy mane of the Frisian. "*Si*, a master and his horse bond in a special way. They must feel something special between them. This is a beautiful pony." Shade slipped his fingers beneath Lorenzo's chin, and gently lifted his face, starring deep into his son's blue eyes.

"Lorenzo, are you sure this is the one you want?"

Lorenzo looked back at his father and nodded his head. "Daddy, I love him already. He's mine. I can tell!"

"*Si*, then you may keep him."

Shade motioned Marco forward. "Take the pony and Lorenzo to the stables, let him ride over there a bit, stay with him."

Shade let Antonio know he wished drinks to be served in the garden. "Lorenzo, Marco will take you to the stables, you may ride him there, but only at a slow pace until I can ride with you, *si*?"

Shade waited until the boy was far enough away he couldn't hear their conversation, then turned his attention to Donatella. "You knew he would never be able to resist that pony, Dona. But I will not accept this as a gift, I will insist on paying you for the pony. Antonio is bringing us drinks to the garden, let us all go and sit, decide the price. No argument."

Donatella slipped her arm into his as she walked beside him. "Oh Shade, you know I don't need your money. And it is the least I can do. Our territories border each other, our covens have worked together for centuries in the vineyards. Surely, you can accept this small token from an old friend."

Donatella looked up at the cold stare from his mate. "Tell him, Kate. It is a gift and a down payment on our future. Lorenzo will rule here one day, and we want to continue the good relationship that exists between our two covens."

Antonio arrived with the drinks and they all took a seat on the portico. Kate stared back at her as she accepted her drink. "I'll follow my mate's lead. Don't try to come between us, Donatella."

Dona's laugh was shrill as she tossed her head back. Taking a seat on the other side of Shade, she accepted the glass of Midnight. "As if I could. He has clearly chosen his mate, although, I must say, I never expected a mortal. His father was so adamant he marry royal blood, but then, Shade had a way of defying his father in all things."

Shade took a sip from his glass before responding, "You will take the money, Dona, we insist. Our son will learn such rewards are earned, not handed to him."

He leaned back in the chair and crossed his ankle over his knee, taking another sip of Midnight. "You, of all people, should know it is important for us to instill those values in him. His life will be privileged as it is. He should not expect everything to be handed to him on a platter. And yes, my *padre* wanted our covens united. We shared borders, and an alliance would have made both covens stronger. Both of our fathers were powerful kings, and I understood my *padre*'s reasoning for wanting us to mate. But, my heart was not there, Dona, never was. My parents' mating was arranged, as were the matings of all of my ancestors before them, but my *padre* had a great love for my *madre*. I wanted the same, and my *madre* understood. My heart was waiting for Kate. She may have been mortal, but no longer. Without her, I am nothing. Together, we have assured the legacy of the Medici. Someday, after he finishes his training as a warrior, and travels the world to learn the mortal ways, Lorenzo will rule here."

Donatella stretched out her long, lean body, breathing deep the sweet night air. "Ah yes, his worldly travels, so important to a young vampire's growth and maturity, are they not, Medici? It is so important to sow those wild oats when we are young. Let us hope young Lorenzo does not completely follow in his father's footsteps. I fear your beautiful Kate will find her lovely red locks will have turned grey if that is the case. I wonder, Medici, what your own *padre* would have thought of our exploits? Do you remember Venice, and your old friend Casanova?"

She laughed with abandon as she downed the glass and poured herself another. "I thought, for sure, I had won you over then, but it was not to be. There was never enough for the young, virile Medici, was there? Always searching for the next conquest."

Kate was watching the sparring match between them and wasn't happy with the direction of this conversation.

Shade nodded, acknowledging the memories. "Ah, my

friend Casanova, he was wicked with the ladies. But he could not best the Medici."

Shade reached over and clinked glasses with Dona. "But this is no news to my *bel rosso*, she knows of my past, Dona, and she also knows those days are well over. I have left all of them behind me. All of them, even you."

Turning to Kate, he slid his hand slowly down her cheek. "You see, Dona, when I found my intended mate, this warrior laid down his heart and soul for the beauty before me. She is loved like no other."

He lifted Kate's hand to his lips, locking eyes with her. "You should think about mating, yourself, Dona. You need progeny to assure the future of your coven. You will always be at risk without a master. The Medici have long provided protection, but it is not the same."

Donatella ignored his suggestion as she watched the display of affection. Shade may laugh off his past, but his mate wasn't laughing. She may know of his exploits, but she wasn't pleased. She took another sip from her glass. "I must say, Medici, you have found a very understanding and forgiving mate. I'm not sure all would be so forgiving. You would don the mask at Venetian Carnival, and even with your handsome face disguised, you would take the women, two and three at a time, both mortal and immortal. Your appetite knew no bounds. And the women were so pleasured. They would always come back for more."

Kate was steaming mad at this woman, who was clearly seeking to cause trouble. She was about to speak up when Lorenzo came running back toward them, breathless. "Mommy, this is the best pony ever!"

Kate caught him in her arms and told him he must thank Miss Donatella for thinking of him. Lorenzo ran and climbed into Donatella's lap, where she welcomed him with a big hug.

"You are so welcome, Lorenzo. And feel free to visit my castle in Umbria anytime. The Alizzi and the Medici go way back. We are two great families that have ruled in Italy for centuries."

Lorenzo planted a wet kiss on her cheek and the woman

hugged him close, her lips close to the child's ear as she whispered, "You look so much like your father, it breaks my heart."

Lorenzo pulled back from her and touched her cheek. "Don't be sad, Miss Dona. I'll visit you."

Kate scooped up the boy from Donatella's clutches. "Let's get you inside, shall we? It's getting past your bedtime."

The boy waved goodbye to Donatella, flashing her a bright smile. "I love my pony. Thank you forever!"

Donatella turned to Shade as his mate carried the young boy away. "It could have been us, Medici. In fact, it should have been us. We should rule here together, with our children."

Shade stood to go inside, turning his back on Donatella. "It was never going to be us, Dona. It's time you go back home. I will have the funds for the pony sent to you tomorrow."

He heard her stand and start to approach, and he spun on her, his face calm but his tone deadly. "Before you go, there is something you need to know. My *madre* was right about you all along. She saw the darkness inside you, and to be honest, so did I. My *padre* was too consumed in securing an alliance to look too deeply. I know I once carried that darkness inside me as well, but no longer. Kate is my light. I won't bother to explain, you will never understand what it feels like to love deeply, and have that love returned unconditionally. I live and breathe for her."

Walking to her, he stood nose to nose, and could feel her breath on his face. "My *madre* went to battle for me, over you. The only time in her life she ever went against my *padre*, and she never backed down. You may have come between them, but only for a time because they died together, loved together, conquered together. You will never come between me and my mate. There was nothing of substance between us, and never will be, so go home, take your memories with you."

Stepping aside, he walked back into Castello, never looking back.

Donatella watched him go, his shoulders broad, his back strong. She'd laid beneath him many a night, and shared him with other women as well, but she knew those days were behind him. She didn't doubt his loyalty to his mate, but there was more than one path to gain what she wanted. Her coven was at risk, and she'd mate with a Medici if it was the last thing she did. "You can't control everything, Medici. Not even you have that power."

He was out of reach of her words, but it didn't matter. She smiled to herself, knowing the young boy would live here soon, without the watchful eye of his mother and father.

Shade took the stairs two at a time and stopped in front of their bedroom door. He calmed his heart rate and his breathing, not realizing how Dona had fired him up so quickly. Stepping inside, he closed the door behind him and leaned against it. Kate sat silently in a brocade chair, staring out the window. She looked calm, but he knew the flames of hell had been stirred up inside her. He wouldn't let Dona come between them. "I am sure you have much to say to me."

"Shade, I'm not angry at you. It's her. I don't know the details of your past, nor do I want to. But it's clear she wants me to know. She knows she can get to me by throwing that in my face."

Standing, she went to him, allowed him to wrap her in his embrace. "I understand she's an ally to the Medici coven, and her territory borders ours, but can we please try to keep her at a distance? I hate that she brought the horse. But Lorenzo responded right away. I don't want our son to be pulled into this drama, so I hope accepting the horse isn't a mistake."

Clutching her tightly to his chest, he closed his eyes and thanked whatever powers brought this beautiful female into his life. "I am sending her a check for the pony, so at least it is not a gift to our son. She knew what she was doing with the horse, Kate. She knows Impavido, and she was counting on Lorenzo wanting to have a horse that looked like mine. I could not take that from him, forgive me. She sees me as a conquest still, she wants to rule here with me, and she is jealous of you."

Kate looked up at him. "Is she a danger? Would she harm

us to get to you? Because I'll kill her now if that is the case."

Shade threw back his head and laughed. His smile was wide as he gazed down at her. "*Si*, you are definitely my fiery haired queen. Do you think I would ever let her bring harm upon us? No, *mi amore*. I put her in her place, she knows where I stand. I doubt we will see much of Dona."

Theresa tapped at the door before opening and Lorenzo flew into the room, wearing his pajamas, his bare feet smacking against the floor. He took a leap and Shade caught him mid-flight as Kate laughed at her son's antics.

"I love my pony, Daddy, I love him!"

Shade winked at *bel*. "I am glad you have such love for your pony, they are a lot of responsibility. You are in charge of taking care of him now. He is beautiful, *si*? Have you decided what to name this pony of yours?"

Lorenzo nodded, his curls bouncing. "Yep, I named him Zeus."

Kate looked at him quizzically. "Zeus, really? That's an odd choice for a horse. Why did you pick that name?"

Lorenzo held both hands palms up. "Because, Mommy, Enzo is making me read "The Odyssey", by Homer, and Zeus is the god of the sky and the thunder. He can make lightning bolts shoot from his hands...like me with fire!"

Kate stared at him, dumbfounded, as she looked at Shade. "He's reading The Odyssey? I didn't read that until high school."

Shade held his son in his arms and beamed with a pride. "Little warrior, I think Zeus is the perfect name for your horse. A horse should reflect its master, and fire is your gift. Brilliant choice."

Shade dropped down onto the bed, as Lorenzo rolled away from him laughing, before he started bouncing on the bed. "Lorenzo, the pony will have to be sent to the States by boat, so he will not arrive home at the same time we do. You have earned the pony with your cards, and he is a great reward, but we don't brag about the things we own. Do you understand?"

Lorenzo stopped bouncing and clung to his father's chest. He could feel the synchronization take place with their heart beats. "I understand, Daddy." He patted his father's chest. "No bragging. Enzo says bragging is a sign of weakness, and a king never shows weakness. I get it."

Shade laid his hand over this small boy. "You make my heart burst with love and pride, little warrior. I love you so much, Lorenzo."

Kissing his son on the cheek, he couldn't believe Kate's love had given him so much, made his life complete, and now he had a small daughter to love and protect as well. "Now, it's your bedtime and your *madre* and I need to go see Sophia."

"Can I go too, Daddy? Can I say good night to Sophia?"

"*Si*. She is your sister, and she will miss you if you do not let her know you protect and love her with all your heart."

Shade lifted him off his chest and Lorenzo shot out of the room before Shade could get off the bed. "He makes my ass feel old and slow, *mi amore*."

She slipped her arm around his waist as they followed their son to Sophia's room. "That makes two of us, and we haven't even gotten started with Sophia yet."

89

Shade had supervised the chaos of loading up everything, and everyone, to leave Castello and return to the States. He remembered a time, not too long ago, when it was just him, and he could teleport anywhere at a moment's notice. Now he had a mate, two small children and one adult half-breed child, two wet-feeders, a nanny, a Lady in Waiting, a protector, and two mortal females in this entourage. His life used to be simpler, for sure, but he'd never been happier.

It had taken forever to get everyone on the plane, and he and Kate took to their bedroom in the back of the fuselage. He'd spent the flight stretched out on the bed, his newborn daughter lying on his chest as he'd slept. She had easily compensated for the inconvenience of flying.

They'd been back home for a week now, and the festivities had continued. Sophia had been presented to the warriors at Bel Rosso to receive their pledge of devotion, and Luca had sealed his blood bond to the child as her protector. Luca now held a great deal of responsibility for the Medici, but Shade was sure he could handle it.

Lorenzo had been driving him mad with persistent questions about the arrival of Zeus. Shade had tried distracting him by spending more time with him in the camp, teaching him how to master the use of the new sword. Lorenzo had written his first letter to Alfie, and had proudly read it aloud to Shade before mailing it.

As Shade dressed in his leathers, getting ready to head to camp and hopefully, get in a good workout, he heard the rapid footsteps, beating down the hall, and he knew exactly the first question that would be fired at him. Shade turned to look at *bel* as she lay on the bed, already laughing and he threw his shirt at her.

Their door was open just a crack, so Lorenzo barreled his way through and launched himself onto their bed, where his mother grabbed him up, laughing. Lorenzo was too excited to stay still and scrambled off the other side of the bed. He ran to his father. "Will Zeus get here today? How much longer, Daddy?"

Shaking his head, Shade sighed and sat down on the chair next to the armoire, tugging on his boots. "You know, son, you have no patience. I know you spent the entire day outside in the stables waiting, instead of doing your studies. Do you have your saddle? Is the stall cleaned and ready?"

Lorenzo looked at him with exasperation and placed his small hands on his hips. "Daddy, course I did. Angelo helped me get his stall ready, and we have fresh hay and my saddle is ready. I bet Zeus is worrying about me and wondering how long he has to stay on that boat. How much longer, Daddy? Can't you do something?"

Shade felt as impatient as his son. He hadn't fed, and it took little to irritate him. Kate was sitting in their bed with the sheet pulled over her mouth, stifling a laugh. He snapped back at the child. "Enough, Lorenzo!"

He rummaged through the armoire, looking for a long sleeved shirt, tossing shirts and jeans to the floor until he found what he was looking for. He pulled the shirt over his head and turned to see Lorenzo and *bel* staring at him. "What?"

Lorenzo retreated to the bed and climbed up to the safety of his mother's arms. He wasn't often scolded by his father, but he'd seen his father's temper unleashed on others, and he never wanted to be on the receiving end of that. Kate slid her arms around her son. "Your daddy is just grumpy tonight. Zeus will be here soon, Lorenzo, and you'll be the first to know." She kissed the top of his head, his hair smelled like sunshine and hay. "Now, go find Enzo, see if there are studies you need to catch up on."

Lorenzo nodded and quietly answered, "Yes, Mommy." He dropped over the side of the bed and left for the door, looking back at his father. "I'm sorry, Daddy."

He closed the door behind him as Kate turned her attention back to Shade. "You haven't fed, have you? You never lose your patience with him. I think it's time you come back to me. Sophia feeds well from Theresa and Gita now. And I'm not sure this household can tolerate you, otherwise. Besides, I've missed you."

He stared at the door. "I hurt his feelings and I didn't mean to. I never want him to be scared of me, like I was of my father. He's been attached to my leg lately, and I know he is just excited, but I am the one with no patience."

He sat on the edge of the bed, his head in his hands. "I need to fix this. Zeus should arrive tomorrow. I don't want to tell him, he will drive Angelo out of his mind."

He flopped back on the bed and took a deep breath, inhaling her. "*Cazzo*, I miss you so much, I feel unable to function without you, *mi amore*."

Kate climbed on all fours to the foot of the bed and lay across his chest. "Then stop missing me, and feed."

His hands slid across her cheeks and into that mass of crimson, he looked into her eyes and felt the depth of his love for her crushing him. "Do you have any idea how hard it is to be away from you, not feed from you? I am not whole without you."

His growl was low and deep in his chest, his beast rising to the surface, knowing her beast was ready, once again, to take him on. He nuzzled into her neck as his fangs punched, long and sharp, and so in need of her they ached. His eyes lit the room in a ruby color that made her lily white skin glow as if a soft pink. Without a word spoken, he sank his fangs into the soft flesh of her neck as her blood gushed into his mouth, and he almost lost his mind. Luca could temporarily satisfy his hunger, but his *bel* satisfied his immortal soul. He fed with mouthful after mouthful as his cock became hard and throbbed for release.

Kate felt almost lightheaded when he fed from her. He must abstain from feeding from her while she was pregnant, and for a period after the baby was born, until the newborn was weaned. The baby fed often but took little. Shade drank from her now with a hunger that had built up after months of waiting. She knew he sustained himself with Luca's blood, but it wasn't the same, for either of them.

The sharp, sweet sting of his teeth into her flesh immediately ignited the fire between her legs as her fingers gripped his shoulders. She rolled over on her back, pulling him with her, so she could feel the weight of him again. She wrapped her legs around his waist, as his cock slid deep inside her, his mouth still sealed to her throat. Her moan was primal as she relaxed her head back, letting him take his fill, and felt him thrusting deep inside her.

Matching the rhythm of her hips, he finally unlatched from her neck, licking the wounds with his hot tongue. "Let go, *bel*, cum with me."

He felt her nails sink into his broad muscular back. He knew how her body responded. He knew every inch of her, like it was his own. "Now, *mi amore*."

He felt her hands grab his hair and yank his head down as she sank her fangs into his flesh and his whole body ignited as he felt her cum, and his body followed, filling her with his seed.

His beast roared, echoing loudly off the walls, leaving no question to anyone in this house that the king and queen were, once again, united.

He pulled her close, wrapping the sheet around them as they lay together, hearts beating fast. She placed her hand on his chest, feeling his heart and breathing return to normal. She sighed in contentment when she heard a loud wail.

Their daughter wasn't happy and was demanding attention, and Kate knew Theresa and Gita would respond. They both tried to block out the noise, but the wails continued, getting louder. Kate felt the pull of the blood bond that would keep her tied to these children for eternity and knew the wailing wouldn't stop until she responded.

Reluctantly, she sat up, breaking free of his warm embrace, and slipped on her robe. "I knew this one would be a handful. I think we better get used to it. Sophia will be nothing like her brother, I'm afraid."

Stepping into a pair of slippers, she scuffed to the nursery that had been set up for the new baby, to find both Theresa and

Gita frantically trying to quiet the infant.

"My lady, I'm so sorry. She won't stop crying."

Kate took the baby from Theresa and placed her over her shoulder, where the baby immediately rooted for Kate's neck and fed. Kate shook her head. "A little jealous, are we, Sophia?"

Shade grunted as she rolled out of their bed. He did miss the days when he'd had her all to himself. He slid out of bed and quickly dressed, following her to the nursery to find their daughter suckling from her mother's neck.

He knelt beside the rocking chair and pulled Kate's hair back, as huge blue eyes looked up at him. "*Si*, she gives us life, does she not, little one?"

He kissed the curly mop of red on top of Sophia's head, and rubbed her back softly as she fed. "You can't sustain us both, Kate. Let her be comforted, but do not let her feed too long. I need to have a word with our little warrior before I go. If you need me, I will be at camp. *Ti amo*."

Kissing *bel* on the cheek, he stood and walked to the door, looking back at them before he left. His heart almost leapt from his chest. "You two are so beautiful."

Kate smiled back at him. "We make beautiful babies. Now, go to Lorenzo. Soothe his hurt feelings."

Shade headed down the hallway past the bedrooms to the room that had been set up as a classroom for their children. He entered the room quietly, and stood at the door, leaning against the doorjamb, observing his son.

Enzo never changed. He looked much the way Shade remembered him when he was a boy, sitting in a classroom in Florence. His hair was grey and disheveled, his glasses worn low on his nose, where he looked over them. Enzo exuded an air of authority and had little tolerance for foolishness in his classroom.

Lorenzo sat still as a mouse and appeared totally absorbed by his lessons as Enzo taught him the history of Italy. Shade cleared his throat and chuckled as Enzo raised his head, looking over his glasses at him.

"I do apologize, Enzo, but I wish to speak with my son alone for a moment."

Enzo nodded, brushing the chalk from his hands onto his pants leg. "He is a good student, Medici, much more attentive than you ever could be."

Shade laughed and watched as the old man stepped outside the door, his suit looking as rumpled as Shade remembered.

"Did I do something wrong, Daddy? I'm studying about Italy. And I'm paying attention in class like you told me."

Crouching down to Lorenzo's level, he slid his hand across the boy's small cheek. "I need to apologize to you, little warrior. You know, I miss your mommy a lot, and we have been so busy, I get grumpy when I don't spend time with her. I took that out on you, and that was not fair. You did nothing wrong, Lorenzo. You make me proud, you study hard. I love you so much, and I need to ask you to forgive me. Please?"

Lorenzo laid his forehead against his father's. "Daddy, you don't have to ask. I already forgived."

Enzo's voice floated in from the hallway. "Forgave."

Lorenzo corrected himself. "Right, I already forgave. I love you too, Daddy."

Shade picked him up from his seat and held him close to his chest, as two little arms went around his neck. "Zeus arrives tomorrow morning. But here is the thing. He will have endured a long trip on that boat. We need to let him get his land legs back, because he has been bouncing around. Let him settle down a bit before we go see him. I need you to leave Angelo alone, so he can take care of Zeus, and when I wake up from my sleep, we will go together to greet him and welcome him properly to his new home. Will you do that for me?"

Lorenzo bounced in his father's arms. "Yes. I'll wait for you, Daddy. And I can feed him too, right?"

Shade smiled at the unbridled enthusiasm of his little warrior. "You better have lots of carrots and apples, because I'm sure he will be hungry after his long trip. Now, I need to get to work, and so do you."

90

They had been home for about a week now, and Cory missed the daily contact with Madison. She'd shared his room at Castello, and every day was an adventure as they discovered Florence together for the first time.

Now that they were back, Cory was busy in the shop, and Madison was busy with her final year of college. They were back to juggling their schedules and trying to find the time to be together. Cory laid out a new piece of leather and started to cut a pattern for an outfit for Aislynn, but his mind was elsewhere. He could hear the warriors practicing outside, the clank of metal against metal, a familiar sound to his work night. His father's voice shouted out instruction as he corrected the young recruits. Cory walked to the door of his workshop and stood in the doorway, watching the young warriors sparring. His dad was easy to pick out among the crowd. As if sensing his presence, Shade turned and locked eyes with him, and Cory motioned to his dad to come join him.

Shade gave a hand signal to Marcello to take over as he left the training field and walked to the shop. He followed Cory inside and closed the door behind him, shutting out much of the sound. "Something, or someone, on your mind, son?"

Cory dropped down on the work stool by the table. "Someone is always on my mind." Cory smiled as him. "But you already know that. Dad, with everything that has happened, and Madison learning who we are, coming with us to Castello, I mean, she's practically family now, right?"

Shade walked around the shop, looking at the bolts of leather stacked against the wall before taking a seat across from Cory. "*Si*, I would say she is *familia*. Did she feed from you yet?"

Cory shook his head. "No. And I don't even know how to do that with a mortal. I mean, she won't need to feed from me, Dad. I can't turn her. She'll never be a vamp, not even a half-breed like me. Will she even have a desire for my blood?"

Shade shook his head. "Son, listen to me, I am not exactly sure about anything when it comes to what you both will feel. You are a half-breed, and she's mortal, so I can't identify with your experience, but I will tell you this much. Letting her feed from you is a good idea, blood bonding, even in a half-breed, will be beneficial. You won't have the same bond as a full-blooded vampire, and of course, she can never be vampire, but you will have something, more than you have now. She will not have the desire to feed from you to satisfy her hunger. She will never feel that. But even if it is once, it will create a bond that goes beyond anything mortals can imagine."

Cory ran his hand over his face. *Another obstacle for the two of us to overcome.* "Yeah, okay. I'll talk to her about it. But what I wanted to ask you is, do you think it would be okay if I went to California and took Madison with me to meet my mom? I've told Mom about her, and she's been asking to meet her. I haven't been to see my mom in a while. I'd have to wait until Madison has her next break in school. She already missed some classes while we were in Florence."

Shade stood up and paced around the room. He knew Cory really wanted this trip with Madison. "Cory, I'm going to be honest with you. Right now, I can't let any of my warriors go with you. We are really busy with this class of recruits, and the trip to Florence has put us behind schedule with their training. Raven is nearby. He can't leave Napa to stay with you, but he's there if you need him. Do you feel comfortable traveling alone? Just the two of you?"

Cory shrugged. "Dad, we'll be fine. No one pays any attention to me. I'm really happy to be a part of this family, but let's face it. All those old vamps in Europe who came to see Sophia could have cared less about meeting me. They only showed me respect because of you. Besides, we'll be at my mom's. It's the most boring place in the world. But I do want her to meet Madison."

Shade ran his hand through his hair, not completely comfortable with the idea of letting him travel without a protector. "I'll let Raven know you're coming. You stay at your mom's, not in the city. And when you visit the city, stay away from your old stomping grounds, and stay out of the underground clubs, deal?"

"Jeez, do you think I'd actually take Madison to the streets where I grew up? The last thing I would want is for Madison to see how I lived. If you hadn't found me, brought me here to live, I never would've approached a girl like Madison. She knows I'm a half-breed, and as far as she knows, I grew up with my mom. It almost sounds normal. She's seen our world, and she sees how I'm on the edge of it, not the center of it, and I think that's what makes it okay for her."

"Go to California, I will talk with Raven. Just let me know your schedule. You can take the jet, and you'll need to get a rental car. I know you can handle this, and I have to let go of the reins at some point. Spend time with your mom. Be sure she knows how much you love her."

Cory walked around the table and hugged his father. "She knows I love her. Thanks to you, we've been able to heal all the wounds we both inflicted on each other when I was growing up. I talk to her on the phone a lot, and she just wants me to be happy. We'll be fine. You worry too much."

Returning his son's hug, he slapped his back. "So, go, enjoy the sun of California because, before you know it, we'll be freezing our asses off here."

As they hugged each other, Shade knew he had to let his son grow up and learn to take care of his own female.

91

Lorenzo sat on the floor outside the closed door of his parents' bedroom. His pony had arrived, and he'd waited all day for his father to wake. The sun would set any minute now, and as soon as he heard any sound from the other side of the door, he'd knock. He laid his head against the door, his ear pressed tightly against the wood, straining to hear anything.

Theresa stood in the hallway, holding Sophia and shook her head. "Lorenzo, that won't make your father wake up any earlier."

Lorenzo whispered, "I know, but I need to be ready."

Shade moaned softly as he slowly woke from the depths of his death slumber and heard the soft whir of the electronic blinds. He felt her body, soft and warm, curled up next to him and he slid his hand through her tangled silken tresses of crimson. He fisted the softness gently in his hand and smiled. It felt good to have her sleeping with her head on his chest again, having her blood energize him and his cock. The thought alone made him hard and instantly, he felt *bel's* hand around his steel. "Good evening to you too, *mi amore*."

Kate giggled as she snuggled into his neck, running her tongue along the pulsing vein. He responded to her advances when they heard a tapping at the door.

Kate dropped her head down on his chest. "Really? I got up with Sophia twice today because she wouldn't stop crying for Theresa or Gita, and now, Lorenzo's already at the door. I'm wondering if we'll ever be alone again."

Shade growled in agitation at the interruption, but quickly switched gears to concern for his children. "Is she all right?"

"She's fine. She's just a child who'll demand what she wants, and right now, she wants me over her nanny or feeder. She's been hard to wean. I need to learn to just let her cry, but it's difficult."

They heard another round of tapping at the door and a

small voice calling. "Hello? Can you hear me?"

Shade looked at Kate and winked, and in a louder than usual voice responded, "*Mi amore*, did you hear something?"

Kate rolled off of him and pulled the pillow over her head. Her voice muffled by the pillow. "I didn't hear anything. I'm going back to sleep."

"Back to sleep, you say? Oh, *si*. Good idea."

Lorenzo tapped on the door again. "Hello! It's your son, Lorenzo. I can hear talking. Can I come in now?"

Shade sighed as he gave Kate one last cuddle. It felt like the nights spent waking up with her in his arms, followed by hours of love making, were a thing of the past, at least until the children were grown. "What is the problem, Lorenzo?"

Lorenzo heard his father speak out to him. "Daddy, you said Zeus would be here today, but I had to wait till you were up before I went to the stables. I waited all day!"

Shade chuckled to himself at the image of his son sitting outside the bedroom door, waiting for some sign his parents were awake. "Come in, little warrior."

Lorenzo opened the door and threw himself onto the bed shared by his parents, landing in a heap on top of them. His mother squealed as Shade began to tickle the boy, and watched as he collapsed in laughter.

Theresa appeared at the door, holding Sophia wrapped in a blanket. "Excuse me, master, but as long as you're awake, this one is getting restless again too."

"Ah, my Princess, give her to me, Theresa, she just misses her *padre*, that is all, *si*?" Taking Sophia into his arms, he smiled down at that beautiful, sweet face. "You miss me, don't you?"

Sophia let out a loud coo.

"They think you are fussy. My princess is not fussy, she is cooing like a sweet dove." Putting her on his shoulder, she nuzzled into his neck and gripped a handful of his curls, yanking hard. "Ouch, okay, okay, I know you are hungry."

Kate lifted the baby from him as she kicked her small feet, her tiny hands fisted and waving in the air, her face scrunched up, ready to cry. Kate shushed her and laid her on her shoulder, where the baby immediately rooted for her neck and started to suckle. Sophia relaxed instantly, as she clung to her mother. Kate stroked her back. "Sophia, you're breaking all the rules already. What am I going to do with you?"

Shade watched as Sophia instantly stopped flailing once she nestled in and fed from *bel.* "*Mi amore,* Sophia should not be taking from you so often, this is not normal, I think, perhaps, we need to call Doc Bonutti. Have him come check her out. I'm concerned. Do you think she needs my blood?"

"I think it's just her preference. But yes, she does need to feed from you as well. She feeds often, from both Theresa and Gita, but she prefers to feed from me and she's very willful, even at this age."

Sliding from their bed, Shade picked Lorenzo up in his arms. "Once we're back from the stables, she should be hungry again, and I will feed her before my death slumber, perhaps it will help. Did you want to come with us to see Zeus?"

Kate stroked the silky, soft red curls on top of her daughter's head as she continued to feed. "You go ahead, Shade. I have my hands full with this one."

Lorenzo jumped from his father's arms, running to the door, impatiently hopping from one foot to the other.

"Lorenzo, I need to get dressed, and you need your boots. I'll meet you in your room, go."

As Lorenzo took off, Shade began to get dressed, pulling on his jeans and lacing up his boots. As he pulled the shirt over his head, Lorenzo barreled back in the room. Shade ruffled his son's hair and gave *bel* a kiss. "Your warriors will be in the stables if you need us."

Kate leaned over the side of the bed, kissing Lorenzo, who grew taller every day. "Have fun, you two."

"Let's go, little warrior, we have a pony to attend to."

Shade took the boy's hand and led him outside and across the field to the stables. Lorenzo kept running ahead, pulling his father by the hand. "Faster, Daddy!"

Shade laughed and teleported across the wide expanse of Bel Rosso, holding tight to Lorenzo's hand. Touching down in the stables, Lorenzo landed with a thud and quickly picked himself up, running for the stall that housed Zeus. The pony had been fed and brushed and given time to acclimate to his new surroundings. His stall was only a few spots down from Impavido's, who didn't look the least bit impressed with this miniature impostor. Lorenzo quickly clambered over the gate and dropped down inside the stall, startling the pony, who backed away a little wild eyed. "Zeus! It's just me, Lorenzo."

"Easy, little warrior, Zeus is in new surroundings, he is a little scared still, and he is not used to you or your scent yet. Why don't you get him a carrot, make friends with him, let him eat from your hand, you know what to do."

Lorenzo went for the carrots as Angelo approached, leaning over the stall beside Shade.

"Any problems getting him settled?"

Angelo shook his head. "No problems, master, the pony has a good temperament. But I was told to give this to the Prince."

He handed Shade a sealed envelope with Lorenzo's name on it. He could pick up Dona's faint scent on the paper, and wondered what in the hell that was about. Tucking it in the back pocket of his jeans, he'd give it to Lorenzo later. "So, little warrior, what do you make of this Zeus, so far?"

Lorenzo climbed up on the gate and extended his hand, palm up, with the carrot, while the pony sniffed, then accepted the offering. "I think Zeus is the best pony ever. He'll run as fast as Impavido. Maybe faster!"

"He has to grow up a bit, I think." Climbing inside the stall, Shade took a closer look at Zeus, checking his legs and his hoofs. "He made the boat journey well. Perhaps, we should take him for a ride around the pasture. What do you think? The sooner the two of you get used to one another, the better. I will lead him out for you. You will train together to learn to ride and jump. Angelo can help you with that in the daylight. You must come to understand his movements, his temper, how he reacts in every situation. He will grow to trust you, in time."

Lorenzo copied his father's actions, checking the pony's legs and hooves, even though he had no idea what he was looking for. "Okay, Daddy. But he already likes me, I can tell. Can we put his saddle on now?"

"Go with Angelo, he will put the saddle on for you, and teach you how it is done. I expect you to help take care of this pony. They require much work and grooming. The pony needs to learn you are his master. Go, now, I am going to check on Pavi while you do that."

Lorenzo followed Angelo out of the stall as he led the pony over to be saddled and bridled. The boy carefully observed Angelo, and followed his instructions, tightening the straps that secured the saddle. He wanted to make a good impression, and he was a fast learner.

Shade opened the gate to Impavido's stall, as the horse bobbed his head up and down, his long mane shaking. Shade stroked the horse's massive neck, calming him with his voice. "Settle down, Pavi, you are still my boy. But you better get used to the pony because you will be riding alongside that one before you know it."

He heard Lorenzo squeal with laughter and looked up to see him astride his pony, ready to do some riding. "Come on, Daddy. Zeus is ready. Let's ride now!"

"You are one impatient warrior tonight." Shade strolled over to Zeus and grabbed hold of his bridle, leading him outside. "You have ridden Pavi with me enough you should know how to hold the reins and control them. Give him a verbal command, as well as the directional command from the reins. He will eventually respond to both. And remember, when he responds to your command, he needs to be rewarded. Pat his neck firmly and tell him he has done a good job. Once he gets used to that, he will do anything you ask, Lorenzo. He will want to please you."

Shade led him further out into the pasture, watching closely how Lorenzo sat in the saddle. "Don't hold the reins so tightly, Lorenzo. Let them loose in your hands until you want him to do something. Now, I want you to make Zeus turn right, so remember to pull back gently on the right rein."

Lorenzo paid close attention to his father's instruction, and he loosened the reins and tugged lightly on the right. Zeus responded immediately, turning to the right. "He did it, Daddy!"

"Good job, now how do we reward Zeus?"

Lorenzo patted the pony's neck and told him, "Good job, Zeus. Now what do you want me to do, Daddy?"

Shade continued to walk faster and faster, leading Zeus by the bridle. "I am going to let go of him, Lorenzo. I want Zeus to make a complete circle to the left, then stop, *si?*"

Lorenzo nodded, and led the pony in a circle before bringing him to a complete stop. Lorenzo beamed at his father as he patted the pony again.

"Did you see that, Daddy? He listened to me. He'll be like Pavi."

"You are an awesome team already." Hugging his son, he adjusted his riding helmet, tightening the strap under his chin. "Never go riding without your helmet. If you do, you will have your riding privileges taken away, *si?* Now, I want you to ride the fence line by yourself, remember to use your thighs and the reins. Zeus will follow the fence. Keep your pace slow at first and then you can speed him up into a gallop after you do a few slow laps."

Lorenzo led Zeus toward the fence line, having complete control of the pony. Zeus made one loop around the pasture before Lorenzo dug in his heels and snapped the reins for Zeus to pick up speed. The pony seemed eager to let off some steam after being cooped up so long, and easily shifted into a gallop. Lorenzo squealed with excitement.

Shade and Angelo stood together at the entrance of the stables, watching as Lorenzo mastered his riding skills. After a few hours, Shade had decided it was enough for one night and signaled Lorenzo to come to him.

"It is time we go inside now, Lorenzo, it is close to your bedtime and we don't want to tire out Zeus his first night at Bel Rosso. I am proud of you. Now, I want you to dismount and walk him into his stall. Get him watered."

Lorenzo felt like he could ride all night, but he followed his father's instruction and dismounted, leading the pony back to the stables. "Thank you, Daddy. This is my best present ever!"

Angelo followed him as they led the pony back into the stall and Angelo removed the saddle. "Go ahead, little warrior. I'll brush him down tonight and get him watered. But next time, I'll teach you how to do that on your own."

Lorenzo nodded and watched as Angelo took control. Rejoining his father, his took his hand and pulled himself up so he was riding piggy-back. "I love you, Daddy."

"I love you more, little warrior. Now, a few rules. Every day, you need to find time to come out here, clean that stall, brush down Zeus, ride and work with Angelo. You need to figure out a schedule, because you have to practice your fire-throwing skills with Skelk, as well as practice with your sword. You have your studies with Enzo, and now this. Zeus is your responsibility. He belongs to you. He relies on you to keep him happy."

As they got to the patio on the back of the house, Shade slid the boy from his back and sat down with him on the chaise lounge. He pulled Lorenzo into his lap and pulled the letter from his pocket. "Lorenzo, this letter came with Zeus. So, before we go inside, I think you should read it aloud to me, *si*?"

Lorenzo took the sealed envelope from his father's hand. "I'm a good reader, Daddy. Enzo says I'm at a twelfth-grade level." Opening the envelope, Lorenzo read the hand written script.

> *Dear Lorenzo,*
>
> *I sincerely hope you will enjoy many years with your new pony. I understand you have named him Zeus. What a proud and noble name for a pony that will be ridden by such a strong, young warrior. You are such a treasure, Lorenzo, and will be so important to your coven. You must work hard and study hard, as you will carry so much responsibility on your young shoulders.*
>
> *Please do not have any fear of leaving your family and moving to Castello when the time comes. I know you will miss your family,*

but know I will be here for you, and you can call on me anytime. The Medici and the Alizzi share a long alliance, going back many centuries, and together, we must continue to be aligned against the forces of evil that would seek to break up our territory. Please write to me often and let me know of your progress.

Yours for eternity,
Donatella'

"Wow, that's a nice letter, isn't it, Daddy?"

Shade listened to Lorenzo read the letter flawlessly; pronouncing each word without trouble, but his heart was stricken. Dona was sly, and she was already working her magic on his son.

"Donatella has a very small coven, Lorenzo, not many warriors. It was a great coven centuries ago, but she never mated, and I fear she has spent much of the wealth her *padre* left for her. The vampires in her coven have drifted off throughout the years, seeking better for themselves. She relies on the Medici and its warriors to protect her. It is true our two families have had an alliance. Because she never mated, she is more vulnerable to attacks. So, yes, she is someone who I imagine will always be around. Do you wish to write to her, because you do not have to?"

Lorenzo listened to his father's explanation of Donatella's situation, and his heart broke knowing she didn't have a family. "But I like her, Daddy. And she needs us, right? I'll protect her."

"I'm glad you like her, but you will have your own coven to protect, and many that will rely on you, so it is a big job. What do you say we get back inside, you need a bath before bed."

Lorenzo folded the letter carefully and tucked it in his shirt. He'd write back to Donatella tomorrow. "Okay, I'm ready."

"Come on, little warrior, let's see what Mommy is up to. By

the way, have you heard from Alfie yet?"

"Yep. He wrote to me too. I will have a lot of letters to write, huh?"

"Just one more duty you better get used to performing on a regular basis, Prince Lorenzo."

As they entered the house, the boy ran ahead to the stairs. Halfway up, he stopped and turned to his father. "What is it, Lorenzo?"

"Don't worry, Daddy. I study every day and pay attention to Enzo just like you told me to, and I practice with Skelk and Marcello. And now, I have Zeus. I like being a warrior. I'll be ready when you send me to Castello, and Marco will be proud of me too. I promise."

Shade stood looking up at this small boy standing on the stairs, and remembered doing the same, begging for some small compliment or words of encouragement from his own *padre*, and rarely getting it. He vowed to never be like his father. "You already make me proud, Lorenzo."

He watched as his son scurried up the stairs, and he knew in his heart Lorenzo would be okay. He'd grow up to be a great warrior, Shade's equal in all things, and lead the next generation of Medici.

92

Shade made his way up the stairs as Lorenzo ran ahead. He could hear his son talking to Theresa about Zeus and their night of riding, and he smiled. Then he heard a loud wailing as he headed toward the nursery. Walking in, he found Gita in a nervous frenzy, trying to get Sophia to settle down and feed.

He gently took his daughter from Gita and laid her over his shoulder. "Go on, Gita, my Princess needs her *padre*."

Gita wrung her hands, and feared she'd let him down, but nodded and left the room.

Settling himself into the rocking chair, Shade cuddled Sophia to his chest. "So, what is the problem here, little princess? Why are you resisting your feeder and only seeking the comfort of your *madre*? Settle down, *Padre* has you, nothing will harm you while in my arms."

Sophia immediately settled and looked up at him, as if she understood his words. Then she scrunched up her face, as she was about to unleash some serious wailing.

"Oh no, no, no, *Padre* does not like tears. Come on now, let's get some powerful Medici blood in your system, and you will sleep like the princess you are."

Pulling her to his neck, she nuzzled and sank her small fangs into his flesh. He closed his eyes and rocked slowly as his progeny fed, drawing her power directly from the source of her Medici roots. Rubbing her back, he felt her body relax against his chest. "There, you see, you just needed *Padre*. Feed, my sweet angel."

Kate stood in the doorway of Sophia's nursery, and watched as the infant had him wrapped around her fingers already. Walking in, she sat on the nanny's sofa bed. "Your princess already thinks she should only drink royal blood. She needs to bond with you, but she'll need discipline and structure as well. I can't feed both of you."

He continued to rock and listened to her lecture him.

Opening his eyes, he looked at her and placed his hand gently on Sophia's head, letting his fingers slide through the soft red curls. "She hasn't fed from me since birth, *bel*, perhaps this will calm her. I understand our *bambinos* need structure and discipline. Lorenzo does just fine. So will Sophia."

As she unlatched, he nuzzled into her soft cheek and kissed her, continuing to rock her as she laid her head on his shoulder, staring at her mother. "See, she is fine now."

Kate looked at him in the soft light of the small lamp, as he held their daughter to his chest. She was so small, and her skin so white against his dark complexion. "She's beautiful, isn't she? Now, tell me about Lorenzo and his first experience with his pony. How did that go?"

"Lorenzo did great. He and Zeus are a good match, and I let him ride alone for a good hour or two. Damn, he makes me so proud. But there was one other thing." Shade paused, and hoped she didn't get angry about the letter, but better coming from him than finding out from Lorenzo. Sophia wiggled a bit and he adjusted her on his shoulder and she sighed.

Kate sat forward on the sofa. "Did he fall? Is he okay?"

"No, *mi amore*, he didn't fall. He will be a strong rider." Shade repositioned the infant in the crook of his arm as she gurgled and closed her eyes. "Dona sent a letter to Lorenzo, just to say she hopes he enjoys the pony and wishing him well in the future. Just a letter, is all."

Kate looked at his face, trying to read his intent. "A letter? I suppose that's appropriate. She did find the pony. You did pay her, right?"

"Of course, I paid her. She is just being kind to Lorenzo. I don't think she has any motive except maybe to stir the pot between you and me. So, don't play her game. Lorenzo thought the letter was nice. He is going to write back to her. I explained her situation to him, his responsibility to the Alizzi coven and he understands. And my princess is sound asleep, so you see, she just wanted her *padre*'s potent blood."

Standing, he carefully placed her in her crib, pulling a soft pink blanket over her. "She is so beautiful. I will have to fight them off when she grows up. Every damn male in the world will want her."

Kate joined him at the crib, looking down at their daughter as she nestled into the soft blanket. Sliding her arm around his waist, she leaned against him. "I'm not jealous of Donatella. I won you from her centuries ago, long before I even existed in this world, and there's no one who'll come between us. But you're right about one thing, this one will give us a run for our money."

93

It had been a month and a half since the funeral, but Braden had them back on the campaign trail in three short weeks. Alec had seen an initial bump in the polls immediately after Rissa's death, a sympathy response from the voters. But his absence in the campaign gave his fellow candidates an edge, and now that he was back, the press was questioning whether he should be in the race. Every reporter wanted to know how he was doing, and if Rissa's death would have any effect on his ability to focus on the Presidency. No one was asking him policy questions and he was having a hard time getting the same attention. The women still approached him for an autograph, or a selfie, but the crowds were noticeably smaller.

After a very disappointing day, he was walking back to the campaign bus with Braden at his side, and Mateo close behind him. As soon as they closed the doors of the bus, Alec poured a large Midnight. "Well, that was a fucking waste of time."

Braden dropped down in his own seat and tried to maintain a positive spin. "Give it some time, Alec. This is new ground. The people don't know how to respond."

Alec gave him a stare that could melt steel. "Oh, they know how to respond, Braden. They're taking their support elsewhere." His laugh was bitter as he downed the Midnight. "Rissa is having the last laugh, controlling everything, even now."

He tossed the glass across the bus and watched as it smashed into the bullet proof glass of the windows. Growling, he looked at Mateo. "What are you looking at?"

Mateo had been with this campaign since the beginning, with and without Rissa, and it was obvious this campaign was going downhill, and Canton had no one to blame but himself this time. He'd been watching Canton's reaction to voters, as well as his mood off camera. What he'd discovered was very simple, the mighty master had finally realized he missed his mate, and his goal of the Presidency was slipping further and further away. Mateo had watched as Alec's anger reached a boiling point.

As the glass shattered, and the Midnight ran down the window, Mateo turned to him. "Was it worth it?"

Alec was out of his seat with his hand around Mateo's neck, pushing him hard against the door. He was nose to nose with him, speaking through gritted teeth, "Don't you challenge me, warrior. You know nothing of a master's life. You were born to serve. You take orders. Or have you forgotten?"

Braden was immediately at his side, pulling him back. "Alec. Calm down."

Mateo growled back at Alec, as his eyes glowed red and his fangs were bared. "You gonna throw my ass down some stairs too?"

Alec hissed at him. "Get out of my face. In fact, get off this bus! You've crossed the line, warrior. How I handle my affairs is not your concern. You're not here to judge me. Go. Now!"

Spinning on his heels, he pulled his cell phone from his pocket and dialed Shade as Mateo teleported out.

Shade had just arrived in camp when his phone rang. Looking at the caller ID, it was Alec. *What in the hell is he calling about?* Just as he went to answer the call, Mateo appeared at the doorway.

Puzzled by the unexpected appearance of Mateo, he answered the phone. "Medici."

Alec immediately started in, "You need to teach your warriors some manners, brother. I just sent Mateo packing. Since when is it okay for a warrior to challenge a master? Is that what you're teaching them?"

Shade hit the speaker, so Mateo could hear the conversation. Shade's eyes lifted to Mateo as Mateo telepathically told him what went down. "What I teach them is how to keep you alive, so tell me what in the hell you want me to do."

"Send me someone who knows how to keep their mouth shut and their opinions to themselves. I don't need the judgment of any warrior. You're paid handsomely for this service, brother, and I think I deserve a little respect. Send me Hyde."

Mateo rolled his eyes and Shade signaled him to leave. "Look, brother, Hyde isn't available right now. I'll meet with Marcello, we will find someone who can take the assignment, and I'll deal with Mateo. Alec, you know you have all the masters in an uproar, not to mention the Council. This campaign, now Rissa's very public death, you're playing with fire. If this goes south, you're going to have to go underground. You understand that?"

Alec dropped down into the seat and waved his hand for Braden to leave. Braden stepped into the private bedroom on the bus and closed the door, giving Alec his privacy.

"Listen, brother, between you and me, things aren't going well. I don't know how this is going to turn out. I'm down in the polls. Every day looks worse than the last. Braden still thinks we can turn it around, but I'm not so sure. I can see it in the mortals' eyes. They feel pity, and they don't feel confident anymore. If this falls through, I don't have a plan B. The possibility of not winning wasn't even an option. Look, just send me somebody, brother. We have to keep going here."

Shade could hear the defeat in Alec's voice, something he'd never heard before. "Relax, brother, keep doing what you have to do, I will have someone there in the morning. You need warrior protection, more than you think. The masters see you falling, everyone is watching you, been watching. I don't need to tell you when a master falls, it doesn't take long for the predators to move in. Get some rest. I got your back, brother."

Alec tossed his phone on the table and covered his face with his hands. For the first time in almost 800 years, he was wondering what he'd do about his future.

94

Dante had taken Cory to Madison's apartment to pick her up for the flight to California. Dante waited in the car while Cory went inside to help her. Cory was excited. He knew his mom was eager to meet Madison. He just hoped the two women liked each other.

He carried her luggage to the door, and watched her scurry around, double checking to make sure everything was turned off.

Madison had watered the plants and informed her landlord she'd be gone for two weeks, and to please collect her mail. She'd packed and repacked in preparation for the trip. She was even more nervous about meeting Cory's mom than she was about going to Florence. "Okay. I think I have everything."

She looked nervously around the apartment, wiping her sweating palms on her long skirt. She grabbed a coat from her closet, and threw her purse over her shoulder, and with one final glance around, she turned to him and said, "Let's go."

Cory laughed and kissed her quickly as he carried her luggage to the car. Dante helped Cory load the luggage, then they all piled back into the car, and took off for the private hangar. Cory could sense her nervousness. "Don't be nervous, Maddie, my mom's really nice. She lives in a simple house. She could have had anything, Dad would have given her whatever she wanted, but she chose something simple to accommodate her. She'll like you."

Madison twisted her hands. "I hope so, Cory. I mean, I know we don't need her approval or anything, but I know you love her, so it's important to me. And she knows everything, right? About the... you know, the vampire stuff?"

Reaching over, he took her hand in his. "Yes, she knows, she was at Bel Rosso, she knows everything about Shade and Kate. She's a mortal who fed a vampire for several weeks when she was much younger. She used to go to the vampire clubs. A lot of mortals are attracted to the clubs and allow the vampires to feed from them. Just don't judge her, Maddie, she did the best she could for me, but I wasn't exactly normal."

Madison laid her head back against the seat. "Cory, none of us are normal. I don't think normal exists. We make our own normal, okay?"

Cory looked out the window, he'd never known normal. "You're my normal, Maddie. You're as close as I've come to ever feeling normal."

"Well, life with you won't be boring, that's for sure."

Dante pulled up to the private hangar and the staff appeared from nowhere to transfer their luggage to the plane. Madison looked at the sleek jet as Dante boarded. "You know, it doesn't take long to get used to this."

She laughed as she took his hand and they boarded the flight. The flight attendant greeted them at the door.

"Welcome aboard, Cory, Miss Barnes. My name is Carolyn. You may remember me from the Florence flight."

Madison smiled at her. "Of course, I remember."

Carolyn helped them get situated and as soon as they were airborne, she brought a glass of wine for Madison and a Midnight for Cory. "Please let me know when you're ready for your meal. The flight will be about four hours."

Madison looked out the window as the ground dropped away beneath them, and she could see the Blue Ridge Mountains getting smaller and fading into the distance as Cory held her hand.

Cory and Madison watched a movie and enjoyed a steak dinner with all the trimmings. The flight went smoothly, as always, as they touched down at San Francisco International. Once on the ground, Dante quickly transferred their luggage to the rental car.

As they exited the plane, Cory laughed. Dante had rented them a nice BMW SUV. "Wow, Dante, I don't think we'll need that big thing in California."

Dante slapped him on the back and wished them well, letting him know he'd be here with the jet when they were ready to return to Virginia. Cory led Madison to the Beamer and they managed their way out of the airport and the gridlock of traffic through San Francisco to Walnut Creek.

"Maddie, can you put this address into the GPS, I'm not sure, exactly, how to drive to her house from here."

He handed her the paper with the address as he maneuvered through the traffic. "We won't have to drive back into the city. Once we're at my mom's, we can take the subway. Plus, it will be fun to walk around the city."

Madison entered the address and then started looking out the window in every direction. She could see the San Francisco skyline as they headed for the Oakland Bay Bridge. "Oh my gosh, Cory. I can't believe you got to grow up in that city. I've always wanted to visit here. They have a great arts community. How far is it to your mom's?"

"We should be there in about twenty-five minutes, according to the GPS, but in this traffic, all bets are off."

She leaned back in her seat as they crossed into Oakland and stayed on the highway toward Walnut Creek. As they approached the city limits, Madison took in the low mountain range in the small town. "Wow, this kind of reminds me of Charlottesville!"

As they turned down the street where Cory's mom lived, the GPS announced their arrival. The quaint neighborhood had children playing in the streets. Switching off the engine, he looked at Maddie. "Well, here we are. Now, I'm feeling nervous."

Madison exited the car into a suburban neighborhood that could be anywhere USA. "Don't go soft on me now, Cory Medici. Come on, let's face the firing squad."

***

Rachael had been pacing the floor and constantly checking her watch. It had been a while since Cory's last visit, but this visit would be special. Cory had never had a girlfriend that Rachael was aware of. At least, he'd never had one he wanted to introduce her to. She knew from their phone conversations this was serious, and he'd already taken her to Castello. That could only mean the girl was aware of what Cory was, and Shade had accepted her into the coven. She saw the SUV pull into the driveway and her son exit the car. She flung the door open and was already down the front steps as the two of them approached. She held her arms open to her son. "Cory!"

Cory looked up as his mom rushed out the door. He knew she'd be waiting for them. Her hair seemed much greyer than the last time he saw her. Every time he saw her, it was a stark reality check that her life had not been easy. "Mom!"

He hugged her tight and noticed her frailty. He'd become so accustomed to the vampires, whose strength and muscle mass were so defined, she felt like a piece of bone china in his hands, fragile and breakable. "You look amazing, Mom. Let's go in, I want you to meet Maddie."

Madison smiled as Cory embraced his mom and followed them inside. She tried to imagine Shade with this woman, and forgot, for a moment, that Cory's mom aged, and Shade didn't. She shook the image from her head. Rachael gave Madison a big hug.

"Welcome to my home. I know it's nothing as grand as Bel Rosso, but it's comfortable here. I made up the guest room for the two of you. Do you need help with your luggage?"

Madison returned the hug. "Thank you. You have a lovely home. And please, let Cory get our stuff. You've done enough already."

"Mom, relax, I'll get the luggage in a bit. Just sit down and talk a while. This is my girl, Madison." Cory took Madison's hand and led her to the couch, where they sat down together. "Oh, Dad and Kate send their love."

Rachael sat down across from her son and his girlfriend, and she could feel her son's happiness radiating off him. She'd thought her son couldn't get any happier when he was found by Shade, accepted as his son, and accepted into the coven. But she was wrong. Looking at him now, it was like he'd found the other half of himself. It was something she'd dared not even dream for him. He'd been rejected by the mortal world, and he'd finally found a place with the immortals. She knew, even in that world, he wouldn't have been accepted had it not been for Shade and the power he held. Maybe, for the first time in her life, she was free of the guilt of bringing this child into the world.

"Cory, I'm so happy for you."

95

Cory and Madison had been taking some day trips into San Francisco, and even riding the ferry over to Sausalito and Tiburon. Cory's mom had come to the city with them one day, but she said she preferred to be at home. Madison liked Cory's mom, although she was quiet and tended to keep to herself a lot.

In the evenings, they'd ride the subway back out to Walnut Creek and have a late dinner with his mom. One evening, his mom pulled out a bunch of photo albums, and they sat down together, looking at old photographs. There were a fair number of pictures of Cory as a baby and as a young child, but less as he got older. Both Cory and his mom seemed more sad than happy when they looked at the old pictures, and Madison noticed Cory was rarely smiling in the photographs.

Rachael ran her fingertips over a picture of Cory as a teenager. "Those were hard times, for both of us. I knew he was different, even as a baby, but I had no resources. I know now Shade would have helped me, helped us, but I didn't know how to find him. There was a big Goth community here, like when the hippies took over the Haight in the 60's. We frequented the underground clubs. There were people there who were really into the whole vampire mythology, believed in that whole thing, and there were some who claimed to be vampires. I don't know if I really believed that at the time, or if I just thought it was a cool place to hang out with my friends. Anyway, that's how I met Cory's father. Once Cory was born, I kept going back to the club, trying to find some of the vamps to help me out, to explain to me what I needed to do for my son, but they rejected me, and him. He grew up so angry at the world, and who could blame him? And then, for him to find his father, by pure circumstance..."

Rachael wiped away a tear. Cory slid his arm around her

shoulder and kissed her cheek. "It's all right now, Mom."

She nodded. "Yes, it is. But if he hadn't found you, Cory, I'm not sure either of us would be here. I don't know how much longer you could have survived on the streets, and if you had died, I think I would have taken my own life. I carried so much guilt over the life I brought you into."

Cory removed the photo album from her hands and gave her a hug. "It's all in the past now, Mom, for both of us. I know I made it hard for you, I blamed you for a lot, but that's gone now. I feel like that was a different person. We've both changed, thanks to Dad."

Rachael nodded and gave him a sad smile. Cory thought she looked tired, and older than her years. "Why don't you go ahead to bed? You don't need to stay up to entertain us. Madison and I can just watch some TV."

Rachael stroked his cheek. "You're sure you don't mind?"

Madison spoke up. "Of course not. Besides, I feel like I walked a hundred miles today. It will feel good to just sit here and put my feet up."

Rachael excused herself and retreated to her bedroom, and Madison slid over on the couch next to Cory. Cory grabbed the remote and turned on the TV, but the volume was low, and neither of them were really engaged in the program.

Madison looked at his delicate profile in the reflected light of the TV. "I'm so sorry, Cory. I had no idea how bad things were for you growing up."

He shrugged it off. "It's nothing. Water under the bridge."

They sat silently for a few minutes, starring at the TV screen, when she spoke again. "Will you take me there? To the club, where your mother met Shade, and where you later found him?"

Cory stared at the TV, as his mind wandered back to the time when he practically lived in the clubs, and all the pain, abuse, and degradation. The things he'd done to survive. "No, absolutely not, Maddie. Why would you even want to see it? That's no place for you, no."

"You don't need to hide your past from me, Cory. I'm not

ashamed, and neither should you be. None of us has any say about how we come into this world. And the more I see of your life, the more I understand you."

Cory stood up, pacing the floor. He threw his hands up in the air, he didn't want to ruin this trip, but he was just going to tell it like it was. "Look, it's not like any club you could imagine. It's run by the vampires, and there's open sex and feeding. Vampires will feed from mortals, and often, they have to seduce them, and then wipe their memory of the event. But in the clubs, the mortals come to them willingly. It's loud and crowded, and things happen there, things I don't want you to see. It's not even like when my mom went there. Times are different, people exchange blood for money, mortal and immortal. I don't want you to be exposed. Besides, I'm not like that anymore, and I promised Dad I wouldn't take you there. He'd kill me if he knew we were even talking about this."

"Cory, you said you found your father there, with Kate. He took Kate there. He must have had a reason, and I suspect the reason was to show her who he was, or at least, who he'd been. If you think this will make me change my opinion of you, I assure you, it won't. Please, take me there, and then we can both put this behind us. You don't have to worry about things you're keeping secret in your life, because there are no secrets. Can't you see that?"

Cory ran his hand through his hair as he flopped down on the sofa next to her. "I love you so much, Maddie. There's nothing of the past inside me anymore. Maybe..." His words left him as he considered her request. "If we go, you have to promise me you won't leave my side, we aren't staying long. You're mortal. They'll assume you're there to offer yourself to them. I don't even know what they might try to do. I just worry as to whether it will be safe enough. I could even run into people I once knew."

Madison squeezed his arm. "We'll be fine. We'll stay together, check out the place, and leave. No big deal. I know it torments you. This is a good way to put it behind you, once and for all."

Cory lowered his head into his hands. "What am I doing? Okay, let's just do this tomorrow night and be done with it. But you can't say a word to Mom, nothing. She'll go off if she knew. We'll tell her we are going into the city for some night life, deal?"

"Deal. We'll spend some time here tomorrow with your mom, then go out in the evening. But, right now, I'm exhausted. Let's go watch TV in the guest bedroom where we can just fall asleep."

He followed her to the bedroom his mother made ready for them, and turning on the TV, they climbed beneath the covers, but they were both asleep before the program was over.

The next day, they went with Rachael to do some grocery shopping and to see the small town of Walnut Creek. After dinner, they got dressed for an evening out and let her know they were going into the city.

"Okay, be careful."

Cory kissed her forehead. "You worry too much."

Cory drove the SUV to the subway station and they rode into the city, where Cory led her into the seedy Tenderloin district. Madison could see the immediate difference in this section of town over the historic Russian Hills and Pacific Heights sections. Cory led her to a nightclub that was painted black on the exterior. She could feel the vibration of the heavy bass from the music inside.

As they approached the club, they stepped in line with young people dressed in leather, with multiple piercings and their visible skin covered in tattoos. Madison already felt out of place in her long boho skirt and fringed suede leather top.

As they approached the doorman, he looked up with surprise. "Cory! We haven't seen you in years, brother. Welcome home."

"Hey man, yeah been a while. I moved away, so we're just visiting. Looks like things haven't changed much."

The doorman released the rope, allowing them to enter, without asking for the cover charge. It was normal protocol for the mortals and the half-breeds who came willingly to offer themselves up to the vampires in the club. Cory remembered the nights he came here, willing to do whatever they wanted, in exchange for money.

He led Madison inside, where they were immediately assaulted by the heavy metal music. Cory could feel the vibrations in the floor. He leaned in close to her ear, his voice still loud in order to be heard over the bone-shattering music. "Let's stay as close to the dance floor as possible, we don't need a table. Whatever you see, don't stare."

Madison giggled. "Come on, Cory, how bad could it be?"

She grabbed his hand and pushed her way through the crowd onto the dance floor. The flashing strobe lights made it hard to see much of anything, but she caught glimpses of people in the booths along the wall, quick flashes as the strobe light illuminated the room before plunging it back into darkness. She caught images of bodies, some of them nude, wrapped around each other, feeding, having sex, and she quickly looked away.

Madison made a space for them on the dance floor as they started to dance to the pounding beat of *Living Dead Girl*, by Rob Zombie. This wasn't the type of music she'd normally be listening to, but she'd heard it at the frat parties. As they danced, a very tall man approached and ran his hand through Cory's hair before bending down and licking his cheek.

He hissed through clenched teeth. "Hello, delicious. It's been a while. How much for the night?"

Cory recognized Drew's voice, as he felt that hot, wet tongue snake across his cheek. He looked at Maddie as she stared in horror at the tall, slim male vampire with the pierced nose, and rings on every finger, covered in leather from head to foot. Drew had been one of Cory's *regulars*. His money flowed easy, and he had a taste for young males. Cory could score big bucks with him. But tonight, Drew's appearance made his stomach churn, and he hated that Madison was seeing this.

Drew licked his lips and ran his forefinger down Cory's arm. "Come, you were never shy. Come to my booth, and bring her along, if you must."

Cory shook his head. "No, Drew, just visiting, not interested. Find someone else. Leave us alone." Cory drew Maddie close, hoping to shield her from the ugliness.

In a flash of insight, Madison realized his life here. He sold himself to the vampires to survive, to be used by them for feeding and sex, and she knew now why he didn't want to come. Madison took his hand and looked the vampire in the eye. She presented a face of bravery she didn't feel on the inside. "He's with me. Come on, Cory."

Madison pulled at his hand and made her way to the bar. The woman behind the bar looked up in surprise at Madison and wondered what the hell this girl was doing here.

"You lost, sugar? This doesn't look like your crowd." Then Tatiana saw Cory and her face lit up with a smile. "Cory! Where have you been? We haven't seen you in years. You doing okay? What can I get for you?"

"Hey Tat, I live on the other side of the States, now. I'm great, and you?"

He gave her a big smile. Tatiana had always been nice to him, she'd give him tips on where to score, and she gave him drinks for free. Turning back to Madison, he inquired, "Whatever you want, what will it be?"

Madison shrugged. "Just wine, if you've got it. White please, not the Midnight stuff."

Tatiana laughed. "You don't need to tell me, sugar. We can spot a mortal a mile away."

She poured a white wine for Madison and a Midnight for Cory. As Cory pulled out his wallet, Tatiana held up her hand. "It's on the house. So, Mr. Medici, who knew? I guess you're living the high life now?"

Cory laughed a bit. "Trust me when I tell you, it was a surprise all the way around. But listen to me; you'll take my money, because I owe you. You always looked after me."

He slid the $100 bill across the bar and gave her a look that said he wasn't taking no for an answer. Tatiana leaned over the bar and kissed him on the lips.

"You always were a sweetheart, Cory, true Medici, like Shade."

Cory shook his head and laughed. "I don't think I'm in the same league as my dad, but yes, my life is very different. This is my girl, Madison. We're just visiting my mom for a few weeks."

Tatiana took in the young girl at his side. She looked sweet and kind. She looked nothing like the mortal girls who frequented this club. She didn't think she was Cory's type, but then she realized, she'd never seen Cory outside this club. Tatiana served up several more drinks to other customers, never missing a step behind the bar as she continued her conversation.

"So, how's Shade? Still playing the role of devoted husband and father?"

"You wouldn't know him now, Tat. He and Kate are really happy, and they have a new baby. He put away his reputation for good, but then, so have I."

He glanced over at Maddie, as she looked uncertainly at the activity in the booths, before looking back at her wine. He took her hand and pulled her close, kissing her sweetly.

Tatiana shook her head. "Well, I have to say, I never thought I'd see the day any female would tame Shade Medici. But I'm happy for you, Cory. I really am."

***

Sitting at the far end of the bar, Max had been scoping out the merchandise. He'd been plying the young, blonde, mortal female with alcohol for the past half hour. He immediately recognized Cory when he approached the bar and he tuned in to their conversation, suddenly more interested in revenge than sex. He looked around the club and it didn't take long to figure out Cory was here alone with the mortal. How convenient.

Max pushed the young girl he'd so eagerly been seducing back into the crowd, telling her he'd changed his mind. Slipping a few seats closer, he kept his back turned, as he listened to their conversation and followed them out when they left the bar. Shadowing himself, he followed them through the San

Francisco night, and teleported above the subway, following them into Walnut Creek. Cory helped Madison out of the SUV, and Max trailed them to the cozy little house. He landed in a tree that sat on the property and contemplated his next move.

"Well, well, well. Good things come to those who wait. You took everything from me, Shade. I think it's about time I even up the score."

96

Max sat in the rented palatial house in Sea Cliff, with views of the Golden Gate Bridge and the San Francisco bay to his right, and the Pacific Ocean to his left. He sipped at the Midnight, as he stared out the floor to ceiling windows at the breathtaking views. He'd come here to escape the tension in the royal palace and perhaps even to save his own life. He knew Fan Chen had no use for him now. Setting the wheels in motion to get rid of Rissa and watching Alec struggle to regain his footing in the presidential campaign had been entertaining and had helped to soothe the anger that constantly boiled up inside him. Seeing Shade's half-breed bastard last night, roaming the city with a mortal, had only served to stir up all the hatred and anger again.

After the Battle of Bel Rosso, and the slaughter that came with the onslaught of the animals that attacked his army of warriors, he knew he could never directly go after Shade again. But the half-breed, that was a different story. The half-breed had no worth. He could never rule Shade's coven, but for whatever reason, Shade had accepted this bastard offspring into his coven. He couldn't get to Shade, and he could probably never get close enough to Lorenzo, but the half-breed was an easy target. In the long run, he knew the elimination of Cory wouldn't have any impact on the Medici dynasty, but he could at least inflict emotional pain on his old nemesis by taking something from him he loved. He emptied his glass as he teleported out. He didn't have a plan. He'd have to follow the half-breed and the mortal and wait for his opportunity.

***

Madison and Cory slept late, and it was almost noon before they woke. Climbing out of bed and shuffling into the kitchen, the smell of coffee brewing drew them both in. Rachael laughed as she saw the two of them with their tangled hair and puffy eyes.

"You two look like you had a long night. Here, have some

coffee. You'll feel better."

They filled two mugs to the brim with the rich, black coffee. Madison added sugar and milk, and Cory sipped at his black. His mother looked at them both. "So, what are your plans today?"

Cory yawned and stretched, "Nothing specific. I think Madison wants to check out some of the clothing shops in the Haight, and there's a great dim sum restaurant over in the financial district we wanted to try. Do you want to come along, Mom?"

Rachael shook her head. "I've got a new sweater I'm knitting I want to finish. Really, Cory, don't worry about me. I like to stay at home."

He polished off the last of the coffee and kissed her on the cheek. "Okay, then. We're going to get dressed and head out. We won't be as late tonight. Should be back by nine, at the latest."

They scrambled to get dressed and out of the house, making their way to the subway.

Madison looked over at Cory as he drove. "Do you think she's lonely?"

Cory scrunched up his brow. "I'm not sure. I think she feels safe there, you know? I mean, it's not like her life was in danger or anything, but before Shade found me, she worked two jobs and could barely make ends meet. After she was pregnant with me, she never went back to college. She had low paying jobs and had to pay for a sitter. We never had any money and we were always getting evicted when she couldn't pay the rent. And then, when I got older, I was always running away. I think this is just the first time in her life she hasn't had to struggle and worry, you know? She has the house, and it's paid for. Dad makes sure her bills are paid and she has an income. She likes to read and garden. She knits and has a few other hobbies, but I think she pretty much keeps to herself. She seems happy to me, now. Or maybe not happy, maybe content is a better word."

Madison nodded. "Yeah, I can see that, content and safe.

That house is where she feels safe."

He parked the car and they jumped on the subway, heading into the hustle and bustle of the city.

***

Max saw them jump on the subway and teleported ahead. He'd have to check each stop in the city to see where they got off. They exited on Cole Street and started walking in the direction of Haight-Ashbury. How predictable. He followed behind them, shadowing his presence as they walked from shop to shop, the blonde mortal making several purchases.

The Haight was full of old buildings, some of them no longer occupied, and a few narrow alleys. The streets were crowded, but as always in the Haight, there was a sizable population of young people, looking bedraggled, sitting on the sidewalks. Street musicians played for money, and tourists gawked. Max thought he could manage to grab these two in broad daylight without a lot of notice or interference. He saw them exit the shop and he followed closely, bidding his time.

The half-breed pointed to a side street, and the young couple took a right. The half-breed was pointing to a house, and Max could hear him talking to her.

"Janis Joplin lived here back in the 60's. It was before my time, but my mom used to point this house out to me all the time."

Max swooped in, taking advantage of the fact they walked onto a residential street without a lot of foot traffic, and grabbed them both, teleporting out at warp speed.

***

Shade was deep in his death slumber, the daylight keeping him down. It was his immortal curse, this forced sleep in the daylight hours. He felt the sudden spike of fear, and the rush of adrenalin that woke him with a jolt. He sat straight up in the bed as his son's blood bond connected him to Cory's intense emotions. His beast emerged as Shade screamed out, his voice rattling everything inside the house. "No! Cory!"

He bolted from the bed and was acutely aware the room was sealed in darkness, and the electronic blinds still sealed the windows. He could feel Cory's panic, but he was unable to see what was happening.

He fell to his knees and threw his head back, his eyes blazing bright red, as his fangs punched through. Closing his eyes, he concentrated all his energy on Cory, and knew his son feared for his life.

Kate was in the nursery with Theresa. Sophia had been cranky today and Kate had made her a paper crown. Whenever she cried, Kate placed the paper crown on the baby's head, and the crying stopped immediately. She and Theresa had laughed so hard, they both had tears on their cheeks. Their laughter was interrupted by Shade's scream and Kate's blood ran cold. Her first thought was of Lorenzo. She quickly handed the baby to Theresa and ran to their bedroom to find Shade on his knees, and the beast emerged.

Kate looked around the room for any signs of danger and saw nothing as Luca appeared at her side and called to him, "Master!"

Kate could hear the sound of little feet running and turned to see Lorenzo barreling down the hall in her direction. She dropped to her knees and grabbed her son, who fought her, trying to get free and run to his father.

"Daddy!"

Kate was in tears now, feeling only his panic and fear, but seeing no danger. She screamed at Shade, "What's happening? Shade, talk to me!"

Shade was aware they'd entered the room, but his attention remained focused on Cory, as the fear inside him built. Looking through a red haze, he stared at Kate as the beast growled out his son's name. "Cory, it's Cory!"

Luca crouched before Shade. "Master, talk to me. Tell me what you know."

Shade shook his head back and forth, his curls now dripping with sweat. "Something has Cory. I don't know what, or where."

Shade stood and turned, he was fully naked, and his sinewy muscles taunt as his eyes lit the room in a soft red glow. "We need help. I need Raven. I need to know where Cory is. I can't go to him!"

Luca called out to Raven telepathically, alerting him to the situation as Kate was still wrestling with Lorenzo, who was fighting her to be released so he could run to his father. "Lorenzo! Calm down. I need you to be a warrior, now. Help Mommy."

Lorenzo settled instantly and looked at her, his eyes filled with fear. "Tell me what to do, Mommy."

Kate looked at Luca, confused. Only Shade could feel Cory, and he wouldn't be able to leave to help him until sunset. "Go back to Enzo for now. Please."

Marcello appeared in the hallway, pulled by his master's fear and he heard Kate's instructions to Lorenzo. Marcello picked up the child and took him back to his classroom. "Come on, little warrior. We need to keep you safe, so your father can figure this out."

Kate approached Shade and stood with Luca. "Lover, tell me what to do."

Shade just shook his head. He had no answers.

They felt the energy in the room shift as Raven landed only a few feet from his master. He took in the scene of his master in full beast mode, and Kate and Luca in front of him. "What the fuck?"

Luca filled him in on what little they knew. "It's Cory. Something's happened to Cory, but Shade can't see where he is."

Kate scrambled for the cell phone on the bedside table. "I'll call Rachael. See what she knows."

Rachael answered almost immediately and she could hear the panic in Kate's voice when she asked about the whereabouts of Cory. Rachael told her Cory and Madison went into the city. She remembered Madison wanted to shop, and she thought they were going to Haight-Ashbury. Now Rachael was concerned. "What's going on, Kate?"

Kate told her they weren't sure, but she had to go now, and she'd call back. Kate hung up and dialed Cory's phone, which went to voicemail. She recounted what she knew about where

Cory and Madison were going. Shade was beside himself with anger, the beast ready to rip anything apart.

She looked at Raven. "Can you find them?"

He shook his head. "Kate, I can get back to Cali in a second, but I have no blood bond to Cory. I won't be able to track him. If you think they were in Haight-Ashbury, I may be able to follow their scent, but that's a long shot."

Kate covered her face in frustration. "There must be something!" She wondered if her gift could help and looked up at Raven. "What about Poe?"

Raven looked confused. "What about him?"

"Maybe Poe can track him. Leave now. Leave! Poe will be waiting for you."

Raven looked at Luca for direction and Luca shrugged. "I got nothing, bro. Until Shade can leave here, we have no idea how to find Cory. Maybe Poe can track him. It's worth a try, and better than doing nothing."

Raven nodded and was gone before their eyes.

***

Max landed in the dark and abandoned warehouse in the naval yards at Hunter's Point. The area had been left abandoned after WWII when it became contaminated with radioactive materials and had only recently begun to have any inhabitants.

He swiftly tied Cory to a support column inside the warehouse, his hands bound behind his back, not that the half-breed offered any threat to him. Cory's strength could never come close to that of a master, let alone a master warrior. He held the blonde in a tight grip against his chest as she struggled to get free. He grabbed her hair and yanked hard. "Hold still or I'll kill you now."

Madison whimpered and stopped her struggle, looking with pleading eyes at Cory.

Cory felt helpless, as he was tied tightly to the column, and it allowed him no movement. He'd been calling out to his dad telepathically, but he knew it was daylight still, and he wondered if they'd ever get out alive. His dad couldn't respond to him in the day, and no one else had any idea where in the hell they were, including him.

He calmed himself as much as possible, trying not to scare Madison any more than she already was. Cory knew this vampire was a warrior. He'd been around enough warriors to recognize that much, at least, but he had no idea who this was, or why they'd want him or Maddie. But he knew one thing, this was about the Medici. "Stay still, Maddie, just do whatever he tells you."

Cory's eyes signaled to her to try to relax. He could barely breathe, himself, but he'd give up his life for her. He just had to figure out how to stall this vampire long enough to give his father time to get here. *Use your head, Cory!* He knew he could telepathically send his father whatever information he could gather. Maybe he could find out who this was, and what he wanted.

"Who are you and what do you want with us? We've done nothing to you."

Max smirked at the half-breed, his laugh an evil taunt. "Well, you're right about one thing, half-breed. You've done nothing to me. You and your mortal toy mean nothing to me. Unfortunately, the same can't be said of your father. He has destroyed me, taken everything, and left me humiliated among my kind. The Battle of Bel Rosso was my undoing. It's a dangerous thing, to leave a vampire alive who has nothing left to lose. I escaped with my life, only to find it was a life not worth living, and every day, I'm aware of his joy and good fortune. I may not be able to touch the Medici, but I can destroy something precious to him. Something he'll never be able to replace, something that will leave him feeling pain and guilt for all eternity, for not being able to save you in time. So, please..." Max stroked Madison's long hair and pulled it back from her neck as he licked the vein, pulsing hard and fast with her fear. "I beg your forgiveness in advance. You've done nothing to me. You are but pawns on my chessboard, and you serve the purpose of taking a king to his knees."

Cory knew instantly this was Max, and the more he talked, the more Cory knew he was looking at his own death. Max would never let them get out alive. His only hope was if his father could find a way to get to them. Cory looked around the abandoned warehouse and transmitted that image to his father. He closed his eyes and focused all his senses. He picked up the scent of the salty water and could hear some sea gulls in the distance. San Francisco was surrounded by water, so that didn't help a lot, but at least he knew he wasn't in the middle of the city. He let Shade know they were on the waterfront, in an industrial area, surrounded by the smell of machine oil, and his captor was Max.

Max continued to toy with Madison, teasing her, as Cory struggled to release the bonds that bound him to the column. His own beast emerged, as his fangs punched through.

"Let her go. Take me, do whatever you want to me, but let her go. I'm the Medici's son, I'm the one you want, not her. You can kill me, but your fate is sealed. My dad will slaughter you."

Cory saw the anger rise in the vampire, and it was just what he wanted, anything to draw the vampire's attention away from Madison, and it worked. The last thing he saw was Madison dropped to the floor as Max backhanded him across the face and Cory lost consciousness.

***

Shade closed his eyes, and took a long deep breath, clearing his mind of everything, so he could focus on his son. "Quiet!"

The noise around him was a distraction, and he needed to focus hard. The room went silent, as Kate and Luca stood waiting. Shade saw images of a dark warehouse, but they were from the inside, so that didn't help him with location. He heard his son telling him they were near the waterfront, and he heard the name that sent a chill down his spine...Max.

Shade knew this attack was pure revenge, and a cowardly one, at that. He looked at Kate as he quietly told her what he knew. It was time to end this once and for all. "It is Max. He has Cory and Madison. I don't know where."

He turned to Luca. "All Medici go on red alert, right now. I want this house locked down, no one comes or goes. I will go alone. No one fucks with my *familia*. This is personal, and I have a score to settle. Move now!"

Luca took off to deliver the message to the camp, as Shade began to dress in his leathers. He wasn't in a panic. He'd prepared for battle many times. This was revenge, and he'd slay Max the second he was able to leave this house. He only hoped it was soon enough to save his son.

Kate had watched in silence as he pulled on the leathers, crafted for him by Cory. She had no doubt about the outcome for Max. Today, tomorrow, or some day in the future, Shade would make him pay for this with his life. But they still didn't know where Cory was, or if they could get to him in time.

He kissed her softly as he walked from the room. "I am going to see Lorenzo and my princess, and then I am getting my weapons. I am going to save my son. I will return when this is over. I won't be back until Max's head is detached."

He stepped with purpose into the hallway, and headed to the children's rooms. His mind was clear, and he had but one purpose. Maximus had tried once to stop him and lost. It had been a mistake to let him retreat. It wasn't a mistake Shade would repeat. He sent a message to his son, **"I'm coming for you."**

97

Kate followed him as he walked to Sophia's room. "Find Raven. I've sent Poe to him and asked him to track Cory. Follow Poe and he'll lead you and Raven to Cory."

He kissed Sophia, and then headed to the classroom where Lorenzo was being held by Marcello, with Enzo in attendance. Shade knelt down as his son ran into his arms, giving him a hug. "I am counting on you, little warrior, to make sure your mommy and sister are safe."

Lorenzo kissed his father and squeezed him tight. "I will, Daddy."

He kissed his son then took Kate in his arms. She fought the impulse to tell him to be careful, knowing it only annoyed him. She'd keep her worries to herself. "Go now, bring our son and Madison home, and bring Rachael. I'll manage things here."

He kissed her as if it might be the last time he ever kissed her, and Kate fought back any tears.

***

Raven and Poe took off for the Haight District. Raven had no idea if the bird could pick up Cory's scent. It seemed like a long shot. The sun had gone down, so if he could find anything for them to follow, he knew he'd be able to lead Shade to his son.

The bird seemed to search randomly, landing on rooftops, and occasionally landing on the sidewalk, pecking and creating a raucous that drew the attention of the people passing by. The bird didn't seem to be reacting to anything, but Raven followed close behind, keeping an eye on him. Poe took off, and Raven picked up the pace, trying to follow him as he rounded the corner and saw Poe in front of a small Victorian style house. Raven rushed to the sidewalk in front of the house, and noticed two shopping bags that had been blown into the yard. As he stood in front of the house, even he could pick up Cory's scent. It was very faint, and Raven was about to enter the house when the bird flew skyward again, cawing loudly. As he watched the bird fly toward the bay, he received a telepathic message from Shade. It was Max, and Cory was being held inside a vacant warehouse near the waterfront. His master would soon be on the way. Raven took to the sky himself, teleporting ahead of the bird, but allowing Poe to navigate.

***

Max waited patiently for the young half-breed to regain consciousness after taking the hard blow to the head. The blonde mortal had screamed and started to run when she saw the half-breed collapse. Max quickly had her within his grasp and dragged her back to the center of the warehouse where Cory was tied up. He turned her, so she was facing Cory, making sure she could see him as he pulled the hair back from her face. In a hoarse whisper, meant to scare her, he leaned in close to her ear, "Poor half-breed, he doesn't stand a chance, and neither do you. But I'd hate for either of you to miss the show."

Cory moaned and slowly lifted his head to see Madison in Max's grips. "Maddie!"

Madison struggled and tried to reach him, and Max only tightened his grip and laughed. Making eye contact with Cory, Max asked him, "Are you watching, half-breed? I wouldn't want you to miss this."

Cory's beast emerged as he struggled against his restraints, but he couldn't free himself, and he looked on in horror as Max stroked Madison's neck before lowering his mouth to the pulsing vein, and slowly sinking his teeth into her.

Madison screamed and struggled. This felt nothing like when Cory fed from her. It was painful, and she could feel her life draining away. This vampire was going to kill her.

Cory struggled, calling to her, "Maddie! Please, don't hurt her. You don't have to hurt her!"

Max looked up with an evil grin, the blood dripping from his chin. "Oh, but I do, half-breed. That is the whole point."

***

Shade landed on the roof of an old building near the bay. It was dark here now, and he'd teleported slowly, staying just behind the setting sun. He looked across the bay to Alcatraz Island, and up and down the coastline. He honed his senses, trying to pick up Cory's scent, but was only inhaling the smell of the salty air, and the fuel oil from a few tankers moored nearby. He telepathically talked to his son as he leapt from rooftop to rooftop. **"Hang on son, I am here, I'm coming, be strong. You are Medici."**

His son didn't answer, but Shade felt his fear, like a stake through his heart, and he had no doubt Max would kill his son. Shade heard the loud caw of the large, black bird as Poe swooped down in his direction. Raven landed on the rooftop next to him.

Shade looked at Raven expectantly. "Tell me what you've found."

Raven caught his breath as his long black hair was caught in the wind. "Poe has his scent. He picked it up in the city and I've been following him. Has Cory been able to send you anymore information?"

Shade shook his head. He couldn't believe they must rely on a bird to save his son and his girlfriend. Poe cocked his head, looking and listening, before he took flight again, and both Shade and Raven followed, leading them further away from the city.

Poe landed on a large warehouse that looked like it was abandoned years ago. The bird pecked frantically at a rooftop skylight, making an intense racket. Raven landed beside him, as Shade signaled he was going to land on the ground. Raven squatted near the window, covered in decades of dirt, and used his hand to clear a section to allow him to peer inside the building. What he saw made his blood run cold. **"Max has Cory tied to a column, middle of the building. He's feeding from Madison."**

Shade felt his body shake as his beast emerged, his eyes now red, with intent to kill. **"Get inside. You get Madison, I'll get Cory. Max is mine."**

Shade slid along the outer wall and found a dock door that had been pried open. He looked inside to see Max holding Madison, too involved in draining her to sense any danger.

Madison was struggling very little, which told him Max was close to ending her. Cory was tied to a support column and begged helplessly for Max to stop.

The next sound was that of breaking glass, as Raven dropped through the rooftop window, and landed right in front of Max. Max looked up, startled by the intrusion, and dropped Madison in a heap on the floor. Before he could respond, Shade appeared, positioning himself between Max and his son. Shade made quick eye contact with his son. His face was swollen, his mouth bleeding from a busted lip. The blood dripped from his hands from his struggles with the ropes, as they cut into his wrists.

Shade and Raven moved at once as Max took a stand against them, his beast ready for battle. Max's eyes glowed red in the darkened warehouse, and it didn't take him long to see the imposing outline of Shade. He dropped into a crouch, ready to pounce. The time for playing was over.

Shade pulled the sword from the sheath on his back as he hissed, "This night, you die, you black bastard. A half-breed and a mortal? You fucking coward! "

Shade swung the sword, aiming for the throat, but Max catapulted himself over Shade's head. Shade spun, with shuriken's flying, and instantly smelled blood as they hit their target. Shade pulled another sword from the sheath on his back and attacked. Max was armed with only a blade and was no match for the swords that were wielded, so expertly against him. The two flipped and rolled, in a game of cat and mouse, but each strike left its mark on Max, as his blood left a path across the dusty floor.

Raven kept an eye on Shade's progress, but quickly moved to pick Madison up and move her away from the fight. He stood over her, legs spread, and sword drawn, waiting to help if his master needed him.

Poe flew through the broken window and went straight to Cory, where he began to methodically peck at the ropes until Cory was freed. Cory wanted to run to Madison, but his instincts told him to stay still and clear of the battle. He dropped to his knees and tried to follow the fight to the death that was taking place in front of him. The battle between the two master warriors was moving so fast it was hard for Cory to distinguish the action. He felt the hot blood splatter across his face, and prayed it was Max's blood and not his dad's.

Dust and debris fell down around them, and the floor began to crack, like an earthquake had hit the building, as the two warriors battled nonstop. Shade felt the slice of his opponent's knife in his arm, as he spun away. In the fraction of a second that the wound distracted him, Max used the diversion to go for Cory. If he couldn't defeat the Medici, he'd at least take his son.

***

Kate knew the babies were safe and retreated to their bedroom, shutting the door behind her. She cleared her head and focused all her attention on Shade. She couldn't follow him, because her duty to the coven was here, but she could stay linked to him telepathically. She'd feel what he felt. She knew they'd found Max, thanks to the guidance from Poe and she sent the bird her gratitude. She felt the encounter between the two masters, as they battled to the death, and Kate knew only one of them would walk away from this tonight. She paced the floor, her heart pounding, and she sent him her strength. She felt the sharp pain across her own arm and knew Shade had been wounded. She dropped to her knees as her beast emerged, and the roar that escaped her shook the house.

Shade felt the energy of his mate's beast merge with his own, as he leapt skyward, both swords drawn as he came down on top of Max, slicing through both shoulders as he dismembered him. Max dropped instantly to his knees in front of Cory and they locked eyes. Cory's eyes turned red and his fangs punched as he growled. "Die, bastard!"

Shade swung the sword with his right hand in a wide arc, slicing cleanly through his rival's neck. The power of the sword sent Max's head into the air, spinning over and over, as his body collapsed in a heap. His beast was not sated, and continued to mutilate the headless body as the blood gushed like a river under his booted feet. He was covered in blood, skin and bone, and yet, he didn't stop. His beast was out of control.

Madison lay on her side on the cement floor and stared blankly at the blood bath taking place right in front of her. She remembered this warrior with the long black hair who'd rescued her, and knew he was from the Medici coven. She felt too weak to sit, let alone stand. She looked helplessly at Cory, as his father slaughtered the evil creature that had been feeding from her neck. The black bird flew around the warehouse, squawking loudly, and she saw the head of the enemy roll across the floor in their direction. She looked on in horror as the head rolled to stop in front of her. Her eyes widened in fear but she didn't have the strength to move. The large black bird swooped down, landing on the severed head, his talons sunk deep into the flesh, as the bird plucked out one eye.

Raven was watching the slaughter when Max's head landed near them, and Poe began to feast upon the severed head until Raven kicked it away, watching the head roll in a macabre unbalanced wobble. His master continued to mangle the dead vampire and showed no signs of stopping. Raven approached his master slowly and yelled, "Boss man, enough!"

Shade appeared not to hear him, as Raven shouted at him again. His master stepped back, a sword in both hands and covered in the blood of his rival as his beast retreated. Shade dropped his swords, as they clanged to the floor and went straight for Cory, picking him up in his arms. Turning to Raven, he barked out commands.

"Teleport Madison to Bel Rosso now. She is in the most danger. I will take Cory. Have the California warriors come and clean up this mess. Send someone to Rachel, have them teleport her to Bel Rosso as well. We move out now!"

Raven moved like lightning, gathering up Madison in his arms and was gone in the blink of an eye. Shade looked down at his son as his blood tears poured from his eyes. He was alive.

Cory was weak with relief, and curled into his father's chest, his head on his shoulder. Cory knew they weren't out of the woods yet. He'd seen how close Max came to draining

Madison, and he wanted to get to her. "Hurry, Dad."

Shade held his son tightly in his arms, whispering in his ear, "Feed from me, son, you need the blood. We are going home."

He heard Cory moan as his fangs hit his vein and he teleported them from one side of the States to the other.

***

Kate gasped and dropped forward on the floor as Luca ran to her, helping her up. "Kate!"

She whispered, "It's over."

Luca could feel the absence of his master's anger but wasn't sure if this meant victory or defeat. His master still lived, though, as he could feel the power of him in his own veins. "What happened?" He gently lifted Kate to her feet.

Kate spoke softly, "Max is dead."

They felt the energy shift as Raven teleported into the room, carrying a barely conscious Madison, with open wounds on her neck, her face pale and colorless. Kate responded to her immediately. "Oh my god. He almost drained her!"

She started to offer herself to Madison to feed when Luca stopped her. "It can't be you. Shade may need your blood. Marcello is here, and no one feeds from him. She will have to feed from him."

Luca summoned Marcello and Lorenzo followed in his footsteps, curious about all of the sudden activity in the house. Marcello took the girl from Raven's arms and Raven supported her head. Kate talked to her in a soft voice, "Madison. You must feed. Feed from Marcello. He's Medici. He's a warrior. His blood will heal you."

Madison stared back at Kate in confusion, wondering where she'd come from, and heard her voice as if it came to her through a long tunnel. She started to close her eyes again. She just wanted to sleep, but Kate was insistent, shaking her awake. "Madison, you must feed."

Marcello laid the girl on the floor and bit into his own wrist, placing the bleeding wound on her lips. "Drink, *mia cara*. Drink so you will live."

Madison felt the blood across her tongue and grasped

Marcello's wrist, sucking hard and drawing strength. She closed her eyes as Kate, Raven and Marcello all loomed over her. With each mouthful of his blood, she felt her body respond. The wounds on her neck began to heal, and her weakness faded.

Shade teleported inside the house, holding Cory in his arms. He bound up the stairs, as he heard another warrior drop in behind him with Rachael. Rachael screamed for Cory and rushed up the stairs behind Shade.

Shade followed the commotion and carried Cory inside their bedroom where Marcello was feeding Madison, and he felt Rachael enter behind him. He locked eyes with Kate. "He is alive, he has fed, but he had wounds that need tending to."

Cory groaned and lifted his head, seeing Madison on the floor with Marcello. He scrambled to be freed from his dad's arms and rushed to Madison. He dropped to his knees and pulled her into his arms. Rocking her softly, he saw the visible fang marks in her neck. "I'm here, Maddie, it's okay. You're okay, we're safe. We're safe."

Cory looked at his dad, his face a picture of the agony he felt inside. "Is she going to be all right? Is she going to live?"

Marcello reached down and laid his hand on Cory's shoulder. "She'll live, Cory, she fed from me. We had no choice, brother. It will take her some time, but she needs to rest, and she'll recover. She may need more blood in a while."

Shade felt Rachael grip his arm, as she almost passed out at the sight of Cory. He steadied her as he hugged her tightly. "Rachael, it's okay. Cory is fine, so is Madison. Just breathe. I think we all need to clean up, and these kids need some rest to heal. Marcello, you can take the camp back to yellow alert. I think we are clear. I only saw Max, and he is dead. I don't think there were others helping him, but let's not take any chances."

Luca and Marcello nodded and exited the room. Rachael still clung to him as he locked eyes with *bel.*

Kate got up from the floor and went to him, her arms surrounding both Shade and Rachael. She looked at Shade and she spoke to him in her head, **"I love you."**

She stroked Rachael's back, and calmed her. "Come on.

Let's get you in a hot bath, and then you need to lie down. Cory's fine."

Emma instantly appeared and helped Rachael to a guest bedroom. Theresa entered to help take care of Cory and Madison.

Raven lifted Madison in his arms and turned to Cory. "Where do you want her?"

Cory led the way to his bedroom as Raven carried the girl. Theresa followed, her pockets filled with the herbal remedies and salves from the old country. Theresa took charge as they entered Cory's suite.

She spoke to Raven, "Place her in the tub, then leave."

Raven set the girl down gently in the tub, then exited the suite. Cory and Theresa worked together to remove her clothes and filled the tub with hot water. Theresa washed her wounds as Cory supported her in the tub. Once she was cleaned, Cory lifted her from the tub and Theresa dried her off and started to apply the thick salves to the wounds on her neck. She directed Cory to lay her on the bed, where Theresa pulled the covers under her chin.

"Let her sleep for now. The rest will help her body heal." Then she turned her attention to Cory. "And now you. Get out of those clothes, so I can see what you need."

Cory started to object, telling her he was fine when Theresa started to remove his shirt. "Don't argue with me, Cory."

Cory stepped out of his clothes and Theresa inspected him for injuries. "Shower now, clean these wounds, I'll wait." She sat on the side of the bed as Cory showered, and watched as Madison slept soundly. When Cory returned, she filled the cuts and abrasion with the pungent salve. "Now, drink some Midnight, and get to bed, yourself. Sleep will heal you."

He downed the glass of Midnight she handed him, and then she practically pushed him into the bed. "No arguing. Sleep."

Cory wanted to go check on his father. He wanted to thank Raven and Marcello, but as soon as his head hit the pillow, he felt the tiredness overtake him. He lay with his arms around Maddie and fell into a deep sleep. Theresa watched as his body took over to heal itself, and then exited the room.

***

Kate looked up to see Lorenzo still standing in the doorway, wide-eyed. "It's okay, Lorenzo. Daddy's okay, and Cory and Madison are safe."

The child nodded his head.

"Go to Gita, please. I need to take care of Daddy."

As Lorenzo turned to leave, Kate laid against Shade's chest as his arms surrounded her. "Come with me."

She led him to their bathroom where she stripped him from his leathers and removed the blood-caked boots from his feet. Shedding her own clothes, she stepped with him into the shower, as the hot water cascaded over them both. Her hands washed him, as he bent his head to her and fed.

98

Madison had lost track of time. She lay curled up in a ball in the safe haven of Cory's bed. He'd stayed by her side, brought her food and drink, and soothed her each time she woke in a panic. She slept sporadically, but every time she slept, she dreamt, and in her dreams, she felt the fangs of that monster at her neck, she saw the carnage left by Cory's father as he ripped that monster apart and the room was splattered in blood. She'd never seen so much blood. Her last memory was of the severed head landing only inches from her face, those dead eyes staring into hers, right before the large black bird plucked out the dead man's eye. She couldn't remember much after that. She couldn't remember coming back here to Bel Rosso.

Kate checked on her periodically, but Madison wasn't ready to talk, and always pretended to be asleep when Kate entered the room. She felt Kate's hand stroking her back, brushing her hair away from her face, her voice soft as a whisper, encouraging her to come back to them. It only made her retreat more deeply into herself, and she wondered if she'd ever want to leave the safety of this room.

Cory had healed from the ordeal. It was slow, but his dad's blood had helped the progress. His heart was breaking for Madison. The terror she felt after everything she'd witnessed had traumatized her, and now, he couldn't reach her. She responded to no one but him, and even he was limited in his abilities to pull her back. She never left his bed, and he'd stayed close to her side. He held her when she woke in panic attacks, dreaming of the kidnapping.

Madison made a small moan, and he gently pushed back the hair from her face. "It's okay, Maddie. I'm right here, everything's fine, you're safe. I won't let anything happen to you."

He looked at her haggard appearance. He'd bathed her every night as she just stared blankly ahead, and then returned to his bed. He was scared for her mental health but had no idea how to reach her. Rubbing her back and massaging her shoulders, he watched as she sank back into her stupor, curled up like a baby in the womb.

Creeping slowly from the room, he went down to the kitchen to retrieve some hot soup and a drink for her. His mind was whirling, he'd not been sleeping much either.

Looking up as he entered the kitchen, Shannon was fixing herself a cup of coffee. "How's Madison today? Any change?"

His hair was a tangled mess, and Cory pushed it out of his eyes, his voice sounding hollow as he answered in a monotone. "No change."

Shannon took a sip from the steaming cup of coffee, and then blew on it to cool it down. "No offense, but you look like shit, Cory. Do you want me to talk to her? Kate says she's unresponsive. Does she talk to you at all?"

He sighed. At this point, he'd try anything to get her to talk. "She wakes in a panic. I bathe her, I have to feed her. She stares at nothing, she doesn't see me. I'm losing her, and in the process, losing myself. No mortal should have seen what she saw or experienced the hell that bastard inflicted on her. I just want her to respond to something, anything!"

Shannon set the mug on the counter and put her arms around him. "Listen. Why don't you go to Luca's suite, take a shower in there, and then get something to eat for yourself. You're no good to her if you fall apart too. In the meantime, I'll go talk to her, okay?"

Hanging his head, his voice sounded low and defeated, "You know, even if she comes out of this, Maddie may want to leave me. I don't want to go on without her. She was learning to understand our world, and now, look at her. This isn't fair."

Shannon guided him in the direction of Luca's suite. He moved like his shoes were weighted down with lead. He wanted to scream, hit something, but knew that wasn't going to fix anything. He was lost too.

Leaving him to shower, Shannon took a deep breath before heading up the two flights of stairs to Cory's suites. The rooms had a stale smell to them. She pulled back the drapes to let in the sun, and even though it was cold out, she cracked open the windows to let in some fresh air. She looked around at the dishes Cory had piled on the coffee table and shook her head. Calling to Emma, she asked her to come in and get the rooms cleaned up.

Emma rushed in with maximum efficiency and started to clean the rooms.

Shannon took advantage of her help, asking for her assistance to change the bed linens. "Let's get her bed changed while you're here."

Emma nodded and scurried off to get fresh linens. Shannon entered the dark bedroom and opened the drapes, cracking open those windows as well. She heard a disgruntled moan from Madison, as she lay with the covers pulled over her head. Shannon sat down on the side of the bed and gently drew back the blankets, exposing the young girl's face. Madison still looked pale and had dark circles under her eyes. Shannon stroked her face but spoke with authority, "Okay, girl, here's how this is going down. You're going to get up and walk with me to the bathroom, where you're going to take a shower. And while you're doing that, Emma is going to get this bed changed. Understood?"

Madison looked back at her with pale eyes and nodded.

"Good, come on." Helping her from the bed, Shannon led her to the bathroom as Emma rushed in behind them. Shannon turned to Emma, "And bring us some coffee when you finish with the bed please, Emma."

Shannon guided the young girl into the shower and turned on the steaming hot tap. She helped her lather up and washed her hair. "We're washing him away, Maddie, all of it. Right down the drain. Max can't hurt you now, understand?"

Madison didn't answer but looked back at her, and that was a start. Shannon helped her from the shower and dried her off briskly, stimulating her skin, helping to get her circulation going again. She pulled a comb through her wet hair, and then used a hair dryer to blow out her golden locks, letting them dry into their natural waves and ringlets. "There, you look better already. Now, come with me."

As they returned to the bedroom, the bed had been made with all fresh linens and blankets, the room dusted and vacuumed. The pillows were stacked against the headboard and Shannon pulled back the covers for her. "Sit up in bed."

Madison did as she was told and climbed back in the bed, resting her back against the stack of pillows. Shannon handed Madison a hot mug of coffee from the tray left at the bedside and took one for herself.

Madison sat on the bed, her back against the pillows and her knees pulled up to her chest, wearing a clean gown. She knew it wasn't her gown. Perhaps it belonged to Kate. She gratefully accepted the mug and sipped at the hot coffee, feeling its warmth slide through her, warming her from the inside out.

Shannon looked at her with a critical eye. "You've been up here hiding away for a few days now. You're going to have to come out sometime."

Madison whispered, "I know."

Shannon looked at her with sympathy. "You know, Maddie, I'm not going to say I know how you feel, because I don't. I know you were scared for your life and scared for Cory's. I know what Max did to you, and I can't imagine it. But you're safe now. We're both still mortal, but to Shade, that makes no difference. From his perspective, we're part of the coven, do you understand?"

Madison nodded her head.

"Good, because that's important. When anyone in the coven is threatened, then all the resources of the coven are brought forth to protect them. You need to understand that Shade would have come for you, even if Cory hadn't been there. Do you get that?"

Madison looked back at her with a blank stare, absorbing that information. Sliding closer, Shannon rubbed her arm. "No one here can promise you that you'll never encounter danger. But no one can promise you that in the mortal world, either. All

I can tell you is you'll always have the protection of this coven. Every person here has a duty to protect you, and Cory, and me. No one life is considered less valued than another. Do you understand? Their strength comes from their bond to each other, their loyalty. It took me a while to figure that out."

Madison nodded slowly. "But when I close my eyes...it all comes back."

Setting the mug aside, Shannon embraced her. "I know. I understand that. But you have to come back to us. Come out of this room, be with the family, and realize we're all here for you. The longer you hide from this, the harder that becomes. Don't let Max steal another day."

Madison nodded her head, but a single tear ran down her cheek. "I'm tired of feeling afraid. I'm just so tired of feeling afraid."

Shannon hugged her tight. "You're going to be all right, Maddie. Trust me, okay?"

Cory returned to the suite, freshly showered and in clean clothes. Shannon smiled at him, as she stood to leave. Leaving the two of them alone, Shannon headed down the stairs. She could hear Kate in the nursery with Sophia and took a detour. Standing in the doorway, Kate looked up.

"Hey. What's up?"

Shannon shook her head and relayed to her best friend her impression of Madison's progress. "I'm not sure how to help her past the fear, Kate. She has to move past that before she can move forward."

Kate nodded, as she handed the squirming baby over to Theresa. She remembered well the immobilizing fear after Cuerpo attacked her, and he never got close enough to touch her. She couldn't imagine what Madison must be feeling. But Shade healed her somehow.

"I'm worried for her too. Cory stays at her side day and night. I check on her several times a day. I don't know what else to do. I'll talk to Shade again when he wakes. We can't lose her. Not after everything she's been through."

The two women hugged, and Kate returned to their

bedroom, climbing into bed next to him. The events of the past few days had taken their toll, but Sophia's needs didn't allow for her to take a break and she quickly fell asleep, waiting for him to rise from his slumber.

The electronic blinds rose in their timely fashion, as evening descended in the mountains of Virginia. The house had become deathly quiet lately, everyone on edge. Lorenzo had been kept busy with his school work, going to camp, and attending to Zeus. Sophia had even been shuffled into a better routine and kept as quiet as possible. As Shade opened his eyes, he lay still; knowing *bel* was asleep beside him.

Max had taken a toll on all of them, and still was, and it ate at him. He should have never let Cory and Madison go to California without a protector, but he'd let Cory convince him otherwise. He almost lost them both. The young woman was so traumatized she never left his room. Shade had tried to talk to Cory, but he, too, was not as responsive, and Shade knew this house wasn't going to get back to normal unless something happened. He'd hoped Madison would heal with time, and things would work themselves out, but he knew, deep in his heart, he'd have to step in.

He hadn't approached Madison since their return. Cory had told him it would 'freak her out'. Throwing his arm over his eyes, he gathered himself before sitting up on the side of the bed, his elbows on his knees and his head in his hands. He had to do something. He wasn't going to stand for this any longer. He was the master of this coven, the leader of this family, and his family needed him to put it back together. He just wasn't sure how and where to start.

Feeling his weight shift in the bed, Kate knew, before looking at him, he was troubled. "Lover? What's wrong?"

Running his hand through his hair, his mind was working overtime to no avail. "My family is what's wrong, *bel*. I have made some mistakes and I placed lives in danger. The choices I made were wrong, and I knew deep inside they were wrong. I have to make them right."

Kate sat up in the bed and laid her head against his back.

"What can we do? Shannon spent the afternoon with Madison. I think she made some progress, but the girl is so afraid. I remember that fear, after Cuerpo, and hers must be a hundred times worse. I don't know how to undo the past. Her body has healed, but it's her mind that holds her gripped in fear."

He sighed in exasperation. "I talked to Rachel, she's okay, but she fears for Cory." Standing up quickly, he shook his head, spoke with purpose, "I let this go too long, I thought it would work itself out, but that has not happened. There is a solution, it's the only one I have. I didn't want to do this, not to her, but I cannot see another way. This has to stop. No one in my household should ever live in fear. No one who loves my son should live in fear."

Pacing the floor, he stood at the window, his arms crossed over his chest, looking at the waning evening light. Turning to her, he locked eyes with his mate. "I am going to dream-walk."

Kate sat up straight. He rarely used his gift. "Will that work?"

He paused before he answered, "Maybe. I need to get rid of her fear, make some of the memories disappear, so they don't keep replaying in her head. I can't erase this memory completely. Too much time has passed, but I can do a rewiring, of sorts."

He walked back to the bed and sat down beside her. "Cory says she is afraid of me, so how do I get close to her? Do we tell her or not?"

"I don't know how it works. Do you need her permission? Will she feel anything?"

"I don't need her permission. I can go to her once she is asleep, but if she wakes, I don't want to frighten her more. I have to be alone with her, no distractions."

"Just go to her, Shade. Do what you have to do."

"I don't know if I can handle her freaking out over my presence. Tell me how to do this, *mi amore*. I can't traumatize her more."

Kate slid from the bed, quickly getting herself dressed. "Get dressed and come with me."

Taking his hand, she led him up the stairs to Cory's suite. They entered quietly, and Kate could tell the rooms had been cleaned and smelled of fresh air. The door to the bedroom was closed and she tapped lightly. Cory answered the door and Kate told him they needed some privacy with Madison. Cory looked confused but didn't question the look of determination on his father's face.

As Cory brushed past him, Shade grabbed his arm, spinning him toward him and embraced his son. "It is going to be okay, son, I am going to help her, just leave me to be alone with her for a while. I am going to fix this."

Cory felt his dad's stress, but he also heard his words. If anyone could get through to her, it would be his dad. "I just want her back, Dad, I want my Maddie back."

Shade ran his hand through his son's hair and hugged him tightly. "I am going to bring her back."

Cory headed down the stairs and never looked back. Shade turned to Kate. "You lead, I follow."

She smiled at him, as he used her common refrain, and she entered the darkened room, approaching the bed as Shade followed at a discreet distance. Madison had returned to the fetal position, covered in the blankets. Kate pulled the blankets down from her face and gently woke her. "Maddie, wake up for me please."

Madison's eyelids fluttered lightly before she opened her eyes to see Kate seated beside her. She was about to sit up when she saw the shadow of a tall man standing behind Kate and she started to panic. Kate shushed her, telling her it was just Shade and she was safe.

"Maddie, I want to leave Shade here with you. Do you understand?"

Madison scooted her back against the headboard and pulled the blankets up under her chin. She looked at Kate with questioning eyes, but she knew in her heart she was safe here. "Yeah, okay." Her voice trembled when she spoke.

Shade stepped closer to the bed and laid his hand on Kate's

shoulder. "It's okay, *mi amore*, go, leave us and close the door. Make sure Cory is all right. Madison and I will be fine."

He looked at Madison, her eyes huge in her head, and he knew he had to make her understand what was going to happen.

Kate left the room, looking over her shoulder at Madison. She smiled at the girl, hoping to instill some sense of security. Closing the door behind her, she joined Cory downstairs.

Madison sat still on the bed, her eyes on Shade. She'd felt intimidated by him since the first time she'd seen him. And now, she saw him again in her head, his sword removing the monsters head, his swords and teeth ripping through him, as the blood flowed. She knew his actions were to protect her and Cory, but the vision of the violence wouldn't leave her.

Shade sat on the edge of the bed. He could feel the absolute fear and horror ravaging her. Taking her hand, she started to pull away, but he grasped it lightly. Stroking her palm with his thumb, he tried to make eye contact with her, but she couldn't look at him for very long.

"Are you frightened of me? I would never hurt you, Madison. I care about you a great deal, but I need you to trust me. I know what you have seen of me, and you know my power. But I have other powers too, powers that can help you right now. But you have to trust me first. You have to want to let go of the fear."

Her tears rained down her cheeks. "I'm so tired of being afraid."

Her tears broke his heart. He slowly drew her to him, pulling her to his chest, as she laid her head on his shoulder.

"It's okay to be afraid. Sometimes, fear makes us stronger. But you are trapped in your fear. I want to help you. I want to take that fear from your memory. I am a dream-walker. I can go inside your dreams and rewire some of those memories. It does not hurt. You feel nothing. I cannot make what happened disappear completely, but I can blur your memory, and stop the scenes from replaying in your mind. I can make this happen for you. But I don't want to do this without you knowing. I do this because I love you, and I love my son. I want you to come back to our family, we miss you. So, please, let me help you. Will you do that for me?"

His voice was deep, hypnotic, and soothed her. His strength was a comfort to her and she relaxed into him. She felt drawn into a trance and knew that was part of his power as well, but she felt safe with him. In fact, this was the safest she'd felt since the incident. With her face buried in his chest, she answered, "Yes."

"That's my brave girl. Now, come lay down."

Slowly helping her lay down, he smiled softly down at her. "I want you to sleep. I will help you fall sleep. You will dream, one more time, but it will be the last time you will see these visions as they were. I will step inside your dreams, and I will alter what you see. You won't wake up until it's over."

Staring at him as he spoke, he locked her tight into his gaze. He laid her back on the pillow, his voice a soft monotone that calmed her, lulling her into sleep. Her eyelids fluttered several times and then closed. He drew her into a deep sleep, listening to the sound of her breathing. Laying his hand on her forehead, he felt her fear, as it rolled out of her like a living entity. For the first time, Shade saw himself through her eyes, as he ravaged Max. Her memory was vivid and detailed, and he walked into the dream and physically changed her vision of him, blurring the images of blood, beheading and gore. He faded the image, like an old photograph that had been left in the sun until the people almost disappeared into the background. The clanging of his sword, and Max's scream, cut short as his head was severed from his body, were replaced with nothing but a white noise she wouldn't recognize. He could smell her blood, as Max fed from her, and he felt her pain and fear as he drained her and her body weakened from the loss of blood. He saw that final image her memory held of Max's head, on a wobbly roll that landed before her, with Max's cold, dead stare looking back at her just before Poe plucked one eye from the socket. The event couldn't be erased, but he'd rearrange the puzzle pieces, so they no longer fit together.

Shade could feel himself being slowly drained mentally, the process taking all of his concentration and mental capacity. Struggling to work as fast as he could, he wanted to make sure every second that haunted her was altered in a way that made it hard for her to remember. He felt his own exhaustion taking its toll, and he let go, stepping out of her dreams.

Madison had fallen into a deep sleep, and the dream started to repeat, but this time, she watched as the colors started to run, and the edges faded, like watercolor paints, one color bleeding into another until the image was blurred. The images became less clear and were harder and harder to grasp. As the dream became more abstract, so did her fear and she could feel her body relaxing as the dream faded. She didn't wake with a start, her heart pounding and covered in sweat. She woke slowly, gently, and she knew he'd taken the fear. The tears returned, but they were tears of gratitude. This man she'd feared had saved her once again.

He heard her sobs, but knew they were tears of relief. As she sat up slowly, she threw her arms around his shoulders and wept. Wrapping his arms around her, he let her cry. "Shh, let it go, Madison. I have you. It's going to be okay now. Welcome back to us. We have missed you."

99

Shade stayed in Cory's room with Madison for a while, both of them quiet. Madison seemed a bit more at ease after the dream-walking. He knew she'd always been intimidated by him, but the battle with Max had totally shaken what little confidence she'd felt with him. As she slowly sat up, he smiled at her. His voice was calm and coaxing as he helped her up.

Scurrying into the bathroom, she got dressed and looked much better when she exited. She stood before him and wasn't sure what to say. He could sense, from her body language and the way she cast a furtive sideways glance at him, that she was still unsure as to how to proceed.

Holding out his hand to her, he was worried still. She had to readjust to their lifestyle, and he hoped she wouldn't always be looking over her shoulder. "Let's go downstairs, shall we? Join the family. Get you some hot food, and let's all sit down and talk."

Shade didn't miss the smallest of smiles, as she took his hand and allowed him to lead her downstairs, into the kitchen. To his surprise, Shannon was there with Luca, making her habitual coffee. Cory was standing and starring off into space but snapped out of it immediately and hugged Madison into his arms. Nodding to Luca, Shade spoke to Shannon as she grinned from ear to ear. "Where is Kate?"

Shannon turned to him and raised an eyebrow. "I imagine she's with the baby, or Lorenzo, or both. The kids keep her pretty busy. Do you want me to get her?"

"*Si*, thank you. We are going to go into the living room, and I want Kate with us. I also need Rachael."

He turned to Cory. "Get your mom. We need to talk, all of us together. This is important."

Before leaving to get his mother, Cory smiled at Madison, giving her a sideways hug as his dad continued to issue instructions.

"Grab something to eat. I am going to go make us a nice fire in the fireplace. When you are done, you and Cory come join us."

Heading into the living room, Shade made a fire appear in the stacked logs with just his thoughts. The heat felt good. He stood in front of the fire, leaning with his hands on the mantel. He was exhausted but needed to make sure his family was whole again.

Shannon ran up the stairs, and let Kate know Shade was calling the family together. She took the baby from her arms, telling her, "Go ahead. She's quiet now anyway."

Kate left the nursery and encountered Cory, exiting the guest bedroom with his mom, and they headed down the stairs together. Kate was glad to see Madison exiting the kitchen, showered and dressed, and carrying a large mug of coffee. They headed into the living room where Shade was standing in front of the fire. Rachael curled up in a large arm chair as Madison and Cory sat together on the love seat. Shade took a seat on the sofa, and Kate curled up next to him.

Kate looked at him, and could see the fatigue in his face. "What's on your mind?'

Cazzo, he was so mentally wiped out. "It seems we are always dealing with our *bambinos*, either older or younger ones, *si*?" He laughed softly. "I see I have an authoritative effect on my *familia*, no one speaks until I start. Not sure if that is a good thing or bad. First of all, let me say that letting Cory and Madison go to California alone was something I was not too keen on. I should have insisted on a protector, and that is my burden to bear. No one could have seen what was coming, not even me. But that threat has been extinguished now. Everyone is healing, and some of us will take longer than others." He made eye contact with Madison, and she nodded.

"But one thing remains heavily on my mind, and that is the safety of Madison and Cory." He paused a moment before continuing. "Madison, I want you to move into *Bel Rosso*."

Startled to hear what he was suggesting, she shook her

head. "But I have school. I'm almost finished. I graduate in the spring. I don't want to quit."

Shade stared at her hard. He liked this young woman immensely, but she would abide by his orders. "Madison, I cannot let you out of Bel Rosso any longer without protection. Moving in here guarantees all of us peace of mind. I do not expect you to give up school, education is vital. So, we are left with some options. One of them is to have a personal protector for you. You move in here, we get you a car, and your protector drives you to and from, stays on campus with you, but out of sight. Give me your thoughts."

Madison blushed. "You mean like a chauffeur? I'd show up on campus driven by a chauffeur like some rich kid? And you want me to give up my place?" She looked at Cory. She hadn't really thought in detail about their future, but she realized now she'd assumed he'd move away from his parents and the two of them would live somewhere else together. "Do you think this is really necessary?"

Cory slid his arm around her shoulder. He was at least glad to see his old Maddie return when her freedom was compromised. "Maddie, you're looking at this all wrong. Dad wants to keep us safe. We can live here easily. My rooms are bigger than your apartment. Having a protector is no big deal. They don't hang on everything you do. They're just around in case something gets dicey, like Luca and Kate. I want this because I don't ever want to be that afraid for you again. I love you. I want us to be together for the rest of our lives. I'm not taking any chances."

Madison looked around the room as they all stared back at her, waiting for her response. "What about my potter's wheel? What about my art? I need to take things into town."

Cory turned to face her. "Those are just details, Maddie, we'll work through all of that. You won't be a prisoner here. Please, listen to my dad; he knows what he's doing."

Seeing the confusion on the young girl's face, Kate knew this was a lot to take in. "Madison, I know this sounds drastic, but we can manage everything. Decide what you want to bring from your apartment and move it here. If you want to redecorate Cory's suite to reflect something for the two of you, then feel free to do that. As far as the potter's wheel, we have plenty of space here. The garage is huge, and enclosing a space for your studio wouldn't be a problem. The building already has electricity, heating and plumbing to accommodate the mechanics who maintain the vehicles. We can give you more room than you have now. As far as a protector goes, he can be as visible or invisible as you want. Luca is my protector, and you can see he doesn't follow on my heels, but I never leave Bel Rosso without Shade or Luca."

Madison felt conflicted. There was a part of her that sought the security, especially after what had happened in California, but she didn't want to lose her independence. "But I can still go to class, right? I can still graduate?"

Kate nodded her head. "Of course. You can come and go as you please. Living here is safer for you now, that's all."

Madison bit her lip and reluctantly agreed. "Yeah, okay, I guess. So, is Luca my protector too?"

Shade shook his head. "No, I think that vampire has his hands full. Two *bambinos* and my *bel* is a bit more than any ordinary protector should be dealt. I want you to have someone you are comfortable with, someone who can blend in to your environment. I think Hyde would be a suitable protector for you. He likes you, and you got on well with him in Florence. Hyde has had several assignments as a protector, and he has done well with each. There is nothing we cannot fix, or make accommodations for, Madison. I want you to live without fear, feel free to come and go. Make this your home. This is not a punishment but a gift. As for the car, you choose whatever you like. Hyde will drive you back and forth, and he can be discreet. Please Madison, will you do this for me, for Cory?"

Madison twisted the ring on her finger, and nodded her head, still unsure of this rapid change. "Okay. I have to give notice on my apartment, and I'll have to tell my parents I'm moving."

Shade nodded with a huge smile. "That's fine. We will have

Cory and Hyde help you move all your things. And I have a beautiful Palomino horse by the name of Biondo out there in the stables that desperately needs some love. She is yours now."

He hugged Kate as he looked to Rachael. "You have been quiet, Rachael. I know we threw you into this, but I wanted you to be involved in our son's life, see that he is fine. But I also am concerned about your safety. This incident has brought a lot to light for me. I want you to also have a warrior on patrol near you. It is easily done with my warriors in California. Raven can head that up. They can be as visible or as invisible as you choose. I want you to feel safe. I owe you so much."

Rachael nodded. "That's fine. I was never in any danger, but I understand. By having mortals close to you, we offer an easy target to those who can't get to you. They can use us as pawns. I'll do it because, in the long run, it protects Cory too."

"*Grazie.* I will have Dante fly you home whenever you are ready. I am sure I speak for Kate and myself when I say, you are always welcome here, stay as long as you wish." Shade laid his head back on the sofa and exhaled. "I am sorry, to all of you. I should never have let the two of them go unprotected. I am still struggling to deal with how I let this happen."

Kate laid her head on his shoulder. "Lover, how could we have known Max was in California? We can't live our lives looking over our shoulder. But this is good. We are stronger when we're together."

"*Si*, we are always stronger as *familia*, working together. I am exhausted from my dream-walking, and I must rest for a while. I hope to hell this does not mean I am getting old."

Kate giggled as she nuzzled into his neck. "Don't fade on me now, warrior! We still have another baby in our future."

100

Sitting in a window seat on the campaign bus, Alec stared out the window without seeing the passing countryside. Braden had been managing the press during the hiatus and painting a picture of the candidate in mourning but also a candidate who was still determined to fulfill his mission and his commitment to the American people.

They'd attended several rallies, and the crowds weren't as large. Many of those that did show up seemed to be drawn more by curiosity. The press was questioning whether he should remain in the race and asking whether it might be too soon for the Senator to get back in the game. There were suggestions that, perhaps, he should 'sit this one out', and try again in the next election. His poll numbers were slipping, and he'd come in third in the Iowa caucus. Before Rissa's untimely demise, he'd been a shoe-in for Iowa. In fact, the press had speculated his path to be the party's nominee was pretty much a lock.

He dropped his head back on the head rest and sighed heavily, scrunching up his forehead. Braden looked up from his laptop to see the pained expression on his face. He signaled for Kelsey to bring him a Midnight, as he moved to the open seat next to Alec.

"You okay? You look pale. I sent you a feeder last night. She texted me that you sent her away."

Kelsey handed him the Midnight, overhearing this interesting tidbit of information about the feeder. Alec accepted the glass and downed the thick wine in a single gulp.

"You can't fix everything, Braden. Besides, you know I don't care for the feeders. Too eager to please, and all the allure of a blow-up doll."

Braden stared back at him, getting annoyed. "Okay, listen to me. I expected this lag in the polls. That doesn't mean we can't turn this around, Alec, but you've got to get your head in the game. You've got to show some energy, some enthusiasm.

You're delivering your speeches like a robot. If you don't feel it, the people won't feel it. What's going on here? Do you still want this?"

Handing the glass back to Kelsey, he bent forward, his arms resting on his knees. "I'm not sure what I want. Even when it was right in front of me, and it looked like a shoe-in, I was starting to second guess myself."

Braden shook his head. "What do you mean? Is this because of Rissa? Do you need more time?"

Alec rubbed his face, clearly agitated. "No. It has nothing to do with Rissa. I'm wondering why I even want this. I mean, what's the point? The vampire community is against this, so it's not like I'll be doing anything to elevate our status in the world. It will be a constant game of subterfuge. That's all it was ever about. Me, obtaining the most powerful mortal position in the world, and hiding in plain sight, fooling them all. It's a game, Braden, a big fucking game. I was bored, and I wanted what I couldn't have."

Braden sighed heavily. "So, what are you saying? You're done here?"

There was a long pause before he answered, as he considered his options. What else would he do, if not this? He didn't have an answer to that. "Not yet."

The frustrated sigh from Braden could be heard all over the bus. "All right, Alec, I'll keep doing my job. But help me out here, brother, and start doing yours."

He got up and moved to the far end of the bus, putting as much distance between him and Alec as possible.

Kelsey brought him another glass of Midnight and slid into the seat next to him. He took the glass without speaking, sipping quietly as he looked out the window. She slid her hand along his thigh, covered in the rich fabric of his hand-tailored suit. "You know, Alec, I'd be more than happy to have you feed from me."

Removing her hand from his thigh, his grip on her wrist was much tighter than it need be, and he watched with pleasure as she winced in pain and tried to pull away. He chuckled at her reaction. "Somehow, my darling, I seriously doubt that. You have no idea what I need."

Kelsey rubbed her wrist and quickly stood up from her seat. The look he gave her sent a chill down her spine. This was a side of him she'd never seen, as she too scurried away, putting distance between them.

Alec returned to looking out the window as he thought to himself, Rissa would have loved the pain. She would have even loved the rejection. She wouldn't have run from him, she would have just tried harder.

101

The bus pulled into the parking lot for the last stop of the day. They had continued to attend rallies with dwindling numbers, and Braden kept pushing him to show more of the 'Alec' the voters had come to expect, but his heart was no longer in this race. His energy was low, as he'd not fed, continuing to reject the feeders Braden sent to him nightly. Alec knew it was taking a toll, and he'd have to succumb to his body's demand, sooner rather than later.

He made his way through the small crowd, and it looked like the press was starting to outnumber the constituents. He stopped to pose for a few pictures as he made his way to the podium and delivered his canned speech. As he spoke to the crowd, he made eye contact with a female reporter, who smiled up at him and winked. He held her gaze as he continued to speak, and several people in the front row turned to see what had captured his attention. The pretty blond reporter made no effort to hide her interest.

As the rally concluded, he stepped off the stage, and into a wall of microphones, as the press hit him with a barrage of questions about his dwindling poll numbers. He delivered his carefully prepared responses, as he eased his way through the throng. Just as he was about to break free, she stepped in front of him.

"Hi. I'm Jessica, and I'm a reporter for the local news station here in Dayton. Any chance for an interview?"

He stopped in his tracks and stared at the mortal. His gums itched as his fangs ached to break through. She was blonde, with blue eyes, tall, slender, and well-proportioned. She reminded him of Rissa. He looked at his watch. "Can you meet me later?"

She looked back at him coquettishly. "Of course, just name the time and place."

"I'm at the Hilton, the Presidential suite. Come after

eleven. My staffers have cleared out by then."

Jessica gave him a knowing smile and answered, "No problem. But just so I'm clear, is this visit on the record or off the record?"

For the first time in months, Alec felt the thrill of the hunt. "Oh, it's definitely off the record."

He climbed back on the bus with Braden and the other staffers as they headed back to the hotel. He knew the drill. They'd all congregate in his hotel suite and go through a debriefing of the day's events, examining what worked and what didn't, and then they'd go over the agenda for tomorrow. Alec was antsy throughout the evening, and Braden kept asking him if he was okay.

"I'm okay, Braden. Could we just wrap this up, please?"

After a few hours, the crowd exited his suite and he was finally alone. He was loosening his tie when he heard the light tap at his door. He opened the door to find the blonde reporter, holding a bottle of wine. "Is now a good time?"

He opened the door for her, as she entered the room with confidence. "I brought us some wine. Can I pour you a glass?"

He closed the door and slowly turned to her. "I have my own blend, but please, pour a glass for you, and get comfortable. I was just about to get undressed, myself."

Jessica grabbed a glass from the bar and poured the white wine for herself. She saw the dark bottle of Midnight sitting on the bar. "Is this your poison? I'd be happy to fix you a glass."

As he pulled the tie free from his neck, he started to unbutton the starched white shirt. "Please."

She returned with the two glasses of wine and took a seat on the ample couch. She'd been following his campaign from the beginning and had been planning to vote for him. She'd been at other rallies in Ohio, and was intrigued by him, but his wife, not so much. She couldn't say she'd spent any time mourning over the loss of his bitchy wife, and then she saw he was on schedule to make a campaign stop right here in her home town, she couldn't resist the opportunity to try to get up close and personal.

She set his glass on the coffee table, as she took a few sips from her own glass, and watched, mesmerized, as the white shirt slid off his broad shoulders. She'd hoped she'd understood his meaning when he said their visit was off the record, but if she had any doubts before, the Senator was making his intent crystal clear.

Alec tossed the shirt aside, and removed his belt, looping it in his right hand as he snapped the belt against his leg. "Have you been a bad girl, Jessica?"

She giggled nervously, wondering what she'd gotten herself into, but was eager to find out. She kicked off her heels and slid her bare legs under her. "I guess it depends on what you mean by bad."

He liked that she didn't appear afraid and was willing to explore. Sitting down next to her, he told her to drink up. She looked at him quizzically before downing the wine.

He waited as she emptied the glass. "Do you want another glass?"

She laughed. "Am I going to need another glass?"

His smile was seductive, his eyes had a glint of pure evil, and she couldn't turn away. "That will depend on you, my darling. Do you have a safe word?"

She looked confused as he took the empty glass from her hand. "A what?"

He chuckled. "Never mind, I never paid attention to safe words anyhow."

Before she was able to process his comment, he'd pulled her across his lap, when he lifted her skirt, his hand cupping the roundness of her ass. He stroked her slowly before pinching the firm flesh and she yelped, excited by his aggressiveness, and yet frightened at the same time. He could feel her sexual desire, and picked up the scent of her sex.

"Too much? Do you want me to stop? I'd hate to stop now, Jessica. There's so much to teach you."

Instinctively, she knew she should end this before it got out of hand. This was more than she'd bargained for, but his voice, his eyes. She felt drawn to him, unable to resist. Against her better judgment, she responded. "No, not too much."

He slid her panties down, his hand caressing the smooth, white flesh. He heard her moan, as her body relaxed, and he took that moment to strike her hard with the belt, the leather leaving a sharp red mark across her ass. She cried out as his hand slides over her mouth, muffling the sound of her cry.

He picked her up and carried her to his bed, where her arms and legs were tied down. She struggled against his unnatural strength and started to scream when his hand covered her mouth again. His face was only inches from hers, as he shushed her. "Do I need to gag you too? Or are you going to play nice?"

She looked back at him, her eyes wide with fear. What if he gagged her? What if she couldn't breathe? "I'll play nice."

His smile was evil as he looked at her, trembling in fear, and her fear excited him. He couldn't remember the last time he'd hunted a mortal, and he'd forgotten what a pleasure it was.

"Yes, you will. You're going to do whatever I want, aren't you, my darling?" He ripped her clothes from her with little effort, and she listened to the sound of the seams tearing away. He stood over her, admiring her nakedness, and she'd never felt more vulnerable.

"Please, don't hurt me."

He removed his own clothes as he climbed on top of her. "It's a little late to be worrying about that, don't you think?"

He took her over and over again, feeding deeply each time he fucked her. Despite her fear, he made her cum, her body responding to his skillful hands and large cock. He fed until he was filled, the hunger finally abated, and then he fell asleep beside her.

She lay beside him, caught in a space between exhaustion and unconsciousness. *He drank my blood. He has fangs. I saw them, I clearly saw them!* It was her last thought before she slipped back into the darkness, her arms and legs still shackled.

102

Braden was an early riser, always had been. He woke before the sun was up, and it was still dark in his room. He felt the warmth of the feeder who'd shared his bed last night. He didn't remember her name. Sitting up, he turned on the lamp on the bedside table, as the soft light illuminated the room. He felt her nestle down under the covers, seeking a few more minutes of sleep.

"Get up, get dressed. I need you to leave before there's a lot of activity."

The feeder reluctantly drew back the blankets and looked at him. "Should I return tonight?"

He was already standing and heading for the showers. "I'll let you know."

Braden could hear the door close in his hotel room when she left. He finished up his shower, shaved, and dried off quickly. He wanted to read the morning papers and check the TV news before he met with Alec and the staffers.

Stepping out of the bathroom, wearing only a towel, he grabbed the TV remote and turned on the news. He stepped outside his door to find the stack of newspapers from across the country he requested be left for him, *The New York Times, The Washington Post*, as well as the local papers.

He started dressing as the news covered local weather and traffic, then stopped and stared at the screen as the 'Breaking News' banner scrolled across the screen. The TV reporter was repeating a story they ran earlier. 'As we reported, our own political analyst, Jessica Broch, has been reported missing. Miss Broch attended the Presidential candidate's rally yesterday for Alec Canton and can be seen in this footage at the rally."

The image on the screen switched to show Alec as he was exiting the crowd, and Jessica stepping in to talk with him. Braden remembered the moment, but he was too far away to hear the conversation between them, and he hadn't paid any attention to it. Reporters approached Alec all the time.

The image switched back to the reporter, with a smiling head shot of the attractive blonde behind him. 'Eyewitnesses saw her leave the rally, but Miss Broch never returned to the station, and has not reported in. Her roommate said she didn't return home last night, and all attempts to reach her by cell phone have failed. The police are handling this case as a missing person at this point in time, and we encourage anyone who has seen Miss Broch to please call the police hotline number on the screen.'

Braden got a sick feeling in the pit of his stomach as he quickly finished dressing. He grabbed the extra key card he kept for Alec's suite, and rushed from his room, trying to walk quickly down the hall to Alec's suite without drawing undue attention. The sun was just coming up as he slid the card into the lock and opened the door.

Stepping into the living room of the suite, he saw the two glasses on the table and Alec's shirt on the floor. He could taste the bile in the back of his throat as his stomach churned, and he rushed to the door of the bedroom. Swinging the door open, he saw Alec, still asleep, her blood still on his face as he was draped casually over her. The girl was deathly white, and Braden rushed to her side of the bed. He could see she was still breathing, but only faintly, her breaths very shallow. He sighed in relief.

He pulled the cell phone from his pocket and ordered Kelsey to gather up a few of the male staffers and get to Alec's suite immediately. Braden started to untie the girl, releasing her arms and legs, and rubbing her chafed flesh, restoring her circulation. She moaned softly but remained largely unresponsive.

"Alec, wake the fuck up!"

Alec slowly lifted his head from the pillow, his head full of cobwebs. He'd not fed that deeply, or slept that soundly, in months. He looked, with some confusion, at Braden, who was bent over his bed, then turned his head to see the girl. "Fuck."

Braden jerked back the covers and shouted at him. "Fuck? That's all you can say for yourself? Get up, get dressed! This girl has been reported missing."

Alec was pulling on his pants when Kelsey and two burly male staffers stormed into the room. Kelsey took one look at the girl on the bed and covered her mouth with her hand. "Oh, god! Is she alive, Braden?"

He nodded. "Yes, but just barely. I think we can fix this if we move quickly." He grabbed one of the males by the arm and dragged him over to the bed. "Score your wrist, and get some blood into her, quick! As much as you can spare."

Turning to the other male, he told him to standby, and step in as soon as the first male was done. Alec was buttoning his shirt and watching nonchalantly as they struggled to save the girl.

"She's just a mortal. Why do you care? They're all disposable."

Braden screamed at him, "Are you fucking kidding me? She's all over the news! She's a fucking reporter, for Christ's sake! The police are involved. Right now, it's a missing person. Now get the fuck over here and erase her memory of last night."

Alec knelt on the bed and placed his hand on her forehead. Her color was already returning, as she weakly drank the blood from the wrist of the staffer. He wiped her memory clean. He knew between erasing her memory, and her blood loss, she'd remember almost nothing of last night.

Standing, he headed for the shower, and caught a glimpse of himself in the mirror, her blood still smeared around his mouth and chin. "Let me know when you get this cleaned up."

Without another word, he stepped into the shower, letting the hot water soothe him, as he held his face upward, letting the water wash the blood down the drain.

Braden was steaming mad. He'd kill him right now if he could. "Kelsey, look around the room, start in the living room. Gather up anything that belongs to this girl. Don't miss anything. Then wipe the place down. We don't know what she might have touched, so wipe down everything. Find a way to get a vacuum out of housekeeping, and vacuum the carpet, and that sofa."

Kelsey nodded and swung into action. "What about her?"

Sighing heavily, Braden shrugged. "If we can get some blood back into her, get her color back and let our blood heal the chafing marks on her wrists and ankles, I'll place her in her car. It's probably in the parking garage, somewhere. We should be able to find it with her keys, be sure to check her purse."

Kelsey found the purse on the floor by the sofa and dug out the keys for the girl's Toyota Camry. Kelsey held the keys up in the air. "Got it!" She tucked them in her jeans pocket as she started to clean in a frenzy.

Braden turned his attention back to the girl, as the second staffer stepped in place, scoring his wrist and placing it over the blonde girl's lips. As she fed, her color returned, and the dark, black circles under her eyes disappeared. She was gripping the staffers arm now as she fed from him. That was a good sign. Braden checked her ankles, and notices the red, raw skin was slowly healing.

Looking about on the floor, he saw the girl's clothes had been ripped. He wouldn't be able to salvage any of those. Sending the first male staffer on an errand, he told him to head back to Kelsey's room, and bring back some underwear and a pair of jeans and a shirt. The staffer hurried from the room as Braden sat down next to the girl on the bed. He pushed the other staffer away.

"Enough. Let's get her cleaned up now."

The staffer looked at him doubtfully. "But, master is still in the bathroom."

Braden looked up with disgust, then headed to the bathroom and opened the door. Alec was stepping from his leisurely shower and grabbed a towel. Alec looked up at the intrusion. "You still here?"

"Fuck you, Alec!"

Braden grabbed some washcloths, and wet them under the faucet, and grabbed a towel on his way out. Together, he and the staffer washed the girl off, removing the dried blood from her neck, mouth, and shoulders.

The other staffer returned with the clothes, and the three of them dressed her. Kelsey kept cleaning but tossed the car keys to one of the staffers who headed to the parking garage, in search of the girl's car. In the meantime, Braden pulled a few wine bottles from the bar, uncorked them, and emptied their contents down the sink. He grabbed up the one bottle that was already opened on the coffee table, wiped it clean, and poured out the remaining contents.

Kelsey had finished the clean-up and gathered up the girl's torn clothes. The staffer lifted the girl in his arms, as Braden pulled all the sheets and blanket from the bed. Shoving them in Kelsey's hands, he instructed her. "Burn these, and her clothes."

"Yes, boss." She hurried out, teleporting down to the basement of the large hotel complex into the massive laundry room and maintenance facilities. Finding the incinerator, she stuffed the damning evidence into the flames and closed the door, teleporting back to the suite. She arrived in time to see Braden telling her to wait here.

Kelsey stopped him. "Don't forget her purse. And her shoes. Here!" She handed them off to Braden, before he and the staffer teleported out with the girl. They landed next to the Camry, located by the first staffer, as the three men placed her in the car, behind the driver's seat. Jessica moaned as she was jostled into position and draped over the steering wheel of the car. Braden threw her shoes on the floor and left her purse in the passenger seat. They inserted the keys into the ignition. As a last step, Braden tossed in the empty wine bottles, closed the car door and hoped for the best.

"Okay, good job. Now get back to your rooms. Get packed and check out. Don't rush. Don't do anything to draw attention. Then get the fuck out of here."

"You want us on the bus today, boss?"

Braden shook his head. "Don't think so. Go home. I'll be in touch."

Kelsey was making a last minute inspection of the suite when Alec exited the bathroom, showered and clean shaven.

He scanned the room and saw the girl was gone. Walking to his closet, he started to get dressed for the day. "See, crisis averted. No big deal."

Kelsey glared at him. He put them all at risk with his reckless antics. She was too angry to speak. Braden reappeared in the room, grabbed the TV remote, and turned on the TV. There was no change in the coverage, still the same story of Jessica Broch as a missing person. Turning to Alec, he could barely control his anger.

"We're done here, Alec. I mean it. I've had enough of this shit. First Rissa, now this? There are only so many missteps I can clean up, brother. Find yourself another campaign manager if you plan to continue with this farce."

Alec sat down hard on the side of the bed, placing his head in his hands. "Wait."

Braden was about to leave with Kelsey when he paused. "Wait for what? You got any other secrets I need to know about?"

Alec shook his head, defeated. "Just end it, Braden. Not today, and not in this town. I don't want there to be any ties to the girl. Let's go to the next rally, and I want you to announce that it's over. Announce that I'm withdrawing from the race. Please. It is the last thing I'll ask of you."

Braden closed his eyes. He'd known Alec a long time, he'd helped him win his Senate seat, and he felt he owed him that much. "Okay, but that's it. I'm done, Alec, I mean it."

Alec answered in a whisper, "I know."

Braden grabbed Kelsey's hand as they turned to leave. "Get packed and check out, Alec. We need to put some distance between us and this city."

Within an hour, all of them were gone, back on the bus, moving on to Columbus, where Braden would break the news.

***

In the dimly lit garage, Jessica Broch lifted her aching head and looked around confused. She was in a parking garage, but she wasn't sure which one, or why. Her head was pounding, and she saw the empty wine bottles in the car. She wasn't a heavy drinker, so it only compounded her confusion. She dug in her purse and found her cell phone. It had been turned off. She had a vague memory of turning off her phone but couldn't remember why. Turning on the phone, she saw a lot of texts and unanswered phone calls, as well as news alerts. She tapped the news alert pop-up first and was startled to read she was the news. She scanned the missing person story and was even more confused. She remembered the rally, she remembered talking to Alec Canton, as she watched herself in the video, but she had no memory of anything after that.

Looking down at her clothes, she knew they weren't hers. Her feet were bare, but her expensive heels were lying on the floor on the passenger side of the car. She read a few texts, all of which were some version of 'where are you', or 'call me!' She had no explanation for why she was in the car, or why she was parked here, or what happened in the last twelve hours. Did she get drunk? Was she in a bar? If that's the case, and the whole city was looking for her, she was afraid she could lose her job. She was already on probation for showing up late.

She quickly hit dial on her phone. "Mom? It's Jessica. I'm okay."

103

The bus pulled into the parking lot of the arena in Columbus. Braden had sent out a notice to the press that they'd make a special announcement there, so he knew the event would have more press than usual. He'd been monitoring the situation in Dayton, where the news reported the missing reporter had been found, and it appeared she'd simply fallen asleep in her car overnight. Braden was glad the potential scandal was behind him, but still angry they'd had to deal with it in the first place. It was extremely irresponsible on Alec's part, and Braden felt like the decision for him to exit the campaign was a sound one. He couldn't fathom the damage it would do to the vampire community if they were all to be exposed while Alec was President. It would probably mean the end of all of them. They walked such a fine line, living in the mortal world.

He'd been writing Alec's speech for him, and Alec had practiced it and was ready. Braden had sent the speech ahead by email to be loaded on the teleprompter, but he kept a folded paper copy in his pocket, just in case.

As they exited the bus, the press was already surrounding them, and Braden pushed them back, telling them the announcement would be made inside. Alec walked stoically through the crowd, barely acknowledging their presence. Once inside, his supporters started to clap and cheer, as he and Braden made their way to the stage. Standing behind the podium, Alec raised his hand to quiet the crowd.

"I want to thank you all for coming and for standing behind me throughout this long campaign. As you're all aware, I lost my dear wife a few months ago. I took some time to heal, and I thought I was ready to resume this fight. But I've found I don't have the drive to continue."

He paused as he heard a collective moan from the crowd, and a few people yelled out, "We love you, Alec!"

"Thank you, sincerely. But the dream of occupying the

White House was not just my dream, it was our dream, and I'm afraid I don't have the same will to pursue it without her. For that reason, I am suspending my campaign for the President of the United States."

As he stepped away from the podium, the press was shouting questions. "Alec, will you resume your Senate seat?" "Senator Canton, where will you go now?" "Do you think you'll run again next election?"

He waved at the crowd, nodded, and with Braden's help, made his way back outside the rally. As they climbed back on the bus, Braden instructed their driver to take them to the airport.

"I'm flying back to Connecticut, Alec. You're on your own from here. The press is going to be climbing up your ass, so you might want to lay low for a while."

At the airport, Braden booked a commercial flight home, and Alec booked a private jet. Braden told him he'd settle up the final paychecks for the paid staffers and close all the campaign headquarters in the other States and would send him a bill for his services when it was done.

Alec thanked him, and with little fanfare, turned and headed toward the private terminals. Braden shook his head before leaving to catch his own flight. As Alec was walking to the terminal, he was mentally calculating how long it would take him to get back to D.C., and knew when he did, there would be a throng of press coverage to greet him. In an instant, he made his decision. "Fuck it."

He teleported out, and a short period later, was standing in the foyer of his Georgetown home. Santos rushed to greet him.

"Master, I wasn't expecting you. I didn't hear your car. Do you have luggage? I can get your luggage."

"No luggage, Santos. Bring me a Midnight, please."

The butler rushed off as Alec walked through the familiar halls of his home and into the family room where he turned on his TV. Every news channel was covering his announcement to leave the campaign, and the pundits were all speculating as to his reason. And just as he expected, the press was waiting for his arrival at Reagan National Airport, even though airport officials had told them they had no flight plan for a private flight out of Columbus, nor had they been notified to anticipate Mr. Canton's arrival.

Santos returned with the Midnight, and Alec was enjoying a long draw from the glass when his cell phone rang. He checked the ID, and saw it is was an international exchange. He scrunched up his brow, wondering who'd be calling him. He hadn't lived in Europe in the last 150 years. He sighed, not wanting anymore drama in his day, as he answered the call. "Alec here."

Malachi was gritting his teeth on the other side of the ocean, where, even here, bad news traveled fast. "Master Canton. This is Malachi. Council has demanded your presence before an official tribune. We expect you here tomorrow."

The line went dead, and Malachi disconnected as soon as his message was delivered. He didn't call for a discussion. The Council was long overdue in reigning in the antics of this vampire.

Alec downed the last of the Midnight. "Pack my bags, Santos. Looks like I'm going to Florence."

104

Not much had changed since the last time he'd visited Council. The massive stone building was located in a compound just outside of Florence, where the Council members all resided. He was allowed to enter by the guards, who were all warriors trained by the Medici, wearing ceremonial leathers bearing the Council crest. He recognized a few faces of the warriors but didn't remember their names. The warriors, who were chosen to serve here, served for life, just as the Council members did. The security was tight, and as far as Alec could remember, there had never been a breach of Council security.

Alec was offered a seat in the waiting area outside the chambers, but he remained standing, pacing nervously. It had been centuries since he'd been summoned to Council. He had no doubt this was over the presidency. The Council had never been happy with his decision to pursue such a high-profile position in the mortal world. In fact, there had been little he'd done that had ever pleased Council, so at least he was consistent.

The massive doors into chambers were opened, as two heavily armed warriors stepped forward, and motioned him to come in. One of the warriors announced him. "Master Alec Canton."

Alec heard his own name echo off the high walls. He approached the long table, with a single chair that faced the dais of the seven Council members, all wearing their signature hooded robe. The robes were each a different color, and the color designated their area of control. The hoods obscured their faces, casting the upper portion of their faces in shadow. Alec had forgotten who was responsible for what but remembered Malachi generally took the lead in these Council sessions.

He sat down in the empty chair and waited for the inevitable. He took note that the two warriors who escorted him in had taken up position behind him. Onyx, in his black robe, stood up behind the dais.

"Master Canton, we regret that we must call this session of Council to address the situation you have placed us in."

Alec looked back at him with indifference. He'd never been one for rules. "I don't understand how what I've done affects you in any way. You didn't want me running for President, and I've withdrawn. What's the problem?"

Onyx pushed back his hood, exposing his face, as his eyes bored into Alec. "My role here is security. Not just the security of the Council but security for our species. The fact that you have gone through your life with total disregard for your fellow vampires, and how your actions have put them at risk, speaks volumes. It is not our business how you handle your mate. Your decision to end her life is your choice, she is your property. But when you have chosen to live such a high-profile life among the mortals, her death becomes something the mortals could question. Fortunately for you, the situation was well handled, and we were not exposed. And now, you end your campaign, but don't think we are not aware of the situation with the mortal. Again, you show a total disregard for the safety of us all. You are not some rogue who runs the streets, you are a master, and with that comes great responsibility."

Alec shrugged. "The thing with the girl was handled. No big deal."

Onyx raised his voice. "It was handled, but not by you! You do nothing but create situations we must work to cover up. First it was your mate, Larissa, and now this! You have no regard for the danger you put us all in! So, now you have resigned yourself to the fact the Presidency is out of reach for you. What now? Your face is known internationally. The mortals believe you to be one of them, and yet, you will not age. Do you even think of these things? Where can you go that you will not be recognized? You disgrace us all! Your coven is gone. You were so self-absorbed, living in the mortal world, and in the meantime they have all dispersed, moved on to other covens. If I could remove your title of master, I would, but that is your birthright. However, it is the decision of the Council that you are to be exiled. Your territory, what is left of it will be re-assigned, and you are henceforth ordered to live underground. Remove yourself from the mortals completely for a full century."

Alec was on his feet, when he heard the two warriors step closer. He looked over his shoulder to see they had weapons drawn. He looked back at the dais and shouted, "You can't do that!"

Onyx pulled the hood back over his head. "We can, and we have." Turning to Florian, in his blue robe, Onyx asked him to read from their bylaws.

Florian stood and flipped open the ancient text, as he read the passage aloud. "Any master, who, by his actions, risks the safety and security of the species, shall, at the discretion of Council, have all of his territories revoked, and must forfeit his coven. Said master may be required to live in exile for whatever time period is determined necessary by Council to restore security."

Alec could feel his face burning he was so angry. "You can't take my territory! Where am I supposed to go?"

Jasperion, in his orange robe, flipped open the ledger containing all maps of all territories and land deeds. "You have already given your territory of California to Master Medici. Given his close association with you, and his management of both California and Virginia, it is the decision of Council that your territory of Connecticut, as well as the District of Columbia, otherwise known as Washington, D.C., will both be transferred over to the Medici. Perhaps, in a hundred years, he may be willing to transfer it back to you. That will be his choice."

Alec slammed his hand down on the table. "Fuck! You're taking everything. What am I supposed to do?"

Malachi spoke softly, "You still have significant financial resources at your disposal. You are a very rich master. Where and how you survive the next hundred years is up to you to figure out. But make no mistake, Master Canton. If you do not abide by the decision of this Council, and you continue to place our species at risk of exposure, we will not hesitate to exterminate you, so plan carefully."

Onyx struck a gavel hard on the dais, as the robed Council members all stood and exited.

Alec called out to them. "Wait. I have questions. Don't turn your backs on me!"

He felt a tap on his shoulder, as the two warriors stepped up next to him, and physically led him from chambers and to the exterior entrance of the Council compound. In a matter of seconds, Alec found himself standing outside alone.

105

Returning to Georgetown, Alec teleported directly inside his house into the foyer. Since the announcement about his campaign, he'd had a number of reporters hanging around near the house, trying to get a statement, and the last thing he wanted to deal with was the press. The house was deathly quiet, and he called out for Santos to bring him a Midnight.

He was sliding off his jacket, as he called out and noticed the hollow echo of his voice. Looking around, the antique low boy that sat by the front entrance was gone, as was the priceless Persian rug. "Santos!"

He hurried into the family room, to find that room was empty of all its furnishings. "Santos!"

In a panic now, he ran back into the hallway, quickly running from room to room, finding them all empty. The rugs removed, the art on the wall was gone. He ran up the stairs, opening the door to the bedroom suite, but he already knew he'd find nothing. Even his butler was gone. Santos had served him for centuries, and Council had even taken him away.

"Alto!" Alec called out to his driver and body guard, but he got no response. He stood in the empty room, the room where he'd slept with Rissa. He could still smell her perfume. His closet was empty, but when he opened her closet, her clothes, her shoes, everything was still there. He stepped into the large walk-in closet, surrounded by her things, and her scent, and dropped to his knees. The blood tears poured down his face, and he clinched his fists. He'd lost everything, but the only thing that mattered was her, and he had only himself to blame. He curled up in a ball on the floor of her closet. From his vantage point on the floor, he saw a silk robe that had slipped from its hanger and lay in a soft pool on the floor. Reaching out, he pulled the robe toward him, holding it to his nose as he inhaled. "Rissa."

His cries went unanswered, and unheard, and he fell into a

sleep, exhausted by the long teleport, and overcome with the realization of the impact of being exiled. When he woke several hours later, the room was dark, and he sat up, momentarily confused. As he got his bearings, he started to pull himself together. He knew he wouldn't be allowed to stay in the house, but he had no idea where to go. He called out to the only vampire he knew would respond, **"Shade!"**

***

Shade sat in his office, reviewing the deeds and land maps sent to him by Council, organizing what was now his newest territories, Connecticut, and the District of Columbia. The news from Council wasn't a surprise. He'd seen masters exiled before. He had yet to hear from Alec, but he knew Alec had resources and could be anywhere by now.

As the evening progressed into night, the house was beginning to come to life, and so was the camp outside. The terrace door hung open, allowing the early spring breeze into the room. It was an exceptionally warm night for this time of year, and he could hear the sounds from the camp, carried on the night breeze, metal against metal as the swords clashed, and the orders were shouted out by his warriors. Above his head was the sound of small feet, rushing from room to room. Shade had already sent some warriors to Connecticut to establish a base of operations there and was just about to check on Theo at the Dead House when Alec's voice wailed loud and clear in his head. He wasn't used to hearing such desperation in his old ally's voice. **"Bro! What the fuck is going on?"**

Alec heard the response in his head. The first voice he'd heard since the doors of the Council compound closed behind him. **"I need your help, brother. I have no place to go."**

Shade closed his eyes, he knew this was coming, it was inevitable. **"Come out to Bel Rosso. Let's have some Midnight, talk, we can figure it out."**

Shade had tried, many times, to warn him of the consequences of pretending to be mortal and ignoring Council. Alec had always squashed those warnings, along with everything and everyone in his way as he climbed his way to the top. And now, it had all backfired, and he had a long way to fall.

Alec sighed with relief. He knew that many of his species had already turned their backs on him, even before he was exiled. Shade had everything now, and Alec had nothing to offer in exchange for the favor he was about to ask for. Shade could easily have walked away from him too. **"I'm on my way, brother."**

Hearing Alec's respond, Shade let Kate know what was going on. **"*Mi amore*, Alec is on his way to the house. This is the big turn I was expecting. Please keep things under control with the kids, if possible. I hate to ask this of you my red headed vixen, but right now, Alec needs our help."**

Kate heard his message, as she juggled Sophia on her shoulder, and Lorenzo was clinging to her leg, begging for attention. *Keep things under control?* She almost laughed out loud. She'd lost control of this situation about four years ago when Lorenzo was born, and now, with Sophia, their life was chaos. **"Yeah, okay. No problem. I'll just lock them in a closet."**

He smiled from ear to ear. He couldn't imagine his life with anyone else. She was born to bear his *bambinos*. **"Bel, I love you. Right now, I have my hands full as well. We just gained more territory, so it is vital I get Alec in hand."**

As he finished his thought, Gi walked in with several bottles of Midnight to replenish the office supply for the upcoming visit. "Good man, Gi. Master Canton should be arriving any moment, if his ass doesn't get lost." Gi nodded and exited, and within minutes, Shade heard voices, knowing Alec had arrived.

Wishing to avoid any encounter with Kate's wolf warriors, Alec teleported directly inside the house, breaking yet another carved in stone rule from the Council. Entering another vampire's home this way without explicit permission was strictly forbidden, and a violation could result in a death sentence if the offended master chose to press charges with the Council. Under his current circumstances, Alec thought he could get away with it. The ancient butler was there to greet him immediately and led him to Shade's office.

"Brother, thanks for seeing me."

Shade stood as Alec entered the room, and the effects of the last few days were obvious on Alec's face. He didn't stand as tall, his shoulders slumped, and his suit looked like he'd slept in it. He looked pale and removed of his pride. His eyes were empty, void of any emotion. "Sit down, brother, before you fall down."

Shade poured two tall tumblers full of Midnight, sitting one in front of Alec before taking a seat in the leather chair behind his desk. He sat the opened bottle of Midnight on his desk, knowing this wouldn't be the last drink they took. "You look like shit."

Alec accepted the glass and downed it quickly, needing the boost of blood and alcohol. "Yeah, well, I feel like shit. They took everything, brother. They told me they were giving you my territories, but when I got home, the house was empty. Santos and Alto, they're both gone. I'm supposed to go underground, but I don't even know where to go. I know some vamps live their whole life underground, but that was never my style. Besides, there's not a master out there who'll even give me the time of day, except you. Help me out here, brother."

Shade eyed him closely and didn't miss how he gulped down the Midnight. Alec never had a problem finding a source for feeding, but an exiled vampire wasn't welcome in many venues. Swirling the thick ruby-colored liquid around in the tumbler, he cleared his throat. "Seems to me I have been helping you since the moment I landed in the States."

Shade locked eyes with Alec, letting his statement hang in the air between them, as he let it sink in. He'd help his old friend, but make no mistake; he was the one calling the shots now. "Everything is gone, Alec, but as I see it, you have two options."

Alec laughed. "Really? Well, that's two more options than I see, brother. So please, tell me."

Sipping from his Midnight, Shade set the glass down, slowly spinning it round and round on the worn surface of his desk.

"Your first option is Colin in Nevada. He roams the underground. He knows you, and I would say you might have a shot there, but to be honest, he is even more depraved than you are." Shade smiled, the corners of his mouth curling up slightly. "But there is another avenue I am willing to offer you."

Alec cringed. He'd hate to go begging to Colin. "Let's hear it. Anything is better than Colin."

"Smart decision. Besides, Colin was always more drawn to Rissa than to you."

Leaning forward, Shade poured Alec another Midnight. "You know California. I have warriors there, and an established base. Raven is my Second-in-Command. I will offer you refuge there, underground, of course. I'll provide protection, up to a point. But let me make one thing perfectly fucking clear, brother. You get out of hand and I'll deal with you, one on one. This is no game. You have one shot to get your fucking life under control. The underground network thrives there. It is up to you to make your own contacts, figure out where you go from there."

Alec swirled the dark liquid in his glass. How did he fall so far, so fast? "Deal, brother. There were always a lot of underground clubs in California. Rissa liked the clubs, but it was never my thing. I can make it work."

Shade opened his desk drawer, pulled out a pack of cigarettes and dug in his pocket for a light. He lit up and threw the pack to Alec. "You have to make it work. If you don't, you are a dead vampire."

Shade took a few drags from the cigarette and stood, walking around the office. "I can tell you haven't fed, I can offer you something before you head out, if you are interested. Feeder compound on the camp premise, I will give you a night there, if it's what you need. "

Alec nodded. "I'll accept your offer. It will take me a while to get settled in California, so I should probably feed."

"I'll have Aislynn escort you down. She is my Lieutenant at camp, and she oversees the feeder compound. Access requires fingerprint ID, so only authorized warriors can get inside. You will probably know the Matron, Velia from Castello."

Alec looked up. "I remember Velia. It's been a very long time, but I remember her. Had no idea she was here with you. Listen, I get it, brother, your house, your rules. You'll get no trouble from me."

Shade looked at the broken master before him. "Do you miss her?"

"Yeah, brother, I do. But she fed from him, from Max. I miss her, but I could never forgive her for that."

Shade sighed. He knew Alec would never have destroyed Rissa without provocation. "Well, let's just say, you got retribution for both of us on that count. Come on, let's walk down to camp, get you set up for the night. You can leave whenever you're ready. Medici stands with you, we remain allies. Be sure of that."

106

After walking with Alec to the camps and turning him over to Aislynn, he walked to the training field, observing this year's new recruits. He was going to need them now more than ever, as his territory was expanding. He'd just sent a large number of his experienced warriors to set up a base in Connecticut. He watched the young warriors train, and could easily spot those who'd learn fast, and be able to rise within the ranks quickly. Normally, he'd take up his sword and join in; challenging some of the more skilled recruits, pushing them to their limits, but tonight, his head wasn't in it.

Meeting with Alec had made him reflect on his own life choices, a surreal reminder of how much had happened in such a short time, and how quickly it could all disappear. He needed to clear his head, and the warm spring night called to him. He ached to be away from the burden of responsibilities that lay on his shoulders. He yelled out his orders to Marcello and strolled back to the house. The stars were clearly visible tonight, as they shone down from the cloudless sky.

As he approached the house, he stopped and looked up at the windows, lit from within in a soft, warm glow, inviting him inside. He knew he should go in, but his body ached to be set loose. He needed some time alone, a break from the chaos of being mate, daddy, master, and warrior. It only took a second to convince himself, and he detoured away from the house, and in the direction of the garage. He stepped around the area of new construction, where Kate had already ordered a section to be enclosed and remodeled to accommodate a room for Madison to place her potter's wheel, with ample shelving to store the raw materials for her work, as well as the finished product.

He grabbed his helmet and straddled the Harley, eager to feel the fresh air in his face. He couldn't remember the last time he'd had a Harley between his legs, and then the memory hit him and his chuckle echoed off the walls of the garage. Their life together had changed so much since that ride into Charlottesville. He strapped on his helmet, eased the bike out of the garage, and kick started the engine. The distinctive roar was deafening. He rode the bike down the long lane that lead to the entrance, and then hit the open road, quickly accelerating.

As the night air cleared his mind, he headed away from the city. As he hit I-64, he headed west, up the mountains. Reaching the top of Afton Mountain, he veered left down the Blue Ridge Parkway, the narrow two-lane road carved into the crest of the mountain that ran the entire length of the Blue Ridge Mountain range, frequently running parallel to the Appalachian Trail. The road ran through the national park, and remained largely deserted at night, allowing him to open the throttle, increasing his speed as he leaned into each curve. He pulled into a deserted overlook and switched off the engine. He removed his helmet, lowered the kick stand on the bike, and walked to the stone embankment that marked the sharp drop off. Sitting down on the wall, he lit up a smoke. Exhaling the smoke into the cool night, he inhaled deeply, drawing in the rich smell of the earth as it awakened to spring.

Looking out over the valley below him was the place he now called home, and in the distance, he could see the lights of Charlottesville. He was surrounded by the beauty of nature, and he'd never thought, six years ago, this would be where he'd put down roots.

He'd come to the States to work for Alec. At the time, he thought he'd be here a year at the most, although he was interested in exploring opportunities to expand his territory. *Fuck, that seems like ages ago now.* The States represented new ground for vampires from Europe. There were covens here, but not many and not well organized, with the structure and discipline like the covens in Europe. But then, he met her. He never saw it coming.

He'd stood against admirable opponents, many his equal, and walked away unscathed, but he couldn't walk away from her. He'd avoided his obligation to mate for more than 500 years, but he was struck down, by a mortal no less, with crimson hair, and large doe eyes. She'd stolen his heart the first moment he saw her. She walked beside him now, as his immortal Medici Queen, and he cherished the ground she walked on. He'd shared everything with her, well, almost everything.

He felt a pang of guilt, knowing he'd taken her away from all she'd known and loved, and turned her into one of them. Would she have made the same choice to be with him if she knew the truth? He shook his head, clearing away those thoughts. He'd decided, long ago, that some secrets were better left buried, because sometimes, love did not conquer all.

Look at Alec and Rissa. Alec had ruled even longer than he had and had risen to great heights in power and wealth, but now was nothing but a shell of a master, with nothing to his name. How easily it could all be stripped away.

Looking down across the valley, he could make out the outlines of the 4,500 acres they now called Bel Rosso. He remembered the first time he'd brought Kate to see the place, the house in need of renovation, and empty except for a mattress he'd thrown on the floor. They had built that piece of land into something magical, something enchanting and peaceful, which called to his soul. This was his home now, in a way Castello had never been.

She had doubled his annual income with her sunflowers and lavender and created a beautiful landscape of color and fragrance. He realized how much she'd grounded him, even as he grew his base of power. He now held title to Virginia, California, District of Columbia, and Connecticut, in addition to the territories in Italy, France, and Greece. His *padre* could never have fathomed such a large responsibility. With Lorenzo, he knew the dynasty was secure for another generation. He could already see the warrior his son would become.

He didn't know everything his future held, but he knew *bel* was his light in the darkness. He'd never be alone with any of his struggles. She gave him courage and strength, and she'd always stand at his side. He couldn't grasp Rissa's betrayal of her mate or the depth of Alec's grief over losing her, even if it was at his own hand. He wouldn't be able to bear the loss of Kate.

But while Alec's life was unraveling, theirs was expanding every day. He had three children to raise, and there was still one more to come. This would be no small undertaking. Lorenzo must be prepared to follow in his footsteps, to lead the coven, and secure its future. Sophia's and Natalia's roles had not been revealed to them, but they were royal blood, and they too would carry great responsibility for the Medici coven, and ensuring the bloodline. His half-breed son, Cory, presented unique challenges, as no vampire had ever integrated a half-breed into the coven before. But Cory had found Madison, and she too was now under his protection, and living under his roof.

He took a long, final drag on the cigarette before stomping it out under his boot as he chuckled to himself. It would be a long time before he and Kate ever got to enjoy the quiet of living in that house as just the two of them again.

Sighing deeply, he reviewed his life, what had been, what was, and what had yet to come. The cobwebs cleared from his head, and he could see the eastern horizon as the sky began to unperceptively lighten, and he knew he didn't have much time. Walking back to the bike, he put on his helmet and fired up the Harley. He took one last look, scanning the rolling foothills over all that was his, this was his Virginia. In the valley was his home and all he held dear to his heart. He'd found the answers he was looking for in *bel*, she was his destiny, and he'd never questioned that. Her role in his life was vital to the continuation of the Medici legacy. He only hoped she wouldn't, one day, feel the price she'd paid was too much.

Lorenzo's Rising – Sample of Book 5

Standing at the window, Lorenzo looked out over the grounds of Castello. The sun was setting, and his father would wake soon. He was ten now, and they'd come to Florence for him to begin officially training as a warrior in the camp, under Marco's direction. He felt both excited and nervous to begin this journey. On one hand, he couldn't wait to join the other young boys, and to train in earnest. Of course, he'd practically grown up in the camp in Bel Rosso, but he'd never been allowed to engage in mock combat with the adult warriors. He did have his private lessons with Skelk to master his fire-throwing skills, and his father's help with mastering the sword. Now he was ten, coming to Castello meant leaving the comfort of his family. His parents and his sisters, Sophia and Natalia, would all return home to Bel Rosso after he was settled in. At least he'd have Zeus here. His father had promised to have his pony shipped back to Florence for him, although, Lorenzo would soon outgrow him.

He'd visited Castello many times since his birth, and his father had made it clear he had strong obligations to the coven. Lorenzo would be allowed to live inside Castello, as opposed to living in the barracks. Other than that one concession, his father had told him to expect no favors from Marco. He'd be treated the same as the other boys in the camp, and expected to excel. Lorenzo's wet-feeder, Nita, would reside at Castello. He wouldn't require the services of the adult female feeders until his puberty, which, unlike mortal children, he wouldn't reach until around eighteen to twenty years of age. He'd no longer have his beloved nanny, Theresa. She'd return to Virginia with the rest of his family. Instead, Carlos had been assigned as his private butler.

Yesterday, he'd met Uberto, who would become his new tutor here in Italy. Enzo too would remain at Bel Rosso, teaching his sisters. Lorenzo felt like he was being ripped from everything, and everyone, he'd known in his highly guarded life. He was aware, now, of how different he was. He'd been taught the differences between the mortal and immortal world, although he'd found that lesson hard to grasp. He'd been made aware of how, and why, it was necessary to protect himself from mortals, while growing up in a household with two mortals. His half-brother, Cory had plans to marry a mortal girl. He understood Cory would never have been able to mate with an immortal. He accepted but didn't understand why his species rejected the half-breed. He couldn't imagine his life without Cory. And Madison presented no danger to him. Cory's mortal mother would come to visit from time to time, and she was always welcomed into their home with loving arms.

There was, of course, his Uncle Luca and Aunt Shannon. His auntie had been turned now and was mated to Luca. For most of his life, he understood Shannon had been mortal. Of course, he knew his own mother was once mortal, even though Lorenzo never knew her as such. One thing was for sure, there were no mortals at Castello, and currently no female warriors either. His Uncle Marco was strictly old school, and this camp was run much differently than the camp in Virginia.

As he watched the sky turn pink with the setting sun, he heard a strange sound, like the clip-clop of horse's hooves echoing down the long hallways of the castle. He turned to see his sister, Sophia, pushing open the massive door to his bedroom. Lorenzo rolled his eyes at the sight of her. Not only was his six-year-old sister wearing their mother's heels, but she had somehow managed to get inside the vault where the royal jewels were stored. Sophia had the coronation crown for the queen, sitting lopsided on her small head, slipping down over one eye, and had on the large twenty carat diamond necklace, which was hanging almost to her waist.

"Sophia! Mom has told you to stay out of the vault."

"Be quiet, Lorenzo, I can wear a crown whenever I want. I'm a princess too!"

Lorenzo had learned already that arguing with Sophia was a waste of time. "Okay, but don't look at me when you get in trouble."

Sophia stuck out her tongue, before turning to clip-clop out of the room, and ran right into her mother.

Kate shook her head in exasperation, as the willful child with red curls was once again breaking the rules. "Hold on, missy. Where exactly do you think you're going?"

Sophia put her hands on her hips. "Are you going to take my

crown?"

"Indeed I am, and the necklace. Now, hand them over."

The child stomped her foot as she shouted. "But I'm a princess!"

Kate knelt down in front of the girl and locked eyes with her. "And I'm a queen. Hand them over now."

With a sigh that could be heard the length of the hallway, the child reluctantly removed the crown and the necklace, returning them to her mother.

"Thank you. Now the shoes."

"Mommy!"

"The shoes, Sophia."

Sophia stepped out of the designer heels, her chubby bare feet dancing on the cold marble floor. Kate summoned Emma who arrived quickly to take the jewels back to the vault.

Kate issued the last request to the child. "Could you please be quiet until your father and sister wake from their slumber? They will be up shortly."

Sophia shrugged. "I don't know why they can't sleep at night like we do. This is very inconvenient."

Kate laughed. "Inconvenient is it? Did Enzo teach you that word? And you know perfectly well why they sleep during the day. Your father and Natalia weren't born with the gift of day-walking."

"Will Natalia have the gift of Animalism like us?"

Kate shook her head. "We haven't seen her gifts yet, Sophia. We only know she's not a day-walker. We'll see her gifts emerge as she gets older, just as we saw yours. Now head back to your room, and put on your socks and shoes. These floors are too cold."

Sophia turned and started to skip down the hall toward her room, singing at the top of her lungs.

Kate called out. "Quietly, please."

Sophia looked over her shoulder and giggled. "I forgot."

Kate muttered under her breath, "I doubt it," and heard Sophia giggle even louder. She stood in the hallway until she saw her daughter enter her bedroom, then turned and tapped at Lorenzo's open door. He'd watched quietly as the drama played out between mother and daughter, a scene he'd gotten quite used to in the last six years.

"Hey, Mom."

Kate entered the room and sat on his bed. Looking at this miniature version of Shade, a boy on the threshold of moving out of childhood, she swallowed hard. He'd been brave about this move to Florence, but she knew his apprehension around all the change. She'd not add to it by making him carry the burden of her own sadness. She couldn't believe ten years had passed so quickly, and now, the next phase of his life he'd live apart from her. "Are you okay?" she asked.

The boy nodded yes, his black curls bobbing, just as they did when he was such an impish toddler. "I'll be fine. Alfie is here, and Uncle Marco. Besides, you'll come visit, and I'll come home from time to time. I want this. I want to train. I have a warrior's blood, and people will depend on me."

Kate smiled at her son who'd been raised with the understanding of his responsibility, the burden he must bear for the coven, and the legacy of Medici. "True, many will depend on you, and you're born to greatness. You'll be a warrior to equal your father, but foremost, you'll always be my son."

Lorenzo felt a wave of emotion and quickly turned back toward the window, the sky now dark, as the sun slid below the horizon. "You'll keep my room for me at Bel Rosso, right?"

Kate stepped up behind him, kissing the top of his head. "Always."

End of Sample

About the Author

Emily Bex is an avid life-long reader, and a first-time writer of the epic six book Medici Warrior Series. As she says, "Why start small?" She worked for over twenty years in marketing, developing ad campaigns, catalogs, product launches and promotional literature. She figured if she could write creatively about products, then surely she could write something about these characters that were rattling around inside her brain. She currently lives in Virginia, but has used her extensive love of travel, both foreign and domestic, to create the backdrop for her characters to play out their story.

View the Medici Warrior Series Here:

https://www.emilybex.com/books/

Make sure to stalk me!

Instagram:
https://bit.ly/3dAaO5k

Facebook:
http://bit.ly/3k5GHUC

Goodreads:
http://bit.ly/3ukYcVU

Twitter:
https://bit.ly/3s6m3GG

Bookbub:
http://bit.ly/2ZBJ9ZM

Website:
https://www.emilybex.com/

More from This Author

*"Blood Covenant combines the hedonistic jet-setting pleasures of **BILLIONAIRE ROMANCE** and the dirty little secret thrills of a **DEAD SEXY VAMPIRE!**"* - Katalina Leon, USA Today Bestselling Author

*"This series is going to **HIT THE CHARTS**... what an epic tale. Thank you Emily from a **NEW FAN!**"* - Cheryl, Amazon Reviewer

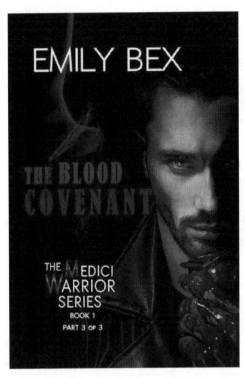

When he met her, he knew how it would end.

Shade Medici, a warrior king and sole male heir to the dynasty, is expected to mate and produce an heir to secure the continuation of the Medici coven. He's waited over 500 years for the right mate, and when he meets Kate Reese, his attraction is more than primal - it's merciless.

She's also mortal.

Kate is fresh off a broken engagement and reluctant to open her heart, but her hesitations are no match for the unrelenting pursuits of the vampire King. Their passion for each other is searing... and not everyone is happy about it.

Namely the ruling Council.

As they fight against deceit, treachery, and those who aim to see their love fail, Shade also struggles to control his impulses as Kate is immersed into his dark and dangerous world, but it's imperative he prepare her for the changes that will be demanded of her should she choose to bind herself to him through the blood covenant. All that scorches and glitters isn't gold, and she quickly learns that falling in love with a vampire King comes at a hefty price:
It may just cost her everything.

"Riveting", "electric", and hailed as "the NEXT BIG THING", The Medici Warrior Series follows the exploits of a vampire dynasty that spans four generations in a multi-genre novel with elements of paranormal, smoldering slow-burn romance, and historical fiction. Get your copy today! Your vampire king is waiting...

JR Ward and Christine Feehan fans will become enchanted with this deliciously dark and scandalous tale by International Bestselling Author Emily Bex. It's everything vampire romances should be made of!

*"The **DANGEROUS ELEGANCE** of these worldly, wine and blood loving Medici warrior vampires and their mates is **TOTALLY ADDICTIVE**. I cannot wait for more."* - Katalina Leon, USA Today Bestselling Author

Immortality beckons.

Unable to escape crushing grief, Kate needs an outlet to channel her anguish. Turning to Luca, she pleads to be trained to fight like a warrior, but such a thing is in direct violation of Shade's commands.

If she can get Luca to agree, her training must be done in secret.

Unfortunately, any training is too little too late. Intent on crushing Shade, the Aries coven is pressing in on him from all sides. Shade's only weakness is Kate, who becomes their perfect bait.

While Kate has been made stronger, as long as she's mortal, her life is in peril. But going through the turning to become immortal would be a big gamble to her survival.

So many decisions, too many obstacles. This second installment in a vampire saga will draw you in from the first page to the spellbinding end.

"Scorching", "riveting", and hailed as" the NEXT BIG THING", The Medici Warrior Series follows the exploits of a vampire dynasty that spans four generations in a multi-genre novel with elements of paranormal, smoldering romance, and historical fiction. Get your copy today! Your vampire king is waiting...

AUTHOR'S NOTE: This is a series that must be read in order. New to the Medici Warrior universe? Start at Book One!

JR Ward and Christine Feehan fans will become enchanted with this deliciously dark and erotic tale by International Bestselling Author Emily Bex. It's everything vampire romances should be made of!

There are new beginnings for the ancient Medici vampire coven.

The sexy, powerful King Shade Medici intends to increase his coven and territories to include the U.S. The new Medici Queen proves she can hold her own beside her king. She carries rare abilities believed extinct by the vampire community. She also possesses something never seen in the vampire world. What will it mean to their kind?

A male heir must be produced to carry on the Medici line. The royal couple has many new plans in business to advance their hold in the States...but not everyone is happy about it. The sprawling Medici estate is a threat to its neighboring coven, controlled by Max. Their lifestyle is Rissa's greatest envy. Secrets will be revealed, old scores will be settled, and many will fall.

"Scorching","riveting", and hailed as" the NEXT BIG THING", The Medici Warrior Series follows the exploits of a vampire dynasty that spans four generations in a multi-genre novel with elements of paranormal, smoldering romance, and

historical fiction. Get your copy today! Your vampire king and queen are waiting...

More From Foundations

The Alyx Rayer Series: Book One, Vengeance Marked
by S.J. Pierce

Her Marked was more than just precious to her, he was precious in ways the world could only fathom. If she failed, she failed everyone. Alyx Rayer's existence in Atlanta, the eternally bustling capital of Georgia, is one of routine and blending in among the worker bees. But her 'normal' life is a facade for a higher calling. She's a three-hundred-year-old soul, sent from the darkness to capture her Marked when summoned by her superiors. Until then, she was to keep her distance. Except... something about him makes it hard to stay away.

While already trapped between honor and desire, a man in a black suit continually shows up when she least expects it, his presence evoking a strange response from the scar she was branded with at birth. Because her superiors never told her what this would mean, or much of anything except what to do when they summon, she can only conclude to try and keep her sanity-and her life-from completely shattering to pieces. This engaging first book of the series is a Paranormal Romance novel interlaced with twists, turns and thrilling suspense that is sure to satisfy readers of any genre.

May not be suitable for YA.

The Guardian League: Book One, Jasper
by TK Lawyer

Lauren was an assignment. He didn't expect to fall in love.

From her birth, Apollo watched Lauren mature, witnessing all her milestones with a strong sense of pride. Advising, protecting and whispering loving words to her, Lauren is strong and perfect. Unfortunately, she doesn't want to live.

A drastic decision one day sets Lauren face to face with her own Guardian Angel- a being she never knew existed. However, he won't leave her alone. He is relentless, encouraging her to better her life when he doesn't understand what it takes to survive on Earth. Despite this "flaw," she is drawn to him in ways she can't explain and Apollo soon becomes as necessary as the air she breathes. He asks for only one thing- to be his, forever.

Will she allow Apollo to love and care for her when many have failed?

Foundations Book Publishing

Copyright 2016 © Foundations Book Publications Licensing
Brandon, Mississippi 39047
All Rights Reserved

10-9-8-7-6-5-4-3-2-1

Fall From Grace
Emily Bex
Copyright 2019 © Emily Bex
All Rights Reserved

Printed in Great Britain
by Amazon

28895792R00377